THE DIVINE TALISMAN

ALSO BY ELDON THOMPSON

The Obsidian Key
The Crimson Sword

THE DIVINE TALISMAN

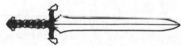

BOOK THREE OF THE LEGEND OF ASAHIEL

ELDON THOMPSON

An Imprint of HarperCollinsPublishers

THE DIVINE TALISMAN. Copyright © 2008 by Eldon Thompson. All rights reserved. Printed in the United States of America. No part of this book may be used or reproduced in any manner whatsoever without written permission except in the case of brief quotations embodied in critical articles and reviews. For information address HarperCollins Publishers, 10 East 53rd Street, New York, NY 10022.

HarperCollins books may be purchased for educational, business, or sales promotional use. For information please write: Special Markets Department, HarperCollins Publishers, 10 East 53rd Street, New York, NY 10022.

FIRST EDITION

Eos is a federally registered trademark of HarperCollins Publishers.

Based on a design by Iva Hacker-Delany
Yawacor map by Tone Rodriguez
Pentania map by David Cain

Library of Congress Cataloging-in-Publication Data has been applied for.

ISBN 978-0-06-074154-9

08 09 10 11 12 ov/rrd 10 9 8 7 6 5 4 3 2 1

ACKNOWLEDGMENT

*To my friends in the beginning, and those encountered
along the way, my heartfelt appreciation
for your faith, tolerance, and support.*

—E.T.

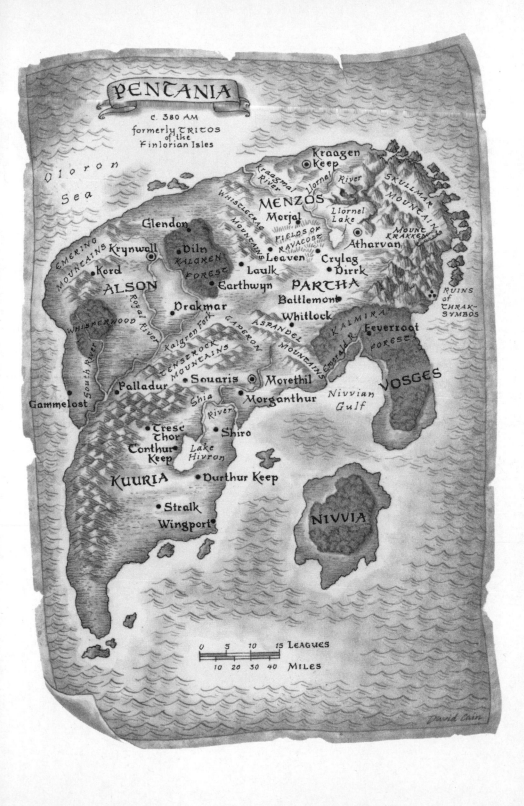

CHAPTER ONE

THE CREATURE SPRANG WITH A rabid snarl, moving quickly to cut off their escape. No longer elven, it bounded after them with the lust of a maddened predator, tearing through brush and forest limbs, feral eyes blind to all but the thrill of its impending kill.

Laressa stumbled and went to one knee. She screamed for her daughter to run on, then spun to meet their pursuer's final charge. A pair of blades shone darkly in the moonlight, slick with blood and thirsting for more. She looked past them, focused on her assailant's eyes as she gripped the wellstone hung from her wrist. Raising it like a shield in the palm of her hand, she bid its power forth.

Light flared and crackled in a thin, forked streamer. Fearing she was too late, Laressa closed her own eyes and threw herself aside, hearing at the same time her daughter's scream.

Upon a tangled bed of vine and root, Laressa's entire body clenched, bracing for the inevitable. She could smell the Illychar's fetid breath, and sense the creature's hatred. After millennia of imprisonment, it would not be denied.

But the terrible moment passed, and still the daggers did not bite. Though her heartbeat was like a drum in her ears, she heard now her killer's snarls of frustration. When she opened her eyes, she found it staggering about, sniffing and blinking in confusion, too disoriented to find its quarry a mere pace away. As it slashed aimlessly at the surrounding foliage, its growls of disappointment gave way to howls of rage.

Laressa hurried to regain her feet. The release would not grant her much time. And even if its effect were to last forever, she had by no means escaped the peril gnashing all around her.

Her next concern was not for herself, however, but for her daughter. She cast about frantically, trying to remember from which direction she had heard the young maiden scream. No easy task, given the chorus of shrieks and caterwauls that rent the night. She had worried upon hearing it that the child had witnessed her fall and meant to return to her. Now, she wished for just that.

That hope, like so many others this night, was engulfed by the horrifying truth. Laressa had managed just a few strides when her desperate search came to an abrupt end. Her daughter's flight had been swift, but no elf was going to outrun a goblin—least of all a pair of the creatures Illysp-possessed and lying in ambush.

Laressa jerked to a halt as she watched the batlike fiends shred their victim.

Part jackals, part whirlwind, they tore at the bloody pulp with hooked teeth and barbed claws, scrambling over and atop one another, painting themselves and the earth red. Laressa told herself that the writhing mass beneath was not—could not possibly be—her daughter. Then the victim arched sharply, and their eyes met.

One of those eyes was missing. The other was wide, its emerald ring drowning against a blood-filled white. Tresses of red-gold hair hung matted and torn. But through them, the lone eye still saw. An arm reached out, covered in deep lacerations, and the mouth opened in a soundless cry. A plea for mercy. An expression of unspeakable pain.

Laressa matched that cry with a terrible, bloodcurdling wail that peaked momentarily above the cacophony. One of the goblins looked to her with a blood-spattered maw. In the next instant, she sent a brilliant bolt of scintillating light smashing into it, igniting it. It screeched as it flew through the air to lie in a charred heap. The other spun away, a black funnel cloud in the moonlit darkness. The light struck it from behind, and the beast disintegrated in an explosive burst of red fire.

Laressa Solymir, keifer of the elven nation of Finloria, crumbled then, her strength and power spent. As she landed upon her knees, her gaze fell upon the wellstone in her palm, the multifaceted crystal gone dark. Her protection against the enemy was gone. She had nothing left with which to defend herself from the bestial darkness come to lay claim.

Looking once more upon her only child, Laressa welcomed its approach.

Somehow, without even realizing it, she crawled forward to kneel at her daughter's side. The girl's mouth groped uselessly, vocal cords torn. Her remaining eye shone with anguish and fright. Laressa knew she had to finish it, but she could not find the strength.

A bloody hand found hers, clamped itself over the wellstone.

Laressa sobbed as the crystal whitened, fed by the child's remaining life strength. Her daughter could only give so much. With tears in her eyes, Laressa forced herself to draw the rest.

A moment, and it was done.

All around, the slaughter continued. Hers was but one of a thousand such agonies suffered this night. She could hear the Illychar sweeping through the forest from all angles, feeding with ravenous delight. The screams of her people did not lie. Before the break of dawn, the once-proud Finlorian nation would be no more. Doomed to a fate they had foolishly thought to avoid. Sentenced to die at the hands of the most relentless enemy their world had ever known.

And it had been *her* duty to prevent it.

The thought angered Laressa. Despite her guilt, despite her pain, that fury lent her strength enough to do what was required. She gripped her wellstone, calling upon its power to light a blaze beneath her daughter's remains. The energy she had drawn from the child was barely enough, and left the stone dark and empty once more. But Laressa would not fail her daughter so completely as to allow her to become an Illychar herself.

When it was over, the finality of what she had done drove Laressa to her feet. Blinded by tears, she ran from the horror, ran from the pain. She ran from the folly, the nearsightedness, that had led to this calamity. She ran from what she had done, and from what she had failed to do.

All around her, the woods thrashed with Illychar pursuit. Their lusty howls mocked her efforts. She sensed their dark forms, hunting her with darker intent. All had been trampled and destroyed, or soon would be. The Illysp knew no other way.

She tripped then and pitched to the ground, gasping for breath, only to choke on a mouthful of dirt. Her heart pounded. From ahead now, and from either side, enemies approached. She was surrounded, defeated. Laressa was too heartsick to care.

Nevertheless, when the first of the Illychar reached her, she cried out, horrified by its frigid touch upon her back. Rolling to the side, she called upon her wellstone's magic, even though there was nothing left. A moment later, she was glad the release had failed, for as she glanced up, her fury was swept away by a wave of relief.

Eolin!

She blinked vigorously, then stared. Eolin, her husband, had come for her. In this, her blackest hour, he had returned to help shield and sustain her. His hand reached out. Even now, his face shone with wisdom and love.

Tears of joy mixed with those of torment as Laressa allowed him to pull her to her feet. Throwing her arms about his neck, she wept in his ear, begging his forgiveness while confessing all: the warnings ignored, her arrogance in thinking them safe, her inability to protect their child . . . She held nothing back, for here was someone with whom to share her agony and failures, someone who could soothe her fears, someone . . .

. . . who had not yet returned her embrace.

A knot of sickening dread stole Laressa's breath, as her wracked mind suddenly recalled that Eolin had been murdered weeks ago. Before she could stop, convince herself that she did not want to know, her jaw lifted, forcing her gaze to meet her husband's eyes. Immediately she recognized the pain therein—the ultimate anguish of an enslaved soul.

A soul gripped in the mandibles of possession.

Eolin's features seemed to melt, his face shriveling into a blackened death mask. The Illychar smiled, as if laughing at the cries of its body's former spirit, and lifted a single hand.

Laressa screamed as it found her throat.

SHE AWOKE WITH A START, shivering through a cold sweat as she inhaled sharply of the musky air. Just like that, she was back in her *denzaan*, her burrow home, safe beneath the earth. Even so, she lunged reflexively for the bracelet that lay upon her bedside table, clutching its wellstone in her palm. Drawing upon the energy stored within that central crystal, she began to calm, her pulse to slow. All at once, the savage images were receding. The Illychar, the devastation, Eolin's possession—all faded swiftly from mental view.

Small comfort. For Laressa knew they would return.

She hung her head, fighting to steady her breathing. In doing so, she remained careful not to close her eyes, lest the phantom horrors be resummoned before they had fully dispersed. She had not the strength to confront them again.

Yet she would have to, she knew. Though she did all she could these days to avoid it, she had to sleep at some point. And when she did, the nightmares would be waiting.

It had been that way for three weeks now, ever since the visit of the one called Torin—the one whose coming had ended her life as she had known it, and left behind this cruel emptiness for her to endure in its stead. For it was his quest that had brought on the rest: Crag's betrayal, Warrlun's retribution, Eolin's murder . . .

Her eyes did close then, seeking to deny a reality every bit as horrible as her dreams. It was the former that had spawned the latter. There was no escape, in sleep or in waking, from her agonies. The only question seemed to be which would lay final claim to her broken spirit.

It would happen soon. The dreams had been growing stronger, more intense, every night. At this rate, madness lay just around the corner.

A welcome relief, some part of her whispered, should it find her before the Illysp.

Drawing several steadying breaths, Laressa slipped from beneath her covers, leaving her wellstone bracelet to hang upon her wrist. As her feet brushed upon the moss that carpeted her earthen bedchamber, its life sent unspoken assurances through her skin. But for how long? How long did even the flowers and trees and grasses have once there was no one left to care for them? For she had seen the end in her dreams, the twisted landscapes of utter desolation, where lonely winds whistled through bare canyons of blackened stone. Where the heavens wept over the charred remains of a blistered earth. It would take centuries, eons maybe, for it to reach that point, for the Illychar to eradicate even themselves. Yet such was the inevitable outcome of their unchallenged reign. Eolin, and then the dreams, had told her so.

She sat for a moment at the edge of her woven bed, her head in her hands, wishing now that Eolin had died before he had shared with her the truth of the Vandari and their legacy. In passing that information on to her with his dying breaths, he had made her the final bearer of that knowledge. He had not done so to burden her with guilt—had begged her, in fact, to let any resulting failure rest with him alone. But there was no separating the two. Laressa, not Eolin, was now last of the Vandari, defender of the Swords of Asahiel and keeper of the secrets of the Illysp War.

The fate of all rested in her hands.

And yet, what could she do? Eolin had had his reasons for refusing to join Torin's crusade, none of which had changed with his untimely death. His bitterness toward the humans that had come to beg his aid was shared by all Finlorians, and with good reason. Why should her people risk themselves to help those who had hunted them to near extinction? Aside from that, their powers of magic were no more—or at least, those of the kind Torin had been seeking. She had knowledge only—of a secret history, yes, but if Torin had been sent by a scion of the Entient Algorath, as claimed, then surely the young king already knew everything she might share. And lastly, even if her people wished to help the humans, and possessed the required powers, how was she to reach them while trapped in this valley by her father's armies?

She had gone over it in her mind for weeks now. Even while grieving, even while wishing upon Torin and his friends the fate they deserved, she had been thinking it through, in search of what she could do—if not to protect *them*, then to protect her own people. For this was not a menace that would be satisfied with laying claim to the shores upon which it had been born. Its cravings were too primitive, too bestial to ever be sated. It would hunger, and it would grow, and no matter the obstacle, it would find a way to spread.

"Mother, you promised you would sleep."

Laressa spun, startled by the voice. In the near darkness of her denzaan's bedchamber, she could scarcely see the outline of the figure that stood upon her threshold.

"I tried, child."

Her daughter touched one of the exposed root tendrils that dangled from the ceiling, coaxing forth more light. Its brightened glow revealed youthful skin, emerald eyes, and long tresses of delicate blond hair. Despite the welcome sight, Laressa flinched, seeing for a moment that same face torn apart by goblin Illychar, contorted by suffering as her life's energy drained away into her mother's wellstone . . .

"You had another nightmare," Annleia presumed, her concern evident as she stepped forward.

Denial was useless. Most likely, she had been awakened, as on previous nights, by her mother's screams.

Annleia sat down beside her and took her hand. "Was it about Father?"

Laressa winced. She meant Eolin, of course, her adoptive father—the only father she had ever known. But Laressa could not help but think of Warrlun, the child's birth father—he who had taken Eolin's life in reprisal for a perceived wrong.

Annleia reached up to feel her forehead. "Are you ready to speak of it?"

She was not. Nor did she think she ever would be. It was unfair, of course. The child deserved to know the full truth behind her father's death. She deserved to know who Warrlun really was, and what had driven him to commit such a savage act. On top of that, she deserved to know about the peril she and the rest of their people faced, in order to come to terms with it in her own way.

But Laressa could not bring herself to share such grave news with anyone—least of all the one true love she had left in this world. To even think of exposing her precious child to these afflicting horrors was more than she could bear.

And yet, how long could she hold out? Annleia and the others who dwelled within this valley already suspected much. Their keifer had been murdered by none other than an agent of Lord Lorre—led here by the lone individual entrusted to serve as guardian to their lands. Given that, how could they think themselves safe?

Rather than confirm their fears, Laressa had done what she could to allay them. Crag's betrayal had wounded her more deeply than any of them, and none could argue otherwise. At the same time, the Tuthari dwarf had made sure that none would be able to follow his trail. Shallow grounds for forgiveness, perhaps, given the damage already sustained. But the dwarf had had his reasons, she had argued. Her life being not without its own misdeeds, she was in poor position to judge another's.

"If you wish to be free of your grief," Annleia admonished, "you cannot keep it trapped inside."

Laressa nodded, but refused to meet her daughter's gaze. She wasn't sure that she *wanted* to be free of it. In some ways, her grief seemed the only way to keep Eolin alive. Though it went against many of the fundamental life principles of her Finlorian people, she was not yet ready to surrender her temporal claim upon the man she had loved.

"You cannot persist like this. Our people need you."

Laressa responded with a look of annoyance before quickly turning away. The girl was only trying to help, not knowing that this matter was beyond her. Or was it? If the truth was more than her daughter could handle, then why was she so afraid to meet the young woman's gaze? Could it be that she feared Annleia might be *too* perceptive, that if she shared even one small thread, the girl might unravel the rest? Perhaps it was not her daughter's weakness, but her own that kept her silent.

"In time, child. I will be well enough in time."

Annleia must have heard the doubt in her voice. "You cannot deceive me, Mother. Nor can you expect to shoulder this burden alone."

Again Laressa tried to evade the other's gaze. But the child hooked a finger beneath her chin and forced their eyes to meet. *Eolin*, Laressa told herself. *She speaks only of Eolin.*

"Your father was a good man," she forced herself to say, in an attempt to escape the other's scrutiny.

"The best," Annleia agreed. "But you are also angry with him. Why?"

Laressa put on her most indignant expression, even as she caught her breath. "I . . . Why would you say that?"

"Because I know you as well as you know yourself. I sense it, in your words and in your posture—with me and with others. Do you feel he brought this somehow upon himself?"

Eolin himself had raised that argument, though it was not one Laressa shared. He had viewed his death as a punishment for allowing bitterness to overrule duty—for taking delight in Torin's travails. He should not have spurned the outlander as he had. He should have at least talked things through with the wielder of the Crimson Sword, to confirm what the other knew and offer any solution Torin and his allies might have missed.

Laressa had not cared to debate the issue at the time. Bad enough that their final moments had been spent revealing secrets that should never have been kept from her. Worse yet would have been to waste breath arguing over what to do about them, and whether her husband's fate was deserved.

"I blame your father's murder on none but those who committed it," she stated plainly.

And yet, that had not stopped her from accepting Eolin's suggested action. It made no sense to let her people perish as a result of their contempt—justified or no. And while a proper sharing of knowledge with Torin may have merited nothing, there was too much at stake not to take the chance.

By then, however, it had been too late. Her first act as keifer had been to send forth scouts on the trail of Torin and his friends—even before she had overcome the raw sting of her grief. But Torin's departure from their lands had been swift; Crag had seen to that. And her scouts had been strictly ordered not to jeopardize themselves by treading beyond the exits of the caves that led from Aefengaard. In accordance with her wishes, they had followed as far as they dared, only to return empty-handed.

"Then why do you torture yourself over what is done?" Annleia asked, refusing to let her dwell alone in her thoughts.

She had not, at first. When the news had returned that Torin had escaped their reach, Laressa had decided it just as well that they be rid of him forever. But that had been before the nightmares, before the roiling waves of heartache had subsided enough to reveal the truth.

"Mother, what is it you're not telling me?"

Laressa felt the threat of tears, of pride and of pity. Not yet twenty years of age, this girl, and already so wise and strong. The child might not have survived with anything less. Though born within this valley, she was an outsider in many respects—the daughter of a half-elven woman and a human male she knew nothing about. In this world, her mixed heritage was a scar, no matter how much they might pretend otherwise. The Finlorians had accepted her out of deference to their king, just as they had Laressa when, as a prince, Eolin had brought her to live among them. Since then, she had taught Annleia not to condemn herself, as others might, for her unique appearance. Human blood may have deprived her of sharpened ears, angled brow, and a pointed jawline. It may have granted her a full head of thick, lustrous hair. But it could never change the fact that she was an elf at heart. In the end, nothing else truly—

Laressa choked on the thought, and pulled away in horror. So obvious. The solution to her dilemma. The answer to her prayers. There in front of her, where it had been all along.

"Mother, what is it?"

No. She would not allow herself to even consider it. They still had the Sword, did Torin and the others, the last unbroken Sword of Asahiel. With it, they would find a way. Anyone who could have hunted the Finlorians here, to their secret location, was resourceful enough to put a stop to the Illysp on his own. As long as he wielded both the divine talisman and the knowledge descended from Algorath, the human king of Alson stood a chance. As did they all.

But Laressa knew she could not leave it at that. For the sake of her people, for the sake of her own sanity, she had to know that something more was being done. Whatever the act, wherever it might lead, however useless and inconsequential the effort might seem, she could not sit idly by if it was within her power to help.

"Mother?"

The smooth, earthen walls of her burrow seemed to close in around her. It was the only way. These walls could not protect her. Nor could the walls of their valley protect her people. If they remained here and did nothing, Aefengaard would become as a mass grave. And a temporary one at that, as, with the Illysp, not even the dead were safe.

Slowly, as if dragging against the weight of the world, Laressa turned once more to peer into her daughter's eyes. The truth was affirmed, and her heart fell. It would seem her people were not quite as powerless as she had believed. All she needed was someone who could pass for human when set to rove the barbaric world of men.

Tears welled. She could not allow it. She could not permit her daughter, so innocent and fragile, to venture into the outer world. Not when any escort Laressa might send—herself included—would only endanger the child further. Alone and unprotected, the girl would surely perish, and, for Laressa, nothing could be so devastating. She had already lost her husband. She would be damned before letting go of her daughter as well.

She meant to look away again, but Annleia squeezed her hand, and those emerald eyes held her. Again Laressa had to fight off the nightmare image of those eyes as the living light left them. Should she send the girl on this quest, she would be condemning her—because of her appearance, no less. And yet, could keeping her here end in anything but a death sentence?

Annleia remained silent, the child's luminous eyes seeming to bore right through her. Perhaps it was not her decision to make, Laressa thought suddenly. Should her daughter not be given a chance to at least discuss her own fate? She was not so young, Laressa reminded herself—nearly the same age *she* had been when deciding to leave her father and run away with Eolin to live among the Finlorians. How might she have felt had Lorre or anyone else successfully prevented her from making that choice?

Besides, she did not wish to wait, as Eolin had, to deliver these secrets with her final breaths. Though she had sworn no oath, and inherited their cause only through marriage and catastrophe, she understood the sacred honor of the Vandari and what they had been called upon to do. Rather than risk letting their secrets die with her, perhaps she should share them now. Armed with a full knowledge, her daughter might even recognize a solution that she had not. Either way, Laressa would not be alone in deciding upon the best course for all concerned.

Even now, she could scarcely imagine exposing her child to such terrible responsibility. But Annleia's eyes seemed to challenge her, pleading for her to trust in her daughter's strength.

The Ceilhigh only knew how little she had left of her own.

Breathing deeply to steady herself, Laressa stared warningly into her child's brave visage, offering her one last chance to escape before the truth descended upon her.

Annleia's eyes shone. *Tell me*, they seemed to insist.

"Dear child," Laressa sighed. "Let me tell you a story."

CHAPTER TWO

Aʟʟɪᴏɴ ʟᴏᴏᴋᴇᴅ ᴜᴘ ᴀs ᴛʜᴇ double doors to the council hall split wide. Around the table, whispered chatter died into stillness.

General Rogun had arrived.

Flanked by a pair of lieutenants, the grim-faced general strode forward with an imperious air. As always, the rattle of spurs ushered his approach, and ceased only when he had come to a stop at the table's edge.

Seated at the opposite head, Thaddreus raised a hand in welcome. "Good of you to join us, General," the First Elder grumbled. "We were beginning to wonder whether you meant to attend your own summons."

A few murmurs swept through the Circle's ranks, whether in support or opposition of Thaddreus's remarks, Allion couldn't tell.

"Please," the old man continued, "take your seat."

Rogun refused, as Allion expected, choosing instead to lean forward and plant his fists upon the table's surface. A posture meant to dictate, not debate.

And yet, the general did not speak. He forced his gaze around the table in a slow and steady circuit, staring at each of those assembled. When Allion's turn came, he felt as if he was being measured for an unpleasant task.

Thaddreus, speaker of the Circle of City Elders, cleared his throat in annoyance. "What is it you wish to report?"

Rogun finished his sweep, then let his gaze fall squarely upon the First Elder. "Our engagements beyond the walls are ended. The Illychar come to sack our city have been sent away in full retreat."

The man's face shone with sweat, and his armor was painted with blood and grime. The chief commander of Krynwall's forces had not merely watched the conflict from afar.

"That is most welcome news," Thaddreus allowed, while seeming not at all pleased, "but word that any page might have delivered."

Indeed, Allion thought, the battle had been well in hand since dawn of the previous day. Rogun had called this gathering with some other purpose in mind.

"The fight was more brutal than expected," the general went on. "My men outnumbered the enemy five to one, but our opponents fought as if the opposite were true."

Allion did not miss his use of the phrase "*my* men," and glanced quickly around to see what the others thought of it.

"Still," Rogun said, "the troops performed admirably, particularly given the number of fresh conscripts and recruits among them."

Thaddreus dipped his head in salute. "They have our gratitude, as does our general. Your rest and theirs is well earned."

"Not quite," Rogun argued, and Allion's stomach tightened. "There is still the matter of our safety here within the city."

A few among them grumbled. Thaddreus's frown deepened.

"But the Illychar have been driven out, as you yourself have assured us," the speaker remarked.

"Those who took up arms against us, yes," Rogun corrected, peering back coldly. "But they chose to dwell among us for some time before doing so. It may be that there are others yet to be rooted out."

That set off a string of murmurs, though Thaddreus moved quickly to cut them off.

"We know you to be a man of action, General. What are you proposing?"

"I mean to implement a citywide cleansing, to weed out any who have fallen prey to our enemies' foul influence."

Just like that, the murmurs gave way to uproar. Allion, like Thaddreus, remained silent, marking carefully the reactions of the other Elders. Some lauded the general's decision, while others cried out in fierce refusal.

"You would have soldiers, many untested, serve as judge and executioner over an entire populace?" Thaddreus demanded.

Rogun weathered the storm of protests, scowling patiently while the arguments bled themselves out. "It is the only way to ensure we do not again face the kind of attack we have just so narrowly survived."

His stern words and pitiless tone had the Elders shouting once more. Allion continued to hide his own uncertain emotions. This afternoon's council was the second Rogun had called since the Illychar ambush two nights past. The first had been unexpectedly brief, meant mostly to get a grasp on events and to reassure everyone of their relative security before the general set forth again on military duties. This one, clearly, was to be spent asking the hard questions and taking the appropriate actions.

But had the general come to *ask* them, or *tell* them what those actions would be? As he looked again to Thaddreus, Allion thought the First Elder appeared uncharacteristically nervous. If so, who could blame him? Rogun controlled the army, after all. Torin was dead. Should the general use this opportunity to impose martial law and demand the crown for himself, who could stop him?

Already, half of the City Elders seemed to be urging just that, by happily agreeing to the general's suggestion. The rest had turned to Thaddreus, balking at the notion and exhorting the speaker to make their voices heard.

"People will panic," Thaddreus shouted. "You will cause greater unrest than there is now."

"Those with nothing to hide have nothing to fear," Rogun countered with dead calm.

"You know as well as I, General, that people do not respond rationally in a climate of fear. How do you think they will react when you begin taking husband from wife, brother from sister, parents from children? They will call it a witch hunt and rise up against us."

"It is the only way," Rogun said again, "to ensure the safety of all."

Thaddreus glowered, but did not respond right away. Fearing him defeated, the dissenting Elders roared again their various protests.

"You would extract from our people a heavy price," the First Elder summarized finally. "With such an invasion of privacy, you take from them their most basic freedoms."

"Privacy or security," Rogun offered. "In this case, it is impossible to have both."

Again the debate raged, with many of the Elders angered by the way in which the headstrong general could so easily dismiss their concerns. Allion wasn't sure which way to lean. Having fought the Illychar himself and suffered greatly the depths of their cunning, he was inclined to side with Rogun. And yet, a *cleansing*, as the general described it, would almost certainly lead to more chaos and bloodshed, as Thaddreus feared. Rogun might not have any qualms about that, but Allion did. Especially when their efforts right now needed to be focused outward, toward the Illychar still laying siege to their lands, not on harassing and containing the residents of their own city.

Besides, Rogun was loyal to none but himself. A hero he may have become in saving Krynwall from an unexpected attack. But he had done so through defiance and manipulation, ignoring a direct edict of the Circle and risking the lives of many in order to wage his own secret defense campaign. Hindsight might validate those actions, but that didn't mean the man could be trusted.

"And where will it end?" Thaddreus asked, as if attuned to Allion's thoughts. "What guarantee do we have that the innocent will not be condemned alongside the guilty?"

Rogun's lip curled—a cruel smile. "Is there something you wish to accuse me of, old man?"

"I feel your very presence here merits discussion, yes," the speaker replied. Though his voice remained steady, his shifting gaze betrayed his nervousness. "Your actions have saved us, but if our people are to stand trial for no offense at all, then why not our chief commander for his insubordination?"

Another outcry ensued. Only, this time, the loudest voices were those who sided with the general, aghast that Thaddreus would even suggest that he be vilified for his heroism. Others murmured an assent, but, with the general glaring down at them, were much less vocal.

Rogun let the notion play out, then smirked with cold amusement. "Should this body wish to waste time in pursuit of such allegations, I will be more than happy to address them. Were it not for me, this city would belong already to the enemy. A wiser man would keep that foremost in his mind."

Grunts and murmurs were drowned out by raucous approval.

"I wonder what our king might say," Thaddreus mumbled when the wave of noise had subsided, "were he still alive."

An obvious slight, meant to remind Rogun's supporters that the general's victory had not come without a terrible price.

But that was not Rogun's fault. Nor did he appear overly troubled by it.

"Even Torin, I'm sure, would recognize the need to comfort our citizens, by demonstrating to all that the conflict is well in hand."

"And is it?" Allion scoffed, raising his voice at last. "Krynwall may be safe for the moment, but our southern lands are evacuating to Kuuria, and we have yet to receive word from those farther out."

For more than a day now, messengers had been riding fast and furious across Pentania, bearing official tidings amid much rumor. News of events at Krynwall would just now be reaching the outer territories of Partha and Kuuria. The only return word had come from the Alsonian barony of Drakmar—and that word was less than encouraging. Apparently, both Nevik, baron of Drakmar, and Ghellenay, baroness of Palladur, had agreed to lead their people south for the protection of Kuuria and the coalition force assembled there. The decision had come after a conference with Commander Troy of Souaris, who had led a mounted division north on Allion's heels when it was believed Rogun—and perhaps Nevik—were planning an ambush against Torin and the crown. On even this count, details were sketchy. Of matters beyond, Allion knew nothing at all. Given the attack his city had faced, it might be that others had already fallen.

"Your friend's death is unfortunate," the general agreed after a moment of contemplation. Even this small concession took Allion by surprise. "For all our differences, the lad showed promise. Regardless, I daresay his loss is not as great as it could have been."

Allion glared, growing hot with anger. "And how is that, would you *daresay*?"

"Torin may have been the son of Sorl. But we all know it was the Sword that truly crowned him king."

Allion's hand slipped instinctively to the hilt of the Crimson Sword, sheathed at his waist. "What are you implying, General?"

"Only that Torin's greatest asset is still with us. Remind our people of that, and they will have less cause to mourn."

"A blade is nothing without its wielder," Allion reminded the other harshly. He would tolerate only so much disrespect, even from the dangerous general.

"Indeed," Rogun agreed, his narrowed gaze sending chills down Allion's back. "And it occurs to me that you are an archer, not a swordsman. Perhaps, for the sake of all, the weapon should be given over to one who can best use it."

Allion fought down a flutter of panic. "Such as?"

"If we are accepting nominations, I would suggest that the blade go hand in hand with the crown."

That raised mutters all around from those who had grown silent. Despite the general's unassuming tone, most understood what Rogun was really saying. Allion himself had known from the moment he learned of Torin's death that the general would make a bid for the Sword—and the throne. He just hadn't expected it to come this soon.

Still, Rogun had just uttered the best argument *against* surrendering the Sword to anyone at this juncture.

"I have no quarrel with that," Allion replied. It was what Torin himself had wanted, should the Sword's more immediate beneficiaries, Marisha and Allion, agree to it. "But we are in no position yet to elect a new king."

"Doubtless, there will be much discussion," Rogun sneered. He returned his attention to Thaddreus. "Only, bear in mind, every moment we delay is a moment in which we grant our enemy renewed confidence. To build upon our victory here, we must act swiftly and without hesitation."

A debate ensued, which the First Elder moved swiftly to quell. "Our regent is right," he offered hastily. "We must not rush a decision of that magnitude. Surely, even the general would have us wait at least until Baron Nevik arrives."

Rogun glared, then relented with a slight bow. Allion wondered what to make of his reaction. Was it only that he did not wish to appear overeager? Or did it suggest a specific confidence where Nevik was concerned? As the land's highest-ranking nobleman, Drakmar's baron would seem to be the general's chief rival. But Nevik had aided the general in his secret plot, after all, and thus far Allion had only Rogun's word as to why. Perhaps the pair had already conspired for this eventuality.

"So be it," the general allowed. "As I understand it, the baron will soon be en route?"

"If not already," Thaddreus affirmed. "He was said to be waiting only until Baroness Ghellenay had arrived at Drakmar to help escort their refugees alongside Commander Troy."

"Until then," Rogun said, "I recommend we appoint a military task force to ensure the Sword's safekeeping."

All eyes turned to Allion.

"*Until then*," he echoed sternly, "the Sword remains in *my* possession, or in the possession of those I deem fit to carry it."

"That talisman is our standard. We cannot risk—"

"You know well that our king willed the Sword to Marisha, and, as regent, I bear it now at her request. On this matter, I will not be challenged, General."

He was hanging by a thread, he knew. Rogun was but a step away from securing the support of the populace, with or without the blessing of the Circle. But Allion was still the land's appointed regent and, as such, had no intention of letting Rogun walk away with things. That included keeping the Sword until such time as he felt comfortable relinquishing it.

He forced himself to match stares with the general while the others observed in strained silence. To his surprise, Rogun was the first to blink.

"As you will," the general conceded, "though my recommendation stands."

Allion breathed a sigh of relief the moment Rogun looked away. Evidently, his strength of conviction had persuaded the general to let the matter lie—for now.

"I require an answer, then, to my initial demand," Rogun said, without a moment's loss of control. "Have I this body's commission to begin testing for the undead hiding among us? Or would you permit them to once again spread their disease?"

Allion turned his gaze toward Thaddreus. The typically calm First Elder appeared angry, desperate even. If seeking comfort, the regent would have to look elsewhere.

"We will take the general's proposal under advisement," the speaker determined, frowning at those who protested. "Until then, I'm sure the army has much to do in tending to the carnage that clogs our streets already."

As it had upon arrival, Rogun's gaze swept the Circle in count of his supporters. A sly smile suggested that he was not entirely displeased.

"We will reconvene tomorrow," the chief commander stated. "I expect the matter will be decided by then."

He spun from the table and marched for the exit, his lieutenants in tow. As soon as he'd gone, the debate resumed, though Allion continued to wonder what choice they'd truly been given.

VORRIC HAZE NODDED CURTLY TO those he passed in the outer hall. His angry visage did not invite discussion. While one or two bid greeting as if to beg further word, most of the noblemen and courtiers and servants that clogged the corridor seemed only too happy to clear his way.

As he rounded a corner, his eyes met those of the sentry posted at his door. The guardsman, engaged in casual talk with a chambermaid, straightened immediately. The woman stiffened as she turned, widened eyes betraying her sudden alarm.

"Elder Thaddreus," she greeted, "I beg your pardon. I was not given to expect your return."

Vorric Haze brushed past the obsequious scrubwoman. Inside, he slammed the door and slid the bolt. He needed some time to himself, free from the duties of the mortal whose guise he had taken.

Time in which to consider his untenable position.

General Rogun was a savior. Those who did not already believe it would not long remain unconvinced. Even now, Haze chafed at the ease with which the general and his supporters on the council had brushed aside the notion of insubordination—or worse, insurrection. Though Haze had known before suggesting it that he would never be able to jail the commander on such charges, a lengthy trial might at least have weakened Rogun's standing and bought the First Elder some time.

It would not be long now before the Circle sided with the general in its entirety. A few of the Elders, he knew, would dissent until the bitter end, but with half of them agreeing already to the idea of a citywide cleansing, these lone voices would soon be trampled. The cry for personal privacy could not withstand the people's growing demand for security. Haze himself would be subjected to the general's tests. And when found to be Illysp-possessed, he would be destroyed.

He stepped to the window, flush with fury and denial. Gazing out upon the city that had so nearly been his, he thought back to how matters had gone wrong. Due to his station, First Elder Thaddreus had been among the first to be taken and reborn. In the weeks that had followed, Vorric Haze had killed and raised more than a dozen himself—including a pair of Elders. His victims had claimed others in turn. They had done so carefully, patiently, as their leader, Kael-Magus—the one known outwardly as Darinor—had instructed.

Perhaps they should have worked faster. But why? With Kael-Magus away, and Allion and Marisha off in pursuit, there had been no one left behind who truly understood what they were up against. The city's defenses were hardly a threat. Rogun and the army had been dispatched to the south. And Evhan, captain of the City Shield, had been the primary seed with which Kael-Magus had sown the infestation. His orders had been clear: Start with Thaddreus, and do nothing to raise an alarm.

And they hadn't. There had been whispers, of course. Even in the beginning, fears and suspicions and false assumptions had abounded. But their execution had been flawless. In the course of supplanting Krynwall's leadership, Kael-Magus had seen to it that those most likely to uncover his plot were either reborn or distracted elsewhere. Using general confusion and various illnesses of the winter season as cover, Vorric Haze had helped to orchestrate a flawless takeover from within.

But Rogun had outwitted them, and in so doing had changed everything. Instead of rising up against an unguarded city, the force Kael-Magus had seeded had found itself in a vicious struggle against nearly the whole of Alson's armies. Recognizing this—and knowing well that his greatest value lay not in his combat skills but as one of the city's ruling advisors—Haze had kept to the side, waiting for the dust to settle. Doing so had spared him the immediate destruction so many of his kind had faced. Yet, with Rogun's military victory and the elimination of Kael-Magus, his own end remained clearly in sight.

He had to escape before the general discovered him; that much was evident. But he was determined to salvage something of Kael-Magus's plan before surrendering all to folly. This war would yet be waged on many fronts, and it had come to him to lead his kind. He would not fail as those before him had.

The afternoon sun burned against his flesh, but Haze felt only the fire of his own resolve. That Kael-Magus had signaled them to attack meant the information gathered by Torin concerning their enemies must have pleased him. The time for posturing had ended. Numbers and weapons and savagery were what mattered now, for ahead lay only bloodshed.

And rebirth.

He would have the Sword, Haze decided, before joining his Illychar brethren beyond these walls. In this, he would counter Rogun's blow. By arming his kind, yes, but more importantly, by depriving their enemies of the hope and strength the talisman fostered. If he gained nothing else, this alone might be enough—enough to make him lord of the Illychar, master of this world.

And he would have no better chance than right now.

But how? Since Torin's death, the former Fason and presiding regent had all but sequestered the blade along with himself and Marisha. The pair trusted virtually no one. And those they did . . .

One by one, Haze considered them—the members of that small inner circle—wondering who he might twist to his advantage. How, exactly, was not yet a concern, only that one or more might be malleable enough to serve him in some capacity, willingly or otherwise.

He turned, lost in private focus . . . and nearly tripped over a water bucket neglected by his chambermaid. In desperate need of strangling *someone*, he almost called to his guard to fetch her.

Then it struck him.

Seeking to unravel the truth of events, the Circle had interviewed dozens of potential witnesses. Aside from Allion and Marisha, only two had claimed any knowledge of Torin's return prior to his death: Pagus, the chief herald, and Stephan, the chief seneschal. Rogun, Haze suspected, had also known, based upon the foresight the general had shown in sending his commander-in-waiting, Zain, through the city's lower tunnels in search of any who might attempt to flee. Such intelligence might have come from any well-placed spy, including one that had been slain in the fighting. But Haze had wondered at the time of their testimony if either Stephan or Pagus—each a *confirmed* witness—might have served as Rogun's mole.

Now, upon focused reflection, Haze knew it. Not Stephan, for the aged fool was much too loyal to his city and king. But Pagus . . . Pagus was young and naive, full of ambition. The boy's narrative had included no mention of Rogun or Zain. Why would it, when some still whispered that Zain himself had assassinated Torin at Rogun's command? Had Pagus played any part in such treachery, he would surely seek to hide it.

The boy had refused to even look the general's way, Haze recalled, while testifying before the council. And though normally buoyant in mood and speech, the herald had been moping ever since beneath a pall of what had looked to be sadness—but might as easily be guilt.

He could be wrong, of course, but Vorric Haze was short on time, and limited in his options. He would make the boy his pawn, then decide how best to use him.

Rogun had won the day. He would not win the war.

CHAPTER THREE

"Are you sure about this?" Marisha asked.

In spite of everything—the fears, the doubts, the gut-wrenching pangs of sorrow and loss—Allion could have laughed.

"There is precious little I *can* be sure about anymore," he said instead. "But Rogun has already begun burning bodies, and I'll not allow him to burn this one."

"His might be the greater kindness."

Allion stopped what he was doing to glare at her.

"To make sure," she explained.

He held his glare, but ignored her comment and its dread implications. A moment later, he went back to his work, tying another rope into place.

"There is no need for this," she pressed. "It is an unwise and unnecessary risk."

"He would have done the same for me," Allion insisted, reaching for another length of rope.

"Torin would never have demanded this of you. Not under these circumstances. And if he had, then he was not the friend you believed him to be."

Allion whirled angrily. "What would you have me do, Marisha? Forsake everything I've been raised to believe? Pretend there's no difference between a consecrated burial and the flames of a communal pyre?"

"It would not be like that. He is still king, and would be granted the utmost respect. Many burn their dead."

"Heathens and savages!" Allion snapped. He recalled the screams of Corathel's men as they were sacrificed to the A'awari flames . . . the ritual slaying of Jaquith Wyevesces . . . his and Marisha's first kiss . . .

His hands clenched into fists. His eyes moistened with the threat of tears. When Marisha's hands reached for his face, he recoiled.

She halted, looking as if he had slapped her.

Rather than apologize, he turned back to the body—wrapped loosely in its burial shroud—and fished out a longer cord from the pile upon the floor. As he had with the knees and ankles, he cinched this one about his friend's waist.

When Marisha spoke again, her voice had changed. "Is this about burial customs? Or is this about us?"

Allion tensed. He wasn't sure *what* was happening anymore, could not seem to think clearly. All he really knew was that his friend was dead, had perished while defending them—knowing full well of their betrayal . . .

"There is no *us*," Allion muttered.

A chill silence settled over him. Already, he regretted the words, but would not take them back. Nor could he bring himself to turn and face Marisha, who he expected to go storming from the king's chambers.

When she did not, he thought that perhaps she hadn't heard him.

Her strained tone told him otherwise. "Should you not wait at least until Nevik arrives?"

"The sooner I am gone, the sooner I can return."

"Have you told your family?"

Allion shook his head. "They would only insist on accompanying me, and I would not have them do so."

"What about Stephan? Or does he not deserve to know?"

The strain was giving way to resentment. Allion did his best to ignore its sting, focusing on his work. "Stephan worries even more than you do. You will do a better job, I'm sure, of keeping things calm in my absence."

"Is there anything else you require of me, *my lord*?"

Her voice was tight, angry. Allion finished tying the final rope in place before rising again to face her.

"Only this," he said, taking up the scabbard and belt that lay propped beside the bed. From the scabbard's throat protruded the jeweled hilt of the Crimson Sword.

Marisha's glare could not mask her surprise.

"I will not risk it on the open road," he explained. "The blade belongs here, with you."

"I am no swordsman," she argued.

"Nor am I, as Rogun kindly pointed out."

"You are whatever is required of you. You always have been."

Allion wished he could believe that. He wished he could reach out and hold her, kiss her, comfort her, then and there, without insult to his dead friend. He spent a lot of time, these days, wishing for things that couldn't be.

"This talisman is our voice. Our people see it as a divine standard—one that even Rogun must respect." Allion sighed. "The general grows impatient. He seeks permission to go door to door in search of Illychar who may yet be hiding among us. There's no telling what he might do should the Circle refuse. Either way, we're but a step away from falling under his thumb."

"Perhaps we should *all* flee, then, while we can."

"I don't believe he yet dares take it by force. He can't risk a civil uprising on top of the threat we already face. The important thing is to make sure it stays within our hands, so that we're able to counter any unilateral moves he might make."

He had no right to ask this of her, he knew. But there was no one else he could trust.

"Rogun concerns me, yes," he added, when still she did not accept the sheathed blade. "But the Illychar frighten me more. As of now, we are all safer behind the city's walls—the Sword included."

Marisha met his gaze, her brilliant blue orbs holding him fast. "Then why insist on doing this?"

There was a softness to her tone once more, a more natural note of kindness and commiseration. Allion looked to the floor, then back at the bundled corpse behind him. "Because he deserves to go home and receive the proper rites. I owe him that much, at the very least."

If she recognized the guilt he was carrying, she did not speak to it. "And if I fail to hide the fact that the body is missing?"

"Then you'll tell them where I've gone, and why."

"Some will spread rumor that he was taken by the enemy."

"You will assure them he was not. Nor will it matter to most, provided you still possess the Sword."

He raised it once more, urging her silently to take it.

Her gaze dipped to the pommel. A hand came up, fingers brushing lightly against the flaming heartstones embedded along the grip and crosspiece. Finally, her other hand lifted, taking hold of the scabbard.

Allion carefully let go.

Marisha shook her head, as if disgusted by her own compliance. Before Allion could think of an appropriate reassurance, her eyes snapped back to his.

"He may be an Illychar already," she stated bluntly.

This time, Allion had no choice but to address the warning. "Should he revive, I'll kill him myself before I bury him."

"Will you?"

"You think I would see him become like your father?" She winced. Once again, he wished it were possible to swallow his hasty words. "I'm sorry."

But it was too late. The budding tenderness had passed, and the harshness had returned.

"And what of the Circle?" she asked brusquely. "I have no seat on that council, unless you care to formerly appoint me to yours—which, of course, you cannot do if you wish to carry out this other task in secret."

"What of it?" Allion asked slowly, softly.

"Should it fall to Rogun's influence, you and I will have precious little ground to stand upon, Sword or no."

She was right, of course. The Sword was theirs by royal writ, but they needed the City Elders, as representatives of the people, to support any stand they might take against Rogun. Had Allion himself not raised this same argument when Torin had determined to embark on Darinor's quest?

"If I set forth this night, I'll be gone no more than a day, returning by dawn after tomorrow. The Circle will hold together until then."

A baseless guarantee, and Marisha knew it. "Amid this unrest?"

"Go to Stephan, if you must. Or Nevik, when he arrives."

"You trust the baron to take our side, then?"

"I trust that if anyone can hold things together, it is you." That much, he believed wholeheartedly, and he stared deep into her eyes to prove it.

She did not respond, and as the silence became awkward, he wondered if he should say something more. He had to do this, if for no other reason than in hopes of laying his own demons to rest. Surely, despite all her protests, she understood—likely better than he. That was her gift: to know people and discern their sufferings better than they could themselves.

"I should check on Pagus," he said finally, unable to match her gaze any longer, "to see if all has been made ready. If you've anything left to say to him," he added, nodding toward Torin's bundled form, "I'll leave you to say it now."

He tried not to sound accusatory, for he certainly didn't blame her in any way for what had happened—between them, or to Torin. If there was indeed betrayal here, it was his alone. Nevertheless, he might have felt better if she were to show just a little less fortitude, and a little more sorrow.

With a light touch upon her shoulder, he slipped past and through the inner doorway, out into the sitting chamber beyond. He had nearly reached the latched door that would carry him to the outer hall when her voice stopped him in his tracks.

"When this is done, return to me guilt-free, or not at all."

Allion hesitated, his hand upon the iron pull. When he turned, he found her standing beneath the arch that separated the royal chambers, clutching the Sword by its scabbard. Light cast by the hearth's flames flickered upon her pale, implacable face.

Having no better response, he slipped the latch, stepped out into the hall, and closed the door behind him.

HEAD BOWED, PAGUS SCUFFED ALONG the gravel paths of the palace grounds. There were no torches along this route, no cressets or braziers to light the way, for it was a winding back course seldom traveled. The lantern he bore was his only aid in the moonlit darkness. And even this he kept shuttered, its glow muted, for he did not care to draw attention to himself.

Every so often, he would reach up with a soiled sleeve to wipe his dripping nose. The tears, for the most part, he had managed to keep in check. Nothing was ever set right by a woman's weeping, his father had always told him, and it seemed now that his father might have been correct. For on this, the second day of his lord king's death, he was surprised he had any left to shed. And all that lamenting hadn't changed a thing.

He'd been unable to help it, however, and none were more taken aback by the truth than he. He was not his mother or sister. He did not cry every time a baby bird fell from its nest or a dog was run over by a wagon. When the Red Death had taken his family, and he had gone to live with his uncle, a royal guardsman, he had been saddened, to be sure, but had acclimated quickly enough to his new life. Life, death—the two were inseparable, and there wasn't much a lad like him could do about either. So why fuss?

But with Torin, something within had seemed to snap, and he couldn't figure why that might be. A lack of appreciation for what the king had done, perhaps. Like most palace servants, he was well accustomed to being ordered hither and fro, kicked around like a lazy cat. He had never really taken offense at such treatment; while others let themselves be cowed or else muttered curses under their breath, he had simply smiled all the brighter and labored all the harder. His reactions had vexed some, but not Torin. The king was the one person, he now realized, to have ever accorded him a measure of courtesy and respect, treating him not as a callow youth, but as a young man whose enthusiasm was to be admired, and whose counsel was always welcome.

Pagus sniffed and slowed, picking his way now through an overgrown stand of brambles that crossed his path to scratch at the bailey wall. The pricks he suffered seemed well deserved. None other than the king himself could have elevated him to the position of chief herald. It was a calling Pagus had done nothing to seek and little to deserve, having performed his duties the same as always. That he had somehow found Torin's favor was a quirk of fate, not something for which he felt beholden. Nevertheless, he could have done better to express his gratitude.

Rather than act in a manner that might have contributed to the king's death.

His path came to an end at a weather-beaten portal in one of the old, abandoned guard towers. Withdrawing a key tied to a string around his neck, Pagus struggled with the lock until its rusted tumblers finally relented. How many times, he wondered, had he used this forgotten trail—its twists and turns and the keys to its gates provided him by the sneaky armorer, Faldron. Tonight, without a word of the truth to Allion as to how it had been discovered, he had used it to help slip Torin's body to an out-of-the-way stable, so that the regent could bear his friend from the city in order to bury him in secret.

Allion had thanked him for his assistance. Pagus had only shrugged, wanting once again to cry.

Never before had he seen the harm his actions might bring. Whispers and intrigues were a part of city life—particularly within a royal household. Why should he not profit from them when someone else would? Even when he'd delivered to Commander Zain the news of King Torin's return, even suspecting it could trigger a coup, Pagus had been untroubled. Not until he'd learned Torin had been killed—whether directly or indirectly because of his actions—had he come to hate himself for what he'd done.

On the verge of manhood, he was naught but a callow youth after all.

His thoughts continued to haunt him down darkened corridors and seldom-used passages, until he came at last to the wing that would lead to his private chambers. Chambers he would still be sharing with a dozen other servants and page boys, he recalled glumly, had it not been for the unrequited kindness of a slain king.

The door was unlocked, and he entered with his head still bowed. It was not until he had shed his cloak and hung it on a peg that he turned to find the intruder seated upon his sleeping pallet.

"Elder Thaddreus," he greeted, after a startled gasp. At the last moment, he remembered to bow. "Forgive my surprise."

"Your surprise is to be expected, though I do apologize if I frightened you."

Pagus brushed aside the concern, though his heart continued to thrum. The man's words did not sound threatening, but his very presence was highly irregular. "To what do I owe the honor of your visit, my lord?"

"I've been looking for you for quite some time. I finally decided to come here to wait."

He'd been found out. Zain or someone else had betrayed him as a spy. His would be a slow, painful death. "How can I be of service to my lord?"

The speaker of the Circle did not move. Pagus wondered how long he had been waiting.

"To begin with, I wonder if you might tell me where you have been."

"Errands, my lord, for . . ." He started to lie, then thought better of it. "For Master Allion, my lord."

"And what would those errands be?"

"They . . . they were of a private nature, my lord."

"Private to whom?"

Pagus began to sweat.

"You needn't fear answer, my boy. I am not your enemy."

Though warm in tone, the words sent a shiver down Pagus's spine. "Of course not, my lord. But I was asked to keep quiet, you see."

"Ah, that I do. Would it help you to know, then, that I already have some idea as to what you were about?"

He considered bolting, but his quarters were small, and he wasn't certain he'd be able to open the door before Thaddreus seized him. Besides, the old man likely had soldiers stationed nearby, ready to respond.

"Have I committed an offense, my lord?"

"That depends. One of my pages claims to have seen you with Master Allion some time ago, pushing a barrow full of linens through the palace. A curious job for regent or herald, it must be said. And it has just been reported to me that our regent is now en route from the city. Would you care to tell me where he is going?"

"I . . ." This time, he went with the lie. "I do not know, my lord. I suspect he is riding forth to greet the imminent arrival of Baron Nevik."

Pagus could have sworn that the Elder's face darkened. The stern brow lowered, and the grim mouth tightened. "And did he take the Sword with him?"

"The Sword?" he echoed, feigning ignorance. "I'm sure I do not know, my lord. 'Tis not a herald's place to inquire about such things."

"Ah, but you are a curious boy, are you not? A boy who takes note of many things he may or may not be meant to see."

It was Pagus's turn to scowl. His taste for intrigues had soured. Whatever game the Elder was trying to drag him into, he wanted no part of it.

"I'm not sure I'm aware of my lord's meaning."

"Mercy, lad!" the Elder exclaimed, leaping to his feet with an urgency and swiftness Pagus had never seen in the old man. The boy hunkered, his back to the door, half tempted to draw his knife. But already, Thaddreus spoke as if to mollify him. "These are dangerous and uncertain times. With the passing of our lord king, our city and government may seem ripe for the taking. Surely I do not have to tell a clever lad like you that there are those who may choose to twist these events to their own advantage."

Rogun. He was speaking of the general who would be king.

"It may be," Thaddreus continued, crouching, "that some have already played us foul. You can see this, can you not?"

Pagus managed to nod. Was the speaker of the Circle suggesting that the rumors of assassination might be true? If so, had Pagus himself been the one to facilitate it?

"I can sense your grief," Thaddreus went on. "I share it. Torin was a fine and worthy king. To grant individuals such as us positions of such high esteem . . ." He allowed the thought to hang. "'Tis a rare leader who is willing to listen more than he speaks. Am I right?"

The Elder's tone had grown soft, reassuring, even as his eyes blazed with cold intensity. Pagus forced himself to respond. "What do you ask of me, my lord?"

"Only that you be my ally in helping to defend the crown against all enemies. There are others, young Pagus, who might continue the work King Torin has begun. But in order to defeat the evil without, we must first weather challenges from within. You understand this, yes?"

"Does my lord speak of General Rogun?"

Thaddreus's taut smile vanished quickly. "It is but a matter of time, I fear, before Rogun lays claim to the Sword, one way or another. We must be vigilant, and protect against that eventuality at all costs. Would you agree?"

Pagus nodded slowly.

"So, I ask again, did Master Allion take the Sword with him?"

The boy could almost believe the other's sincerity. At the same time, he suspected what was really being asked of him, and did not like it. Though he couldn't be sure that his spying had played any part in Torin's fall, he was loath to risk harm upon anyone else by returning to his informant's ways.

"Aye, my lord." He tried to look the other in the eyes while saying it, but failed to do so. "Aye, I believe he did."

When he looked up again, Thaddreus's features had tightened with renewed anger. Or so he thought. A moment later, the old man was all gentle seriousness once more.

"I see. Well, then, I ask you this: Keep an eye out, lad. For both the Sword and its wielder. The general is not a bad man, but he will do bad things, hurt innocent people, to accomplish what he believes he must. Help me see that the Sword is kept safe and not put at risk in any way. Can you do that for me?"

Again the intensity of the old man's gaze forced Pagus's to the floor.

"Look at me, boy!" The old man grasped him by the arms with a savage strength.

"Aye, my lord. Aye, I will keep watch."

"And let me know where both are at all times."

"Aye, if that is your wish, my lord."

Thaddreus stepped back. "Good. In gratitude, and to see that you keep your oath, I offer you this gildron."

He pressed the promised coin into Pagus's palm. The boy could not even bring himself to look at it.

"There are more where that came from, I promise. That one merely seals our agreement. A goodly sum, as you know, but a small price for our continued freedom. Yes?"

"Aye. Thank you, my lord."

"Do not disappoint me, boy."

Pagus stared up at the old man, hoping to make him leave. "I will do my best, my lord."

Thaddreus grunted, then gripped his shoulder in what passed for acknowledgment but might as easily have been a warning. Pushing him aside, the First Elder reached for the door, then vanished down the hall.

For a while after the other had gone, Pagus held his coin in silence. Finally, when the old man's footsteps had faded, he flung it across the room and fell to his mattress in tears.

CHAPTER FOUR

Allion clicked his tongue and cracked his whip, urging his wagon team onward. The gate guards had barely looked at his cargo. To them, it was just another load of rotting corpses being driven from the city.

He was, perhaps, being overly cautious. Torin was *his* friend, and he the king's regent. It might have been that, had he explained himself, no one would try to stop him. But he wasn't taking any chances. There had been many who protested as their slain ones were being dragged away to be burned, on order of the army and of the Circle—an order that Allion himself had done nothing to fight. From what they'd been given to know, it was the only way to protect those fallen from rising again as Illychar. Some did not yet believe, and saw only that those precious to them were being desecrated, denied a proper mourning and burial. But Allion, still haunted by the final look in Evhan's eyes, understood that they had little choice.

Even so, he would not allow his friend's remains to share the fate of these others. This was not Torin's home; he had never belonged here. His life's road complete, he would be laid to rest where it had begun: in Diln, beneath the boughs of the Kalgren Forest, among friends and loved ones. And this was not a matter Allion would chance to debate. The inherent risks, he had decided, were manageable enough.

An evening breeze, unseasonably mild, rustled his cowl and brushed his cheeks. Spring was well on its way. Or perhaps it was only the heat of the fires that warmed this night.

The first came into view as he continued east around the hill. Its red glow painted the sky like a molten sunrise, and already he could see the tips of the flames spitting from their bowl, forked limbs clawing toward the heavens.

At a branch in the switchback roadway, a soldier gestured in the direction he should follow. Allion nodded without showing his face, and whipped his horses past.

From there, he but followed the long line of wagons and barrows pouring down and around the ragged hills that formed Krynwall's base. It was a sobering sight, to see just how many had fallen.

The burnings themselves were no haphazard affair, but a regimented effort carefully planned and closely monitored. The closer Allion got, the more soldiers he encountered. There were blazes that had been tamped down until the winds changed, to avoid blowing ash and smoke across the city. Some were just being lit, while others raged so hot that the tenders allowed no one within fifty paces. At a main checkpoint, Allion received orders as to where his load would be deposited. Using a cloth to cover his nose and mouth, the hunter rode on.

His eyes stung and his throat burned when at last he came upon a new pit, freshly dug, into which bodies were just now being laid. Laborers and taskmasters of countless number and untold variety swarmed the pitted landscape, which smelled of rot and burning flesh and tilled earth. Diggers and woodcutters and pyre-builders and flame-bearers and others went about their work with stoic resignation. Those who handled the bodies did so, for the most part, with proper dignity. The soldiers acting as overseers would tolerate no disrespect, Allion supposed, where it concerned those they had battled alongside.

The civilians, sorted and separated from the men-at-arms, were carried off to different pits. The treatment of these appeared much the same, only with less solemnity and few prayers or rites to speak of. The priests and their acolytes, it appeared, could only attend to so many souls at one time.

Better to have died a commoner, however, than an Illychar. The latter, referred to by most as "reavers," came in all shapes and sizes—though in quantities much smaller than Allion would have hoped, given the overall number of dead. Elves, mostly—Finlorian. But Allion spotted a pair of ogres and even a goblin among them, as well as several whose original race he could only guess at. These were handled with nothing short of disgust—kicked and tossed like vermin, spat and even pissed upon, showered with taunts and curses and wards to protect against the spread of their evil. A baseless prejudice, really. After all, while in some cases difficult to tell, there were many of their own kind—such as Evhan—who had been confirmed as Illychar. From what Allion could see, most of these were being treated with pity, rather than contempt, as if their human shell made them somehow less vile.

"Oy! You going to lend a hand, or let your arse blister while we do all the work?"

Allion turned to regard the stranger, a giant of a man with twisted features and a gnarled bent. After waving in apology, the hunter tied off the reins to his team, double-checked the brake, and climbed over the bench to assist with the unloading of bodies from the wagon bed.

His load had already been sorted before leaving the city, wrapped in canvas and marked according to station. Fasor all—members of the City Shield. He had not wanted to give the workers—or soldiers—reason to look down upon him.

The decision seemed to have the desired effect.

"Stout lads, these, and brave," the crooked giant observed solemnly. "Shame to see so many struck down in their prime."

Allion wondered how exactly the man had determined this, since the faces of the fallen were covered. Most likely, he was speaking in general terms. Either way, Allion was not going to disagree.

"We'll overcome," he replied huskily. "We Alsonians always do."

The other grunted and clapped his shoulder, without causing so much as a hitch in their efforts.

When naught but bloodstained straw remained, the giant and his team of unloaders moved on to the next wagon drawn up in line. Allion saw them off with a workmanlike nod, climbed back upon the bench, and took up his reins.

Time to be about his real business.

He turned not toward the city, but continued down along the road wending east. He had driven no more than twenty lengths when a voice cried out.

"You there! Halt!"

A battalion commander, Allion realized, and quickly reined his horses and wagon to a stop.

He bowed low as the colonel drew close, a personal regiment of a dozen or more in tow.

"I beg pardon, sir. Is there a problem?"

"You've just completed a delivery, no?"

"Yes, sir. A team of Fasor killed within the walls."

"Then where are you taking this cart?"

"I—I was returning it to my sister's farm for the night," Allion stammered.

The colonel shook his head. "All carts commissioned for deliveries are to return to the city immediately for reloading. Upon decommission, they are to be destroyed."

Allion's stomach lurched. "But my sister—"

"Your sister can apply for compensation for commissioned articles. But my orders are clear. I will not risk spreading this contagion."

It was difficult to fault the man for such precautions. And yet, Allion cringed, recognizing full well that a dangerous turn had been taken, and fearing where such paranoia on the part of his countrymen might lead.

"On whose authority was this order given?" he asked, as innocently as he could manage.

"The highest you'll find," the colonel responded.

Within his cowl, Allion's frown deepened. The Circle had issued no such edict before his departure. "Does the army mean to burn all drivers and handlers, too?"

"Only them that challenge orders," came the curt reply.

It made little sense, Allion knew, to treat this like a form of plague spread by contact. But neither was this the time or place for that argument. All of a sudden, he regretted his decision not to attempt to sneak Torin out through the secret passages beneath the city. Those segmented pathways would have been virtually impossible to navigate with his friend's deadweight, and much of the network had been placed under heavy patrol by Commander Zain. But if he'd known in the beginning that this would be the result of his efforts . . .

"Your choice is simple," the colonel added in his clipped tones. "Either return to the city at once, or we destroy this wagon, here and now."

His ruse was up. He would have to reveal himself—and likely his true purpose—if he meant to escape. Even then, he had no doubt that Rogun himself would take part in the final decision before he was allowed to leave.

He was about to draw back his hood when the thunder of an approaching rider stole his—and then the colonel's—attention.

"Colonel Venmore," the messenger greeted, after pulling his steed to a thrashing halt. "Commander Zain bids you gather as many as can be spared to join him at once at the head of the Hanoan Promontory."

"What is it?"

"A delegation under Drakmar banner approaches, sir. The commander has been ordered to welcome it in full force."

The colonel glanced back at the work taking place around him. "I don't have time for welcoming committees," he muttered.

"Sir?"

"Strike that, Corporal. Inform the commander that we are on your heels."

"Upon your command, sir."

"Given."

The nameless rider twisted his mount's head and put heel to flank, spurring it back up the rise.

Just like that, Allion was forgotten, as Venmore turned to his aides and runners and issued the necessary orders.

"You there," the colonel added before turning away, and Allion knew—without a great deal of surprise—that he was not to be let off so easy. "I would see you back here within the hour with another load. If not, and I learn that this cart has traveled anywhere other than straight back to the city, I will hunt it down and burn it with both you and your horses strapped to the traces. Is that clear?"

Allion bowed in his seat, letting the colonel believe that his threat alone was sufficient to ensure compliance.

To be safe, he drove halfway back to the city before daring to veer off onto one of the lesser roadways that would circle the city west and north before carrying him around to his ultimate destination in the east. The roundabout route would add an hour or more to his journey, and would be difficult to navigate in the darkness, but there was no help for it now.

More than once, he glanced south along the line of slopes and ridges, down to where hundreds of torches lit the night almost as brightly as one of the giant funeral fires. He was fiercely tempted to go and demand answers of Nevik, but better that he use the diversion provided by the baron's arrival to make his escape.

His thoughts darkened by recollection of the task that lay ahead, Allion hunkered in his seat, driving his wagon—and its hidden cargo—into the night.

MARISHA STEPPED OUT ONTO HER balcony as bells tolled the Raven's Hour—the last before midnight. Though it had been a long day, her restless thoughts and churning emotions would allow her no sleep.

Even at this distance, she could smell the smoke from the fires that wrapped the city on three sides. So much death. So much suffering. Would it ever end?

Worse, she had contributed to it. She had spent more time with Darinor than anyone. She should have been the one to figure out the truth of his Illysp possession. Had she not been such a little girl, blinded by her devotion to a beloved father she'd not seen in more than twelve years . . .

But that was not the whole of it. For it was not just love that had blinded her, but personal need. The need to learn who she was and who she was meant to be. Having learned the truth of her heritage as one bearing the blood of the Entients, she had succumbed to that need like never before, defending her father—the only one who could hope to teach her about herself—against all suspicions and challenges. Had she not been so selfish, he might have been exposed much sooner, and the deaths of thousands avoided.

But "what if" and "might have been" were of no help to anyone now, and so she tried not to dwell on them. She had two choices: become a slave to her devastation, or pick up the pieces and move forward as best she could, encouraging others to do the same.

She had chosen the latter; the alternative could grant only desolation and madness. What she hadn't anticipated, and found much harder to accept, was Allion's withdrawal from her for doing so. Though he would never say that he blamed her for Torin's death or her father's treachery, he had regarded her these past two days as if she were no more than a reminder of his pain. This, more than anything else, had stung her to the core.

She believed she recognized the actual source of his feelings. Though it was her fault as much as his, and though Torin had shown no animosity upon learning of it, they had in fact formed a forbidden relationship in the king's absence. Not quite lovers, but near enough. In consequence, Allion was being devoured by guilt, and the more she tried to assuage that guilt, the more sullen and angry he had become—as if her overtures for strength were a temptation he must resist. What she considered moving on, he perceived as callousness toward Torin, her onetime betrothed.

Nothing could be farther from the truth.

Hence her decision to let him go forth on this hazardous and potentially foolhardy venture—not because she'd been persuaded by his arguments, but to demonstrate her love and respect for both men. A terrible sacrifice on her part, trusting him to return safely on his own. Whether Allion recognized it or not, he was all she had left. Yet he was no good to her or the kingdom a broken man. Unless he could come to terms with his grief, he might as well be dead.

The stars blurred as tears came to her eyes, but she gripped the stone balustrade and blinked them away. Though it had pained her to say it, she'd meant what she had said about burying either his guilt or himself along with his friend. For there was still much to be done. They knew not the whole of her father's Illysp-driven plan, nor quite how to combat it. They could not even be certain of what things he had told them were true, and which were lies. This war was bigger than Allion and Marisha, more important than their personal quest for love and happiness. No matter what became of his feelings for her, the hunter, as a keystone soldier in the conflict to come, could not go around carrying such anchors as he now bore.

Without quite meaning to, Marisha drew forth the Pendant of Asahiel from where it hid against her breast. Clutching the gleaming heartstone, she lifted her gaze to the heavens and prayed once more for Allion's safety, asking that this act of laying his friend to rest be enough to heal his wounds and bring him peace—and, should it please the Ceilhigh, that they be given a chance to find the joy they deserved, when the time was right.

So intense was her yearning that she did not recognize, at first, the knocking upon the door behind her. When it came again, louder and more insistent, her thoughts drew suddenly back into focus. Who could be calling upon her at this hour?

With her next breath, a chill seeped through her. *Allion*. Something had happened to him. What else could it be?

Fighting down a sense of panic, she belted her robe and strode toward the chamber door, tucking the Pendant away. Her only hesitation came at the doorway to her adjacent bedchamber, where she glanced through to see the Sword hanging from one of her bedposts. She started to go for it when the knock sounded yet again, and the voice of her guardsman carried through the oaken portal.

"My lady?"

Neglecting the talisman, she moved up against the door to answer. "I'm awakened, Bearer. What is it?"

"Ah, my lady. Forgive me, but you have a visitor: the young Master Pagus. He claims it cannot wait."

Pagus. Allion's only accomplice in this night's endeavor. Her heart beat faster.

"Shall I send him away, my lady?"

"Let me hear his voice."

"It is I, my lady."

Taking a deep breath, she removed the bolt and opened the door a crack. Pagus stood just beyond her sentry's warding pike, eyeing her urgently.

"You may admit him, Bearer."

"As you will, my lady."

A moment later, she bolted the door and asked the question to which she feared an answer. "What has happened?"

The chief herald shifted nervously. "Forgive me, my lady, I thought . . . I mean I—"

"Pagus, look at me. Is Allion all right?"

"Master Allion is fine, my lady, or was when I left him. But . . ."

"But what? What have you come to tell me?"

He met her gaze at last. "Elder Thaddreus, my lady. He came to me just a few short hours ago, was waiting for me in my chambers, actually. He asked . . . My lady, he asked about the Sword. He wished to know if Master Allion had taken it."

She glanced again to where the weapon hung in the adjacent chamber. Pagus's eyes followed. "I see. And what did you tell him?"

"I lied, my lady. I told him that it was with Master Allion. He expressed concern that the blade be kept safe. But I . . ." His eyes fell.

"Tell me, Pagus."

"I believe he is up to something, my lady. I cannot say why, but I have a terrible feeling. It was the way he looked at me. He wanted so badly to know where it was—the Sword, I mean. He claims Rogun will try to take it, but I'm not sure that is the sole reason for his interest."

He stared at her for a moment, then looked to his feet as if feeling suddenly foolish.

"I'm sorry, my lady. I should not have disturbed your rest. But I couldn't sleep. I thought you should—"

"You were right to tell me, Pagus," she said, cupping his chin with her hand. "We've no one but ourselves to count on. While the speaker's concern for the Sword comes as no surprise, it troubles me that he should try to use you so." She smiled reassuringly. "Go now. Get some sleep. Let me worry about the speaker and any others who may take an interest in what does not belong to them."

The boy nodded uncertainly. "Yes, my lady."

She ushered him toward the door and drew back the bolt. "Off to bed, then."

She had only barely cracked the portal ajar when it flew inward, smacking Pagus in the chin and sending him sprawling back into her. A stream of bodies came pouring through, clad in armor and with weapons drawn. No sooner had she landed on her back than the tip of a sword was leveled at her throat.

She glared at her assailant—a city guardsman—then looked to the doorway, where the body of her sentry was being dragged inside by a pair she recognized as City Elders. Blood washed his throat and chest, glistening in the firelight.

Then Thaddreus entered, closing the door gently behind him.

Marisha tried to cry for help, but the shifting swordsman smothered her shriek with his gloved hand.

"If she screams again, kill the boy," Thaddreus ordered coldly.

She looked to Pagus, certain she had been betrayed. The young herald, sitting upright with the tip of a pike pressed against the back of his neck, stared back at her with frantic eyes.

"If *he* should do so," Thaddreus added, addressing one of the dagger-wielding Elders, "cut off her feet."

Four henchmen in all: the pikeman warding Pagus, the swordsman at her back, the City Elder at her feet—Ashwar, if she wasn't mistaken—and the other, Emric, who had helped drag her sentry inside. The latter stood beside Thaddreus, her guardsman's blood upon his dagger.

"Better still," Thaddreus decided, "gag them both while I search the chambers."

Marisha's thoughts raced. Fool that she'd been, she'd left the Sword hanging in full view. She had only seconds in which to act before Thaddreus—or perhaps the man who had once been Thaddreus—lay claim.

The blade at her neck fell away as the swordsman stuffed a rag in her mouth and, with a heavy cord, roped it in place. Now was her chance, but if she were to resist, would she not be sentencing Pagus to death?

Her gaze shifted back to the boy. Seeing the conflict in her face, he made the decision for her.

"No!" he shouted through his own gag, lunging from beneath the pike and drawing his knife.

As the others looked to the boy's distraction, Marisha rolled to her knees and elbowed her captor in the mouth.

Pagus's muffled cry spurred her on. "Run!"

Her hands and feet dug at the carpet as she raced toward her bedchamber. Thaddreus had a step on her, but he too had stopped to look back on his captives. His hesitation allowed her to barrel past with a shove, leaving him to stumble and trip on his robes.

Once inside the next room, she seized the Sword and tossed aside its sheath. Thaddreus had recovered by then, but skidded to a halt, gripping the inner doorframe lest he impale himself upon the Sword's tip. Awash with the euphoria the talisman unleashed within her, Marisha advanced, forcing him back into the receiving chamber, her first thought that Pagus needed her.

The young chief herald had done a remarkable job against those trying to kill him. The swordsman assigned to her, along with Elder Ashwar, had come up behind Thaddreus and were ignoring the lad, but it was still two to one against him. As she rejoined the fray, Pagus tore his knife from where it twisted in the side of the pikeman, then slipped a strike from Elder Emric before gashing the man's leg from behind. Whirling around in the same movement, Pagus plunged his blade into the Elder's heart.

The dagger came free, and the boy searched for his next target. He froze, however, upon seeing Marisha with the Sword. In that moment's delay, the pikeman seized him from behind, pressing the haft of his weapon against Pagus's throat and pinning the lad tight against his armored chest.

Pagus thrashed and squirmed as Emric, who should have been dead, rose from his knees. The Elder did not strike right away, but looked to Thaddreus. When Thaddreus nodded, Emric reversed grip upon his own dagger and threw a forearm across the boy's stomach, blade leading. Pagus's belly opened, and steaming entrails spilled forth.

Marisha screamed against the gag in her mouth. Pagus's eyes watered as they remained locked on hers. His knife slipped from his hand. When he tried to speak, only blood poured from his lips.

The pikeman held firm until the body went slack, then let it slump to the floor.

"See what you have done, my lady?" Thaddreus teased, retreating toward the fallen boy while all four of his henchmen fanned to either side.

Eyes still fixed on the ghastly sight, Marisha kept the Sword raised and held her ground, even as the noose tightened.

"Surrender the blade, and the same need not happen to you. We can make it quick, and for the most part painless. Else we can suffocate you with your own screams."

Marisha reached up to tear at the gag, but it was too tight. Meanwhile, the guardsman who had tied it tested her defenses. The Sword swept out, driving him back, before arcing around to discourage Ashwar, on her opposite flank. Both men sneered, yet their hatred was unmistakable.

She let the gag be, knowing that she would never loosen the knot with a single hand, and gripped the Sword with both.

Thaddreus continued to mock her. "Come, my lady, you are no swordsman."

Neither are you, she thought, recalling her earlier exchange with Allion.

But her own doubts weighed on her. She was a healer, not a fighter. She knew the basic forms of dagger and shortsword, but her meager skill did not encompass broadswords. Even with two hands upon its hilt, the Sword of Asahiel felt much too big for her, its heft and reach awkward and unwieldy. Were it not for its divine influence, she was certain she would already be dead.

She tried at once to banish the thought. She knew from experience—both hers and Torin's—that the blade acted as an extension of the bearer's will. Only the gods could tell her how, exactly. But she understood well enough to know that the weapon's power would not compensate for her own uncertainty.

"Perhaps you mean to hold us at bay until help arrives," Thaddreus taunted. "If that is the case, I fear you are in for a long night."

Again he was right. Whatever sentries might have spied them at this late hour would have given little thought to their dealings. A trio of City Elders, escorted by a pair of Fasor, was hardly cause for alarm.

Her adversaries closed further. The sound of her own breathing sawed in her ears, harsh and ragged. Her question as to whether these were traitors or Illychar had been answered. Against the five of them, what chance did she have?

A wielder of the Crimson Sword never tired. And yet it seemed to grow heavier in her hands as the cold truth bowed her shoulders. *Allion*, she thought hopelessly, *forgive me*.

"Take her!"

Somehow, she rose to meet their charge. In a whirlwind of motion, they came at her, various weapons cleaving the air at odd angles. The swordsman died first. He knew there would be no trading blows, and so executed a high feint before driving his weapon around in a low arc. Marisha ignored the former and cut short the latter, sending his blade off in pieces and his head rolling after.

Daggers whistled past her ears as she dodged and spun. Ashwar fell, clutching his severed leg. The pikeman tore a hole in her fluttering robe, but missed her flesh. When the tip struck the wall, she split its shaft with a downward arc, then swept around and whipped a stroke across his back. Crimson flames erupted along the blade as it sliced through leather and mail like sodden parchment, skin and bone like air. The cut was so swift and clean that the torso did not slide from its perch until the legs had toppled.

The flames licked blood from blade and retreated within, leaving the talisman unblemished, its radiance undimmed.

Emric struck her with a lowered shoulder, slashing wildly. She fell back a step, onto a central rug. Another slash drew blood from her forearm. She could have prevented it, but sensed in the instant before it happened the small price it would exact. Marisha paid it gladly in order to raise the Sword high and bring it crashing down upon her assailant's head.

A perfect strike would have cleaved the man from crown to groin. But her focus on him had been so strong that she hadn't considered her feet. A sudden jerk by Thaddreus tore the rug out from under her, causing her to stumble. Her killing stroke slid sideways, exiting at Emric's waist as she fell. When her hands separated in an instinctive effort to catch herself, that which clutched the Sword struck the edge of a table.

The blade skittered from her grasp and hit the floor on the other side.

The savage euphoria left her as if the wind had been blasted from her lungs. The warmth from the Pendant seemed but a distant reminder of its rush. She rolled to her feet, but slipped in a river of blood. Thaddreus was diving for the Sword again. She scrabbled desperately, even flung aside a vase and toppled an impeding chair, but was too late. Her fingers brushed the blade as Thaddreus seized it by the hilt and snatched it away.

He crouched there for a moment, gaping as if astounded by the waves of power now coursing through him. As he rose, Marisha found herself backing away in helpless denial.

"It is more wondrous than I'd imagined," Thaddreus wheezed.

Marisha knew what he meant. Witnessing the blade, bathing in its aura, was nothing compared to handling it. Even that, she knew, was an experience largely affected by the glory one attributed to it—explaining why strangers in a room might not even recognize its presence, and a man who knew nothing of the talisman could carry it without feeling a thing.

The former First Elder, it seemed, knew well what he had attained, and was enraptured by the prospects.

"Ceilhigh be praised," he said. "With this, their world becomes mine."

Marisha had no response. She considered trying to rush past him for the exit, but a step in that direction brought his focus back to her.

"My world might have a queen," he suggested with a lewd smile.

She stepped away from him, back toward the balcony. Bodies twitched throughout the chamber. Ashwar, whose leg she had taken, clawed at the floor in anguish and fury, struggling to rise. She had killed the rest, but had failed to slay Thaddreus. And with that, she had failed all.

The First Elder came forward, and Marisha hastened her retreat. Before she knew it, she stood outside upon the terrace, pressed up against the balustrade.

"Don't be foolish," Thaddreus hissed. "'Tis not as you fear. Eternal life, for but a moment's pain. A just trade."

Tears and sweat stung Marisha's eyes. All she could think of was what a fool she had already been. She never should have allowed Allion to leave. She should have fought better, been stronger, when she'd had the chance. Now, her only option seemed clear.

She risked a quick glance over the stone rail. A deep pond lay far below, but its area was small and ringed with boulders. Should she jump, she just might make it. But if her aim proved poor . . .

The mere thought made her dizzy, so she forced her gaze back to her chambers. Thaddreus had reached the edge of the terrace. Beyond, Ashwar stood now upon his remaining leg, unthreatened by the loss of stagnant blood dripping from the wounded stump.

She looked to those who could have aided her. Her sentry slumped lifelessly against the far wall, blood spilling from his mouth and the deep slice across his throat. Pagus, as brave as he was foolish, lay facedown in a heap of his own intestines. Their deaths, it seemed, had merited nothing.

Still, Marisha refused to go quietly. She would rather her body be destroyed in communal fire than become an Illysp vessel.

Thaddreus lunged, seeking to trap her. Before she could reconsider, Marisha swung her legs up and over the rail, casting herself to the wind.

CHAPTER FIVE

T̲HE TENDONS IN HIS WRIST strained as Allion tightened the final strap, cinching the leather band about the frame of the simple litter. When satisfied that his canvas-wrapped cargo was securely fastened, he stepped back to survey his work. All at once, his eyes began to moisten with emotions he could no longer seem to control. He had driven most of the night to reach this point, a long, lonely progression of hours spent in pained remembrance and soulful reflection. His thoughts were ragged, his emotions raw, and he had not yet begun what he had come here to do.

He stepped toward his wagon, parked aside the forested road. The bulky cart could carry him no farther, but had served its purpose well. The litter had been tied to its undercarriage, while Torin's body had been stowed in a hidden lockbox, cleverly concealed beneath the bench seat. Only a trained eye would note that the seat's primary storage bin was shallower than it should have been, or be able to uncover the trapdoor to the secondary compartment, accessible only from below. An unlawful design, clearly built and used for smuggling. When asked where he had acquired such a wagon, Pagus had claimed that it had been bequeathed along with store and tools to a young friend of his, Tam, upon the death of Tam's master, an armorer by the name of Faldron.

A good lad, Pagus. Enthusiastic and resourceful. So focused had Allion been on their task that he had neglected to tell the boy just how much he appreciated the helpful efforts. He would be sure to do so, he decided, just as soon as he returned to Krynwall.

He crawled beneath the wagon long enough to close the trapdoor to the smuggler's box, then unfastened the digging spade that had been lashed in place beside the litter. Finding no better place for it, he shoved the long-handled tool beneath the leather straps he'd used to tie Torin to the litter, then set off to retrieve his horses, which he had set to rest and graze in a tiny glen just off the roadway. Neither seemed too happy about resuming this journey, but Allion cared little for their complaints. With one hitched to the litter and the other tied off behind, Allion left the empty roadway and set forth through the trees.

It was a dense, uneven trail he followed, grown denser in the many weeks since it had last seen regular use. Darkness pressed him, but he knew this route well enough to walk it in his dreams.

He tried not to listen to the litter as it scraped and bounced along the overgrown path, focusing instead on the potential approach of any enemy. While one hand held his mount's lead rope, the other gripped his hunting knife. It was one of the main reasons he had sought to do this in private. He hadn't wanted to endanger Marisha or any members of his family by allowing them to come. If the Illychar gathered at Krynwall had been driven forth, there was a good chance he might stumble upon them here, in the concealing reaches of the Kalgren Forest. As he stood little chance of defeating even one of the possessed creatures by himself in his ragged state, his best hope was to simply escape their attention.

He had done well enough so far. The highway leading east had been deserted. All farmsteads had been abandoned. Birds and wildlife had been scarce—hauntingly so, here within the forest. Perhaps that meant the Illychar were still about, hunting for prey. Or perhaps even they had moved on.

Allion was not certain he cared either way. Though he carried his bow and arrows, the weapon was not even strung. Part of him wished that his enemies would come and take him—relieve him of his misery and pain. In a way, he envied his fallen friend. For Torin, the struggle was already ended. For the rest of them, it had scarcely begun.

And what was he to fight for? He cared little about Krynwall. He cared even less about any hidden treasures the future might have in store. Chasing his dreams had brought nothing but grief and betrayal. Performing his duties had resulted only in loss. Weary of fighting, he simply wanted things to be as they had been before.

He paused as he realized where he stood—upon the rim of a small clearing that lay within a wooded hollow. One of their favorite archery grounds, Allion recalled, and the one in which they had first heard Queen Ellebe's startled cry. This was where it had all begun. Her arrival—and their rush to respond—had led to the rest: Torin's quest, Diln's destruction, the drawing of the Sword, the unleashing of the Illysp, Torin's death . . .

Allion clenched his eyes against the flood of imagery. The truth, so terrible and fresh, still seemed to lack a solid edge. It was more like a flame, bright and scorching and difficult to grasp. Even now, he could scarcely fathom how that single event had triggered so much death and devastation.

His lead horse tossed its head. The trailing one whickered impatiently. Flush with sorrow and regrets, Allion marched on.

He tried to see the forest as it had once been. It was easier out here, removed from the village center that had been burned to cinders and trampled into the earth by those who had hunted them. Having returned well after Torin's team had gone through and buried the remains, Allion had been spared much of the toil and grief his friend had endured in laying so many friends and loved ones to rest.

Now it was his turn.

It might have been easier had he been able to understand how Torin had died, exactly, or what his death had won them. Certainly, his victory over Darinor represented a tremendous counterblow to the Illysp conquest. But was it enough to alter the final outcome, or would they only find another leader? Regardless, what greater price could Allion be asked to pay?

An internal scream silenced the hunter's tortured reflections. This wasn't about him. As forbidding as his own future seemed, there would be time enough to confront it later. His mission now was to mourn and bid proper farewell to he who had already paid the ultimate price. Justice, some might call it, in that Torin himself had unleashed this scourge. But such a debate would seem to dishonor the man's memory. For the next few hours, at least, Allion meant to think only of his friend's better qualities.

He reached his destination as a new dawn spilled through the trees, spreading diffuse light and meager warmth over a swollen stream and its forested banks. There was no need to search for the perfect plot. Each member of their erstwhile community selected his or her own at the age of eight—deemed the first age of accountability—by planting a tree that would grow as they grew, and mark their final resting spot. Torin's lay beneath the canopy of a fire poplar planted near the edge of the stream. While half its boughs reached out over the water's edge, the other half sheltered a grassy rise atop the southern bank, where Torin, as a child, had taken that first small step toward becoming a man.

Allion smiled wistfully as he gazed upon the sheltered grove. From the banks of that stream, he and Torin—Jarom, at the time—must have watched half their youth flow by, while dreaming of adventure in faraway lands. Their fantasies had been filled with monsters and maidens and triumphs on an epic scale. But that had been long ago, before they had outgrown such childish reveries and been compelled to experience the dark and harrowing reality of them. They had been so naive, so innocent and carefree.

So long ago.

Amid the rushing of crystalline waters, Allion heard again Marisha's pleas to stay, to allow Torin to go to the fires instead. He was glad now that he had ignored her. In the solemn hush of these familiar surroundings, he was more certain than ever that this was what Torin would have wanted, to be returned to his true home, to lie forever among his original people. Despite the risks involved, it seemed such a small favor to grant.

His smile vanished as he forced himself to the work at hand. He untied the horses first, watered both, then led each to a separate sentry position some thirty paces off. Leaving each hobbled and with a nosebag of feed, he then returned to the gravesite, shovel in hand.

Ignoring his own hunger, Allion knelt upon the site and bowed his head in silent prayer. When finished, he wiped his eyes, set shovel to earth, and began to dig.

He dug slowly at first, mindful of the strength that would be required, and determined to execute this task with proper and noble dignity. But by the time the first bead of sweat fell, Allion felt himself losing control, succumbing to the memories and emotions that were so much a part of his labor. Never again would they sit side by side within this grove to discuss their hopes and dreams. Never again would his boyhood friend dip his toes into the cool water, grinning as the waves lapped at his ankles. That boy was slain, and all that remained for Allion was to dig . . . dig . . . dig . . .

With unbridled fury, the hunter attacked the earth, hacking at its surface. It would share his anguish. It would know the horror and emptiness of his loss. With each memory, Allion's wrath increased. The long days at work and at play . . . the nights of mischief in Glendon . . . the time they had run away . . . And later, the coming of Queen Ellebe . . . the hunt for the Crimson Sword . . . their battle at Kraagen Keep against the dragonspawn . . .

Allion could not stop the onrush, and it fueled him when all physical strength had fled. It forced his muscles to respond, to lash out again and again until blisters formed, burst, and formed again. The burning within his shoulders and arms became unbearable, yet he would have welcomed its eternal agony for but a moment's reprieve from that in his head and heart. So much to mourn, so much to reckon with, and for hours, Allion had no choice but to face it all, to challenge every demon his grief could muster.

Until finally, almost suddenly, it came to an end.

As the last shard of their former lives left its scar and skittered away, Allion found himself staring blankly through the mud, sweat, and tears that stung his eyes. He leaned heavily upon his shovel, its haft smeared with the blood from his hands, and gazed at the floor of the pit in which he stood. It was finished. He had nothing more to give. A hollow ache remained, a hole within that he would carry to his own grave. But the time had come to bury the worst of his feelings and be done with his grieving.

As Marisha had told him, life must go on.

He took a deep breath, a refreshing taste of the early spring season, and looked to the heavens. The sun shone high in the sky, almost directly overhead. Midday already, and his task was only half finished.

As he climbed from the pit, however, and looked to Torin's bundled form, Marisha's other concern became paramount once more. How could he be sure that Torin was truly being laid to rest? There was a chance, after all, that the king was already being possessed, suffering through the three-day incubation period that all Illysp faced—during which the host's original soul was torn from the Olirian afterlife and shackled once more to its physical coil. Assuming, of course, that what they had learned of their enemy from Darinor was true, Allion might merely be burying his friend as an Illychar—a creature that would not perish from hunger or lack of breath—leaving him imprisoned in an earthen grave for eternity.

And yet, waiting around to see if his friend would revive—so that he could kill him again—only increased the time in which an Illysp spirit might take possession. For all Allion knew, he carried a host of the fleshless spirits with him. He might mutilate the body in some fashion, but he could not bring himself to do so. If even a headless corpse might rise again, as Darinor had claimed, then what good would it do for Allion to desecrate the body by hacking it into pieces, only to have those pieces somehow retain Torin's living awareness? What sort of torment might that be?

No, he reassured himself, short of cremation, which he still refused to consider, the best he could do was to bury his friend quickly and trust to the mercy of the Ceilhigh that the young king had not already been poisoned. Perhaps, when this war was finished and the world rid of Illysp, he might return and dig up the grave to make sure Torin's remains were truly at peace. Until then, he had done all he could.

The rest went faster than expected. Cut from the litter, Torin's body was interred in the earth that had nourished it in life. Though he was no priest, Allion took it upon himself to bestow all rites customary to his people, as he had seen them delivered. Torin's life in the hereafter, he assured himself, would be better than this one.

As he tamped the last of the soil back into place, Allion looked to the grave's marker. A dozen years after its planting, Torin's tree had grown tall and strong. And it would continue to do so, the hunter reminded himself, though the human life it represented had moved on.

He set aside the shovel and again lowered himself to his knees. Time to beseech the final blessing of the Ceilhigh, and to offer his own apologies for the wrongs he had committed against his friend. The latter, he thought sullenly, could take some time.

He had accomplished the first, but had only barely begun the last, when one of his horses gave a cry. Allion froze. He heard voices, and the thrashing of bodies through the brush. It seemed his time was up.

His bow and arrows lay beside the empty litter. Allion moved quickly to retrieve them, slinging the quiver over his shoulder and locating a thick trunk behind which to hide. By the time the intruders reached his clearing, leading their own mounts afoot, the hunter peered at them through the foliage with an arrow drawn.

There were only two of them—human, they appeared—dressed in the royal livery of Alson. Marked as messengers by the sash each wore. Neither had yet drawn a weapon.

"He was here all right," one of them said.

"Clearly," the other snorted. "But off to where, then, with his mounts behind?"

They did not appear to be Illychar, which left Allion to wonder if Colonel Venmore had made good on his oath to track down the insubordinate wagon driver. After waiting a moment to reassure himself that they were alone, he released his arrow. It struck the earth at the toe of the messenger nearest him, drawing a startled shout.

"Stay your weapons!" he commanded, another arrow already loaded and ready to fire. He let them see this as he stepped out from behind his shelter.

Both men's hands froze upon the hilts of their swords.

"Master Allion," one of them offered, peering through the evening dusk, "is that you?"

"Tell me first who *you* are," the hunter replied, "and what you are doing in my woods."

"My lord, we are come from Krynwall. We bear a message for His Lord Regent Allion."

"And what message would that be?"

"Are you indeed Master Allion?" the other of them asked.

"My proof will be this shaft through your throat. Deliver your message."

"My lord," the first replied hastily, "there has been an accident—at Krynwall, my lord. It happened late last night, not long after you left."

Marisha. Allion's throat constricted. "*What* happened, Corporal?"

"We do not know, my lord, only that Master Stephan begs you hurry home at once."

Allion tried to tell himself that it could mean anything. But Stephan had learned of his departure—and likely his destination, for these riders to have found him. That meant that Marisha—or Pagus—had told him, and neither would have done so unless the need were dire.

"That is all of it? You are sure?"

"Yes, my lord."

An *accident*, they called it. News deemed too terrible to be delivered secondhand.

"We ride for Krynwall," he agreed, spurring himself to action before his heart could sink further. He had been a fool to come here. Marisha had warned him. Why hadn't he listened?

The messengers helped him to retrieve his horses. No mention was made of the shovel or litter left behind in the grove, nor of the wagon he chose to abandon once they reached the main road. With all haste, Allion galloped westward in the murky light of a forbidding sunset, driven by an uncertain horror, and with those who had delivered it in tow.

Vorric Haze waited until Allion and his messengers had left before venturing forth from his place of concealment. Once again, his knowledge and intuition had served him well. He had known that riders would be dispatched in search of Allion to inform the regent of the murders in Marisha's chambers. Having escaped the city with his own contingent ahead of time, the former First Elder and now wielder of the Crimson Sword had been well on his way by then. They had headed east, for that was where an army of their brood lay in wait—an army of which Haze now intended to take command.

But that had not been his only reason for taking the eastern road. In truth, he had already come to suspect what Allion was about, and the direction in which the regent had headed. When finally those bearing the sash of royal dispatch had galloped past, with Haze and his escorts tucked out of sight along the woodland road, the Elder had led his team in furtive pursuit, presuming that they would lead him to his quarry.

They had.

"We should have killed them," one of Haze's guardsmen grumbled.

There were only two of them now—Fasor undiscovered as Illychar. Held in reserve while Haze had confronted Marisha, the duo had joined him in setting forth from Krynwall. There might have been three, but Haze had decided to put an end to the one Marisha had crippled.

Still, even odds should he have decided to attack Allion and his escorts. But he had deemed it an unnecessary risk. He had not come here to claim Allion, but the former wielder of the Crimson Sword—he who might be able to share with Vorric Haze a measure of its secrets.

He explained none of this to his disgruntled guardsman, only glared in warning before continuing on through the trees. Except for the stream, the grove was silent, serene. A fresh and unprotected grave lay in a wash of filtered moonlight. A litter lay nearby, and next to that, a single shovel.

Haze picked up the shovel and handed it to the questioning guardsman. "Dig," he commanded. To the other, he said, "Stand watch." When both looked to him for further explanation, he replied with a withering scowl. "I would have a word or two with your former lord."

CHAPTER SIX

CORATHEL HELD HIS BREATH AS he held his salute. This was the report he had been anxiously awaiting for two days now. But given the grim set of his scout's jaw, he was no longer certain he wished to hear it.

"Report."

"Sir. Atharvan is besieged, and in desperate need of reinforcement. I estimate her enemies' number at twenty thousand, sir."

The chief general of the Parthan Legion felt his stomach knot. Just as they'd feared. Worse, even. When his scouts had returned with word that the western cities of Laulk and Leaven were all clear, he had dared hope that those fears might prove unfounded. It would seem he had given to hope too soon.

They had commenced their homeward trek from the Gaperon two nights previous, prepped and ready to march even before receiving the message from Allion urging them to do so. Darinor had played them false. The mustering of Pentanian armies into a central coalition, intended to draw the enemy into battle at a place of their choosing, had been a ruse, it seemed, meant to strip the various homelands of their defenses. Krynwall had already been ambushed. There was no telling which city—or cities—would be next.

Now they knew.

"Have you anything further?" the chief general asked.

"No, sir. All else is quiet, sir."

Of course it was. Most of the major cities and holdfasts lining central Partha had been annihilated by the swarms of dragonspawn unleashed by the Demon Queen. And this latter threat had emerged before they'd had a chance to even begin rebuilding. Survivors throughout Partha had flocked to the capital city of Atharvan, to the east, or sought refuge behind the walls of Laulk and Leaven, to the west. Outside of that, his country was a wasteland.

"Have any of the others reported in, sir?" the scout asked him.

No. Nor could the chief general be assured that they would. Of the scouts he had sent out, less than half had returned. Waylaid at the very least. More likely ambushed and killed by rogue packs of the enemy. Giving him an incomplete view of what they faced, and making information such as he had just received ever more difficult to come by.

"Yours is the first we've heard of the east," he admitted. "I expect reports from the others soon."

The rider nodded, though his hopeful countenance fell.

"Dismissed, Corporal. Take your rest." *You're going to need it.*

"Yes, sir."

Corathel sat astride his mount for some time after the scout had left, watching his forces march past on either side. If any looked to him, he did not see it, for his own gaze was fixed upon the plains to the east. He had thought to keep them moving throughout the night, thinking to return home as quickly as possible—to get them behind Atharvan's walls before allowing them sleep. But this news changed everything.

"Sergeant," he called, summoning the lieutenant commander of his personal regiment to his side.

"Sir?" the man greeted, pushing his way through the buffer of marching soldiers his chief general had placed between them.

"Call a halt, and summon my lieutenant generals for a command council. Have my tent erected here on this ridge."

"Yes, sir."

BY THE TIME HIS COUNCIL convened, the chief general knew already what he must do. After sharing with his division commanders the word from Atharvan, he delivered his orders.

"Your men are to receive a half night's rest. After that, the Second, Third, and Fourth Divisions resume march to the east. The Fifth marches north to reinforce Leaven. The Sixth will do the same for Laulk."

As expected, the orders touched off a minor debate among his most senior officers.

Lar, the soft-spoken giant who commanded the Fourth Division, was the first to speak. "With respect, sir, Laulk and Leaven have been reported clear. Why divide the legion when, by the sounds of your report, all will be needed at Atharvan?"

"Because we don't know that either will remain clear for long, and I would rather have our armies inside the walls when the enemy comes."

"Atharvan shields more than Laulk and Leaven combined," Fifth General Dengyn reminded him, "not to mention the king himself."

"I'm aware of that, General. But I will not favor one city over another, picking and choosing as to which shall be spared."

"Either way, we weaken our overall strength by splitting our forces," added Bannon, lieutenant general of the Sixth Division. "And you ask us to do so not once, but twice."

"For a time only," Corathel corrected. "If possible, I want those two western cities rolled into one. When you have reached Laulk, your division, General, is to escort her people east through the mountains to join those at Leaven."

That made sense to everyone, since all assembled knew Leaven to be more defensible than her sister city, and no nearer the conflict since this conflict surrounded them.

"Shouldn't those of us headed to Atharvan be on the move?" Jasyn asked with typical eagerness. "It'll do us no good to arrive after the city falls."

"You know as well as I that our lord king can hold out for a couple of days, even with the limited garrison we left behind. I will not race my men into battle only to deliver them faint from forced march and lack of sleep."

"Perhaps I could lead an advance cavalry company, just to relieve pressure."

Corathel shook his head. "Patience, my friend. There will be battle aplenty before the week is done."

The Second Division's commander frowned, but withheld further protest.

"As good a plan as any," Maltyk offered in support. "Until we know more, I see no better alternative." The Third General's voice was the last to be heard, but put an end to further discussion.

"You know your assignments, then," the chief general concluded. "Advise your units. We strike camp upon the Vulture's Hour."

ALLION STRODE BRISKLY DOWN THE castle corridor, step for step with the page sent to escort him. He could have throttled the lad for not simply giving him a destination and letting him be on his way, but this was one of Rogun's own. On top of that, soldiers lined the walls of this lower passage, stone-faced sentinels hand-selected for their loyalty to the general.

The hunter gave little thought to what it might mean. He had not slept in over a day now, and only a few fitful hours in the last three. Emotionally drained and physically exhausted, it was all he could do to recognize where he was and to keep his body upright. Only one thing allowed him to do either: the need to know what had become of Marisha.

At long last, the page stopped beside a door warded by no fewer than four watchmen—this in addition to the score or more they had passed en route. Their captain returned the page's salute, glanced at Allion, then moved at once to unlock and open the guarded portal.

The page turned to the weary hunter. "I shall inform the lord general of your arrival," he said.

Allion ignored him. For as the door opened, he caught sight of Stephan, who knelt beside a bed in which Marisha lay motionless.

He said nothing to page or guardsmen, but rushed inside, only vaguely aware of the door being closed and locked behind him.

Stephan rose to meet him. "My lord, praises be, you've returned."

Allion brushed right past, his heart in his throat and fresh tears in his eyes. "Is she . . ."

"Resting, my lord."

A soft laugh burst from the hunter's lips, part sob, part sigh of relief. He gazed down upon Marisha's slumbering form. Dark circles ringed her eyes. Her skin seemed paler than usual, and her lips were tinged blue. A pile of blankets and heavy quilts covered her.

"What happened?" he whispered.

"She nearly drowned, my lord." There was sadness in his tone, but a touch of bitterness as well. "The Ceilhigh alone could have saved her from that fall.

And were it not for the sentries who happened by on patrol . . ." He shook his head as if to clear away the thought. "By rights, my lord, she should have been killed."

Allion touched her forehead, then gently brushed a hair from her lips. It was so hard not to wake her, to reach beneath the covers to grasp her hand, to kiss her and tell her how sorry he was.

"If only the others had been as lucky," the chief seneschal added solemnly.

"What others?"

"Corman, my lord, and Brae and Donal."

City Shield, Allion recalled. His men, from a time not so long ago, when he had served as their captain.

"Elders Logrim and Kamis, as well," Stephan continued, "and . . ."

When he did not finish, Allion turned to find the seneschal wiping his eyes.

"And Pagus, my lord."

A sudden warmth billowed through him, flush with horror and denial. "What? No."

Stephan composed himself and nodded. "He tried to defend her, my lord, against Thaddreus and those under his command."

"Thaddreus?" Allion's head swam. He could hardly believe it. "*Elder* Thaddreus?"

Stephan nodded. "An Illychar, judging by his deeds, and the others—all but Pagus and Corman—with him. They—"

"Why was I not sent for earlier?"

Stephan seemed startled by the rebuke. "My lord?"

"Your riders claim this happened not long after I left. Why did it take them so long to reach me?"

"My lord, I was busy with preparations for the arrival of Baron Nevik and his retinue. It was some time before I learned of the struggle in my lady's chambers. Even then, I knew not the extent of it, nor where word should be sent, since my lord did not bother to let me know he was leaving."

The steward's plump cheeks had grown redder than usual—in embarrassment, perhaps, or indignation. Allion suspected the latter, given the man's reproachful tone. The hunter decided to forgive his friend's frustration, however, for the reprimand was well deserved.

"As soon as she revived," Stephan went on, when it became clear Allion did not mean to chastise him, "the lady insisted that riders be sent to fetch you. For even the swiftest horse, Diln is a half day's ride, my lord."

"You have done what you could, then," the hunter allowed. "For that, you have my thanks."

It was not exactly the apology he felt Stephan was looking for, but as close as the steward was going to get.

"My lord, Elder Thaddreus escaped, and the Sword with him."

Allion blinked, then felt a new hole open up inside him.

At that moment, Marisha coughed, and both men spun back to her. Allion, who had closed his eyes against hearing any more, opened them now as Marisha's fluttered wide.

Her blue orbs found him. "Allion?"

She shifted within her cocoon. Allion placed a hand atop the mound of covers where he had seen *her* hand begin to rise. He knelt and kissed her forehead.

"I'm here, Marisha."

A wan smile loosened her lips, but quickly faded. Tears welled within her eyes. "Pagus . . ." she tried, but couldn't finish.

Allion hushed her. "I know, Marisha. I . . ." He knew not where to begin. There was so much he wished to say to her, so many apologies he wished to make. His grief for Torin had blinded him to what was most important: those still fighting for a chance to live. He realized that now, and wanted to swear to her that he would not make that same mistake twice.

Marisha wept silently for a moment, then asked, "Did you get to . . . ? Is Torin . . . ?"

"Torin is home now. I won't be leaving you again."

Her features tightened with sudden urgency. "The Sword—"

"That doesn't matter." And it didn't. Not to him. Not in that moment. "We'll be all right, Marisha, with or without it."

"My lord," Stephan interjected quietly, "there is more you should know."

Allion tensed, wishing suddenly that the other wasn't there, but forced himself to nod. "So tell me."

"My lord, riders and emissaries have begun to return with word from abroad. Kuuria is secure, and western Partha, my lord. But Atharvan is under attack, surrounded as we were. Only, they have no armies to protect them, and are begging aid."

"And what is the Circle's response?" Allion asked with resignation.

"My lord, the Circle no longer rules Krynwall."

The hunter turned his head. "What?"

"The Elders are no longer in control, my lord. General Rogun has established martial law."

Allion looked back to Marisha. Her somber expression confirmed the truth. One day. He'd been gone only a single day, and in that short span, his worst fears had been realized. The Sword gone, the city fallen from within, Marisha nearly killed. And yet, could he really have prevented any of it?

Just then, the door to the chamber opened, and a pair of guardsmen stepped in. Another pair followed, and another, forming up to either side to create an aisle between them. Through this aisle stepped Commander Zain, and finally, General Rogun himself.

The door closed. A temporary silence hung in the air.

"Master Allion, welcome home," the general greeted. "And Lady Marisha, I'm pleased to see you awake."

Neither replied. Allion glanced at Zain, who flashed him a weasel's smirk.

"I trust you find your quarters suitable?" Rogun asked.

Allion cast about, noticing for the first time the fine appointments given to this makeshift infirmary suite.

"I am quite comfortable, General, thank you," Marisha replied.

"And well protected," Allion added, somewhat dryly.

"I would not risk a repeat of last night's tragedy," Rogun remarked, standing there with arms crossed. "Surely you do not disapprove."

Allion dipped his head in stoic acknowledgment. There seemed little point in quarreling over the issue. Whatever his grievances with the general, he did appreciate the aid rendered Marisha, though it would seem he had made a captive of her—of all of them—in doing so.

"Judging by your brooding," Rogun continued, "I presume our good seneschal has already briefed you on recent developments."

"I've just learned that the army has taken control of the city."

"In the absence of king, regent, and First Elder, the people have demanded it, and the remaining members of the Circle are not so foolish as to fight it."

There was a difference in the general's tone, an almost gleeful quality that seemed to soften the normally harsh edges. No doubt, the man was feeling rather smug at having finally become the city's chief authority.

"And here we are," Allion dared, "the last of those who might dispute it."

"Not the last, I assure you. The loudest, perhaps. You understand my predicament."

"Are we to remain prisoners, then?"

The general chuckled—an eerie sound, coming from him. "I gave you a chance to prove your strength. Look at the result. From now on, I intend to run matters as I alone see fit. Had I done so sooner, we would not be in this mess."

Allion could not easily disagree. The general had done them much good—in great part because of his absolute faith in himself. The hunter would have liked to share in that faith, but still felt the general to be too headstrong and dismissive of others. Wise and experienced, perhaps, yet Allion found it difficult to trust a man who claimed to know the best for all.

"You are tracking Thaddreus, then?" he asked pointedly.

"An elite squad has been sent to recover the Sword," Rogun assured him, "dispatched the moment I learned of Marisha's plight. Something I should have been apprised of immediately," he added, glaring at Stephan.

The glum seneschal bowed his head dutifully, but offered no apology.

"And Partha?" Allion pressed.

Rogun shook his head. "I have sent my response. It is too late to be sending troops back and forth across the open plain. The Illychar that pressed us here at home might easily regroup. The best way to protect ourselves at this juncture is to guard our own walls, and let them guard theirs."

"Then their pleas go unheard?"

"Reports are that Partha's own legion is already en route. A shame they were ever drawn away," Rogun observed incisively. "But that is their folly, not mine. I'm afraid they shall have to reap the results of it, as it is beyond Alson's limited resources to lend aid."

"You cannot be serious!"

"I am ever serious, especially in matters of war. That is my business, as it has been my family's for generations. I would not expect a village huntsman to fully understand."

There it was at last, that hallmark scorn that had been missing. As usual, it set Allion's teeth on edge.

"I am no mere huntsman," he snapped, rising from Marisha's bedside to face the general archly. "I am Allion, regent of Krynwall—"

"Whose powers were voted to me in absentee, by the surviving members of his own council. Should you deny my command, I am within my right to have you jailed for treason."

Allion felt his blood boil. He glanced again at Zain, Rogun's right hand, who wore a look of vague amusement. He was half tempted to launch himself upon the haughty commander when he felt a soft touch upon his wrist. Turning back, he found that Marisha had worked an arm free of her blankets. Her silent expression told him that this was not the time.

"Believe it or not, I have no desire to do so," Rogun declared. The scorn had slipped away, though his gruff candor remained. "However, the situation is difficult enough as is, and I'll not tolerate further dissension from within. Should you wish to challenge me, I'll gladly entertain you, but not before this war is ended. Is that understood?"

Allion glowered, but left it at that. In truth, he could live with the general's small opinion of him. He only wanted to do what he could to help—and to make sure none were abandoned.

"And what does Nevik have to say?" he asked, recalling the baron suddenly.

"Ask him yourself, if that is your wish. Only, bear in mind the futility—and consequences—of any attempt at revolt."

Marisha's grip on his wrist tightened.

"I have been so warned," Allion replied.

"Good. Then we are finished here. You are free to come and go as you please, though I suspect you will wish to stay close to the lady, and thus have ordered chambers prepared for both you and Stephan nearby. My guardsmen will be happy to see to anything that may have been neglected." He bowed his head to Marisha. "Lady, I bid you a swift recovery."

With that, he turned on a heel and marched back through his aisle of soldiers. Zain smirked again before following. The door opened upon the general's knock, and the entire procession filed out in reverse order.

"I'm sorry I let things get out of hand," Marisha said when the three were alone again.

Allion spun, taking her hand and gripping it reassuringly. "The fault is mine." He glanced at Stephan. "All of it."

Marisha smiled weakly. "We will be all right. As you said."

He nodded. "Just the same, if you will forgive me, I think I'll go and arrange for that word with Nevik."

CHAPTER SEVEN

Darkness.

Its folds enveloped him, comforted him. Within that vast emptiness, he knew only warmth and peace—a timeless calm that permeated his soul and swept forth beyond the bounds of his limited consciousness.

Then it stirred. Silent ripples churned and gathered. A tingling, soft at first, grew steadily more acute, stealing his numbness. He felt a crack, and the darkness shattered.

The light pierced him, and he lashed out against it. Then a burning within. He cried out, and was horrified by the sound. A stink assailed him. He snorted, but it was all around, penetrating, driving away the shards of retreating darkness. His cries became a desperate bellow as his world flew apart.

Color and shape drew into focus. He was seeing. Before him, a face, wreathed in starlight. The face of a man.

It spoke. "Welcome, brother, to the realm of flesh."

He bucked forward, straining with unfamiliar limbs. A force restrained him. He howled and gnashed his teeth, driven by a feral frenzy he did not understand but did not bother to deny. His senses, raw and biting, tormented him. The burning at his core. The stench clouding his thoughts. If only he could kill this man before him, it might all go away.

And yet, already the sting was lessening, his horror softening, as realization lay claim. Lungs, nostrils, to go with limbs and teeth. The sensations they wrought no longer frightened him. A man himself. Seated within a forest, his back to a tree. Pinned there by another pair of men who gripped his arms, each to one side. He blinked, felt muscles relax. The pair to either side released him and stepped away.

He turned back to the face before him, the one he would have ripped asunder. It grinned. "Who are you?"

He considered. An ache tore at his stomach as he probed a mind not his own. *Torin*, it yielded. He recoiled, searching elsewhere. All at once, he knew the answer.

"I am nameless," he heard himself whisper.

Torin had been the name of this body, but that was not who *he* was. He had yet to be defined. He was Illysp no longer, but Illychar, reborn into this mortal coil. *His* coil.

He glanced at his companions, those who had restrained him during his birth throes, then glared at Vorric Haze—the one who had once been called Thaddreus. That much he remembered easily now, along with the rest of his Illysp past. The memories and experiences returned as if they had never been lost. The centuries of entrapment, caught between this world and his own. Their sudden and unexpected freedom. Kael-Magus, and the scheme concocted to ensure their freedom forever. Biding his time among so many others, waiting for the perfect vessel to make his own. The confrontation in the tunnel . . . Kael-Magus's destruction . . . Torin's fall . . .

"Yes, brother," Vorric Haze hissed. "You remember well, don't you? But that is not what I wish of you. I already share your *former* memories. What I desire now are your *new* ones."

Again the brush with a mind that did not belong to him, and again he recoiled. He knew now what was being asked of him, but he was not yet ready.

"Few come to know their host this soon, I realize," Haze continued in a tone of false regret. "But our time here may be short. I need you to do so now."

Still he hesitated. Even as an Illysp, he had "seen" the process enough times to know the agony to which Haze meant to subject him.

"Start small," Haze encouraged. "For instance, we all know your former name to be Torin, son of Sorl. But tell me, who was the man who raised you?"

He shifted focus from his own, innate awareness to the one that lay unexplored. Another fierce and sudden pang assaulted him as he tore free the name Haze sought.

"Esaias," he croaked.

"Esaias. Good. Now tell me more. Tell me about the Sword."

The Sword of Asahiel. The divine talisman that had helped drive their kind back into the bowels of Thrak-Symbos and seal them away for millennia—unable to return to their own world; unable to fully claim this one. The one that Torin now wielded. Except that . . .

Haze pulled back his cloak, revealing the gem-studded hilt belted at his waist. The Illychar grinned menacingly. "You did not expect to claim Torin's coil *and* his weapon, did you?"

The Nameless One glowered. He had known, of course, that there would be a period of separation. He hadn't truly believed that the blade would be buried with the king's body. But yes, he had fully expected that, once revived—be it in a royal crypt or among his enemies—he would find a way to make the weapon his once more.

"Granted, you have something I do not," Haze allowed. "A knowledge and familiarity that I can only gain with time. But war beckons, brother. The sooner I learn the weapon's secrets, the sooner I can use its powers for all of us. You can help me by sharing any insights your host may have already gleaned."

He was not so easily swayed. Haze had none but selfish interests at heart. That was how it worked among their kind. The strongest, most ruthless endured; the weak were destroyed. By giving in to Haze's demand, he would in fact strengthen all Illysp in their war against the flesh-wearers. But he would also be weakening himself against his brother when the time came to take back what belonged to him.

"Your swift infestation has spared me much delay," Haze offered with genuine approval. "By the same token, you owe me a debt of thanks. For, without me, it would have taken you some time to free yourself from this earthen prison."

The Elder gestured to a pit—an open grave—in the floor of the moonlit grove. Severed bindings and a discarded shroud lay nearby.

"So tell me."

Resistance would win him nothing. The rape of its host's memories and experiences was the most gratifying aspect of an Illychar's existence—the ultimate conquest of another living being. Already, he hungered for it. There was no question as to *if* it would happen, only *when*.

But there was a price to be paid. Illychar who underwent the process too quickly or too soon often drove themselves mad. Given the pain wrought by just those few, simple brushes with Torin's former self, he was inclined to make himself—and Haze—wait.

Then the Sword was in Haze's hand, and its radiant tip at his throat.

"Do it now, or remain nameless forever."

One of the others snickered. Another's pain was an Illysp's pleasure—even among their own kind. He would have felt the same had their positions been reversed.

But he saw no way to make that happen, and so surrendered to Haze's demand and his own feral hunger. With a snarl upon his lips, he turned his savage focus inward.

He began slowly, like a predator circling its wounded prey. Torin's mind lay fallen, not defenseless. Mental probes picked experimentally, exposing various images of people and places. For each, he suffered a wracking, physical response—a pinch in his chest, a stab in his gut. The deeper the probe, the deeper his pain.

But with each taste, his hunger grew. He tolerated the pain at first, then challenged it, gritting aside its feeble counterattacks. The stolen treasures to which he lay claim were well worth the price.

A memory of this forest, Torin's homeland. He did not just glimpse this vision, but allowed himself to savor it. He was there, as the boy Jarom, racing through woods of summer gold alongside laughing companions. A girl, Hidee, smiled at him—

So intense was his body's reaction that his eyes popped open and his vision spun. He had slipped too deep, beyond mere image to the emotion that accompanied it. An old emotion, vague and inconsequential to Torin, but fresh to *him*. Fresh and powerful. A child's longing, yet experienced as though by a child. It was too much. He told himself again he was not yet ready.

His vision regained focus. Vorric Haze, he saw, was not about to allow him pause. But the other's threat mattered not. For as the sharp sting of that simple emotion slipped away, he knew that he must have more.

His lust consumed him, and the pain became its own reward. He welcomed it, mocked its inability to defeat his efforts. A twisting, gut-wrenching torment paralyzed him, causing muscles to clench and his stomach to heave. But he would not stop now. Each memory became his own. Every sight, every sensation, every raw emotion Torin had known. A crippling onslaught of love and hate, joy and sorrow, triumph and failure. A lifetime of hopes realized and dreams dashed, all in one fell swoop. The knowledge and experiences of another, made his own.

In some small, distant way, he realized they were destroying him.

And he reveled in it.

All too soon, it ended. At full fury, he made short work of his prey. As his assault waned, a void closed round, in which nothing remained but indigestible fragments.

And the ecstasy, of course—ultimate, indescribable. All that the young mortal had ever been or aimed to become, shredded and consumed with bestial efficiency, devoured and assimilated into his own awareness. Had he known—truly known—the savage pleasure this would bring him, he never would have hesitated to complete his transformation.

Nor was it fully finished. The hollow ache he might otherwise have felt was assuaged in that he still had the fragments. He had understood from others that it would be so. For some reason, there were invariably a few memories that escaped an Illychar's initial onslaught, a few treasured images and emotions held most dear by their original host. Rarely did these more closely guarded visions prove to bear any practical significance; their value was often of a private, sentimental nature. Whatever the source of their resistance, even these wasted away and were devoured in time. All that Torin had managed to hide would eventually be his—a future conquest to be regarded with savory anticipation.

When he opened his eyes again to the natural world, he did so with the entirety of Torin's faculties, mental and physical, at his disposal. His feasting had made him master of this coil and the enslaved, former essence that churned inside. He lacked only one thing more: the name by which his deeds in this realm would become known.

Haze leaned near. "So then, tell me what you know."

Images whirled through his head, summoned as if they had belonged to him all along. The most recent were of Cianellen, Allion, Marisha. He understood now why Torin had truly collapsed in those tunnels, and knew that Allion was alive, raised in his stead. He felt a smile form upon his lips, for the recollection of the king's sacrifice—of which no one else knew—amused him.

The expression seemed to anger Haze. "Your time grows short, Nameless One."

Already, his new life hung by a string. With Kael-Magus gone, Vorric Haze clearly meant to assume the mantle of leadership among them—and as wielder of the Sword, was in the best position to do so. Though it chafed him to admit it, he had to appease his brother before he could ever hope to satisfy himself. That was going to prove difficult, knowing that he lacked the answers Haze sought.

"The Sword's power is . . . mercurial," he replied. He had to be direct enough that Haze did not kill him on the spot, yet evasive enough to imply hidden worth. His brother would expect nothing less.

"Go on."

"It is not sentient, yet it seems to sense your goal, and will amplify your ability to achieve it."

"What of its inner fires? How do I summon them?"

He chuckled derisively. "Had Torin known the answer to that, do you believe he would have fallen?"

The lines in Haze's forehead deepened. "Perhaps the next Illysp to inhabit this coil will respond better," he said, and drew back as if to stab forward and drive the Sword home.

"He did, however, witness the eruption of those fires more than once. Perhaps you can solve a riddle he could not."

Haze spared him, but continued to scowl. "Speak quickly."

"It defends itself," he claimed, peering beyond the surface of the gleaming blade to stare at the crimson fires swirling hypnotically within, "at all costs."

"From magical assaults, yes. And the wielder with it. I have already heard that this is how he destroyed Spithaera."

An inexact account, but no matter. He saw no reason to divulge the full truth of that final conflict, or tell of the Pendant's existence.

"And do you know of Leaven's jailor?" he asked instead.

"Would you suggest I seek to pry one of the heartstones from the blade's hilt?" Haze teased, knowing, evidently, that it would destroy him.

"I only suggest, brother, that it is not just magic to which the Sword responds, but physical assault. A clue, perhaps?"

"You raise more questions than answers," Haze determined. "If your next words do not please me, they will be your last."

"He spoke with the Vandari."

Haze stiffened at the name, but arched an eyebrow in obvious interest. "And learned what?"

Very little, though he could ill afford to admit it.

Before he could summon a more pleasing lie, Haze tensed, then whipped about to dodge a crossbow bolt, which drove with a thwack into the trunk beside his ear.

"Coils!" his brother hissed, angry yet eager.

The Nameless One glanced at the Illychar Fasor to either side of him. Each had taken a bolt in the chest, but that did not stop them now from drawing their swords. Already, their opponents were bursting through the brush, soldiers wearing light mail and the colors of Alson's Legion of the Sword. An elite cadre of swordsmen and marksmen, fanned out in a half-moon arc meant to keep its quarry pinned against the nearby stream. Across that body of water, a secondary trio of crossbowmen appeared, cutting off any retreat.

He scrambled to his feet, casting about for a weapon of his own. His gaze snagged upon a discarded shovel, and he dove toward it. It came to hand as an enemy soldier bore down on him. He looked up, and their eyes met. If the soldier had any hesitation about striking down his former king, the Nameless One did not perceive it.

He ducked the soldier's swipe and came up swinging. The flat of the shovel's blade cracked against the man's mail hood, spinning him about. Euphoric, the Illychar took that moment to snap the haft of the shovel across his own knee, providing a weapon for each hand. As his enemy recovered, he used the metal scoop to deflect a second swordstroke, then lunged forward with his weight behind the empty shaft, driving its splintered end into the soldier's throat.

The chain links of his gorget prevented the wood from stabbing through. Nevertheless, the soldier choked and dropped his blade to clutch his wounded neck with both hands. A poor shield, as the Nameless One took aim and buried the tip of his spade just a bit higher, in the soft flesh below his enemy's chin.

The nearly decapitated soldier was still thrashing as a comrade rushed to his aid. The Nameless One snatched up the fallen sword in time to parry the first blow, then rang back a pair of his own. He battered his opponent relentlessly, reveling in the vibrations of steel on steel, snarling with bestial delight. Fear crept into his assailant's eyes, which widened when his blade tore through the man's heart.

He ripped free, the taste of blood in his mouth, desperate for more. When no adversary approached, his gaze swept out in search. Bodies lay throughout the grove. One of the Fasor was down. The other had happened upon a crossbow and was trading volleys with the marksmen across the stream—just two of them, now. Despite being outnumbered by the pair, and though riddled with bolts, his Illychar brother seemed to have that battle well in hand.

Vorric Haze, however, appeared hard-pressed. Half a dozen swordsmen encircled him, with a set of crossbowmen lending cover from afar. The Sword had kept him alive, and yet he had done little real harm. Too much offense, and not enough defense against his opponents' carefully coordinated attacks. Where he should have held fast and let them close round, he instead wasted time chasing after one or another, thirsting for blood. Invariably, his target would dance away, refusing to engage the Sword, and while Haze's attention was focused in pursuit, the others would close from the sides, scoring nicks and stings. He who scored most deeply would then draw the Illychar's ire; rather than finish the man he'd been after, Haze would start a fresh pursuit, and the process would begin anew.

It would take quite a while to bring Haze down in such a fashion, but if they could bait him long enough into chasing after their shifting feints, that combination of blades and quarrels might actually succeed in finishing him.

The Nameless One gritted his teeth at a fresh stab of pain, and looked down to find a bolt in the fleshy part of his leg. A bolt intended for Haze, he was sure, but that didn't matter to him.

With surging bloodlust, he dashed across the tiny clearing, leaping the open grave from which he'd been dug and roaring past a swordsman who turned to meet his attack. Weapons clanged, but he charged on by, unslowed by injury, undeterred by pain. It only reminded him that after millennia of longing, physical life was now his.

He dove into the trees, howling with rage, caring not for the bolts that whizzed past as others turned aim to their comrade's defense. The doomed crossbowman looked up while cranking his own bolt into place. He should have dropped the weapon and gone for his dagger. Before he could raise it to fire, a meaty hack took his head.

Less than five paces away, another was prepping his next bolt, features tight with concentration. But the Nameless One had only to retrieve the fully loaded crossbow from his latest victim, take aim, and squeeze the trigger. The soldier's focus gave way to shock as the quarrel punched a hole in his brain.

He turned, then, charging the remaining marksman with sword in hand. A hastily fired bolt missed his heart, striking his shoulder instead. His yelp became a growl. He clenched his jaw and bore down. The marksman drew a blade, a shortsword. The Nameless One feigned a cleaving stroke that his opponent raised his guard to meet. Only as their bodies were about to collide did he lower his own weapon, while reaching up with one hand to seize the man's wrist. The borrowed longsword bit deep, ripping a strangled cry from the impaled soldier's lungs.

He swept the bloody ground like a rabid animal, foaming at the mouth, vision glazed with mind-numbing fury. He happened upon the other's crossbow and a belt full of unused quarrels. He fitted one to the string, stomping on his adversary's throat when the dying man tried to rise. As the man gurgled and squirmed beneath him, he searched for a target.

The marksmen on this side of the stream were gone. Within the grove, Haze had brought the number of swordsmen down to five, but the rest still had him fighting according to their strategy. Lunging and retreating, they continued to work the Illychar into a hapless frenzy. Had the old man known anything about group tactics, he would have recognized what was being done to him. Instead of trusting the Sword, he was fighting to bend it to his own will. The Nameless One seethed. Put *him* in the same position, and this battle would already be over.

And then they had him. Two in back and one in front had positioned Haze between the pair on either flank, setting up a killing combination. The Sword arced out to the right, chopping through a descending broadsword, but instead of spinning back to thwart the other, Haze drove on in search of blood.

The Nameless One had seen it coming, and his crossbow was already leveled at the soldier's neck. It was a quick shot, off the mark. His quarrel struck the other in the side—not enough to slay him, but enough to thwart the lethal blow on Haze's exposed back.

Haze seemed to realize this as he turned at the other's cry and took advantage of the soldier's temporary paralysis to cut him clean in half just below the chest. The Elder actually nodded at the Nameless One and his empty crossbow before being pressed back into battle.

The outcome had been decided. The four remaining soldiers, including one who relied now on ancillary blades, could not stop Haze on their own. But the Nameless One was not nearly sated by the blood he had already spilt. Tearing the bolt from his shoulder and his sword from the corpse at his feet, he bounded forward to join the melee.

Madness gripped him as he crashed his way into the center of the soldier ring. Back to back, he and Haze hacked and stabbed, stepping over the bodies of their victims, circling within the midst of those weaving blades. When first one and then another fell beneath fiery strokes of the Crimson Sword, he expected the remaining pair to flee. They did not. And when both focused on Haze, the Nameless One drove his sword tip through the back of one's skull, so that the blade emerged somewhere on the other side of the fool's face.

By the time he had gained the leverage to tug his weapon free, his brother was tearing the Sword across the final man's stomach. The soldier stood there stupidly for a moment, then slumped to his knees, cradling his intestines.

Haze stared at the man, his chest heaving with triumph. The Nameless One joined him.

"What say you, brother?" Haze wheezed, though he could not have been winded with the Sword's power coursing through him. Nor would his Illychar body have suffered in any case. "An arm for each of us?"

The Nameless One was surprised by the invitation, but happy to accept it. With a vicious grin, he hefted his sword overhead.

Not to be outdone, Haze rushed to land his strike first. Both blades descended at almost the same moment, racing toward the helpless man's shoulders.

A sheath of flames enveloped the Crimson Sword as it dove effortlessly through armor and clavicle. The Nameless One had to work a bit harder, even as he shifted his angle at the last moment in order to strike at Haze's wrists.

As hands and Sword hit the ground, Vorric Haze fell back, gaping at his bloody stumps. The Nameless One did not wait, but lowered a shoulder and drove his brother sideways, knocking the stunned Illychar into the open grave pit.

While the other fell, he bent and took up the Sword, prying Haze's fingers from the hilt. The waves of power, both fresh and familiar, billowed through him, awakening his senses as they should have been all along, and causing him to close his eyes in sweet rapture.

He kept them closed as Haze's howl tore through the woods, exulting in its anguish, before opening them as the cry expired.

"You should not have forgotten your suspicions against me, brother. The Sword can do little to aid the unwary, or fully defend a wielder who is too narrowed in his focus. You would have learned this in time, I'm sure."

Again Haze howled, though the Nameless One ignored him in order to face the Illychar guardsman who limped near. His hair and clothes were dripping wet—evidence of a swim, perhaps. A dozen bolts protruded from his flesh like spines.

The guardsman seemed to realize this after taking in the scene. Showing no concern over what had happened to Haze, he reached down and tore one of the bolts free.

"All clear," he snarled, and flung the quarrel aside.

Only then did the Nameless One recall the bolt still buried in his own thigh. He removed it with a twist and a yank, grunting as the barbed head took with it a small chunk of meaty flesh.

"Then the time has come to be on our way."

Haze roared again and tried to scramble from the pit along its access slope, only to fall when he tried to use hands that were no longer there.

"Here, brother," the Nameless One offered, crouching to retrieve the severed hands and fling them into the pit. "Take these."

Spit flew from Haze's lips. "I'll gnaw on your bones before this is done!"

The guardsman approached. The Nameless One brandished the Sword in warning, though his eyes remained fixed on Haze.

"What do you mean to do with him?" the other asked.

"He tried to take what was mine. So let him have it," he decided, kicking a handful of dirt into Haze's face.

The guardsman grinned, moving to fetch the broken spade still lodged in the neck of the Nameless One's first victim. Haze did not need to see this to know what was intended, and reacted frantically.

"I suggest you hold still, brother, lest you find yourself lying there in carefully dismembered pieces."

"I am not your enemy!"

"So prove it now. Accept your punishment, and perhaps I shall return someday to set you free. The alternative will be much less pleasant, I promise you."

The guardsman snickered as he returned with the broken spade and began shoveling loose earth upon his former leader. Electing a glimmer of hope over none at all, Haze seemed to ignore the task itself, fixating on he who had ordered it.

His stare might have melted iron from ore, but the Nameless One only basked in the heat of its glow. With the Sword in hand, he gave feel to the carnage around him and wished there were more to kill. No matter. He knew well enough where his allies and enemies could be found—and battle joined. With power such as this—

The thought terminated abruptly, forced aside by a blinding revelation. Power such as this was only the beginning. For as he watched Haze's entombment, he was reminded of another weapon, one equal in measure, perhaps, to the Sword itself. Should he be able to unearth that weapon and bend it to his will, he might transcend the designs of gods and avatars alike. There would be no limits to the horror he would inflict, no bounds to his savagery.

His visions carried off with him, until he became convinced they represented no mere fantasy, but an attainable goal. Haze was immobilized, buried to the chest in freshly packed earth, when the Nameless One finally came to with the need for action.

"Your name, brother?"

The guardsman paused. "Dral Morga."

"Dral Morga. I go to fetch a horse," he said, expecting that the mounts this squad had ridden would be found nearby. "When you have finished, depart this area at once. Seek those of our kind driven into these woods. Summon all you can, all our scattered forces, and bid them rally to join those awaiting us to the east."

Morga nodded. "And who shall I say commands us?"

Again he searched for a name to properly describe himself. This time, he found it easily.

"Itz lar Thrakkon," he replied.

The Boundless One.

CHAPTER EIGHT

"Then you are not Rogun's man?" Allion asked, looking Nevik directly in the eye.

The baron of Drakmar sighed. He had just finished explaining to Allion his role in Rogun's secret defense campaign, and the reasons for it. With the lines of communication running through his lands in southern Alson, it hadn't been difficult to see false word concerning the general's whereabouts ferried back and forth between Krynwall and the Gaperon—leading each group to believe that Alson's legions were with the other. In so doing, he had provided Rogun the cover needed to smuggle their troops back into the capital city, where they had lain in wait for just the sort of ambush the Illychar had eventually executed—a trap that could have been launched *against* the crown as easily as for it.

"I am my own man, Allion. I did as I believed I must. If I erred in doing so, then the best apology I can make is to take action now to undo my mistake."

In truth, he hadn't been given a great deal of choice. Rogun might have easily overpowered the beleaguered barony had he so chosen—which, in fact, had been Allion's initial fear. But Nevik claimed that he had not sided with Rogun for that reason alone. He had done so because he, like everyone else, was suspicious of Darinor, about whom they knew so little, and of the renegade Entient's unconventional strategy. To his ears, Rogun's reasoning was much more sound. Should the Illychar mass elsewhere, the troops secreted away at Krynwall could always redeploy. Better to placate the general in this, a logical course, he had decided, than to denounce him and risk spurring him into even more forceful action against the crown.

"I wouldn't say you erred," Allion replied with a sigh of his own. How could he? Were it not for Rogun's actions—and Nevik's support—the city would already belong to the Illysp. It was the idea of betrayal, more than the actions themselves, that had troubled him. "I fear for our future, is all."

"As do I. Rogun is an uncompromising leader. But my father always respected him, despite their many disagreements. While I cannot say I favor all of his views, at this point, there is no one I would sooner charge with Alson's defense."

"You agree that something must be done to help the others, then?"

"I do," Nevik admitted, "though I see not how. You'll not get Rogun to budge on the topic of troop deployment. I tried to convince him to leave a battalion behind in the south to help reinforce our own citadels as he meant to reinforce Krynwall. He refused. Having heard of what happened here, you can see why I leapt at Troy's offer."

The baron had explained that, as well. Like most, he had found himself in recent weeks at a crossroads. Half his people had already fled north to Krynwall or south to Souaris, having recognized, as did he, the slim chances of defending themselves against this new scourge—especially given the chaos so recently endured. Drakmar's garrison was small and sapped of strength, with many of its soldiers desiring to leave as well, rather than remain to protect stubborn stragglers. In short, the baron had claimed, Drakmar was a barren atoll, and the tide was rising.

When Commander Troy had come to him with a mounted division in tow and demanded accountability for Nevik's false courier reports, the baron had resigned himself to traveling south to explain himself to King Thelin. Before they could set forth, however, word had arrived from Krynwall of an Illychar uprising that had been crushed and scattered—redirected south, in great part—and Torin slain. At that, Troy had pointed out the obvious: Drakmar could no longer risk defending itself. The commander had offered to guide the remainder of its citizenry south to Souaris. Nevik himself could join their coalition, else add his troops to Krynwall's. Whichever he chose, he could not be expected to remain.

Nevik had been only too happy to accept. Their people had fled south before, during the wizard's invasion, and in truth had never really settled back in. His father had always taught him that lands were less important than those who tended them. Still, he would not abandon Palladur, their fellow barony to the west. Troy had agreed to wait, should her people come without delay. Word had been sent; Palladur had concurred. By dawn, Nevik imagined, the united peoples of southern Alson would be en route to Kuuria under military escort. Trusting Troy to make it so, the baron himself had ridden north, with a regiment of personal guard, to witness the fate of Krynwall firsthand, and to lend what guidance he could in the absence of the king.

And yet, as quickly as he had come, it would seem too late. Given Thaddreus's treachery, Rogun had quickly torn through what remained of the Circle's resistance. Clearly, they were not yet safe—within or without. Preying on their collective fears, the general had convinced them to let him rectify that, by whatever means he saw fit.

"You have served your people well," Allion agreed finally, "and in a time of great crisis. Though it may not be fair to ask this of you, you are Alson's rightful king—"

"Am I?" Nevik asked hollowly.

The baron's gaze slipped to the fire that warmed his sitting chambers, contained in the hearth before which the pair of them stood. As brightly as it burned, the flickering light failed to penetrate the many dark furrows creasing the young man's brow. Nor could it dispel the inky pools gathered beneath his bloodshot eyes. Allion might have urged the other to rest, had he not known himself to look about the same.

"Not even Rogun can deny it," he assured the baron with more confidence than he felt. "If you were to formally stake your claim, the people would welcome it. Rogun would have no choice but to . . ."

His words slowed to a trickle, then stopped altogether as Nevik shook his head.

"You presume too much, my friend. That the people would offer me the crown, or that I even wish to wear it." The baron eyed him pointedly, then moved to cut short his forthcoming protest. "I would accept the burden, of course, if I truly thought it would help. But who is to say that Rogun would then offer his support? Should he refuse, where would the army's allegiance lie? I might be able to jail him, but is that what this land needs? Which commander would replace him?"

Allion closed his mouth, which he realized was still hanging open.

"No, my friend, a challenge such as you suggest might only lead to greater internal strife, with little to be gained in return. As I said before, while I do not agree with all of Rogun's decisions, Krynwall is safer with him in charge. This 'cleansing' of his is necessary, I believe, after what happened with Darinor and now Thaddreus—though we will have to wait and see how the people react. And his refusal to divide the legions at this point makes sense from a military standpoint. Hard acts, yes, but *were* I king, I'm not sure I would undo them."

It was Allion now who averted his gaze, though only for a moment. "Then what *will* you do?" he demanded softly.

Nevik reached up to lean forward upon the mantel. "For now, I shall offer to do as General Rogun asks of me. Perhaps in doing so I can further gain his trust, and use that to the eventual advantage of our people."

"And if he has no use for you?"

"Then I will journey south to verify that my people find safety in Kuuria. If I hurry, I might catch them before they reach Souaris." He paused. "And you?"

"I cannot sit here and do nothing when I know others are threatened," Allion responded. He tried not to make it sound like an accusation. "I shall head east, I think, in pursuit of Corathel, to lend what aid I can."

Nevik frowned. "Alone?"

"If I had troops of my own to command, they would already be en route. Perhaps I can find a volunteer or two among the City Shield, should Rogun permit it."

"I would feel better if you did. Either way, we'll ride together, among my personal regiment, until our roads diverge." Before Allion could decide if thanks were in order, the baron fixed him with a solemn stare. "Whatever doubts you may harbor, do not forget that Torin was my friend, and you like his brother. I am your ally in this, to whatever end."

Allion watched the firelight play across Nevik's bearded cheeks, and found no crack in the baron's expression. Unable to fashion a proper response, he merely nodded. For a moment after, both men peered into the flames, as if they might find their flagging strength within.

It was Nevik who broke the silence. "What of the Sword?"

Allion winced. All of a sudden, he regretted the demanding stance he had taken with the baron when he had first invaded the man's chambers—as if to insist upon an apology for the choices the other had made. If anything, *he* should have been the one to beg forgiveness, for *his* choices were the ones that had already had a profoundly negative impact upon their struggle.

There was no sign of reproach in Nevik's tone or bearing, only a workmanlike resignation, which made the hunter feel all the worse.

"As much as I'd like to personally repay Thaddreus for what he did to Pagus and Marisha, I think the matter is best left to those Rogun has already sent."

Nevik's brow lifted in obvious surprise. "You are certain of this?"

"As certain as I can be," Allion replied, surprised himself at the ease of his decision. "I feel an utter fool for having let it slip away, but the Sword was never meant for me. If Rogun desires it, then let him be the one to worry about it."

There was more to it than that, of course. Truthfully, he had grown tired of chasing after that single talisman to the detriment of all else. Up until now, what had it truly won them? He saw it as a standard and little more—a distraction when there were already lives at stake. He had felt that way from the very beginning, when Torin—Jarom—had insisted upon hunting for the legendary weapon. After nearly losing Marisha because of it, he would be just as happy if he never saw the damn thing again.

The look Nevik gave him suggested that the baron suspected at least some of the angst behind his reasoning.

"Should I be given the chance, I would of course do what I could to retrieve the weapon," Allion added, "but for now, I'd rather focus on the more immediate needs of those in peril."

Nevik searched his face a moment longer, then nodded slowly. "I suppose we should have our talk with the general, then—unless you'd rather rest and wait until morning."

Allion laughed mirthlessly. "I do believe the midnight hour has come and gone. The sooner we speak with him, the sooner we can make plans to be on our way."

"Agreed." The baron pushed himself from the hearth. Before he turned away, however, he asked abruptly, "You have family here within the city, do you not?"

The hunter nodded. "Parents and siblings, as well as other friends who survived the attack on Diln. Why?"

"On their lives, I swear to you, I'll not abandon Krynwall. I will see to it that Rogun remains sensible in his course. If he does not, he shall wish otherwise."

Once again, Allion could only stare at his friend in mute bewilderment.

"That is the reassurance you would have of me, is it not?"

The hunter swallowed and bowed, chastising himself for having ever doubted the young baron's loyalty.

Even though, deep down, he knew Nevik's vow would prove easier to make than to keep.

"You ACTUALLY MEAN TO DO this, then?"

Htomah regarded the other innocently. "Do what?"

"Come, Htomah," Quinlan said, closing the room's portal with a wave of his hand, "do not presume me a fool. We both know what you are up to." His gaze fell upon the leather satchel half filled with personal artifacts and provisions.

Htomah scowled before turning back to his work. "Then you already know the answer to your question, do you not?"

"I know what you are planning. But I do not believe you foolish enough to actually carry it out."

"Have you brought the others, then?"

"You know they will not force you to stay. That is not our way."

"Then why should you?" Htomah grumbled, carefully arranging another set of possessions to be left behind forever.

Quinlan stepped closer. "My friend, you are acting in anger. The council—"

"Of course I am angry!" Htomah snapped, whirling upon his comrade. "You would have me sanction blindness and idiocy with a smile upon my face?"

"I admit, their ridicule is unnecessary."

"Their ridicule I can tolerate. You know me too well, Quinlan, to believe me troubled by that."

"Well then, if you would but take time to consider—"

"*Time?* I have taken all that there is and more." He should have departed the moment Torin had perished, but had waited. He should then have left when the Sword fell into Thaddreus's hands, but had delayed long enough to see if Rogun could recover it. Having watched that attempt fail, he had had enough. Waiting had afforded them only greater loss, so he would wait no longer.

"If matters are as dire as you fear," Quinlan remarked, "then why act now, when it is already too late?"

"Because *something* must be done. We helped sow the seeds of this calamity. We cannot simply turn our backs to the chaos that has flowered as a result."

"So you have urged us in council. If you'll recall, not all have disagreed. There is a proper course to be taken here, and the action you are now contemplating is not it."

Htomah smiled sadly upon his fellow Entient. Quinlan's protests were born of a genuine sympathy, which he did in fact appreciate. But even his friend did not fully understand. The time for debate and propriety had long since passed. Darinor's treachery had put them in a hole from which mankind might not be able to recover. The others refused action now because they had refused action before; to reverse their stance would be to admit that they had been mistaken all along. Pride had made them intractable—a fault often found and criticized in their human charges, yet they did not see it in themselves.

Even now, when it could very well destroy them all.

"As you plainly note, I am well beyond mere contemplations. You, my friend, may be happy to sit and observe and hope for the best, but I will no longer stand idle after all that I have witnessed."

If only he had been able to see more, things might have been different. But there were limits to their Third Sight, and Darinor had hidden his tracks well. Though Htomah had spent countless hours in the scrying chamber, the renegade Entient wore a cloud against such intrusions, and could thus be observed only in the presence of another. Focused primarily on Torin, Allion, Marisha, and a handful of others, Htomah had evidently missed the clandestine meetings with Evhan and other Illychar. Even as the infestation spread to Thaddreus and others within Krynwall, Htomah and his brethren had no real idea that Darinor himself was behind it. Only near the end, upon Torin's return from Yawacor, had they come to realize the ominous truth.

By then, the others viewed it as but one more setback in a series of escalating events. Had any number of these dreadful occurrences happened all at once, Htomah was certain that his fellow Entients would view the matter as he did: a catastrophe that demanded their personal intervention. Instead, they had conditioned themselves little by little to accept each new loss as it came their way. Darinor an Illychar, Torin killed, the Sword stolen, Torin possessed and now wielder of the Sword once more . . . At this point, Htomah could scarcely imagine a singular tragedy severe enough to convince his brethren of the peril they faced.

Nor was he fool enough to wait for it when he might be able to do something to prevent it.

"And what do you intend to do, exactly?" Quinlan asked him.

Htomah bristled at the thinly veiled mockery in the other's voice. "I will find a way to counteract the renegade Darinor's ruthlessness—as well as this latest disaster concerning the Sword."

"A curious strategy, given the cost of becoming a renegade yourself."

Htomah ceased leafing through a set of his journals, dropping them into a drawer and slamming it shut. "You think me helpless now, do you?"

"I do not believe such a vague plan to be worth expulsion and exile."

"Hence the difference between us, my friend. For I am not so concerned with personal cost as I am with the cost to this world and those we oversee—and yes, even to all of you, my brothers of this order. It is all at risk, and if, through some small sacrifice, I can help to preserve it, I will."

"I should like to think, at the very least, that you had a more specific task in mind."

Htomah frowned and resumed his bustle, putting things in order while gathering those few small items he felt might be of use to him in his journey. He was not certain how to interpret that last statement. Was his fellow Entient—one of the few sensitive to his cause—offering to join him should he be able to chart a logical course for them to follow? Or was he merely trying to trick Htomah into revealing his intentions so that it might be easier for the others of his order to thwart them?

"Do not concern yourself with me or my plans," he replied finally. "Maventhrowe has forbidden me human contact. If I can, I will abide by that decree, and perhaps earn leniency as a result. Though, I stress again, reinstatement to a doomed order is not my foremost concern. I shall do as I must."

He approached his friend, tossing a handful of tiny pouches into his satchel and cinching it shut. Quinlan's features tightened thoughtfully—defensively, perhaps. Else he might have been trying to determine if what Htomah had shared with him could be considered a clue.

Either way, the moment of final choice was upon them.

"Do you intend to alert the others?" the elder Entient asked his friend bluntly.

Quinlan looked positively torn, then shook his head bitterly. "As you say, it is no business of mine."

Htomah marched past, then stopped to place a hand on the other's shoulder. "If this is farewell, I shall miss you. Try not to think ill of me." Even to him, the words sounded hollow and inadequate, but they were all he had.

"I will continue to keep an eye on events in your absence," Quinlan offered. "Will I be able to look in on you?"

Htomah came to a stop before the chamber portal. "I think not. Not for a while, at least. Perhaps when I am ready to attempt a return."

With a wave of his hand, the stone that filled his doorway vanished, clearing the way for his exit.

"I will also do what I can to persuade the others of the necessity of your course," Quinlan assured him, "should it be within my power to do so."

"It will not. But I thank you for your kindness. Be well, my brother."

"And a safe journey to you, my friend."

Htomah nodded, glancing once more about his private chambers. His next step carried him into the hallway, where it felt as though he had already left behind all that was familiar, and entered the unknown.

CHAPTER NINE

Nightmares.

He had lived them before. So many, in fact, that he could scarcely recall the life he had known without them. The battles against demons and dragonspawn. The coming of Darinor and the Illysp—which he himself had unleashed. His journey to Yawacor in search of the Vandari, slipping from one conflict to the next against wizard, witch, warlord, and worse. The return he had not really wanted to make, forcing him to leave behind those he had grown to love. An unbroken string of trial and tribulation, death and disappointment, culminating finally in the loss of his dearest friend. By the end, he'd been only too willing to escape these nightmares and the world that had spawned them.

And he had.

And would now give anything to go back.

This isn't happening, he told himself. A litany he had been repeating for hours as he rode east through a once-familiar forest, drawing after him an ever-increasing brood of Illychar. A feeble denial, like the daylight during a sun's eclipse. But it was his only ward against madness, his only hope of bringing this nightmare to an end.

He had even believed it, for a time. When the blanket of darkness had been yanked away, and his physical senses returned, he knew himself to be dreaming. *Death will not be cheated,* she had warned him, and he had accepted it as truth. Having willingly paid its price, he knew that his awakening could not be what it seemed.

Nor was it. Though his senses had returned, he no longer commanded them. His gaze, his movements, his expressions—none obeyed him, but rather were forced upon him, as if driven by the will of an unseen influence taken root within. At some point between his life and his death, something had gone terribly wrong.

He had realized soon enough what that meant.

So he had resisted it, telling himself that it couldn't be, willing himself back to slumber and comforting darkness. But Thaddreus and the others would not let him go. They spoke to him as if he were someone else, and he heard himself respond in kind. He had fought for the words *he* wanted to say, but there was not enough left of him to do so. His tongue, like the rest of his body, was no longer his. He was nothing more than a consciousness, a soul, a living essence. Whatever the name for it, he was but a shadow of his former self. Enslaved by a coil over which he had once held dominion. Chained to a nightmare of his own making.

Then the rape had begun. Had he the capacity, Torin might have wailed at the vile intrusion. He knew nothing of the other's thoughts, yet could feel its scathing infiltration of his deepest heart and mind—had shrieked soundlessly as the creature laid bare his knowledge and experiences and the emotions that went with them. A few of these he had managed to hide, those he had clung to most desperately. But the remainder—nearly all of what had shaped him in life—he'd been compelled to share with the parasitic entity that had seized control of him.

Shame. Fury. Indignation. And his only recourse was to endure it all.

This isn't happening.

And yet it was, Torin realized, no matter how fervently he denied it. He'd had plenty of time to consider it during the long ride east. A living nightmare like all the rest—the worst yet, perhaps. But railing helplessly against the truth did not make it a lie. He was Illychar, a prisoner in his own body, abhorrent to himself. Already, the savagery of his actions was beyond anything he had believed himself to be capable of. Nor could he fully absolve himself by blaming it on his parasitic companion. Part of him had reveled in the killings, in the sheer strength and brutality of them. Part of him had been all too happy to maim and torture Thaddreus for separating him from the Sword for even a short while. Had he not been so conflicted in how he felt about his own actions, perhaps he would have been able to put a stop to them.

And how much worse lay in store?

It would have been better for all had he been buried alive. That's what this new existence felt like anyway. Incapable of movement. Incapable of speech. Trapped in a state of utter helplessness, emptiness, and fear.

In either case, Allion should have burned him rather than buried him. For who else would have returned him to Diln? Who else would have had both the cause and opportunity to bury him in that grove beneath his life's tree? Such foolishness could only be Allion's. The man believed so staunchly in the specific tenets of his parents' faith. Surely, the Ceilhigh would not have rejected Torin in the afterlife simply because his mortal remains had not been properly consecrated and laid to rest. And even if they had, and his soul been left to wander, would that not have been preferable to this?

Nevertheless, his frustration was not with Allion. On the contrary, it gave him his one ray of hope, knowing that Autumn—Cianellen, she had called herself—had kept her word. With his death, Torin had bought his friend life—as it should have been. And if anyone could devise a way to stave off the Illysp, to discover and expose any inherent weaknesses, it would be Allion.

Besides, would he have acted any differently? Though his faith in the ritual demands placed upon departed souls was not as strong as his friend's, he had risked much to preserve Allion's body in those tunnels, when it would have been easier to destroy it by fire and carry on. He might have done so had he taken the time to consider the potential consequences, rather than refusing to accept that his friend was truly dead. Then again, he might have done exactly what Allion had so obviously tried to do for him.

Not that such questions mattered now.

He broke free of the forest as a fog-smothered dawn seeped over the eastern horizon. A crisp breeze greeted him, blown down out of the Whistle-crags. Coupled with the winds of his steed's passage, it caused his body to shiver. Rather than hunker against its brush, however, he felt himself rise in the saddle as if welcoming the sensation. A smirk came to his lips; evidently, his controlling self felt somehow invigorated.

He supposed that it was. After eons of craving, it likely took pleasure in any feeling whatsoever. For Torin, it was but one more level of suffering: aches he could not rub, pains he could not soothe. His Illychar self, he had thought, was simply ignoring them. It was not. It was reveling in them.

Ahead, the road curved, skirting the eastern edge of the Kalgren while veering south toward the Parthan border and the city of Laulk. But just as Torin was supposing that to be their destination, he jerked his reins to the left, cutting off across the open range so that he continued to head directly toward the mountains. He glanced back. The Illychar rallied from the woods continued to follow in packs and strings. Torin felt only mild surprise at their ability to keep pace. As elves and goblins, they were as fleet afoot as any horse. As Illychar, their stamina seemed without fail.

The terrain roughened noticeably, a rugged flatland peppered with bits of stone and fields of wild grass. At this reckless speed, his horse was sure to catch a foot in an animal hole or else go tumbling down a hidden ravine. When that happened, he was liable to shatter his own neck and paralyze his other self along with him. He knew he should hope for just that, yet remained terrified at the prospect.

But the Illychar he'd become showed no hesitation whatsoever. He drove his mount as he drove himself—beyond thirst, beyond hunger, beyond pain—without any regard for his body's normal, physical limitations. A vessel to be used, that's all a coil was. It needed no maintenance in a typical sense; since it was already dead, it required neither breath nor water nor food. Traumatic injury could destroy it, yes, and the parasitic spirit within. But Illysp were ruled by the primordial sense that only the strongest, most savage survived. Restraint, in most any circumstance, was tantamount to weakness.

That was how Torin had interpreted it from Darinor, anyway. And thus far he had seen nothing to suggest otherwise.

Aside from their overall scheme of conquest, of course. If Torin understood correctly—and he was not yet certain that he did—then their latest foray into this world was based very much on the principles of restraint. Instead of outright slaughter, they had relied greatly on manipulation and subterfuge. Rather than kill him and steal the Sword straightaway, the renegade Entient who had served as the Illysp's leader had held his kind in check while sending Torin in search of those whose powers might be used against them. A plot whereby any such powers would be delivered directly into Darinor's—

and thus the Illysp's—hands. In the meantime, the mystic had been carefully positioning armies on both sides for the war to come. Only when Torin had learned that the Vandari and their talismans were no more had the bridled Illychar forces been set loose.

How much patience must that have taken? he wondered. How much more terrible would their wrath be now that it was finally unleashed?

By the same token, what else might Darinor have lied about? Little, it would seem. For had he done so openly, he would have risked being exposed had Torin returned with an army of Vandari magi in tow—those who shared a full knowledge of the original Illysp War. Clearly, however, there were things Darinor had neglected to tell them. But were these omitted truths cause for hope or even greater despair? And either way, how might he help to reveal them?

A ridiculous question, given that he was now one of the enemy. For if Darinor, with all his knowledge and power, had failed to resist or overcome the Illysp spirit within, then what chance did *he* have?

It was a crippling thought, so he pushed it from his mind. Having surrendered his denial, he had only this to cling to: the grim determination to contribute somehow to his people's deliverance and his own destruction. Impossible as it seemed, he would find the answers first, and then figure out a way to act upon them. Anything less was too terrible to contemplate.

As if attuned to his stubborn will, his other self looked back to check again on the packs of Illychar serving as entourage. Not the dozen or so he had fought in the tunnels beneath his home city, but scores. Though driven from Krynwall, they bore no sign of that defeat, only a feral urge to take up the struggle once more.

The struggle that he, as wielder of the Crimson Sword, had promised them.

Torin felt his courage wilt and his own mouth smile in response. Bereft of hope, he rode on.

AROUND MIDMORNING, HE BEGAN TO receive some of his answers.

He rode slowly now, fighting steep mountain trails riddled with clefts and gullies and rockslides. He had broken his first horse some time ago—had simply left it behind for the wolves and vultures while taking one of the trailing remounts. This second steed, too, had eventually crumpled beneath his weight and received the same unceremonious treatment. At that point, he had heard himself order—amid growls of disgust and derision—that the animals be kept fresh, for he still had a long journey ahead of him.

The sun had burned away the fog, yet he still felt the chill here upon the slopes, at the upper edge of the treeline. His breath clouded before him. His army of perhaps a hundred scraped along behind. The rim of yet another valley climbed precipitously ahead.

A pair of Illychar emerged from the rocks in front of him. Ogres. Massive and misshapen, with slack jaws, walnut skins, and glazed-eyed expressions.

Sentries of a sort, Torin decided. There had been others along the way. He ignored these as he had the rest, riding forward with an imperious air. They growled, but let him pass.

Then the trail crested and the valley beyond was revealed. He should have gasped at what he saw, but grinned instead. An army of thousands filled the sun-baked cauldron, an Illychar swarm that dwarfed any Torin had seen thus far. Some lounged about. Many others were fighting—and in some instances, even killing—one another in combat exercises. They turned as one to greet him, restless all. A reserve force, he thought, though he could only guess as to the exact motives of his predatory spirit and its kind.

Without any discernible reason, he paused then, there upon the valley's rim, to gaze upon the eastern horizon. For a moment, he wasn't sure what he was looking at. A hazy gray smudge colored the air far beyond these jutting cliffs of the central Whistlecrags, darker than the sky above. The Skullmar Mountains, Torin realized suddenly, that monstrous range of peaks that lined Pentania's eastern coast and dominated her shores. A pale glimpse only, yet for some reason, it held his stolen gaze in thrall.

And then he was moving again, kicking his weary steed to hasten its descent. As those below continued to rise up, he felt an urge to look back and make sure his entourage still followed—as if their paltry numbers could even begin to dissuade this new group from attacking. Instinctive as it may have been, the effort was in vain. Evidently, his Illychar self did not share his concern.

Though the creatures ahead fought toward him in an eager press, they were restrained by a number of others who acted as commanders and overseers among them. It surprised Torin that this would be so, though perhaps it should not have. They had obeyed Darinor, had they not? And Thaddreus. And now him. They were creatures of an unruly, individualistic nature, but they were not fools. Each still had a life to defend, and a common goal to achieve. The true infighting, he supposed, would not come until all enemies were dead, and a collective supremacy assured.

A forward contingent detached itself to stand before the main body. Torin aimed his steed in its direction.

As he neared, the group kept growing larger—not in number, but in size. Giants, he recognized, having met the creatures recently in his battle against Lord Lorre. Proportioned like humans, but with an average height closer to ten feet. King of the Sahndamar family of races, of which mankind was a part. With longer, thicker hair; stronger, denser muscles; and vaster, more acute intelligence.

A score in all, by Torin's count—difficult to ascertain when his eyes would not focus as he wished them to. They stood in ring formation, tusks bared, weapons drawn, surrounding a pair in the center. Only as Torin neared and slowed his horse's gait did the walls part to permit him inside.

One of them, a male, barked and grunted. The larger, a female, threw an arm against her companion's burly chest as if to silence him.

"Kethra Dane," Torin greeted her, ignoring the other. "Kael-Magus spoke of you."

"Where is he?" she demanded, responding in the Entian tongue.

"Destroyed, by the one I now possess. I am his successor. I am Itz lar Thrakkon."

The male giant snarled some form of challenge. He started forward, but again the giantess held him back.

"A bold name, and a bolder claim. What do you bring us?"

The words, low and guttural as they sounded, did not seem to constitute an open threat. And yet, Torin realized that her ring of guards was closing now around him, cutting him off from any potential help.

"I bring orders." Though raspy with thirst, his voice was strong, confident. "Your vigil here is no longer necessary. I bid you to battle."

A few huffed or grunted eagerly at the prospect. But the one called Dane did not appear to share their enthusiasm.

"And where would you send us, exactly? Our scouts tell us that the western target is already lost. Kael-Magus has failed us."

"In part," Torin conceded. "The flesh-wearers have indeed foiled us at Krynwall. But there are other cities, here in the east, that are ripe for the taking, provided we act quickly."

The giantess's eyes gleamed with a feral hunger, but she looked far from mollified. "The plan was to topple the northern capitals, not rattle the bulwarks of some minor outpost. Had we not been left here to relay commands, and been allowed instead to participate—"

"You were ordered to remain here for precisely this reason, to respond to the unexpected. Too much was uncertain—much that has now been made clear."

Astride his horse, Torin was at just about the right height to have his head ripped from its shoulders. Dane's male counterpart looked ready to do precisely that. Yet even *his* gaze now narrowed with interest.

"The Vandari?"

"Why else would Kael-Magus have signaled the attack on Krynwall? Why else would that command have been sent through this camp and on to those awaiting word to assault Atharvan?"

The giants surrounding him glanced at one another. One or two even offered a thoughtful murmur. Farther on, the hordes of suppressed Illychar churned restlessly, itching to know what was being decided.

"You are disenchanted that you were not called upon to join the fight then and there," Torin added. "You had expected to be sent east or west as battle dictated, not left to wither while at least one of those battles was lost."

"We could have ransacked Krynwall," the male brute snorted in agreement. "Kael-Magus was too cautious."

"Perhaps. Or perhaps I would now be seeking to gather you up as I am the others who were scattered. Either way, it bears little consequence now, given my favorable tidings."

Another string of grunts and murmurs. This time, even Dane's lip curled back in a snarl.

"Favorable? We were to take only two cities, and one of those is lost. Now you tell us Kael-Magus is destroyed. You bring us a handful of strays, insult our strength, and claim to be our new leader. You speak as only a human can," she added, "wearing arrogance as some kind of shield. How well will it protect you, I wonder, when I ask Rek Gerra here to grind that feeble coil of yours into splinters?"

Gerra smiled menacingly.

"That will prove difficult," Torin replied, "when I have relieved him of his shaggy limbs."

The smile vanished. Gerra lunged, unrestrained this time by Kethra Dane. One long stride brought him into striking distance. He did not even draw a blade, merely slapped his fist in anticipation. Then a great arm reached out, as if to seize Torin by the throat.

Torin's horse shied instinctively. As it did, his will and that of his controlling self seemed as one. Reaching into his cloak, he grasped the concealed Sword hilt with a stabbing motion, and sliced upward through the scabbard's side, so that in one swift movement, he had the blade's tip pointed against Gerra's chest.

Rek Gerra froze as the Sword punched through a round armor plate and penetrated his breastbone. A shallow nick, but one that held everyone's rapt attention—Gerra's most of all.

"I would rather he keep them, of course, at least until this war is won. But I'll leave that to him."

Gerra seethed, his arm still cocked. The rest stared with awe at the crimson flames that writhed around that small portion of the blade embedded in the commander's chest.

"You see? Krynwall matters not. I *am* Krynwall, and more. As feeble as you may find my coil to be, it is that which freed us from limbo, and that which wields the fires of Asahiel. It is my hand that shall lead us to victory."

Torin saw hatred in Kethra Dane's eyes, fueled by pride and jealousy. But he saw also an undeniable reverence for the power he held, and a grudging respect where only disdain had lived before.

"Then the games are truly ended?" she asked him.

"To the Maelstrom with Kael-Magus and lurking in shadow. His ruse is no longer necessary. The time has come to battle for our survival." He turned his gaze to Gerra. "For those who wish to do so."

The giant lowered his arm and clenched his jaw in bridled fury, begging to be turned loose, desperate for the chance to kill.

"Will our brethren follow such a command?" Torin asked archly.

"To the sea itself," Gerra snarled, then bowed his head, "Itz lar Thrakkon."

Torin smiled. "That won't be necessary. Not yet, anyway. We shall start here, I believe, to the south. The twin cities of Laulk and Leaven."

"Outposts," Kethra Dane grumbled again.

"Then you will storm them quickly," Torin snapped. "And after doing so, will continue south toward Kuuria."

"What of Atharvan? If the humans have surprised us there as they did at Krynwall—"

"They have not," Torin assured her. "Their armies were rerouted as Kael-Magus planned. If our forces there need aid, I will see to it personally, along with the select few I have come to gather from your ranks."

"You do not join us?" Gerra asked.

Torin looked to the giant and withdrew the Sword from his chest. "Your command, Rek Gerra, Kethra Dane, is more than sufficient. I have a greater mission to undertake," he revealed, and once again his gaze drifted skyward to the stain of the Skullmars far to the east. "One that will not only seal our triumph upon these shores, but may even allow me to sow our seeds beyond."

The giants stared at him, then glanced at one another in surprise. As they did so, Torin hefted the Crimson Sword high for all to see. There was a murmur, and then a roar, like the approach of a tidal wave, as thousands upon thousands of Illychar recognized his sign. Within moments, the entire valley shook.

"You have waited eons," he said to his commanders, shouting to be heard above the tumult beyond. "You need wait no longer."

Rek Gerra spun toward his hordes with a ferocious grin. A moment later, Kethra Dane went with him. One by one, those who formed her guard ring offered nod or salute to Itz lar Thrakkon before setting after.

While inside the Illysp lord's body, Torin's soul trembled.

For he had come to suspect what lay to the east, amid the Skullmars.

Mount Krakken.

And the final resting place of Killangrathor.

"Htomah has gone."

Maventhrowe did not seem to have heard him. Hunched over his work-table, the head Entient continued to sketch upon a piece of goatskin parchment with his inkless quill, its movements unslowed. When finally he spoke, he did so without looking up from his work. "Has he now? Gone where, would you say?"

If he was concerned, or even surprised, his steady tone did not betray it.

"I know not, exactly," Quinlan admitted.

"Have you attempted to scry him?" Maventhrowe asked, over the scratching of his quill.

"He clouds himself from view."

"Because he fears we will try to stop him."

Quinlan watched the head Entient work, waiting for him to say something more. He may as well have waited for the winds to grind the mountain around him into sand.

"Forgive me, my esteemed brother, but it seems—"

"Htomah was made aware of the consequences of such action. If this is the fate he would choose for himself, so be it."

Quinlan took a deep breath. "I do not accept that."

At long last, Maventhrowe set down his quill and looked up from his drawing, crystalline blue eyes piercing from beneath a brow of busy white. An expression of vague amusement tugged at the corner of his lips. "And pray tell, how might you intend to rectify matters?"

"If it would please you, I seek permission to depart Whitlock long enough to see our wayward brother safely returned." Remembering his courtesies, he gave a slight bow.

"And how would that please me, should I lose two brothers instead of one?"

"Should I succeed, you will have lost no brothers, honored one. Nor will our kind have interfered where so many upon the council have agreed we should not."

"And you feel Htomah intends such interference?"

Was that not obvious? "I can fathom no other reason for his unauthorized departure."

Maventhrowe leaned upon his elbows and pressed his fingers together as if in thought. "Tell me this. Would you, too, risk expulsion, should you fail?"

Quinlan felt his stomach muscles tighten. "I would."

"I see. And yet, you are not up to the challenge."

"You say?"

"You are powerful, Quinlan, but scarcely Htomah's equal. If he felt strongly enough to have selected this course, he will not easily be persuaded to abandon it. Nor will you be able to force him. You will have failed, and our order will thus have been doubly weakened. You know this to be true."

He knew it—had known it before summoning the courage to make his request. Their order did not tolerate rogue behavior. To defy the will of the ruling council meant exile. As it had for Algorath, so long ago. As it did now for Htomah. The whole had always been greater than the one. There could be no exceptions.

And yet, Maventhrowe was far and away their most senior brother, with a will and a voice that had proven strong enough in the past to steer the others in almost any direction. If he could persuade Maventhrowe, he might just stand a chance of persuading the rest.

"What if I were not alone?" he asked.

Maventhrowe had been reaching for his quill as if the matter had been decided. He now paused. "Others?"

"Suppose I can convince another to accompany me," Quinlan rushed to explain, before the idea had fully formed. "The pair of us would stand a better chance of success, and three would not be so easy to expel. The council would have to at least consider permitting our return."

The head Entient regarded him silently. "Two."

"Two?"

"In addition to yourself. It will take at least three of you to subdue Htomah. Of this I am certain."

Quinlan drew another deep breath. "Two it is, then."

"Senior members," Maventhrowe clarified. "Those upon the council. It will do you little good to drag along a pair of acolytes."

He felt his glimmer of hope fading. "Any further stipulations?"

"They will, of course, have to agree to the same terms: All come back, or none. And it must be before any of you, Htomah included, makes forbidden contact."

Impossible. He would never find two of his senior brothers willing to accept that risk for Htomah's sake. "And when I have them?"

"Then we shall speak again, in full council, and I will see to it that you are afforded the opportunity you seek. Consider carefully, my brother, for there will be no second chance."

Quinlan nodded, his heart heavy, but his determination intact. "That is all I ask."

CHAPTER TEN

Amid a pelting rain of stones and arrows cast by the enemy below, King Galdric stalked the outer wall of his capital city. His ministers and advisors had asked him not to, of course. But after four days of having such pleas ignored, their protests had become little more than grunts of resignation.

Four days. In some ways, it seemed impossible that they had held out even that long. The Illychar that swarmed the broken slopes upon which Atharvan was built numbered in the tens of thousands. How and why so many had massed together to descend upon his people all at once was not something to which he had an answer. Yet there they were.

He had his suspicions, of course, and they began with Darinor—the mystic who had lured his legion away, leaving this city and others with nothing more than a skeletal garrison. Do so, Darinor had promised, and the Illychar would ignore them, giving chase instead to the soldier coils that could most satisfy them. In this way, and this way alone, could they hope to protect their citizens while directly engaging what *had* been a strike-and-disperse enemy.

Either Darinor had been wrong, or he had deliberately misled them. If any knew the truth, Galdric had not yet learned it. Thus far, none of the messengers he had sent forth through the escape tunnels had managed to return. And if any news had been sent from lands beyond, then it had not yet found a way past the hordes outside to reach him.

There was a chance, he knew, that the other cities were as hard-pressed as his.

An arrow from below whizzed past his naked ear. His royal guardsmen were upon him in an instant, shields raised, cocooning him with their own iron-shelled bodies. Shouts rang out, and defenses upon the wall were redirected to deal with the threat. Only after it had been addressed—that particular fire snuffed—was he freely permitted to continue on his way.

It was like that all along the battlement, soldiers scurrying from one point to the next, as if plugging holes in a collapsing dike. Less than three thousand, set to guard a city whose population had more than doubled in recent weeks—swelling to more than half a million. Many of those had been put to task in one fashion or another, but not nearly enough, and not in the capacity truly needed. Indeed, the king feared that children and grandmothers would be asked to wield blades before it was over, and even that might not be enough to alter the inevitable outcome.

"Sire? Sire, are you hurt?"

He shook his head and waved his commander aside, then resumed his march upon the battlement. Bad enough that he should *feel* like an invalid. He certainly didn't need to be fawned over like one.

And yet, he understood his people's need for a figurehead, and so stopped short of dismissing his guard unit altogether. That was why he made these rounds, after all—not only to see for himself how the defenses fared, but to lend encouragement to those whose strength of heart could not be allowed to wane.

In truth, he took from them as much as he gave. He had been a fighter since he could remember, a man who never felt so alive as he did when pitted against a challenge—man or beast—that might take it from him. But he also knew when he was outmatched. Had these Illychar taken the time to construct even the most rudimentary ram or tower or catapult, Atharvan might have already fallen. Instead, they battled as if only vaguely interested in the city or its inhabitants. And perhaps that was the case. Perhaps they were only biding their time, waiting for the true spoils—the soldiers of Partha's legion—to return.

After all, what need was there to actually conquer the city? Time favored the attacker—particularly one that required neither food nor shelter. And as long as the Illychar held the city in their noose, any soldiers who *did* come would face a frightful dilemma: engage the undead creatures on open ground, or else abandon their loved ones—the young, the elderly, the infirm—to a fate worse than death.

Yet, for three days now, the entire city had been praying for just that: the return of Corathel and the Parthan Legion. Without that or other military aid, they would eventually be overrun—or else starve and *then* be overrun.

He came upon a pair of garrison soldiers carrying a wounded man between them. All—even the brave soul with an arrow in his gut—paused to salute their king's courage in striding so brazenly upon the battlement's front line.

Galdric shook his head. "Don't stop here, you fools. Get that man aid."

Before they could carry on, however, the king laid a hand upon the wounded lad's shoulder. "You'll have a scar to match one of mine."

The wounded man brightened. Galdric pressed on.

At last he reached the corner of the northernmost parapet. There he stopped, in the evening shadow cast by a pocked and weathered merlon. To one side, a pack of long-dead elves fell screaming as their scaling ropes were sliced away, into a surging crush of their companions below. Creatures from another age, he thought, before wondering how long it might be before the same would be said of man.

He shifted focus then, turning eye to the vast array of cliffs and canyons that split the northern landscape for as far as he could see—a scene of rugged, breathtaking majesty. His people might yet make use of those canyons, of course. The slopes and plateaus that served as Atharvan's foundation were riddled with caves and tunnels—some of which constituted large, well-tended bolt-holes through which the city could empty at a rate of thousands per hour.

Most poured into the bottom of those northern canyons, where ancient trails and fast-flowing rivers might lead to safety.

And yet, he remained hesitant to use them. Outnumbered as they were, his people stood a better chance behind their walls than out on the naked, unknown plain. Thus far, his ministers and advisors had agreed. Until they saw clearly what they were running *into*, far better that they entrench themselves here.

But there was another reason the idea of an exodus troubled him—one that had not yet been openly discussed. Put simply, this was his home. He had gazed north upon these same lands his entire life, lands that belonged to Partha but had been lost to the seceding Menzoes. For nearly three hundred years, his forefathers had been fighting to reclaim those lands. Even during the years of truce, the longest of which had lasted more than a century, the Parthans had never stopped seething over what had been taken from them.

And now it was his. All of it. From the canyons that used to form his northern border, clear to the Oloron Sea. It was not his armies that had ended the age-old stalemate. Nor had Menzos's demise been formally recognized, or her lands given over to Parthan rule. But more than half of the refugees now cowering within his walls were of Menzo descent. They were his to do with as he pleased. And while he felt no great sense of fulfillment in how it had happened, he could not help but think that he stood here today at the height of his nation's power, the pinnacle of his life's achievements.

Compelled already to consider leaving it all behind.

"My lord! My lord!"

Galdric turned to find a red-faced messenger racing toward him, dodging and twisting to slip past any who got in his way. Immediately, the king's personal guard formed up to intercept.

"My lord," the messenger gasped as he came to a choking stop against that armored wall. "I bear word . . . from the watch . . . upon the south tower."

Galdric studied the sweat-streaked face, the frantic eyes, steeling himself for the report.

"My lord, they're here!"

CORATHEL TWISTED THE SHAFT OF his spyglass, bringing the image beyond into sharper focus. Prepared though he was, his intestines knotted at the sight. The Illychar were packed against the base of his home city like a swarm of ants, crawling and writhing against her walls as if to chew through her very foundation. The chief general was reminded at once of the battles he had fought not so long ago against the dragonspawn. Through risky baiting maneuvers and sheer fortune, he had managed to spare Atharvan the destruction that so much of the rest of his land had faced as a result of that former threat. This time, the fight had begun at her very gates.

"Are the reports accurate?" asked Lar, a soft-spoken rumble at his side.

Corathel handed his lieutenant general the spyglass. "See for yourself."

To his credit, the giant of a man did not flinch or gasp as he scanned the

dusk-shrouded vista that stretched away to the north and east of their position—looking at a wall of enemies that would not be breached.

"Difficult to gauge numbers in this light," he offered at last, lowering the
spyglass. "Nor do they arrange themselves in measurable formations."

"They fight as one," Corathel agreed.

"Like the 'spawn."

A grim silence overcame them. The chief general almost wished that he
had brought Jasyn along instead, for the always eager commander would have
had something to say to paint things in a more favorable light. But he had left
Jasyn, Maltyk, and the rest of the legion behind for precisely that reason. He
had wanted his first look at what they were up against to be unclouded by
fervor of any kind. He needed facts before opinions. Lar, always the last to
become unsettled, had seemed the best choice from among his chief lieutenants.

"They don't seem to share the dragonspawn's capabilities," the Fourth
General observed after another long look.

"We can thank the good graces for that. Were it otherwise, I fear we would
already be too late."

Lar grunted. "Even so, their numbers are more than sufficient to have
breached the walls by now."

Corathel took back the spyglass and had another look for himself. Those
in front continued their attempts to scale the city's walls and bulwarks, seeking to reach the defenders above. But the vast majority farther back seemed
almost calm, listless. Many were not even focused upon the city, he realized,
but out prowling the hills beyond, as if lacking interest in the prize before
them.

After another moment, the chief general turned his back to the distant
scene, dropping down behind the shelter of their ridge.

"Perhaps at least some of what Darinor led us to believe was true," Lar
remarked.

Corathel nodded absently. He had been considering the mystic's treachery
for days now, ever since Allion's message from Krynwall. The new assumption, of course, was that Darinor had manipulated their forces away from
the major cities so that those unguarded cities might fall to the enemy with
scarcely a fight. But what if the Illychar were interested in the cities and their
inhabitants only as bait? What if the true goal was to harvest the bodies of
soldiers for their Illysp brethren, as Darinor had claimed?

"If we attack them here and now . . ." Lar ventured.

Corathel looked at the lieutenant general and finished the thought. "We
give them exactly what they want: a fight in the open, and the opportunity to
swell their ranks with our dead."

"Yet if we leave . . ."

"We risk giving to them those who cannot fight for themselves."

Another heavy silence.

"Perhaps Jasyn had the right idea," Lar suggested. "Perhaps we might use a mounted force to lure them away."

"And how long before they return? Besides, we've both encountered enough of these creatures in weeks past to know how swift they are. If they flee, we lose our chance to engage them. If they give chase, we'll never get away."

"You mean to grant them their battle, then?"

"It's what we ourselves have been striving for, is it not? A direct confrontation? They are not dragonspawn, as you've pointed out. I suspect it won't be all that different from slaughtering Menzoes on the Fields of Ravacost."

"A struggle we never actually won," Lar reminded him.

"True. But we cannot simply stand here and watch while the city is overrun." He gave his lieutenant a moment to argue, then pressed ahead. "We'll confer with the others first. In the meantime, I want a signal relay set up that will allow us to trade messages with those atop our city's watchtowers. Mobile units, of course. Let us tell them what we intend, and hope that our king has a better idea."

CHAPTER ELEVEN

Krakken's maw loomed before him, the slack-jawed gape of a titan at rest. Surely, the black cleft was but one of many such rifts in the mountain's stone skin. But having followed the unmistakable trail of thousands of dragonspawn to its source, there could be little doubt that this was the opening he sought.

As the light of yet another day slipped away over the sharp cliffs that walled this particular valley, Itz lar Thrakkon, the Boundless One, tried to imagine this fissure and others as they had recently been—jagged scars that helped to give vent to the tumultuous forces caged within. But just now, the mountain was quiet, oblivious to those come to gather at its threshold.

Helpless to resist the plundering of its depths.

He continued forward then, Sword in hand to light the way. Those who had accompanied him all the way from the Whistlecrags hesitated only briefly before following. Thrakkon could sense their upturned eyes, their gazes rooted upon the magnificent summit that yet rose thousands of feet above their heads. He could feel their solemn apprehension. For they had come to disturb not a dozing titan but a slumbering god.

Thrakkon, however, would not be cowed. Were he to succeed in this endeavor, he would come one step closer to breaking the shackles fixed upon him by this world's creators, transcending even their immortal designs. In doing so, he was about to prove himself stronger than they.

To that end, he was relying more on his bodiless brethren than on those whose heavy steps crunched against the piles of obsidian stones beneath their feet. The Illychar would serve as laborers, yes, but it was the Illysp—clinging to his mind and theirs like a swarm of gnats—who faced the greater task: that of bringing to life the creature who would help to ensure that their kind were never again shut out from this world.

As the dank, suffocating chill of the cave closed round, and the winds from outside funneled ahead with a mournful wail, it was difficult not to be reminded of that time. The barren emptiness of that tomb within the earth, trapped between this new world and the one from which they had been loosed. He might have gone back, of course—he and the others who had not yet claimed bodies material to this realm. But even for them, there was naught but a storm-tossed void to return to. Their world had long since been stripped of its own resources, its desolate future already decided. Despite their defeat at the hands of the flesh-wearers, it was *this* world that offered them hope, a chance to begin again.

So he had remained, like so many others, to watch over the centuries of butchery that had taken place amid their Illychar brethren. With no one else upon whom to unleash their hateful frustrations, those with coils had turned against one another in a chaotic bloodbath that was without end. For no sooner did a body fall than it was possessed anew by one of the innumerable Illysp desperate to taste the pleasures of flesh—chiefly, the ability to inflict pain and otherwise exercise physical dominion over others.

But Thrakkon, nameless at the time, had resisted. Though he, too, hungered, he did not wish to waste his only opportunity at physical life on one that would provide only short-term gratification. He and those like him had managed therefore to control their common craving, to satisfy themselves with merely viewing the ceaseless brutality, when they so urgently yearned to participate.

And then, without warning, their imprisonment had ended. It had taken them some time to realize it, and to break off the cannibalistic self-slaughter. Once they had, many had ventured forth recklessly, heedlessly, in search of a freedom they could scarcely remember. But not all. Other, wiser ones—those better able to manage their own hunger—had recognized this for what it was: an opportunity to overcome their mistakes of the past, to make sure that this time their freedom would last forever.

So it was that they had lain in wait for those they knew must come, those who had locked them away to begin with.

Even they, however, had not foreseen the utter folly of the one who had come alone, the one they later learned to be the gatekeeper. Darinor, scion of Algorath—the same Algorath who had helped lead the battle against their kind so long ago—had come to inspect the seal, to see with his own eyes whether it had actually been broken. By the time he had learned the truth, he had delved too deep to escape their ambush. Despite a ferocious struggle, the renegade Entient was killed.

And Kael-Magus was born.

Thrakkon smiled. With Darinor's fall, they had learned almost everything about how they had previously been defeated, and what they must do to avoid a repeat of that fate. With Kael-Magus to pave the way, they would soon know ultimate victory.

The smile faded. Thrakkon had been covetous, at first, of their new leader. He had been one of the many to attempt to infiltrate and possess Darinor's fallen shell. All those years of patience and starvation, waiting for the perfect coil to come along, and when it had, he had failed to lay claim.

He might have surrendered then, and settled for another, but had not. Instead, he had remained with Kael-Magus, one of many to do so, waiting once again for the right kill, or for the mystic himself to fall a second time. Only at the very end, when Kael-Magus had been utterly destroyed, had he been forced to abandon that vessel and find a new host to cling to. He had latched onto Torin, lurking helplessly about the man's mind, whispering inaudible curses and doing what he could to sow seeds of mental despair.

Yet when Torin himself had fallen, the fury and outrage Thrakkon had felt at the loss of Darinor's coil had become a stream of unalterable focus. If any offered an acceptable substitute, it was the body of he who bore the Crimson Sword, he who had journeyed to Yawacor and met with the Vandari, he upon whom the flesh-wearers believed they depended most. The Illysp spirit Thrakkon had been had not hesitated, but had dug deep, with savage will and insatiable need, fighting off a host of others to lay claim to the slain king.

With one hand still gripping the Sword, Itz lar Thrakkon ran the other through his close-cropped hair. *His* hand. *His* hair. Though hardly the destiny he had envisioned for himself, he had little reason to be dissatisfied with the result.

Of course, he still would have preferred Darinor's coil to this one. The renegade Entient had borne strength and knowledge the likes of which a pure mortal like Torin could scarcely fathom. Had *he* been able to gain control of those powers and chart their course from the very beginning, how much better off would they be?

But that was the animal in him—always hungry, never sated. In truth, Kael-Magus had done an almost unerring job of plotting their emergence this second time around. Playing the guise of Darinor to near perfection, he had seen to it that almost all of their primary goals were accomplished. His only significant failure had been his inability to finish off Torin and the rest of those at Krynwall once the young king's mission to Yawacor had been completed. Instead of riding forth from a captured city with the Crimson Sword in hand, he had been exposed as an Illychar, and had paid for his victories with his life.

Which was, perhaps, the best possible outcome. Had the renegade Entient taken hold of the Sword, his rule might have proven unshakable. As matters stood, Kael-Magus had done him the favor of setting everything up and then stepping aside forever—leaving Thrakkon to oversee the ensuing conquest, and saving him the trouble of challenging the renegade Entient later on for supremacy of their kind.

For hours, such reflections consumed him. As the frigid darkness of the scabrous corridor stretched endlessly ahead, Thrakkon continued to contemplate Kael-Magus's scheme—both its triumphs and shortcomings—and how he might build upon those gains. He considered his past and his future, agonies endured and glories to come. Now that the latter was upon him, the centuries of isolation and banishment seemed worthwhile, for that same span of time had served to weaken this world. The Vandari were gone. The last of the Crimson Swords was in his possession. The men of these shores were weak. What opposition remained?

The question prompted a recollection of Crag, the Tuthari dwarf who had accompanied Torin from Yawacor to seek out his cousins upon these shores. But Thrakkon already knew what the fool would find. The Illysp had gained possession of some Hrothgari dwarves weeks ago, and thus understood the threat posed by a potential massing of Crag's embittered people.

Itz lar Thrakkon was not concerned.

Yet what else might he be missing? He searched his new mind, grinding away at those hidden memories, jaw clenched against the pain it caused him. Perhaps there was something more in there that Torin knew, some secret discovery that might be brought to bear against them. Much of what the man had kept from him had taken place in Yawacor, after all. Thrakkon could discern that much based on the gaps in what was now *his* memory—like threads missing from a tattered weave. And some of those slender gaps did indeed extend up to and through Torin's visit to Aefengaard. Given the overall fullness of his recollection, he doubted that Torin's secrets had anything to do with the Finlorians or their powers. And yet, it would only be prudent of him to make sure.

But try as he might, Thrakkon could come no closer than before to wearing down those prized nuggets. Despite being consumed with a soul-wracking turmoil, Torin wasn't giving these up just yet.

It was a strange sensation, having another essence locked within him. He did not know if Torin was actually conscious; if so, the man's current thoughts were closed to him. But he could feel a general presence, a tortured writhing that indicated an awareness on Torin's part of the fate he had come to, and of events taking place. As eager as Thrakkon was to accomplish his goal here, that deep, silent part of him in which Torin still resided was a gnawing sense of reluctance, horror, dismay—all of which suggested at least a primordial understanding of their purpose in visiting this mountain tomb.

For that was what Mount Krakken had become, really: a monolithic cairn housing the remains of Killangrathor, the last of the most powerful creatures to have ever inhabited this world. The dragon had made the mountain its home millennia ago, when, at the close of the Dragon Wars, it had fled the fury of the Vandari and their Swords of Asahiel. Having no heart to eradicate the mighty species altogether, the Finlorians had allowed the dragon its self-imposed exile. Here the creature had simmered as ages had come and gone, dreaming of the annihilation of the lesser beings that ruled its earth, yet accepting its bitter fate as even its god had accepted His.

In all that time, only the vain and the foolish had taken it upon themselves to pursue Killangrathor's death. Without fail, each had found his own instead.

But that was before Spithaera had launched her conquest upon these shores. Knowing of the dragon's ability to harness the latent magic of the mountain itself, she had stoked the embers of Killangrathor's smoldering hatred and enlisted his aid. Though unable to coax him from his den, she *had* convinced him to give birth to an army capable of laying waste to the world beyond. In doing so, he had made himself the focus of a hunt sanctioned by the Entients—a hunt that had ended ultimately, almost inexplicably, in the dragon's demise.

To this so-called Demon Queen, Itz lar Thrakkon owed a considerable debt.

Onward he burrowed through the ancient tube, its curtains of darkness cleaved by the Sword's penetrating glow. His band of Illychar followed dutifully. He could hear the huffing of their breath—a reflex, not a need—and the scuffing of their footfalls upon the jagged stone. Otherwise, they kept silent, doing nothing to interrupt his musings. In that relative stillness, he was well aware of the presence of the others, the Illysp. Their wordless whispers bespoke a feral eagerness, fostering in him an urgent need to hurry. Understandable, given that they had come to contend for perhaps the most magnificent coil of all.

A gamble, yes, on Thrakkon's part, helping to give birth to a potential rival. But the Boundless One was wagering that as long as he wielded the Sword, he could keep Killangrathor under control. In life, the dragon had both hated and feared the magnificent weapon, having witnessed its fury in the slaughter of its kin. Regardless of the spirit that ruled Killangrathor's actions, that wariness would remain, and—as long as Thrakkon did not turn his back or show sign of weakness—would hold the creature in check.

Giving him the vessel he required to dominate this world on a global scale.

A wonder, really, that Kael-Magus had not attempted this course upon hearing the tale of Killangrathor's fall. Too busy with his own schemes, perhaps. Too subtle for his own good. He might have doubted his ability to harness the creature's fury, or lacked Thrakkon's ambition of moving beyond these shores. A shame, then, that one of their kind should limit himself with such narrow vision.

Or perhaps he feared simply that it wouldn't work. As of now, Thrakkon himself could not be certain that it would.

But nothing would stop him from trying.

Flush with anticipation, the lord of the Illysp strode on.

WHEN AT LAST HIS TREK ended, it did so abruptly, tunnel walls and ceiling giving way to a gulf of unending darkness.

The heart of Mount Krakken.

The crypt of Killangrathor.

His focus sharpened, and an eagerness overtook him, spreading from within his gut. The Sword's fires quickened in response. Its crimson light strained against the smothering blackness, a candle in an abyss.

Rather than delve forward into that fathomless void, Itz lar Thrakkon angled to his right, seeking the cavern wall where it met the tunnel that had brought him. He found it after a few steps, rising skyward into infinity. With the fingers of one outstretched arm brushing lightly against its cold, jagged surface, he edged cautiously ahead.

Shattered boulders and bits of rubble littered the uneven floor. As he had heard it, the mountain had nearly caved in upon itself during and immediately after the dragon's final frenzy. Some chunks were so large that Thrakkon was forced to navigate around them, while other, smaller pieces slid precariously beneath his feet. Several times, he had to let go of the wall and pick his own path through the darkness, tetherless in the unknown.

His pack of giant Illychar huffed along behind him. He marked their progress at all times, with senses heightened by the Sword. He wasn't about to disregard *them* the way Vorric Haze had so carelessly disregarded *him*.

He passed a number of broken ledges and crumbled landings, any number of which could have been the one from which Allion, the archer, had staged his initial assault—before being brought to earth amid a heap of stone by a single switch of the dragon's tail. How laughable it seemed, then and now, that those two young men had ventured here intending to slay the beast—as if their need alone would somehow grant them the power to do so. A testament to mortal foolishness. And yet, a fine example of what might be accomplished, Thrakkon thought, by those who cowed not to the threat of failure.

By one like him.

He did not see what he was searching for, but kept on, certain from the descriptions given him that the trail he sought lay somewhere ahead. Though it felt as if he had gone too far already, better to keep to his chosen path than hazard blindly into that devouring gloom.

His patience was rewarded when, without sign or warning, his course intersected a depression in the earth. It cut across the ground like a river frozen within its banks. In essence, he had found precisely that: a stream of once-molten lava chilled into solid form with the death of the creature that had stoked the mountain's flames.

He stepped out onto the hardened flow, following it east. His pace quickened after that, for the level surface was relatively smooth and rubble-free. Clearly, whatever debris had fallen here had swiftly melted and joined the sluggish current. And by the time that current had ceased altogether, the mountain had long since grown still.

His anticipation mounted with each successive step. The cavern's chill wracked his body, sapping warmth from flesh and bones. His breath clouded. The stench was atrocious, thicker and more pungent than it had been in the tunnel. But none of that would slow his progress along the broad, curving track.

Hardened tributaries branched off at various angles—the petrified remains of those smaller streams on which the river had fed spilled from clefts in the cavern walls. Thrakkon ignored these, following only the slight bends of his primary course as it channeled onward, cutting a clear and certain swath.

And then it ended. Like the tunneling passage that had emptied into this cavern, so too did the river widen suddenly, stretching away to either side in a vast pool of solid magma. To the right, beyond the limits of his sight, he would find the cavern wall serving as its rear bank.

He turned to the left, seeking its forward shore.

His steps had slowed again, though the pool's surface was as clear of obstacles as the river had been. Yet a wariness had overtaken him, a trepidation over what he might find. He had traveled a long way for this, trekking for days and nights over barren and treacherous landscapes—when he could have soaked himself by now in the blood of his enemies. He did not want to believe that it might all come to naught.

In the glow of the Sword, the pool's surface gleamed red, seeming almost livid once more. Its shore stretched along to his left, intruding now and then with spits of earth blanketed by loose fragments of stone. Most of these were but shallow humps that he simply stepped or climbed over. Only a few were tall or broad or sharp enough to cause him to pass around.

Another of these loomed before him—the strangest formation yet. Two steps later, he froze. This was no jutting finger of boulder-strewn shoreline.

He had found the dragon's head.

For a long spell, he forgot to breathe, awestruck by the sight. A feeling like knives traced his spine. Every image his mind had conjured of this moment had proven woefully inadequate. Even in his fallen state, even with just this small portion of him exposed, Killangrathor was everything Thrakkon had dreamed, yet more than he could have ever envisioned.

The head lay cradled upon the black stone of the cavern floor, snout up-turned by the rugged slope. A stretch of neck was visible, arcing downward into the magma pool. Though locked in his final position of evident agony, Killangrathor yet wore a hateful grimace, an eternal expression of unbridled contempt.

Thrakkon smiled.

He started forward again slowly, respectfully, only vaguely aware of those behind him—those whose awe exceeded even his own. The globe of light cast by the Sword strengthened and spread, feeding upon his exhilaration. He saw it all now as it must have been. A tumultuous mountain wracked by Killangrathor's throes. Cavern walls shifting and grating, moist with intense heat. At the feet of the monster, the young Kylac Kronus, his unique blades unsheathed at last. The stone-rending thunder of the dragon's denial. Its dreadful wails as it sank slowly, ever so slowly, into the molten pool. Magma churning harmlessly against dragonflesh. And yet, settled upon the pool's surface like oil upon water, the liquid waste of the creature's own magic. Its hissing and steaming as it devoured Killangrathor's body like acid, before finally stopping his mighty heart. The continuing rain of boulders . . . Krakken's final rumble . . . the almost feathery descent of the dead dragon's outstretched wings as they settled down over what would become the creature's grave.

Thrakkon knew well the story, for Torin had had his friends share it a dozen times over in agonizing detail, searching for some clue that would help them to comprehend Killangrathor's unfathomable frenzy. Unfathomable to *them*, at least. With his Illysp knowledge, Thrakkon believed he understood the dragon's suicide. Nor did he much care if he was mistaken. His concern lay not in how the creature had perished, but in how it might be reborn.

He stood directly beside it now, close enough to see the individual, plate-like ridges of its stone-skin flesh. Hooks and spines and tufts of hair riddled the black hide, which appeared to have suffered little rot in this cold environment, despite the passing of nearly two full seasons. Then again, for all he knew, it might take centuries for a dragon's flesh to decay, even if left to blister beneath a sweltering sun.

He *hoped* for this, in fact. He had placed a great deal of faith, when deciding to undertake this mission, on the resiliency of Killangrathor's coil. Were that faith to prove unfounded—were he to find that the acids had eaten away not just skin but the muscles and ligaments and tendons beneath—then this entire venture might prove to be a colossal disappointment.

Though he could see no farther than a few paces, his gaze swept out across the expanse of the dragon's burial plot—trying to fathom the entirety of what lay entombed beneath. He could not. The head alone was taller than him. Turning back, he judged that the crown of his own head came no higher than the monster's clenched eyelid. Standing there, he felt a twinge of admiration for Kylac, who had dared come this close to the foul-smelling beast while it yet lived, wading through the crushed bones of past dragon-hunters to do so. Thrakkon wondered if—had he lacked the Sword—even he would have been so audacious.

He shook the thought aside. There were only two questions that mattered now. The first was likely being tested already. Though it was ever difficult to be certain, he no longer felt the Illysp swarming over and around his own mind. His impressions and impulses and inner voices were his own, not prompted by another. Each of his bodiless brethren, he felt sure, had long since begun attacking the dragon's lifeless coil, seeking to imbue its essence within. But could any of them succeed in doing so? Could an Illysp's capacity for reason even begin to match and overwhelm the depthless awareness of the dragon's former spirit?

Either way, it wouldn't matter, if what lay beneath this pool had been stripped of its capacity for muscular function. So the final question was, did enough of the creature remain to be put to use?

Thrakkon knew of only one way to find out.

He marched back out onto the frozen magma, determination overcoming awe at last. He traced the line of the neck, using that to guide him toward the area in which the main body might lie. After a dozen paces, he found the scapular arch of the beast's wings. The wings themselves lay spread upon the pool's surface where they had come to rest. Though it took quite some time, Thrakkon strode a full circuit around each, inspecting them closely for damage. The membranes were riddled with holes where acids had eaten through. Were they the sails of a ship, they would have needed patching to prevent them from tearing further in the wind. But no woven cloth, he suspected, could match the strength of Killangrathor's skin, even at its thinnest. And overall, the wings appeared free of structural damage or advanced decay.

As he had hoped.

Only one task remained to him then, and he had wasted too much time already. He moved back to stand beside the neck, his giants on his heels. Down flew the Sword—an overhead chopping motion—into the bed of lava rock. The blade, sheathed in the fires sprouted from within, slipped easily through the hardened stone. A second blow, at an angle to the first, created a loose wedge that he motioned for one of his Illychar to pry free. By the time the giant had heaved it aside, Thrakkon had chopped free another wedge, and another, hacking into the petrified magma as he might the wood of a tree.

After several moments, he paused to survey his work—to make sure that in all his hacking, he hadn't cut or damaged the dragon itself. His examination confirmed his suspicions. So long as he maintained focus on his intended target—the surrounding rock, and *not* the dragon—the Sword would obey his will and guide his hand.

Still, he needn't take any unnecessary chances. He waved a pair of his giants forward. With pick and hammer, they chipped away at the chunks of lava rock still clinging to a previously buried stretch of the dragon's neck that Thrakkon had uncovered. When one of the brutes struck too deep, Thrakkon simply smiled at how Killangrathor's natural armor deflected the blow.

The Boundless One looked around at those he had brought with him. Ten giants in all, armed with pick-axes and hammers and hearty limbs with which to haul loose stone. It would seem now to be more than enough.

"To work, all of you," he commanded. "We've a dragon to unearth."

The remaining Illychar grunted and snarled, drawing their weapons and tools. Thrakkon found a new spot in which to safely dig. Within moments, all had been put to task.

In the red-tinged darkness, the heart of Mount Krakken thrummed with life, walls ringing with the echo of their labors.

CHAPTER TWELVE

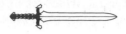

Allion frowned, but held forth his wrist, allowing the sentry to check for his pulse. "How many times must we be examined?"

The sentry released his arm without a word and took hold of Marisha's. Allion felt a twinge of indignation on her behalf.

"Heartbeats both," the soldier announced, as if they did not already know themselves to be free of Illysp possession.

Allion glared sourly, then looked to the page—dispatched upon their arrival—who was racing back to them.

"The chief general will see them," the lanky youth huffed, "provided they have been cleared."

The sentry, a scarred veteran who appeared better suited for the front lines, glared at the lad as if begrudging him his youthful mobility. Only then did it occur to Allion that the gruff soldier might be even less happy about his present duty than they. He looked back to the new arrivals and nodded them on. "Good to have you with us, sir," he grunted as Allion marched past.

The hunter turned his head at the comment, but the sentry was focused now on returning the salute of the outrider who had accompanied them. The rider barely glanced at his former charges before continuing on his own way.

Allion faced forward again as Marisha took his hand to pull him along in pursuit of the page boy, whose lengthy strides were leaving them behind. They had been relieved of their horses and supplies upon arrival, at about the same time word had been sent to Corathel of their request to see him. So they had nothing but themselves to worry about, and no excuse for lagging.

The legion's base camp buzzed with activity. The deeper they proceeded, the fuller and faster that activity became. Those whose faces Allion could see wore looks of dour and focused intensity. Not a laugh or smile was to be found.

Despite the noisome bustle, Allion thought at times that he heard the distant clangor of combat. His imagination, surely. According to the outrider who had brought them in, the camp was kept leagues away from the fighting—and on the move to ensure that it remained so. Allion saw plenty of evidence now to support the claim. Everything from racks to tables to awnings was mounted to or stretched from wagon frames. There were no tents, no barracks, only open-air pavilions to protect against the sun. A war *caravan*, really, rather than a camp.

Their guide swerved and dodged almost artfully ahead of them, maintaining stride despite the many whose labors crossed his path. Allion and Marisha did their best to keep pace. More than once, as they slipped past any number of makeshift infirmaries, the Lewellyn healer was drawn by the moan or cry of a wounded man begging or receiving treatment. In each case, Allion was forced to give *her* a gentle tug in order to continue on.

At last, the page brought them to the side of a wagon loosely warded by sentries, where Allion spied a pair of figures he identified immediately. Both Chief General Corathel and Second General Jasyn had their backs turned, bent over a folding tabletop hung down from the wagon's wall on a set of chains and hinges. Neither man was wearing his full armor, but both appeared sweaty and filthy enough that they must have shed it only recently. Together, they were pointing and gesturing at a sheaf of parchment unfurled and weighted at the edges. While they did so, the chief general was having a gash in his forearm sewn shut by an attendant.

The guards came together to slow their approach.

"The new arrivals I spoke of," the page reported, "welcomed by the chief general."

"So they were," Corathel said. Allion looked up the small rise to find both generals peering down at them. "You may permit them, Sergeant."

The guardsmen looked Allion and Marisha over briefly before stepping aside.

As the pair from Alson stepped forward, Jasyn, layered in a sooty grime, greeted them with a bold grin. "Allion, Marisha, welcome to our festival of fools." He bowed low before clasping the hunter's forearm and accepting the healer's embrace.

"Good of you to come," Corathel added, pulling away from his attendant's ministrations long enough to grip the hunter's hand. "Though you must be mad to have ridden this far without an escort."

"We rode much of the way with Baron Nevik of Drakmar," Marisha reassured him. "He offered a detachment when we separated, but Allion and I thought we'd be safer without drawing the extra notice."

"Tell that to my shrinking stable of messengers," Corathel replied. "In any case, you're here and, mad as you be, exactly the kind of men we need."

"Sir, your wound," the attendant reminded him.

"Please, let me," Marisha requested, frowning at the angry folds of skin and ugly line of stitches. "It has not even been properly cleaned."

"He tried," Corathel admitted. "I've little enough time as is."

"A decision you'll regret when it rots off from the inside, and you are forced to fight left-handed." Her scowl deepened. "I'm afraid I must insist, Commander."

The general matched her stare for a moment, then shook his head in defeat. "Fetch her what she needs," he ordered his attendant, who offered a quick salute, then scampered off to comply. "Anything else, my lady?"

"Whatever we can do to help," Allion interjected. "How goes the battle?"

Corathel snorted, glancing back at the parchment atop his hinge-board table. The paper was covered with arcs and lines and other symbols—a crude map of the ever-shifting battlefield.

"I'm afraid we can scarcely call it that," he admitted. "The reavers have proven stronger, more stubborn, than even I had imagined. The scattered packs I fought before this showed none of the cunning and organization we face now. If they relinquish ground—as they so often did as smaller units— they do so only to bait us into a trap. And their overall strength as a group this large is much greater than I had anticipated, magnified in ways few could have guessed." He eyed the hunter squarely. "Thus far, our strategies have proven worthless."

Allion glanced at Jasyn. Even *his* smile was gone.

"We've had moderate success with our cavalry units," Corathel continued, "and shielded ourselves well enough with trenches and breastworks, where our sappers have been given a chance to build them. But we've done little overall to scatter or divide this horde, and, worst of all, we've been utterly unable to secure the dead—theirs or ours."

The widening rift in Allion's stomach split suddenly to become a chasm. "General, if you don't—"

"We're aware of the consequences, my friend. I've seen it often enough over the past weeks on a smaller scale. Believe me, it has become our first priority. But when it comes to the fallen, the enemy are worse than rabid dogs, defending each kill like a mother wolf, and dragging them off to where we cannot reach them. As a last resort, our oil and fire regiments have been tripled in number, and are working double time. The field itself is a bloody furnace."

Corathel coughed and spat. Allion had seen the smoke that had blackened the skies, but had presumed it to be from controlled pyres of burning Illychar, not fruitless efforts at destroying their own men. Either way, he understood the infernal toll such conditions took upon men who needed air to breathe— and the lack of effect upon those who didn't.

"A corpse can be more difficult to light than you might expect," the chief general resumed when his fit had passed. "And the reavers are not afraid to use their own bodies, if necessary, to help put out flames. Indeed, each of them fights as if impervious to pain or injury of any sort until struck with the blow that finally lays them low."

It was a dire assessment, made more so by the grave bearing of the typically stouthearted commanders standing before him. They did not appear ready to surrender, but neither did they seem at all confident of their chances.

The hunter took a deep breath. "Our services are yours," he repeated. "What can we do to help?"

"Conjure an army," Corathel answered quickly—and with too much seriousness.

"We've tried. At the time of our departure, Rogun remained unwilling to budge."

"Nevik, however, is on his way to Kuuria," Marisha added. "He has promised to prevail upon the Kuurian army—as well as General Rogun—to lend aid where it is most needed."

Once again, the chief general simply shook his head. "I don't blame Rogun or anyone else for keeping their troops close to home. Who's to say this enemy won't flock to their cities the moment they rush out to save ours?"

At that moment, the attendant returned with a small satchel slung over his shoulder. Marisha went to him right away, and the two began a quiet conference of their own in search of the proper medicines and materials. Allion watched her until the chief general's voice forced his attention.

"In any case, the pair of you know your individual skills better than I. You are more than welcome to lend a hand however you see fit."

Allion nodded absently, realizing only now how little he had to offer. At the time of his departure, anything had seemed better than sitting around Krynwall under Rogun's thumb. But what difference had his arrival made?

"Runner," Jasyn barked suddenly, causing all to turn. "Why are you still standing there?"

The lieutenant general's gaze, Allion found, was fixed upon the page, forgotten by all, though he stood with rapt attention just paces away. Stranger still, that attention seemed to be focused on none other than the hunter himself.

"I—I'm sorry, sir," the page stammered. "But is it really him?"

"Him, who?"

"The dragon-slayer, sir."

Jasyn's broad grin returned, and he cast Allion a wink. "He means you."

"I fear I did little more than serve witness to the deed."

"Bah!" Jasyn exclaimed. "No need for modesty at a time like this. Go now, lad. Spread word that the dragon-slayer fights among us."

The page saluted Allion sharply, holding it in place while beaming with unconcealed admiration. "Yes, sir!" he said. To the hunter, he added, "It is an honor, sir."

Allion dipped his head in acknowledgment, not sure whether he should attempt a Parthan salute, and feeling too awkward to say anything else.

Remembering belatedly to salute his superior officer as well, the page set off down the rise, past the sentries, and out into the camp.

"You should hear the reverence with which they speak of you," Corathel remarked. "Jasyn's right. If nothing else, your presence should do wonders for morale."

"I should have killed me a dragon a long time ago," the Second General posed ruefully. "I'd not be able to keep the maidens at bay."

"Oh?" Marisha said as she returned to them with a cleaning cloth and some sort of unguent in hand. "From the tales I've heard, you already have that affliction."

Jasyn bowed low. "My dear lady, you cannot believe every piece of gossip that blows through a military encampment."

"Even when that gossip comes from the Second General's own lips?"

"Especially then," Corathel grunted, then winced as the healer began to scrub his wound.

Jasyn's smile was of mock innocence. "Well, as much as I'd like to hang around to defend my reputation, some of us have a war to tend to. With my lady's leave?"

"See to it you take better care than your commander here," Marisha admonished him.

"The general spends too much time watching the backs of others, rather than his own," Jasyn replied. "I am much less prone to that particular ailment."

"If you say so," Marisha said, trying to match the other's facetiousness.

"I want that sling battalion moved to the northwestern rim," Corathel ordered his lieutenant, "and the arrow battalions brought up from the south. Also, I want a fresh report from Maltyk. I'll catch up with you atop Gaermont Ridge."

"As you request, sir. Come, Allion, let us show you a better view of the little hornet's nest we've stirred up, shall we?"

Allion looked to Marisha. He had sworn not to leave her again, and he had meant it.

"Go," she said. "I'll accompany the chief general when we're finished here. I've no doubt we'll find men who could use my attention on the front lines."

Still he hesitated.

"She'll be in better hands than you," Corathel assured him, though it seemed all playfulness had ended. "Don't allow him to convince you to do anything as foolish as he did the last time."

The chief general, Allion decided, was only partly serious. As much as he had disagreed with their decision to come after him when he'd been captured by the A'awari, Corathel remained deeply thankful for what they had done, and would not go so far as to ridicule them for it.

"We'll be waiting for you both," Allion replied earnestly, then turned to follow a smirking Jasyn.

His chest ached as he did so. Perhaps it was the fear of abandoning Marisha. Or perhaps it was the knowledge that he would soon catch his first glimpse of what the Illychar were truly capable of. For if they could cause one such as Corathel to render such grim appraisal after just a day and a half of fighting, what hope did his people have?

Gritting his teeth against the thought, he hurried on to find out.

NEVIK'S NERVES DREW TAUT AS he crested the rampway of the fifth and final gate, passing at last into the highest level of the mountain city of Souaris. Up until now, he had done a reasonable job of containing his anxiety. Now that only the Palace of Kings lay before him, seated atop its jutting plateau, all of the concerns he had so assiduously managed to avoid seemed to descend upon him at once.

Odd, feeling like a criminal as he made his return. When last he had left these famed battlements, he had done so as one of the city's heroes. Battling alongside High Commander Troy, he had stood proud in the defense of a city not his own, the legendary City of Man, against the greatest scourge their kind had ever known. Never mind that he had fought for himself and his own people—tucked away within her walls—as much as the Souari who called the city home. Never mind that had it not been for the unlikely triumphs of Torin, Kylac, and Allion, the city and all of its inhabitants would have suffered a calamitous defeat. No, despite any of that, all the grateful citizens of Souaris seemed to remember was that Baron Nevik of Alson was an outsider who had nearly given his life to help shield theirs.

And now he had returned, a purveyor of lies that might have threatened their nation, all so as to protect his own.

They couldn't know that, of course. The general populace would have no awareness of the false reports delivered to King Thelin and his high-level commanders. But his own conscience cared little for such trifles, and a people's ignorance did not equal forgiveness.

Besides, Thelin himself *did* know. And it was the king he now had to face.

Surprisingly, Thelin had not sent for him. Nevik had presumed that Troy would march him before the Souari ruler the moment they reached the city. Instead, the high commander had gone to meet with his sovereign alone, while leaving the baron behind to help oversee the accommodations granted his people. Nevik had done so for a time, until the continuing silence and his own guilt had gnawed holes inside him. Only after making his request for a royal audience this very night had that messenger returned with the mounted escort that now led him to the king.

Leaving his lieutenants and advisors to assist Ghellenay in the supervision of their people and hers, he had set forth straightaway, determined to account for his actions once and for all. However, as he'd made his way through the ascending, half-moon rungs toward the city's elevated reaches, his thoughts had soon shifted. With the climb up each successive gateway ramp, he recalled the frantic retreat he had made alongside those seeking to survive the most vicious battle in the history of a city that had seen more than its share. The scars from that conflict had scarcely begun to heal, and here they were, on the verge of reliving it all again.

More than that, he had continued to marvel at the sheer volume of refugees come again to beg the city's shelter. Even here, within the royal zenith, his escort had to carve a path through a sea of disillusioned souls—men and women of all ages and from all corners of Pentania—who had crammed within these walls to escape a common nightmare. When word of the Illychar had first begun to spread, back before anyone had even known what to call them, the Culmarils—King Thelin and his wife, Queen Loisse—had made it known that no one seeking Souaris's legendary shelter would be turned away. In truth, many of those herded here by the invasions of wizard and demon had never left, and those who *had* were quick to return. Few had forgotten the utter devastation of those prior threats. Fewer still were willing to wait around to see what horrors this one might manifest.

Nevik had heard some of the rough census counts, which had the city swelling to three and four times its normal capacity. But seeing it for himself was a visceral experience unlike any he had imagined. While many had chosen to divert to other Kuurian cities like Stralk and Tresc Thor, an almost equal number of citizens from those lesser strongholds had been received. Judging by the baron's own arrival—and the thousands who had accompanied him from southern Alson—the situation promised to worsen before it improved.

Yet, rather than stem the incoming flow, the Souari were scrambling to accommodate the continuing inundation. According to the coordinators he and Ghellenay had met with earlier, refugees were now being tucked away in the mountain tunnels behind the city, taking advantage of an immense warren of caverns as ancient as the land itself. Food, water, light, medicines, and other necessities would be delivered as efficiently as possible. And a system of rotation was being designed so that those underground would not remain so forever. Extreme as it seemed, it was the last course available, for there was only so much space that could be shared with the armies who would protect the city against the inevitable invasion.

That the people had so readily accepted the idea spoke to their desperation.

It would also explain the vast number making their way up into the mountains from the lower levels of the city. Nevik took one last, lingering look at the slow-moving crush before rounding a bend onto the causeway that would carry him to the top of the plateau and the Palace of the Kings. At that point, he tried to put aside his misgivings at the sight of a prideful, warrior-like city become an asylum for the cowering population of an entire continent. Despite countless hours of reflection, he had yet to craft an apology that suited him. Not because he regretted his actions, but because, as Troy had pointed out, he should have trusted them with the truth. Never had that seemed so clear to the young baron than now, as his moment of reckoning with a very powerful—and very beleaguered—monarch drew near.

HE IS A BARON, NOTHING MORE, Nevik told himself, as he paced the marbled floor of a royal antechamber. After being led through a maze of halls and corridors decorated in the stark, militaristic style for which Souaris was known, he had been left here to make himself comfortable. An attendant had provided food and drink—both of which remained untouched—and stoked a fire to help keep him warm. As if his fitful pacing were not enough to fuel his anxious sweat.

For there was no deceiving himself. Though correct in the strictest sense, this "baron" of Souaris was perhaps the most powerful ruler in all of Pentania. With the deaths of Emperor Derreg and his eldest son, and the turmoil surrounding the Imperial Council, most of Kuuria's nobles were imploring

Thelin to take the empire's reins. While Thelin himself had urged patience during these troubled times, the latest crisis had only caused those pleas to intensify.

Nor had Souaris ever truly been a mere barony. At the time of the Proclamation of Man, when the empire of Kuuria had been formally founded, King Bannok had been the favorite to serve as first emperor, with the great City of Man as his ruling seat. But the Souari ruler—the guiding force behind the creation of the League of Man and the penning of the Proclamation itself—had refused the honor. Only with Bannok's support had King Morgan been elected emperor in his stead, and Morganthur, the city of Derreg's forebears, named the imperial capital.

There had been many changes within and without Kuuria in the nearly four centuries that had followed: the independence of Alson and Menzos; the Treaty of Duran; the dissolution of the League of Man; the formation of Kuuria's Imperial Council—an outward appeasement by Derreg's father that had in fact been used to strengthen the emperor's rule; and, of course, the construction of Morethil, the city with which Derreg himself had replaced his realm's ancestral capital. But one thing that hadn't changed in all that time, amid all the various upheavals, was Souaris's reputation as the first seat of man's power upon these shores, and the respect accorded its unbroken line of rulers.

Barons though they might be.

"Sir!"

The sharpness of the tone snapped Nevik from his turbulent musings and spun him round with clenched breath. Thelin's aide stood in the doorway, with a scowl to match his irritated voice—causing Nevik to wonder how long the man had been trying to hail his attention.

The face and tone smoothed. "My lord will see you now."

Nevik gave a slight bow, then strode forward, summoning his wits and his courage as he followed the sweep of the aide's arm through the inner doorway.

"My lord, the baron of Drakmar," the man presented, upon entering behind him.

Nevik scarcely heard him. The baron had lost himself once again, this time to the startling appearance of the ruler seated before him. At first, he assumed the other to be an impostor. For the Thelin he faced was but a ghost of the man he had known just months before. Gray hair had turned white and wispy. A weary countenance hung from his brow like the wax of a melting candle. Eyes of steel had sunk inward, their wells thick with shadow in the room's gently flickering light.

With the glow of the moon through an unshuttered window, Nevik wondered if he had ever seen a living man so pale.

"Thank you, Leyem," the apparition managed. "That will be all."

The aide bowed and stole from the room, closing the door. Realizing that he'd been staring, Nevik forced his gaze to the floor.

"Sit," Thelin bade him, indicating another of the chairs adorning his private sitting room.

Nevik, still too disoriented to speak, found his legs and did as entreated, sinking into the padded cloth and feeling suddenly exhausted himself. At the same time, his gaze roamed the chamber, searching for sentries and finding not a one.

"You keep no guard, Your Majesty?"

The king found the strength to raise an eyebrow. "Do you intend me harm?"

"Of course not, Your Majesty. An observation only." His voice resonated powerfully in comparison to the other's, making him even more self-conscious.

"My soldiers these days have more important things to do than watch over a wasting old man. Besides, in these environs, one seldom knows who can be trusted, and is often safest when alone."

Nevik searched long and hard for a fitting response. "Is Your Majesty unwell?"

Thelin replied with a strange hacking sound—a cough, perhaps, or a burst of mirthless laughter. "I am no Illychar, if that's what you imply. I only wish I possessed their strength."

"Your Majesty, I did not mean to suggest—"

"Your eyes speak volumes, young baron, that your lips do not. Your father, as I recall, had the same difficulty: much too honest to be politic."

"I admired my father greatly."

"I knew him not as well as I should have liked." He waved a hand in a dismissive gesture. "But he is not here, and you are. So tell me, what can I do for you, Baron Nevik?"

Nevik gaped. "Your Majesty, I've come to apologize for my part in Rogun's deception, to beg your forgiveness for—"

"Commander Troy has informed me of what took place. You were doing what you could to defend your people, were you not?"

"Yes, Your Majesty, but—"

"At no real cost to mine, that I can discern."

"The general and I disobeyed a royal edict."

"And were correct to do so, as we now know. Edicts mean little if the ones giving them are as ignorant as those asked to follow."

The baron could scarcely believe what he was hearing, and was almost as surprised by his reaction to it. Should he not be grateful that Thelin was so willing to absolve him of an act that had bordered on treason?

"From what Troy tells me," the king continued, "you have received quite a tongue-lashing already. Whether a greater or lesser punishment is deserved, I cannot say. Now that your people are here, under my protection, I can trust you to defend mine as you would yours, can I not?"

"You can, Your Majesty."

"Then you will forgive me if I claim to have more troubling concerns than those already past."

Nevik bowed his head in due deference. The king need not have admitted as much, for his doubts and fears had made clear their torment upon him.

Nevertheless, the baron wished to make sure the other was fully informed, and so ventured carefully, "I presume the high commander told you also of the theft of the Crimson Sword?"

Thelin exhaled slowly, his chest rattling with the effort. "He did. And though I pray Rogun can recover it, I must confess that I remain uncertain as to how it might deliver us from this particular foe."

Nevik understood that no news, however horrid, could inflict a pain the Souari king had not endured already. Both of his children had been lost. The near annihilation of his city, previously thought to be impregnable, had severely nicked the iron confidence of its citizens. And the current drain upon his resources could not be overestimated.

Even so, the baron was fast growing frustrated with the continued sense of battered resignation exuded by the once-proud ruler. Those who had come to Souaris had done so because they believed it to be the first great bastion of mankind—led by those who would be the last to falter. Yet here sat Thelin, haggard and defeated, causing Nevik to wonder if he had made a mistake in leading his people south.

"With respect, Your Majesty, we survived the dragonspawn. And matters are not yet as dire as they were then."

"No? At least that was a corporeal threat. You slew the beast before you, or it slew you. Preferable to what we face now, don't you think?"

"Your Majesty, think of Krynwall, of Atharvan. It would hardly seem fair to suggest . . ." He hesitated, not sure how he could phrase his argument without causing offense.

"Our sufferings do not match theirs. Is that what you would have me believe?"

"I only ask that Your Majesty take heart in the fine job you and your people have done in responding to this crisis."

Thelin managed a wan smile. "You saw it yourself, did you not? There are more than a million people crammed within or stuffed back behind the walls of my city—at least five times our normal populace. More flow in every day. One cannot walk without stepping on someone else, and we have not the means to comfortably support even half their number."

"Yet all seem to be handling it well," Nevik insisted.

Though it seemed to require a great effort, the king shook his head in disagreement. "Tempers grow short, my friend. This city is like a tinderbox waiting for the flame to drop. Already we've had people murder one another over the most trivial of matters. Less than a week past, an elderly man was beaten to death by a young lad who had been refused a drink from the man's waterskin."

"People are scared."

Thelin leaned forward, fixing Nevik with a half-crazed stare. "Three days later, that same lad was himself slain—by the very old man he had killed!"

Nevik groped for a response, and failed.

"A back-alley account, but there have been many like it—more than enough to suggest the obvious. The Illysp are among us. They hover about like flies, precipitating violent acts, then stealing our dead out from under us. Those with bodies—the Illychar—hide the freshly fallen until they are ready to rise again. We have hundreds of patrols whose only purpose is to follow such reports, to see the dead sequestered or destroyed, and to root out those already claimed. They are not enough. Civilian gangs have been formed, whose eager assistance I fear will only lead to greater bloodshed. If perhaps the number of soldiers and civilians were reversed . . ."

He shook aside the helpless notion, then fell back again into his chair.

"And that is the simple part. Assume for a moment that we could in fact keep pace and burn our dead into dust. How are we to prevent an invisible assailant from entering our walls? How do we know these Illysp are even substantial enough to be kept out by walls? We know nothing, Nevik. We suspect much, we can guess more, but the truth is, we know only that which Darinor imparted to us. Much of this is true, I don't doubt, but how much is false? And how do we distinguish one from the other?"

Nevik continued to hold his tongue. He understood now what was truly eating at the king. The lack of knowledge. The uncertainty of when, where, and in what form his enemy would strike. Worse, the baron could do little but agree. They had been crippled from the outset by the mix of truth and untruth with which Darinor had left them to grapple. Their only hope—again, according to their enemy—had been those whom Torin had been sent to find. But Torin had returned empty-handed and was now dead, leaving them naught but unanswerable questions.

The silence between them lengthened. As much as Nevik wished to lend the king strength, he first had to rediscover his own.

"This burial is not our way," Thelin remarked absently.

Nevik looked up, but the king did not meet his gaze. What was he suggesting? Seemingly, that this defensive posture, in the long run, afforded them nothing. But what options might they have?

Before the baron could probe the other's thoughts, Thelin raised a question of his own.

"Your people. Have they been well received?"

"They have, Your Majesty. Ghellenay will see to it that they cause no stir."

"Ah yes, the *baroness* of Palladur. I understand the two of you have grown close."

Nevik flushed at his slip of familiarity. It still seemed strange to him at times, knowing her to be the cousin of his father's mortal enemy. And yet, working alongside her these past few months had been nothing less than a boon to his shattered spirit.

"We have done what we can, Your Majesty, to put the enmity of our fore-bears behind us."

Thelin nodded, a hint of a gleam in his lightless eyes. "Good it is to see onetime rivals joined in common pursuit. It gives me hope."

Nevik nearly scoffed, for he saw little enough of hope in the king's glum visage. "And the queen?" he prompted instead. "How fares she?"

Thelin's head turned, his gaze focusing as if to spy her through whatever walls lay between them. "I find it truly amazing, how easily she finds peace in these times."

"She has great faith in her lord and husband, I'm sure."

Rather than brighten at the notion, Thelin frowned, shriveling further beneath the crush of some unseen pressure.

"I should let you to your sleep, Your Majesty," Nevik offered hastily, worried now that his visit had done more harm than good—to both of them.

"It is not you that prevents it, I assure you. But do go to your people. Be sure to let me know if any of their needs are not met."

"We shall do our best to aid Your Majesty, rather than burden him."

The king nodded absently, then turned his gaze to the open window as a coarse wind blew through. A candle upon a nearby table guttered and went out. Thelin made no move to relight it.

Nevik studied the man a moment longer, then bowed again and made his way from the room.

Leaving Thelin, king of Souaris, to brood silently in the moonlit darkness of his chambers.

CHAPTER THIRTEEN

CORATHEL FELT HIS STOMACH LURCH as he tumbled from his mount, followed by a bone-jarring crunch as he hit the earth. For a moment, the world became faint, and he sensed it turning around him. A thunder rocked his ringing ears. The cries of men. The hammering of hooves.

The storm of battle.

He found his sword, then pushed himself to his feet, making himself as thin as possible as armored horses continued to roar past. A wonder that he hadn't already been trampled. Better to suffer *that* risk, however, than to have taken that javelin in the chest.

Behind the passing cavalry came a charge of foot soldiers, howling now as they broke into a run. Realizing that they were to have been at his back, Corathel turned. A horde of elves was racing toward him, having sifted through the lines of his mounted vanguard. He and a host of others injured or unhorsed in the initial crush were caught now in a no-man's-land between the two forces about to collide, rising amid the dead like wind-stirred blades of trampled grass.

Though dazed and battered, he managed to raise his sword as another spear came flying, deflecting its shaft so that the tip only grazed his bronze shoulder plate. An elf then lunged at him from the side. The general stumbled, but put his sword in the creature's stomach while blocking its strike with a swipe of his armored forearm. He need scarcely have bothered. The elf carried no weapon; its hand had been severed, and its legs were badly broken. Though it thrashed and hissed, it was as good as dead.

Still, he had to kick the sputtering thing away in order to free his blade for the next opponent. By then, his soldiers were pouring past him in droves, sweeping across the battlefield with lethal intent and seasoned proficiency. It appeared their maneuvers this day had worked. Thanks to a diversionary strike from the west, and the use of a canyon trail snaking up from the south, they had gained the plateau with three full companies—one mounted, two afoot. More than half a battalion in all, and plenty, he believed, to attain their next objective.

He glanced about for his horse. When he did not see it, he ran forward to join the assault. Elves dodged and skittered, their lithe forms swift and graceful. Yet they lacked the armor of their Parthan counterparts, and were, for the moment, badly outnumbered. Slipping one blow only put them in line for another. With chain and plate and iron shields to repel the elves' lightweight weapons, Corathel's troops happily traded the nicks and cuts from spear, arrow, and dagger for the crushing, cleaving impact of sword, hammer, and mace.

Their advantage would not last long. Sooner or later, the enemy would get itself turned around to confront the surprise threat. For days now, the legion had attacked Atharvan's foothills in this manner, with a series of feints and runs, draws and flanking maneuvers. No matter the strategy or the angle of attack, they had yet to make a serious gash that had not quickly been filled.

But this was a first—catching the enemy off guard on such a large scale—which gave the chief general hope. On this, the fourth day of fighting, his men were in serious need of a major victory. Battle had all but ground to a stalemate. With one after another of their assaults repelled, the bulk of the legion had settled a stationary defensive line along the western front. They had been forced to in order to allow troops to rest and regroup. What he and his lieutenant generals had hoped would be a swift and decisive offensive against a smaller enemy force had become anything but. As it now stood, those superior numbers—and weaponry—were all that was keeping them alive, negated by an enemy that neither needed nor offered any reprieve.

"Goblin!"

The warning shouts came only a moment before the creature came ripping through the lines before him. Corathel's muscles clenched, eyes wide with both horror and fascination. Of all the savage forms taken by the Illychar, goblins were perhaps the worst: nothing but a whirlwind of tooth and claw and crushing strength. Their leathery hides did not bleed easily—and that was assuming you could pin one in place long enough to get a clean strike. If you took the time to aim your attack, you were already too late.

So he barreled in as the others did, hacking heedlessly at what seemed to be a vortex of whipping tendrils, then racing past. His blade tore through some part of the beast, so he must have caught it looking elsewhere. Only blind luck determined whether you took a piece of a goblin, or it took a piece of you. He certainly hadn't killed the thing, but hoped he had at least helped to slow it down so that those coming behind him could.

Either way, he did not stop to check. The primary goal was to continue driving forward until his force encountered one led by General Jasyn from the west. Clear the plateau, *then* sweep up the dregs. If successful, they would have secured a critical stretch of high ground from which to carry forth their continued assault.

Most of his men needed no reminder of this, killing as many as they could while surging onward, trusting those who followed to keep the survivors off their backs. He did spot one team fighting to bring down an ogre, but its members were quick enough to abandon the brute when he ordered them on. As the largest and strongest of the enemy, ogres were difficult to fell and sought after by many as trophy kills—a sport for which there was no time. Or perhaps his men simply feared leaving one of these rampaging monstrosities to attack them from behind. Slow as the beasts moved, Corathel himself would have much rather had an ogre huffing down his neck than a goblin—or even an elf. Regardless, the only true issue, in those terrible moments, was to prevent his forces from stalling.

He maintained such focus instinctively, even in the midst of battle. He'd been at this enough times that his tactician's mind never seemed to rest. Or maybe that was the problem. He'd gone without sleep for three consecutive shifts now, fighting longer than he should have and drawing up plans instead—even while lying in his cot. His thoughts seemed a permanent part of the maelstrom by which the legion had been engulfed, and raged now with single-minded purpose.

A semblance of a guard ring had formed loosely around him, comprised of men rallied by his commands. He hadn't summoned their protection, but they granted it instinctively, shielding him from the worst of the bloody chaos. Bodies continued to hurtle past or else fall to either side. Their screams cut the midday sky.

Another goblin tore across the field to his left, while a third carved a swath to his right. The press ahead thickened with the growing reaver response, and, with fatigue setting in, the Parthan charge began to slow.

They battled on, each man forging his path one kill at a time. From farther back came the crackling roar of blazes being lit, accompanied by the shrieks of fury and indignation of those enemies who watched coils being destroyed. It also marked a sign of progress, for Corathel had ordered that the fire teams hold back until the forward rush had crossed the westerly line of Fahren Cleft. He had not wanted to draw the enemy's full attention too soon, nor set ablaze the ground of their only escape. As of this moment, they had passed the point of no retreat.

With renewed strength and ferocity, he and his men bore down against the foes in front of them. Corathel had lost count of the number he had killed, and though his lungs and shoulders burned, he held his sword high, ready for the next.

The cavalry was just ahead now, wheeling and grinding amid choking clouds of dust. Corathel's heart leapt in recognition of their finishing maneuvers. The battle was nearly won.

The notion fueled his spirits, even as he stepped over and around the bodies of the fallen—more of which were Parthan than had been in the beginning. The movements of those around him—and indeed his own—had grown increasingly leaden. Attacks were weaker, defenses slower. More and more, men had to pause to catch their breath, awaiting the next confrontation rather than seeking it out. Their mortal bodies had only so much to give.

But they could not relent now, not with victory at hand. So Corathel continued to bellow amid the tumult, barking commands and shouting encouragement. Those nearest him relayed his words and his growls outward, until the field resonated his sense of conviction. Slowly, sluggishly, their lines drove on.

At almost the same time, however, he began to detect cries of dismay echoing back from the front lines. As they grew in strength, he knew something wasn't right. He tried to see what was happening ahead of him, but saw little more than a thrashing wall of knotted limbs and weapons, screened through by curtains of dust.

The northern edge of the plateau loomed before him, walled off by a mountain bluff that served as its spine. The reavers had been decimated and were fighting a helpless struggle now in scattered pockets. They had nowhere to flee.

The cavalry, he then noticed, was doing its best to form a line to the west. Corathel angled in that direction. Jasyn's force had arrived! Their plan had succeeded.

So why the defensive posturing?

And then he realized.

These were not Jasyn's men.

They closed upon the cavalry line with a sickening crunch, Parthan weapons hacking with abandon at horse and rider alike. Corathel had known it would happen eventually. Though he had done everything he could to prevent it, the reavers had, by this fourth day, hoarded away a fair collection of the Parthan dead.

The time had come to battle his own.

Instead of celebrating a hard-fought and much-needed triumph, Corathel felt the worst sickness he had ever known take hold. He had seen his slain rise again on the plains to the south, in the forests of the Kalmira, and in the jungles of Vosges. It had been a sorrowful experience, akin to watching a friend go mad or losing a dog to the foaming disease. But on a scale such as this—in which it was not just a matter of putting down one or two unfortunate souls, but concentrating a full-scale assault against hundreds who had once been like sons to him—the truth seemed more than his heart could bear.

He carried on anyway, burying such feelings as soldiers did, in order to fulfill his duty. Brothers that they were, he would not see them enslaved. It became the new rallying cry sent forth among his troops: Bring them down. Set them free.

But words alone did not restore broken confidence, or heal a man's shattered faith. His troops had been prepped for this eventuality, and were responding as expected, but they, like he, lacked the passion and assurance with which they had cut down the nonhuman creatures for which the reavers were known. No matter how they chose to view it, this was something quite different. Given their already ragged state, the chief general could no longer be certain they would overcome.

And yet, they had little choice. The wall of fire set at their backs by those charged with destroying their trail of carnage would not be easily breached. Their best option was to press forward, trusting that Jasyn's force was still en route, and that it could seal off the swarm of Illychar that doubtless would be surging right behind. That it had yet to arrive—given its earlier start and a shorter distance to cover—was a foreboding sign.

"Sergeant!" he shouted breathlessly, pleased to find the commander of his cavalry company amid the throng.

The soldier did not hear him at first, too busy directing matters of his own. Within moments, however, Corathel's troops had successfully established a western phalanx that would allow the cavalry to disengage from the new threat—as the general intended of them. With the help of his ever-growing command ring, he finally managed to secure a hasty conference with the cavalry's leader within a pocket of relative stillness.

"Sir! We feared you fallen."

Corathel did not waste time recounting his fate, but issued hurried orders for the valor sergeant to begin the reverse sweep against those who by now were forming up at their backs.

"And Sergeant, send word to the fire teams. I want spot blazes only. No more oil lines. It may be our own necks we're roasting."

The company commander nodded. "Will you not have my horse, sir? I can remain here with the front lines."

The general shook his head. "I mean to make sure we hold until Jasyn arrives. Go."

The conference ended. As the valor sergeant wheeled his lathered mount to the south, Corathel and his protective flock rejoined the western fray.

Already, the lines were splintering, as weary and heartsick soldiers fell beneath the unnatural strength and rage of their former comrades. Corathel recognized the danger in letting that happen. For once the two armies mingled, there would be almost no telling friend from foe. Every raised blade would become a potential threat. Hesitate and be slain, or strike indiscriminately and kill the living along with those undead.

Exactly the type of chaos on which the Illychar would continue to breed.

His voice rang out, ordering the desired formations, making certain they held together. As long as the reavers continued to lunge at them as ravening individuals, accidental deaths could be kept to a minimum. Should his men break apart, or the enemy begin to mirror their movements . . .

To his horror, some of the reavers chose that very course, mimicking his strategy, demonstrating the same understanding of warfare that their stolen vessels had shown in life. Low-level commanders shouted orders, and the others seemed willing enough to follow them. Their organization was spontaneous and rudimentary. But the mere fact that they remained capable of—and willing to execute—a common strategy did not bode well.

With dwindling hopes and no rest in sight, Corathel and his troops dug in.

ALLION LOWERED HIS BOW AS Corporal Janus did the same. The others in their squad swiftly followed suit.

"What do we do now?" the hunter asked.

The squad commander only shook his head.

"Is there a problem?" Marisha demanded.

Allion glanced back at her. She and half a dozen others had formed a team of frontline healers, tending hastily to the most grievous of wounds suffered by those being dragged from the battlefield, then sending them on for full and proper treatment. In order to remain near her side, Allion had joined the squad assigned as protection, allowing the physicians and nurses to do their work with less risk of falling victim themselves, so near the fighting.

Like other such teams, theirs had been assigned to a fixed location, where, for the most part, they had remained behind the army's defensive earthworks, too busy with the wounded returned to them by friendly soldiers to venture out in search of more. Even so, Allion and his fellow bowmen had not stood idle sentry, but had busied themselves by carrying out ranged attacks against pockets of the enemy.

"My archers can take no further offensive action here, my lady," Janus answered.

Marisha, arms wet with the blood of her charges, came to stand beside them. Allion heard the slightest gasp as her eyes fixed upon the group their squad commander referred to: a cluster of what appeared to be Parthans fighting among themselves.

"What are they doing? They cannot—"

She stopped abruptly, and Allion knew that she had realized the truth. There were elves and other Illysp-driven creatures among the warring troop. It only *looked* like Parthans battling one another because so many of the Illychar were in fact former comrades-in-arms.

"They came streaming down off that northern ridge," Allion added softly. "Our men did not seem to know what hit them. The flank crumpled almost instantly."

"We can no longer tell theirs from ours," the corporal lamented. "And at this range, I dare not fire blindly into their midst."

Marisha swallowed bravely. "It will have happened elsewhere, too."

Allion turned to his commander. She was right. They could see but a small portion of the overall battlefield, but what happened here was surely a sample of the greater conflict unfolding around them.

"Just in case, I must notify my platoon commander," Janus declared. "To give warning and learn how he would have us respond."

Marisha glanced back to where the last of the wounded under their immediate care was being carted off. Were it not so, Allion thought, she might never have noticed this new dilemma, so absorbed was she in her work.

"Our entire team may as well move on," she determined.

"Ours was a stationary assignment," Janus reminded her. "There will be plenty of wounded streaming in when this skirmish is over."

"There are wounded everywhere," Marisha argued. "And skirmishes in which your men's bows might yet make a difference. Why should we wait for either to come to us?"

Though he, too, felt utterly helpless, Allion knew that abandoning their assigned position was not that simple. Not in the eyes of a mere corporal, anyway, who was accustomed to following orders until given new ones.

"I'll not willingly abandon our checkpoint," Janus replied.

"Leave a runner," Marisha pressed. "We'll head south along the line. He can call for us when we are needed."

"My lady—"

"Remain, then. But Allion and I are moving on to where we can better serve."

She looked to the hunter for confirmation. He gave it with a swift nod.

"I cannot force either of you to stay," Janus observed. "I only wish I could join you." He bowed curtly, then turned to the rest of their team, those under his command. "Stand down, all of you. Take what rest you can. Runner, urgent word for Sergeant Caresh . . ."

Already forgotten, Allion nodded a quick farewell to the squad members, then hastened after Marisha. He might have been content to take a measure of rest himself, but knew better than to suggest as much to the determined healer. Nor did he dare chide her for pushing herself so hard. That strength was just one of the traits he loved in her.

He only hoped that when they reached the next checkpoint, or the one after, his talents weren't rendered as useless as they had been at this one.

"SIRE, I HAVE THE NUMBERS you requested."

Galdric started to turn from the parapet wall, but could not pry his eyes from the fighting below. "Report," he replied automatically.

"I was asked to stress, sire, that these are estimates only, compiled—"

"The numbers, Corporal." He felt a rash of irritation that the ministers had not come themselves to deliver the figures they had been asked to gather. Perhaps they remained hesitant to join him atop the battlement. Or perhaps they merely felt they had better things to do.

"Unofficial counts put the enemy's number at twenty thousand, sire. With three full divisions, the chief general arrived with thirty thousand."

"And now?"

The messenger cleared his throat. "If our various spotters are not grossly mistaken, and if all has been accounted correctly—"

"Corporal!" Galdric snapped, wheeling away from the crenellated wall to face him at last. "Figures alone will suffice."

"Five thousand dead, sire, on either side. Ten thousand total."

"And of the ten?"

"Between three and four now fight against us."

The soldier gave a bow, likely a result of the shock Galdric suddenly realized had registered upon his face. A third of their initial advantage had already been lost. After just four days. The morrow would make it worse, as those killed on the second day of the conflict rose again. Even if the spotters were wrong, even if the legion were able to destroy a greater portion of the fallen than they had in the beginning, it seemed obvious where this battle was headed.

"Assemble the council," the king commanded, his voice as heavy as his heart. "Tell the ministers that I will meet with them at the close of the hour."

"As you will, sire."

After seeing him off, Galdric turned back to the wall, feeling adrift in his own body. A bloody sunset painted the eastern sky, like a velvet curtain being drawn across his world. The decision they had all been dreading had come. They could not wait until the enemy's numbers surpassed their own. If any were to survive this unholy slaughter, they had to act swiftly.

"Are you all right, sire?" the leader of his ever-present guardsmen inquired.

"We shall see, Captain," he replied, continuing to gaze upon a landscape of crags and valleys teeming with death and bloodshed. "We shall see."

"SIR, THEY'VE LOWERED THE FLAGS."

Corathel blanched, his ashen hue matching that of the despondent runner. All activity within the command tent came to a sudden halt. Even Marisha, Allion noticed, seemed paralyzed, her needle frozen in the chief general's side.

Jasyn scoffed. "Impossible."

"I beg forgiveness, sir, but I confirmed the signal myself."

"Check again," Jasyn said coldly, then turned to Corathel. "Sir, it must be a mistake."

To Allion's eyes, the chief general wasn't so sure. The man's gaze had fallen into his lap. When Marisha resumed her work, he no longer seemed aware of her needle threading its way through another gash in his skin. Too stunned to make his own denial, perhaps, though Allion would have wagered differently. To him, Corathel's look was one of heavyhearted resignation.

"What does it mean?" the hunter asked.

No one answered.

"Marisha?"

She paused again, as if to gather herself, then faced him squarely. "They mean to evacuate the city."

"Never," Jasyn insisted stubbornly. "The king would sooner die than abandon Atharvan."

"So I would have believed," Corathel admitted, staring at his boots in obvious dismay. "Then again," he added, his gaze finding Jasyn's, "he may not be so willing to sacrifice an entire populace."

"We might yet recapture her outer grounds," the Second General argued. "It is too soon."

Allion wondered if Jasyn's remarks were born of valor or sheer stubbornness. By all reports, the lieutenant general had nearly perished that day—along with Corathel, for that matter. Despite a valiant effort, their midday incursion had failed. They had claimed the desired plateau, but had been unable to hold it against a resurgent crush of Illychar. Were it not for a battalion led by Jasyn punching through at last, none would have escaped the heights. As it stood, they had suffered the heaviest number of casualties of any single day since this conflict had begun.

There was no reason to believe that tomorrow or the next day would bring better results. Surely, the lieutenant general was as weary and heartsick as the rest of them. Yet the fire still raged within him.

"It is not our position to judge such an order," Corathel admonished his friend.

Jasyn burned, but did not speak.

"We might send a division upriver," Maltyk suggested hopefully, "to help shore up the city from within. Perhaps that would affect His Majesty's decision."

Corathel seemed to consider. "Had we attempted that course in the beginning, when Lar first suggested it, we might have managed. But it could take days to construct the required barges, and a day or more to fight the currents running through those canyons." The chief general shook his head. "I will go myself to verify this report. If confirmed, our new strategy will be to cover the exodus of those within. I want initial plans drawn up accordingly, ready for approval upon my return. See to it, gentlemen, that preparations are made for us to hold for as long as it takes."

He stared at each of his lieutenant generals, first Maltyk and then Jasyn, until he had received their reluctant nods.

"Runner, report to General Lar at once, apprising him of the situation."

"Yes, sir."

"With any luck," Corathel muttered, "we'll see our people away without destroying ourselves utterly in the process."

CHAPTER FOURTEEN

THRAKKON WORKED CAREFULLY TO CARVE away the dried lava rock that still filled the gaps between one of Killangrathor's mighty foreclaws. Such detail was all that remained. The once-churning pool of lava had become a massive crater in the cavern floor. Within, the dead dragon lay all but fully exposed, crouched upon the bedrock like an onyx sculpture mounted atop a granite pedestal.

Though the darkness had revealed only segments at a time, Thrakkon could see it all in his mind's eye—and found it magnificent. More than a hundred paces from head to tail, with a wingspan to match. Armed with horns and ridges, and riddled with spines. Most importantly, the beast was intact. Disfigured, yes, especially around its hindquarters. Wherever the dragon's magical wastes had touched, iron flesh hung in tatters, the muscles beneath horribly scarred. In some areas, the acids had burned holes clear to the bone. But nothing had been severed, nothing melted away entirely. Thrakkon had seen corpses in worse condition resurrected by his kind before.

Of course, none of those had been dragons. The possibility remained that a being of Killangrathor's fathomless nature would prove uninhabitable by an Illysp spirit. For all his hopes and efforts, this entire endeavor might yet amount to nothing.

He should know soon enough. In the engulfing blackness of Krakken's core, it was impossible to measure precisely how much time had passed. But he and his team of giants had been toiling without pause for what seemed like days now—time enough, he thought, for the incubation to have taken place.

Since it hadn't, they continued to labor, chopping away at the stony materials that kept the dead dragon rooted in place. With boundless stamina and concentrated focus, Thrakkon himself had used the Sword to remove tons of rock without once harming the treasured remains beneath. His giants, meanwhile, had helped to chisel and sculpt away much of the rest with their picks and hammers—weapons that nicked and scraped but caused Killangrathor no significant damage. The surrounding floor was piled high with excavated chunks of debris, and a dusty haze filled the air, lit in patches by the torches of the other teams.

Again the Sword flared and pulled free. Thrakkon motioned to the giant at his side to clear the rubble from between the dragon's fingers, and slipped around to the adjacent gap.

He had taken just a few swipes toward clearing this next trench when a tremendous crack filled his ears, and the ground shifted beneath his feet. Upon regaining his balance, he found that the monstrous fingers had clenched, shattering the stone between them.

Thrakkon and his giant glanced at each other before springing away.

The Boundless One looked to his right as he clambered up the crater's edge. Killangrathor's lips were curled, his black teeth bared. His jaw remained sealed to the floor on which it rested, as did the rest of his body along a sloping, serpentine line. But only for a moment. Even as Thrakkon watched, the dragon's head wrenched free of the binding stone, arching backward as if in terrible pain.

The creature drew breath and roared. The walls of the cavern shook. Giants within the crater dropped their tools *and* torches and scrambled for safety, trying to slip away unnoticed. Many were too slow. For with a single, earth-splitting heave, Killangrathor propelled his ravaged torso upward, pushing himself upright to lean back on his haunches.

Before going berserk.

Darkness prevailed, but the Sword enabled Thrakkon to sense what he could not fully see. A gargantuan elbow flew back, and a giant went hurtling. The other clawed hand tore free, then smashed down again upon a fleeing trio, grinding them swiftly into pulp. Another giant reached the crater's rim, only to be crushed by a mound of boulders dislodged by Killangrathor's frenzy.

These and other fragments bounced and skittered, shaken from piles, raining from the dragon's flesh. A thunderous cacophony arose as they rolled and scraped and grated across the cavern. Killangrathor seemed not to notice, though their jagged edges battered him, filling the crater as if to bury him anew. His wings, still braced and cemented at their tips, snapped skyward. With a single flap and another roar, the dragon climbed into the air, ripping both knees from the earth at once and tucking them close against his chest. Perfectly balanced above the balls of his feet, he crashed again to the floor.

As the fury of his movements continued to ripple through the earth, Killangrathor, now fully liberated, reared back and spewed a geyser of flames toward a ceiling lost in darkness. Its light filled the chamber, casting all in a flickering glow. Before that light had faded, the dragon stepped forward, neck swaying, claws flexing, teeth gnashing at the suffocating air.

Then its gaze fell upon the Sword.

Its aura shone through a thick cloud of dust as chunks of rock continued to tumble about the cavern floor. Killangrathor froze, eyes burning with inner fire. He then settled back into a protective crouch. Hunkering like a cornered animal, Thrakkon thought, poised to either fight or flee. A snarl like grinding boulders escaped the creature's lips.

Thrakkon had done all he could to prepare for this moment. He had known before ever reaching the Skullmars that he would have to face the undead dragon down before he could ever make use of its might. Now that the moment had come, he wondered if he had made a mistake.

Killangrathor leaned forward, an obsidian hulk in that well of darkness. Thrakkon raised the Sword higher, his roiling anxiety strengthening its glow.

"You have chosen a fine vessel," he said, voice choking on the gritty air. "The greatest, perhaps, our kind has ever known."

The dragon huffed. A decay that smelled centuries old washed over Thrakkon, but he steeled himself against its warm, fetid brush. Should he waver now, he might never get another chance to establish his dominance.

The surviving giants had finally escaped the dragon's crater. Several were wounded, clutching or limping along on bruised and broken limbs. All were covered in a dusty grit. None, Thrakkon noticed, came to form up around him, choosing instead to keep to the farthest edges of the Sword's light.

"But let us not forget," Thrakkon said, "who brought you here, who made possible this rebirth."

A growl, deep and guttural. The massive head leaned closer, eyes narrowing.

Several of the giants shuffled backward, deeper into the concealing darkness. As if they could ever run far or fast enough to escape Killangrathor's fury, Thrakkon sneered silently. Flush with the Sword's power, he stood his ground, reminding himself of the rewards he would soon reap.

"Defy me, and I shall rid you of that mighty coil, and give it over to another."

The dragon snorted and drew back like a serpent readying to strike. Thrakkon wondered if he had gone too far. He was relying on Killangrathor's innate fear of the Sword to keep the dragon in check. But the Illychar before him had not yet had a chance to devour its host's mind, and that disorientation made it doubly dangerous. For while its Illysp knowledge was enough to recognize the Sword as a threat, Killangrathor's deeper fears remained buried yet beneath an Illysp's wanton, untamed savagery.

As the moments lengthened, however, Thrakkon's confidence grew. Killangrathor did not need to reveal his thoughts; the Boundless One knew them as surely as he knew his own. The dragon would kill him, would feel the taste of his blood upon its tongue and the splinters of his bones between its teeth. But not yet. As much as it would relish the act, the Illysp that had claimed the beast surely recalled by now the greater goals at hand.

"Our enemies await," Thrakkon soothed. "Is it not time for them to taste our vengeance?"

Another grumble, like the crackle of falling trees. But Killangrathor seemed to relax and settle back, as his sense of awareness increased. Thrakkon smiled. If the beast accepted his rule now, it was only because it believed it would get a better chance to turn the tables in the future. But that was all the Illysp lord required.

The dragon reared suddenly. Thrakkon's smile vanished, and he took a reflexive step in retreat. Killangrathor's entire body shuddered and thrashed violently, shaking off a rocky crust that still clung to his acid-eaten flesh, flinging shattered bits of stone in all directions. Thrakkon sidestepped the larger chunks that flew his way, and weathered the rest. When the storm had ceased, the dragon hunkered down again in a nonthreatening posture.

Thrakkon's smile returned.

Killangrathor stepped from the crater then, looming ever larger as he emerged from that pool of darkness. Boulders crunched and shattered beneath his monstrous feet. Thrakkon refused to move, and wondered if the dragon meant to confront him after all

But at the last moment, Killangrathor shifted his head with an arrogant twist. His great bulk followed, brushing past with that scent of age-old rot. Without a stray glance, the dragon turned its attention toward the gaping exit tunnel and the promise of glories beyond.

Thrakkon, smirking boldly into the fiery depths of his gleaming weapon, signaled for the others to follow.

THE JAGGED CORRIDOR STRETCHED ONWARD, and Torin hoped that it would never end.

A feeble notion, but he had tried everything else. With every ounce of willpower he could muster, he had struggled for days now to regain control of his body, if only for a moment. Long enough to hurl himself from one of the many precipices they had edged along during the northern hike to Mount Krakken. Long enough, while exhuming Killangrathor's remains, to direct a strike through the prone dragon's neck. Long enough, once the beast had been raised, to attack, hoping that a fight between the two of them would leave one or both destroyed utterly.

He had failed. At every critical juncture, and at all times in between, he had gained not the slightest sway over his Illysp captor. Soon, the entire world would suffer for his weakness.

The mere possibility of Killangrathor's resurrection had been dreadful enough. The reality, far worse. Ahead, the beast wormed its way through the darkness. Even crouched and coiled, with wings and spines pressed flat, the dragon's form raked the sides of the corridor, chipping and scraping at the many random outcroppings. Torin could scarcely imagine the desperation that had driven the creature through this passage and into Krakken's heart all those centuries ago. All he sensed now was strength and fury and a mind-numbing capacity for destruction.

The desperation was entirely his.

He marched behind at a safe distance, eyeing carefully the red-tinged path ahead. At his heels were four of the five surviving giants. The fifth had been hobbled by a shattered leg bone and unable to keep pace. Doubtless, he, too, would emerge, crawling if he had to over the sharp terrain, and over the many leagues of broken trail yet to come. No Illychar was going to simply lie down in defeat.

Torin might have taken consolation in Killangrathor's swift annihilation of the others—few of whom were likely to be raised up again. But what were five giants compared to a single dragon? What were fifty? If the legends he'd been told of the ancient Dragon Wars held even a hint of truth, Killangrathor might well slaughter every other Illychar around him and still prove unassailable by the hosts of mankind.

Again Torin cursed his inability to put a stop to it. All of his fervent denials had won him nothing. He remained as helpless now as he had in the moment of his awakening. There was nothing for him but to bemoan his fate.

Yet he refused to do that—to accept the unacceptable. He was not entirely powerless, he reminded himself. There were still pieces of his past—memories and experiences—that Itz lar Thrakkon had not taken from him. And if he could withhold these, then he had to believe that he would find a way to exert his will over that of the other.

The sooner the better. For confronting the dragon would be easier in these cramped quarters than out in the open, where it might wing away at the slightest provocation.

Either way, chances seemed better that the tunnel itself would never end.

THAT WISH, LIKE ALL OTHERS, proved vain.

With startling abruptness, seven thousand years of self-imposed banishment came to an end. After hours of being trapped in that tunneling passage, choking on the beast's stench, ears ringing with the huffing and crunching of its movements, Torin might have been relieved. Instead, he knew only horror as Killangrathor burst like a child from the womb, into the open air.

Torin slowed his pace, squinting in the shadowed half-light that rimmed the inner edges of the cave mouth. The dragon, however, strutted full and clear into the valley beyond, swelling and stretching to full size. Wings extended, spines bristled, and its serpentine neck arched skyward, emitting a bone-rattling roar like an infant's first wail.

The sound shook stones from the valley heights and chilled Torin to his core. Yet he found himself smiling at the display. His horror, it seemed, was Thrakkon's ecstasy.

High overhead, the noonday sun ducked behind a thin, passing cloud before reemerging in all its blinding splendor. Killangrathor hissed at its rays and continued to stretch wide. His acid-eaten flesh, Torin thought, looked much worse in the full light, raw and patchy and blistered. He wondered if the wounds hurt, and hoped they did—for all the good that might do him.

At last he stepped from Krakken's dark threshold and felt the warmth of the sun upon his own flesh. Nearby, a knot of ropes and belts lay beside a flat boulder. Torin had wondered why he had ordered his giants to bring along the materials, only to leave them behind at the cave entrance. Now he knew.

Treading carefully upon a loose carpet of obsidian shards, he climbed atop the boulder with a pair of belts in one hand and the Sword in the other.

"Our feast grows cold," he shouted.

The dragon's neck whipped around with alarming velocity. Had he been able to control his own body, Torin surely would have toppled from his perch. But Thrakkon stood tall, uncowed, even as the dragon's fetid stench washed over him in nauseating waves.

He lowered the Sword, and held the belts aloft. "Will the mighty Killangrathor carry us to the slaughter?"

Torin studied the hatred that burned in the dragon's eyes, steamed from its nostrils, and quivered ever so slightly in its curled lip. He would have fanned that ire if he could, though Thrakkon's insult was likely enough. Killangrathor would never suffer being ridden like some mule. The confrontation Torin had hoped to instigate had come.

He waved the Sword at his side—tiny movements, like a pennon in a lazy breeze. A reminder, he supposed, lest the dragon act upon its obvious urge to snap his tiny frame in two. Still, he couldn't believe that it hadn't happened already.

"Together, we shall finish what began ages ago. And when this land's rivers run red, and we have fattened ourselves on those who oppose us, the true conquest will begin. For if you will, Killangrathor, I would have you free us of our shackles and bear us in search of glories hitherto undreamed!"

An echo of the message he had been carrying for some time—as cryptic as it was vain and absurd. But the dragon Illychar must have understood something Torin did not, for the great beast finally snorted and settled back upon its haunches, as if accepting of Thrakkon's proposal.

Again, Torin's hopes fell. He signaled the others forward. They came hesitantly at first, but as one giant and then another began to scale the creature's ravaged hide, the others took to it with greater enthusiasm. They settled in among the long row of spines that ran from the crest of Killangrathor's neck to the tip of his tail. With ropes and belts, they tied themselves to these natural anchors fore and aft. Should the dragon choose to rid itself of its passengers in midflight, it would not do so without considerable effort.

Perhaps he should not have been surprised, Torin thought, moving now to join his companions. He had glimpsed already the concessions these Illychar were willing to make to see their common goal of survival in this realm achieved. Only, he had counted on Killangrathor behaving differently. A creature such as Killangrathor served no one, the Entients had told him, even when it might appear otherwise. Which seemed to suggest one of two possibilities: Either the dragon had cast lots with the Illysp willingly, or, perhaps even more frightening, its will had become as irrelevant as his own.

The beast snarled, but made no further complaint as Torin sheathed the Sword in a sling across his back and clambered up the dragon's side. Bony knobs and ridges in the scaled flesh made for easy handholds. Within moments, he had settled in at the head of his line of giants, at the base of Killangrathor's neck. The spines there were taller than himself, and as thick as his legs. He belted himself at the waist to the one behind him, and tethered a line to the one in front to help maintain balance. He doubled all with safety ropes, should one or more loosen or fail. Coarse as it was, a thick line of dragonhair served to cushion his seat. Were it not for the smell, he might have been comfortable.

Without warning, Killangrathor rose from his crouch. Torin's stomach lurched, and he gripped at that tangled hair with white-knuckled fists. He looked up to find the creature leering back at him, as if to say their time was up. Spreading its wings, the dragon cast its shadow over half the valley floor. A few experimental flaps summoned a chilling wind filled with sand and dirt. Torin felt himself squint, but Thrakkon refused to release his grip in order to clear the grit from his eyes.

The dragon reared and shrugged, testing their bindings, perhaps, or their courage. Its body shifted and rolled like a ship at sea as muscles knotted and released. Torin's remained clenched.

Then the monstrous creature squatted low before catapulting skyward, roaring and flapping and climbing toward the unfamiliar sun.

Frigid winds raked his flesh, clawed his eyes, and chafed his ears. His stomach churned, and his head roiled, dizzied by the rush of images racing past below. Already, his hands and legs ached from clinging so tightly to the beast he rode.

Despite his discomfort, Thrakkon felt truly invulnerable.

Flight itself offered a sensation unlike any other, both sickening and exhilarating. But it wasn't the freedom of soaring high above a broken earth that filled the Illysp lord with rapture. It was knowing that he did so having conquered a dragon—the mightiest creature this world had ever known. Their game of dominion may have only just begun, but Thrakkon had won the crucial first toss. Everything he meant to achieve had suddenly become attainable. After this, no dream was too great.

He forced himself to relax his grip, to trust in the straps and buckles that held him fast. He closed his eyes, reveling in the violent rush of wind through his hair and across his cheeks. Such power, such majesty. To be wielded as he saw fit. Should the Eleahim unite against him, he would divide and scatter them once more, maybe even set fire to the Maelstrom that had birthed them. He could think of none that would not be made to cower before—

His thoughts and world seemed to buckle as Killangrathor dove sharply, pinning him against the spine at his back. Thrakkon opened his eyes, muscles knotted anew with unspoken panic. What was the dragon about?

He thought to cry out, to draw the Sword and threaten to kill them all. But Killangrathor already seemed intent on doing just that, racing like an arrow almost directly into the earth below. At such an angle, and at this accelerated pace, it was as though the beast meant to shatter its own neck.

Surely the creature had something else in mind. Refusing to let his alarm show, Thrakkon simply clung to the dragon's gnarled backbone, searching for some clue as to Killangrathor's designs. He had assumed the dragon would test his patience and his authority at every conceivable juncture. He just hadn't anticipated the first of those tests to come so soon.

As the floor of a barren valley loomed nearer, Thrakkon went from praising his own glories to questioning his decision in raising the dragon from its deathbed. He should have known the beast would never be tamed. Better that he had decimated its corpse to save himself the challenge.

With eyes narrowed in defiance, however, Thrakkon finally saw the truth. An animal stood among the rocks below, growing swiftly in size and clarity. A horse, Thrakkon realized—the very mount he had ridden as deeply as he could into the Skullmars before the narrow paths had made it useless. He had left it for dead at that point, allowing it to stumble about the foothills until starvation worked its course. The steed had proven more resilient than he would have thought.

Though not for long.

It seemed too late for Killangrathor to halt his descent when the dragon did so, swooping now to skim the earth. Massive jaws opened wide, scooping up the frightened mare with piercing impact. A single, piteous whinny was all the horse could muster before Killangrathor jerked it effortlessly into the air.

Thrakkon's makeshift harness suddenly seemed a flimsy thing, groaning with the strain of the dragon's every movement. But his gaze remained fixed upon Killangrathor's awesome maw, where his former mount dangled, tattered and bleeding, impaled upon crooked rows of stalagmite teeth.

Then the jaws closed, teeth grinding, and the doomed creature fell away in ruined chunks.

Despite his frustration, Thrakkon marveled at the horrific display. Hovering above the mangled carcass like some nightmare vulture, Killangrathor seemed every bit the master Thrakkon considered himself to be. A lesson for his benefit, he was certain, and one he would not soon forget.

With the power of the Sword pulsing upon his back, Itz lar Thrakkon met the unspoken challenge with cruel understanding and savage delight. The stakes had been set, then, and the battle lines drawn. An ongoing struggle against the flesh-wearers, against an unruly dragon, against the world entire.

A smirk split his wind-ravaged lips. This promised to be fun.

CHAPTER FIFTEEN

Kᴉɴɢ Gᴀʟᴅʀɪᴄ sᴡᴇᴘᴛ ɪɴᴛᴏ ʜɪs solar, pleased to find his counselors already assembled.

"A draught of the hemgrape, if you would," he said to his steward. "Better yet, bring me the flagon."

The king looked to the others, stood or seated about the chamber with cups of their own, and with servers standing by. Heads bowed in greeting.

"Have the ministers been made comfortable?" he asked of his returning steward.

"To the best of my abilities, my lord."

Galdric took the flagon and drained its contents in one long, satisfying pull. The sweet red slid down his throat like liquid velvet, its sharp aroma clearing his head like a fresh winter breeze.

"I'll take another," he said, passing back the empty container. He wiped the sweat from his brow, then found and faced Eban, the city's chief minister. "How goes the exodus?"

"As well as one can expect, my lord." Eban had a gruff voice for one so refined. "The latest tallies have six in ten safely downriver, and the next wave set soon to embark. The bargemasters report open waters, and advance scouts have swept the canyon egress, reporting all clear upon the western range."

Galdric nodded his approval, and again to thank his steward as he drained another wine flask. "How long before the city is clear?"

"At the current rate, her streets will be empty before midnight. However, we expect that rate to slow as we come upon those who resist."

"They have until dawn, then," Galdric determined. "I'll not risk my garrison beyond that for the sake of a few mules. How many would you say there are?"

"Of which, sire?"

"Mules. The ones who will not go."

"Less than one in ten, my lord. Though doubled if you include those trying to convey more than their allotted possessions."

Fair numbers, given the circumstances, and in line with what Galdric had witnessed himself throughout the day. In an effort to boost morale in a dispiriting venture, the king had taken to the streets with his personal retinue, helping to ease fears and beg cooperation. For the most part, his people had responded admirably, clearing their homes without panic and in accordance with the restrictions imposed. It was only natural, however, that the city's administrators and enforcers be called upon to contend with those who refused to go quietly—or not at all.

"And how fares the legion, my lord?"

Galdric looked to Hamus, a minister of public works, who was the opposite of Eban—a brute in terms of size, but with a strangely tremulous voice.

"The legion has found its stride," the king responded encouragingly. He had checked throughout the day and just moments ago with the watch. Now that Corathel's troops were fighting evasively, rather than trying to fragment and destroy the Illychar horde, the number of casualties had been greatly reduced. "The new tactics will allow them to hold out for much longer than they could have before. With a little luck, sirs, we may see ourselves through this yet."

He managed a smile as a show of pride. In his heart, matters were a little less clear. Though undeniably pleased by the day's events, he could not help but be shamed by his own cowardice. In the streets, there had been those who shook their fists and shouted curses and even thrown vegetables at his ring of guards. They had been few in number, and too craven to show themselves afterward, but the attacks had cut more deeply than Galdric had been willing to show. Hours later, the wounds still bled.

"The choice was well made, sire," Eban agreed, and the others nodded, causing Galdric to wonder if his inner turmoil was visible through his facade. The reaction of his advisors seemed like a reassurance, though perhaps they were merely being congratulatory.

Either way, the chief minister was right. He had made the only decision he could. Abandoning Atharvan now did not mean he must do so forever. Preserving her citizens and himself would enable them all to fight another day. He would take what solace he could from that.

And hope that a new battle was not far off.

"A toast then," he proposed, raising a fresh flagon delivered by his steward. "To a swift retreat, and a safe journey south. Would that I could see the faces of our enemies when they realize we have gone, but I shall settle for staring them square in the eye the next time they think to catch us unawares."

The gathered ministers raised their cups, offering grunts and cheers. Together they drank, and Galdric closed his eyes, choking on the taste of his swallowed pride.

"My lord," Minister Ordem broached carefully, "with regard to the treasury. The articles you listed have been secured for transport. But the crews charged with burying the rest have requested—"

A sound like shattered thunder buried his words, rippling through the walls and the ground beneath their feet. Those assembled steadied themselves, frowning in bewilderment. A tremor, perhaps, or a landslide. But the very uncertainty told Galdric otherwise. For he and his people were well accustomed to such shiftings of the restless earth, and this was like no quake he had felt before.

A shadow passed across the lowered sun, casting the king's solar in momentary darkness. Then came the distant screams of thousands of voices raised up at once, followed hard upon by a clamorous ringing of the city bells.

. . .

SCREAMS USHERED THEIR DESCENT. BUT it was fire that hailed their arrival.

It spewed downward in a blistering stream, and the world below seemed to melt in a shimmering wash. Thrakkon had to close his eyes, so intense was the cloud of heat that lifted skyward in its wake. When he opened them again, a tower was crumbling, its granite blocks become like glowing embers. Mortar and stone and timbers descended in a flaming crush, sending ash and cinders billowing outward. The tallest edifice Thrakkon could see, reduced to rubble in a single, fiery blast.

Killangrathor beat his wings to hover in place, and gave another staggering roar. Bodies flailed and tumbled amid the collapsing debris, joining those that had vanished beneath. The fortunate ones had been incinerated. But there were others. Thrakkon could smell the boiled fat dripping from their charred flesh, and listened to their anguished cries. Such pain. Such blissful . . . succulent . . . harmonious . . . pain.

Before the dust had settled, Killangrathor winged onward, passing over an almost limitless sprawl of domes and bunkers and squat stone towers. Bells pealed throughout the city, tolling a useless warning. Their echo reverberated off jagged bluffs and carried down shallow canyons, where tiny figures raced about like ants. Atharvan had been designed to withstand the sort of quakes and slides that had shaped the mountains upon which she was built.

But nothing could withstand this.

Another intake of breath, and another flame gout, this one directed into the top of an open bell tower at close range. The watchman dove over the waist-high wall, choosing to plummet rather than burn. Killangrathor denied him by reaching down with that serpentine neck and snatching the man out of midair. With a flick, he sent the watchman soaring even higher, well above the position of the setting sun. When the man drew breath to scream, the dragon unleashed yet another concentrated flameburst.

Not even ash remained.

"We want their coils!" Thrakkon shouted in fierce reminder. Though he shared the dragon's ecstasy, their goal here was not to reduce the entire world to soot and cinder.

Not yet.

Killangrathor responded by arching his neck and spraying a wave of fire skyward, from side to side, as if to ignite the very heavens. When at last the impressive display had expired, leaving only sparks amid a shimmering veil, the dragon tucked its shaggy chin, surveyed the sea of structures below, and dove.

Slopes and ridges fell behind in a dizzying blur. Thrakkon clung tightly to his perch. He saw where the dragon was headed. It was the first target he would have aimed for, as well. After days of siege, the city's curtain wall stood strong, its gates and battlements keeping the Illychar hordes at bay.

No longer.

The primary gatehouse loomed ever larger as they hurtled toward it. At the last moment, Killangrathor twisted, feet extended like a striking hawk. With a grimace, Thrakkon braced for the impact.

But the dragon's muscles shielded him, squeezing and flexing and absorbing the titanic forces that rippled through his monstrous body as beast and bulwark collided. Though thick and strong, the stones of the barbican turned to powder beneath Killangrathor's bulk. Floors collapsed, walls caved, supporting timbers splintered and fell away. Armored bodies, iron chains, and vats of oil rained down amid the wreckage.

The dragon flew high, winging around for another pass. Soldiers scrambled atop the surrounding ramparts. Stones and arrows and other missiles arced skyward. Those that struck ricocheted harmlessly off Killangrathor's flesh. The creature flew low, grazing the battlement, smashing men and weaponry beneath his chest, cutting through merlons and even a watchtower with his outstretched wing.

He landed atop the ruined gatehouse, legs kicking, claws flexing. Stone and iron and flesh—all shattered and crumbled when caught in his merciless grip. Arms swiped, and his giant head shook. In a thrashing frenzy, he simply shredded the city's main portal, ripping through the iron doors, kicking aside the twisted portcullis, pulverizing anyone or anything that got in his way.

Bits of rock, shards of iron, and other materials bounced and skittered about the dragon's hide. Thrakkon was cut and bruised in a dozen different places. He cared not. He was too busy reveling in Killangrathor's onslaught, in the unrestrained fury *he* had unleashed.

The dragon leapt free, then, to land atop the wall beside the tangled breach. It stood high and roared, beating its wings in challenge. Thrakkon looked around. One of the giants strapped behind him had been skewered by a wall spike. Another's head dangled upon a shoulder by a flap of skin. A dangerous place to be, atop the dragon's back. Though safer, right now, than any other.

He turned his attention outward. Upon the broken hills fronting the city, and across the folded plains beyond, the swarm of Illychar sent to sack Atharvan had strung itself out in desperate pursuit of the flesh-wearers come to retake their besieged capital. He was pleased to see, however, that many were already turning back toward the city. Fill its streets. Slaughter its citizens. That ought to force the majority of its soldiers to respond.

"More!" Thrakkon roared.

Killangrathor needed little prodding. The dragon hopped to the earth outside the wall, using its tail to swat aside banks of schilltrons, rows of abatises, and other breastworks that helped to dissect the broken escarpment—clearing the ground for a more direct approach. He then resumed attack upon the wall itself, ramming it with head and shoulders and swipes of his powerful arms, pulling it down in ragged chunks.

The soldiers of the city's garrison did not know whether to fight or flee.

Their confusion only added to the chaos. Thrakkon grinned at their feeble efforts to do either. Ants upon a hill, he thought again, and Killangrathor the lizard come to devour them all.

Within moments, a throng of lesser Illychar had swarmed up around him, hailing the titan's efforts and rushing through the gaping clefts in the shattered wall. When they began to pour past like a rising tide at the dragon's feet, Killangrathor roared and barreled onward, into the city proper, to lead the way. While the Illychar gushed and swirled down streets and squares and plazas, the dragon carved a path of its own—mashing, pounding, grinding—leaving only death and rubble in its wake.

Strapped in place, clutching tightly to the monster's back, Thrakkon continued to ride the wave of destruction, smiling upon its rolling crest.

GALDRIC STARED OUT THE OPEN window, gripping the stone sill as he watched his city be destroyed. Billowing clouds of smoke and dust lent the scene an unnatural, dreamlike quality. But the rumble of toppled buildings and the screams of victims left in the dragon's wake were more horrid than any nightmare he had previously known. Even before the initial shock had worn away, he decided that he had seen enough.

"Captain," he said, trying and failing to loosen his gaze from the growing devastation.

The guardsman croaked in response. "Sire?"

"Rally the Castleguard." His own voice sounded strangely calm and distant, as though it belonged to someone else. "Have them prepare the palace for full siege."

"As you command, sire." The captain turned to his runners.

"And send another to make my armor ready."

He sensed the soldier's momentary hesitation, but by the time he turned, his orders were being relayed.

Eban, however, gaped at him in astonishment. "My lord, you do not mean to confront this creature."

Galdric looked around at the other ministers, all of whom wore the same horrified expression. "I will not give it free rein, if that's what you suggest." His own horror and fury were buried beneath an odd resignation, allowing him to speak in his usual, measured tones.

"M—my lord," Hamus stammered, "we must flee while we can!"

"And leave the rest to fend for themselves? I think not, counselor." He turned toward the door, through which the captain's runners were already racing.

"Sire," Eban blurted after him, "Hamus is right. There is no sense in fighting a battle that cannot be won."

"So they cautioned me before I slew my first boar at the age of ten. And again when I snapped the neck of the stag that gored my father. I have speared sharks, wrestled bears, and broken more horses than half of our cavalry roughriders. Every time, I was told it could not be done. But I tell *you,* counselor, there is no beast that cannot be conquered. Not one."

His glare flicked from Eban, to Hamus, to Ordem, and the rest. None could match it. None dared challenge his claim.

"Make your escape at once," he commanded, without rancor or hostility. "See that my sons are escorted safely from the city, and that our people receive the guidance they need. I shall catch up with you on the road south . . ."

"Please, my lord. I beg you reconsider."

". . . once I have mounted this dragon's head atop my palace wall."

CHAPTER SIXTEEN

Horns blared and bells tolled, trying vainly to steal the dragon's attention. Perhaps the beast could not hear them over the raucous din of its ongoing assault. Or perhaps it was too clever to be lured by their trap. Whatever the reason, it seemed in no rush to respond to their desperate summons.

Galdric held steady at the head of his assembled regiment, resisting the urge to sally forth against the beast. While he truly believed that no creature was invulnerable, he knew he would need every advantage available to him if he was to bring this one down. And that meant remaining here, upon his chosen battleground. If he was patient, the dragon would find him.

Easier spoken than done. For while he hunkered there in that walled courtyard, with twoscore Castleguard and the squat, angled face of the palace at his back, soldiers and civilians alike were being slaughtered like gnats in a chaotic bloodbath. Even if they managed to slay the dragon, Atharvan was lost, its squares and streets teeming with Illychar. Survival would be difficult, escape nearly impossible.

But neither much concerned him in that moment. His sons were en route with the others underground, as safe as he could make them. All that mattered now was the challenge before him. At worst, he meant to buy his people time with a valiant last stand. At best, to become a legend.

For this was no mere diversion, but the ultimate battle between man and beast. One final chance to prove his strength and gild his legacy as perhaps the greatest hunter his people had ever known. An opportunity to make both his forefathers and his progeny proud—with a display of courage that would cause even his fair Deliah to smile in her tomb.

The trace of a smile pulling at his own lips vanished as a sudden explosion rocked the ground beneath his feet. Peering through the open portcullis of the palace courtyard, he had a clear view of the King's Mile, a sloping avenue that fell away at the foot of the palace. Lined with guildhouses, cathedrals, and other stone structures of timeless magnificence—and filled now with the rubble of a bell tower at the end of the row.

A pair of riders tore frantically around the corner of the collapsed structure, whistles blowing. Galdric did not need to see their faces to witness the terror etched there. Shattered blocks rained about them, amid splintered beams and mangled iron struts. The forward rider ducked his head, and his lathered mount bore him through. But the trailing steed turned its hoof on a bouncing stone. Both horse and rider crashed and tumbled headlong upon the cobbles.

Before either could recover, the dragon was upon them, its black bulk emerging from the broken bell tower and plugging the breach at the bottom of the King's Mile. While its mighty arms gripped a pair of buildings on either side, its great neck lashed out. The rider was flung against a near wall with bone-shattering force, and fell limply to the side. The horse, which tried to rise on its broken leg, was shredded.

Still the remaining rabbit blew his whistle, charging hard upon his courser. There was no further need, Galdric wished to tell him, but the soldier was clearly panic-stricken. The dragon hastened its pace, its horned shoulders gouging the buildings to either side, its wings spread above the rooftops. Paving stones cracked and buckled beneath its clawed feet. With the creature's shadow falling over him like a cresting tidal wave, the soldier bore down upon the palace gate. Galdric feared the man had forgotten about their trap, and might inadvertently expose it too soon. He even considered closing the portcullis, to force the rider to avert. He need not have bothered. For the rider remembered himself, and at the last moment yanked hard upon his mount's reins, just before entering the courtyard.

Unfortunately, he was too late. The dragon would not be denied. With a serpentine thrust, its head lunged after them. The stone bailey blocked Galdric's view, so the king did not see what exactly became of them. But the whistle stopped, and blew no more.

Now that both rabbits had been silenced, the dragon turned its attention to the bells and horns that rang from the palace itself. Galdric signaled for quiet, and within moments the clangor had died to echoes. In the relative stillness that followed, the sounds of pain and slaughter throughout his city became ever more acute. Yet none of these was more keen than the crackling snarl of the beast before him.

It looked in on them from above the bailey with eyes like livid coals. Galdric peered deep into those flaming embers—as he had so many other wild beasts. It knew it had been baited, and that knowledge gave it pause. Though several of his men shifted nervously behind him, most held fast through either discipline or terror. That they had not yet scattered was surely another clear warning that something was amiss.

When the dragon began sniffing, Galdric feared their ruse was up, the trap wasted. His mind raced, given over to his own bestial instincts—to what he would do in the creature's stead. It would take to the air. It would circumvent the courtyard by winging in from above.

He was still calculating an appropriate counter when the beast surprised him. There came a human cry—a command from an unseen source—though he could not make out the words. The dragon responded by rising up and beating its wings, roaring in challenge. It came forward then, not over the wall, as he feared, but through it, as he hoped. Galdric tensed. A fitting end, he reminded himself, no matter the outcome.

Blocks and mortar crumbled. Winches and chains and the spiked iron grate, hefted high, snapped apart and fell away. The dragon tore it down like waves would a ridge of sand. A few pieces tumbled into the sludge that awaited, but the beast seemed not to notice. Galdric could not help but marvel at the creature's sheer power and unrestrained tenacity, and knew suddenly that he had not given nearly enough thought to this course.

But he refused to run. Though awed, never in his life had he bowed before a physical challenge. He would not do so now.

In a final, frenzied burst, the dragon punched through the palace gatehouse, shrugging aside the cascading remnants. The courtyard awaited, dusty and leaf-strewn. Once more, the beast hesitated, scanning the empty battlements before lowering its head and sniffing at the earth. As it did so, Galdric saw something he hadn't noticed before.

There were riders upon its back.

Their presence surprised him. Before he could even wonder what to make of it, however, the one in front—a human—shouted and kicked his heels as if spurring a horse. The dragon hissed, but strode forward, eyes narrowing at those assembled upon the palace steps.

One breath, Galdric thought, and it could destroy them all.

Nevertheless, he held his plumed helm high, daring them on. He hoped the beast or its chief rider might somehow recognize his significance. He prayed they would not back down.

His defiance had the desired effect. The dragon bristled and growled. Its stride had just begun to lengthen when the first foot sank abruptly through the false layer of dirt and leaves and into the black sludge beneath. The creature easily kept its balance, but by the time it looked down to see what it had stepped in, the second foot splashed down. When the first did not immediately pull free, the dragon's weight and momentum caused it to pitch forward. When it reached out to halt its fall, one hand and then the other became stuck in the mire.

"Now!" Galdric roared.

He wasn't sure they had the beast, but he could not afford to hesitate. Even before he had donned his armor, his men had been ordered to raise the tar gates and flood the courtyard. A defensive mechanism implemented by his great-grandfather, who had nearly lost the palace not once but twice to civil riot. By harvesting thousands of buckets of the sticky mineral pitch from a natural seep within the city, and by hollowing out a vast section of the main courtyard, the elder king had crafted a trap certain to stop any mob in its tracks. It took time to trigger, of course, but the buried conduits in which the bitumen was stored were kept heated to encourage flow. Once the sticky substance had pooled, nothing was getting through.

Or so his engineers assured him. None could know, for until now it had never been used. Galdric only wished his great-grandfather were alive to see for himself how effective his unique—and costly—sludge pit really was.

Though it was, perhaps, too soon to tell. The depth of the tar was more than twice that required to entrap the strongest ogre. But even this was insufficient to fully cover the dragon's toes. Given the breadth of its clawed feet, and with all four legs ensnared, the creature indeed seemed unable to pull free. But if it were to gain some kind of leverage . . .

Galdric's men, according to his command, were not waiting to find out. Boulders and missiles rained down upon the beast from the suddenly swarming battlements. Soldiers and armaments alike, hidden within turrets and covered trenches, had emerged in full force. The dragon, caught below, was at their mercy.

The beast roared and bucked, but could not quite tear free. It surely could have, had it focused on one limb at a time. But that required patience, and the dragon's rage was all-consuming, leaving it to thrash and squirm and draw heavy strings of tar that simply sucked it back down again. Its neck and tail whipped and swayed violently, but neither could reach the enemies that surrounded it.

Its head shot forward then, to snap at those upon the palace steps. Galdric recoiled. Its breath was like the wind from a funeral pyre; the snap of its teeth rattled his bones. He remembered his signal, though, lowering his raised arm and crying out. His Castleguard responded. From the shadowed portico, a volley of iron-tipped spears flew past, launched by the Hornet's Nest. The widow-maker ballista was twenty feet wide, its missiles loaded in three staggered rows. Threescore heavy spears in all, fired with enough force to penetrate an oak eight inches thick.

The dragon grunted as they peppered its face. Most of the spears were deflected. Some splintered against iron ridges and knobs of bone. A few managed to barely penetrate the softer hide around lips and throat, to dangle like spines from barbed tips.

The beast blinked, then threw its head back and roared. Most of the clinging spears fell away, unbloodied. Galdric had hoped for far greater damage, but had not been foolish enough to rely on it. Nor was he truly dismayed by the failure of his soldiers upon the battlements, whose continued strikes did little more than fill the courtyard with debris. Having witnessed a measure of the dragon's power, he would not have wagered the outcome of this battle on strength of arms alone. His entire purpose was to antagonize the beast, that he might spring his final trap—the one on which everything depended.

Sensing the dragon's fury, he gave the command to displace, and was glad he did. For the creature had had enough. Its head lowered as before, only this time it spewed a river of flame into the breach from which the Hornet's Nest had fired, to reduce the stinging battle engine to cinders and molten metal. Galdric nearly smiled. The weapon's certain loss had been a necessary casualty. To reach it, his enemy had stretched its neck across the chopping block. Time for the axe to fall.

Another signal, relayed via spotters above to those unseen below. He did not see the pins released, the hasps unlocked, the braces removed. He did not see the hammer blows that drove the loose wedges of stone, the supporting columns that toppled, nor the counterweights and pulleys that screamed as one set rose and another fell. But from outside, he heard the groans, felt the shifting of forces, and raced to join his men within the nearest flanking alcove.

From that sheltered position, he had a clear view of the palace face as it sheared away from the rest of the structure. Thousands of tons of steps and arches and colonnades, of corbels and trusses and bas-relief, rigged to collapse. All became one giant avalanche of granite that slid now into the courtyard, burying the dragon to its shoulders beneath a mountainous cairn.

A cloud of dust billowed skyward. The dragon's wings flapped desperately, stirring airborne grit throughout the courtyard. Galdric squinted behind a shielding arm. He could scarcely see. But then the flapping of the wings subsided, and his men above the ramparts raised a heartfelt cheer.

There was no time for celebration, the king knew. Perhaps the beast's neck had broken. Or perchance it would suffocate under all that rubble. But he wasn't counting on either, easier possibility to end his troubles. They still had to find a way to capitalize on their temporary advantage.

He emerged cautiously from the alcove. The creature continued to writhe, its tail to switch—proof that the dragon was not yet dead. Would that he had tar enough to immerse the beast, or time and sappers enough to bring down the flanking walls and complete the burial mound. Alas for options he did not have.

"Lines and anchors!" he shouted, and his men above and below scrambled to obey. Ballistae launched heavy ropes across the yard, at the end of harpoons that others hurried to stake into the earth and bury with stone. More soldiers appeared from bunkers within the walls, lugging chain. With luck, they could create a net large and strong enough to weigh the rest of the monster down until he could find its vulnerability.

A gargantuan effort, for with every shift and twitch and restless wingbeat, anchors would snap and men would go flying. The others kept at it, though, doubling and tripling the lines, wrapping them around blocks for greater leverage. A race they had little chance of winning, Galdric noted, despite their overwhelming numbers. But the only chance they had.

"Sire, look!"

Galdric turned. Through the choking haze, a crimson glow, centered around the dragon's foremost rider—the human. A radiance that seemed to emanate from a blade gripped—

The king felt a flutter in his chest, and for a moment his breath failed him.

"Archers," he whispered.

His captain-at-arms relayed the command, bellowing and gesturing. Within heartbeats, a fresh rain of fire hammered down upon the dragon's back, aimed at its tethered passengers. Though strapped in place, they remained elusive targets—like aiming for a man's little finger. The beast they rode continued to flex and jostle erratically, the shifting spines acted as shields, and a random wingbeat would deflect waves of arrows at a time. In addition, the wielder of the Crimson Sword seemed to know precisely when to dodge or recoil to avoid a would-be strike.

Galdric decided to wait no longer. They had the Sword-bearer trapped—King Torin himself, perhaps, though it did not matter. An Illychar now wielded the Sword, and would soon be made to turn it over. A weapon with which to slay this dragon, if any could. A means to redirect their fortunes in this war.

With the blood coursing through his veins, he could scarce feel the ache of worn joints and the scars of old wounds earned throughout decades of physical contest against nature's minions. He was a young man once more, though time-tested and battle-hardened. His sword was strapped across his back; a loaded crossbow hung in a shoulder harness beneath one arm. Even if it came down to bare-handed combat, he was ready. His entire life had been in preparation for this moment.

The dragon's hide felt like boiled leather stretched over plates of studded iron. Though his spiked gauntlets could not penetrate, their scrape and claw helped him to scrabble up the scaled shoulder. His personal guard were right behind him, struggling to keep pace. The archers now held their fire, and likely stood gaping in disbelief—awed by his strength and his resolve.

He settled into position. The monster squirmed beneath him, but he gripped a spine for balance. Blocks rolled and tumbled from their broken mound, loosened by the dragon's struggles. His new target lay only paces away. The human Illychar had made no move to cut himself free; he simply sat there, Sword in hand, smirking. But Galdric sensed the rage behind that false smile, knew the fury demanding release.

The Parthan king drew his crossbow from its sling. Flush with exertion, he slid aside the safety latch. He felt the wrenching, rolling motions of the serpent pinned below him, and attuned himself to their chaotic rhythm. He then raised his weapon and took aim.

The Sword flashed first, a horizontal swipe that cleaved the tip of the spine in front of the bearer. The dragon wrung itself in torment, twisting violently to one side. More than half of Galdric's men tumbled from their perch. Some landed upon the boulder mound, while others slipped into the tar pool. The king himself dropped his weapon and wrapped both arms around the nearest spine. The crossbow dangled by its stock, tied by a thong to its sling, but the bolt fired and was lost.

He had no chance to reel the weapon in and reload. The dragon's reaction to that tiny bite from the Sword made its earlier thrashing seem like gentle nestling. With its current spasms, Galdric was certain the creature would sever its own spine. A favorable outcome, to be sure, especially when he lost his hold and went tumbling. He nearly caught himself as he skidded down the beast's wing, but a whipping flap sent him over the edge. He dangled for a moment, grasping at a clump of hair, then dropped with a sucking splash into the black sludge below.

He landed feetfirst before slumping back on his seat, arms thrust back to arrest his fall. Drawing breath, he considered himself fortunate. While some of his men drowned in the thick, oily pitch, its two-foot depth came only to his chest.

A fairer fate may have been to share theirs, he realized, as he tried to move and failed. Already, he felt the tar oozing through the seams in his armor. He lay beneath the dragon's wing, facing toward its tail and the ruin of the courtyard gatehouse. He looked to the nearest side wall. Castleguard were trying to throw ropes and extend poles to those like him who still had a chance. But unless he were to grip one or the other in his teeth, he saw no way to take hold.

Some of his men were shouting desperately—both those mired and those attempting a rescue. Galdric kept silent, fighting to remain calm, though he felt their panic. That panic only intensified when the cries reached a sudden crescendo. He did not have to turn his head to know what had happened; he felt the reverberations through the earth, and heard the grating, rumbling clatter. Tar sloshed around him in slow-moving ripples that stilled almost instantly. The heavens shook with a mind-shredding roar.

A shadow fell over him. Galdric looked to the faces of his soldiers—those clinging uselessly to ropes and anchors at the dragon's tail end. An unnatural stillness gripped them. He saw the truth in their eyes before he turned to face it for himself. As he twisted his head, still topped with that plumed helm, he found the dragon's black teeth mere inches away, its flaming eye glaring down at him.

He thought to lie back while he could, to duck his head and let the sludge take him. Make the beast root through the tar for its meal. But he would not go to greet his wife in shame. Instead, he faced that eye squarely, seeing his own reflection, and refused to look away.

No matter the outcome.

The blackness snapped at him, serpentine swift. He caught its foul stench, and felt a crushing pressure around his throat. Then the pressure was gone, and even darkness lost claim.

THRAKKON SNEERED AS THE COMMANDER's headless corpse sprayed blood atop the ooze. He wasn't sure what the soldier had done to merit such a swift and painless end. Better to have left him to starve and be dragged from the pit later as an Illychar. But he had grown weary of the other's tricks, and was content to see him gone.

Even so, he might have taken another piece of the dragon in reprimand, were he not wary of pushing the beast too far. Though he had incited its wrath, he did not wish to draw it.

"Enough!" he bellowed, and Killangrathor seemed to agree. While enemy missiles rained anew, the creature again tried to pull its hands from the tar. When it could not, it lowered its head like an animal set to gnaw itself free.

Instead, dragonfire streamed. With a thunderous pop, the air above the sludge burst into flames, ignited by the intense heat. Thrakkon closed his eyes, hunkering against the singeing blast. When he forced them open again, he was enveloped by an oily black smoke. It filled his lungs and caused him to choke. The tar itself was afire now, bubbling as it burned. Entrapped enemies shrieked and wailed, flesh and armor melting. The rest scattered, unable to withstand the wash of heat.

Thrakkon might have joined them if he could. The dragon's body shielded him from the roaring flames, but he could feel his own flesh broiling. The Sword was of no protection. Were he to remain much longer amid that fiery pool, he would be nothing but a roasted husk.

"Up!" he commanded, and laid the naked edge of the Sword's blade against Killangrathor's flesh.

The dragon howled and beat its wings, fanning the smoke into black curtains. It reared back, hands tearing free of the heat-softened mineral pitch. Soon after, one foot and then the other pulled away. For a moment, the creature lurched and twisted in midair, shaking free of the feeble rope strands that sought to anchor it. Hovering above the flaming courtyard, it sprayed fire upon the battlements. It directed another stream below for good measure, incinerating a clutch of soldiers hiding within an alcove, then carried itself and its riders clear.

"There!" Thrakkon shouted, pointing to a squat tower built atop a nearby plateau. As usual, Killangrathor seemed to know what was expected of him, and chose to obey. Trumpeting its arrival, the creature settled down to roost.

Through scorched and stinging eyes, Thrakkon peered down upon the thick black column rising from the ruined courtyard. Beyond that lay the broken swath they had cut through the city's heart. There and elsewhere, tiny figures raced through the streets, fleeing the tide of Illychar welling up from below.

Beneath him, Killangrathor cleaned himself, using fire to melt tar residue from hands and feet. Thrakkon ignored the beast while continuing to survey the damage. Much of the city remained unscathed. Should he so choose, the butchery and destruction might continue for hours. But he saw no need. The thrill had already faded, tempered by the ease of his conquest. Besides, Killangrathor had proven an unwieldy weapon. Using the dragon to flush out survivors would be like using an axe to pick one's teeth. His lesser brethren were perfectly capable of finishing off this particular carcass, and better suited to doing so.

Time now to bring another to its knees.

But which? This land was full of cities whose walls could be laid low—not one of which held any particular value over the rest. A few might hold out for days or even weeks, but he knew how his brethren worked, how insidious and relentless their methods. Whether or not he paved the way, all would fall before their onslaught.

He considered one target in particular: Whitlock, the stronghold of the Entients. If there were any who might attempt to rally and defend this doomed flock, it would be those who considered themselves the shepherds. But Whitlock was buried somewhere within the Aspandel Mountains; though Torin had once been granted entry, he would not easily find it again. Nor would it be an easy task to penetrate its many unknown wards.

A challenge he meant to undertake, surely. But not yet. As of now, there was only one target that mattered to him, one people whose slaughter could slake his hunger for vengeance. For it was not the pitiful men laying claim to Pentania's shores who had defeated his kind so long ago, or condemned him and his brethren to millennia of entrapment. Those who *had* hid now across the ocean, believing themselves safe.

They were not.

It was the only move that made sense, the primary reason for which he had risked so much in unearthing Killangrathor's remains, and dared now to harness the beast. For all the power, all the glory, all the dominion he meant to claim henceforth for himself and for his kind, he would forever be haunted knowing that *they* still lived beyond his thrall.

The sooner they fell, the sooner he would have his revenge.

When finished cleaning his feet, Killangrathor stretched his great neck around to pick at some of the ropes and chains still caught upon his spines.

"Leave them," Thrakkon commanded.

The dragon glared, ravaged lips curling to reveal those giant obsidian teeth.

"We can use them, provided you have strength enough to bear a few more in our hunt across the seas."

Killangrathor answered with a crackling snarl, and let the tangled lines be.

"Good. Then what say we leave this carrion land to its crows and vultures? I have a taste for Finlorian flesh."

The dragon straightened. A wave of knotting muscles rode up its back, causing its spines to bristle. Its wings stretched and its head reared. As its gaze fell upon an army of flesh-wearers massing beyond the distant city wall, it hissed in hateful warning.

"I see them," Thrakkon soothed, tightening his grip on the Sword. "Come. Let us bid proper farewell."

CHAPTER SEVENTEEN

"Marisha!" Allion shouted, searching desperately amid a sea of Parthan troops. "Marisha!"

He'd been at her side, pinching the artery in a soldier's leg as she cleaned the wound, when an alarm had sounded. A clutch of Illychar had broken through one of the warding flanks. Though far from the city, well behind friendly lines, their camp was under attack. Leaving another to assist her, Allion had raced off to answer the call to arms, bidding her remain until he had returned.

But that minor skirmish had escalated into a heated battle. When finally it had ended, he had returned to find Marisha gone. According to the sergeant whose platoon now occupied her ground, an even larger Illychar force had been sighted in the immediate area, moving swiftly through a series of forested ravines. It was only a matter of time before they sought to scale this or another nearby ridge. Marisha and the others had been ordered to displace, and had headed south toward better protection.

Allion had obtained precise directions before setting off in lone pursuit. But the tracks he followed took him headlong into another battle. He hadn't waited for this one to conclude, firing only a few shots while begging after the healing caravan. A junior officer had gestured vaguely to the east, back toward the city. Anticipating no better lead, Allion seized upon the one given.

But the caravan he'd found had been the wrong one. After that, everywhere, it seemed, another conflict or dead end had awaited. Marisha could not simply have disappeared; Allion assured himself of that much. Even so, panic ate at him. He had vowed not to let her out of his sight, and was left to curse himself for doing so.

Before long, he had begun to catch wind of terrible rumors. The city had been breached. The enemy was inside her walls. The bulk of the divisions was mobilizing to respond. Any who could not join in battle were being ordered to secure a retreat.

The hunter had needed but one guess as to which group Marisha would have joined. Though unarmed and unarmored, she would be at or near the center of the conflict, working to save as many as she could.

"Marisha!" he yelled again. His voice was growing hoarse, but he dared not lower his cries. Soldiers jogged forward on either side, but he pushed past their staggered lines, scouring their columns. His neck ached from twisting back and forth. His legs felt like lead, and his lungs burned. Sweat and grit clawed his eyes. But he would not stop looking—not while he still drew breath.

The terrain rose beneath his feet, then leveled off onto a broad steppe. He caught sight of the city, off in the distance, and his chest tightened. Through hazy curtains of smoke and dust, he saw that at least some of the rumors were true. Atharvan's mighty gatehouse was a mangled heap of iron and rubble. Giant clefts had appeared in the outer wall, through which black bodies surged like floodwaters. From within the city, screams climbed columns of smoke to the merciless heavens.

For a moment, he wondered if the other rumors—the impossible ones—might also be true.

But he did not have time to dwell on it. Beneath those floodwaters, an entire sea of Illychar awaited, and was even now streaming toward them. Allion's legs nearly buckled when he realized how near he was to the front lines—with but a range weapon and a hunting knife. He would have stopped and fallen back had he known for certain that Marisha might not still be ahead of him, and armed with even less.

Instead, he carried on, pushing forward, shouting her name. Those around him misunderstood his purpose and lifted shouts of their own, hurrying pace to match his stride. Before he knew it, the hunter was but a speck of foam upon a cresting wave, borne high and chained to its rush.

Though shielded behind the foremost ranks of his comrades, Allion was tossed backward by the initial collision. Bodies hurtled past one another, weapons raking, flesh ripping. A whirling funnel cloud—a goblin—forced a seam to the hunter's left, leaving a spray of blood in its wake. Elves filled the gap and spread forth in jagged lines, cutting deep with their flashing blades and their rictus sneers.

The men of Partha surged forward, however, pushing from behind, squeezing those in the front. Allion tasted dirt and blood as he was jostled to and fro, and it was all he could do to keep his feet. The crush bore him one way, then the next. Were he to fall, he might be trampled before he ever had the chance to rise.

As it was, he could scarcely breathe, pressed from all sides. He clenched his bow, useless as it was in these tight quarters, and thought back to his first battle, the Battle of Kraagen Keep. There, he had been little more than an observer, an untested youth who had been shoved gratefully to the outer ranks of the tumult, where his skills might serve a purpose. Here, caught in the thick of it, he could do little but wait for his turn to fall.

An ogre lumbered near, and bodies went sailing. It wielded a cudgel of twisted oak taller and heavier, Allion guessed, than the average man. The weapon leveled a cluster of soldiers, creating a void in the press. The knot in which the hunter was entangled stumbled in that direction. Several at the edges toppled, unable to maintain their balance. The ogre strode forward, its great foot crushing their skulls and smothering their screams.

Allion twisted and fought, trying to worm his way clear. A friendly blade sliced his arm. Another might have claimed his head, but he managed to duck, spilling the arrows from his quiver in the process. He continued to find his breath only with labored gasps while, all about, swarming soldiers rocked with the effort of keeping the enemy at bay.

Entrenched within this frenzied bloodbath, he gave little thought to the dark cloud that stole the sun from overhead. It wasn't until heads began to turn as one and a common shriek arose from both enemies and allies that he wrenched his neck and gaze skyward.

This time, his legs *did* buckle. That weakness saved him. For as he fell to the earth, a hurricane wind gusted overhead. Those who remained standing felt not only the wind, but the massive claws that raked past, smashing and skewering bodies, grinding them into the earth or else carrying them away like the teeth of a giant plow.

Just like that, the surrounding press slackened. Blood fountained around him from those who had been decapitated. Bodies and weapons lay scattered like storm wreckage. Most of those who had survived were on their knees, staring at the monster that continued to cut its way through the battlefield, ridged tail sweeping after.

Killangrathor.

Allion had heard the rumored cries. It was a new enemy that had opened up the city—a dragon, some had said. But the hunter had refused to believe them. Even after seeing the ruin of Atharvan's outer wall, he had told himself that it must be something else. There *were* no dragons, none save the one he and Kylac had slain.

Killangrathor.

The truth paralyzed him as he watched the mighty beast lift free of the steppe. Crushed bodies rained down as the dragon released those caught in its grip and shook free of those impaled upon its claws. Beneath, a gory swath lay across the battlefield like a great, oozing gash. Scores, perhaps hundreds, dead, in less time than it would take to fell a deer with a clean shot to the heart.

Killangrathor.

He knew it even before he saw the creature's face—revealed to him as it came around for another strike. Once again, those trapped in the path of the monster's swooping assault were given no chance to disperse. Like the prow of a great ship crashing through the ocean's waves, the dragon plowed indiscriminately through the ranks of men and Illychar alike, shredding bodies, scattering limbs, casting souls deep into the realm of the dead. Allion watched on hands and knees, without blinking, without breathing, while others dispersed or cowered around him. Others might flee, but Allion knew there would be no escape. Returned from its self-imposed death sentence, the world's most awesome living creature had come to settle a score.

It had come for *him*.

So it seemed even after the winged titan barreled past, off to his right. It may not have seen him this time, but surely it was combing the field, seeking him out.

The field itself had already been reduced to utter chaos. The Parthans who had gathered to assault were fleeing in waves, or else rushing for the nearest boulder or ravine that might provide some semblance of cover. The Illychar looked every bit as confused. Many cheered the dragon's efforts, despite the number of their own slaughtered by its gusting strikes. Even these, however, did so while dashing for safety, unwilling to risk being swept aside during the next pass.

Allion alone seemed unable to move, knelt there amid the carnage while those around him scrambled away in all directions. His gaze remained fixed on the dragon, which swerved high before turning back with a whip of its serpentine neck. The spiteful lock of its jaw, the sneering expression, the fluid and mind-numbing power of its movements—all were as Allion remembered them. Had there been any doubt, there was its flesh, savagely scarred—clear evidence of the acids that had claimed its life. Its wings were like a moth-eaten shroud, riddled with holes and tears to the point that flight should have been impossible. Yet Killangrathor flew anyway, as if refusing to acknowledge this limitation.

When it comes to the functioning of an Illychar, the physical condition is less important than the mental . . .

Darinor had told them as much, weeks earlier, following the ambush of those goblin Illychar on the plains of Partha. It was then that Allion had first begun to fathom the depth of the horror they faced.

Only now did he know what true horror was.

The dragon looked ready to swoop again, but instead lowered itself with slow, steady wingbeats. Allion managed to peer around, feeling suddenly naked and exposed. There were plenty of dead and wounded heaped up around him, hiding him. Beyond that, friend and foe mingled chaotically—fighting, yes, but mostly seeking retreat. A sizable force of Parthan soldiers continued to press toward the city, as if to hide among the Illychar ranks, but for all intents, their counterassault had been broken.

His eyes fell upon a massive, bloodstained cudgel, and he wondered how much more merciful his death could have been. Alas, the ogre that had wielded it was nowhere to be found.

Killangrathor roared, and Allion fell forward, covering his ears. The beast's stench washed over him and caused his leg to ache—the one he had broken in the monster's lair. Though his eyes were clenched, he could see the dragon's hateful visage, those flaming eyes fixed upon him. His body shook as though it might crumble into pieces.

"Brethren!" a voice hailed, and despite his terror, Allion froze in confusion. Surely, it was not the dragon who spoke.

"I give you rein upon this land!"

Somehow, the hunter turned his neck and opened his eyes. Faster than his thoughts, his gaze found and locked upon a line of riders clinging to Killangrathor's back. The one in front held aloft a radiant sword.

"May your fury be relentless! Your vengeance swift!"

No.

"Let your darkness cover its shores!"

It cannot be.

"As thick, as engulfing, as that which claimed us!"

Torin.

"Let none be spared, and know that none shall be!"

Allion wanted to wail in tormented denial. But a numbness had stolen through his veins, turning muscles to sand and rendering him mute. Thaddreus. Thaddreus was the one said to have taken the Sword. Torin was safely buried. He had paid his price already. Killangrathor might have risen, but not Torin, not—

"There are victories yet to claim! Glories yet to reap! Go forth, my brethren, and take what you will, while I carry our reprisals to the ends of this earth!"

No. This was not his friend, but some maniacal impostor. Torin was not one to crush an insect without provocation, while this one . . . this one wielded its power like some demented—

"Bear my name!" the fiend shouted. "With every kill, every coil claimed, remember the name of he who gave you your freedom! The name of your lord!"

A ruse. A trick of the mind—

"I am *Thrakkon*! Itz lar Thrakkon! And my age has come!"

Killangrathor roared again, and spewed fire upon the wind. The grating rumble wracked Allion's spine, yet still he did not look away. He would not do so until he had convinced himself of his eyes' mistake. Tears bled from their corners, drawn by raking breezes, but the image before him remained unchanged. And so he stared, fraught with denial, gripped by nightmare, determined to make it all go away.

Another roar welled up from those below, as hundreds and then thousands of Illychar took up a common cheer of bloodlust. It resonated across the wartorn land, rising up from ravines, echoing upon the mountain slopes. Allion could sense their summoned courage, their stirred frenzy, and knew that what tiny measure of hope remained to those of his world was lost.

The Sword twirled in the impostor's hand, a movement he had seen Torin execute countless times. The fiend then pumped his sword arm into the air, as if to remind all whose victory this truly was.

Finally, the Illychar calling itself Thrakkon jerked on a leather hold tied to one of the dragon's spines like a horse's bridle. Somehow, Killangrathor sensed that pull, and responded. The creature lifted higher into the air—ravaged wings flapping, its neck and tail writhing. Claws twitched as if anxious to claim more victims of its own, and its mouth snapped shut like a spring-loaded trap. The grinding of its teeth was like that of stones in a rockslide, and reverberated in Allion's bones.

The creature faced west and began to straighten. But a shout from its lead rider caused it to coil and turn to the east. With a final survey of the battlefield, the titan propelled itself toward the Skullmars, spurred by the savage cheers of its Illychar brethren and by the cries of terror from the fleeing Parthans it passed overhead.

Allion traced its departure in mute horror, watching it dip now and then to swipe at the combatants below. Whenever it did, bodies flew like ocean spray, and the waves of those nearby receded. Even after it had lifted away, high above the city and off into the mountains, the hunter stared after. A part of him recognized that he was still in danger, but the greater portion did not seem to care. As the sounds of battle drew nearer, he told himself that he must flee. Yet his mind would not focus; his body would not respond.

The Sword. Killangrathor. Torin.

"Allion!"

The voice sounded real enough, but reality no longer held any meaning.

"Allion!"

He felt himself blink. The dragon was but a black speck amid the jagged teeth of the Skullmars. At this distance, it could have been anything. A crow, perhaps. A fly.

"Allion," Marisha breathed in relief, skidding to her knees beside him. Her hands fell upon his jaw, the sides of his neck. He peered right through her. An apparition, like all the rest. He looked again for the dragon, but it was no longer there. Perhaps it never had been.

"Allion, look at me," she begged, her fingers tightening. A palm pushed his cheek, turning his head, forcing their gazes to meet. Sapphire orbs burned into him.

"Torin," he whispered. "He . . . I . . ."

"Allion, are you all right? Are you hurt?"

He couldn't begin to answer her question. How had she found him, anyway? Was it even her?

"We don't have time for this," someone else grumbled. "Get him up, now."

Allion turned. Corathel. A pair of Parthan soldiers approached, bending to take hold of his arms.

"Leave him be!" Marisha snapped. She looked him over, then cupped his cheek. "Allion, look at me. Can you stand?"

"It was him, Marisha. It was him."

"We saw," she replied quietly. "We all saw."

"You were right."

"Shh, never mind that now. Allion, we're not safe here. We have to go."

The clangor of arms surrounded them. Killangrathor's assault had cleared the area, but battle yet raged, surging across the steppe in twisted knots and wriggling lines. He could see at once that there was no predicting its random flow—only that the enemy would soon claim all.

"The faster we move, the more we can save," Corathel urged, extending the hunter a hand.

Allion understood then what was at stake. Though it seemed to him that all was already lost, the determination in the chief general's eyes said otherwise. But there was desperation there, as well, in the faces of his soldiers—even in Marisha's. The hunter felt a stab of shame at his own weakness, which gave him the strength to nod to Marisha before reaching up to clasp the general's hand.

"You'll find the bulk of my people on the southern shore of Llornel Lake," Corathel said, after pulling him to his feet. "If the pair of you can find your way there, and help oversee the exodus, I'd be grateful."

"What is it *you* intend?" Marisha asked with alarm.

"The same as before. To draw the enemy for as long as I can, and allow as many as I can to escape."

"We'll assist you," Allion offered.

"You will indeed," the general agreed, "by doing as I've asked. My task will no doubt prove the easier of the two. It is the innocents that concern me most, and tending to the safety of others is what you, my lady, do best. Look to the welfare of my people, I beg you."

Allion could feel Marisha's gaze upon him. *Not without you*, she seemed to be thinking, and he felt the same. Each had suffered a taste now of what it would be like to lose the other. Even a moment's separation, it seemed, was too much to allow. However this ended, they would face it together.

He gave her hand a squeeze.

"We'll find your people," Marisha assured the general, "and gather those who've been scattered. Just be sure not to remain here any longer than necessary."

"Jasyn has already been ordered to marshal the retreat and rendezvous at Leaven. I'll be on his heels." He looked away, and Allion sensed the lie. "Corporal Gage, your squad is to escort this pair north. Follow the Gunarian Trail. Obey them as you would me." The corporal saluted. "The rest of you, after me."

Corathel paused to accept Marisha's embrace, then gripped Allion's shoulder. "There will be better days ahead."

And worse, the hunter thought, clasping the other's arm for what he feared would be the last time.

"Strength to you both," the general said, then spun away, shouting orders as he set off across the carnage-laden field.

"Form up," Gage barked to his men, who encircled Allion and Marisha. More than one, Allion noted, cast a wary eye to the east, along the line of Killangrathor's departure.

"My lord, my lady," Gage said urgently. "With your leave?"

Allion felt a tug upon his arm, only then realizing that his gaze, too, was lost to the Skullmars and its monsters.

Torin.

I'm sorry.

Then he, too, was moving, traversing blood-soaked ground with an uncertain stride, the cacophony of battle in his ears, and the stench of dragon in his nose.

BEFORE THE NEXT MARK OF the sun, Corathel, too, was on the run.

For nearly an hour, he had done as planned, executing a desperate series of feints and counterstrikes against the enemy's tail, allowing his troops—as individuals and small, shattered companies—to disengage and make their retreat. It was the chaos alone, on both sides, that had enabled him to do so. His own regiment wasn't large enough to attract the enemy in any significant numbers, only to distract them momentarily before slipping away again through the maze of shallow canyons that lay like a spiderweb across the southern stretches at Atharvan's feet.

But time and the enemy's focus had turned irrevocably against him. As fate would have it, he had nipped finally at the wrong heels. A pack of reavers he could not possibly hope to confront directly had taken up after, and thus far would not be shaken loose. They were Parthan, fortunately, rather than elf or goblin, giving his men a chance, at least, to outrun them. *Un*fortunately, their leader, Colonel Vinn, seemed as familiar as he was with the splintered landscape through which he sought now to escape. This time, there would be no slipping through some hidden defile and waiting until the danger had passed. These pursuers were both patient and determined, knowing precisely who it was they chased, and unlikely to let them go in favor of easier prey.

"Splinter west!" he shouted, and the designated squad peeled away, down along a secondary trail. The command had already been given *not* to return to the field of battle. By now, those nearest the city had been swallowed up by the melee and could not be saved. Those upon its outskirts were on their own, just as he was.

Not only that, but these men were at the end of their strength. They had bought cover for the others for as long as they could. To seek to buy any more would only cost these men their lives—their souls.

If it hadn't already.

Vinn shouted and snarled behind them, but seemed content to let yet another breakaway contingent go. Corathel smiled grimly at his former comrade's narrow-minded focus. The colonel seemed quite willing to sacrifice all other spoils so long as he claimed the general himself. So be it. If necessary, Corathel would readily make that sacrifice.

But he was down to just a pair of squads—a score of men in all. And these, he knew, were unlikely to abandon him, even if commanded to do so.

So they continued on, ragged in their formation, stumbling over the uneven terrain. Several had dropped their heavier weapons. Others had even tossed aside bits of armor. Swiftness was all that mattered now, and the ability to endure—the ache of lungs, the cramp and burn of limbs, the instability of muscles driven already beyond normal capacity. Fear alone kept them one step ahead of their pursuers, and even fear had its limits.

Corathel cringed as Hadric slipped and went down. Kaleth followed, tripped up by his comrade. The others looked to the general, who gritted his teeth and ran on. The lusty cheers of Vinn's company may as well have been a blade in his spine.

"Almost there," the general croaked, his throat thick with dust and raked by exertion. Between gasps, he added, "Stay with me, men. Show me your strength. Show me your will. Show me!"

He saved his remaining breath, focusing on the fire in his legs, reminding himself of how much tougher they would be for having survived this ordeal. Like steel, tempered in the forge. Like bloody . . . burning . . . steel.

So intense did his focus become that he very nearly missed the final fork, the one they needed if they were to have any chance at all. Fortunately, he felt Joakim, on his left, lean that way. Corathel cut after, shouting the command to veer. As he did so, he reached for the scarlet rag upon his belt, and waved it high overhead. He would know within moments now, one way or the other.

His eyes, pinched with agony, scanned the slopes on either side of the narrow gorge. He saw no sign of those to have been stationed above, only empty boulders stacked one upon the other in wondrous formation. His heart fell.

Then he heard the whistle, and the first grating rumble. Still running, he saw now the sappers in Parthan uniform, with their wedges and their hammers and their pry levers. The trap to his right had already been sprung. The one to his left seemed as though it might resist, the boulders refusing to dislodge. But then the anchor stone slipped free, causing those above to topple.

Within heartbeats, the gorge resounded with the roar of cascading boulders, each helping to trigger a larger rockslide that bore down from either side. Though he continued to run, Corathel heard the screams of Vinn's vanguard, reavers who were caught and crushed by the tumbling stones—chewed up and then swallowed by these broken bits of dead earth.

Only when the grinding had begun to die away and he heard the cheers of those above did Corathel dare to look back. He allowed his pace to stagger and slow. The wall of boulders was roughly forty feet high, climbing halfway to the gorge's rim. Whether they chose to scale the mound or dig through, the reavers were sure to lose a fair amount of time in doing so.

But they would in fact continue the hunt, Corathel was certain. Already, Vinn's furious shouts raged above the ebbing tumult. Should the chief general and his men waste any of the time given them, their frantic retreat might yet count for naught.

He offered a salute to Corporal Lagge and his sapper squad, while those around him caught their breath or patted one another in relieved encouragement. He then signaled for their rescuers to disperse, and turned his attention to those trapped alongside him in the gorge.

"We're not out of this yet," he reminded them, though he did so with a dogged grin. "Come. Let us find our way before our enemies find theirs."

They set off at half stride, rejuvenated by the success of their narrow escape. Shuddering to think of the numbers lost this day, Corathel thought instead of those whose lives he had helped salvage. Were he of a mind to do otherwise, he would have long ago gone insane.

The gorge narrowed and twisted ahead of them, empty of the waters that had once carved its basin, yet for the most part worn smooth. The echo of Vinn and his troops carried after them for a time, but was soon lost to the crunch of their own boots upon the graveled earth. A few of the men even managed to jest with one another, finding humor in the bleakest of situations, as many a battle-hardened soldier was wont to do.

That all ceased the moment they turned a bend to the south, to find that they had indeed celebrated their escape too soon. Chuckles turned to gasps, buried by the hiss of steel as Corathel and those among him drew swords and daggers—whatever remained to them. Hemmed in place by the sheer stone walls and the dam placed at their backs, they had little choice. For a pack of reavers filled the gorge ahead, dozens of them, blocking the road south—the only road left.

And not just any reavers, Corathel realized, while his stomach roiled and spat. Though backlit by a setting sun, he saw enough of their black silhouettes to recognize them as elves, savage in appearance, armed with spears and blowguns and giant longbows, clothed in little more than vines and tattoos and horn-shaped piercings—and led by one who wore a ring of sharpened stakes around the crown of his bald head.

CHAPTER EIGHTEEN

THE SUN HUNKERED UPON THE western horizon, cradled among distant peaks like a trough of molten lead. The wind grew sharp, and shadows lengthened. In the stillness of the settling dusk, amid the barren mountain heights, it seemed as though all the world was at peace.

Knowing better, Htomah took little comfort as he sat silent upon a slab of rock, waiting for the other to come. It had been a long week, trekking throughout the day and throughout the night to reach this point. Though meditations allowed his body and mind to refresh themselves without the need for sleep, his muscles and joints were not accustomed to such prolonged periods of strain. Worse, he traveled blind. His physical senses were far more acute than those of any pure mortal, but it had been years—decades—since he had gone so long without a visit to the scrying chamber. Lacking his Third Sight, he felt as lost and vulnerable as a deprived suckling.

He might have regretted his decision, yet found he did not. He would be given cause to do so before this was finished, he was certain. Thus far, however, his doubts and fears had only spurred his resolve. An Entient had little business outside their den, to be sure. Had they only remembered that in the beginning, it might be that none of this would have happened. Yet now that it had, and he had committed himself to this course, he was buoyed by his indignation toward those who had mocked his concern and scorned his efforts. Fools all, himself included. But at least he was willing to admit it, and to labor in some small way to counteract his folly. Should he fail, it would serve the rest of them just.

He heard the other nearing now, and so stowed his brooding contemplations in order to focus on the moment at hand. He was here to win the other's aid, not give him cause to think that it was already too late.

To that end, he did his best not to appear threatening, drawing back the hood of his cloak and placing his hands upon his knees. Cold breezes scraped his flesh and raked his hair, but he forced himself to remain still.

Even so, the figure that came stumping up the narrow trail froze when it spied him. With its stout and gnarled frame, it looked not unlike a boulder wedged against those on either side. Then its axe came to hand, slid free from a sling upon its back. Its crooked limbs belied the smoothness of the movement.

"Peace, good dwarf," Htomah offered in greeting. "I am no enemy."

His startled visitor cast about, looking for others who might be lurking amid the boulder-strewn ridge. "And just how ya be knowin' *that*, without knowin' who *I* am?"

"You call yourself Crag, do you not?"

The Tuthari's features tightened, eyes pinching with increased suspicion. "My own name ain't no mystery to me."

"Mine is Htomah. I am a friend to Torin."

"Are ya now? Name don't strike as one he ever mentioned."

"Perhaps not. To be fair, I was not a very good friend. Though, as I recall, he did speak of the Entients."

Crag spat. One eye squinted fiercely, giving his lumpy face an even more mangled appearance. "Might have. That be true, what would one of 'em be doing out here?"

A fair question, no matter who he had been. Humanoid or beast, few were those who traveled these desolate mountain paths. Elsewise, the dwarf need not have been so wary. "My purpose in being here is much the same as yours: to visit with those who long ago chose to dig their homes beneath this land, rather than contend with those swarming above it."

He felt Crag hesitate, though there was no outward sign. "Claimin' to know my business, too, then, are ya?"

Htomah bowed respectfully. "Affairs being what they are, I have had cause to observe Torin for some time. I know much of what passed between the two of you."

The dwarf responded with a low grumble, deep in his throat. "Ain't meet to spy on people—magical or otherwise."

"Be that as it may, I had hoped we might help one another."

Crag let his axe slip down to butt the earth, leaning a hand upon its head. "Way I hear it, help such as your kind offers ain't much help at all. And that's allowing ya are who ya say ya are."

"Do you require proof?"

"You're the one what stole upon *me*, more or less. What is it *you* require?"

Htomah sighed. Already, this little parlay was growing tiresome. Crag seemed not to care about meaningless details, which worked to their advantage, given the shortage of time. But things might move faster still if he would loosen his mistrust and adopt a less combative stance.

"I suspect that the Hrothgari will want little to do with me," the Entient admitted, "and even less with what they will undoubtedly view as man's war against the Illysp. Thus, I would *ask*," he added, with deferential emphasis, "that when we meet with them, you might suggest they consider elsewise."

"Already told Torin I'd see 'bout securing any aid they might offer. Threat ain't just to man, no?"

Htomah shook his head. "It is to your kind and mine, as well. But matters are worse than Torin—than any of us—knew. And they have only grown worse since your arrival upon these shores."

"That so?"

The Tuthari would not know, of course, having crossed this land upon a wilderness course, veering clear of the highways and settlements where tidings and rumor were sown. He had seen Illychar for himself—that much was made clear by subtle changes in his eyes and his posture. But it was equally clear that he had yet to develop any true appreciation for the threat they posed. Once again, it was up to Htomah to convince another that his own fears were not merely phantoms.

"Torin was ambushed at Krynwall," he stated bluntly. "He slew his enemy, but fell soon after."

"Fell. Dead?"

And possessed, Htomah thought, but merely nodded instead. He was not sure he wished to tread that road just yet.

Crag's pinning gaze slipped briefly to his own hand, flexed now upon the head of his axe. "You *observed* this, did ya?"

The Entient nodded. "I am sorry to bear the word."

"Not as sorry as I am to hear it. That one and I, we had unfinished business."

"Unfortunately, that is not the worst of it. The talisman he carried—the Sword of Asahiel—has fallen to the enemy, its power to be wielded now against us."

For a moment, the dwarf was silent, though Htomah could hear him grinding his teeth in thought. "And what do ya expect *I* should do about it?"

"As I said—"

"I heard what ya said. Need a few pawns, do ya? Where's the rest of your clan?"

"My clan?"

"Seems to me, you're the ones what wield sorcery and all. Why come to lay it all on a people not your own?"

Htomah managed a sad smile. "My *clan* thinks the matter unworthy of their current attentions. They did not send me to raise others to do battle in their stead. I have acted alone in this, become an exile like yourself. I go to the Hrothgari because they number among the few to have not yet joined this struggle in earnest, and because I think they might make a difference. I go to them because there is no one else, and I fear what may happen should we not contain this fire before it spreads any further."

Crag reached up with his free hand to massage his growth-laden brow. "And what do I get out of it, should I throw in with you? I ain't exactly one of 'em. I've come a long way just to be tossed out."

"I can lead you to them, and shall, should you but agree to help impress upon them the need to action."

The Tuthari snorted. "Good chance I can find 'em on my own."

"And an equal chance that they are even now burying themselves ever deeper in response to this threat—perchance never to emerge again. Would you risk it, given the small favor that I ask?"

"You do me greater honor than I deserve," Crag chortled wryly. "What makes you reckon I've the words what with to persuade 'em?"

"You are Tuthari, the last of a once-proud nation. Your very presence is a cautionary tale. If you would but share with them the fate of your people, it ought to be enough."

"And if it ain't? What sort of wasting disease am I to be stricken with if they turn you out?"

It was Htomah's turn to laugh without mirth. "My good dwarf, the plague upon us now is the worst, I dare hope, that any shall ever know. Should we fail, my only reprisal would be to leave you and your kin to suffer its course."

A vague threat, and nothing new at that. But Crag seemed to relax somewhat, trusting him better for it. A sad world they lived in, Htomah thought, where kindness was believed to hide a darker menace than one openly revealed.

"Well, seein' as ya knew where to find me in the first place, I don't reckon I'd have an easy time slippin' away. Mayhap we travel together a spell. I'd know more of who ya claim to be, and how our mutual friend met his end."

Htomah bowed his head. "As it pleases you."

Crag gave another snort, as if to suggest that nothing about this pleased him. "And just how long is this shared journey of ours apt to take?"

"Not more than a day, I should hope. Would you prefer to spend this night *above* ground, or below?"

"Why?"

Htomah stood—slowly, so as not to trigger concern in his skittish companion. "Because an entrance to their domain lies beneath the very slab upon which I sit."

THRAKKON BENT LOW AGAINST THE shrieking winds, gaze pinned to the white-capped seas below. At this height, the ocean was naught but a frozen wasteland—an iron-gray void as vast and unchanging as the skies through which he flew. Nevertheless, he dared not remove his gaze for a moment, remaining ever watchful for that which lurked beneath the glistening swells.

Killangrathor's mighty wings lay stretched to either side, gliding upon the currents of an invisible stream. Behind him, strapped like he to the dragon's spines, were a pair of giants and two dozen goblins. A paltry number, it now seemed, given the way in which they hunkered breathlessly, sharing his anticipation.

Yet there had only been room for so many to accompany him, and of all the races, goblins were the most lethal, the most relentless. A waste, at first glance, strapping one winged beast to the back of another. But for all their flapping, flailing fury, goblins were not true flying creatures. Though capable of riding the winds in short bursts, none could soar as high or as far as Killangrathor—upon whose strength they now all depended.

Later, however, their hunting talents would be put to good use. A goblin was worth ten elves or more. Thus, following the slaughter at Atharvan, Thrakkon had flown directly into the Skullmars, to a valley in which a swarm of the creatures lay in reserve. There, he had tossed aside the carcasses of the giants slain by Killangrathor's frenzy and taken on as many goblins as would fit. He had considered sending the rest out from the mountains to join their brethren, but had decided against it. Even now, euphoric with his successes, he felt it was only prudent to maintain the rear guard Kael-Magus had established. Should his enemies be so foolish as to attempt an attack on the nest from which his kind had emerged . . .

Thrakkon relished the thought.

His incursion force secured, they had flown throughout the remainder of that night and all of the following day, watching league after league of earth slide by below. An exulting sensation, consuming days' worth of travel in mere hours. Back then, the terrain had changed by the moment, grassy plains alternating with rocky highlands while sprouting forests, mountains, lakes, and more.

Unlike now, when all there was to see was the occasional island or empty atoll.

More than once, he had been tempted to bear down upon another of the cities they were leaving behind, just to make sure that none would hold out against his Illychar armies for long. But that might mean more casualties to his team and more time wasted mining replacements. His brethren could handle what was left to claim throughout these lands. And if not, he would finish it for them upon his return.

Another night had carried them to Pentania's westernmost shoreline. By dawn, they had edged out over the cliffs and sands and seas, veering higher amid the windswept clouds. All at once, the doubts had returned, and Thrakkon had been forced to remind himself of the necessity of this course. He did this not merely for revenge, but because the Finlorians' was the true threat—if indeed any remained. He understood the risks, pressing in this manner, but he would not suffer that even one of Finlorian ilk was left alive to challenge him. Unlike his predecessors, he would not squander his hard-earned advantage.

On the other hand, his fears whispered, the Vandari were no more. The last had perished as a result of Torin's visit. The remaining Finlorians were but a pathetic whisper of a mighty past. They possessed magic, no doubt, but their numbers and power were no longer significant. It was not too late to turn back, to let this meaningless struggle go.

But Itz lar Thrakkon would not be shackled by his fears, nor made to settle for what had already been achieved. Where others had relented, Thrakkon would continue to prove his superiority. And when this challenge, too, had passed, he would find himself another.

In that very moment, the monster struck.

For hours they had waited, watching expectantly, knowing it would not be contained. Nevertheless, when the geyser erupted, Thrakkon's hand flew to the Sword's hilt, and beneath him, even the mighty Killangrathor flexed in startled terror. Thousands of feet it climbed, without sign of slowing. From the center of that billowing column, its face appeared, hideous and ravaged as it thrust skyward into the unfamiliar sun, borne up by an eel-shaped torso of staggering immensity.

Its maw groaned wide, almost greater than Thrakkon could comprehend, leaving him to peer down into a gullet large enough to engulf mountains. Taller and larger it loomed, numbing his mind, sapping his confidence. He felt suddenly as though he rode a sparrow, rather than a dragon. Armored in reefs of coral and limestone, draped in forests of seaweed, the behemoth might have been mistaken for a divine manifestation of the very earth.

Risen up to swallow them whole.

The dragon beat its wings, hissing in defiance. Thrakkon and his fellow passengers could only watch, mesmerized, as the leviathan lunged ever higher, reaching in hungry pursuit—an eruption so swift, not even Killangrathor could hope to climb away in time.

But the dragon did not have to. Suddenly, impossibly, the ocean-bound creature reached the end of its chain. At the height of its ascent, titanic jaws snapped shut like the collision of drifting landmasses. A striking serpent denied, it fell away then, back toward the sea. As it did so, it unleashed a sound no serpent could make, bellowing a roar that seemed to stretch the very fabric of the heavens.

As its unfathomable mass slipped back into the seething ocean, tides tore at one another in an effort to seal the resulting rift. A second stream of geysers exploded skyward, slapping at one another with enough height and force to wet Thrakkon's lips with salty spray. Only upon their descent was the breach in the ocean's surface sealed, its hidden horror buried once more.

For several moments, Thrakkon eyed the distant landscape as it shimmered beneath them, marveling silently while its surface continued to roil. A catastrophic encounter. For unless the creature below could mend the tides it had unleashed, its violent emergence was liable to raise waves that would destroy entire villages and carve a new face onto the seaward bluffs of distant lands.

Thrakkon delighted in the thought. Even as the ocean calmed, he knew its wind-combed surface to be a facade. Though hundreds of leagues lay behind them, and thousands more lay ahead, the devastation was en route.

Even more exhilarating than the thought of hundreds being caught unawares by the abrupt and merciless fury of the sea, however, was the cherished dream of untold millions falling prey to this behemoth's feral hunger. Not even Killangrathor had the capacity to shred as many coils or sow as much fear. And while there should have been no doubt in the Illysp lord's mind, the centuries of languor had clearly left this beast of the deep as anxious as any of Thrakkon's kin to feed.

He continued to search the waves, eager now for the agitated titan to show itself again. When he realized that it wouldn't, he settled back upon his perch and relaxed his grip on the Sword. His companions eased around him, though he could sense their savage pleasure, akin to his own.

Killangrathor stretched his wings and glided tirelessly westward, pleased by his own insolence. Thrakkon, meanwhile, wiped the taste of the ocean from his lips and continued to smile down upon the sea as it glimmered in the noonday sun.

Fear not, he promised his angry friend below. *Your time comes soon.*

CHAPTER NINETEEN

"*H*OLD! THAT'S FAR ENOUGH NOW."

Htomah stopped. The words had been spoken in Gohran, but he knew that tongue as well as any.

He turned slowly, and Crag beside him. Neither was surprised by the trio of Hrothgari staring back at them from the murky depths of the tunnel. The patrolling sentries had been trailing them for some time now—with all the stealth of a herd of goats. Even Crag had sensed them, though when the Tuthari had turned to mumble a warning, Htomah had placed a reassuring hand on his companion's knotted shoulder, preferring to let the trackers reveal themselves in their own due time.

"Strength to you, friends of the shadow-earth," the Entient replied in the Mountain Tongue. "We bear you no malice."

The dwarves continued to scowl. All three were outfitted in layers of wool and leather, with iron bands about the arms and wrists. Their heavy cloaks had been pushed back, to reveal the countless gems and minerals with which their tunics and belts and bracers were studded—radiant in the light of glow lanterns hung about their necks. The lanterns themselves were filled with luminous minerals set to shining by thornweed firebrands—the ideal wick in that they burned extremely slowly while giving off virtually no smoke. By contrast, the acrid smoke from the torch Crag had insisted upon carrying filled the narrow corridor.

The sentries to either side held spiked hammers at the ready. One of them murmured to the one in the middle, commenting on the size of Crag's battle-axe. Htomah marked the concern, but did not speak to it, keeping his gaze locked with that of the trio's toifeam.

"You belong to the surface," the leader grumbled. One hand rested upon the hilt of his own hammer, slung at his waist, while the other twisted a knob on his glowstone lantern, adjusting its tiny shutter and redirecting its light toward Crag. "And you are not Hrothgari."

"Nor are we *skatchykem*," Htomah assured him, using the word their people had adopted to describe the Illychar—*harvested dead*, translated loosely into Entian. At the very mention, the third dwarf warded himself with the sign of the Smith. "He is Tuthari, cousin and kin from across the seas. I am Entient. In another time, King Vagorum counted my father a friend."

Again the first dwarf, whose yellow beard shone green in the blue-tinged light of his glow lamp, turned to his leader with a bitter word. The toifeam, however, held forth a palm to silence his protest.

"King Vagorum no longer rules us."

"Vagorum blows forever amid the bellows winds of Achthium's Earth-forge," Htomah acknowledged, "fanning the flames of a thousand stars and more. King Hreidmar watches now over His people of this realm. With your permission, we would pay him homage."

"With what? You bear no gifts that I can see."

"Why, I bring him this good dwarf, for one, the last of a scattered flock." He paused as Yellowbeard snorted, and turned his glare upon that one. When he spoke again, he added an echo to his voice that seemed to multiply upon the jagged walls. "What is more, I bear knowledge of the plague that has found its way to you, and fell warning of what shall happen should your people fail to rally against it."

The toifeam stared, unblinking. The dwarf to his left, a redbeard, allowed his cloak's folds to slip forward around his mineral-studded leathers, as if to hide himself in the tunnel gloom. Even Yellowbeard, it seemed, had run dry of responses, glaring sullenly, hands flexing upon his weapon's haft. In the resulting stillness, Crag's torch crackled.

"And does this Entient have a name?" the toifeam asked finally.

"I am called Htomah."

THE TOIFEAM LED THEM AFTER that. He did not offer his own name, nor did Htomah ask for it. Crag kept silent the entire time. The Tuthari did not even complain when they demanded that he extinguish his torch and its choking cloud of smoke. Htomah had warned his companion that the Hrothgari would not take kindly to besmirching the air within their tunnels, but Crag had refused to travel blind in that inkwell blackness, despite the Entient's claim that he could lead them just as well without any exterior light source.

Yellowbeard and Redbeard marched along at the rear, hammers in hand. Htomah paid little mind to the grim gazes they leveled at his back. He did not fault them their mistrust. Though the Illysp had not spread throughout this underground domain nearly to the extent they had elsewhere, the Hrothgari had seen enough to recognize the nature of their threat. When brother was slaying brother, there seemed little reason to trust those who clearly did not belong.

Aside from that, Htomah had lived his entire life in shadow, dealing with matters that even long-lived mortals like these of the Gorgathar family could scarcely comprehend. Thus, he was no stranger to others' mistrust.

Guides notwithstanding, his journey continued as it had before, through a twisting maze of cramped tunnels that, for the most part, were naturally laid. Now and then, sections had been smoothed or reshaped by dwarven hands, allowing passages to intersect more directly, or to steer away from dangerous chasms. But, for the untrained eye, it would be difficult to determine where nature's work had ended and the Hrothgari's had begun.

They had hours to travel yet, though he and Crag had been scuffing along for nearly an entire day already. In truth, he had been surprised to come across this particular band of sentries so near the surface. While the Hrothgari made numerous routine excursions to the world above, this was most definitely a sentry patrol, and not one sent to scout, map, or forage. This was a people not easily alarmed, yet what little they had seen of the Illysp had alarmed them. Good. Perhaps that meant his pleas would not go unheard.

One way or another, he had to make them see. For if the Hrothgari failed to act as he would have them, he was not sure where else he might turn. He could attempt to consult Ravar, but that would constitute an unconscionable risk, given what little he knew about the creature's role in this. Long had the Entients known of His presence, yet even they could only guess at His designs. That His awakening was somehow tied to the emergence of the Illysp seemed evident. Whether linked for good or for ill had, thus far, been impossible to discern.

A fool he was, Htomah thought again, for not taking action sooner. A wiser man might have set a corrective course the moment the Illychar were unleashed and Ravar had begun to stir, rather than observing it all from afar as some kind of natural oddity. The distance his kind kept from the affairs of this earth had been meant to lend clarity to their vision, not cloud it.

None of which could be helped now, he reminded himself. For all their vaunted insight and understanding of universal mysteries, none of them could unmake the past. Better that he keep his focus upon the challenges that lay ahead.

It remained difficult to do so, however, as he marched along those subterranean corridors, many of which seemed so much like his own. Thinking of Whitlock only caused him to wonder if he would ever see the vaults of his home again, or if he, like Algorath of old, had made himself a permanent outcast to all he had once held dear. Such courageous defiance. Had he not heard the tale of the other's noble yet necessary sacrifice, he might never have dared to follow form. But his own would mean less than naught if he did not find a way to make a difference, as Algorath had. Ideals might stir hearts and open minds, but it was deeds that changed the world.

The darkness continued to press them, as if spilled forth from the caves and pockets branching off to either side. In addition to extinguishing Crag's torch, the Hrothgari sentries had dimmed their own lanterns, damping the flues to conserve the flaming thornweed wicks. Those at his back were mere slits, while the toifeam's scarcely revealed the path at their feet.

That suited Htomah just fine, who saw better by tuning his vision fully to the underground spectrum, rather than fighting between that and natural light. With only the soft mineral glow ahead of him, he was able to detect every pit and crag and alcove as surely as he would in the harsh light of the sun.

Would that he could see their future as clearly.

HE WAS STILL SEEKING SOLACE when, hours later, they came upon the Hrothgari city of Ungarveld.

It took some time to win themselves entrance, as their toifeam was forced to share with a set of stern-faced city warders all that Htomah had imparted back in the tunnels. The Entient had to resist the urge to intervene, for the dwarf captain had misremembered much of it, and forgotten the rest—or else did not think it important enough to mention. According to him, they were but intruders caught prowling the upper tunnels, fled from the skatchykem above. That they might in fact be who they claimed did not seem to have any bearing on the matter, one way or the other.

Eventually, the warders parted as had several other sets encountered earlier, though these ones had insisted their hands be bound before traveling any further. In truth, Htomah had been surprised not to have been thus constrained from the first, and so had submitted without complaint. Crag had glared sourly at these distant cousins of his—and at Htomah—as if wondering now whether his voyage from Yawacor had been a mistake. But once again, the bitter Tuthari had kept his tongue and thoughts to himself.

That resentment gave way to awe, however, the moment they stepped from the tunnel and into the cavern that housed the city proper. Clearly, the Tuthari had never seen anything quite like it. Their guides had brought them in along a side route, near the uppermost tier, giving them a rather splendid view of the subterranean hollow and all of its unique marvels. The walls themselves were dazzling, shot through with veins of luminous minerals, studded with gold and gems and glimmering crystal formations. There were homes, carved into pockets along all sides; terraced roadways, reaching throughout the complex like a thousand frayed strands; and forests of stalagmites and stalactites, including the wondrous and mighty Achthium's Spear itself. But what amazed his Tuthari comrade more than anything, Htomah suspected, was the sheer number of dwarves, young and old, who bustled about, wearing gem-studded belts and bands that left them striped with iridescence in the blue light of thousands upon thousands of glow lamps. Craftsmen, tradesmen, and artisans of every variety. Miners, cultivators, and herders. Male, female, and even children—whose merry laughter rang upon the walls in stark disregard of all the world's ills.

Htomah smiled sadly. That the Tuthari should be moved by the sights and sounds and smells of a thriving dwarven culture should not have come to him unexpectedly. A long time had it been since Crag had known such peace— decades since his own people had been harried and scattered, forced to endure famine and war and slaughter. To have been the only one to survive, to wonder if he might never again meet and talk and laugh with one of his own kind . . . to him, this world, buried as it was, must have seemed like paradise.

They started down a narrow, switchback trail marked now and then with steep steps hewn into the stone—a route of quick, direct access to the cavern floor. Though Crag might have preferred to march the long, winding perimeter, exploring up close the many hidden wonders of which he could gain only a vague sense from afar, that seemed to be precisely what their guides wished to avoid. Htomah, of course, knew that this central cavern was not the half of it, but merely the threshold to a vast network that lay beyond. The Hrothgari had always been an industrious and enterprising people, defined more by their labors than by their homes and parks. Beyond this central living area, one would find myriad sources of harvest: grassy fields sown on beds of lichen and grazed upon by goats, springwater grottos and streams filled with blind fish and shell creatures, forests of mushrooms, caves from which crushed ore and sulfur and mercury and gemstones were mined, jungles of thornweed, rivers of magma, foundries of iron and steel, crystalline gardens, and so much more. Being herded underground like cave dwellers had forced this people to stretch their talents and adapt themselves in creative ways. Given the size of Crag's eyes as he attempted to absorb just this small portion of their world, Htomah worried that those eyes might pop right out of the Tuthari's skull were he to be shown the rest.

They encountered few others along their path of descent, just the occasional patrolling warder and a lone tanner hauling a rolled bundle of bloody goatskin up the staggered heights. Like all dwarves, the old whitebeard was put together like the most gnarled of oak trees—malformed by human standards, yet in no way hampered by the twist and bulge of limb and joint. He nodded warily as they let him pass, then trundled on without huff or groan, despite his heavy load and a waddling gait.

When at last they reached a broad shelf near the cavern floor, they were ushered through a busy marketplace, drawing grim gazes and guarded whispers. The muttered oaths, Htomah noted, were filled more with concern than with any real invective. He might have offered them reassurance of some kind, but thought it best to remain silent and continue playing the role of obedient captive. To them, his very appearance was ill omen enough. Let them believe that whatever threat he posed was well contained.

Near the center of the market grounds, a cluster of pits awaited, covered over by iron grates. A small crowd had begun to gather, but gave way for the nameless toifeam to open the lid to one of the cells.

Crag eyed the pit distastefully, then locked another glare upon Htomah. *Is this really necessary?* he seemed to ask.

"We do not have time for delay," the Entient agreed.

"That is for His Glory, King Hreidmar, to decide," the toifeam replied. "If you would have us trust you, I suggest you show us the same courtesy."

Yellowbeard gave Crag a prod with his hammer. The Tuthari stumped down the rugged slope, his hands still bound behind him, followed by Htomah.

"Mind your skull," Yellowbeard called out, a moment before the ceiling grate slammed shut.

"The king will be notified of your request," the toifeam assured them, while Yellowbeard slid an iron linchpin into place. "Make yourselves comfortable."

Even seated, the Entient had to bow his head to prevent it from knocking against the bars. A minor annoyance. He had been forced to stoop or crawl throughout much of this trek, and could bear such petty torments with ease. He felt worse for Crag, who he knew had not come all this way to suffer such indignities.

"I had hoped for a warmer welcome," the Entient offered in apology.

Crag said nothing for a moment, then replied, "Best I've had in years."

They did not converse after that. What words that needed to be shared had passed between them during the long hours prior to their capture. Htomah had not for a moment fooled Crag into believing he had revealed all there was to know, but the dwarf seemed to understand the futility of pressing him for any knowledge he had not readily volunteered. Likewise, the Entient was not fooled by Crag's stoic response to the tale of Torin's confrontation with Darinor and subsequent death due to the smoke he had breathed in that fiery smelter. The Tuthari was clearly driven by a strong sense of duty, and troubled by the thought of a debt he would never get a chance to repay. Htomah had argued that the dwarf had already done much more for Torin than Torin had done for him, but, for Crag, that did not seem enough.

Soon after their sentries had left, Hrothgari milling about the area had come to look down on them, shaking their heads and murmuring and casting looks meant to arouse shame. Suitable punishment, Htomah supposed, for most who found themselves cast hither. But in this case, their dour judgment felt misdirected and undeserved.

Though it might be said he deserved worse.

He did his best to be patient, to respect the wishes of those who had placed him here and await their coming. It would have been much easier, in some respects, to throw aside the lid to their prison and take the king's audience by force. But it would not be by force that he might win the allegiance of an entire people. As the nameless toifeam had suggested, he first had to win their trust.

But his patience waned quickly as one hour and then another slipped by, with naught to do but listen for the distant drip of Achthium's Spear as it marked the passing moments. And with each drip, he heard in his mind the screams of another soul lost to Illysp possession. Like a shepherd sitting upon his staff while wolves butchered his flock.

The faces above came and went. Though he kept his head bowed and his eyes low, Htomah sensed the onlookers for who they were: curio-seekers of little import. If any of influence had learned of his imprisonment, they had yet to show themselves.

He had begun to contemplate a transposition, which would allow him to take temporary control of one of his viewers and thus discreetly check on whatever progress the king might be making, when he detected the coming of a sizable company, swift and direct in its approach. With a twitch of his fingers, he cast an invisible jolt through Crag's flesh, nudging the snoring Tuthari from a restless slumber. As the dwarf regained his bearings, the crowds above continued to shuffle and part, making way for what Htomah believed to be the king's envoy.

He was not disappointed. When a pair of well-armed warders had cleared aside the last of the random observers, the Entient's upturned gaze was met by that of Warder General Vashen herself—primary commander of the Hrothgari military and first defender of Ungarveld.

At long last, an auspicious sign.

He matched her stare while waiting for her to speak. The warder general's cheeks were smooth and hairless, though a long beard of forked braids decorated her chin. Its strands were soft and silken, as opposed to the scouring mesh that clung to the males' faces like brambleweed. A signature collection of knobs and spurs grew upon her brow and elsewhere upon her hearty limbs. Her scarred lips formed a ragged frown.

Her gaze turned toward Crag, who held his breath in response to her appearance, then settled again upon Htomah.

"Your sire's name—"

"Aethelred." Htomah had anticipated the question, thus answering before it could be fully asked.

Vashen scowled at him over a pair of blue eyes almost as bright as his own. "King Hreidmar would speak with you."

Moments later, they were free from their pen and on the move once more, encircled by warders as they made their way through the lower city. They drew quite a lot of notice this time. Their escort was a score in number, bristling with weapons and echoing a heavy, rhythmic march. But then, there was little need for discretion when the whispers had already traveled the length and breadth of all but the farthest reaches of Ungarveld. Hreidmar and his general were making it clear that the intruders were being dealt with.

Their snaking route brought them eventually to the King's Warren. A series of curving passages carried them upward through the rock and emptied at last within an openmouthed audience chamber overlooking the city's main cavern. Here, they were left to wait yet again, bound still, while General Vashen stumped off down another corridor, leaving more than half of her patrol to stand guard.

This time, the wait proved brief. Crag had only barely taken a seat upon one of the encircling stone benches when another dwarven company approached. One of the warder sentries ordered the Tuthari to rise, which he did just before General Vashen, a dozen fresh guard units, and King Hreidmar himself crossed the chamber threshold.

"Be seated," the Hrothgari king bade them, peering up at Htomah from within his ring of warders, "else I'm likely to crick my neck, staring up so high."

The Entient accommodated the gnarled ruler, settling beside Crag upon an elaborately sculpted bench—bathed like everything else in that blue-tinged mineral glow. Lights from the cavern beyond shone through the terrace opening like crystalline stars.

Hreidmar pushed through his throng of guards to stand boldly before the pair. Warder General Vashen remained at his shoulder, glaring in warning.

"You carry a dwarven name, bairn of Aethelred," the king remarked, his focus still locked on Htomah.

The Entient bowed in acknowledgment. Even seated, he was more than a head taller than the Hrothgari monarch. "In honor of the dwarf who defended my mother's life, enabling me to be born safely into this world."

The king raised a bushy brow, though he did not ask to hear the story. "I thought it a lie, perhaps, meant to curry favor."

"Trust won by lies is no trust at all."

Hreidmar pulled at a bejeweled beard striped red and black. "Then tell me true, what reason have you to sully our halls?"

"I am he who helped unleash the skatchykem upon your proud people. I am here now to liberate you from my foolishness, and that of man above."

Vashen continued to scowl. The king himself betrayed more amusement than concern.

"So let us hear it."

As he had with Crag, Htomah proceeded to tell the Hrothgari king all he needed to know concerning the Illysp, beginning with the Entients' role in the quest that had resulted in their release. He spoke of Darinor, and the way in which this scion of the renegade Algorath had played them all for tools. He spoke also of Torin's final stand—what the Alsonian king had won, and what he had lost. He told them of his own sacrifice in leaving Whitlock, and of the sacrifice he had come to ask the Hrothgari people to make—a sacrifice not without reward, he pointed out, emphasizing his ultimate goal of returning their kind to the surface. Hreidmar seized upon the notion.

"What you speak of is something my kin have dreamt about for centuries," the king allowed when at last he chose to respond. "We have done what we had to do to subsist down here, but why should we be deprived of sun and sky? Why should we be forced to root around like gnomes in the dark, feeding upon trogs and skitters and other burrowing creatures? Alas, our entire populace would not fill even one of man's cities. We survive largely because he no longer believes we exist."

"The Illysp know better," the Entient reminded him.

"Quite so, and yet have paid us little heed, if the story you tell be true. Leaving me to wonder if mayhap this plague you speak of is in answer to our prayers. Unleashed by man, you say. Well, let it consume him, or at the very least bugger his numbers, to give us a fair chance to emerge once more."

Htomah shook his head. "A grave misjudgment that would be. For this plague does not consume, but strengthen, making man the very essence of his most primal urges. Nor do his numbers dwindle, for every man fallen does rise again, along with countless more already interred in the earth. If you would emerge, you must do so now, to fight alongside those not yet poisoned. Wait, and it will find you—an unimaginable swarm, possessed of a single-minded cruelty you cannot fathom."

The king chewed upon that for a moment, then turned to Crag. "And what is *your* story?"

"The one ya seem to fear," the Tuthari admitted, clearing his throat. "Name is Craggenbrun, bairn of Ragglesband. I've seen man's cruelty up close, and ain't likely to forget it. Stick your neck out now, and there's a fine chance he'll lop it off."

Hreidmar glanced at Htomah with fresh amusement. If the Entient had brought Crag along in an effort to win sympathy or support, he had misjudged the Tuthari grossly. In that moment, Htomah was thinking much the same, but did his best not to look surprised or betrayed.

"When war broke between our races," Crag continued, "we stood our ground long as we could. When forced to flee, his armies chased us down. Wasn't enough that we were beaten. He viewed our kind as vermin to be eradicated. To my knowledge, I'm the last what got away. Been in hiding ever since, alone mostly, and among those smart enough to secret themselves away at the first."

Htomah resisted the urge to silence the dwarf. He realized Crag had made no promises, and he in turn had demanded none. Even so, he had not expected such outright opposition.

"Then you carry different counsel than your friend here," Hreidmar observed.

Crag shrugged. "Ain't my place to tell your folk how to live, and only barely my concern. I sailed with Torin to this land in hopes of finding a people to dwell among. But that was before I understood just how bad things were. Way I see it, ain't much hope for the lot of ya. I'm thinking now it'd be wiser of me to make my own way."

"You don't think we can defend ourselves?" the king asked with a frown.

"Against this threat? No more'n my own stood against theirs."

"But you said—"

"I said ya stick your neck out, might be it gets lopped. But it might also be that man's willing to accept whatever aid is offered. Seems to me, quick death with a chance at life—a life ya claim ya want—is better than a slow, certain death, which is what ya face here."

Again Htomah had to fight to keep his expression neutral. This time, however, it was his pleasure he sought to hide from a suddenly disgruntled king.

"You've a rather loose tongue, Craggenbrun, and speak less fact than judgments that may or may not have been fed to you by this one."

"Little to gain and less to lose," the Tuthari huffed. "Mayhap I'm wrong, and your forces can weather this scourge." His eyes flicked to Vashen, then back to her king. "But I've had near twenty years to reflect on the mistakes my people made, and the biggest is the one I see your own about to repeat."

Hreidmar stroked his beard. "Oh? And what would that be?"

"Refusing allies. Trying to subsist on your own. Do that, as we did, and—in my *judgment*—the mighty Hrothgari will share the Tuthari's fate."

CHAPTER TWENTY

THE SENTRIES AT THE EDGE of camp peered at him as if he were an apparition born of the swirling mists. Corathel smiled at their shock. That he might already be a ghost was something even he would have to consider. For he could think of no surer way to explain his unlikely string of narrow escapes.

He continued forward, overcome with relief, anxious to learn how many more had come to rendezvous.

Then the guardsmen caught sight of those who accompanied him, flexing their bows in response. The chief general froze, raising his hands.

"Hold!"

It was all he could manage before one of the arrows was loosed, directly toward the Mookla'ayan chieftain—he of the crown of stakes embedded in his skull.

Swifter than thought, one of the flanking elves snapped forward, catching the arrow by its shaft. Mercifully so, for instead of dodging, the chieftain had puffed up as if to shield his trailing clansmen. He held himself that way now, with the arrow's tip not but a finger's breadth from his tattooed cheek.

Corathel might have sighed in relief, but scarcely had time to blink before the response he feared was unleashed.

In a bounding swarm, a dozen Mookla'ayans lunged forward, weaving from side to side to engage the startled sentries from all directions. The bowman who had not yet fired his arrow did so now, only to gape as it went sailing harmlessly into the night-cloaked forest. The other drew his knife with a sharp, sudden rasp. Just as suddenly, it was torn from his grip, following a wild slash. In the next heartbeat, both soldiers were on the ground, limbs twisted painfully behind them, with half-moon blades held against their necks.

"No! Stop!" Corathel was finally able to shout. He turned toward the chieftain, the one his men had taken to calling "Owl." The elf clicked and gestured. Grudgingly, his savages relaxed their holds.

Corathel hastened forward, flanked by men of his own. One of the Parthan sentries looked at him with confused gratitude. In the other's eyes, he saw only horror and mistrust.

"At ease, soldiers. It is I, your chief general." He pulled up his sleeve, offering them his pulse. But neither could take his eyes off of the towering chieftain who strolled up beside him. "Ceilhigh be praised," he added with a sigh, "but these are our friends."

. . .

RATHER THAN RISK A REPEAT of hostilities throughout the encampment, the chief general sent the more accepting of the two sentries to fetch Lieutenant General Jasyn to him. He demanded of the remaining sentry a full report, clenching his jaw as the news was delivered. What remained of the legion had arrived just hours ago. Their numbers were better than he would have anticipated, given the slaughter and chaos that had marked their counterassault at Atharvan. The Second General had done an admirable job marshaling the retreat.

All of which might account for naught. Leaven was already besieged. At best, their count was half that of the enemy, and though other scattered companies could be expected to funnel in, following the markers as he had done, the same might be said of the reavers. No matter how he looked at it, they had not the numbers for another battle upon the plain.

A preliminary assessment, the sentry admitted, reading the chief general's distress. By now, the lieutenant commanders and their scouts might have better word.

The sentry-turned-herald was gone just long enough to make Corathel wonder if he had deserted when the Second General and his squad came upon the brush-covered hill where the rest of them waited. As Jasyn entered the rugged glen claimed by the chief general for his central command, one of the lieutenant's personal guard offered to examine Corathel, to verify that he was who he claimed to be.

"No need, Sergeant," Jasyn replied. "No reaver ever looked so haggard."

"I was about to say the same of you," Corathel offered, clasping the other's arm in greeting. "When was the last time you slept?"

"My days may be numbered. I'm not about to waste what moments I have left in nightmare."

"Preferable to the waking truth, I should think."

"In your boots, I can see why," Jasyn agreed. His gaze shifted to regard the band of wild Mookla'ayans with evident distaste. Most of his squad were already doing the same. "How in the Abyss do you explain them?"

"Would that I could. They came upon us as if in ambush, but were it not for them, we might never have escaped the reavers who hunted us."

"Allies?"

"It would seem so."

Jasyn gnawed at the inside of his lip. "Nevertheless, the men have become skittish enough. Would it not be better to send these savages on their own way?"

"I tried, but once we left Atharvan behind, they seemed insistent on following us. And I lacked the men to persuade them otherwise."

"You have them now. Give the word, and I'll call for a battalion at once."

Corathel shook his head. "I care for the sight of them no more than you do. But it would seem a poor show of gratitude. They've shielded us more than once against Illychar attack, else you and I might not be having this conversation."

The chieftain, seated nearby, looked up as if knowing they were talking about him. Corathel turned away, oddly embarrassed. Jasyn's expression remained sour.

"What do you suppose they want?" the lieutenant general asked.

"My company lacks a translator, so I can only guess. But Stake-brow there is clearly their leader. I haven't been able to make out his name—sounds different every time. 'Hoo-hoo Hen'? 'Ooo-ooo Wren'? Most of ours call him 'Owl,' given his hooting. The rest choose not to refer to him at all. What I *have* heard, more than once amid the rest of his gibberish, is *Jarom*."

"Torin, Jarom?" Jasyn asked, arching a brow in interest.

Corathel nodded. "Who else? Leads me to wonder if he might not be the one who led our Alsonian friend's expedition through the ruins of that elven city."

"You were told of that, were you?"

"That and more, when first Kylac introduced me to Jarom and Allion, back in Leaven. Why?"

"The story you shared with the rest of us made no mention of the savages. I didn't learn of their involvement until our trek through that forsaken jungle to rescue you."

Corathel saw no need to apologize. "As I recall, we were fighting swarms of dragonspawn at the time. You'll forgive me if I neglected a few meaningless details."

"Not so meaningless, perhaps," Jasyn said, turning his gaze back to Owl.

"For our purposes here, it is." He felt his face darken. "The city. How bad is it?"

"No sign of any dragon yet," Jasyn offered cheerfully. His eyes lifted toward the starlit skies, and Corathel's reflexively followed. "Other than that, the Queen is as heavily besieged as her King, with reavers crawling up her skirts."

Queen of the East, Leaven was called, larger and grander than any but Atharvan. But if the King had already fallen . . .

"Did our divisions make it inside?" Corathel asked.

"The scouts sent near enough to make sure have not yet returned—and I'm doubting now that they will. But my gut tells me Dengyn made it. Maybe Bannon, too. Otherwise, she'd have already fallen."

"You've sent riders on to Laulk?"

"Awaiting word. The one we have now, however, is that the passes are already filled with Illychar."

Which meant that there would be no quick escape as had been attempted at Atharvan. Leaven's only bolt-holes led through the mountains to Laulk—likewise the reverse. Either both cities were surrounded, or General Bannon had managed to escort Laulk's citizenry east to Leaven as commanded. Whichever, the Queen, if not her sister, stood now upon an island, and with no way to stem the rising tide, could only pray for the waves to be diverted.

"Whatever her defenders," Jasyn continued, "be they one division or two—or merely her own garrison—they fly the red."

Of course they did. Every city in Pentania, it now seemed, was begging reinforcement—those that hadn't already succumbed. And it had fallen to him, with but the dregs of his once-mighty legion, to answer them all.

He looked around his temporary campsite, here among the shadowed slopes and ravines of the lower Whistlecrags. He had gathered barely a hundred men in his flight from Atharvan. Half or more of those were savages he'd been taught since birth to regard with only contempt and loathing. Of the roughly thirty thousand he had marched into battle only a week ago, less than a quarter had gathered here, to hide amid rock and crag and tree lest their enemy sniff them out.

While every day, every hour, his opponent grew stronger.

"General?"

The task before him was impossible. The wisest course would be to take those who followed him now and continue on to Kuuria, hoping the horror that had claimed his lands had not yet devoured theirs.

His gaze found Owl's, depthless, implacable. It reminded him of his father's. Suddenly, in the back of his mind, he could almost hear the man's voice.

How do you climb a mountain?

A favorite phrase, used whenever Corathel had complained of an insurmountable challenge. His own, trained response echoed automatically. *One stride at a time.*

"Sir?"

"Maltyk and Lar, I'm told they are here?"

"Nicked and bruised, but as capable as ever," Jasyn assured him.

"Send for them at once. I have a plan, but we must execute it before dawn."

It was a lie, of course. He had no plan, only cold hard truths. Still, he knew they must be met head-on, and there were only so many ways to do so.

While Jasyn's runners fetched the others, Corathel received a more detailed account of the size and condition of their forces. It was not much to work with, but it would have to suffice. Their numbers might be minuscule compared to those of their enemy, but they were too large to avoid detection for long. Whatever they chose to do, they could not remain here.

By the time Third General Maltyk and Fourth General Lar had joined them, Corathel knew what course they must take, and set the idea forth quickly.

"We can do our people little good from out here," he stated bluntly. "Atharvan showed us that. If we mean to make a better showing than we did there, we must do so from within the walls, where at the very least we might rest and regroup." He waited for one or more to raise protest, but none did. Their silence spoke volumes. "You say the bulk of the enemy assails the main gate?"

Jasyn nodded grimly. "And to a lesser extent, the western road."

"Leaving the southern portal mostly clear."

"By comparison."

"Then our strategy seems plain. A diversion out front, to draw their attention to the east. If this swarm responds as did the one at Atharvan, its members will forsake the walls to hunt those on open ground. Move swift and quiet, and the bulk of the legion just may find time enough to win entrance through the south while the enemy is occupied."

"What of the diversion force?" Maltyk asked.

"Mounted, of course. As the main force reaches the portal, I want a full-bodied wedge planted against the wall, pointed southward and split down the middle to form a safety corridor for those funneling after. The diversion force will buy as much time as it can, then race around to the south, to follow the rest of our troops. The shield lines formed by the wedge will deflect the reavers giving chase, and allow our riders inside. Afterward, the shield lines themselves will fall in, in reverse formation—tip first, base last, until all have entered and the portal is closed."

"And if the shield lines fail?" Lar posed, his voice a quiet rumble.

Corathel eyed him squarely. "I trust you to make sure that doesn't happen. Thick at the anchor, thin at the tip, to help redirect closing enemies southward, away from the portal. Should you find yourself unable to build the wedge, or if you find its echelons failing too soon, get as many as you can inside, and close the gate. Forget the cavalry unit, if you must. The gate is your first priority. Better that my company should perish than the entire city be breached."

"*Your* company?" Jasyn noted.

"You didn't think I'd let *you* lead it, did you?" the chief general replied, forcing a reckless smile.

Jasyn shook his head. "It's a long ride from the main gate to the southern portal—at night over rugged terrain. Should you stumble, or the reavers to the south hold their position rather than be sucked out to the east, you'll be finished."

"Perhaps, though we might argue all night about which group faces the greatest danger. Is it the diversion force, or those first to the portal? Those at the southern tip of the wedge, few and easily blunted; or those at its base, who must hold the longest and will be the last to find safety within the walls?"

The Second General stroked his normally smooth chin, fingers scraping against the dark stumps of hair that had sprouted across his face.

"At least I'll be on horseback," Corathel pointed out, "with a better chance of escaping into the night, should it come to that."

"You can hope," Maltyk muttered darkly. "The animals brought with us have eaten and rested no more than the men."

A desperate maneuver, without question. But it was all the chief general could think of. Were they thrice the number and half as ragged, little or nothing would have changed.

"Hope is for those whose fate lies in another's hands. As of yet, I control my own. All else are but risks I choose to accept."

"Assuming this works," Lar interjected, "and we manage to reinforce those within, how do you propose we get back out?"

Corathel shook his head. "We'll bridge that river when we come to it. Agreed?"

They did, and no more complaints were uttered. Instead, their discussion shifted to focus on logistics, assignments, and other details. Very little breath was wasted on safeguards and contingency plans, none of which truly mattered. Should they fail, those strong enough to run would do so. The rest would be without further concerns.

The Nightingale's Hour was upon them by the time all of relevance had been settled.

"What of the savages?" Jasyn asked in afterthought. "Are they to play a role in this?"

"That will be up to them," Corathel answered, with a glance toward Owl. "I've not the time to try to make them understand our intent, or to glean theirs."

"A shame Allion isn't here. He might be able to tell us more about them, and what they may want."

Corathel nodded. "He may yet, should our paths cross again. Until then, if they're willing to risk their lives to protect ours, they're welcome to it."

"Are you certain you can trust them?" Maltyk asked warily.

The chief general barked a laugh. "No more certain than I am that Torin and his dragon won't drop upon us from the sky. But at this point, no risk we take could be worse than sitting still, awaiting further betrayal."

That cruel reminder of the larger battles yet to be waged served to tie his lieutenants' tongues. But it also fostered in them a rising anger, and a determination to fight this night's battle as though it were their last. He saw it in their faces, and felt it in his own.

"Are we in full understanding, then, of what must occur?"

"The plan is sound," Maltyk said.

"We'll make it work," assured Jasyn with an eager smile.

Lar gave a slow and steady nod.

"Good. You have until the Woodcock's Hour to make your soldiers comprehend it. After that, we move."

THIS IS WHAT YOU WISHED to see, is it not?" King Hreidmar asked him.

"It is," Htomah replied, running his hand along the mole's iron-shelled body. He ducked inside the open rider bay, to examine the pump-lever mechanism used to propel the carriage, as well as the various cranks and gears that operated its grinding face. "You have some that are larger, yes?"

"We might," Hreidmar allowed guardedly, stroking his beard. "Care to tell us what you're thinking?"

"I am thinking that these vessels of yours might be put to better use than boring tunnels beneath the earth."

"How so?" Warder General Vashen inquired.

"They help you to dig through rock. What might they do to a wall of enemies, I wonder?"

The king and general glanced at one another.

"Perhaps the thought never occurred to you," Htomah said, though he knew that it had. "I make no judgments, one way or the other. I only say, I should like to see what these creatures look like in the light of day."

Down here, in the blue-lit dark, the creature looked like a giant beetle, with a conical nose built of diamond-edged teeth and a thousand metal pincers on rotating rings of steel. A tool—a weapon—that even now its creators had been reluctant to reveal. This was one of their earlier designs, seldom used. Some of the newer ones were ten times its size, and could be driven twice as fast, with better wheels, thicker walls, and larger bays that were fully enclosed, capable of bearing a score of dwarves or more.

"It is a tunneling device, not a siege engine," Hreidmar maintained.

"Some modifications would be required, to be sure. But even the smallest boat can be rigged to cross the largest ocean."

He had not revealed to them, of course, just how much he knew about their drilling machines, or how he knew it. They were mistrustful enough already. Instead, he had chosen to plant theories and suggestions as to the types of tools and engines that might prove useful, and to make inquiries based on what he claimed was physical evidence encountered during his trek through their halls.

"We're not crossing any oceans," Vashen pointed out. "And no wind would push these monsters. It requires teams of our strongest dwarves, working in shifts, to propel even the lighter moles the length of a mile through open space. Through stone, we may burrow but paces in a day."

Htomah pretended to consider. "What might you say if I told you that I could ease the burden of your drivers, using steam to help push the rods and turn the wheels?"

"Steam?" Hreidmar snorted. "And sorcery, I suppose."

"A mechanical process," the Entient assured him, "no more complex than the crank and pulley and bellows used already by your people in myriad ways. If I were to show your engineers the design, I am certain that they could construct the parts and fit them to your existing moles in the time it might take the rest of your people to make ready to depart."

Again the king and general shared a frown, while Crag and the attending warders remained silent in that earthen tunnel.

"Why would you show us such workings, when they might only be turned against your own kind?" Hreidmar finally asked.

"Because our fates are linked in this, as I have already explained. Because you are the only ones who can make use of my knowledge before it is too late. Because I trust you to use it to the betterment of all. Are these not reason enough?"

Another silence, as the Hrothgari king searched deep within his eyes for any hint of deception. "We haven't the capacity in our existing moles to carry a tenth of our populace."

"Nor have we the time to properly refit more than a few of these creatures," Htomah agreed, laying his hand upon a steel-rimmed panel. The rivets along its seam protruded like bony knobs. "It matters not. What we can do, we shall do, and let that suffice."

The dwarves stared back at him, unconvinced.

"Will your engineers have a look at what I would show them?"

Hreidmar combed his beard with gnarled fingers. "We shall *all* have a look."

They set out then, back the way they had come. All in all, Htomah had to be pleased with his progress. Thus far, Hreidmar and his people had committed themselves to nothing, but they were obviously intrigued. Intrigued and fearful. Not so much so that they would do anything irrational, but enough that they were willing to take a risk or two to avoid the sort of fate Htomah and Crag had promised them was on its way. Taken individually, nothing in his words or Crag's—or in their minor skirmishes with Illychar—would have convinced them such risk was necessary. But taken together, these events had painted an image Hreidmar and the others were too wise to ignore.

Things would go faster, of course, if they would accept the Entient's wisdom in the spirit with which it was offered, rather than second-guessing the motive behind his every word. The plan with which he had come had been fully formulated long before the Hrothgari ruler had deigned speak with him. But this was a proud and cunning people that refused to be manipulated. His stratagem would seem much more palatable should they devise it for themselves, with his own involvement limited to promptings, rather than directives.

Still, it frustrated him to feign ignorance when time was so critical. If their enthusiasm did not ignite soon, he might have to find another way to fan its flames.

At the mouth of the tunnel, they were met by a trio of warders—the same trio, Htomah noticed, that he and Crag had first encountered when making their way from the surface. General Vashen, marching with another pair a step ahead of Crag and Htomah, did not seem pleased to see them.

"Thaggon," she said, addressing the previously unidentified toifeam, "what is it now? You were ordered to resume patrol of the Hunarrian Loop."

Thaggon ignored her. The Hrothgari warder, along with his companions Yellowbeard and Redbeard, turned their gazes instead upon Htomah. As soon as he saw their eyes, the Entient froze. For while their orbs might look the same to anyone else, he saw clearly the telltale sapphire glow marking a transposition.

"Well met, my brother," Thaggon said to him.

"Quinlan, is it?" Htomah replied.

"And Jedua and Wislome," the other answered in his dwarven guise.

It might have been worse. At least it was not Maventhrowe himself who had come for him. Still, he had no right to believe he could escape the three of them.

Vashen and her forward escorts wore stern masks over their evident confusion. King Hreidmar, who trailed amid his ringing entourage, came to a stop now with all the rest. "What goes on here?" the king asked.

Even Crag, Htomah noted, was regarding him with suspicion. He had no more allies. The trust he had worked so hard to earn was gone, as quick as that.

"You shame yourselves, my friends," he said, "to use these noble vessels so."

"A sordid act," Quinlan agreed, "but one you compelled us to undertake. You move quickly, dear brother."

"Not quickly enough, it seems."

"General," Hreidmar snapped, "who are these dwarves?"

Vashen was no longer sure. "Thaggon. Look at me."

"Forgive me, Warder General, Your Glory," Htomah offered, with a nod to both Vashen and her king, "but your brave warders are under a mystical influence."

Hammers and axes and polearms slipped from their slings. The three Entient-dwarves raised their hands.

"No!" Htomah threw his own arms wide to hold all in check. "No harm need come to them. My brothers mean to release them at once."

"Just as soon as we have escorted you from the city, and into our own hands," Quinlan said.

"Is this how your kind works?" Hreidmar asked, with venom in his tone. "Should we fail to do your bidding, do you mean to force it upon us?"

Htomah fought to remain calm, though he felt a fury rising. "You know better than this, Quinlan."

"We have come to save you, my brother, from your own impetuousness. Maventhrowe has allowed that you may return, but you must do so now."

"Whatever happened to allowing a brother to choose his own path?"

"This path you have chosen bears too many consequences that cannot be predetermined. Consider the risks—"

"Spare me your counsel, my brother. I have heard the arguments, and you have heard mine. At one time, I thought you sympathetic to my plight."

"Your frustrations are shared," Quinlan said. Despite the gruff Gohran tongue, Htomah could almost hear the compassion in the other's voice. "But you have violated—"

"What? What have I violated? I seek to finish a task that we all began and left unfinished. What vows have I broken?"

Thaggon's mouth twisted, while his lumpy brow wrung with uncertainty. The rest of the dwarves in the tunnel remained still, gripping their weapons while they glared at their stricken comrades.

"You were forbidden human contact," Quinlan said finally. "You agreed—"

"As you can plainly see, I have made no human contact. Or would you further insult this people with such base disparagements?"

Behind him, King Hreidmar actually snorted with laughter.

Thaggon's eyes shifted to meet those of Yellowbeard and Redbeard—Jedua and Wislome. Neither had anything to offer. "My brother, I beg you. We have staked our own futures upon yours. If you do not return with us now, it may be that none of us ever will."

Htomah refused to weaken, to show just how deeply saddened he was to bear their fates along with his. Would that he could send them on their way and face the consequences of his actions alone. But that was not his choice. His was to carry on as he felt he must, or surrender all and let the plague he had helped loose run its course. Though it might mean permanent exile— his *and* theirs, he had heard nothing yet that could persuade him to let that happen.

"I swear to you, my brothers: I have every intention of doing what I must within the parameters set forth by our guiding council. When finished, I shall return with you willingly, to face whatever punishment befits my crime. But do not ask me to do so before I have accomplished the task I have undertaken. I would sooner waste away my remaining years in utter solitude than abandon our flock and all others for the sake of my own vanity. Should you doubt my resolve, now is your chance to test it."

"And ours," Hreidmar grunted unexpectedly. Htomah glanced back as the king strode forward, a bejeweled war hammer in hand. "Bunch of cravens," he spat at Quinlan and the others. "Afraid to face us in your own skins? What are you, skatchykem? Tells me this one has more mettle than the lot of you. Take him, if you will, but you'll do so through us."

Though careful not to show it, Htomah felt invigorated at the other's sudden fervor. Perhaps Quinlan's coming had done him good after all.

The Entient controlling Thaggon's body took a long look at the Hrothgari king. His gaze remained cool and steady. Such threats, Htomah knew, would have little effect on the outcome of this contest. When the eyes of Quinlan, Jedua, and Wislome found him again, the elder Entient found himself holding his breath.

"Then let us have a look," Quinlan suggested finally, "at what precisely you intend."

CHAPTER TWENTY-ONE

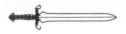

BLACK CLOUDS HID A SOILED moon. The stars were out, but their light shone faintly, like candles behind a silk curtain. Leaves and limbs swayed softly overhead, sifting the dim radiance.

Beneath this screen of mottled darkness, Corathel trod carefully, leading his horse by its halter along the ravine floor. A column of the best riders remaining to him trailed after, fourscore in all. Their faces were grim, painted dark with mud and coal. Their eyes were gleaming pools of captured twilight, shifting furtively in their sockets. If anything like their chief general, their entrails were wound tight around hollow stomachs, their lungs squeezed with apprehension.

Some had witnessed already their last sunrise. It was left only to learn which ones—if not all. Until then, the gnawing anxiety seemed a torment from which even death might be welcome.

Corathel pushed aside a low-hanging tree limb and continued along the overgrown path. A veteran of more battles than he could remember, it bothered him that he should be beset by the doubts and fears of a wet-nosed greenhorn. He had long ago become inured to the harsh realities of warfare—of death and dismemberment and scars both mental and physical. And yet he could not recall having ever been more afraid.

Perhaps because he understood now that death could not save him. Death could be romanticized, celebrated even. But he could think of no solace to be taken in becoming an Illychar, a slave in one's own mortal shell. Though he hadn't spoken of it, he had seen the looks in the eyes of his men risen as reavers—the helpless horror, the begging for release. A fate that might endure centuries, an eternity. The mere thought was enough to drive even the bravest, the most callous, mad.

The ravings of a weary mind, he assured himself. Were he to see rainbow-colored squirrels frolicking amid the trees, he might not give the matter another thought. Best that he do the same here.

The track they followed twisted and wound roughly eastward through the foothills south of Leaven. They were more than a mile off, but dared not move closer until ready to spring their attack. Even at this distance, they could hear the muted sounds of battle, as the reavers maintained their siege throughout the night. As at Atharvan, the undead savages had as yet constructed no engines with which to force the gates or bring down the walls, seeking instead to scale the heights with ladders and grapnels. Were it not for a dozen less favorable factors, he might have taken that as cause for hope. As it was, he saw it only as a way for the Ceilhigh to prolong their little mummers' show of monsters and men.

He cast his gaze to either flank, where the lithe forms of Owl and his Mookla'ayans slipped nimbly, almost invisibly, through the brush-choked trees. Every time he glimpsed them, he had to remind himself that these were not his enemy, but serving him as wards and scouts. He wasn't certain what they meant to accomplish once the fighting began. On the open roads of the foothills above, they would be unable to match his horse's pace. Despite his earlier words, he had tried again to rid himself of them, for *their* sake if not his own. He had even gone so far as to attempt a diagram of his strategy, to convince them to depart or else remain with Jasyn and the bulk of the legion. Alas, they continued to dog him like the stink of his own garb, refusing to leave him be.

But he had too many concerns to dwell on that one, so he ignored it as best he could. Just one more potential reason for the sickness in his gut.

The ravine forked again, crosscut by the rise of another hill. This time, he turned north through the crease. Stones and deadwood and skittering rodents filled his path. Sage and bramble scratched at him with their thorny claws. Corathel pressed forward as quietly as possible, edging, rather than hacking, through the unruly tangle. Were it only the armies above he had to worry about, such caution was likely unneeded. But if those armies were to employ scouts of their own, or if some stray reaver should happen across his position while seeking to join its bloody kin, his troops were as likely as not to be crushed where they stood.

That it might not matter was yet one more possibility he pretended not to consider. After all, they only had so long before the thousands who had sacked Atharvan finished claiming their dead spoils and joined their comrades, here or elsewhere. The odds promised to grow longer before they evened. Worse, he yet had no news of affairs in Alson, to the west, or Kuuria, to the south. It was quite possible that the miracle he assumed one or the other must eventually send might never come.

The Shrike's Hour came and went, making way for that of the Vulture. Corathel spent it as he had those preceding it, in slow, stubborn trek and persistent denial of the many questions and perils over which he had no control. The Sparrow, marking the spring turn between midnight and dawn, was almost upon them when at last they reached the edge of their cover and saw the truth of what they had come to face.

In the sudden breeze, his sweat became like a cool, damp cloth applied to his fevered brow. Looking up from the gutter of that scrub-strewn slope, still half a mile off, he had a clear view of his enemies' backs as they writhed and surged against the black bulk of Leaven's curtain wall. Between fifteen and twenty thousand, by his scouts' reports, though from this vantage it appeared as if it might be twice that—like an overhanging snowbank that could crumble at any moment, burying his cavalry command beyond any trace.

A chill wracked his spine. To his left, he heard the sound of soldiers retching. When he looked, he saw only Owl and his flock, gathered now at his heels. The sight made him want to retch himself. He might have let himself do so, had he believed it would do anything to dispel his nervousness.

He waited a few moments longer, then gave the signal to mount. Leather creaked, traces rattled, and horses tamped and whinnied, as the silent order was relayed. Courageous men, the chief general thought, to follow him so, trusting in he who had delivered them from hopeless straits before to do so again.

If only he shared their faith.

But he showed no hesitation as he made his final checks and awaited the readiness signal from his squad commanders. When given, he buried his doubts and put heel to flank, leading his column from its place of concealment—slowly at first—to begin the long climb up the hill. A rabbit on the wolf's trail, to be sure, but he had its scent, and there was no turning back.

Halfway up, they passed the Wormroad, cutting its arc around the city's southern face. By now, the enemy had begun to turn and mark their approach. Owl and his Mookla'ayans had spread out before him, and their presence no doubt confused matters. Or perhaps the reavers simply didn't believe that those they preyed upon could be so bold.

It took them only a moment to realize the truth. And when they did, the nearest sheared off from the main horde like river waters through an opened irrigation trench. All of a sudden, the battle had commenced.

Chief General Corathel unsheathed his sword, pressed his steed into a gallop, and charged headlong to meet them.

"WE MOVE," JASYN SAID, THEN launched himself from cover.

He dashed ahead in a crouch, scrambling over scrub and stone like an uncaged lizard. Wound tight as he was with anticipation, it was all he could do not to fly up that barren slope and leave his squad behind. As it was, he did not pause to ensure they followed him, but merely trusted them to obey.

The path ahead had not yet completely cleared. A handful of reavers were still rushing around from the west, in pursuit of those who had already set off to the east. But he didn't have all morn. Those who would make it inside Leaven's walls would do so before dawn. Those upon whom the sun arose would find themselves in desperate search of some other shelter, else rotting where they lay.

Over the last few hours, the legion had been stealing carefully northward, slinking from shadow to shadow, moving into ready position for when Corathel sprang his surprise. Judging by the enemy activity, all was going to plan. Before any could enter the city, however, the way first had to be made clear. The Second General had taken it upon himself—he and his small team— to open the door through which the rest would follow.

Despite his eagerness, he was forced to wait a few moments longer, hunkered in shadow, before entering the final stretch, a dead man's land reaching out from the south gate. He grinned at his soldiers, sword in hand, while a trailing ogre lumbered by along the Wormroad to join the far-off commotion. With a nod and a raised eyebrow, he silently suggested taking the beast down, then feigned disappointment when they shook their heads.

Cravens, he mouthed in mock reprimand.

When that danger had passed, he cast left and right and skittered into the open, making straight for the gatehouse. To do so, he first had to cross the rutted Wormroad, then clamber down and across a dry moat filled with stakes. A few bodies lay across it, amid a debris of severed ropes, broken climbing poles, and the splintered shafts of arrow and spear. Many were oiled and charred, along with their onetime bearers. Merely a glimpse, he knew, of the carnage that lay elsewhere, beneath the areas of principal assault.

He did not waste time in search, but supposed that every arrow slit and crenel contained eyes and worse trained upon him. The reavers may have missed his approach, but the watchmen atop the wall would not have. He could only pray they would treat with him before some itchy greenhorn feathered his partial plate or the padded leathers beneath.

His foot hit an oil slick as he crested the far bank, which nearly sent him tumbling back into the nest of jagged stones and sharpened stakes below. Fortunately, one of his soldiers was able to offer brace and spare him a nasty fall. By the time he righted himself and turned forward once more, a viewing slat in the iron postern had slid wide. Torchlight and a husky voice greeted him from within.

"Who approaches?"

"Jasyn," he wheezed, "lieutenant general of the Parthan Legion, Second Division, come to reinforce Leaven. Who commands the gate?"

"Colonel Ragenon, garrison commander."

Jasyn glanced skyward, straining for a glimpse of those looking down on him from atop the barbican. "Is the colonel himself present?"

"We can bear him word—"

"No time. Look alive, lad, and tell your gatekeepers to lower the bridge."

"How many have you brought?" a second guardsman asked suspiciously.

"Some eight thousand in all," Jasyn replied. His head swiveled, searching for any reavers who might happen upon their position. "Minus a patrol for every moment you keep us locked without."

"We received no signal," the first guardsman protested.

"Will you submit for examination?" the other added.

"Come, man. Does my arm look slender enough to fit through that peekhole? Should I shove it through, your comrades will be checking my pulse while I squeeze your throat. Else we can skip such courtesies while you open the gate."

The pair shared a whispered word, then glared back at him a moment before the slat slammed shut. Jasyn looked around for a usable rope and grapnel, wondering if they would dare shoot down one of their own lieutenant generals should he attempt to scale their wall.

When he didn't see one, he took to banging on the iron postern with the pommel of his sword, letting that serve as his voice. He continued until he heard a screech from the main portal behind him, and one of his men tapped his shoulder.

"Sir."

With a rattle and groan, the immense granitewood drawbridge began to lower from the gatehouse maw. Jasyn's patrolmen stepped aside, clearing its path. As it neared the bottom of its descent, the general found himself looking through the portcullis bars at a full platoon of garrison soldiers. In searching their grim faces, he found hope and wariness in equal measure.

Before the great bridge had fully settled, he squeezed through the gap and pressed the side of his neck against the bars. Quicker, that, than unbuckling the bracers upon his wrists.

"Step forward, then," he urged, "and verify my claim."

The gate captain, perched at the head of his assembled regiment, nodded toward a pair of guardsmen. The same he had met with a moment earlier, Jasyn realized. The two glanced at each other before the fat one stepped forward, removing a glove. As his fingers reached for Jasyn's pulse, the lieutenant general snapped at him like a rabid dog. The guardsman withdrew with a start.

Jasyn laughed at the other's twisted nerves. "Quick now. We haven't got all night." Again he presented his neck, and this time allowed the cowardly sod to press his clammy fingers against its flesh, just below his jaw.

"Begging your pardon, sir. You must understand—"

"Give me torches," Jasyn commanded.

"Eh?"

"A pair of torches, now!"

The fop managed to signal for those nearby to grant his request. With a torch in either hand, Jasyn faced southward, peering down the slope into the dark tangle in which the legion waited. Stood atop the lowered bridge, he waved the flaming beacons back and forth, crossing them overhead. Almost at once, the distant treeline seemed to come alive, as soldiers began to emerge.

He turned back to the gate. "The portcullis now, if you please."

By the time it was raised, the first wave of soldiers was scampering across the bridge, boots thudding upon the thick, ironbound planking. Once that initial detachment had shown the way to still be clear, Jasyn gave the signal for the main body to approach. It did so in a continuous, unbroken stretch, Third General Maltyk at its head.

"They offer you any trouble?" Maltyk asked.

"Watchmen," Jasyn snorted, handing his comrade one of the torches. "Useful as a legless mule. All they do is bray." He then focused his attention on the trailing lines, and bellowed, "Form the wedge!"

. . .

CORATHEL'S BLADE FELL IN A flash, cleaving his opponent's naked skull. The wound erupted, blood spraying. The man hung there for a moment, wriggling like a stringed puppet, his mouth clenched in fury. No savage, this, but some nameless rancher of these very highlands—one of countless common folk of Partha the chief general had spent his life protecting. Dying now, on the edge of his sword. Beneath a beetle brow rigid with denial, the rancher's eyes seemed to glisten with gratitude.

With a wrench of his sword arm, Corathel's blade came free and the dead man crumpled atop his pole-axe. The general felt only a passing guilt. It was either kill or be slaughtered upon the tip of that weapon like one of the rancher's cattle.

His greater feeling—as he parried the lunge of another's spear—was fury. At the Illysp, who would imprison men so. At whatever fell gods had granted them this power. At Torin, for unleashing them upon his world. If he could, he would banish them all back to the Abyss, in exchange for the souls of those innocents already taken.

He wheeled and spun, then leaned forward as his mount reared, flailing its hooves at a pack of enemies drawn near. For a moment, he feared he had plunged too deep, that he would be cut off from the rest of his unit. The mere thought brought an ache to his chest.

But then Owl and his Mookla'ayans were there, half-moon knives slashing. Poisoned darts filled the air, and the forward waves slowed and staggered. Corathel seized his opening, jerking his steed's head back to the east.

Not all were so fortunate. To either side, he listened to the screams as his men were torn from their mounts, and horse and rider both were buried under by a relentless pursuit. With each foray, he seemed to lose a few more. But the reavers were still streaming eastward from around the city walls. Until he had lured them all out and strung them across the open plain, he dared not make his own break to the south.

The next squad of cavalry was barreling toward him. *His* squad, Corathel realized, the head of their company, gathering speed for what would be its third charge. Corathel should have been among them, wheeling and striking alongside. But with each circling pass, he had lingered longer and longer, to fight among the succeeding squads, which rushed in and out in staggered waves. Somehow, he had slipped all the way from the head of his force to its tail. Were it not for the Mookla'ayan guard, this most recent pass would have been his last.

Even so, he considered rejoining the forward ranks as they went thundering past, into the teeth of the trailing storm. But he could feel his horse flagging beneath him, driven as much by its own fear and desperation as its rider's commands. However brief, they both needed respite.

They slowed to a canter as the crunch of bodies and clangor of arms signaled the next raking collision between Parthan and Illychar. Corathel turned back to gauge the number unhorsed. One in four, it seemed. Too many. In the beginning, they had managed to strafe the enemy front with nary a casualty. But his men and their mounts had wearied, and the enemy had grown wise to their tactics. Though the reavers continued to string themselves along in reckless pursuit, they were wise enough now to form up when the waves of cavalry made their charge, raising pikes and spears and pitchforks in defense, then striking out when the beasts presented flank or tail.

Too soon, the chief general despaired. He had not given the legion enough time. Not enough by half.

The next squad roared past, shouting a salute to their general as they raced to relieve those ahead of them. Corathel responded with raised sword and a raucous cry, flanked by a small handful of riders and his Mookla'ayan guard, loping alongside. *Their* numbers were dwindling, too, he realized, though he had never been certain of their original count. Threescore, perhaps, trimmed now to two. Lose many more, and he might lose them all.

Another wave went past, and another, each seeming smaller than the last. As he came upon the knoll on which the resting waves perched, he saw in their valiant faces that they were ready for his command—to charge again, to die, if necessary, on his order. Corathel steeled himself, determined to not be swayed, one way or the other, by their faith and dedication.

In looking back at the city, southwest of their current position, he saw that the rear ranks of the Illychar were even now pulling away from her eastern gate and leaving her walls behind. One more cycle, he thought, should be sufficient. One more, and their work would be done.

But when he turned to give the command, it stuck in his throat. One more charge was all they had left. There would be no more cycles of strike and withdraw. Few would be able to rally again at a point such as this—and even if they could, each retreat forced them farther and farther from the city. If any returned to claim a new staging ground, it would likely become their last.

To lead men to their deaths was cruelty enough. But this would be another sort of condemnation altogether.

"Upon next strike, make for the Wormroad," he ordered Jenarin, the next squad commander in line. "Do not look back until the teeth of the south gate are behind you."

"Sir," Jenarin acknowledged with a salute, then asked, "Have we given them enough time, sir?"

"You men have done your part. Time now for our comrades to do theirs."

A moment later, the appointed timekeeper reached his tally, signaling the departure mark. Jenarin saluted his chief general once more, and called to his men.

"Final run, lads. Make it count."

They set off at a canter down the rise, leaving Corathel to wonder which, if any of them, he would see again.

He wondered the same when the next squad followed them, and the next after that. All too soon, the man given to mark time for his own squad—the one he had most recently attached himself to—gave his signal.

"Barak will lead you," he ordered. "I'll wait here for the last."

The men did not question, but started off in pursuit of the appointed veteran—a valor sergeant once, though it seemed his entire company had been scattered or killed during the massacre at Atharvan. A capable man nonetheless.

One by one, the squads not yet ordered to make for the gate returned. And one by one, Corathel turned them on ahead, to follow after the others. Twice he had to move himself and his Mookla'ayan guard to a farther knoll, to maintain distance from the ever-lengthening reaver swarm. All the while, he kept his eye upon Jenarin and those sent after, who veered south as though in full retreat, before cutting sharply west along the Wormroad. Reavers farther back, along the southern fringe, began seeping in that direction, as if realizing the riders' intent and moving to cut them off. But the vast majority continued to push north and east, toward the chief general's position and the headwaters of the cavalry's flow.

When the last squad to turn back toward his position disengaged from the Illychar front, Corathel raced down to meet them. Of the ten men originally assigned to that unit, only three remained. It might have been better for them had they tucked in and joined the squad before them, or simply bolted. Instead, they were returning along the rally course, buying time for those ahead of them to get away.

They redirected quickly enough when he came upon them, waving his sword in a circle overhead before pointing it to the south. He doubted they could hear his shouts, but they recognized his signal, and fell in readily beside him.

The chief general had barely regained his wind. He could only imagine the others' exhaustion. His horse strained, its eyes wide. With the bulk of the cavalry racing westward, and the majority of reavers redirecting in pursuit, he wasn't sure he and the riders bestride him had the speed to turn the corner and gain the Wormroad before their enemies sealed it off.

He cut a tighter angle, nearly spilling from his mount as a spear hurtled past his head. The forward Illychar were too close. At their present trajectory, those racing east would intercept him long before he had to worry about those farther back who were sweeping south.

Once again, Owl's bloody savages saved him. Though they lacked the speed to match his horse at a gallop, they had followed him south just a short distance before turning west into the very heart of the horde. He wanted to scream at them to clear away, to warn them that no more squads would be coming to relieve them.

He chose instead to save his breath.

The Mookla'ayan diversion bought him seconds only, but they were the seconds he needed. Veering sharply along a boulder-strewn escarpment, he and his trio of riders gained the Wormroad mere heartbeats before the reavers spilled down as if to wash it away. Had the enemy done so along the full of its length, he would have been finished. Fortunately, like any breaking wave, the Illychar throng was doing so from one end to the other—in this case, east to west, as the trailing ranks were the last to learn of the cavalry's movements.

But word traveled faster than bodies. By now, even the rear ranks of Illychar seemed to realize that the enemy that had teased them out from the city was charging westward, in the very direction from which they had been lured to begin with. The entire host was redirecting accordingly, as if pushed along that course by a gusting wind. Would that he were a ship at sea, Corathel thought, able to harness that wind with sails upon his back.

Defenders atop the southern wall were doing what they could to occupy the maddened enemy, sending down a steady rain of hot oil and flaming arrows and crushing stones. At this distance from the wall, however, their barrage seemed to have little effect. The enemy ahead of him—that which had chased Jenarin and the leading riders—seemed to be cresting overhead, ready to break. He could scarcely see the squad he trailed, but did not favor their chances against the looming darkness. The most he could say for them was that the odds of their escape were better than his.

With the road ahead like a river of sluggish black waters in the meager twilight, Corathel settled in for the final ride of his life.

That road leaned and twisted as it crossed the foothills beneath the city, filled with ruts and scree and rain furrows as Jasyn had warned. More than once, he raced past horses and riders broken from a fall. Some lay motionless. Others hobbled about or could be seen crawling south into the woods. He yelled at them to get away, but could do no more.

Time and again, his own mount faltered. He clung to it as best he could and urged it recklessly onward. He kept waiting for the Illychar wave to wash over him, but for some reason, it did not. It was as if the farther he went, the more something else drew its attention.

Then he caught sight of the wedge, stretched out from the southern gate as he had commanded. Its angled face was like a dam against which the Illychar threw themselves, churning madly. The riders ahead of him were even now ducking around its tip, cutting north toward the city behind its blockade.

A hundred paces off. Maybe more. With the finish in sight, Corathel found his strength renewed. He willed what he could of it to his steed, as its lean muscles flexed and pulled.

The rider at his tail went down, torn from his mount and washed away in a surge of crushing violence. The overhanging wave was closing upon him, the reaction and pursuit of the enemy host overcoming the speed of his mount at last. *No*, he thought angrily. They had come so far. They were almost home.

His terror-stricken mount seemed to sense it, flinging mud and stone at their pursuers with its pounding hooves. Enemy missiles flew at them in return. Corathel ducked low, warding off their attacks with a battered shield. Stones thudded against his partial plate and against his horse's lathered hide.

Before him, the legion's phalanx was weakening. He saw Lar at its point, giant Lar, swinging that mighty axe and bellowing commands, making sure that the tip did not fall inward too soon. Though the Illychar threatened to spill over its southern edge, the Fourth General realized how close they were, and was making every effort to counter the swarm, to draw its focus and give the last of the cavalry the precious time it needed.

Corathel bore down, demanding of his steed one final push.

Then an arrow struck its hindquarters. The destrier faltered, but churned on, refusing to surrender. Corathel grimaced as a spear or sword scraped his leg. Behind him, he heard the agonized shriek as another of his men went down, followed quickly by yet another. He glanced wistfully toward Lar's position. So close, he thought, as the leaping bodies of his enemies cascaded over him.

Death roared in his ears as their weight bore down upon him. A suicide charge it had been, and so it would end.

His brave mount carried on for a moment, amid a chorus of howls and a knot of thrashing limbs. It then lurched suddenly to the side, spilling him to the earth and into the darkness awaiting beyond.

CHAPTER TWENTY-TWO

A WARMTH AT HER WRIST DREW her from her slumber. Her eyes opened. Dawn had not yet come, though a brightening through the forest canopy told her that it was not far off.

The warmth was from her mother's wellstone. Her gaze shifted to find the central crystal aglow in the palm of her hand. Its color was faint, its inner pulse slow and steady.

A warning nonetheless.

Her chest tightened, and she forced herself up from the bed of moss upon which she lay, pushing aside a silken blanket. She smelled smoke at about the same time she saw the gentle aura of a nearby flame, casting its flickering light upon the trees at her back. She had been lying on her side, but rolled over quickly now to have a look. Her breath caught to realize that a hooded figure sat on a log beside the fire, poking the flames with a stick.

The figure made a muttering noise, before a raspy voice cut through the quiet of the tiny glade.

"So she awoke, the fatherless wanderer and orphan-to-be, whelped by her of elf and man."

Annleia blinked, then cast about, searching for others. She sensed them, but could not see them, as though they kept watch from the shadows.

"Sent by those who did not exist," her visitor croaked, "in search of a man who once had."

Annleia felt her skin prickle, each word like bark scraped against stone. A female voice, she thought, though she was not yet sure. The stranger's head remained bowed toward the flames, its face invisible. She clasped her wellstone tighter.

"Forgive me," she offered, her own voice sounding stronger than she felt. "I did not mean to trespass."

"Yet trespass she did in a world unfamiliar, from one path to the next, with scant inkling of which to take." The figure twitched, its cowl twisting to the side, and made a guttural sound Annleia did not understand. "Until the one she sought found *her*."

Again Annleia searched the surrounding shadows, unnerved more by the many she could *not* see than by the one she *could*. That changed when the stranger reached up with gnarled hands to draw back its ragged hood.

Annleia gasped. A woman, she decided, though she might have been part troll. Her face was grotesque to look upon, the skin as mottled and growth-ridden as a shagfire oak stricken with white fungus. In the crag of her brow—

beyond the crooked stretch of her jutting nose and a stringy veil of matted hair—shone a pair of catlike eyes, cold and piercing.

"Who are you?" the Finlorian lass heard herself ask.

The withered crone twitched again, at the neck and mouth, to mumble in the ear of the rotted, weasel-like carcass draped across her shoulders. "Necanicum, she was known to some, by others not at all. It was not her name the Orphan needed, but the gift she carried."

"Gift?" Her wellstone continued to glow softly in her palm. Despite the alarm generated by this Necanicum's unexpected presence, the wild woman did not seem to pose any real danger.

For a moment, Annleia feared the crone meant to gnaw upon the head of that poor, desiccated creature, so intense was her spasm. There were others, as well, draped upon her humpbacked frame. Furs, they should have been, but each bore some piece—limb or head or tail—that had not been properly skinned, and left instead to shrivel like unpicked fruit.

When the episode had passed, Necanicum drew a deep, rattling breath.

"Given the Teldara by the Immortal One, prior to his fall. Delivered by Necanicum as the spirits foretold."

Annleia sifted through the crone's words. Ravings, they seemed, though she could not make herself believe that. That there was some mysticism at work here was obvious. What it all meant was not as clear.

"When did you meet this Immortal One?" she asked.

Necanicum muttered to herself before offering her reply. "The sisters led him through her woods, in search of those who did not exist. She knew not where he might find them, only that he would. And his sickness with him."

"Sickness?"

"The one that would claim the world, his and theirs, one way or the other. By fire or by water, it had to be cleansed. And the Leviathan made certain, for that was His penance."

A chill crept up the column of Annleia's spine, and she realized she was shaking. Riddles they were, but plainly spoken, easily understood by one who held the key.

It was time to make sure that she did.

"The Immortal One. Did he call himself Torin?"

Necanicum poked sharply with her stick. All of a sudden, the tiny campfire erupted, spewing green-tinged flames toward the dome of leaves. It settled thereafter, but remained green in color, burning with twice its initial strength.

"The bearer of the Sword, the stirrer of souls, the waker of the dead and those that should have been," Necanicum croaked. "He called himself aught, yes, but was helpless to answer. The sickness ruled him, and in its throes, he harvested only chaos, bathing the world in fire and blood."

Blessed Ceilhigh, Annleia thought to herself, *I'm too late*. She felt a sweat building upon her brow. "And was he stopped?"

"He was, if the end the Teldara spoke of be true. But all events cast a shadow, and not even the spirits knew which would vanish when that sun did rise."

Two outcomes. Two fates. She still had a chance. "What must I do?"

"Upon the wall she fought, and beyond it she waited, when her power was filled. She might have felled him outright, yes, but protected him instead from those who would. For his fate would become hers, and theirs, until the oceans claimed all, unless she poisoned him first."

The crone raised a shaking hand to her breast, to clutch at a wooden phial hung from her neck. She muttered to herself, then tugged sharply, snapping the leather thong that held it in place.

"The fire did not harm her. Only in *its* light could she see."

Annleia stood. Though she could scarcely bear the heat, she forced herself to move closer to the flames, naked feet treading softly upon a dew-dampened earth. The closer she got, the more she could smell the wild woman's terrible musk: an odor of age and death and magic.

"In its light," the crone repeated, bending over the fire.

Annleia bent with her, gaze drawn to the phial clutched in Necanicum's hand. Before she could get a good look, the hand formed a fist, a gnarled mass of crooked fingers and swollen joints, wrapped in a leather skin hairy and spotted and wart-ravaged. Clawed yellow nails—cracked and caked with filth—dug into that flesh as the crone's grip tightened. Annleia glanced at the wild woman's eyes, and found them closed. Her lips moved, but this time, her mutterings were silent.

Then her hand thrust forward, into the flames. Annleia gasped and recoiled. Her next thought was to tackle the woman, to draw her from that mystical blaze. Then she realized—

The hand did not burn.

"In its light."

Annleia peered deep. In the heart of the fire, Necanicum's fingers uncurled, revealing the phial.

"Did she see?" the crone asked.

She did. Though the phial was carved of ebony darkwood, in the light of that blaze, its sides appeared as glass—clouded, yes, yet clear enough that its contents were revealed.

The Immortal One's gift.

Still, she did not understand how she was to use it. "I am to poison him with this?"

She looked up to find Necanicum's gaze, and could not look away. Up close, the crone's orbs were like chiseled gemstones, their edges cut into myriad facets. Annleia felt as if not one, but a thousand eyes were upon her.

"A venom," Necanicum confirmed. "The purest to be found. Warded until the time was right. For it could be used but once, by she who wielded no power of her own, but who controlled the ebb and the flow."

The eyes released her, allowing Annleia to glance at her wellstone. Her gaze slipped then, back to the phial.

"But how am I to administer it?"

The crone responded to her own shoulder—a stern reprimand, it seemed, for her silent companion. She then turned back to Annleia, and her wrinkled, crusted, wart-filled lips parted in what might have been a smile. "Necanicum did tell her."

And so she did. The process was complicated. Though Annleia listened attentively, she was not sure she could remember it all—or that even if she did, she would be able to execute the task without mishandling some vital stroke or measure. Her first thought, when Necanicum had finished and Annleia stood staring at the opaque phial that lay now in her own palm, was that she should not be asked to do this alone.

"We could travel as one," she suggested, though a part of her shuddered at the thought. "We could perform this task together."

Now that she had surrendered the phial, Necanicum sat back, eyes closed, murmuring gently to herself as if slipping into a slumber. The flames between them weakened into small yellow curls.

"Necanicum?"

"Necanicum had neither the speed, nor the strength, that was required. Nor was it she who sang sway to the gosswyn, or would carry it hence."

"Carry it hence? I am to keep the flower?"

"Until its time," Necanicum whispered. "All in its proper time."

"Necanicum," she said, frightened at how quickly the crone seemed to be fading, "you are sure this will put an end to the . . . the sickness?"

"Ends come and go and come again. The Leviathan would make sure. The Leviathan . . ."

Though close-related, that seemed almost another challenge entirely. "If I should fail . . . Necanicum, if I should fail, can the Leviathan be stopped?"

The crone's lips moved, but only whispers slid forth. Her head began to sag.

Annleia was about to go to her when another savage twitch brought the wild woman to life. When she finished muttering, her head snapped upward, those dreadful eyes freezing Annleia in her crouch.

"On their battle, the world hinged. For it was he who wielded the fire, and the Leviathan that wielded the waves. One would be stayed, but not without treachery against the other. Either way, time grew short, for the Harvester moved swiftly."

"Where will he find me, this Harvester?"

Necanicum looked away, eyes darting from one end of their sockets to the next. Her strange gaze swept the glade in fits and starts, as if the wild woman herself had become suddenly reluctant.

"Necanicum?"

"He had but one trail, one path to retrace. One road upon which to sow the seeds of wanton destruction."

A chill spread across Annleia's shoulders before crawling through her stomach. *No. No, no.*

"She followed that road," Necanicum continued, "until she came to its fork."

"Which way did he turn?" she asked anxiously.

"Not his fork, but hers. Two fields he planted—one known to her, the other a city by the sea. She was forced to choose. She could return to deliver warning, or she could administer the poison, but she could not do both."

Beneath her continued denial, Annleia felt the threat of tears. *Orphan*, the wild woman had called her, more than once. *One trail, one path to retrace.* Despite her enigmatic manner, Necanicum was presenting her with one of two decisions: Press forward to put an end to Torin's butchery, or go back to warn her people. *She could not do both.*

"And what choice did she make?" Annleia asked, her voice quavering.

Necanicum met her gaze at last. Beyond the madness reflected in those wild orbs, Annleia thought she detected a gleam of pity.

"Her own," the crone rasped, and once again, her ravaged eyelids began to droop. "It was not for Necanicum to decide. A courier she was called to be, and served her purpose. She could fulfill no other's."

The tears came. Annleia wanted to dismiss it all then and there, to tell herself that the old woman might be wrong—about part of it, if not all. If she hurried, perhaps she could return to tell her mother of this strange encounter. Perhaps together, they could find another way. Or else, she might just be swift enough to catch up to Torin afterward, at whatever time and place the crone believed their paths must cross.

But in her heart, she knew otherwise. Had there been any possibility that this meeting was some ruse or mistake, she would not have been overcome as she was. She knew magic when she felt it. Necanicum's thoughts had been wild and at times erratic, but never muddled. The crone was a messenger—sent by whom, she did not know, but nature and the Ceilhigh themselves did not always divulge the reasons for their methods. Unless she awoke to learn that this had all been a dream, she had no reason to doubt what had occurred.

Nor what she must do.

She peeled her eyes from the phial resting in her palm, looking back to her visitor. "Necani—"

She halted. The crone sat motionless upon her log, chin tucked low against her breast. There was a coldness emanating from her that had not been there before. Annleia glanced at her wellstone. It, too, had chilled.

Still, she rose to make sure, hesitating only briefly before laying her fingers against the crone's terraced brow. She found it clammy. Down upon the neck she felt, then the wrist. Necanicum offered no resistance. Her eyes remained closed, and no breath entered her lungs.

Annleia stepped back slowly, looking skyward as the sun's first streamers slipped through the trees. In her ears, the little fire that Necanicum had built crackled and spat.

But the dawn's rays provided no strength, and the murmur of the flames seemed only to echo those conferences the wild woman had kept to herself. There was no one to answer her remaining questions, none to tell her how to proceed.

A child I've been to have come even this far, she thought ruefully. She had set forth with such stubborn bravery, naivete her shield. Now, with her mother's wellstone in one hand and Necanicum's phial in the other, this adventure—both wondrous and frightening from the outset—suddenly seemed much too real.

And the responsibility too great to bear.

She sniffed, and wiped the last of the tears from her face. Her people were not helpless, she reminded herself. Her mother was wary and wise, and knew already of the danger they faced. Necanicum's use of the term *orphan* did not necessarily mean that her mother would perish on the morrow or the next day or anytime soon. *Orphan-to-be*, the crone had said first. Well, could not the same be said of most children?

What she knew with dread certainty were the things her own mother had warned her of, and what Necanicum's gloomy prophecy had only confirmed. She had to find Torin—or rather be there when *he* found *her*. A city by the sea, the crone had said. Upon the road she already followed. There had been no mention that if she did turn back, she would actually be able to *save* her people, only *warn* them. A terrible, terrible risk, either way. But if she did not poison the Harvester while provided this chance, she might not get another opportunity to do so. And when the end came, as promised—by fire or by water—where would her people hide then?

She found no comfort in the decision, but she would have to be strong, as her mother and queen had bade her. Like Necanicum, she had been given *her* purpose, and could fulfill no other's.

She looked back to the crone while gathering her own few possessions. It seemed cruel to leave her out in the open, to be pecked at and torn apart and strewn about by scavengers. But if she did not have time for both the world at large and her own kin, then she did not have time to bury one poor wild woman. Whatever affliction had claimed Necanicum in life would have to look after her in death.

With her pouches and blanket and the phial of poison secured, Annleia bid a sullen farewell and strode from the glade, leaving the crone's fire to flicker weakly at the dead woman's feet.

THE LASS IS GONE.

Necanicum opened one eye, then the other. The glade was empty, the fire before her naught but a wisp of curling smoke.

"Did you happen to note whither?" she asked them.

South. She means to do as we counseled.

She snorted. "For now. Seems to me she might change her mind easily enough."

You did well.

"And would have done better had you kept silent," she snapped, her chin at her shoulder.

It is crucial that nothing is left to chance.

"All is chance," she argued. "You play your games, with me and with others, but you cannot control half so much as you would like."

It seemed they had no response to that—or at least, not one they wished to share. She harrumphed and began patting around her person, checking to make sure all of her items were in order.

She took none of your things, they assured her, *only what you gave her*.

"Then her elders taught her respect, which is too much to be said of some."

She continued her own inspection, if only to vex them as they vexed her.

Whither shall we go now?

"Home, should I not be able to escape you before we reach it. Elsewise, some place where you'll never find me."

You know you cannot leave us, even if you truly wished to.

Necanicum sighed heavily. She knew.

Rising was a laborious affair. Her coldsleep had chilled her within as well as without, causing bones to ache and joints to stiffen. As if the pains she dealt with already were not enough. Still, it had struck her as necessary at the time. Had she permitted the child's questions to continue, they might have gone on forever. Or worse, the whelp might have insisted upon trying to drag her along. Necanicum had come far enough at the bidding of others. Whither she went now would be *her* choice, and at *her* pace.

Not that she lacked sympathy for the lass. In truth, she had shared more than they had asked her to, ignoring their protests as she had done so. A risk, to be sure, but she did not wish the child to be blind to the consequences. Either road offered horrors enough. At least she had attempted to spare the lass from feeling manipulated and betrayed.

For she knew well enough what that was like.

She used her staff to scatter the charred brands of her fire, then tamped the area with her feet, sprinkling the words of cleansing over that and the log upon which she had rested. Doing so helped to wake her dormant vessels and speed the flow of blood through her veins. By the time she finished, she felt almost fully restored.

Her eyes swept the glade, lingering momentarily upon the patch of moss where the child had lain. Without the phial at her breast, she felt as if she had forgotten something, and wondered if there was more that she might do—or should have done.

It is her *turn now*, they reminded her, almost gently. *The lass has courage. We have left the matter in fair hands.*

Even they were uncertain—that much she could feel. But there was little use in forcing them to admit it, or in dwelling on what could not now be changed. Whether or not the child successfully abided their counsel, they had done all they could.

For her, there was naught but the long road home, and she had best be upon it.

On the chance that her home should remain by the time she reached it.

CHAPTER TWENTY-THREE

CLOUDS CHURNED OVERHEAD, THREATENING ANOTHER storm. It made little difference, Allion supposed, as he was still soaked through from the last. His clothes hung heavy and sodden, his skin chafed raw where the leather and wool rubbed against his thighs. He slogged on despite the irritation, through a muddy field whose fallow rows gave it the look of a wind-chopped sea. Indeed, his weariness was such that, at times, he felt as if the earth rolled and swayed beneath him. A low-hanging fog covered it like misty spray, and its restless murmur filled his ears, a sound in which to drown.

He forced his eyes wide, to wake himself before he slipped beneath the imaginary swells. The murmur stemmed not from ocean waves, but from the sea of refugees swimming alongside in a ragged stream. Few spoke, in hopes that silence would keep them safe. But the rustle of their movements could not be helped: the swish of fabric, the scrape of litter, the creak of wheel, the rattle of traces, the huff and snort of horse and mule and ox, the squish of mud beneath the plodding footfalls of man and beast . . . Nor were the voices completely silent. By now, Allion had heard it all: angry mutterings, oaths of vengeance, whispered reassurances, sniffles and sobs and the occasional wail. With this many in tow, the hunter might as well have announced his crossing of this land with pipes and drums and bells a-toll.

But chiding them would do no good. Nor could he fault them their passions. Two and a half days following the slaughter at Atharvan, shock still hung thick over the heads of this tattered throng. But they had dozed and awakened enough times now to realize that this was not some nightmare to be burned away by the sun. Friends had been lost, families torn apart. Even though much of the city's populace had fled before the dragon's arrival, few had escaped without losing someone they knew. They were now widows and widowers and orphans, clinging to strangers and onetime rivals in search of strength and solace, seeking an understanding that would not be found.

Allion felt as hollow and lost as any of them.

He glanced at Marisha, who held the hand of a child found hiding in a wood the night before last. Five years old, perhaps, without parent or sibling. Though not from the city, the boy was but one of many among them who were similarly dispossessed. Over the past two days, a fair share of those separated had been reunited with family or neighbor. The network of city ministers had done a remarkable job, all in all, of organizing the exodus. But according to census officials, Atharvan had been home to more than three hundred thousand heads prior to the Illychar siege, swelled by as much as a third more by refugees throughout both Partha and Menzos. With such numbers, and given the hasty manner of their departure, it would be some time before they were able to properly sort the living from the dead, and the abandoned from the loot. They had offered to place this particular child with the others unclaimed, but when they had attempted to do so, the poor young mute had clung to Marisha so feverishly, and trembled so terribly, that she had asked them to let the boy be.

As always, she tried to do too much, lending her skills when and where they were required, toiling day and night. The Pendant gave her strength, she assured Allion, whenever he voiced concern that she, too, needed rest. Be that as it may, he continued to worry what might happen should she persist in ignoring her own limitations. To that, she was fond of telling him that she was only doing what they all must.

He would grow silent afterward, having no suitable response. Truly, it seemed that limitations were all they had. Whatever their exact number, they were woefully unprotected. Outriders rode ahead, behind, and upon their flanks, while other soldiers, both mounted and afoot, patrolled the throng's perimeter. Chief General Corathel had sent two battalions north as soon as King Galdric had signaled his intent to empty the city, and the king himself had made sure to assign a fair portion of his garrison to those exiting her tunnels. In addition, Allion's had not been the only squad that had found its way north following the slaughter, to meet those who had floated down the rivers to the southern shore of Llornel Lake. Each day thus far, in fact, had brought more scattered regiments to them. Even so, estimates held that those trained with the use of weapons comprised less than one in thirty of their overall ranks. Hardly enough, the commanders grumbled, to see this flock delivered all the way to Kuuria.

For they had learned already that Leaven, the nearest city to which they might have fled, was closed to them, besieged by Illychar. Fewer than had assaulted Atharvan, the scouts claimed, but far too many for them to battle or circumvent. A brief council held by Atharvan's city ministers and military commanders had raised the next best hope: to veer south and make for the Gaperon, hoping their pleas for additional protection would be answered and met along the way.

And if Kuuria, too, is overrun? Allion had wondered. But it did them no good to wander too far down that road of thought. The scouts would continue searching for the safest path, and the host's leaders would keep them on it. Until such time as all avenues were closed, their best hope was to keep running.

Or crawling, as it were. Given their pace, he was somewhat astonished to have made it as far as they had. According to their scouts, the bulk of the enemy swarm had not yet set out in search of those who had managed to escape. Rather, it seemed to be waiting at Atharvan until its spirit kin laid claim to the bodies of the fallen, making certain that the humans were not allowed to circle back and put those incubating coils to the torch. By making this choice, the Illychar had given Atharvan's refugees a few days' lead—the best explanation as to why they hadn't already been overrun.

Even this small piece of fortune, however, was a dagger in Allion's gut, a stark and chilling reminder of the fate he had brought upon Torin—and the world in turn. Had he committed his friend's body to ashes when urged to do so, Torin would have had no chance to retrieve the Sword and unearth Killangrathor. Had he destroyed that single coil, he would not now be fretting over those being claimed at Atharvan. Thousands might have been spared. General Corathel, King Galdric, and all the many others whose fate was unknown might yet be safe. This people would still have their city, their leaders, their former lives.

The horror his selfishness and arrogance had permitted was almost more than he could fathom.

So he tried not to. As best he could, he put aside the haunting doubts and accusations that tormented him at all times. It was of little use now, ruminating over mistakes made and opportunities passed. Instead, he tried to focus on their current situation, on what he might do to encourage this people and maintain his vow to Corathel to help keep them safe.

An easier task, he brooded sullenly, were he still the dragon-slayer. But the tales brought by battlefield survivors of the beast that had destroyed their city had spread quickly among those who had fled Atharvan long before Killangrathor's arrival. Though some refused to believe, they were far and away the minority. Wherever he now went, Allion met with cold gazes, guarded whispers, or awkward reassurances—from soldiers and civilians alike. It could only be *his* dragon, after all, that had joined the reavers. The people knew of no others but the one whose death had won him their gratitude and praise not so long ago. A great victory gone sour, it now sat rancid in his belly. Where he might have paraded among them as a champion and bearer of hope, as Corathel had likely intended, he chose instead to remain silent and aloof, lest he incite their fear, their wrath, or their damnable pity.

"You're making more of it than there is," Marisha had told him, when he had suggested that his presence might be doing more harm than good.

"I am the salt in the wound, if not the blade itself," he had argued.

To which she had shaken her head and replied, "It is your own guilt, unnecessary and undeserved, that eats at you. And it serves no useful purpose. For your sake and theirs, you must let it go."

Let it go. Simply accept the fact that Killangrathor was alive and loose and possessed of an Illychar fury. Accept that the spirit of his friend, the one he had gone to such lengths to consecrate and preserve for the infinite splendors of Olirium, was chained to a shell of hatred and madness. He had condemned them both—and all others now doomed to fall beneath their onslaught of shadow and fire. How could she expect him to live with that?

A raindrop struck his brow, followed swiftly by another. He glanced up—and tensed to see a winged shadow soaring overhead. A hawk, he realized, forcing down the terror risen to his throat. *While I carry our reprisals to the ends of this earth*, Torin had said. The man was gone, and Killangrathor with him. Or so Allion prayed. For if the dragon were to spy their flock and catch it out in the open like this . . .

He closed his mind to an image born of that upon the steppe outside Atharvan, when Killangrathor had mowed them down like withered stalks in a harvested field. Only, this time, it was not soldiers, but mothers and babes and other innocents whose blood painted the dragon's claws . . .

Despite that danger, Allion much preferred traveling as they did now over open ground, where he could at least see the enemy coming. When surrounded by brush and woods, the rogue Illychar that yet roamed these lands as packs and individuals could drop upon them out of nowhere, as they had learned more than once already. And cover overhead often meant roots and undergrowth and broken trails underfoot, which further hampered their pace.

A source of much debate and continued discussion: the path they should take and how best to traverse it. Some had proposed separating their multitude into smaller parties that might hope to avoid attention. But dividing their civilian populace also meant dividing those who defended them. For now, the consensus was that their minimal strength was best kept marshaled. Ten could defend three hundred better than one could defend thirty.

Of course, that thinking might change on the morrow, or the hour, depending on word brought in by the scouts. It was like traveling through a tunneling dark, never knowing what might be lurking around the next bend.

He turned his head as a horse loped past, mud sucking at its hooves. Moving with purpose, Allion thought, though its rider called no warning. The hunter's eyes followed, blinking against a thickening rain.

The outrider fell in with the small contingent accompanying the nearest platoon commander, positioned near the rear of the vanguard on the left flank. Allion watched their conference from perhaps twenty paces off, wondering if it meant trouble. Of course, he wondered the same of all communications that he saw passing up and down among the soldiers of the outer lines.

His suspicions deepened when he saw the sergeant giving orders to Corporal Gage—he who had escorted Allion and Marisha north from Atharvan—and watched Gage signal for a team to ready mounts. At that, Allion tugged at Marisha's sleeve and hastened ahead to see what he could learn.

"Scouts sent to inspect a nearby holdfast missed their time of return," the corporal confided to them. "I'm to take a squad in search. Would welcome your bow, if you're willing."

Allion looked to Marisha.

"I go with you," she said.

"Not with that pup, you don't," the corporal noted sternly.

It wasn't difficult to read Marisha's thoughts. Allion had seen the child's reaction to earlier attempts at separation. A harmless attachment, on the whole, given that most of Marisha's time was spent within the mob's interior, where those suffering physical ailments were gathered and treated. There, the child could attend easily enough. But if Marisha remained shackled to the child, and Allion chained to her . . .

"We'd best stay here then," he said, which he believed pleased the woman, though her mouth did nothing to show it. "To plug the gap you and your men leave behind."

Gage nodded with curt understanding before swinging astride his mount. "Keep a sharp eye. Be back 'fore long."

The squad rode off at a trot, doing its best not to raise any undue alarm. Heads turned, and a few murmurs arose, but, by and large, they slipped away without causing a stir.

The muddy field gave way to an apple orchard, its trees just now beginning to flower. Their fruit would have been much more welcome, Allion thought. Alas, the harvest season was yet months off, leaving them to settle for the delicate beauty of white petals tinged pink with fresh bloom.

"Allion, wait."

He turned back to Marisha, and found the nameless boy who accompanied her anchored in his tracks. The child still gripped her hand tightly, but refused to be pulled forward. His wide eyes were fixed upon the nearest row of apple trees, his skin as pale as their blossoms.

"What is it?" he asked her.

She shook her head. "Is it the trees?" she asked the boy. He did not respond, though he began to shudder violently. Marisha looked upon Allion plaintively. "Perhaps we should go around."

"Around?" The hunter scanned their surroundings. "Scouts say this is the swiftest cross to the southern road. We're not going to reroute this flood on the fears of one small boy."

Indeed, the river of refugees continued to flow past them as they stood there, filling the orchard's lanes like rainwater down a boulder-strewn gulch.

"Perhaps we could find room in a litter or wagon," she suggested. "One with a cover, so he won't have to look upon whatever it is that frightens him."

Allion frowned. "You know already what little room there is in those." The wounded were being conveyed in those wagons and litters, along with the crippled and many of the elderly, who lacked the strength to keep pace otherwise. "Were it just the boy, perhaps, but he doesn't seem willing to let you out of his sight—and I'm not willing to let you out of mine."

"Perhaps he'll let me carry him," she said. She knelt and gripped the boy's shoulders, seeking to draw his gaze.

The hunter would have offered the same, but suspected that neither Marisha nor the boy would allow it. So he waited patiently—as others strode past with nary a glance—while the healer brushed the child's soft hair and whispered to him soothingly. After several moments, when he had seemed to calm, she hugged him close and hoisted him up into her arms.

She rocked him gently, whispering still, and turned forward once more. With her first step toward the trees, the boy buried his face in her shoulder.

Allion could see the lad trembling, his arms so tight about Marisha's neck that it seemed he might choke her. But the healer nodded that she was fine, and so they rejoined the camp's flow.

Its passage seemed louder here, sounds echoing amid the trunks, netted by the branches and leaves. Allion kept one eye on Marisha, to make sure she and the boy were all right. With the other, he searched for birds and ground animals—rodents or squirrels or a mouthwatering hare. But he saw only insects—and few enough of those. He hoped that those sent to forage their distant flanks would not find the land so completely deserted. The ministers he'd spoken to had claimed sufficient food stores to keep this host fed for up to six days. Unfortunately, they had already been on the march for three, and had yet to cross Partha's lands by half. If forced to march all the way to Kuuria, as now feared, further emphasis would have to be placed on rationing and supplementing their existing stores.

They churned on without event, until the monotony and Allion's weariness began again to dull his senses. This time, instead of sailing an ocean, he was aflight amid mountain slopes, buffeted by windblown snows—great icy flakes tinged with pink. He wasn't certain of his destination, only that he could not rest until he had reached it. And wherever it was, it remained a long way off.

Then he heard the thunder, distant peals that nevertheless threatened his winging course. The winds strengthened, seeming to wail.

"Allion. Allion!"

His eyes snapped wide. Marisha gripped his arm, her face urgent. The other still held the boy, who shook now as if they really were caught in a snowstorm.

The crowd was astir, and small wonder. From somewhere ahead and to the northwest, on their right flank, came the clangor of weapons and the blare of horns calling for additional arms. In response, the civilian throng was gathering tight and edging south through the trees like a herd beset by predators.

"Come," Allion said, taking her by the arm and joining the crush. It was either that or be swept under by it. He could tell by the size and swiftness of the swell, the intensity of the crowd's terror, that whatever had caused this wave was perhaps the largest attack they had faced yet. Child or no, he might have cut against the rush, to join those battling upon the northern fringe, but there was also the southern flank to consider. He had promised to look after the position abandoned by Gage's squad—and it was time to do so. While the small packs of Illychar encountered over the past few days had shown no capacity for coordinated attacks, Allion couldn't help but wonder what this people might be running so heedlessly into.

His fears proved true when—from almost on top of him, it seemed—an elf dropped from one of the apple trees. Had he been its target, he would have been dead before he knew what hit him. Instead, it was a man beside him who spun and fell back into his own pushcart, blood pulsing from a flayed throat.

Allion slipped from beneath his ready bow and notched an arrow to the string. By then, the elf was gone, having killed again before scrabbling up the tree's trunk and leaping from its branches to those of another.

The hunter let that one go, for there were more, he now saw, dropping like rotted fruit. He caught one through the throat as its spear found a woman's heart, and shot a second through the cheek, disrupting a swordthrust that would have gutted an old man.

They were not all elves, either. A scythe came whistling around a narrow trunk, gripped in the hands of a man who months before was no doubt using it to harvest wheat. His flesh was pale, but not yet shriveled or putrid. Perhaps after a few thousand years . . .

Allion's arrow plunged into the man's eye socket. If the coil did last that long, its eventual wearer would not be using that orb to see. He turned back to Marisha then, who was rushing with the child back toward a group that had halted its retreat and was forming up around the base of an empty tree. There, she put the child down and drew her knife, shoving the boy safely behind her.

All around, others were doing the same, healers and farmers and tradesmen coming together and brandishing what weapons they had. Shrieks of terror and wails of sorrow were giving way, he noticed, to furious shouts and spontaneous commands. Carts and wagons were thrown together to form makeshift barricades, from behind which longbows hummed. A shattered people, perhaps, but not one that would surrender what little they had left without a fight.

A bloody mess ensued, continuing unabated for several long, frantic moments. As many fell under friendly fire, Allion feared, as under the blades and shafts wielded by their enemies. Little by little, however, their formations tightened, becoming more organized. Soon after, their superior numbers began to overwhelm those who came at them, killing the most reckless marauders and sending the rest back into the mists. A company of legion soldiers from farther back along the line streamed forward, some ahorse, all armed and armored. Their arrival hastened the Illychar departure and swiftly secured their breached position.

Not swiftly enough, Allion noted, surveying the carnage. Scores lay dead, and many of those wounded would soon join them. He spotted only a few elves, known to be Illychar. Among the humans, it would take longer to discern which bodies had belonged to friends, and which had been foes. A small-scale slaughter, perhaps, but one that overwhelmingly favored the enemy in terms of cost.

A hand took his. He found Marisha, blood smeared upon her knife. She had not been kept from the fighting. From the north, the sounds of battle still rang, but these, too, had slackened. It seemed the hour was won.

The cries of grief and denial began at once, long before the moans had a chance to subside. Even as soldiers hacked apart the most stubborn of the fallen Illychar, husbands mourned wives, mothers their children, sisters their brothers. Many more dashed about, seeking those who were missing, just now realizing, in some cases, that those who had marched beside them were gone.

"Come," Marisha said, tugging firmly, determined as always to save those she could.

Allion resisted momentarily, waiting to make sure that the blood-soaked ground had in fact been made safe. One body looked much the same as the rest, and he feared that one she might bend to help would in fact be an enemy, waiting to slit her throat.

"What's wrong?" she asked.

Though he had only meant to stall, he realized suddenly that someone was missing. "Where's the boy?"

"With the others," she said, turning to point.

But when she looked back, she must not have seen him, for she began to cast about worriedly. Allion did so with her. Together, they hurried over to the rally point where she was certain she had left him.

"Right here," she insisted, an edge of despair creeping into her voice. "You," she said, tugging at an old man's sleeve. "There was a boy among you, blond curls, this tall." She gestured. "Did you see where he slipped off to?"

The old man grunted and shook his head, eyeing her dagger and pulling free of her clutching grasp. She might have gone after him, but Allion put a hand on her arm, drawing her about.

A sickening warmth stirred in his gut, yet somehow he made himself show her what he had found. Marisha gasped, then rushed ahead, pushing through those that came between her and where the boy lay facedown—draped like a bloody rag atop a corpse.

She dropped and seized him by the shoulders, turning him about. To their relief, the child resisted, wrenching free to embrace the body he had found. A woman's body, Allion observed, too pale for one who had just died, with hair that might have been the same color as the boy's own, were it not for the dirt and blood that caked and clotted its tangled strands.

Marisha covered her mouth in horror. "Allion," she whispered, "do you think . . . ?"

The woman's skull had been smashed. Half her face was missing. But that which remained had the same color of eye, and her tunic was of the same coarse wool, dyed blue and green like the boy's own. It was impossible to tell for sure, but Allion knew what Marisha was thinking.

This could well have been the child's mother.

Certainly, the boy's tears seemed to suggest as much, his wracking, voiceless sobs telling them plainly that at the very least, the Illychar *resembled* someone dear to him. And in the eyes of a traumatized five-year-old, perception meant as much as truth.

Marisha covered the lad, lending what silent support she could. Allion realized then that he, too, was trembling, and made a fist to steady his hand. He felt a hardening within, as though his sorrow and pain were a mortar cured by the heat of his rage. He would accept no blame for *this*. Whatever his role in the Illysp's emergence, he refused to hold himself responsible for such atrocities. Killangrathor, Torin, the Sword—none of it need ever have happened. Had he and Jarom followed directions in the very beginning, had his headstrong friend not insisted that finding the Sword was the only way to oppose the wizard—

"That one dead?" a voice asked brusquely.

Allion whirled. The collectors had arrived. "Butchers," they'd been dubbed, and with good reason. The ministers and commanders had agreed: Flames would draw more attention than they dared. So too would the clouds of carrion-eaters come to feast on any left out in the open. The only way to deal with their slain was to chop them up and bury the scraps—beneath the earth, or beneath mounds of stone, whichever was more readily available. A cruel and shameless desecration, but better that than letting Illysp take them.

"A moment's pity, I beg you," Marisha pleaded.

"A moment may be all they need to strike again," one of the butchers replied callously, taking the dead woman by the wrist. "The whelp can come and watch, if he'd like, though I wouldn't recommend it."

"There's plenty of dead to gather," Allion snapped. "This one can set aside for now."

"So says half we come across," the butcher's partner argued. " 'Fraid pity's out of season."

Allion could have throttled the men for their uncompromising gruffness. But his own anger was misdirected, and he knew it. For he understood now where all of this had truly begun, and who must answer for it.

He put a hand on Marisha's shoulder, and drew her gaze. There were others who still had a chance if given immediate attention. They were wasting time here—though he prayed she would not make him speak such coldhearted words.

She didn't, choosing instead to pry the boy's fists from the dead woman's clothes and pull him aside. One of the butchers had already signaled to a nearby "griever"—priests and clerics, mostly, whose unenviable task it was to console the inconsolable, and to clear the way for the butchers to do their grisly work. This one was a great burly man who nevertheless spoke to the quivering boy in soothing tones as he bore the child away.

Marisha looked after him for a moment, then set her jaw and moved to attend her own tasks. *It will be all right*, Allion wanted to tell her, but knew that it wouldn't. Not until all of this suffering had been accounted for. Not until those responsible for it had been destroyed utterly.

As he strode wordlessly on Marisha's heels between a pair of trees, he couldn't help glancing back at the collectors as they hauled off that dead woman—and at the many other teams piling corpses amid the lanes of that orchard. As her tangled hair scraped across the ground, gathering mud and leaves and fallen apple blossoms, a simmering vow began to build within the hunter's mind.

Perhaps the Illysp would never be stopped. Perhaps this scourge would indeed continue until it had claimed each of them, reducing those with bodies to slavering demons, and the rest of them to ashes or useless scraps of flesh. But if the gods granted him the power to fulfill just one oath before he met his own end, he knew now what that must be.

By his own hand if none other, Torin would be destroyed

HE WATCHED HER STROLL AWAY from him with an ache in his breast, and his gaze trailed longingly after. Then she turned, so suddenly, so unexpectedly, and gave her little dance, her lithe frame frisking in place to a silent melody. Her smile flashed—a wondrous, dazzling smile meant only for him. The expression she wore was as mischievous as it was beautiful. Lips parted, and her words spilled forth: "Welcome home, Immortal One."

Though spawned by his own imagination, the message caught Torin by surprise. The memory itself was more than familiar, an image he must have relived a thousand times over. Unalterable, save for the words. Those were different every time. Gazing now with a fiend's eyes upon the dark, forested cliffs appearing through the clouds below, it was not difficult to imagine what had caused her to speak these ones.

Yawacor.

Home.

An unbidden feeling, yet easy enough to trace. His time upon these shores had been marred by strife and bloodshed and failure. And yet, he had discovered here persons and places that had resonated so strongly within that it seemed as if they must have somehow been a part of him all along. Upon departure, he had known only regret, the burning need to see what more he might be leaving behind. To see these shores again was like watching the first rays of sun cut through the clouds after a storm, touching his soul with warmth and peace.

An absurd notion, given his reluctance to set foot upon these lands to begin with. Even more so, given the conditions under which he made his return. Yet he welcomed the feeling nonetheless, basking in the wonder of hopes refreshed and memories bestirred. For they were all he had that remained his own, his only protection from the pain.

He had been relying upon such memories for some time now—more and more each day. Unable to cope with the mayhem unleashed and murders committed, he had slipped deeper within, where the horror of his own deeds was less likely to reach him. It was here that Dyanne waited, she whom his Illysp self did not yet know anything about. Images of their brief time together flitted through his mind. And with each visit, each memory relived, he felt a little less the monster he had become, and more the person he wished to be.

He had to be careful, for he could feel the Illysp gnawing at these precious recollections as it had the rest, seeking to expose and devour Torin's most esteemed secrets. His ongoing thoughts were clearly his own, else the demon would surely have discovered his memories of her by now. But each time he dug these treasures out of hiding, to admire them in the light of his current mind, he feared the Illysp might catch him unawares, and steal them away for itself.

He only wished they could be put to some better use. As a salve for the things he had done, there was no peer. But salves were used only to dull pain, not heal the wounds that had caused it, or to stymie further attack.

Without them, however, his thoughts were a roiling tempest that threatened to consume him. His emotions were like lightning without thunder—powerful, violent urges for which there was no physical release. Grief, guilt, horror, hatred—his constant companions as his Illysp counterpart, the one dubbed Itz lar Thrakkon, controlled his every action.

People—allies—were dying by his hand. The land of his childhood was aswarm with Illychar, and Torin, who should have perished while fighting among his kin, had instead become their greatest enemy, delivering one of their mightiest cities in one swift stroke. Like a hunter killing only for sport, he had then left the spoils to rot. A blessing, perhaps, though it felt like another curse, that he would not even be there to see the struggles of his friends played out.

Of wounds, there was no end.

Nor was it finished. The Illysp within might not know of Dyanne. It might lack the names and faces of others he had met, and of places visited while traversing this land. But it knew of his time among the people of ancient Finloria. It would have some idea of where they might be found. *I have a taste for Finlorian flesh*, he had heard himself utter, following his assault on the palace at Atharvan.

He knew well enough what he had come here to do.

Once over land, Killangrathor sharpened his descent. The line of the Dragontail Mountains grew larger. Many of the peaks were still topped with snow. All wore skirts of emerald, soggy from the incessant rains. Strapped behind him among the spines of the dragon's back, his small army of goblins tensed with fiendish anticipation. Recruited from a swarm being used to guard the mountain pathways to Thrak-Symbos, they and the countless Illysp clinging invisibly to their minds—and his—would be all they needed to spread the spores of this plague across this land. Itz lar Thrakkon had painted a vivid picture with his words before setting out. And Torin had listened in mute denial while speaking every one of them.

For more than a week now, those words had haunted him, tearing at him like the winds of their passage. If only those winds had ripped him from his perch and cast him into the seas below—maybe into the gullet of that ocean-bound monstrosity that had surged up like a rabid dog straining against its leash. It had made only the one appearance, however, and Torin had soon surrendered any hope that it might bring an end to his travails.

After that, as he marked each day by the rise and descent of the sun at his shoulder, he had given to pray that his own relentless pace might do him in. But he had come to understand well enough the fruitlessness of that. He went without water, without food, without rest, yet felt his flesh toughening, tightening, bones and muscles and skin strengthened by their continuing ordeal—like meat dried by the sun. Raking winds and freezing temperatures did not affect him. The harder his Illysp counterpart pressed him, the harder and more resilient he grew.

If he was to perish before he caused any further suffering, it would not be for lack of his body's care.

Which left him as before—helpless, tormented, as reviled by himself as by any others who might curse his name. How had he allowed this to happen? Why did he allow it to persist?

For he remained convinced that the power was his to relieve himself of the bestial spirit taken root within. He had spent his entire life believing that almost anything was attainable. Given the desire, and a willingness to sacrifice, no obstacle was too great to overcome. So which did he lack? Why could he not find the way?

A man of stronger will would be able to do so. A man of stronger will would have told Dyanne how he felt about her. As insignificant as they must have been to her, it seemed he could recall every moment of their time together. Even the smallest traits and gestures had been branded upon his memory: the swish of her hair, the purity of her laughter, the soft gleam of her maple eyes.

This particular scene was his favorite—when, after their flight from Necanicum's poisoned woods, Dyanne had dressed his wound and offered her little dance, her playful smile, and a kindhearted jape. In that moment, harmless enchantment had given way to helpless fascination. Ever since, his heart had belonged to her, and woven through all else that he meant to achieve was his yearning to catch her eye as she had caught his, and to share with her his feelings of limitless devotion.

Despite plenty of opportunities to do so, however, his courage had failed him. He had told himself that he was only being true to Marisha. He had told himself that whatever his feelings, they were of little consequence when matched against the urgency of his quest. True enough, but excuses nonetheless. It was cowardice that had ruled him, leaving his emotions painfully concealed.

Ever since, he had dreamed of this, his return. The chance to relive his past and to rectify the error of his ways. To confess his feelings, risks be damned. Could the disappointment of being spurned be any worse than the misery of wondering what might have been?

And yet, it was much too late for that. It might seem otherwise in the rapture of this moment, of seeing and tasting and feeling again whatever magic graced these shores. But the opportunity he had lost could never be reclaimed. He had no delusions as to what would happen were he to ever be reunited with Dyanne. Itz lar Thrakkon would recognize her, his feelings for her would be revealed, and the Illysp would kill her if only to revel in Torin's suffering.

As close as he had come to realizing his dreams, he could come no closer.

So he took his comfort where he could, hiding within his memories, relishing his return to a land he had feared abandoned forever, picturing the words he would say to Dyanne should he ever see her again.

While praying, for her sake, that he never would.

CHAPTER TWENTY-FOUR

The gates of the Bastion were opened wide, though she found few enough lined before them to make the passing. The soldiers and inspectors milling about beneath the great stone arch far outnumbered those with business in the southern lands. Given the word of those she'd encountered upon the road, most were merchants and suppliers summoned by Lorre himself to help repair and provide for his new city and the army that occupied it.

A city by the sea, Annleia thought, the crone's words a haunting echo amid the soft rumble of crashing waves.

She still wasn't certain she had made the right decision. So much was based on intuition and a wild woman's prophecy. But the phial was real enough. If she believed in one, she dare not disregard the other.

Yet nearly a week had passed since Necanicum had met her in those northern woods. And the more she rehearsed that account, the less likely it seemed—and the less capable she felt of accomplishing her task. Worse, that task all but demanded she take actions here that might jeopardize her mission going forward, should the wild woman or her prophecy prove false.

And with the fate of her people—the fate of the world—resting on her every movement.

"The gates ain't coming to us, lass," the old man prodded gently.

Annleia turned from where her gaze had settled upon the mist-shrouded coastline to the west. A gap had widened between her and the looming gatehouse, the last stretch of road between her and the Bastion. The tail of the preceding caravan stood now beneath its shadow, while those behind her, no doubt hoping to gain entry into Neak-Thur before sunset, were eyeing her and the open space with varying degrees of confusion and irritation.

"Your pardon," she begged, smiling in apology at the aged scrivener whose name she had already forgotten. He had come upon her no more than ten minutes past, greeting her kindly and inquiring politely as to her business. *To visit with family*, she had replied, before turning that and other questions back on him. Though it had been difficult to concentrate on his responses, it had seemed the easiest way to dodge any further inquiries.

She stepped forward, sandaled feet scraping upon the graveled mud, keeping clear of the deeper puddles and sinkholes. Her blood itched in warning. This was her last chance to turn about. Her breathing quickened, and her legs grew heavy. Her gaze swept the battlement above, its patrolling bowmen and ready armaments. Again she heard Necanicum's rasping voice. *Upon the wall she fought . . .*

Then a clerk motioned, and the guardsman at the head of the line nodded her on. She felt his eyes clinging to her as she passed, but paid him no mind. Stiff and uncertain, she managed nevertheless to approach the row of small folding tables set roadside beneath a tattered gray canvas, which offered moderate protection from the evening rain. All the while, her gaze fixed upon the looming gatehouse, counting the spears beneath its arch and lingering upon the iron teeth of the raised portcullis.

The clerk to whom she'd been assigned finished scribbling in his register and blew upon the parchment.

"Name and origin," he prompted, dipping his quill.

Annleia glanced sidelong at the others, and summoned her courage. "I seek a man by the name of Torin."

The clerk glanced up in annoyance, though the expression melted somewhat as he studied her. He was a grizzled thing, much older than most of his fellow clerks, with a tail of gray hair and a gaze that, while not unkind, brooked no foolishness.

"That would be your business, which I ain't asked for yet."

"Can you tell me when last he came this way?"

The clerk snorted. "Well, let's see," he said, making a cursory scan of his register. "Not today, by the look of it. But then, mine ain't the only quill at work. You like, I can call a carriage. You and I can visit the master of census, take a long, hard look at the logs. Maybe dine afterward at His Lordship's table on truffles and fresh roast and spun sugar. That be to your liking?"

"I see no cause for mockery."

"Nor do I have time for yours. The Southland has its fill of rogues and vagabonds, and there are plenty of good folks still waiting behind you. So why don't we move this along, hmm? You can try your charms on the *city* clerks, and I can get on home before my missus feeds my dinner to the hounds."

"Is there perchance a watch commander I can speak with?" she asked, looking around.

"Look, lass, my job is simple: Ask questions, and make note of your responses in this here ledger. If you don't like it, the road travels both ways."

"A watch commander, if you please."

The clerk slapped down his quill in disgust. "Very well. If that's how you wish to play it." He raised an ink-stained hand, and a pair of laughing guardsmen approached.

"Problem?" one of them asked, while the other continued to chuckle.

"Lass can't decide if she's coming or going," the clerk grumbled, gesturing irritably.

Annleia lowered her hood, shaking back her tangled tresses. "Is one of you the watch commander?"

"Denron," the taller one said, eyes running down her body as if to strip her of her sodden cloak. "This here is Broyle." The eyes came back to hers, and the soldier straightened. "How might we be of service?"

"I've come in search of a man whose name you all know. But this poor clerk cannot recall it. Perhaps you can."

Denron grinned. "Should it please you, I'll do my best. What's the lucky lad's name?"

"Torin."

"Torin, eh? I got me a cousin by that name."

"I'll make it my own," Broyle offered, "for but a moment's favor."

The pair snickered. Annleia smiled thinly. "My noble sirs are too kind. But this Torin wields a Crimson Sword."

"Crimson, gold—I'll paint it any color you'd like," Broyle said.

Denron rapped him in the chest, full of mock chivalry while suppressing his own laugh. "That's enough, Broyle. After all, it ain't every day we have maidens fair come from the country hoping for a glimpse of the outlander king. Or was it more than a glimpse you be wanting?"

"Is he still here?" she asked. For a moment, she even gave herself to hope.

"There, see? That's how they all act. Would that someone should spread rumor as to make such a legend of me," Denron told his companion mournfully. "Especially when we know it ain't the color, but size that makes the sword." His hand rested proudly on the hilt of his weapon.

"And a soldier's skill in wielding it," Broyle added.

"So soothes your sister when you catch her look of grave disappointment."

"Had your mother squealing readily enough."

The clerk bristled. "You see, lass? There's your choice. Either put yourself in the hands of these clods, or let me make note of your name, origin, and dealings—so that you can go about them unfettered."

"Most generous offers, all around," Annleia replied. "But I fear my name and dealings are of a private nature. I've come in search of Torin of Alson. In his absence, I would have a word with Lorre."

That set the guardsmen to howling. "His Lordship, it is now?" Denron asked, while Annleia looked around at the many stares she was beginning to attract. The soldier made an act of clearing his throat, and spoke in a deep tone. "'Beg pardon, Your Lordship, but we have this nameless waif come from the uncharted north, who seeks your company. What's that you say? Send her in? As it please Your Lordship.'"

Broyle roared, and Denron gleamed with pride at his own foolery. Even the stolid clerk was shaking his head with a helpless grin.

"Come, lass," Denron went on, taking note of the other guardsmen beginning to flock toward them. "You've gone and caused a stir. Let's continue this elsewhere, shall we?" His gloved hand took hold of her arm.

"Unhand me, sir." Her fist tightened upon her wellstone, giving her words the crack of a whip. Startled, Denron let go. "Should you wish to have further use of it—and it sounds as if you have myriad need—you will not touch me again."

Another chorus of laughter, only, this time, Denron bore its brunt. "Careful," someone shouted, "that filly's wild." Another added, "Give a holler if you need help breaking her in." The soldier weathered their hoots and their taunts, though his beardless cheeks reddened, and his smile now seemed forced.

"It don't have to get ugly, lass. Ain't no one saying you can't trot right back the way you came. But the Southland ain't without law any longer. You choose to pass through these gates, you can do so quietly at my side, else kicking and shrieking, dragged through the mud by those pretty gold locks."

"Quiet would suit me just fine, sir. But unless you mean to escort me to those I've come to see, then my search continues for one who shall." Her gaze captured his, and it seemed he was rendered mute. So she turned away and started past, toward the gatehouse and the line of gathered soldiers. "Is anyone here brave enough to deliver me to your overlord?"

While the gate soldiers blinked or laughed, Denron managed finally to respond. "All right, enough play—"

"What goes on here?" a new voice demanded. She sensed Denron freezing in place, while the rest of the guardsmen split ranks to make way for a horse and rider who pushed in among them from the mouth of the Bastion.

The newcomer's frown vanished as he caught sight of her, standing there in the rain at the edge of the clerks' pavilion, surrounded by guardsmen and the curious stares of at least another score of onlookers. The sheepish smile that played upon his lips gave him an almost boyish quality, as did the nervous hand that reach up to brush at a tousled mop of muddy curls. His eyes, however, shone with anything but innocence.

"Just a lass what seems to have lost her way, Commander," Denron replied. "Thought it'd be fun to make trouble for the registrars."

"The sort of trouble that requires the attention of an entire brigade?" the commander asked, eyeing her warily. "She don't look it from where I sit." His horse gave a snort.

"She threatened Denron, sir," Broyle offered. "And started making demands upon His Lordship."

Murmurs and sniggers passed through the assembly.

"You men, to work," the commander snapped. "Get this rabble moving." The guardsmen were slow to obey, breaking apart only reluctantly, and keeping their eyes and ears upon the exchange. The commander did not seem to notice, his focus upon the pair still flanking her. "Denron draws threats like the honeysuckle draws bees. I see no reason for that to stop traffic through my gate. What is her complaint, exactly?"

"I seek a man named Torin," Annleia replied, and watched the young commander stiffen in recognition. "Or one who can tell me where I might find him."

"And who makes this inquiry?"

"A friend."

"I see. Well, *friend*, despite what tales you may have heard, the Torin

I'll wager you speak of does not dwell among us. Nor anywhere upon these shores, by common reckoning."

"Then I'm afraid your good soldiers are right, and I shall have to visit with your overlord."

The commander smirked, as amused as his underlings at the very notion. "The overlord is a busy man. And *I'm* afraid any such petition must bear with it a name."

Annleia stared until his smirk lost its strength. Her response was soft, yet forceful. "My name would mean nothing. But send notice that the child of Laressa has come to see him. Tell him his *granddaughter* would have a word."

"His Lordship has no family that most are aware of," the commander observed, as he led her along a quiet section of the battlement.

Annleia would never have guessed it, given the reaction of this Commander Bardik and his men. After a moment of stunned silence, the soldiers listening in had ducked their heads and hastened on about their work. There had been no more wanton eyes, no more bawdy jests. The commander had looked for a moment as if he might challenge her further, but decided, under the circumstances, that he would be pleased to escort her to the city himself. He'd offered her his name and rank, and ordered Denron and Broyle to return to their posts. Before going, Denron had begged her pardon for any offense he may have caused.

"Doubtless, my grandfather has many secrets that he has not entrusted to those who serve him," she replied, eyes forward upon their stone-laid path.

Bardik accepted that without argument, step by step beside her. They passed a pair of patrolling sentries, split to look out over parapets north and south. The pair nodded at their commander, casual in their salute. Bardik responded in kind.

When those had been left behind, and it was naught but the two of them again amid the rain- and windswept battlement, the commander offered quietly, "You don't look like an elf."

Annleia felt herself stiffen, though she did not let it interrupt her stride. How much did this one know? She forced herself to laugh. "And why would I?"

She did not look at him, but could feel him regarding her in silent contemplation. "I've spoken with a pair of Torin's companions who traveled north with him from Neak-Thur," the commander confided. "The story they tell is . . . remarkable."

"Is it?" she replied offhandedly. "Well then, I shall want to have a word with them, also." Would that she had known earlier. She might have started there and left Lorre out of this—at least a while longer.

At the same time, she supposed that a meeting with the overlord was unavoidable. Not only for the reasons demanded of her, but for reasons personal to who and what she was. Quest aside, she wanted, needed, to face this tyrant about whom she had heard so much and yet knew so little.

"I fought alongside him, you know," Bardik prodded after another silence.

"My grandfather?"

"Torin. Here, at Neak-Thur, in the battle *against* His Lordship's occupation."

"A man of uncertain loyalties, are you?"

"One might see it that way. In this world, a man does what he must to survive. But then, sometimes we resist things we don't understand. Later, we're left to rue our own ignorance, and wonder how much easier it might have been had we only been more accepting."

"I'm not certain of your meaning, Commander. Is it your purpose to proclaim your newfound allegiance to my grandfather, or apologize for it?"

It was Bardik's turn to laugh. "What I'd like to know is *your* purpose in coming here. Have you come for reconciliation, or vengeance?"

"I've not come to put a dagger in my grandfather's back, be that your hope or your fear. I've come to save him, if I can—and you, and the rest of us—from a threat that cares nothing of man's petty struggles for resources and boundaries. Serve whom you will, but know that a larger storm has brewed, and lightning takes no side when come to rake a battlefield."

She met his gaze, using the effect her eyes seemed to have on these men to drive her warning home. Bardik stared, unfrightened, yet without the gleam of mockery she might have expected.

"His Lordship will be so advised," he answered finally. "Is there anything else you might tell me?"

"Much and more. But I feel my grandfather should hear it first. Should his response dissatisfy me, rest assured I shall be seeking allies wherever I can find them. Though I cannot be sure as to what difference any of us might make."

The commander frowned as if befuddled, and hurried on without question as she hastened her pace. So far, so good, Annleia told herself. Should every man she meet prove as easy to sway and manipulate, there might yet be hope.

The gateway from which they had begun was centrally located amid the Bastion's half-mile stretch from the coastline reefs to Neak-Thur's curtain wall. Thus, it did not take them long to reach the city, where they had to pass through another, smaller gatehouse to continue their trek. It might have gone faster. When setting out, Bardik had called for another horse, thinking to ride directly for the city's main gate, across the coastal plain south of the Bastion. But Annleia had asked to walk the wall, claiming that she felt more comfortable afoot than ahorse. In truth, she had seen this as an opportunity to familiarize herself with the structure's layout—its armaments and stores, bunkers and stairs. Was there any chance that this was indeed where her confrontation must take place, she wished to be ready.

She did the same atop the city's curtain wall, which ran a crooked, southerly line along the lower slopes of the Dragontail Mountains. Not nearly as well defended, she noted, although that seemed to be changing. She questioned

Bardik about it, who explained that while the former Council of Rogues had dedicated its strength to the Bastion in hopes of keeping the Northland at bay, Lord Lorre was more concerned with fending off those from the Southland who might yet attempt to retake their city. A fine shield the Bastion had been, but a forward shield was of only so much use against an enemy crept up behind you. Still, it remained an important gateway in that it allowed His Lordship to regulate all foot traffic passing either north or south, and thereby help to control the distribution of people and resources in either land.

There was much more she might have asked of him concerning the infamous overlord, but she did not wish to seem uninformed or tentative. So she remained concise in her words and detached in her interest, clinging to an aura of self-assuredness. She would learn what she needed to about her mother's father soon enough.

BARDIK LEFT HER WAITING IN an antechamber, under the dead-eyed stares of a pair of troll sentries posted in the outer doorway. The door to the inner chamber lay open, though its depths lay shrouded in darkness. Without, the furnishings were sparse, the walls windowless save for a series of tall, thin arrow loops through which a meager starlight barely penetrated. She was told that a server would be sent for, but the one that came provided only a platter of overripe fruit and a flagon of ale. The hearth sat cold, the only fires in a set of low-burning braziers. As she paced the reed-woven mat laid amid the saltstained benches, her breath clouded before her.

What have I done? Even though she had steeled herself for this eventuality, the prospect of presenting herself to her infamous grandfather within this cage of stone terrified her. Ruthless and intolerant. Callous and vindictive. She knew of no softer terms used to describe him. These were not words her parents had ever used, but they were the only ones that could accurately portray the man's deeds over the past two decades. If the word delivered by Lorre's agent during Torin's visit to Aefengaard was genuine, then it might be that the enmity he had long harbored against the Finlorian people was a thing of the past. But that was difficult to believe, particularly when that messenger's sworn protector had thrown away his life to make sure that Annleia's adoptive father forfeited his.

By all accounts, Warrlun's treachery had been his alone—the jealous rage of a husband and father that needed no further encouragement. But she had no proof that her birth father wasn't acting under orders, or that Lorre was in any way displeased by the result. Surely, her mother would not approve of the risk she had taken in coming here and revealing herself so openly.

She looked again to the trolls, wondering if they had been left to ward her, or imprison her. Would they even care if she attempted to slip past? Their unblinking stares unnerved her. At the same time, she preferred their dispassionate gazes to many of those that had tracked her progress through the avenues of this city and the halls of its castle. Some she had seen, others she had actually felt: men with lewd smiles that crawled upon her skin like worms, women with barbed frowns of suspicion and envy that cut like the thongs of a flail. She had ignored them all as best she could, marveling at their shallowness, and wondering how many other women drew such attention—and if they sensed it as readily as she. Regardless, as uncomfortable as she felt waiting here, she was not looking forward to repeating that trek.

She turned toward the wall of window slits, putting her back to the outer door and its guards. From time to time, a gust of wind would whistle through the narrow openings, to fan the flames of the braziers. The air seemed somehow colder here, along the coast, than it did up in the mountains, where lay her valley home. Granted, that valley was deep and sheltered, ringed by sheer mountain bluffs and heavily wooded. Beyond these stone walls lay only fierce winds carrying frigid ocean spray across a ravaged coastal plain. *Two fields he planted.* She wondered if either would survive the chaos to come.

Before she could reflect further on her home and whether she ever should have left it, she heard footsteps in the outer hall. These were not the whispered scrapings of a slippered steward, but the heavy clop of hard-soled leathers, crisp and measured in their approach. Their cadence slowed and halted, however, just beyond view of the empty doorframe—almost as if the wearer had decided not to show himself. Then a man rounded and entered, stepping right past the troll sentries, who glanced at him but never flinched.

Annleia knew straightaway that she was gazing for the first time upon her grandfather, Lorre.

He stood there for a moment, staring back at her. Even at a distance, she saw him to be a stern man, and proud. Her eyes were not as keen as those of a full-blooded elf, but she did not need perfect lighting to recognize the tightness in his jaw or the cold gleam in his eyes. His stiff posture and hardened countenance told her much that words might try to hide. In that moment, she decided that all she had heard about his strict and unforgiving nature was true.

When he spoke, the room seemed to grow colder still, its chill settling in Annleia's stomach. "Have you been waiting long?"

A lifetime, she thought, but shook her head. "You do me honor, to have come so quickly. I expected another escort."

That she knew him for who he was did not seem to surprise him. Yet there was an awkwardness about him that she hadn't sensed initially. Nowhere near what there should have been, perhaps, but enough to suggest that he wasn't entirely inhuman.

He looked to the darkened doorway at his left. "I can have my steward prepare the inner chamber. Else we can return to my study . . ."

"This room should work as well as any, I think."

Her confidence was growing, while his seemed to be slipping. She wasn't quite what he had expected, she decided. For some reason, that thought pleased her.

His extended silence, however, began to eat away at her carefully held composure. Narrowed eyes regarded her bluntly, viewing her as he might any other potential assassin. Had she been so, the strength of that stare might have been enough to drive her to confession.

At last, he gave a signal, and the pair of troll sentries stepped wordlessly from the antechamber. Their sandaled feet slapped heavily against the stone tiles of the outer corridor as they made their retreat.

The two who remained stood their ground on opposite sides of the room, Annleia with her back to the narrow windows, and her grandfather near the chiseled doorframe. His stance was such that he might have been hewn from the same materials, harsh and rigid. A full-sleeved, black leather jerkin wrapped a frame lean and tall, devoid of adornment or sigil. Were it not for the cropped white hair and the wrinkled skin of his face and hands, she might have mistaken him for a statue of unweathered basalt. The few steps that separated them felt like a gulf.

"Laressa sent you?" he asked finally.

"The decision was mine."

"A bold one. Did she not tell you that I am a man to be feared?"

"Do you intend me harm?"

"No doubt, you've been given reason to believe I might. Why not pretend to be someone else, a stranger to me?"

"Someone else might have been left waiting, else received no audience at all. My purpose in coming here is too important, and our time too short."

Lorre folded his arms across his chest. "*That* again, is it? My lord commander of the Bastion tells me you speak of a gathering storm, a threat to all. As I recall, Torin spoke similarly, when he came through here."

They had found a way past the awkwardness, it seemed. By focusing on Torin, they could avoid the many deeper questions between them. "He is central to this struggle," she admitted. "It is why I seek him."

An uncertain look passed across his face. Disappointment, maybe? Had he hoped or believed that she had come primarily to forge a familial relationship? Or to mend relations between him and his daughter, perhaps?

A twitch, and the look was gone. "I'll admit, I am not one to be cowed by omens."

"You are a warrior, are you not? The warning I bear is not meant to cow you, but to rouse you in preparation of what is to come."

"I am always prepared. Were it otherwise, I would have perished long ago."

"Not against this."

Light from the braziers flickered upon his face, a dance of fire and shadow that made his expressions, however slight, difficult to read. "And what is it, exactly, that you would have me fear?"

Annleia told him then of the Illysp, of the folly and conceit of her ancient ancestors that had opened the rift between this world and theirs. She told him that in drawing the Sword of Asahiel, Torin had set free those that had been bound. His search upon these shores had been for those who might help him close it again. She knew not how much of this Torin might have already relayed to the overlord, but judging by her grandfather's disinterest, it bore repeating, to make certain he understood.

"Torin's quest did not end well," she announced bitterly, though if Bardik knew the tale, then it was likely Lorre did, too. "I once had two fathers. I now have none." She paused, allowing for a response, searching for a reaction, but received only stony silence. "For his part in these murders, Torin was cast out—prematurely, perhaps. For assumptions were made as to what he did or did not know. And if the Illysp are to be banished anew, I must see to it that Torin and the Sword are found, and nothing more left to chance."

Her grandfather clung to his silence, but this time, she was determined to outwait him, to receive an answer to her unspoken question.

"I've heard in great detail from those who survived Torin's northern trek," he admitted finally. "I would have you know that I did not commission Warrlun's assault on . . . on the elf king who served as your father, and would apologize for it. Whatever ill I have done in my life, I never meant to cause your mother pain. I only wish . . ."

"Pain is a part of life," she allowed, when it seemed he knew not how to finish. "Without it, we would be unable to know pleasure."

Lorre gazed upon her with a glimmer of pride and a shadow of regret. Perhaps he thought her too young to have learned such a bitter truth. "Nevertheless, it should not come at the hands of those who care for us."

"And rain should fall only when we wish," Annleia replied with a stoicism she did not feel. Tears were no shame, but she was not yet ready to share hers with him. "If deeds could be undone, I would have scant cause to be here. What matters now is my search, and anything you might share to speed me in it."

She felt him clench, and wondered if she had wounded him. "I'm told that once he left your valley, Torin set sail for his own land. If these Illysp are as you describe them, perhaps he is dead already. I can offer no comfort other than to say that he lived when last his companions saw him."

"These companions, I'm told they dwell here within the city?"

"In willing support of my cause."

She wasn't sure how to take that. Had they been enslaved? Tortured? The thought might not have crossed her mind, had he not been so quick to defend himself. "I would speak with them, if you will permit it."

"You have only to command," he said, bowing stiffly. An unfamiliar act, she supposed, to go with unfamiliar words. He seemed almost as surprised by his response as she. "Will you . . . remain with us awhile?"

"My options grow short," she admitted. "If this is truly the end of Torin's trail . . ." She had thought to tell him of Necanicum's charge, and of her suspicion that this was where she might be called upon to carry it out. For if so, she would need his cooperation—and that of his troops—if she was to be given a chance to execute it properly. But she still had doubts of her own, and was quite certain that her grandfather would only think her mad. Better to keep quiet for now, and wait to see if a clearer choice presented itself after speaking to Torin's former companions. "I cannot stress how critical it is for me to find him," she finished finally.

The warlord's frown deepened, as if sensing a secret that concerned him. "I'll do what I can, if it means so much to you. Perchance there is rumor to be gleaned from port settlements north and south. Else we might put forth a message to be carried overseas. I command no fleet, but the high sailing season is drawing nigh, and few are those merchant captains who wouldn't empty their hulls to win my favor."

A finer offer than she might have hoped for, Annleia thought, and one to consider. That he was willing to succor her in this, despite his obvious skepticism, was not something she could easily dismiss.

"It would mean a month, at the least," Lorre confessed, "awaiting response. But you are welcome here for as long as you care to remain." After a moment's hesitation, he added, "Along with any others in need of protection."

"His Lordship is too kind," Annleia replied, ignoring the subtle reference to her mother and Finlorian people. The notion was impossible, and her grandfather knew it.

The braziers crackled and spat, reflected flames glinting in the warlord's eyes. "We will continue this on the morrow, then. I will have my chief steward prepare chambers for you, and will arrange for that word with Torin's companions. You may choose to wait here, if you wish, else follow me."

"If it please you," she offered with a bow, "I would be honored to attend His Lordship."

Lorre grunted. He did not seem to know what else to say. Annleia stepped forward. She felt his discomfort, radiating outward. His arms unfolded from his chest, and for a moment she feared he meant to embrace her. She stopped, a pace away, near enough to smell his sooty musk, to see each crease in his pale, leathery cheeks, and to sense the many scars, both visible and hidden.

"Come," he said, as if her scrutiny troubled him.

She followed him out, and kept pace down the wide, stark corridor. The breeze of their passage stirred the powerful odor that clung to him—not just of smoke, but of heavy tobacco, like cinder and ash, mixed with the brackish scent that seemed to permeate even the stone of this seaside fortress. She made no mention of that or anything else, preferring the silence between them. He was still ruthless, she reminded herself, a man who had dedicated the latter portion of his life to vengeance and bloodshed, and who, if her mother was correct, would make no apologies for it.

And yet, the fear and nervousness had gone out of her. For all his cunning, his influence, his physical control, this was not a man who would ever find true peace. Too driven was he, too full of passion. Despite all she knew of him, Annleia could only guess as to how such passion had become so rancorous. But she saw plainly its virulent effects, how it ate at him within and without. Her mother—Lorre's child—believed that his wife's death had triggered in him an obvious need not just for retribution, but for personal atonement. Either way, his attempts to defy and subjugate and win freedom through forced tolerance had only intensified his anguish, sapping rather than nourishing his spirit. A ruthless murderer to some, a staunch and respectable leader to others. To Annleia, however, the austere overlord was but a victim of his own misguided hate, worthy of her compassion.

The chief steward was an aged fellow who greeted her kindly and vowed to ensure her every comfort. Almost as soon as they had been introduced to one another, her grandfather took his leave.

"Wait," she called after him.

He paused, his seamed face a stern yet dutiful mask.

"You never questioned my claim," she observed. "How did you know me for who I am?"

His steely gaze bore into her. "You have your grandmother's eyes," he said, then turned and stalked away.

CHAPTER TWENTY-FIVE

Word passed quickly through the ranks of the grinding throng: breathless whispers, muttered curses, cries of terror, and groans of dismay.

Souaris was aflame.

Allion would have felt no different had someone sheathed a dagger in his gut. From a distance, the strange columns had the look of vast pillars seeking to support a sagging sky. But as he rode nearer in the open bed of that creaking wagon, tending to the wounded, the dawn's light grew stronger, and he saw them for what they were: towers of soot worming up and away in the shape of twisted funnel clouds, to bathe the world in perpetual darkness.

Marisha's hand slid into his, and he gripped her fingers tightly. He did not have to see her face to know her thoughts, and feared showing her his. It simply couldn't be. They had not come all this way, survived all those skirmishes, pressed on day after day when it seemed there was no hope, only to be denied now the refuge they so dearly required. All knew Souaris to be mankind's first true bastion upon these shores—and, if necessary, the last. Despite the horrors they had endured at Atharvan, and later on the road south, Souaris would see their strength renewed, their faith restored.

All of which was slipping away before his eyes, lost to the heavens amid those spreading stains of smoke.

A fool he had been, blind and vain, to believe the Ceilhigh watched over them—that some magnificent council of divine creators had reserved for mankind special favor and dominion over all. He should have known better. They were elven gods, after all, resurrected by man when he had come to these shores. And any gods that had allowed one people to be destroyed would not hesitate to abandon another.

"The city is secure!" a rider bellowed, swimming backward against the civilian flow. "Souaris is secure!"

This time, Allion *did* look to Marisha, and saw his own hope reflected in her eyes. He tried to catch the crier's attention as the man surged past, but failed to do so. There were others amid the throng, shouting the same message and urging the crowds to pass it along. Trying to forestall a panic, the hunter thought. He could only pray the word they bore was true.

He sent forth one of Marisha's pages to find out.

"'Tis true, my lord," the lad gasped upon his return from the forward lines. "There's fire within the city, aye. But the blazes are controlled, and the walls are not breached."

Maybe not, Allion allowed privately, although these days, blazes of such size meant one thing only. Perhaps Souaris still stood, but some ill had befallen her. Of that, he had no doubt.

Even so, he smiled bravely, and clapped the young page's shoulder, urging him to help spread the good news. The smile he gave Marisha was more knowing, but he saw no need to voice his suspicions here.

Day and night they had traveled, for more than a week now, resting only when they believed it safe to do so. Too often they had been wrong, and had been roused from their dreams to face a living nightmare. Each time, they had banded together—men, women, and children—to weather the ambush and beat back those small flocks of scavengers come to peck at their flesh. Each time, Allion feared it to be that final attack, executed not by strays and rogues, but by an army that would devour them whole. And though it hadn't come yet, each small bite taken by the enemy had left them that much more haggard, bloody, and disheartened than before.

Worse yet were the cancers that had eaten at them from within: hunger and sickness and despair. Men who stood side by side when the reavers came would rob, cheat, and even kill one another at the slightest insult or provocation. With so few soldiers to keep the peace, it was left to the refugees to govern themselves. And that was like fighting wildfire with boiling oil, for as often as not, men to either side would let the combatants be or else take sides and join the struggle.

It might have gone better, had they a true figurehead among them. But by now it seemed certain that neither Galdric nor any of the king's royal house had escaped. Nightly councils were led by a smattering of low-level city ministers and presided over by Colonel Boldin, a battalion commander and the highest-ranking soldier among them. Allion was not without voice, since, as far as anyone here knew, he remained regent to the throne of Alson. But, much like his "dragon-slayer" moniker, that title now meant little. And even if it were otherwise, in order to command respect, a man first had to respect himself.

Given that, their leadership had done a remarkable job of keeping them together, and of avoiding the larger armies of Illychar said to have massed at Leaven. The force that had destroyed Atharvan was no longer in range of their scouts, but at last report had finished sweeping up the dead and had been driving west toward the Whistlecrags. If the remnants of the Parthan Legion rumored to have holed up at Leaven did not escape soon, both they and the citizenry they sought to protect were as good as dead.

The day had not gone by in which Allion had not considered the fates of Jasyn, Corathel, and the others. It was their courage, as much as anything else, that kept him going. More than once, he had decided that the Illysp could claim him. Let his own soul be damned, so long as it ended his present misery. But then he would recall how Corathel and his men had given their lives at Atharvan so that Allion and the thousands like him might escape. And when he remembered that, he would burn with shame at his own weakness, and remember that he had not come this far to die. To that end, he could have left himself rotting upon that distant battlefield, or upon any of the smaller ones encountered along the way. To surrender now would be to destroy all he had endured, render all his sufferings meaningless, and make a mockery of his friends' sacrifice. He was not about to let that happen.

He had heard similar talk throughout the camp. For every naysayer, there were those who called to memory the bravery of the fallen, the heroism of those who had allowed them to make it this far. There were thousands less fortunate than they, others would remind them. Praise be to the gods that they still had breath to bemoan their fate.

But those voices had grown quiet as the days and trials and weariness compounded, to form a morass in which hope suffocated and time held no purpose. With dour faces and feral longing, their ragged column had pressed forward in fits and starts, harried at all times, driven onward by a relentless fear of death. Only the shared dream of the security to be found at Souaris had kept the better part of them from turning against one another like a pack of rabid dogs. To learn that even the legendary City of Man was not immune to this horror carried with it a bitterness that few were prepared to taste.

The reassurances now being spread, however, seemed to be having the desired effect. While a few continued to mutter, and many more eyed those smoke plumes warily, most were heaving a sigh of relief at the word brought back by the forward spotters. Allion even saw a few smiles and heard a few celebratory laughs. *We've done it*, they cried. *Safety at last*. Though he wasn't so certain, Allion understood their elation. For the time had come to either celebrate or surrender. Desperation had carried them this far, but it could carry them no farther.

The closer they drew, however, the harder it became to hold their smiles. Ash and soot blanketed the sky, casting all in dusky hues. It was not yet mid-morning, and already the world looked as though it were bathed in sunset. Allion tried to focus on the tasks given him by Marisha, but more and more, his stomach churned and his heart's cage seemed to shrink. He spoke assurances to any who asked his thoughts, even to those whose wounds were clearly mortal and who had no need to concern themselves with what another morrow or two might bring. He tried to tell even himself that his dark mood was unfounded, that he was sulking over things that could not be helped by more worry. But his insides refused to listen.

"Lord Allion! Lord Allion!"

He raised his head at the cry, scanning the nearby crowds whose marching feet stirred dust along the scrub-grown highway. A rider was weaving among them.

"Where is Lord Allion?"

Heads shook, and shoulders shrugged, but others turned and pointed. Allion stood in the back of that healer's wagon, clutching the low wall for support as it jostled along. He raised his other hand in signal.

The rider shoved toward him through the press. Questioning gazes followed.

"My lord, you've been summoned to the van."

"For what purpose?"

"A Kuurian envoy has come, led by a High Commander Troy. My lord, King Thelin himself has asked to speak with you."

TROY HAD BROUGHT MOUNTS, FOR him and Marisha both. When asked how he had known they would be coming apair, the high commander had offered them his typical sly smile and replied, "Just in case."

Their pleasantries had been warm and heartfelt, yet brief. There was much to be shared and more to be learned, but King Thelin would conduct that briefing, and had requested their presence with all haste. Troy's manner had been calm and confident, clearly intended to put them at ease. At the same time, there was a strain in the commander's eyes that Allion wasn't certain belonged. And though he saw no bandages beneath the other's armor, its links were scraped, its plates dented, and the warrior seemed to wince every time his horse fidgeted beneath him. Marisha had asked if he'd been hurt, to which Troy had offered good-naturedly, "At a glance, my condition appears better than yours. Come, and all your questions will be answered."

They had ridden hard, back toward the city, leaving the throng of Parthan refugees behind. Despite all his many fears, Allion had been overcome with awe as Souaris rose up before him, tiered battlements clinging to the faces of the mountains upon which they had been built. Atharvan had been huge— larger than Souaris, perhaps, in its sprawl. But Souaris cast the more forbidding shadow, with half-moon walls impossibly tall and impossibly thick, looming so far overhead that even from a distance, Allion had to crane his neck to glimpse those who manned the well-armed parapets.

The central gate of the lowermost wall had engulfed them with its vastness. Allion had been able to smell the strength, the timelessness, of that great corridor. For the first time, he felt a truer sense of the conflict his friends had endured in facing down thousands upon thousands of Killangrathor's dragonspawn as they roiled and surged like ocean waves against these man-made breakers. A conflict no less vast and deafening and horror-filled than his own trials in the dragon-father's lair.

Soon after, all he could smell was the rank closeness of the air that had been partially trapped behind that massive barrier. Winds swirled, but could not drive out the heavy odor of man and beast and all of their combined endeavors. Allion had tried not to breathe too deeply, hoping that the air would cleanse itself the higher they climbed.

It had not. After passing through the first tier, filled primarily with soldiers, they had entered the second, flooded to capacity with faces like those he had left upon the highway. Here, their pace had slowed, as it had become more difficult to part the sea of civilians than those of military discipline and training. Men and their possessions, mothers and their children, slow-moving elders and slower-moving carts, beasts of burden and free-roaming pets—all shuffled or scampered across their path or otherwise came underfoot. They

did their best to clear a path, but the sheer number of comings and goings—
and the lack of open areas in which to turn—made that difficult.

The third and fourth in that series of arced rungs were no better. Not until
they had climbed the central ramp to the fifth—those great, collapsible ramps
used to such great effect in battle—did space open up again, giving way once
more to a preponderance of men-at-arms and a lack of civilians. It had struck
Allion as odd to find it so. That there were refugees enough to spill down into
the lower fighting rings made sense. That they should fail to make use of the
city's highest and innermost defensive area did not.

Then had come the stench, and he had scarce been able to think at all.
Even Troy and his twoscore riders had covered their mouths with their cloaks,
and both Allion and Marisha had been compelled to do likewise. The hunter
feared he might retch nonetheless. He knew that smell, but never had he encountered it so thick and foul. Sure enough, it was here that the great fires
raged, those they had spotted from afar. Ash rained down upon them, and he
had cringed to think of what it was made of. The glow of flames painted the
inner battlement, danced upon the walls of buildings, and writhed against
gray mountain slopes.

By then, he had known for a certainty that something terrible had happened, though he hadn't yet guessed what it was. All he knew was that there
would be no rest from their travails. Whatever reprieve they found here would
be temporary at best.

These were the thoughts that weighed upon him as he climbed the steps
to the Palace of Kings on road-weary legs. He had been more than two hours
now in the saddle, perhaps three, so it should have felt good to stretch his
own muscles again. But those muscles had been worked already beyond their
limits, and might not feel good ever again.

Their trek through those stark and age-weathered halls continued without
delay. The grim gazes of servants and guardsmen marked their progress. Only
Troy accompanied them now, preceded at all times by a herald or page. The
king was in council, they were advised, but had left orders for them to be
brought to him at once.

Indeed, Allion had scarcely found time to brush some of the ash from his
shoulders before the towering doors to the council hall cracked open and the
herald who had gone ahead to announce them beckoned them forward. He
glanced at Marisha, bright and brave as always, be it from her own inner fire
or those which burned within the Pendant, hidden at her breast. Together,
they followed Troy past a half dozen unflinching sentinels, into the chamber
beyond.

The hall was immense, with vaulted ceiling, tiered galleries that rose up
on either side into shadow, and a great central table flocked by massive stone
chairs. Each chair was elaborately sculpted, though none grander than the
one raised up and planted at the table's head. Fire-tinged sunlight streamed
through tall, slender windows set in the far wall behind the king's seat, bathing all in a sullen red glow. The perimeter benches and gallery seats were

empty, as were a handful of the council chairs. The rest were filled with men in robes and furs and jewels—lords and lordlings, perhaps a dozen in all—each with a lone attendant. All, lords and retainers alike, glared back at him with stern brows and solemn faces.

"Come," bade the man standing at the table's head—King Thelin, Allion presumed.

Troy marched forward, seeming to favor his left leg. "Your Majesty, lords of Kuuria, I present to you Allion, lord regent of Alson, and Marisha, betrothed of that land's former king."

Allion winced. Even now, when it no longer mattered, he felt a twinge of guilt at how his relationship with Marisha had unfolded.

He was given no time to dwell on it.

"To our Imperial Council, I bid you welcome," Thelin intoned, with only the slightest hint of courtesy. This council had been dealing with grim matters, Allion decided, and his own arrival had done nothing to brighten their somber mood. "Sit with us, if you please."

His firm tone made it a demand. Allion took Marisha's arm and led her forward. He glanced at Troy, who motioned to the nearest pair of empty seats. Allion sat Marisha in one before sitting himself down beside her. Troy assumed the attendant's position behind them.

"Your riders tell of Atharvan's fall," Thelin said gravely. "We would hear of it from your lips, and of the journey that has brought you here."

Allion glanced at Marisha, who nodded. He wasn't certain why he was being tasked with this. Before this moment, he had never met this king, nor any of the Kuurian Empire's lesser lords. Nor did they seem disposed toward formal introductions now. Nevertheless, he cleared his throat, drank gratefully from the cup and flagon of ale passed down to him, and, with a weary sigh, granted the king's request.

He began from the moment of his separation from Nevik, pausing to see if Thelin had some word to offer on the state of the baron or those from Alson he had traveled south to join. Thelin only stared at him pointedly, jaw locked, mouth set. So he proceeded to tell of his first reunion with Corathel outside Atharvan, of their early attempts to scatter the Illychar horde awaiting them, of the royal decision to evacuate, Torin's later arrival, the city's downfall, and their harrowing escape. He told of how, with minimal rest and with families unaccustomed to such toil, they had cheated death for nearly two weeks while traversing some seventy-five leagues, preserved not by speed or stealth, but the sheer size of their throng—the determination of three hundred thousand souls not to be taken by the smaller packs of predators that had struck occasionally and otherwise eyed them hungrily. He finished by sharing with his listeners what few tidings their scouts had concerning Leaven, and of the sweeping enemy force that was or would be en route—to the west, perhaps, or here to the south. When neither Thelin nor any of his councilors responded, he went on to express how grateful they were for Souaris's welcome, and vowed to serve in whatever manner necessary, to the betterment of all.

Still he met with only frozen silence. He sat back in his stone chair, wishing for some sort of padding, wondering what else the king expected him to share. Marisha sandwiched his nearest hand between her own, and turned her soulful blue eyes upon him, offering what comfort she could.

"There you have it," Thelin declared at last. "The worst of what we have been hearing confirmed. And from the mouth of the dragon-slayer himself. Borne out, judging by her silence, by the daughter of Darinor—the man whose treachery might have claimed us all, were it not for this pair's help in unmasking him. Is this not so?"

Marisha had grown taut—indignant, perhaps, or pained. Allion felt it in her grip, and heard it in her icy reply. "We have been forthright from the beginning. All you've heard from us is true."

"As you understand it."

"As it is," Allion growled. He didn't care where he was, or who these people were. He'd endured enough already without having to tolerate their derision of the woman he loved.

"That was not a slight, lord regent, but a reminder, to us all, that we have only now begun to gain the true measure of our enemy. The moment your father was exposed," Thelin explained to Marisha, "everything we thought we knew was cast in doubt." He turned to the others, his nation's lords and councilors. "And yet, we have seen enough to suggest that most of what Darinor told us concerning this enemy was true. That, along with what we have all just heard, would seem to end any renewed debate."

What debate? Allion wanted to cry out. "With Your Majesty's forgiveness, perhaps we can be of greater help if you were to share with us the matter before this grand council."

Thelin, who had remained standing throughout Allion's long narration, leaned back from where his fists had been planted against the table, and claimed his seat. "This war has ended," he said stolidly. "The enemy has won."

Allion glanced round the table, seeking some further hint from those assembled. Marisha was more direct. "What are you saying?" she asked.

"I've proposed an exodus. The Imperial Council has agreed. The time has come to abandon Souaris."

Allion gaped. "You mean, surrender without a fight and—"

"I mean preserve the lives of those we yet can," Thelin snapped. "While I guarantee you that my people, at least, would sooner die than abandon their homes, I will not allow that to happen, not if there is a chance to survive elsewhere."

"You cannot possibly—"

"You forget yourself, lord regent. I count you friend, though we have never met, for the valor you have shown, and your close knowledge of these affairs. But do not discount my own, or presume to tell me what I cannot do."

The hunter had heard it whispered that Thelin had been the past few months in mourning, overcome with grief at the loss of his young heirs. From the tone of the king's letters, received during Allion's time as regent, those rumors bore at least some truth. Weakened, they suggested of the monarch, a shell of his former self.

Allion saw none of that here. Whatever had happened within these walls had evidently put the fire of battle back in King Thelin. Not such a terrible occurrence, then. But if he had already capitulated, what did it matter?

Trying to think of another approach, Allion asked, "Where would you go?"

"Overseas. Wherever the fastest winds will take us. If there are gods who preside still over this earth, the Illysp will find no way to follow."

"Your Majesty—"

"The city is fallen, Allion. I feared the possibility, but your tale tells me it is true."

Before the hunter could regain his tongue, Marisha spoke the words upon it. "I don't understand."

"Neither did we, when the fighting began. Our attention was focused outward as always, to an enemy upon the horizon, an enemy foolish enough to spend its strength against our walls." The muscles in the king's neck tightened. "The foolishness this time was ours. While we burrowed amid our mountain tunnels, making room for the countless thousands come to shelter here, our invisible foe was doing the same, exploring for itself our vast underground network. There it came upon our catacombs, the vaults and crypts of the veterans of this city's wars—kings and generals, heroes and champions, some of whom had lain in stately rest for more than five centuries."

Allion stiffened in his chair while the blood drained out of him, knowing already the remainder of Thelin's gruesome tale.

But a fever had overtaken the king, and he pressed forward, relentless. "They came back!" he growled. "Even without organs that you and I consider vital, an army of our preserved dead emerged from those dry and frigid depths, composed of warriors, legends, from throughout our famed history. Some of the oldest corpses, fortunately, were too far gone to be of any use. But thousands more rose up against us, including countless slain in our recent war against the Demon Queen. Tell me, could you find the strength to slay your own father and desecrate his remains?"

Thelin had lunged forward in his chair, palms gripping the white granite until his knuckles appeared to be part of the sculpted armrests. His maddened eyes glared at Allion from across the table, while a dreadful silence engulfed the room.

At last, the king sat back. "As you saw, the pyres rage even now. They will do so for days to come. All passageways to our remaining tombs have been sealed, though none can guarantee for how long. The battle was won, though you cannot begin to fathom the cost." He shook his head. "We do not have it in us to weather another such attack."

The others remained silent, cowed even. Allion was not truly surprised. Thelin's was the only voice that mattered. The Imperial Council would have crowned him their new emperor weeks ago, had he allowed it. And likely, these lords and barons were far more terrified than their king by the events unfolding around them. If Thelin had decided it was time to go, then none of those here would offer true challenge.

Yet Allion could not bring himself to accept what he was hearing. "Your people's legacy is here, upon this land, within the walls of this gallant city. After all you have suffered and achieved, how can you now admit defeat?"

Thelin sighed. "I've been asking the same question now for weeks—of my queen, of my countrymen, of myself. Thousands had to perish needlessly before I understood. These piles of mortar and timber and stone, these are not our legacy. The pride and spirit of our people is. Given a chance, we will cultivate new lands, build new homes, and that part of our legacy will endure. Remain here, and there is nothing but the inevitable loss of our own souls to this vile infestation."

"The Illychar are mortal," Marisha argued. "Their coils can be destroyed."

A few murmurs arose, but Thelin's signal quickly silenced them. "But can we do so fast enough? With what you've seen, my lady, can we truly hope to halt their spread? Suppose we could. What of the Illysp who sow the seeds? Henceforth, will every back-alley cutthroat take the time to immolate his victims? Or will the plague rise up anew? And pray tell, what happens to those possessed, our loved ones, after they are mutilated and burned? What cause is there to believe the Ceilhigh will bless and keep their blackened souls?"

Allion looked toward the windows, to the stain of fire and smoke risen from the very heart of this city, and was reminded of the swirling ash, the choking stench, the stinging eyes, all of which afflicted him to a lesser degree even here, within the thick walls of this perfumed chamber. Those blazes would seem to underscore the king's arguments. The Illychar needed not half their current strength to camp outside and wait for the city's inhabitants to starve. And the Illysp, who seemed to pass as they willed, would never truly be contained. The Sword had been lost, and with it, any hope of locking these foes away, even if they *could* be rounded up and driven back into their hole. In his search for the Vandari, Torin had claimed to have found a dead end. On what ground had Allion planted his stubborn hopes?

Thelin was shaking his head, his pale skin and grizzled stubble matching the color of his gray-and-white doublet. "I've denied it for as long as I can. Should I deny it any longer, our fate will be that of Atharvan. And where Souaris falls, no other city can stand. On the morrow, or next month, or a year hence, all will belong to the Illysp, along with the souls of any who must needs cling to these cursed shores."

"And what makes you think you can escape?" Allion asked dejectedly. "Will you truly leave it to the gods to determine whether the Illysp will follow?" Even as he said it, however, he looked to Marisha, who placed her hand upon his arm, gripping it with a sudden hope.

"They won't," she breathed.

"You know this?" someone asked.

"We know nothing for certain," Allion cautioned, still staring at Marisha. But he, too, remembered now the talk they'd had upon that lakeshore, so many weeks ago. "Though Darinor did claim that they fear the sea." He turned toward Thelin. "He had us believe that this is why the Finlorians fled, and he did not deny that we might find similar resort."

"Darinor was the enemy," the unknown lord reminded them, a brutish fellow with pinched eye and tangled yellow beard.

"It matters not," Thelin asserted. "It is our best hope—a chance, at least, to begin anew."

Allion recognized now the spirit behind this notion. It was not a retreat, but their first true counter. Until now, every move they had made had been at Darinor's insistence, or in response to their own fear. The hundreds of thousands come to gather here had not done so to fight, but to hunker behind protective walls. The idea of an exodus, of setting sail across a treacherous sea, was Thelin's way of fighting back at long last, of choosing the most likely front and having the courage to attack it in full force.

Nevertheless, it remained a desperate maneuver, the logistics of which screamed folly.

"It would take a fleet of ships, ten thousand or more—"

"Word has already been sent to the coastal cities in the south," Thelin responded flatly. "I have assurances from Wingport's governor that all will be made ready, should the final order be given. The capacity will be found," he vowed, "if it means I myself am the last to leave."

Allion had heard too many declarations of hollow bravery to pay that one much notice. "So it may be. What of those to the north? Will my own countrymen be left to rot?"

"A good number of yours are already here," Thelin reminded him, showing little reaction to the rebuke. "As for those at Krynwall and elsewhere throughout Alson, word of the possible exodus was issued to your General Rogun the moment we sent our first feelers south."

The hunter snorted. "Rogun? He'll never believe it."

"Your Baron Nevik said the same," Thelin replied with a wan smile. "Which is why he set forth with my courier to personally assure the general that what I've told you this day is true: that all, even the proud Souari, have decided to seek our futures elsewhere. Rogun will follow our lead and guide your people safely overseas, else see them slaughtered."

Allion ground his teeth. "I don't suppose there's been any word on how the baron of Drakmar fares."

Thelin shook his head. "It is too soon to tell."

The hunter wished to say more, but found his frustration withering beneath the king's incontestable glare. "The decision is already made, then?"

"We met here to discuss *how* it would be done—holding out hope, of course, that your tidings would show us another way."

And they did not, Allion fumed helplessly. Looking back, their lives here had ended the moment Torin had unleashed this bane upon them. The Illysp could be combated, but never defeated. His own experiences forced him to acknowledge it. This course was not chosen *by* them, but *for* them. All that remained was to plan the best means for carrying it out.

Thelin's tone softened, as if the man sensed the despair he had caused. "I know not what chance we have of freeing everyone from this land and conducting them safely overseas. Nor can I predict the trials that await us if we are to succeed. What I know is this: For a sacrifice to have meaning, there must be those who benefit in result. It is too late for that to happen here."

A chorus of grunts and nods from those assembled murmured in support of the king.

Once more, all Allion could think of was those pyres, and of the thousands of civilians who had doubtless been among the slain—those incapable of fighting, who had come here with the faith that they would not have to. Those whose final thoughts would have been that their trust had been misplaced. Such a sentiment would spread, infecting the living as well as the dead, and would be a morale-weakening disease which, when hope was everything, could destroy them all.

A crushing thought that only added to his own sense of defeat. Yet that was not what he saw in Thelin's eyes. In Thelin's eyes, and in the eyes of those seated around the table, he saw again that this *was* their fight. Clearly, they had wrestled with this for some time, to be so stern in their conviction. Who was he to tell such men they were wrong?

He thought again of Corathel, of what had likely been the general's final stand there at Atharvan. If this was truly how their war against the Illysp had to play out, then he would find no better opportunity to emulate Corathel's courage, Corathel's selflessness . . .

And, in all likelihood, to meet Corathel's end.

"We have but days, perhaps, before the Illychar are upon us," he reminded them all, "and this exodus will take time." He glanced at Marisha, then faced the king of Souaris squarely. "You'll need a diversion."

CHAPTER TWENTY-SIX

LARESSA SAT ALONE UPON HER daughter's favorite overlook, peering up at moon and stars on a rare, cloudless night. Lush foliage glistened around her, damp with misty spray from a ribbon waterfall that cut through a nearby cleft in the black mountain wall. Insects and nightbirds chirped and twittered, adding resonant layers to the steady thrum of cascading waters. An occasional soft breeze brushed her neck, her cheek, like a lover come to whisper in her ear. When she closed her eyes, she could almost imagine Eolin was there.

But Eolin was gone, and their child as well. She was truly alone again, in a way she hadn't been for a very long time. Not since she was ten, when she had lost her mother, had she felt so forlorn. Her father had been unable to help her, unable to understand. His resentment toward the Finlorian people had blinded him to the fact that she was still very much one of them. A half-breed, yes, who had never lived among them. But her mother's blood ran strong in her veins, and seeking to deny that part of her heritage had been like trying to hush a squalling child. There had been no way to truly silence it, not without destroying herself in the bargain.

Then Eolin had come, opening her eyes, teaching her to see herself and the world in a way she had never dreamed. Drawn to this new awakening, she had been prepared to sacrifice all else in its pursuit—her father, her husband, her human way of life.

Before long, she had been forced to do precisely that.

Yet she had never regretted her decision. If need be, she would make the same sacrifices all over again, mistakes and misunderstandings be damned. She had found greater happiness here, in two decades of hiding among her Finlorian brothers and sisters, than she ever could have in the world at large. While some spoke wistfully of their nation's former majesty and of a divine right to reclaim it, Laressa saw little romance in the notion, craving none of the vindication or contentment such a resurgence might bring.

And yet, she could not refute those murmurs growing among her people that change was upon them. On a night such as this, the world seemed bright and beautiful, safe and serene. A mirage. For somewhere beyond the jagged rim of this thorn-shaped valley, her enemies hunted. Beyond the rivers and streams and fertile greenery prowled those who would take it from them. No matter her reassurances to herself and others, their safety had been compromised, the location of their home discovered by outsiders who now roamed free. It might be that the armies of her father—or any number of lesser hunters eager for sport—were already on their way, to finish the job Warrlun had begun.

A pale concern compared to the Illysp. The nightmares had relaxed some-what since her daughter had set forth. Though Annleia herself had insisted upon it, allowing the child to depart in search of Torin's trail had been the most difficult decision Laressa had ever agreed to, far more heart-wrenching than the one made so long ago that had seemed to tear her in two. With that sacrifice, she had done *something*, at least, to address the issue, and therefore ease her sense of guilt.

But it wasn't enough. Though dulled, the nightmares—and the guilt—persisted. The *Demwei* continued to respect and obey her, but more and more, these guiding statesmen seemed to sense the dire secret she kept from them. Though they be leaders of her people, they were not Vandari, Laressa told herself in private justification. Had Eolin wished to share his knowledge of the Illysp with them, he would have done so long ago—or else permitted them and their priests to attend when he had finally shared that knowledge with her. That much of him, she decided, belonged to her and her daughter alone.

Besides, it mattered not *who* threatened, be it Lorre or the Illysp or both. What mattered was the threat itself, the fact that it existed at all.

Many of her people agreed. Why wait for an enemy to take form? They should leave Aefengaard now, lest any among Torin's company return. Prepa-rations were under way to do just that, to vanish into the caves and mountains before their only true exit was blocked. Laressa had not been so foolish as to suggest that there was no need for readiness. Her only goal had been to pre-vent a panic, to hold her husband's people together, to remind them that blind action might well create perils where there were none.

After all, where were they to go? It had taken years, with the aid of the Tuthari, to find and settle this location. How could they hope to discover a similar haven on their own? And even if they were to do so, how could they be assured that their movements would not be spied, their tracks discovered, by those who hunted? Would it not be better to stay put and trust to the conceal-ment that had served them so long and well?

But it hadn't, as she of all her kin needed no reminder. She had already lost those most precious to her. If no enemies returned, and no more given cause to suffer, she herself would find little solace. A justice, perhaps, that Warrlun had taken from her all she had taken from him. As cold and cruel as the notion held by some of the Vandari, long since dead, that the Illysp were a punishment sent by the Ceilhigh in response to the Finlorians' arrogance. Either way, the peace she had known and loved these past twenty years was shattered, aided in part by one she had trusted to preserve it. Such scars ran too deep to ever truly heal.

Despite the dwarf's hand in her betrayal, she wished Crag were still here. She missed his strength, his blunt and steadfast nature. He might have known better how to handle the situation, to make a decision rather than dancing with ever-changing possibilities. If nothing else, she wished for the chance to tell him that she harbored no ill will against him. He had done nothing out of malice, having taken every precaution to uphold his vows and protect their

secrecy. And loath as she was to admit it, the dwarf had done right in bringing Torin to them. The fault for Eolin's assassination lay as much with her as
with anyone. Had she ever bothered to trust the Tuthari with the name of the
husband she had spurned . . .

She shook her head. It was pointless to entertain such regrets. Doing so
was of no help to her people. She hoped Crag was well, that he had found
what he was searching for in terms of home and kin. But she herself had banished him, and she knew him well enough to realize that he would never again
violate her wishes. As bad as she felt at how matters had ended between them,
she understood that they could do no more for one another.

Her gaze slipped from the stars to the valley below. Like her thoughts,
her eyes seemed to wander of their own accord. Try as she might, she could
not maintain focus. But then, that was why she climbed every night to this
overlook: to escape her cares and responsibilities, to let her senses roam wild
amid nature's inimitable majesties. It never truly worked, of course. Whether
she was alone or in the presence of others, her worries were relentless. On
most nights, the rains poured and the winds swirled about her, making the
trails slick and the trek itself hazardous. Perhaps if she were to slip and fall,
her concerns would find no further purchase.

A defeatist thought, and one that aroused shame within her. She was just
so tired of being hunted. Were her life alone at stake, she would run no more,
but lie in wait for whatever fate her callous creators held in store. What else
was there to take from her?

A shadow passed overhead, drawing her attention from the smooth sea
of night-cloaked treetops and back to the depthless expanse of the heavens
above. A raptor of some sort, circling the mountains on its nightly hunt. There
were flocks of them ordinarily, great solitary predators wheeling and diving
and shrieking at one another as they battled for prey. Even—

She stopped herself, looking about the valley rim. Odd, that there should
be only one. But she saw no other flashes of movement, and heard no cries of
challenge. She listened, and realized that the night itself had grown quiet. The
insects still chirped, but the chorus of birdsong had faded almost to silence. It
was as if they had crawled back into their nests and hollows, else taken wing
when she was not paying attention.

A cold shiver began to take root, tracing the edges of her spine with cat-
erpillar legs. She searched the skies, but the raptor was gone, a mere speck
beyond the tufted slopes come together at the valley's northernmost edge. A
fast-moving bird, to have covered such terrain so quickly, though perhaps it
was only her angle that made it appear so.

Then it cut back, heading south. She wondered if it had seen her, though
she dismissed the irrational thought almost at once. It would take one mighty
large bird of prey to consider attacking . . .

She lost that thought, too, as it continued its southern approach, growing larger with each beat of her heart. Her own perch was upon a western
ridge. But it had definitely spied *something* that had captured its interest. Its

path was much too direct. She looked forward along its course, and saw the Veil, that great curtain waterfall covering the cave mouth that served as the gateway to Aefengaard. Given the distance, she could scarcely hear its rumble, though the thin falls at her shoulder echoed shrilly now in her ears, like a song of shattered glass.

Then came a sound such as Laressa had never heard before, pealing throughout the heavens, raking stones from the heights. The earthen slab beneath her shook with its rumble. The trees below erupted with shadows, as those birds and animals she had believed to be hiding—and others that had been sleeping—beat at one another in their haste to find new shelter. With her heart twisting in her stomach, and her throat in her chest, she managed somehow to force her gaze skyward once more—

As a black shade fell from the heavens, screeching like a missile of hell-slung death.

This is it, Thrakkon thought, euphoric, as the wind of their descent shrieked in his ear. *Our vengeance is upon us.*

All night they had scouted, and throughout the long hours of the following day, flying sweeping patterns over the northern Dragontails and the forked ranges of Trollslay and Wyvern Spur. Somewhere between, in the untamed forest region known as the Splinterwood, lay the Finlorians' hidden valley of Aefengaard. Torin's memory, though riddled with holes, told him as much. In one of these wooded pockets of stone, their quarry waited.

Yet Torin had spent so much of his trek underground, in the blinding dark, that it was difficult to gauge *where* he might have exited. And this bird's-eye view was so unlike the path he had taken. From this height, each mountain and valley looked much like the next, with little or nothing to distinguish it from those that crowded round. Thrakkon might have urged Killangrathor lower, giving them a better chance to peer through the forest canopy, but did not wish to give wind of their presence too soon. For all he had to go on, the Finlorians may as well have been fish hiding beneath an emerald sea.

So while he and his dragon searched with their eyes from above, Thrakkon had focused his thoughts inward, sifting again through Torin's memories and renewing his assault on those that remained hidden. The effort was like searching a grassy field peppered with gopher holes of buried knowledge. Trouble was, there was no telling how deep a particular hole went, or what he might find at the bottom. Some useless name perhaps. A jest shared, or a slight received. There seemed to be no rhyme or reason to it. Often, the secret treasure was further warded, like the brilliant mineral formation inside a stone egg, and chiseling through that outer shell was like digging anew.

There had been a festival of sorts that Torin had attended on his journey to the north. The bandit who had betrayed them in the mountains was there. A woman, a serving wench, had made eyes at him . . .

Thrakkon turned elsewhere.

Before that, a city whose name eluded him. A battle had been waged. He could not recall its conclusion, only the bitter taste of defeat, and days thereafter in chains . . .

Another battle, this one in a dark and twisted wood. Prior to the other, Thrakkon believed, for he fought alone, against a swarm of trees come to life around him. Or had there been allies at his side? He could almost sense another presence, but could bring nothing about it into focus . . .

So it had gone, hour after hour, until the sun had been driven back into its own hole, and moon and stars had filled the sky like the embers from its fire. Still Thrakkon had found no marker or bearing in Torin's memories, only meaningless fragments of a life gone by. He grew dejected. The Finlorians could have already moved on. They could be anywhere. At this pace, it might take weeks or months—

Then he had spied the waterfall, and a sudden pain twisted in his gut like the blade of a spear. Hunched forward against the ropes that bound him, he had gritted his teeth in ecstasy. *The Veil*, he recalled. A memory half hidden among those he had not yet been able to crack. *The curtain over the doorway to Aefenguard.*

He had ordered the dragon to swing about at once, and flown down for a closer look. That was it. It had to be. From this vantage, the valley looked almost nothing like he remembered it. But the falls . . .

Then, Killangrathor's roar, a layered bellow both deep and shrill that rattled the bones of those who clung to him.

The dragon had their scent.

They descended now in a dizzying rush, to strike the forest like a bolt of lightning from the cloudless dark. Down they plunged through its shadowed layers, tearing through trunks and boughs alike. Shattered tops and broken branches raked and stabbed at the dragon's skin, only to snap or be turned aside. Enraged, Killangrathor swiped and clawed and beat his wings in a thrashing frenzy. Pressed tight against the dragon's back, surrounded by pelting debris and a crackling thunder, Thrakkon felt as if he rode within the heart of a tornado.

It ended as abruptly as it had begun. Killangrathor's feet struck the ground, sharpened toes digging trenches in the earth. From its crouched landing position, the dragon reared high, its movements swift and terrifying. A lash of its tail scattered a council of firs at its rear, while its head reached high upon its serpentine neck, roaring in challenge.

A flutter of leaves and needles filled the air, along with a cloud of splinters and the smell of fresh sap. Thrakkon grinned savagely at the devastation. But it was not the blood of the trees he had come for.

The Crimson Sword flared in his hand. Killangrathor sensed it, twitching back to glare at him with a burning eye. Itz lar Thrakkon merely smiled.

The dragon faced forward suddenly, sniffing. Thrakkon sensed them, too. He searched the darkness ahead, gaze darting amid the trees. The Sword helped him pinpoint their location. There, a pair of eyes gleaming softly in the darkness, as wide as the moon whose dim light they reflected. Another beside him. And another, all around, vague shapes limned in soft starlight, frozen in awe of the devil descended among them.

Killangrathor roared, and they scattered, all in different directions. Swift and powerful as it was, not even the dragon could attend to them all.

A few quick cuts, and his harness lines fell away. The others were slashing free as well. Killangrathor hunched low, hissing as he waited. Thrakkon slid down the monster's hide, and sensed his minions scrambling after him. Not all, however. When he looked back, he found a pair of goblin corpses still strapped limply into place among the dragon's spines, jagged lances of woodland debris protruding from their bodies. Most of the rest, he now realized, also bore cuts and scrapes from Killangrathor's reckless descent through the trees. Thrakkon himself had been gashed across the arm, and found a splinter wedged in his brow. He flicked it away as he regarded the others: two dozen goblins, minus the pair dead, and a duo of giants. Despite their injuries, all appeared ready to inflict some damage of their own.

Thrakkon had scarcely taken stock before Killangrathor snorted and forged ahead, roaring that savage, stuttering cry. His great, armored bulk shoved forward through the forest wall, scattering leaves, shredding boughs, and splintering even the trunks of giant trees. A shower of woodland fragments pelted his body, shafts of broken hardwood and bleeding evergreen careening off plates and ridges of bony flesh.

The rest looked after him, then turned to Thrakkon, taut with feral anticipation.

"Kill them all," Thrakkon said.

LARESSA SKIDDED DOWN THE FINAL stretch of slope, feet sliding out from beneath her upon a blanket of loose stone. She landed hard, on her elbow and then her back. Pain flared, though her sharp cry was lost amid the cacophony of screams.

She scrambled up at once. Biting her tongue, clutching her elbow, she ran on. The woods rang with a chorus of shrieks and moans and whistles. She staggered toward the worst of it, her heart racing. Her people were dying. She had to warn them, had to signal the escape.

A line of bodies hurtled past, swift and silent as a hunter's shadow. The last in line froze when it spied her.

"My queen!" he cried. The others paused, but he shouted and waved them on, then leapt through the underbrush to kneel quickly before her. "My queen, you must come at once."

Tears and sweat stung her eyes. Ciaran, she recalled dimly. In another time and place, when Finlorian royalty had meant something, this stripling would have served among the guardian lords, and she would indeed have been his queen. In the present light, however, Laressa saw him with naught but pity, and herself with only shame and contempt.

"My queen, we—" He paused as he studied her. "My queen, you're hurt."

Her eyes peered past him, through shrouded woodland colonnades, to where it sounded as if the forest itself was being devoured. "What have they seen?" she asked him. Her voice sounded thin and whispery. "What have they told you?"

"We are under assault, my queen. The Demwei have commanded all to flee."

"Go then," she said. "See to your charges. Help as many as you can get away."

"That includes you, my queen. We must make for the Veil. There is no time—"

"Nor will there be, for any of us, if the enemy finds us all to be running in the same direction." She hadn't realized it until she'd spoken the words, but she knew now where she had been headed, and what she must do. "Go," she said, softly now, but with authority. "You must keep moving. Tell them all to run, and to not look back."

His eyes fixed upon hers, bright with youthful bravery and conviction. *He does not know. He has no idea what we face.* "My place is beside my queen," he said stubbornly.

"Your place is to serve. Do as I say."

She waited until he bowed, then ran on, through a profusion of underbrush grown suddenly dark and sinister. Other forms continued to race past, flitting through the trees. Some were weeping or clutching one another. Some cast frantic glances behind them and bowled over others in their haste. She could taste their fear now, along with her own, a tang of blood and sweat upon the air. Ahead of her, trees whipped and swayed, as something huge grated among them. The screams grew louder, more desperate.

She came then upon the dragon's wake, a mangled swath of trampled woodland. Trees that had taken a thousand years to grow had been snapped or stripped or shoved aside as if no stronger than virgin stalks. Dust and leaves and spores and splinters filled the air in a choking cloud. There were other forms tearing past her now, whirlwinds in the dark. When they shrieked, it felt as though their claws were already upon her back and buried in her ears. *Goblins*, she realized. Gods without mercy, there were actually goblins among them.

One flew by her position near enough that she could smell the rotten fetor of its leathery hide. An elf was bounding by, and felled before she could draw breath to shout a warning. Blood sprayed as the doomed elf was swept up and away as if by an entire colony of flesh-eating bats, then cast aside as the spinning goblin tore into another.

She turned to her left, and the goblin was forgotten. For there stalked the dragon, an obsidian hulk that both slithered and smashed, fluid grace and brute strength rolled and hammered into one. Elven corpses lay scattered around it, some in pieces, some as pulp, some only as fleshy stains. Many lay smashed and crumpled amid the ruin of the forest, impaled by splintered shafts or caught between the branches and trunks of felled trees. Their moonlit eyes seemed to stare in judgment of her soul.

The dragon charged, lowering its head and straightening its neck like a ram. A cedar welmwood toppled beneath its rush, flinging bark and heaving soil as roots snapped or ripped free of the earth. Cries of terror welled up from below. A burrow. Realizing this, the dragon seized the mighty trunk with its forelimbs and heaved it aside, exposing the nest of halls beneath. Elves huddled or flailed or scampered, exposed like beetles beneath an overturned stone. A pack of goblins swarmed in to finish them.

Laressa watched it happen, crouched amid seedling shrubs beneath the slant of a juniper deadfall. Though paralyzed with horror, she nearly jumped from her skin when Ciaran squatted beside her, a dozen of his fellow guardians at his heels.

His eyes, she noticed, no longer shone with brash innocence, but were rimmed wide with terror and disbelief. Yet he found the courage to say, "Whatever you mean to accomplish, we are with you, my queen."

His voice was hoarse, and his gaze a madman's twitch, flitting at each new sound. She wanted to scream at him, then at herself. What *did* she mean to accomplish? Her people had no weapons, nothing at all with which to stem this carnage. They could run, or they could hide. They could fill the heavens with their prayers. With a hundred wellstones, she might have sapped a measure of the dragon's strength for use against the goblins—or drawn from the latter for release against the former. Alas, hers was but a handful of such talismans still possessed by the Finlorian people, relics of a former age. And Annleia had taken hers south in any case, as a ward against the unknown. Annleia, who was now safest among them. Or might this slaughter suggest that her daughter had failed and was already dead?

The dragon turned westward, following a flight of elves who leapt through the forest like stricken deer. All were running to the same place. All were making for the Veil.

"Come, then," Laressa said, her own voice thick in her throat. "Let us slow that creature down."

They followed without question as she retreated south and west, running what she thought might be a likely intercept course. She sent a pair of her guardians to make sure. The hynara tree. They must see to it that the dragon found them at the hynara tree. That was where they would make their stand.

The brave guardians accepted their task and took to it in full stride, gathering up pouches of stones from a stream whose waters now ran red. Laressa filled a pouch of her own, and had Ciaran and her remaining guardians do the same.

Her band grew as it raced along in loose formation, drawing stragglers to its ranks. Most pleaded with her as Ciaran first had: to flee while she yet might. But when she would not, others refused as well, determined to stand beside their queen. Their loyalty was touching. If only she could believe it would make a difference.

She was not as nimble as her Finlorian brothers and sisters, and her elbow still ached, yet she climbed the hynara with little difficulty. It was the tallest and thickest in the valley, an ancient ironwood with grooves in its bark that could fit a man sideways. The broad base was gently sloped, with knobs and curls that could be used as steps to the lower branches. The limbs themselves shot outward in such profusion that fifty elves could have climbed at the same time. A shame she had less than a score.

Nevertheless, they scurried up those great sticky boughs without complaint, scaling branches as they might the rungs of a ladder. At roughly two hundred feet—high enough, she hoped, to place her above the dragon's direct line of attack—Laressa scurried out toward the end of a snaking limb thicker than her entire body. Others climbed even higher before moving toward the tree's needled perimeter, where they might have a clearer attack line of their own.

Most had barely settled into position when the dragon came bursting into view at the far end of the narrow glade, opposite the hynara. One of the guardians sent to lure the beast squirmed in its black fist. The other raced ahead, twisting now and then to chuck a stone at the behemoth's face. With the open space before him, the second guardian—Farial, she now saw—gave himself over to a full sprint, bounding through the tall grass. A goblin raced to cut him down, but the dragon roared, and the goblin wisely shied away. Hunting strides became attacking strides. In two lightning-quick steps, the dragon reached out and snatched up Farial as he had Denarr, who continued to writhe in the monster's grasp.

Then both fists closed, and the pair of guardians exploded like crushed eggs.

Laressa led a chorus of shouts from the hynara, flinging her own stones in challenge. A hail of rocks joined hers. None landed anywhere near the dragon, but it looked up and growled at them all the same. *Topple us, if you can*, Laressa thought. *See if you take down* this *tree*.

The dragon hissed, crouching down upon its haunches. It then sprang forward, launching another battering-ram charge. *Let its neck shatter*, she prayed. *Let our roots hold strong*.

The collision drove tremors through the length of the tree and rattled more than a few of her small host from where they perched, sending them bouncing down through the branches like fallen seed cones. The resounding crack was such that Laressa feared her own skull had split. The great hynara listed and groaned, convulsing already with aftershocks. But the roots maintained their hold, and the tree stood fast.

Laressa opened her eyes, not realizing she had closed them, and peered down through the hynara's quivering mesh. Her mouth filled with blood from having bitten her tongue, but in that moment it tasted like victory.

The dragon's most prominent horns swept back from its skull like the spines running down its serpentine body. But smaller spikes topped its crown, and where those had simply shredded the welmwood she'd seen it attack earlier, the hynara had absorbed their punch and swallowed them whole. Twist and yank as it might, the dragon could not seem to wrench free of the juicy ironwood.

Ciaran noticed it, too, and was the first to recover himself and bounce a stone off the dragon's neck. Others soon followed. Laressa released her full-body death grip upon her branch and added her own stones to the mix, shouting taunts with lusty glee.

Their pelting attack, of course, did nothing but annoy the dragon further. Yet it was enough for Laressa, who at long last had an outlet for all of the doubt and fear and guilt that had ruled her since Torin's coming and Eolin's death. Every throw was a triumph, every cry a burden cast aside. And every heartbeat in which the dragon struggled was that of a kinsman saved.

The creature below seemed to realize this as well. With its skull pressed tight against the fissured trunk, it pushed and heaved and shook. Its arms reached up among the boughs, raking and snapping. Elves tumbled to the earth, where goblins dove in and snatched them up, like black crows feasting at the foot of a lion.

The dragon's furious assault quickly stripped and scarred the proud hynara beyond recognition. Branches lay piled at its feet, or hung limply from the central bole by stretched threads of bleeding sapwood. Strips of bark coiled at the base of long furrows dug by the monster's claws in the trunk itself, while several of the fallen elves were now sticky smears upon its rough skin. Even above the attacks, the tree continued to shed nests and cones and needles, shuddering with the damage wrought below.

Yet still the hynara held its stubborn grip upon the beast, swaying with the dragon's flailing, but refusing to fall. The monster responded by tearing gashes in the trunk, deeper than those of any woodsman's axe. Its tail whipped and cracked, sending powerful ripples the length of its body and into the tree. Laressa soon knew what must happen, and could do nothing to prevent it. She could only clutch her branch and shout for her kinsmen to do the same, warm with dread, cold with denial.

With a final hacking, slashing, driving frenzy, the dragon unseated the hynara from its rooted pedestal. The great tree leaned forward, its unfathomable weight drawn down over the empty wedge carved from its base. The beast might have crushed itself, but grappled and twisted. Laressa felt the trunk splinter and turn, and shut her eyes. Amid a rending, splitting, crunching chorus, the mighty council tree, as old perhaps as the dragon itself, rejoined the earth with a jarring crash, taking Laressa with it.

She held initially, but the first bounce broke her grip and sent her sailing with arms and legs afire. Branches clubbed at her like an army of wooden staves, while twigs and needles scraped and poked like the claws of an angry mob. When finally she landed, the breath went out of her, and for a moment she thought she would never draw breath again.

But her lungs responded. Dust and slivers forced her to cough. The ground still quaked and rumbled, and the hynara's final, anguished moan still echoed in her ears. Every other sound had grown muted, as if heard with her head underwater. She smelled blood and uprooted earth, mold and pitch and sweat.

Her eyes opened, revealing a blasted mesh of limbs and needles all but eclipsing a star-filled sky.

She felt then the sudden twists and violent yanks passing like death spasms through the remains of the fallen tree. The world spun, but she managed to sit upright. A thousand pains lanced through her, beckoning her toward darkness. Beyond the tree's ruin, she glimpsed a towering black hulk and remembered the dragon. The spasms were its continuing struggle to remove its half-buried skull from the hynara's death grip.

A massive foot pinned the bouncing deadfall in place. A moment later, the dragon's horns finally wrenched free. It roared, though not as loudly as before.

She felt and heard goblin claws scrabbling amid the wreckage. She fought to roll over and onto her knees, but her legs refused to draw up beneath her. She began to crawl, not certain where she was crawling to, understanding only that she was not safe where she lay. Her elbow ached, and her arms and fingers had been scraped raw. She wondered when all of that had happened. A small stream dripped steadily from her mouth. When she paused to touch it, she felt her teeth through a hole in her lip. She did not remember it being there before.

Bodies dangled amid the branches like linen hung to dry. She crawled past their sightless, gaping forms, wondering why they did not move. The dragon was still there, huffing and crunching. And the goblins . . . The Veil. She was headed toward the Veil. Her kinsmen, too. Why did they wait? They still had a long way to go.

She followed the twisted length of a tree limb that lay flat upon the ground, seeking its tapered end. She continued past, brushing aside curtains of sticky needles. A light flared ahead of her, crimson in its glow. *That must be the way*, she thought, and pulled herself toward it.

The light arced and whirled, a mesmerizing display. A flurry of vague forms danced around it before falling aside. Then it slowed, burning as a single shaft. It drew nearer.

A massive tremor rocked the ground as an obsidian boulder fell suddenly beside her. She looked. Not a boulder, but a mountain. *The dragon*. Its carrion breath washed over her.

She lowered her gaze, back toward the light. It moved toward the dragon, and the beast shied away with a muffled hiss of hate and frustration. She watched the creature stalk off in another direction, mowing down a field of grass before plowing headlong into a dark wall of trees.

She turned back toward the light. It was directly above her now, emanating from the blade of a—

As the Sword's aura washed over her, so too did a flood of memory and realization. The Sword of Asahiel had returned, its wielder come to save them. Annleia must have succeeded. She must have found Torin and convinced him to give the Vandari a second chance. Together, they might rid the world of this pestilence after all.

His face looked familiar enough, but when he smiled, Laressa felt her heart grow cold. All at once, her body became rigid and unresponsive. This was not Torin, she realized, only another nightmare.

Knowing that, she glared at him defiantly. *End it*, she thought. *End it and let me wake.*

His lips moved, but her fading sense of sound had vanished altogether. Odd; that had never happened before. Though his words escaped her, his cruel smile remained, as he raised the Sword, blade pointed downward, in both hands. She eyed him grimly, but without fear. She was tired of being cowed by phantoms.

Then the blade struck, through her back and through her heart and through the earth upon which she lay, and a wall of fire consumed her vision.

The Sword's power swept through him, and Itz lar Thrakkon had never felt so alive.

Burn, elf. Burn within, and be born again.

Laressa Solymir, wife to Eolin and thus queen of the Finlorian Empire, stared up at him with a trickle of blood running down her chin. Her eyes had lit up the moment the blade pierced her flesh, calm daze giving way to horrid comprehension. Her life was ended, her true suffering not yet begun.

As it would be for all of them, Thrakkon sneered. He waited for that invisible curtain to cloud his victim's gaze before yanking the Sword free. Its flames retreated, and her broken body lay still. The sweetest kill that he had tasted.

He left her for the Illysp, and went searching for another. The valley yet teemed with them, and his hunger was far from sated. He sensed them fleeing, sensed them huddling, sensed them stiffening as they were hewn down. A night he had dreamed of for centuries. Indeed, he had been yearning for so long, it scarcely seemed real.

His goblins were anywhere and everywhere, though he had kept his giants close at hand. He signaled to them now and set off on Killangrathor's trail, to hunt those the dragon had flushed but failed to kill. Dregs now, compared to their queen, but he would have them all.

For hours, the Illychar hunted and slew and hunted some more. Thrakkon did not bother to count the number that fell before him—those who would soon learn the horror of being entrapped, enslaved forever, as their ancestors had left his kind so long ago. Not half the number he desired, whatever it might be.

Even so, the taste had grown bland long before the dawn came, bringing with it red-tinged clouds and a cleansing rain. While the initial onslaught had been thick and intense, the Illysp lord had become bored with the tedious process of rooting out those individuals who had not perished or fled early on. As satisfying a victory as it had been, he hungered already for a greater challenge.

He dwelled upon that for some time, seated upon a broken stump as he watched Killangrathor rooting at the cave mouth behind the Veil. Mud and boulders fell from the heights, cast aside by the dragon's claws. Every now and then, Killangrathor would worm his head past the cascading waters and into the opening, to roar in hatred or fill the darkened depths with gouts of flame. Better to burn them all, the dragon seemed to think, than allow even one to escape.

Thrakkon would not disagree, but it seemed a poor use of time. There would be no shortage of strays and vagabonds to be hunted down when the larger battles were won and done. Only hounds and beggars chased table scraps when there were full courses yet to be had.

Their objective here had been accomplished. But where could the next feast be found? They had come a long way—too far to be fully satisfied by such a swift and easy massacre. Now that the Finlorians were dead or scattered, what target would be most likely to bring this land to its knees?

He wished he knew more about this Yawacor. He wished Torin were not still able to keep so much of it from him. Surely, by now, his host vessel's former spirit understood the futility of resistance. Why not surrender its remaining treasures and learn to revel in its new power?

The sort of gnawing question Thrakkon had no patience for. A fish did not question why it swam, nor a hawk why it soared. Each made the best of its appetites and abilities as nature intended, and let the rest be determined by its strength.

At last Killangrathor flew down to join him, a dark hulk glistening with water and mud and blood. Their own battle had not yet ended, but Thrakkon had too much to gain yet from his use of the beast to consider bringing that conflict to a head. The dragon seemed to share his dilemma as it settled upon a nearby ridge, glaring openly, leaving Thrakkon but one guess as to what the creature would do were it not so wary of how the Sword itself, so devastating and mercurial, might respond.

When the goblins, too, began to regroup, Thrakkon knew his time for contemplation was ended. He had to keep moving, had to keep them from growing restive. To the south, he decided. That was where Torin had fought his great battle at the edge of the ocean. A bold move, given that city's proximity to those cold gray seas. But he would show no fear. Not now. Not ever.

He only hoped that he would find there a more formidable foe.

He took to his feet. As he did so, his chest clenched sharply, suddenly. The goblins stirred. Killangrathor raised his ugly head. The cramp held as if it might not let go, before passing as all the others. Thrakkon grinned and held the Sword aloft as his minions peered at him expectantly.

"To Neak-Thur," he said, relishing the taste of the name as the agony of drawing it from Torin's memory subsided. "Before our next feast grows cold."

CHAPTER TWENTY-SEVEN

HE CONTINUED TO RIDE IN his dreams.

The enemy surged after him, a shrieking, thunderous press that closed from three sides. The beat of his horse's hooves hammered in his head. He felt the presence of the city wall looming somewhere in the dark, but could not see it. Lar held the line ahead of him, at the tip of the shield wall, but never seemed to draw any closer.

It occurred to him that he might be dead. Though he could not recall his own name, he seemed to remember that the enemy wave had already overwhelmed him once. But if that were so, why did he still ride?

Perhaps that was the true nature of the Abyss, to toil endlessly in the final moments of one's life, repeating forever that last, failed conflict. Gods knew, with the number he had killed—either at the tip of a blade or with the commands of his voice—his soul deserved no greater comfort than those of an eternal hell.

Yet he could still feel the reins in his hand, still taste the dirt in his mouth. Stabs and cuts stung and throbbed. The darkness might mean he was dreaming, but he dared not slow to find out. The reavers were nearly on top of him. He could smell their rancid flesh. Their hands were upon him, cold and clammy, drawing blood with every swipe. He drew breath to scream—

His eyes flew open as he lurched upright, fist clenched. He heard a startled cry. A crash and a clatter of wood upon stone. A splash of warm liquid—his enemy's blood, perhaps, or his own. He gritted his teeth.

His gaze fell not upon an assailant, but upon an attendant, her doe's eyes wide with shock. She held no weapon, but a wet cloth. An upturned bowl lay upon the floor, in a puddle of warm water. More of the same soaked his sheets. He was not armored. He was not even clothed.

He sensed movement from the other direction. A second attendant was dashing from the room even as a robed chamberlain and guardsman entered. They caught the girl, who only turned and gasped.

"My lord," the chamberlain wheezed. "Pray calm, my lord, you are safe."

Corathel, he realized. *My name is Corathel*. He turned back to the attendant in his clutches.

"They come to bathe you, my lord. She means you no harm."

The general released his grip on her pale, skinny arm. "Pray pardon, milord," the girl murmured, scurrying after her companion.

He said nothing, but looked back around to the chamberlain and guardsman, who stared at him through the open curtains of his four-poster bed. The lighting was mercifully dim, though the chamber stank of herbs and potions, salves and bloody bandages, thick incense and trapped candle smoke.

"Is my lord well?" the chamberlain asked.

Corathel blinked. "Water," he croaked.

The chamberlain dismissed the nurses with a reassuring whisper, then turned himself to pour a cup from a flagon beside the general's bed. While Corathel drank, the chamberlain asked the guardsman to close the chamber door and resume his post outside.

"Leave it open," Corathel said. He motioned with the empty cup for a refill, and the chamberlain obliged him.

"Not too much, my lord. You've had naught but spoonfuls for these eight days past."

"Small wonder I thirst," he said, before draining the cup. When he finished, he looked around. "Is this Leaven?"

"The governor's own house, my lord. You were injured. We feared you might not wake."

Corathel ignored the words, his attention drawn by a shuttered window. Through its wood slats, he could still hear the furor that had plagued his dreams—but distant, like the churning rush of the Merrethain River beyond the walls of his boyhood home.

"I'll summon a page," the chamberlain offered, "and send for the healers."

"I stink enough of healing already," Corathel complained. "What I need is some fresh air."

"My lord, I beg you, do not exert yourself so soon. I shall open a window, if you like."

Despite the man's protests, Corathel moved to rise. Shifting his legs, however, filled his head with clouds that nearly stole his vision. The horrors of the Abyss rose up to meet him . . .

"So be it," he agreed, settling back upon his mound of pillows. "But send also for my officers. I want reports."

"As you command, my lord. Rest, now."

The chamberlain rushed to comply with his demands. Corathel felt slightly better with a breeze blowing through the open window, though the light stung his eyes. It was morning yet—the Lark's Hour, perhaps, or the Snipe's. Of which day, he could not guess.

He thought again to haul himself from his feather-stuffed coffin, and so slid his legs—carefully this time—toward the edge. Again the dizziness swelled within, and with it a multitude of throbbing pains. Corathel struck the mattress in frustration, then threw back the sheets to have a look.

Both legs had suffered damage, but the right one . . . Corathel winced at the horrid sight. Amid the many cuts and scrapes were the scars of leeching, the bruises left behind by tourniquets, and an array of foul-smelling poultices. The color was wrong, and when he peeled back the largest of the poultices, laid upon his thigh, he found a foul ichor oozing from the gash beneath.

"What must we do to make the gods take you?" asked a familiar voice. "Salt your soul and baste your flesh in honey?"

Corathel dropped the poultice and looked to the doorway as Jasyn entered the room. "That was fast."

The lieutenant general strode to his bedside, leather boots heavy upon the floor, the pieces of his partial plate clinking. "As it happens, I was on my way to check on you before heading to the wall."

"My lady mother would be pleased, I'm sure." He offered his hand, and Jasyn clasped it in greeting.

"Looks better than it did," the Second General observed, nodding at his exposed leg. "Might be you'll get to keep it after all."

Corathel grimaced at the prospect, though he'd recognized at once the grim possibility. "I think I'd rather part with my head."

"So you've told me in the past, and so I relayed to them butchers in healers' robes. I made it clear, any man who intended to take *your* leg, first had to give me *his*."

The chief general smiled. "In that case, I thank you."

"Don't thank me yet," Jasyn said, dragging up a wooden chair. He sat himself in reverse position, his arms folded atop the chair's low back. "The rest of my news might not be as well to your liking."

"I thought myself dead already. Unless you tell me I'm a reaver, things are not nearly as bad as I'd feared."

"Understood. Even so, your thanks go to Lar. He's the one who scattered that pile of reavers and made sure that you were hauled inside before commanding the wedge to fall in as instructed. Had it been my choice, I might have left you there, just to make sure you learned your lesson on why we generals do not serve as rear guards."

"Says the man who I'll wager was the last to enter the city and raise the bridge."

"Wager won, but then, if I didn't commit the occasional lapse in judgment, the king would have made me chief general long ago."

"Ceilhigh save us. What were our losses?"

"Of your cavalry regiment, nearly half. Of the main body, one in ten. Closer to two in ten, if you count the wounded. Not so terrible, considering."

Corathel would not deny that assessment. The loss of eight hundred men was nothing to scoff at. But had the enemy offered him those tallies at the outset, he would have accepted them gladly. "What of the Fifth and Sixth?" he asked. "Are Dengyn and Bannon here?"

"They are, with their divisions intact. As we suspected, the reavers clogging the egress west through the mountain pass are those who chased Laulk's citizens eastward. Bannon arrived with the savages on his heels."

The chief general felt a stab of recollection. "How about *our* savages? Do we know what became of *them*?"

Jasyn shook his head, confirming Corathel's fears. "They did not appear until the last of the shield wall was pouring into the city. They never would have made it."

"You shut them out?" That dismayed him more so than his own guess, which had them perishing much earlier and farther to the east, when they had engaged the enemy so that *he* might reach the Wormroad.

"*Their* choice, sir. I'd have held the portal for at least a handful of them, had they tried to fight their way through the Illychar ring. But they turned about, as if realizing what must happen should they make the attempt. I know not whether any escaped."

He wasn't sure why he had even dared hope, or why he found Jasyn's news so distressing. They were only Mookla'ayans, after all. Still, when they had given their lives for his . . .

"I'm sorry, sir."

Jasyn was no happier about it than he, judging by the lieutenant general's somber expression. But there was little enough to be done about it now. "It's for the best, I'm sure. A Mookla'ayan within the walls might have been enough to incite a citywide riot."

"May not take that much."

Corathel frowned. "What do you mean?"

"A week ago, the people were hailing us as saviors, praising our courage and cunning. Word in the streets was that the chief general himself had come to liberate them, with reinforcements enough to crush the enemy without."

"And now?"

"They've come to realize what we knew coming in, that our numbers, even when added to those of the Fifth and Sixth, are insufficient to break the siege."

"Can they not merely be grateful that we hold against it?"

Jasyn shook his head, seeming suddenly, uncommonly haggard. "Just two days after our arrival, the reavers we battled at Atharvan caught up to us. Our spotters' estimates vary widely, but the twenty or so we fought there has swelled to more than thirty on soldiers alone. Another horde, somewhat weaker and slower, arrived half a day later, numbering another thirty, by my guess."

Weaker and slower. "Civilians?"

"It looked that way. They moved on, heading south, but I daresay that group has unnerved this populace more than the fifty thousand or so who remain."

Without being told, Corathel understood why. Fighting savages was one thing; fighting one's own was quite another—as he himself had learned. This people had received a glimpse of the fate befallen their nation's brothers and sisters—thousands of innocents just like them. In doing so, they had seen the horrifying truth of what awaited them all.

"They say now that if Atharvan fell, then Leaven has no chance."

"Thirty thousand," Corathel muttered. "It might be ten times that number had His Majesty not evacuated when he did, or had the main body of refugees been overtaken."

"True enough, but scant cause for hope when we ourselves remain trapped, with twenty-eight holding out against fifty."

What more did they expect of him? Corathel wondered. A suicide run like that which got his forces in would never work to get their entire populace out. And even if it did, his soldiers could not begin to protect them all out in the open against so many. The safest place for them was behind these walls, where one man upon the ramparts was worth five or ten below.

"What else are the people saying?" he asked.

Jasyn sighed. "They say we missed our chance, that we should have fled the city, south to Kuuria, before Leaven was surrounded. They say the odds against us will only worsen. Ours was the last aid that will arrive, they fear, and now seems paltry indeed against the enemy's growing reserves."

Corathel snorted. "They seem to have the right of it. Do they offer any solutions?"

"Some say we should surrender, if you can believe it—that if we do so, the reavers may show mercy. Others suggest bribes and parlays, thinking their freedom might be purchased. And there are those who insist that we must fight free now, whatever the cost, if *any* are to survive."

"What, no thoughts of torching the entire city in order to save our souls from possession?" Corathel scoffed.

"The notion is out there," Jasyn admitted, "though it has yet to win any real fervor."

"Have they no faith in us whatsoever?"

Jasyn shrugged. "Some whisper that you perished in battle, and that the rest of us have no notion of what to do in your stead. The governor is a fool, they say, but common folk are quick to puff themselves up with such chatter. My concern is what happens should they decide to act upon it."

"You think they will actually rise against us?"

"Against us, against one another, against their fear . . . I cannot say but that a man has his limits. And where one breaks, others will follow. You've seen it as often as I."

"The governor must reassure them."

"With what, the truth? As you say, they have almost as much of that as we. And should he lie to them, they will learn it, and he will lose their cooperation all the faster."

Corathel's jaw clenched. His wounds throbbed, though no more than his head. Even these most minor exertions had left him faint and exhausted. He did not yet have the strength to deal in any active way with all that Jasyn was telling him.

"We've talked, of course, of lengthening curfew, increasing city patrols, and jailing the most vocal dissenters," the Second General went on. "But our troops are pressed sore as is upon the walls, and many fear that further restrictions upon the people will only fuel their unrest."

Corathel laughed, though it triggered a whole new set of pains. "Leaving us to watch our backs against the very people we have come to protect."

"The bulk of the Queen's subjects still support us," Jasyn assured him. "I don't mean to suggest otherwise. Only to warn that if she falls, she's as likely to do so from within as without."

"Point taken. Have you any other good news for me?"

"Nothing you need fret over as yet. By the pallor of your skin, I've troubled you too long already. And Maltyk is likely wondering by now why I've not arrived to spell his command."

"I would hear *his* views, as well. And those of the other generals."

Jasyn nodded as he rose. "I'll send pages, to make certain they received your chamberlain's message."

"Go, then. Or have you forgotten what ill fortune it is to visit a fellow soldier's sickbed prior to battle?"

His friend grinned, all knavish enthusiasm once more. "It's good to see you awake, sir."

"And you at all," he tendered in reply, then added, "If you must die out there today, try not to stop halfway. This bed's not nearly as comfortable as it may appear."

"Only because you lack the proper company," Jasyn suggested wryly. He gave a wink before taking his leave.

Corathel had much to ponder when the other had gone. His mind rolled back through their briefing, and at each step, he thought of further questions he might have asked, or counsel he might have given. He hoped his injuries had not dulled his wits permanently.

At the same time, much could be assumed, and many of his own thoughts were better left unsaid. He only hoped the city would hold itself together until he was given another chance to contribute to its defense.

The idea brought him full circle, back to Jasyn's initial greeting. Indeed, even he had to marvel at his latest revival, all the more unlikely given his recent string of narrow escapes. It was beginning to seem as though he could not be killed . . . which caused him to wonder if, after this, he had any luck left. Were this a game of dice, he would have gladly quit with gains in hand.

But there was no walking away while the game wore on. So he took heart where he could. Despite all that lay ahead, his plan to come this far had been a success. The majority of his troops had survived a seemingly hopeless incursion. Though mournful of the fallen, he would have the rest at his side to fight another day.

Tortured still by the lingering images and sensations of his ghostly dream-ride, Corathel supposed he might be happier should that day never arrive.

CHAPTER TWENTY-EIGHT

Simmering in the fire of his misery, Torin sought to lose himself in his surroundings. The gray morning enveloped him, skies swollen with the promise of rain. A stiff wind tore at his bloodied jerkin, slicing through its thick fibers to scrape with icy claws upon his numbed skin. He and his fiendish company flew low to the ground, skimming the tops of trees whose damp boughs shuddered in the wake of his passing. The fissured slopes of the Dragontails were a wall to the east. Torin tried to see in them the tranquillity of an immutable earth, to partake of their boundless calm.

Yet nothing could quench the flames devouring him from within. The pain was too great, the shame overwhelming, and the terror seizing his heart refused to let go.

What he had done to his people, reprehensible. To Laressa, beyond forgiveness. What he was about to do . . . anguish.

If only he could shriek forth his sorrow and self-loathing. If only he could confess to the world his remorse and hatred for what he had done, to call down a divine vengeance upon his own head. It had been *his* sword arm that slew Laressa, *his* commands that had spurred the slaughter of her people. He alone had butchered the Finlorians. He alone was responsible for their annihilation. Just as he would soon be responsible for the destruction of all that he loved, all that he had left to treasure in this wretched existence.

He could not believe he had let slip the name of the city toward which he now flew. His hold upon the remaining pieces of his past was weakening. With every diabolical deed, Itz lar Thrakkon's strength over him grew. More and more, Torin felt himself being torn asunder, surrendering to the Illysp's will. But, for all he knew, he still had friends at Neak-Thur, friends he had vowed to set free. Despite his bitter defeat upon its outer fields, the city itself had become a symbol in his mind, representing this land and those inhabitants he had grown to cherish.

If ever he meant to resist and overthrow his Illysp master, now was the time.

He had tried at once to withdraw the city's name, before realizing that it mattered not. Thrakkon already had an idea of where it lay, and a sense of its significance upon these shores. Even if Torin could find a way to influence the Illysp's vile aims, he knew of no other target that might satisfy the creature's hunger.

His hunger.

He'd been given little chance to do so, in any case. Three days, he had expected, for surely Thrakkon meant to wait for the Finlorian dead to rise again before venturing south. Instead, he had found himself mounting Killangrathor before the blood of the slain had dried, winging up and away with his pack of giants and goblins, not one of which had suffered casualty beyond the two lost during the dragon's descent. And how *could* they have? Laressa and her people had not even been armed.

South he had flown, before the sun had finished rising, fighting with every fiber of his twisted essence to alter the truth. *North!* he had screamed into the vast hollow of his mental shell. *East or west. There is nothing at Neak-Thur. Nothing and no one.*

But Thrakkon only gritted his teeth and snarled at the wind. The Illysp did not hear him, or if it did, ignored his pleas. He had to bring the other down, Torin knew, had to bring *himself* down before he could cause any more harm.

The hopelessness of that led him to deny that any of this was happening. As the Finlorian dell bled into the mists behind him, Torin told himself that the elven massacre was but one more episode in a long, perverse nightmare. Men did not rise from their graves. His was an eternal slumber as his body went to worms wherever it had been laid to rest. The remainder was merely a mind's refusal to let go, to accept that the struggle had ended and that nothing more would be achieved.

But even that thought caused him pain. For it meant that Dyanne was truly lost to him. Did she even remember him? he wondered. Did she ever think of him, as he thought perpetually of her? What might she be doing at this very moment?

He might not have to ask, he answered himself, bitter with self-derision, were he there at her side. He could have stayed. Even if she had never grown to care for him, he could have been near her, gazing unnoticed upon her beauty and charm. He need not be suffering this desperate, childish yearning. He'd had only to open his mouth, to say the words, to speak his heart and mind and respect her right to respond in whatever manner she chose. It might have given him closure, at least. It might have allowed his soul a more peaceful rest.

He had been too cautious, fearing that anything he might say would only drive her further from him. Unwilling to accept what he might lose, he had refused to lay wager on that which he might gain.

But what had they truly shared? In all the time he had known her, their conversations would not have filled a day. What was it that he guarded so closely as to paralyze himself against seeking more?

He remembered Traver, a mere rogue who had elicited from the woman more words and smiles in a matter of hours than Torin had in weeks. Even now, he burned at the recollection of seeing her beside him—the attentions she had granted him. Why hadn't he been able to draw her eye in a similar way?

Not that it should matter, then or now. His opportunity had passed. Only his memory of her remained, a parade of images that sparkled and shone like the glimmering facets of a spinning jewel. She was gone, returned south by now to her forest home, to rove the Widowwood among her kinmate and sister and friends. Enjoying freedom and happiness in a region far removed from the chaos and slaughter that he—

He smothered the thought at once, seeking to bury it in the deepest recesses of his shattered mind. For the same part of him that would not let him dwell on the unattainable would suffer no sway from his delusions of death and slumber. Dreams did not offer the shriek of wind, the sting of raindrops, or the smells of earth and sea. That part of him that would not be deceived understood how and why he had been born anew, and knew as well that as long as he bore knowledge of Dyanne's existence, he endangered both her and her fellow Fenwa. Though they represented a beacon in his world of darkness, the only way to spare them, he knew, was to somehow forget them forever.

By then, the smell of the sea was strong enough that he could taste it. They continued to skirt the mountains, which huddled tight in their eternal council, hunched backs and snow-capped shoulders turned against the world. An intruding fog pressed them from the west, shrouding the land below in swirls of spun cotton. Torin hoped it would be enough to hide their destination from view.

But fell winds had other ideas. Driving from the west, they chased the fog and trapped it against the mountain foothills, there to cower in caves and crevasses and hollows. A black rain began to fall from churning gray clouds, forming beaded curtains against the horizon, but serving to further dissolve the fog below. Whitecaps roiled against a stony coastline, flinging spray toward sandswept fields of sword grass beyond. With the way the lines of mountain and sea were converging . . .

Thrakkon must have been thinking the same, for Torin's gaze traced those lines south until it snagged upon a shadowy gray hulk that tumbled like a rockslide out of the mountains, clear to the ocean shore. But no rockslide stood so straight and tall and narrow, uniform from foot to base. Tiny shadows moved upon it and in a line underneath, like ants scurrying across a bleached piece of driftwood. And there again, just beyond, nestled in a southerly line upon the Dragontails' western face, a pile of the same. Twigs and branches, loosely stacked, aswarm with ants and the tiny sparks of their watch fires.

Only, ants did not build watch fires.

The realization pierced him within. He wasn't ready. He hadn't yet—

Neak-Thur.

Somehow, the long-anticipated sight caught him unawares, stirring memories both fond and foul. It had been here that he had traveled with Dyanne and Holly, here that he had battled alongside General Chamaar, Gilden, Arn, Bardik, Jaik, and so many others—battlefield comrades left to rot in Lorre's clutches. It had been within the dungeons of Neak-Thur that he had met and been misled by Saena, and in the halls above where he had finally been charged by her overlord to complete the hunt that had brought him to these shores. He had left knowing that within these walls were more scores to be settled than he could count—resolutions set aside for the sake of his greater quest. He had sworn then to return, and return he had.

To destroy it all.

In the distance, Torin saw a flash amid the midday clouds, followed swiftly by a rumble of thunder. *Strike me!* he thought, pleading. Let a stream of lightning serve as his chariot to the Abyss. But Killangrathor only hissed and beat his wings, while Torin's own lips drew back in a predatory smile, the cruel sentiments of his Illysp master shining through to smother his own.

How weak he had become! His tortured essence thrashed and screamed and shook, overcome with grief and guilt and helpless, agonizing frustration. Atharvan, Aefengaard, and now Neak-Thur. How could he put a stop to the slaughter when he could not even control the expressions of his face?

Killangrathor's speed quickened in anticipation, and the first cries of alarm rang out from the doomed city. The clangor of bells and the moan of horns resounded over the restless groan of the sea. Torin's gaze fixed upon that slate-gray expanse of wind and waves, as if expecting it to rear up and swallow him whole. Would that it might, he thought—even if it meant taking half the land with him. Alas, though the ocean heaved against the jagged shore, shimmering dully in the light of a cloud-choked sun, the iron rocks held it at bay.

He turned, then, as a missile whistled past. Giant spears, he realized, launched from ballistae mounted atop the Bastion. The massive bulwark bristled with these and other armaments, its sole purpose to defend the Southland against assailants from the north. For a moment, Torin took heart, thinking that Thrakkon and his minions would not find these soldiers such easy prey.

Below, however, the ants were already scattering. A line of travelers, Torin realized, upon the highway. Killangrathor veered low enough that Torin heard their screams over the gale of his own swift passage. With a tail whip, the dragon sent wagons and carts and bodies sailing, like filling the air with a shovelful of sand.

Torin felt himself grin, then urge the dragon up again. Another volley of spears came at them, but Killangrathor beat his wings to swat the missiles away. While those upon the ground raced for what cover they could find, soldiers upon the battlements scrambled into and around one another in a sudden flurry. Some fled while others armed themselves. Some continued to ring the alarm while others could only gape in horror. All, above and below, was chaos and confusion.

Amid a continuing chorus of screams, Killangrathor crashed feetfirst atop the yawning gatehouse, raking with claws still caked in elven blood. Soldiers scurried for cover, but found none, as the dragon plowed through ranks of men and limestone bunkers alike. Merlons shattered and crumbled, while bodies and blocks and mortar tumbled to the earth in broken chunks and ragged pieces. Killangrathor's feet bit deep into the edge of the rampart, carving gouges wherever claw met stone. His wings spread wide, and his roar mocked the heavens' feeble thunder. A lightning strike unleashed by his tail opened a gaping cleft in the battlement's surface, and caused a phalanx of swordsmen to vanish.

The tremors of the attack swept the length of the Bastion, clear to where it connected with the meandering curtain wall of Neak-Thur itself. Through eyes no longer his, Torin saw upon that mountainside the sprawling, randomly constructed buildings of the city proper, and but a few of the untold number of inhabitants jostling madly within. Carcasses all, he reflected, set to lie crushed amid mounds of rubble upon the next fogswept dawn.

Torin would have *shut* his eyes, had he been able, though doing so would not have saved him from the screams—cries that resonated with his own horror and denial. A powerful wind gained strength from the south, bearing with it a thickening rainfall. Dark clouds hung brooding over the city, though a break above the Bastion allowed the sun to shine clear and bright, momentarily, over the carnage below. In the midst of these meaningless sensations, battered by a tempest of emotions, Torin, lord of the Illysp, sat helplessly, drowning in the fury of it all.

ANNLEIA GRIPPED THE STONE SILL with a white-knuckled grip. The glass she peered through was streaked with rain and bowed by wind, clouded with salt stains and rimmed with algae. But the image it showed her was clear enough. Not in her darkest fears had she imagined this. Below and to the west, where the Bastion cut its line toward the sea, her grandfather's patrolmen were being swatted like flies by a beast few believed could exist. Such power, she marveled. Such magnificence. For a creature of such immensity and strength to move as it did . . . To tear through stone as if it were sand, while possessed of such supple grace and devastating swiftness . . .

Saena, standing agape beside her, gave a pained squeak and covered her mouth as a clutch of charging soldiers went flying, flung skyward like debris at the edge of a tornado. The beast roared, and their window shook, more than a mile removed. The very stones of the citadel seemed to tremble beneath their feet. Horns blared, bells tolled, bodies shrieked and pointed and raced panic-stricken through the streets. Already, soldiers were marshaling, the first waves forming up on the city walls and before its gates. And all Annleia could do was stand there at her window, mesmerized by the dragon's fluid movements and serpentlike reflexes, a horror black and dreadful and awesome and majestic and undeniably beautiful . . .

Nor was it alone, she realized abruptly. Upon its back, attached like growths to its spines, were riders, dark and tiny and unknowable. Save one.

"Come," she managed. The voice sounded strange and distant, as though it belonged to someone else. "Take me to my grandfather."

Her companion, who had been speaking so readily mere moments ago, did not respond. Annleia had to turn her own back to the window, blocking the other's view and staring her in the face, before Saena so much as blinked.

"My grandfather," she insisted again, quietly.

Saena nodded.

Her chamberlain sputtered a protest, but they brushed him aside. The corridor was much like the streets outside, with runners and pages and officers and servants dashing in either direction. Saena hesitated, but Annleia pushed her out into the flow, where she finally seemed to remember herself. They swam upstream at first, against the thickest of the currents. Her chamberlain followed at her heels, begging that they remain in her suite until His Lordship called for her. Annleia ignored him.

Lorre was not in his map room, where Saena claimed to have left him before setting forth to answer Annleia's summons. The troll sentry warding the chamber only stared at them blankly, but a passing runner claimed to have seen His Lordship heading down the east stair, toward the armory.

Saena led them in that direction, though they found themselves pinched in the narrow, winding well amid a crush of others heading to or from that castle region. While squeezing her way downward and trying not to fall, Annleia prayed that she was not too late, wishing now that she had told her grandfather more of what she knew—and needed—while she'd had the chance.

They found him with his back to the doorway in one of the lower war rooms, surrounded by a pack of his highest-ranking officers. Their muster around the great oaken table broke as Saena entered, and once more Annleia and her guide were forced to writhe past a wave of mail-clad bodies. Amid the press, she saw Dyanne and Holly, they who had been the first to share what they knew of Torin's journey to Aefengaard, and who had bade her speak with Saena—who had remained with Torin when they had left him—to learn even more. The Nymphs nodded at her and Saena on their way out.

Lorre himself remained, sharing a last-minute word with one of his generals while a giant fitted him with a rippled backplate and helped him buckle it in place.

The general looked at her, a clean-shaven lad, all bulging muscles and youthful confidence. They had not yet been formally introduced, and though she'd heard many a maid whisper his name, she could not seem to recall it just now. He offered her a grim smile regardless.

Lorre turned and caught sight of her. His frown deepened. "You have your orders," he told the general. "Any questions?"

"None, sir." The warrior saluted. "It will be done as you say." He bowed to the women as he took his leave.

"You just missed the latest report from my spotters," Lorre said, shifting in his cuirass as he adjusted its straps. "Our dragon bears riders."

"It's him, isn't it." Her tone was without question.

"You knew he was coming here."

"I had cause to suspect."

Lorre's seamed face darkened. "I'll not ask how."

He thinks me a witch, she realized. *A caster of charms and spells, not to be trusted.*

The warlord looked to his giant. "My blade."

"You cannot kill him," Annleia blurted. "You *must* not, I mean."

"I spared him once already," Lorre snapped. "If this is how he repays me, I'll not do so again."

"He is Illychar. He must not simply be slain. If I am not allowed to poison—"

"I know not what elven curses you came here to weave, but I want no further part of their magics and their misdeeds." With his sword in place, the warlord pulled on his studded leather gauntlets. "Or was it not they who unearthed this abomination to begin with?"

Annleia kept her tone and gaze steady. "Do as you will with the dragon— as you *can*. But if you would truly purge your lands of this *elven* scourge, you and your men must leave Torin to me."

"Torin?" Saena gasped, as if just now realizing who they spoke of.

Lorre picked up his helmet and tucked it beneath an arm. "You are not my captive," he reminded her, turning heel to the war room and setting off to join the sally. Though crowded by his retinue of giants, she and Saena fell in quickly alongside, like minnows chasing sharks down the narrow hall. "If you would deal with him before I do," the overlord added gravely, "then I suggest you do what you can to reach him first."

CHAPTER TWENTY-NINE

Killangrathor stalked the Bastion, leaving ruin in his wake. Bodies lay strewn amid a wreckage of broken merlons, shattered weapons, and mangled siege engines. Great blocks of granite and limestone cracked beneath the dragon's scarred feet. To one side, a soldier crawled toward the battlement's edge, chasing the lower half of his torso. When a brush from the dragon's tail sent the man's legs over the edge, the soldier stopped, peering helplessly at his mutilated body's weird, gruesome descent.

From atop the dragon's back, Itz lar Thrakkon savored the smell of carnage around him: the stench of bowels and brains and bloody meat being exposed to the salty air. Moans and screams sang in his ears, while the rains pattered, the winds shrilled, and the sea groaned. The goblins behind him screeched their approval, painted with dust and grime, speckled with shreds of flesh and splinters of debris. The battle-lust was upon them, and the day's slaughter had only just begun.

Ahead lay the city itself, a walled hive of insects waiting to be crushed. A handful of soldiers stood before the gatehouse at the intersection of Bastion and city wall, clinging to their toothpick weapons with wide eyes and petrified muscles. Too stubborn to run, perhaps, or too frightened. It mattered not which, Thrakkon reflected, as Killangrathor bore down upon them.

Before they reached that tiny tower, a bray of horns turned their attention to the south. From the city's arched gateway streamed a black procession of troops, thick as a locust swarm. Killangrathor looked upon them and snarled. A bold counter meant to draw their attention from the city itself, Thrakkon decided. These were undoubtedly Lorre's armies, and Lorre, as he recalled, was a crafty one. Perhaps they should ignore this bit of bait.

Yet he sensed the dragon's hunger as it continued to glare upon that growing horde, the tower ahead all but forgotten. The beast could scarce refuse such an audacious challenge. Thrakkon smirked at the dragon's fury, and at his own caution. No ruse or strategy would help the warlord this day. Let the city stand for now. Walls could not turn and flee.

He squeezed his knees against the ridge of the dragon's back and jerked them in a southerly direction, as if prodding a horse rather than a creature some thirty times its size. But Killangrathor was ever responsive, and did not need to be urged twice. His tail swept toward the gatehouse as he spun, swatting those assembled and tearing a low gash in its stone face. With a bone-rattling scream, he then leapt from the ravaged Bastion and into the air, wings spreading to catch the wind.

. . .

ANNLEIA JUMPED WHEN THE HOLE opened in the stone wall before her. The troops massed ahead of her flinched as well, many crying out in shock as the tip of the dragon's tail ripped through like a bolt of black lightning. Even their general recoiled, ducking reflexively behind his massive shield as debris from the rift rolled and clattered around him.

"Steady!" he shouted.

She could feel the weight of the dragon's movements beyond the gate. Claws scraped, stones split, and when the creature roared, the wall shook and the floor shuddered. Annleia closed her eyes, then forced them open again, clutching a spear in one hand and her wellstone in the other, taking comfort as its edges dug into her flesh.

With a final crunching, grinding sound, the beast was gone, its weight and shadow no longer there. A call bellowed down from the watchtower. "Clear!"

The general grimaced at his troops. "Sound the sortie." Then, to the tower, he yelled, "Raise the gate!"

An outer portcullis lifted, the inner doors unbarred and flung back. The general was the first through the breach. Gilden, his men had called him, and the name rang in Annleia's memory as that uttered by all those heartsick maidens. His men followed dutifully, bristling in their blades and armor. For a moment, Annleia forgot how to move, weighed down by her borrowed mail and helm, feet rooted by her fear.

Then she was being pressed from behind, and that impetus carried her forward. Outside, she was greeted by clouds of grit and a wind-driven rain. Her stomach churned at the devastation, at a battlement littered with bloody, broken rubble. Most of those who had survived the dragon's initial assault did so groping and writhing, begging their brothers for help or the gods for mercy. Here a man lay with mashed limb, there another with entrails leaking from his sides. Farther west, toward the sea, the damage only grew worse.

She moved toward the parapet, dodging bits of wreckage as she stepped out of line, eyes searching. The dragon was winging south, a low-flying thunderhead amid rain and mist. An army awaited it upon the plains, sallied forth from the city's main gate. Madness, she thought, as she listened to the anguished cries all around her. Her grandfather couldn't hope to—

A barrage of missiles began streaming out from the city wall and its outermost ward—launched by catapult and ballista and mangonel. Just like that, the dragon was under heavy attack as it flew through a hail of boulders and spears and buckets of burning pitch. Most missed their mark, sailing high or low or wide. The rest pelted the beast's hide, but did little damage that she could see. A boulder smashed against its face, drawing an angry hiss, but the creature flew on, undeterred.

With wings spread wide, the dragon fell shrieking upon her grandfather's host, legs leading like the talons of an eagle. Already, that host was scattering, splitting down the center and bleeding away at the edges. The terror of those soldiers was palpable. Their screams were like needles in Annleia's ears, and twisted in her stomach like bits of shattered glass. Orcs, she realized, and shivered with pity.

The dragon roared in turn, frustrated by their cowardice, fighting to catch them all as they sheared off in groups before scrambling in all directions. A gout of flame lit the sky, coloring it fierce shades of yellow and orange. For a moment, rains appeared as fire and clouds as coals, flickering down upon the frantic masses. *Run!* Annleia urged silently. *Run!*

A horn blew at her feet, loud enough to near startle her over the edge. The last of Gilden's men were racing down the steps and ramps along the Bastion's southern face—those that hadn't been damaged beyond use. Lord Commander Bardik had led a similar sortie through the Bastion's lower hall, to emerge now from the central gate. Together, both regiments were forming up, their backs against the towering wall. No more than a thousand in number, yet calling the dragon on.

The monster had heard their summons, and had whipped around to face them across that league-long stretch of coastal plain. The swarm of orcs had already been routed. Annleia doubted now that they could have been anything but a diversion—a feint used to lure the enemy along that strafing line of siege engines. Perhaps this company she had quietly fallen in with meant to do the same. Doubtless, her grandfather was testing the creature's strength and aims, buying time for the bulk of his army to mobilize. She wondered if he'd been watching as she had, and seen the same results. She wondered if he had any notion at all of how to even slow the beast.

Hissing contemptuously at the fleeing orcs, the dragon took again to the skies. For a moment, Annleia thought it meant to fly the same course, and weather the same assault it had before. But as the first missiles flew, the creature veered into the teeth of that storm, skimming low upon the curtain wall to shatter stone, smash siege engines, and mutilate the bodies of those who operated them. A sustained flameburst turned a line of catapults into giant candles, leaving men to wail beneath drippings of cinder and molten iron.

A second battery took aim. Before the dragon reached them, all six fired at blank range. This time, the beast actually seemed staggered by the barrage.

It recovered much faster than the soldiers manning the catapults could reload.

Grinding its jaws, the dragon scattered the nearby soldiers with a flogging display that tipped two of the massive catapults on their sides. It grasped a third with its feet and hoisted it over a courtyard teeming with soldiers. Those beneath its shadow scurried for cover, trampling one another in an effort to clear a path. Annleia winced as the engine crashed among them, crushing scores, and reducing the catapult itself to splinters.

Then the monster broke free, to take aim at the heart of their little northern phalanx. Now was her chance. General Gilden and his men—they had nowhere to run. To the east lay the city wall; to the west, the reefs of the sea. They might spread themselves upon the plain, but the dragon would only fly circles until it had killed them all. If she did nothing to help them, their end would come soon.

But what power was she to use? She could not imagine any she might draw upon that would do more than tickle that dragon's flesh. She'd seen what little use the powerful siege engines had been. Were she able to harness the strength of a hundred swords all at once, would she even be able to scratch it?

A rumble of thunder turned her gaze to the heavens, where lightning flashes danced amid the clouds. Perhaps she could summon a bolt to—

Too late, she thought, as the dragon finished its hawklike descent, roaring in challenge. Rather than clear its path, the host led by Gilden and Bardik surged ahead to meet it. Crouched at the edge of the parapet, Annleia could only gape as the two collided, watching knots of men fade to screams beneath the creature's bulk. She expected it to take flight after that, and for a moment, it reared up as if to do so. But this company refused to run, its members charging the beast from all sides.

Amid a sea of blades, the dragon hunkered down and took up the attack.

The slaughter was more terrible than she had feared, beyond anything she might have envisioned. Men's armor became as silk and lace, for all the good it did them, their heavy shields like parchment. With tooth and claw and horn and tail, the dragon ripped through their scrambling ranks or sent them flying like dandelion spores. If a man thought to evade an attack, he was too late. Bodies were trampled, hewn, hurled aside. Their mashed remains filled the craters of the dragon's footprints, or remained pinned like ornaments upon its horns, teeth, and claws. There was no time for the beast to preen itself, for there were too many enemies before it, too many more to be slain.

When she thought she might retch, Annleia looked away, her gaze trailing to the south. There, from the arched mouth of the city, yet another army was sallying forth. She saw horses this time, and men so tall they could only be giants. Behind this vanguard came the hulking shapes of catapults twice the size of those now burning along the city's inner rim. The heart of her grandfather's force, she supposed. Gilden's foray was little more than another distraction, as she'd feared, allowing Lorre the time he needed to mass his own troops. A fine job the warlord had done in tempting the dragon back and forth across the field, but the games were done, and no force he might muster could possibly make a difference.

Another thunderclap tugged at her gaze, but she ignored the temptation. Any lightning she summoned now would strike Lorre's soldiers as well. And it was far more likely to harm *them* than the dragon, to say nothing of the man she had come to claim.

She looked for him, then, having all but forgotten her purpose in even standing there at the edge of that maelstrom. The dragon moved quickly, snapping left and right with the swiftness of a striking serpent. She could not count the number of those strapped to its spines, let alone examine their faces for one that matched Torin's description. She looked only for the Sword of

Asahiel, for the crimson glow attributed to it in legends. If Torin wielded it, surely he would have drawn it by now.

But she did not spy it, only the frenzied thrashings of an invincible beast beset by a diminishing cloud of gnats. It left her to question Lorre's lookouts, Necanicum's strange prophecy, and her own decision to be here. It left her to wonder at the madness of a world fast slipping away.

Upon the wall she fought, and beyond it she waited, when her power was filled . . .

But how? If she lacked the power to stop the dragon, how was she to drive Torin beyond the wall? And if she *did* find the strength to defeat the beast, what power would she possibly have left?

The cries of battle matched the tempest in her head. *Two fields he planted.* Had her own people already fallen? Rain lashed her cheeks, flooding her eyes like tears. The thousand or so below had been reduced by half, yet still they pressed on, clambering over the deadfall of their comrades, shouting as if to give themselves strength. Why could she not find her own?

A hand clutched at her, so sudden and so tight that she cried out and dropped her spear. An Illychar, surely, come to put an end to her misery.

It wasn't. Only a wounded man. One of those crawling about in front of the gatehouse from which she had emerged, at the junction of Bastion and city wall.

"Help me," he pleaded.

But he was beyond it; she sensed that at a glance, even before she realized that the severed leg he thrust at her was his own. Were it not for the tourniquet about his stump, he would already be dead. Even so, he was dizzy with blood loss, his eyes already glazed. The greatest mercy would be to draw from him what small life remained, to absorb his last strength and apply it toward the greater cause.

Yet if the hundreds who had already perished had been unable to thwart the beast, what would a few beats of this dying man's heart win them now?

Then it struck her, that which she must do—that which she must *attempt*. For it seemed certain to fail. She couldn't possibly draw enough to make a difference. If she *could*, trying to contain that power would likely destroy her. And yet, it was the only course that made sense.

She bent to the soldier, but found him unmoving, staring at her from beneath a bloody brow. She closed his eyes with a brush of her hand before standing tall. Others were moving upon the battlement, picking through the rubble for those who might be saved. One who was dragging a fellow soldier called to her for assistance, but she pretended not to notice. There wasn't time. The dragon was nearly finished here. She had to do her part before it flew away once more to assail her grandfather's throng to the south.

She scrambled toward the gatehouse, stumbling over loose chunks of rock and half-buried soldiers painted white with dust. The ladder to the tower was inside. She climbed quickly, the rungs slippery beneath her sweating palms.

Her mail felt like an apron made of sandbags, weighing heavy against her. Her thick boots felt just as awkward. Twice, in her haste, a foot slipped out from under her. Somehow, she managed to hang on.

The watchmen above were gone—whether fled or gone down to join the battle, she couldn't say. A blessing in either case, since she hadn't the words to explain.

Alone atop the tower, she tossed aside her helm, grateful for the breezes that brushed her face. The rains seemed to be slackening, but the sky flashed, and thunder boomed. It was the lightning she needed. Not to ignite or destroy, but as a conduit, to spark and conduct the transfer she required.

The dragon continued to battle below, surrounded by the sprawled, twisted shapes of its victims. Making note of its position, Annleia palmed her wellstone and reached both hands toward the volatile heavens, searching anxiously for the next flash.

ITZ LAR THRAKKON ROCKED AND twisted in his makeshift harness, wrenched fore and aft and from side to side by the sharp, sudden movements of his mount. Whip, spin, lash—Killangrathor's frenzy rolled through him like colliding waves. The straps that held him to the beast's spine chafed and pinched, slicing at the skin beneath his jerkin. But for every scrape he suffered, half a dozen of his enemies were bludgeoned or torn or flung wide, never to rise again.

Save as Illychar.

So he grimaced against all discomforts, relishing the pain. One hand clenched the leather loop in front of him for balance. The other gripped the hilt of the Sword—sheathed at his side—keeping him flush with energy and awareness, attuned to any imminent danger. He'd had to duck a spear or two when flying south along the city wall, and now and then a throwing axe would go spinning past his head. But by and large, the threat thus far had been rather one-sided. Killangrathor stood taller than the height of the Bastion, and his wide, shifting bulk made for a mighty shield. The ants below would have to come crawling up the dragon's body before they could hope to do its riders any real harm.

Scant chance of that, though the insects seemed determined enough to try. As the number of carcasses grew, so too did Thrakkon's admiration for the reckless fury of these foes. They could not hope to slay the beast; any one-eyed fool could see that. Yet even after watching wave upon wave of their comrades fall, the next would come roaring in. Almost Illysp-like, he marveled, fearless and savage and unrelenting. Not just *willing* to die, but *eager* to test themselves according to nature's rules of strength. If deserving, they would survive. If not . . .

Their bodies continued to pile and sprawl, littering the ground about Killangrathor's clawed feet. Beneath those feet and between the dragon's toes, the earth had become an ooze of mud and blood and grass and sand, thickened by a pulp of iron and steel and leather and bone. Farther out, the untrampled dead lay upon one another in twitching heaps, with the maimed and the battered writhing among them. Those whose wounds appeared less grievous hunched or crawled in search of new weapons, as if to rejoin the fight. A fine army they would make, when born anew.

Regrettable, in a sense. For Thrakkon could easily imagine how much greater the devastation might be were Killangrathor to forgo the preservation of coils and the scraps thereof for his fellow Illysp. Loosen the dragon's reins, and it might turn all the world into a bloody, smoking slough.

The horns blew yet again, another call from the south. Thrakkon and Killangrathor looked together, ignoring for a moment the feeble buffeting carried on by the scores around them—scores that a short time ago had been hundreds. At last, it appeared the baiting and posturing was finished. The force arrayed just outside Neak-Thur's curving entrance corridor dwarfed the orc horde dumped forth earlier. Tens of thousands they were, arranged in lines and columns and wedges, wheeling along more of their heavy weaponry besides. Thrakkon's stagnant blood stirred in anticipation. If those preparing now fought anything like these had . . .

Killangrathor snarled, jaws dripping with the blood of his victims. Thrakkon smiled, envisioning already the scale of slaughter to come. Perhaps he would even find a chance to spill some of their blood himself.

He sensed the lightning only an instant before it struck—scarcely enough time to turn and cringe as it shot toward him in a scintillating burst. It hit a nearby gatehouse first, white hot, before splintering onward. The reflected energy appeared blue in color, and danced momentarily between dragon and tower with a sharp, blinding crackle. It seemed to focus on Killangrathor's face, his eyes, but before Thrakkon could be sure, the bolt retreated, so fast as to riddle the mind.

Killangrathor snorted and shook his massive head, flinging rain and blood from his tufts of fur. The movement caused the beast to buckle, and, for a moment, Thrakkon feared it might have been injured. He saw no smoke, but the light had left a giant flare in the middle of his vision, so he wasn't yet seeing much of anything. Still, he should have been able to smell it: the singeing of hair, the charring of flesh. On both counts, the dragon and its riders were unscathed.

He looked to the gatehouse, blinking irritably. Around the edges of his blind spot, there was naught but an empty barbican. Killangrathor, however, continued to droop and sway like a dazed sot. *Something* had happened, and it didn't bode well.

Their enemies seemed to sense it. Most had fallen back, blinded like he by the strange energy blast, else kneeling in exhaustion. Some looked to the skies, as if wary of further lightning strikes. But the rest resumed their maddened press, emboldened by the dragon's queer behavior.

Fools.

As their blades hacked and pricked at him, Killangrathor righted himself. His roar seemed a rasping thing, his movements stiff and sluggish compared to what they had been moments ago. But he remained a dragon, and Illychar at that. The lightning had stunned him, surely, yet he would not be stopped.

Thrakkon drew the Sword. A risk, should he lose it to one of Killangrathor's sudden twists or jerks—and of little use against Lorre's troops while mounted so high above their heads. But perhaps it would spur the dragon from its stupor. Perhaps it would remind his enemies of the uselessness of their efforts.

Almost at once, his returning sight focused on a familiar figure slipping near. The man was thickly muscled beneath his partial armor of black leather and sewn rings, though he moved with the grace and agility of one half his size. Bulging legs carried him deftly over a slick mound of corpses that blocked his path. He bore a battered shield and a heavy broadsword spattered here and there with blood—that of his comrades, or his own. A thick sheen of it covered his cheek and one of the shaved sides of his head.

Gilden, Thrakkon recalled. The memory caused him no pain, for he had uncovered it some time ago. Torin had admired this one, this "Lancer," as he'd been known. A formidable warrior with whom Torin had battled *against* Lord Lorre, here now to throw away his life in the warlord's service.

Thrakkon kept waiting for the dragon to turn, to catch the traitorous soldier in his approach. An errant tail whip caused him to duck, but its spikes missed his head. A swipe followed that took out a group upon Lancer's flank, but Lancer himself popped back up from behind a mound of dead. The dragon had turned its back to him by then, to deal with a press from the other side.

Lancer came bounding forward, his weapons gripped firmly. Thrakkon sought the man's eyes. They gleamed boldly even now, in the face of imminent death. He slipped at the last moment, but that misstep only saved him from a vicious wing slap. By the time he righted himself, he stood unnoticed by the heavily occupied Killangrathor, with a clear opportunity to strike.

Thrakkon grinned. *What now, traitor?*

Lancer didn't hesitate, settling quickly for the nearest target. With fully summoned force and fury, his blade chopped down upon the dragon's smallest toe.

And broke it.

EVEN FROM ATOP THE GATEHOUSE, amid the wail of wind, the clangor of arms, the huff and snarl of man and beast, Annleia heard the crack. She'd been watching Gilden's approach through a wide crenel, down on one knee as she fought to contain the forces roiling through her. For an instant, she felt certain it was his blade that had shattered.

The dragon's bellow told her otherwise—a sudden trumpeting of shock and dismay. She felt a jolt from her wellstone at the same time. Gilden appeared as stunned as any by the damage he had inflicted. As the dragon whipped its head around to find him, he managed to raise his shield, only a heartbeat before a backhanded swipe sent him hurtling. He flew twenty paces, stopping when his back crunched against the wall of the Bastion. Dead or unconscious, he slid down to lie at its base in a rumpled heap.

With renewed vigor, the warrior's comrades took up the fight, howling their bestial cries. The dragon roared, though it seemed almost a whine. A broken toe. It amounted to no more than a scratch. But the creature should never have suffered even that much. To have proven vulnerable . . .

Annleia hunched over her wellstone. Her head swam, and her stomach turned. The crystal itself pulsed, searing her palm like hot iron. Her eyes watered at the strain. She hoped she was right. She *had* to be right. For she saw now the Sword, drawn by the lead rider, who was lashed to a spine at the base of the dragon's nape. Torin, she presumed. Whoever, the Sword was sure to protect him against any magical assault. Had she considered that from the first, she might have found her answer much sooner, before so many had to die.

Grimacing, she pushed against the parapet. She swooned when she reached her feet, but managed to hold steady. Some of the dizziness was passing. Still, she found it difficult to focus. *Upon the wall she fought, and beyond it she waited* . . . Beyond. But which direction? She had come from the north, as had Torin, she believed—she feared. Yet the battle was *south* of the wall. Which was "beyond"?

An absurd little detail, its vagueness easily overlooked amid all else she'd been called upon to remember. And yet the rest would mean nothing if she guessed wrong.

From the south, a fresh thunder began to build. Lorre's army had started its charge, a great black stain creeping across the battlefield. A hypnotic procession, so great and vast and terrible, like a giant flow of mud and boulders grinding down a mountain's slope. She only hoped it had the strength to do what was required.

In that moment, she made her decision. Turning her back to the carnage below, she stumbled toward the gatehouse ladder. Her head spun. The stones rolled like waves beneath her feet. The power begged its release, threatening to tear her apart. Annleia ignored its pleas, bit down against its demands, and prayed for sufficient strength of her own.

THRAKKON LOOKED UP AT THEIR frenzied approach: a screaming horde of humans, giants, trolls. A vast and formidable army, bearing down upon him.

The Boundless One might have laughed.

But his smile was no more, burned away by a rising fury. The enemy at Killangrathor's feet had been reduced to dregs, yet still refused to be brushed aside. No explanation he could muster would account for how Gilden had wounded his prized mount—not given a thousand such strokes. That single blow had rattled Thrakkon's confidence, and given his foes a false sense of hope.

He was tired of their insolence, had grown bored of their pathetic defiance. The time had come to crush that undue faith, once and for all.

Killangrathor must have thought the same. With a final snap and snarl, the dragon lurched forward, leaving behind the decimated band at the wall's edge. Its first few steps were clumsy, staggering things. It beat its wings as if to rise, but they flapped and dragged strengthlessly, as awkward as those of a hatchling. Killangrathor roared in frustration.

But he did not let it stop him. Loping along on his broken toe, wings lifting and lolling uselessly at his side, he rumbled onward. Sodden earth churned beneath his claws, turning up ash from the pyres of those slain upon this field weeks ago. A mounted vanguard drew near, their leather and iron and steel as wet and dark as the morning storm clouds now beginning to break apart overhead.

The scale and measure of Lorre's forces seemed to grow as they approached. While scanning their ranks, Thrakkon wondered fleetingly if he should have waited at Aefengaard until his own had been swelled by the Finlorian dead. He had considered it, but their vast numbers would be traveling afoot—and only *after* their three-day incubation. Journeying alongside them would have slowed his conquest and allowed advance warning of his impending arrival.

He snarled the doubt away before it could fester, and tightened his grip upon the Sword. Boulders were raining from above, a cover volley launched by the mammoth engines to the south. Killangrathor grunted at those few missiles that found their target. One turned a tailward goblin to splatter and snapped the small spine to which it was strapped. When that happened, the dragon let loose a yowl.

Bolstered by the creature's pain, the enemy closed with a screaming, sprinting flourish.

Killangrathor plowed headlong through the center of their wedge, hissing at those who veered to either side. With arms spread and wings outstretched, he cut a wide swath, shedding men of their steeds and filling the air with mashed and broken bits of both. Lances shattered or fell aside or missed their mark as those who wielded them lost their final joust. Others actually found a home in the dragon's skin, to dangle from its thick hide like splinters.

The shrieks of his foes were splinters in Thrakkon's ears, though he relished every one of them. Too many had escaped to either flank; Thrakkon could not decide if it was the riders or the horses themselves that had refused to engage.

Most were reining up and wheeling about, as if to harry from the rear. Killangrathor let them go, continuing on until he met the foremost waves of foot soldiers in a scraping, grinding clash. Blades and cudgels hacked at him as he tore southward, a prow through tempest seas. Blood and weapons and bodies filled the air like spray and foam. Thrakkon tasted it upon his lips, and felt invigorated.

Again, however, the enemy offered little true resistance, splitting toward the flanks rather than holding strong down the center. Understandable, given Killangrathor's monstrosity. Ten thousand or a hundred thousand, it made no matter. But based on the fight at the wall, Lorre's troops were too bloody stubborn to realize that. Thrakkon had expected more of a fight.

He looked back, though with the Sword in hand, he knew already what he would find. Sure enough, the parted waters were flowing in at all angles. The dead filled his wake like pieces of driftwood, yet did little to block the closing tide. Lorre had commanded them to surround the beast. They thought to bury it beneath their frenetic press.

A pair of siege towers loomed ahead, stacked one behind the other. Killangrathor lowered himself and quickened his pace. The trolls who hauled the heavy carts let go of the ropes and push handles and stood their ground, their shoulder-squeezed faces expressionless. Thrakkon searched the heights for bowmen or hurlers, but found them unmanned. No trap, he decided. Merely another test of strength.

Amid a shower of splinters from the first, the second tower toppled to the moist earth.

But when Killangrathor emerged from the wreckage, he stumbled and slowed, tangled by ropes and beams and twisted bands of iron. The dragon kicked and thrashed and carried on, but the collision had clearly exacted yet another toll. Once invincible, the creature continued to show signs of wear.

The enemy crowded round, swarming like vermin, raking and scrabbling with their little teeth and claws. Incensed and bewildered, Killangrathor lashed back. A dozen here. A score there. He swept them aside, crushed their fragile shells, made them ooze and squirt and squeal in sharp-toned agony.

Still they came, hurling weapons, battle cries, and their own bodies in spectacular defiance. As one after another flung himself at the beast, only to be trampled, gouged, or thrown aside, Thrakkon marveled anew at their collective madness. How had Lorre fostered such courage and confidence within this mixed band of mortal races? Or was it some innate passion shared by all, an animal instinct to which Lorre had merely found the key?

Whatever their inspiration, whatever their reasoning or lack thereof, they continued to battle as if unaware of their own weakness, oblivious to their own mortality. They seemed to think they might win.

Killangrathor was no longer pressing forward. He spun and swiped and slashed, but stood engulfed by the swarm. Rats these were, Thrakkon decided, and as rats they would perish.

"Fire!" he bellowed. "Give them fire!"

A gout burst forth, but even that was not what it had been. A stream, rather than a river. Those nearest were set aflame, causing them to dance in their overheated armor. It should have melted them where they stood.

"Again!" Thrakkon roared. "Immolate them!"

Killangrathor tried, hacking up another fire lance he couldn't seem to sustain. Again. And again. Small pyres arose on all sides, but most of the dragon's strikes simply dissipated in the wind, climbing skyward in trailers of steam and curtains of heat.

The monster raised a howl to those heavens, through which cracks of sunlight continued to grow. Below, his enemies surged. Knives and spears and hand axes came flying at his face. The dragon actually shied as if stung by the blows. Many showed as nicks and scrapes in his thick-scaled flesh.

Impossible. Thrakkon was horrified, disgusted, aghast. What had that lightning strike done?

With unwavering hatred, Killangrathor lowered his head. Fire belched forth, but a hundred blades hacked upon his neck, stretched full-length upon the ground. An enemy giant managed to leave a gash. The giant paid for the strike with its life, its hairy body snatched up by snapping jaws that whipped around before it could free its blade. And yet, another of the brutes stood ready at its side. When Killangrathor reared back and shook the first giant to pieces with his stalactite teeth, he did so with an immense axe blade lodged in the top of his snout.

"Catapults!"

Thrakkon turned toward the shout, the Sword enabling him to draw focus amid the otherwise senseless din. He recognized Lorre at once, commanding from a nearby rise. The warlord was unmistakable in his black plate and cruel visor. Torin had failed to kill the man when given the chance. Thrakkon would not make the same mistake.

But then the rocks came sailing in, a battering hailstorm that peppered Killangrathor and those around him. Thrakkon had to twist savagely to avoid being hit. The engines were almost directly on top of them. Ballistae strikes followed hard upon, while the catapult arms were drawn back. Spears riddled the dragon's face and chest and shoulders. The beast swatted them away, but as many or more stuck.

"Up!" Thrakkon urged, raging against the straps that held him. He spurred the creature and gnashed his teeth. "Fly!"

Killangrathor could not. Instead, he roared and shook and plucked at the quills that had found their mark, his entire body rippling with a terrible frenzy. Lorre's men hemmed him all about, though the ranged strikes had claimed the limbs and lives of their comrades, and a second wave threatened to do the same to them. The dragon could be harmed, overwhelmed, made to fall. The race was on to deliver the killing blow.

Thrakkon considered delivering it himself after a second volley of boulders cracked two of Killangrathor's ribs, deeply bruised the creature's right leg, and snapped one of the finger bones in its left wing. Instead, he gazed upon the thousands of enemies still clambering toward him, and turned the Sword upon the leather bindings of his own harness. He paused, waiting for his giants and goblins to slice and claw free of theirs. He then leapt from his perch, tumbling and skidding his way down the shifting slope of Killangrathor's body, into the fray.

He landed in a sprawl, facedown in the muck, but was on his feet before the first enemy could reach him. He cut that one in half, and the next that followed, before ducking instinctively. The dragon's tail swept overhead, bloodied spikes missing his skull by a hairsbreadth. Its flaming eyes glared back at him.

Cast it, worm. Your lot against mine . . .

The beast turned away. Those siege engines had become its first concern, and it slithered south to deal with them.

Thrakkon spun north, his Illychar fanning out amid the enemy like wolves through sheep. Most of Lorre's troops remained focused on the dragon, paying little heed as its riders slipped by. Thrakkon might have stood there and killed every one of them, so intense was his rage and denial. But he knew also that there were too many to deal with just now. A score against twenty thousand. Killangrathor was to have made all the difference. Killangrathor—

After punching through the northern edge of Lorre's throng, Thrakkon looked back. The dragon continued to wade through the hacking waves of enemies, tearing them to froth. But its roars had become part whine. A mangled wing protruded from its side, while dozens of bloody shafts jutted from its skin. Fast and fluid no longer, it now limped and shambled, dragging its injured bulk. Thrakkon could not recall a more wretched sight.

He jogged on, his pair of giants at his side. Few of Lorre's soldiers noticed; fewer still bothered to give chase. Those who did were intercepted by the goblins that encircled him. He was still their master, he assured himself. He was still Itz lar Thrakkon, lord of the Illysp, the Boundless One.

The catapults were firing again. Thrakkon could not help but look. Killangrathor was upon them. The first projectile—a spiked iron ball—sailed past his head, to roll and crush its way through a pursuing wall of Lorre's men. Killangrathor overturned the second with a furious heave. It toppled against the third, causing yet another misfire. A giant stood by to reload, but Killangrathor crushed the creature underfoot, its bowels erupting through a ruptured torso.

One left. Killangrathor lunged toward its drawn arm, jaws wide with raging contempt.

Its fell strike could not have been delivered at closer range. The spiked ball launched from the catapult's nest simply pulverized the roof of the dragon's mouth, shattering teeth and cartilage and bone. A shower of blood and marrow splattered inward, outward, everywhere.

Killangrathor reeled, then tottered, then forgot how to stand. Though he pitched to the earth, he refused to succumb, flopping and convulsing in sickening fashion as the armies of Neak-Thur swarmed in.

Thrakkon turned and ran, leaving him to his throes.

CHAPTER THIRTY

Only the Bastion could stop him.

A small force awaited him at its base. Threescore, four, it was difficult to know. The living, the wounded, the dead—all were interspersed, working to sort themselves, one from the other.

His own ranks had been lessened as well. Both of his giants remained, but only ten of his goblins—less than half. The rest were carving blood trails of their own through Lorre's force as it scrambled to finish off the dragon. Some had been overtaken by the natural bloodlust of their host creature, and refused to flee. Others had suffered wounds during the battle, and were more easily trapped. In either case, few were likely to cut clear of the thousands who pressed them.

So be it. They would serve as cover. And those few who accompanied him would be more than enough.

Killangrathor himself remained the largest distraction—still fighting, clinging stubbornly to his unnatural life. Lorre's men blanketed his thrashing form like a belligerent swarm of ants, each trying to take its little piece, working together to make sure the monster did not rise. Every time Thrakkon cast a backward glance, his jaw clenched.

By now, the remnants of Gilden's company had spied his approach. An alarm went up. Soldiers set their wounded comrades aside and took up their blades and cudgels once more. Despite their evident weariness, despite their catastrophic losses, they formed their lines as best they could amid the mounds of dead—all under common shroud beneath the wall's shadow. With bold shouts and reckless sneers, they urged Thrakkon in his charge.

Those who crossed his path fell aside in a flash of crimson fire and spurting blood. Iron and steel, wood and leather, flesh and bone—one and the same to the Sword of Asahiel. Its aura shone brightly as it sheared through shields and weapons and the limbs and torsos of those who held them. Its edge never dulled; its stroke never wavered. It allowed him to sense his foes' routines almost before they did, to anticipate and thwart their feeble maneuvers.

In less than a moment, he was beyond the front line, and hacking his way through a reserve wall of those who could barely stand. Thrakkon killed them all the same. He knew no pity. Those who stepped or crawled or reached out before him died.

The ground itself was a sucking, slurping mire, littered with human compost. He slipped more than once, and tripped a time or two as he made his way through a rubble of bodies and weapons and crumbled blocks of stone.

But none of that proved more than a temporary inconvenience. He would let nothing and no one stand in his way.

By the time he reached the gatehouse, he had outdistanced most of his brood. Only two goblins were on his heels, with another just now freeing itself to follow. Savage as his kind were, none but he wielded a divine talisman. Nor would Gilden's dregs be daunted by a mere giant or even a handful of goblins—not after the horror they had faced in Killangrathor.

Of Gilden himself, he saw no sign. Dead, he hoped. Better still, alive, only shattered, paralyzed, choking on lungfuls of blood while riddled with a thousand searing pains . . .

While cherishing that thought, he did spy another he knew. *Bardik*. Another of General Chamaar's turncoats. He recalled, as Torin, that Lorre had promised to deal unfavorably with any captives who refused his rule. Might Chamaar himself have gone over to the warlord's side?

He cared not except that these were men Torin had known, men he had grown fond of—and therefore men Thrakkon would have taken special pleasure in killing. He would have finished Bardik then and there, but the former Wylddean wedge commander was a good thirty paces off, leading a counter against one of his giants. Just now, Thrakkon had other, more critical aims.

He plunged ahead, into the gateway tunnel, where a sizable flock of wounded had been gathered—tended to in part by folk caught out on the highway upon Killangrathor's sudden arrival. A knot of healthy soldiers stood ready to defend both. Thrakkon took heads and arms from all, passing through in a hacking, spinning, blazing blur. He tossed the Sword from hand to hand, then held it again in both—whatever was required to bring it to bear at the desired angle. More blood, more screams.

The portcullis was lowered. Its rust-flecked iron bars were spiked and studded and as thick around as his arm.

He chopped through them as if cutting twine.

A soldier made a charge at him. Thrakkon yanked the ruined grate from its seating and flung it in the man's path. When his foe pitched forward, the Boundless One punched the full length of the Sword up through his chin.

He drew it out through the front of the man's face. Brains splattered at his feet like boiled oats. No others came. His goblins were shredding Lorre's men, one scourgelike slash at a time. Blood sprayed against the damp stones lining the Bastion's gullet. Feral shrieks echoed from its throat.

Thrakkon ducked through the hole in the portcullis. The doors beyond had been closed and barred. Ironbound granitewood, so thick and heavy that a capstan was required to work them open and shut. Carving his way through required as much effort as a butcher's knife taking wedges from a wheel of cheese.

His body was sweating when he emerged, though his strength was undiminished. His lungs filled and emptied reflexively. A sickly sweet carnage packed his nostrils, so that, for once, the breath of the sea was not so overwhelming. He looked to the west, glaring upon it: endless waves grinding against a rutted shore. Farther out, beyond the spires and rock nests and gushing tidewaters, the mighty ocean shone like rippled steel.

He gave it his back and left the highway, cutting north and west toward the mountains. The road was no good. Too easy to run him down by horse. He needed the forest, the trees. There, he would be safe. He could run longer, faster, farther than any pursuit Lorre might muster. He could run forever.

The notion burned as hot and bright as the Sword's fires. He should not be running at all. How had this happened? Not even the Sword could soothe his dizziness at this inconceivable turn. Killangrathor felled, his Illychar brood slaughtered, scattered—waylaid at the very least. And Itz lar Thrakkon, lord of the Illysp, wielder of the Crimson Sword, sent from battle in full retreat.

The din of that ongoing struggle spurred his flight over hummocks and hollows of sand and grass, and around ponds and sinkholes of every size and shape. Rays of sun peeked here and there through the shifting clouds, as if to shed light on his position. A few stalwarts appeared atop the Bastion, and with their bows spawned a rain of arrows that fell mostly in his wake. Thrakkon dodged the remaining shafts easily enough, before quickly outpacing them.

He checked the distant gatehouse continually for any who might follow—be they friend or foe. Thus far, the Bastion held tight-lipped, refusing to spit any forth.

Overanxious he had been, and overconfident. He should have waited at Aefengaard. He should have paused to think matters through. That extra host might have made all the difference.

Or would it? He could still hear Killangrathor's wretched calls of fury and confusion, echoing upon each gust of wind. Thrakkon was similarly mystified. A sorcery, perhaps. But whose? How?

Questions bespoke helplessness, and so he thrust them from his mind. Reaching the fringe of trees that sprouted at the base of the Dragontails, he took another look back at the Bastion. Cries of death and pain and Illychar frenzy still wailed from the gap in its mouth, but nothing physical emerged. A sally port to the east, at the base of the joint between Bastion and city wall, was similarly silent. Thrakkon studied that one for a moment, taking time to peer up at the tower above—the one struck by lightning. Seeing nothing upon its heights that he hadn't before, he sheathed the Sword and buckled its scabbard to his back.

He clambered up an eroded bank, pulling himself up by the tails of protruding roots. At the top, a mesh of rain-washed brush awaited. Arising beyond, dirt and fungus and trees. A final look west availed him nothing.

Alone, he entered the woods.

Spittle and curses fell from his lips as he scraped and clawed his way through the netting tangle. Gloom surrounded him, within and without. Aged trees loomed overhead in silent superiority, judging. He could have felled them all and carved them to splinters. Give them a taste of his wrath, and see what became of their pride then. But the raging clangor he had left behind still filtered through their trunks and boughs, along with the muffled roar of a billowing surf. He could not escape either fast enough.

Ahead, the forest was still and silent, its denizens fled far and fast from the unfathomable horror of Killangrathor's assault. *His* assault. He had brought death and worse to this faraway land. He had brought Illysp. After all that he had endured—centuries of patience, of deprivation . . . He had achieved so much so quickly, and somehow squandered it all in a blink.

A branch slapped at him, so he tore it from its bole. Ivy snagged his boots, so he kicked and scraped and ripped it up by the roots. A bitter laugh escaped him. With the dragon, he'd been able to slay hundreds at a stroke. Without? Reduced to snapping tree limbs and rending ground cover. Lord of foliage. Bane of beetles and deadwood. That ought to make every living creature throughout the world tremble.

His own kind would be mocking him, if they could. The Illysp still clinging to his mind would heckle his failure aloud had they voice with which to do so. And the rest, those hovering thicker than flies upon Neak-Thur's battlefield, knew him now to be vulnerable. None that arose as Illychar would be as quick to fear and obey him as before.

He crested a ridge and started down into a deeply shaded dell. Perhaps it was time to confront this minion of the watery deep. Even Killangrathor was but a flea in comparison. Tame that one, and all else would be forgotten. If not . . . well then, he would be sure to awaken its full fury, and learn what the beast was truly capable of.

He would dominate this world yet, or see it destroyed.

But he could not savor the vision. Its taste was stale and hollow, fouled by the rancid taint of defeat. Killangrathor was gone, and without the dragon, Thrakkon was marooned, shackled to this wilderness land, a victim of his own far-reaching greed.

A large deadfall crossed his path. Rather than climb over, he stopped, striking it with both fists, his entire body rigid with denial. Its rotten flesh cracked and peeled away, falling to the ground in sodden, slivered chunks. He hit it again, and again, his fists scarcely making a dent. The trunk was four feet thick. A thousand naked blows would not clear it from his path. He reached over his shoulder for the Sword—

And hesitated, opening his eyes to the truth. Years, decades it might take for the bones of this ancient giant to crumble away. Without the Sword . . .

The notion gave him pause. Beneath, a sapling had taken root, and was feeding upon the dust of its forebear. And another beside it. And more, all around, covered in mulch. Thrakkon looked again at the fallen tree, and a vicious grin crept slowly across his face.

The dragon was slain perhaps, though he could not grasp how. But destroyed? Never. Fire would not char its bones. And Lorre's vermin could dull their teeth for weeks while trying to gnaw through its limbs. Three days. In three days, Killangrathor would rise again.

An Illysp had failed him, nothing more. That frail spirit had perished as it should. The next would prove stronger. Or the next. Or the next.

And the Finlorians. He would have them as well. Strike south with them, and he would have his revenge—with those he had despised most now fighting at his side.

The realization finally helped to settle him. He had lost nothing that could not be regained. Neak-Thur would still fall. Cities and creatures and lands beyond would suffer his terrible retribution. He had wasted time, was all. He had plenty enough of that.

He left the Sword in its scabbard, and vaulted atop the downed log. A patch of ferns lay on the other side, at the edge of a stream that cut along the hollow's floor. Its waters glistened darkly, filled with sharp, slick stones and overgrown with leafy brush. He couldn't quite tell where the ferns ended and the water began.

In the moment it took him to decide where to safely drop to his feet, there came a flash of light, and a shock of energy like a hammer blow in the small of his back. For an instant, the world around him vanished.

It came rushing back as he hurled forward, almost clear across the stream. His legs splashed heavily. His right knee smashed against an underwater rock. The taste of leaf and vine and soil filled his mouth, while his breath fled in a single, shocking blast.

His veins were afire, swelling, billowing, until he felt they must rupture. His entire body. Even his eyes bulged. He closed them tight lest they burst from his skull.

He snarled and tried to push himself off the ground. But his right arm folded awkwardly, painfully, at the shoulder, unable to hold his weight. Torn from its socket, he realized. The fall had not done that. It was the blow itself, the energy . . .

Thrakkon rolled to his left and sat up, opening his eyes to a blaze of white. Every tiny piece of him was dancing, like countless needles threading through the flesh beneath his skin. When he opened his mouth, he retched in his own lap, a gush of vile fluids that must have been festering for weeks in Torin's belly.

When it was finished, however, he could see. Lights swam like a swarm of bees, but he was able to make out the log, the slope down which he had trailed, the dell's rim above—

And a shadow. A human figure with hands upraised, holding an object of light that pulsed like a midnight star.

He made a grab for his weapon, only to wince with the realization that his sword arm would not function well enough to draw it. He grasped the right arm with the left and gave it a shove, trying vainly to wrench it back into place. Pain flared, but nowhere near as bright as the shadow-person's light as it lanced toward him. He knew he must dodge, but the forked streamer flew faster than thought, and caught him full in the chest.

It thrust him back against the earth, tethered to an invisible rack. He was being drawn and quartered, every limb and digit outstretched. Heat roiled and built until he feared it would erupt as flames from his skin.

He made his left hand fumble for the clasp of his baldric, knowing he must free the Sword so that he could get at it with his working arm. At the slightest tug, the leather strap tore like spiderwebbing. Some of the burning dissipated. He sat up. The shadow-figure was no longer at the dell's rim. He could hear it scampering down the slope. He heard insects chewing at logs and stumps, and worms burrowing in the earth. He could smell all through thickened layers of both bloom and decay.

He spun, snapping his legs beneath him in a crouch. The Sword slid from its sheath and flared in his hand, so bright that he had to avert his eyes. Its own smooth warmth swept through him, caging the unknown flux. The foreign power would not be dispelled, but the fires of Asahiel harnessed its jolts, removed its thorns, bringing it under control.

Thrakkon turned his head—a whiplike motion. There, on the other side of the log, a woman with golden curls pressed and matted about a sweat-streaked brow. She wore a focused expression, though her emerald eyes were bright and full of strain. He could smell every inch of her, as if suddenly possessed of an animal's senses. He growled as an animal might.

Her hands raised, and he saw her weapon: a crystal of some sort, large and flat, clutched in her palm, hung from a chain about her wrist. His eyes narrowed. He had seen such before, though not with his mortal eyes. An ornament from centuries past. The device of an age forgotten by most, but not by him.

Her lips moved silently. Her fingers clenched and then spread. Thrakkon hissed and hefted the Sword. No sorcerous power could—

The blue-tinged bolt streaked unerringly past his defenses. The Sword flared as it struck his body. It lifted him off his feet and threw him far. His back hit a stump, which turned him aside to land facedown again on the forest slope.

Thrakkon could not even cry out, so intense was his pain. The forest roared around him. Every beat of a fly's wing, every scratch of a beetle's leg, sang in his ears. He heard a rattle of fresh rain upon the woodland canopy, the gurgle of stream waters, and the eternal murmur of the distant ocean, rumbling its discontent.

Somehow, the Sword was still in hand. Were it not, he might have slipped away. But its rush continued to envelop him, to steady the waves of the sea in which he swam. Tides of fire, still billowing, still rising within. His teeth were clenched, and every muscle taut. His human coil could not contain this power, so thick, so potent. Why did the Sword not purge him? Why had it not protected him in the first place?

His legs were shaking now, and his arms and torso as well, jerking in convulsion. A landed fish, he must have seemed, wracked by seizure. His instinct was to rise again and fight. But he could hear her coming, the one who had done this to him. And he sensed that he might not survive another blast from her cursed stone.

He made himself go limp. Even so, he felt his muscles flexing and then re-laxing of their own accord, as if hooked to the strings of some puppet master. The thought infuriated him, but he would not be drawn from his feigned stupor. Let her think him finished. Let her believe the struggle was won.

He heard her hesitate in her approach, eyeing him warily from afar. *Come!* he screamed silently. *Finish me!*

He could not restrain himself any longer. Even with the Sword, each in-stant was agony—piercing, swirling, writhing within him. If he did not give it release—

She was moving again, stepping quietly, carefully, across the creek and through the brush on the other side. *Yes*, he urged through gritted teeth. *Just a little closer . . .*

She stepped around his flank, marching a wide circuit. His body continued to spasm, but he made his face seem as lifeless as possible.

He could feel her eyes upon his back, his face, the Sword. She slipped toward the weapon, keeping her gaze rooted upon his expression, searching for a reaction. She meant to kick the talisman away, he knew, to rid herself of any further threat.

He must let her do so, he realized angrily. He could sense her crystal, primed and ready, still flush with whatever power was being used against him. If he did not relinquish the Sword . . .

Her foot swept out. A gentle nudge at first, followed by a swift kick. He forced his fingers to relax, though the muscles were as tightly coiled as those of a man in the rigid stage of death. When his hand no longer brushed the hilt, his body seized and spasmed anew.

She hovered over him momentarily. Without the Sword, he no longer knew where exactly her hands were—or more importantly, the crystal. But he could still smell her fear and caution. It was in those beads of perspiration, the tightness of her breathing, the uncertainty of her movements . . .

At long last, she knelt before him, reaching out to feel for a pulse. He knew not what she meant to achieve with that. Did she not know he was already dead?

She relaxed slightly, exhaling long and slow. He held himself a moment longer—

Then sprang to his feet, clawing out with his left hand. Swifter than even he could believe. Faster than he had ever been. He caught her with her head turned, looking back toward the Sword. She spun back with a startled intake of breath, and brought her trinket to bear, but his own hand clamped over hers.

The crystal seared his flesh, further igniting the fires within. With a howl, he ripped it from its chain and flung it aside. She squealed as her only weapon ricocheted off the fallen log at his back and plunked down to lie at the bottom of the shallow stream.

Once again, his own strength took him by surprise. Yet even that small use of it brought welcome relief, dispersing some of the energy that raged inside, enough to clear his thoughts. She hadn't harmed him at all. She had *fed* him.

That was why the Sword had failed as a shield: Her attacks had not been intended as destructive blasts. Though the infusion of power had proved almost as lethal, she had held back for some reason. He cared not why. Only that it was *her* turn to suffer.

She seemed to sense it. She lost her feet in her haste to escape, but turned on hands and knees, and lunged for the Sword. He caught her by an ankle and tossed her like an empty pouch, laughing at the ease of it. His strength had increased fiftyfold. Bleeding away with every motion, yes, but plentiful enough to finish the task before him.

He scooped up the Sword using his left arm. The other was still displaced, hanging from its vacant socket. No matter. The Sword glowed, while the energy she had stunned him with rode lightning through his muscles and veins. He had the vigor of a giant, an ogre, a *dragon*.

His opponent was scrambling for her life, scurrying like a lizard toward the stream's edge. Her lungs wheezed, and he heard her heart thumping in its cage.

Thrakkon sneered and started after.

Her hand plunged into the waters. The crystal used to channel her magic glimmered amid the algae-coated rocks. But the streambed ran deeper than it appeared. Though she fished frantically, the artifact remained beyond her reach.

She glanced back. Her face was painted with grime, the skin beneath flush with fear. Merciful she had been, or merely daft. Thrakkon was neither.

He flipped the Sword, reversing his grip upon its gem-studded hilt, intent on skewering her where she lay. He pulled back to strike—

And froze, openmouthed, as a flaming poker punctured his chest. He looked down, but there was nothing there, only a sudden, piercing thought in his head.

Dyanne.

For an instant, he did not understand. Then the rain of memories began.

A girl Torin had cared for. In the Widowwood. On the journey north. The thread that had been missing. Revealed at last, so that the tapestry of Torin's time upon these shores was finally complete.

Thrakkon cared nothing for any of it. Yet the thread wove through him, a blaze of fresh pain that bound him head to toe. He tightened his grip on the Sword, then doubled over as a cramp seized him. It was *she* who had battled with him against Necanicum's demons—she and Holly. *Her* hands that had tended his wound. *Her* playful words, delivered in that smooth, sweet voice.

Rubbish and less. Thrakkon fought to push it all aside. Though his enemy had seemed momentarily startled and confused, he heard her groping and splashing anew through rushing water. He was uncertain as to what that might mean, but recalled that he had meant to kill her. *Yes. The Sword. Finish her.*

But the images continued, released like a tidal wave from Torin's closely guarded mental clutches. His surrender against Lorre . . . the dance at Vagarbound . . . Dyanne's touch . . .

Thrakkon wanted to scream, but his body was clenched too tightly to permit it, struggling to cope with the abrupt surge of buried emotion. A girl. A sack of human flesh like any other. Yet Torin's feelings for this one had paralyzed him and set him afire all over again. And all he could do was wait for the flood to pass.

He felt himself stumbling, falling backward. Their battle in the mountain passes . . . their final farewell . . .

Still it went on. The unspoken words . . . the waking dreams . . . the heart-felt yearning . . .

His enemy stood before him, dripping wet, crystal in hand. Thrakkon spat and slavered. No. *No!* He would not accept this betrayal from his own skin. He would rend his heart, put out his eyes, claw the entrails from his stomach, to regain control. He would do the same to her. He wasn't going to fall. Not like this. Not to one who stank of Finlorian descent.

Yet *this* pain went somehow deeper than muscles and tendons. It was in his blood, in his bones, clear to where his Illysp spirit had taken root. The crystal pulsed, and all Itz lar Thrakkon could manage was to gnash soundlessly, helplessly, in final, frenzied denial.

I'll shred your coil and feast upon—

A flash. A jolt. A chasm of unconsciousness that consumed the severed thought.

Shackled by a darkness blacker than itself, the Boundless One followed after.

She awaited him within the darkness, and when he found her, his world filled with light.

They were seated together, on the grassy slope at the edge of a wide, gently flowing stream. The boughs of a tree spread over their heads—his life's tree, planted in his youth. *Home.* He was back home, in the forests of Diln, sharing with her his favorite boyhood haunt.

This was no memory. He had relived those often enough to know. Besides, she had never visited Diln. He had met her in Yawacor, and there bid her farewell. They shouldn't be here. This had never happened.

A dream, he realized then, and felt something that might have been a shiver. He had not dreamt since before his death. As an Illychar, he had known no sleep, only images of events that had been, and variations thereof tweaked forcefully by his tormented mind, in search of solace that would not be found.

But he had relinquished all of those. He remembered now. In a desperate attempt to overwhelm his Illysp parasite, he had set them free: every loving thought, every longing sensation, his most treasured memories and emotions. In doing so, he too had been set free.

To dream.

As he focused on the water's rush, he realized through the corner of his eye that she was staring at him. He glanced away nervously, then carefully looked back. She was still gazing at him, admiring him.

He turned his head to fully face her. Before he could speak, she leaned toward him, her lips meeting his in a soft, delicate kiss.

His eyes closed, and a welcomed darkness took him. His chest heaved, burning with exaltation. At the same time, his mind spun with wonder. She had never shown a hint of affection toward him. A token of gratitude it must be, for having done his part to fell the monster he had become—for having spared her people the butchery brought to so many others.

It mattered not. With this simple gesture, his ultimate desire was made consummate, enabling his soul to fly forever in mindless bliss. With but a single kiss, his life had been given order and meaning and joy undeserved.

Within the depths of his own shapeless existence, Torin smiled.

And at long last knew peace.

CHAPTER THIRTY-ONE

CORATHEL LEANED HEAVILY AGAINST A weathered merlon, closing his eyes as a wave of dizziness swept over him.

"Are you unwell, sir?" his young attendant asked him.

The chief general grunted. He had sought to escape his flock of captor-healers altogether, but their persistent urgings had led even the governor to insist he be accompanied by one of their brood.

"Steady as the wall beneath our feet," Jasyn answered, covering for him until the spell had passed. "And likely to last as long."

The attendant wasn't convinced. "Perhaps the general should return to his rest."

Corathel ignored him, fixing his gaze upon the Illychar swarm below. Having finally won his freedom, he had no intention of relinquishing it. The past four days had seemed an eternity—lying helplessly abed while the city around him struggled to withstand the ongoing siege. Jasyn and others had advised him often, and kept him well stocked with registries and diagrams and reports of every tactical nature. But none of that could match the feeling of a sword in hand or the ring of combat in his ears. What *they* called healing felt to *him* like wasting. It was battle he needed in order to stir his blood and make him whole.

Jasyn understood, and so had helped him forth to join the morning rounds, promising those who objected to keep the chief general from harm's way. As if he were so foolish as to charge headlong into combat when he scarcely had the strength to mount a horse or climb a flight of steps.

"What you see here is what you'll find around the length of the curtain wall," Jasyn offered.

Corathel nodded. Their plan had been to march the city's entire perimeter, but his lieutenant was tacitly offering to cut that trip short should he not feel up to it. While loath to admit as much, the chief general believed that might not be a bad idea. He feared his presence thus far had done as much harm as good. Throughout the city and upon the wall, soldier and civilian alike had greeted him warmly, with cheers and salutes. But behind their proud smiles, he sensed the strain that Jasyn had warned him of upon his first waking. Pale and drawn, he must seem to them as much ghost as man—a grim omen to those who wanted to look upon him as their savior.

They had received no new word from either Alson or Kuuria. Nor had they been able to slip any fresh riders past the enemy lines. With thick concentrations outside the gates, and tens of thousands prowling a constant circuit, the reaver stranglehold was complete. Leaven was highly defensible, a city long shadowed by civil war and fortified to withstand it. But no city could stand forever—not against an enemy that did not hunger or thirst or tire. If an ally did not come to break the siege . . .

"I would see the gatehouse," Corathel said, pushing back from the parapet and the chaos that raged below.

If only he could push aside the foul truth as easily. Whether bedridden or patrolling the battlements, he remained a prisoner, biding his time while anticipating some form of miracle. His daring incursion had won this people a moment's hope, only to foster further disappointment. Despair surrounded them now, worming its way insidiously into their hearts. On a battlefield, a man could lose himself in his fury and find his end before he saw it coming. Trapped behind these walls, there was nothing for many but to wait and wonder and envision the many dreadful forms that death might take.

He did his best to mask these concerns, as did the men who continued to greet him as he passed. Jasyn's retinue of guards made sure that none pressed him too enthusiastically. His body ached and his leg throbbed. Every limping stride twisted the imaginary blades buried beneath his flesh. Nearer the parapet, real blades hacked at scaling ropes, felling enemy climbers. Arrows, stones, and other debris were used sparingly, for any missile hurled down upon their enemies became a weapon in their hands. Oil and fire were used instead—the only armaments an Illychar truly feared. The stench of both— and the poisonous smoke they bred—hung thick in the air.

"What's this, now?" Jasyn murmured, as they looped around from the south and caught sight of the tower above Leaven's east gate.

Corathel looked. The barbican was astir, as were the twin watchtowers that flanked it. But the activity did not appear any different from that left behind. "Is something amiss?"

Jasyn pointed east, beyond the gatehouse. A morning mist still clung to the low-lying hills, filling hollows and ravines as if they were cauldrons, and boiling out onto the slopes. Black shapes writhed within, as Illychar surged toward the wall or battled among themselves. Wherever Corathel searched, their frayed lines covered dozens or even hundreds of paces . . .

Except on the eastern road. There, the line stretched a league or more *away* from the city, its farthest point lost in mist.

"Where are they going?" he asked aloud.

Jasyn shook his head. "Perhaps our lookouts can tell us."

Corathel hastened his pace—until finding that it made his limp more pronounced. He settled then for keeping an eye to the east as he shuffled along bestride his escorts. The reavers farthest out continued to bleed off toward the rising sun in a long, unbroken string. They did not appear to be departing with any real haste—as if drawn by curiosity rather than bloodlust. Nor were their numbers sufficient to distract the hundreds assailing the main gate, or the thousands of others who clamored against the walls or fought for position. Even so, a dozen possibilities, both hopeful and horrid, had raced through Corathel's mind by the time he reached the tower steps.

They were not the first to take note of the strange exodus. Atop the watchtower, they found Ragenon gazing eastward through a spyglass. Lar, standing head and shoulders above the city's garrison commander, nodded at their approach.

"Chief General, sir," Ragenon greeted, lowering his instrument. "I'm pleased to see you on your feet."

Despite his gracious words, the commander seemed startled by Corathel's ragged appearance—one of a hundred such looks the chief general had suffered that morning.

"What have we found?" he asked, frustrated by his own labored breathing.

"Perhaps you can tell us," the colonel said, offering him the spyglass.

Corathel wiped the sweat from his brow before taking the well-worn instrument in hand. Its leather casing was stained and cracked, its brass fittings gone green. Scratches in the glass showed clouds where there were none. More than once, he pulled it away to check the horizon with his naked eye.

"What do you make of it?" Ragenon asked finally.

"Smoke."

"Yes, but from what?"

At his shoulder, Jasyn snickered. "Fire, be my guess."

"Multiple columns," Corathel decided, squinting through the glass. "Three, four, maybe more."

"Reavers caught wind of it during the night," Lar reported. "Watchmen found their stream an hour ago—a trickle compared to this."

"Been growing ever since," Ragenon added, scratching at his beard. Its coarse hairs, red and thick and unruly, gave him the look of a face wreathed in flame.

"Not fast enough, for my taste," Corathel muttered.

"Could it be reinforcements?" the colonel asked hopefully.

Jasyn snorted. "From the east? More likely theirs than ours."

Indeed, while their own prayers for support had gone unanswered, the Illychar ranks had continued to swell over the past few days, as their prolonged assault drew rogues and strays from the lands east of the Whistlecrags—lands deserted by the peoples who had fled Atharvan.

"But we've not seen the reavers make such use of fire," Ragenon observed. "They do everything they can to stamp it out."

"Might be our dragon has returned," said Jasyn.

"Or the King's refugees," Lar rumbled. "They might have been waylaid when setting forth from Llornel Lake."

Corathel disagreed. "Colonel Boldin should be well south of us by now." *If not, only the gods can help him.* "This has to be something else."

"But what?" Ragenon pressed.

The chief general shook his head. "It matters not. Friend, foe, or something in between, it has captured our enemy's attention. We should make ready, should it continue to do so."

Ragenon frowned, his beard of flames consuming his mouth. "Make ready. For exodus?"

"We've agreed that if the chance should present itself, we must lead this people south, to join with those who shelter now at Souaris."

"What if this is a ruse, meant to lure us from our stone cage?"

"Our enemy already possesses the strength required to overrun us in due time. They need not resort to such tricks."

"Then let us suppose this distraction is genuine, and not some ploy. Even if every last reaver at our gates races off to meet it, how long will we have? What if we aren't swift enough in our escape?" When Corathel did not answer, Ragenon's argument gained momentum. "And what of the road south? If we should find it blocked, what then? That was a sizable force that veered off days ago—thirty thousand or more. Common folk, yes, but plentiful enough to bottle us up until these others can rain down upon our backs."

"Valid fears, one and all. Do you have a point, Colonel?"

"With all due respect, sir, it seems a terrible risk. Are we not safer here?"

"Today, yes. Another week or more, perhaps. But beyond that . . ." Corathel trailed off, allowing all to listen to the din of battle raging below. A constant roar, it seemed, punctuated now and again by a shrill cry—like gulls upon the seashore. "Make no mistake. Here, we are but cornered playthings, alone upon a shrinking island. If we do not set sail for higher ground, we will surely drown."

"If the Kuurians will not come to us," Lar agreed, "we must go to them."

Ragenon glanced at the imposing Fourth General, then turned back to Corathel. "Given a clearer opportunity, I might readily agree. But I don't see it here, as yet."

"Then look closer, for it may be the only chance we get."

The red-haired colonel looked instead to Jasyn, and then again to Lar, but saw little help coming from either. Corathel knew his lieutenant generals well enough to sense when they were of the same mind. Had they any protest, they would have uttered it by now.

Ragenon crossed his arms, his expression smoldering.

"The people have prepared already for this eventuality," Corathel reminded him. "We need only give word that the time may be at hand."

The garrison commander shook his head. "I'll advise the governor. His Honor will wish to have a say."

"His Honor is a sensible man. I shall be glad to hear his counsel."

A formality, Corathel knew. In a military crisis, a Parthan governor was beholden to the will of legion command. And this particular governor was more pragmatic than prideful. He had remained at Leaven during the last city-wide evacuation, but that was because the West Legion had initially planned

to hold her gates. If Corathel were to insist that the entire city must empty—
and that he and the army would do so alongside—His Honor would be quick
enough to comply.

Ragenon saluted, then led his entourage in departure. He rounded, however, before reaching the first step. "A final question, sir, if I may."

Corathel nodded.

"Pray tell, if we Parthans abandon our last city, who is to say the Kuurians
have not already done the same?"

The chief general scoffed. "At present, the Kuurians have more strength
than we do." He peered again through the borrowed spyglass, then returned
it to the lookout standing post to one side. "And as one who fought among
them, I promise you: Thelin will never yield Souaris."

By midday, word had reached every niche and corner of the city, and expectations had begun to build. The mists had burned off, and with them,
more than half of the enemy horde. The smoke stains spotted that morning
had grown larger, become visible to the naked eye as a single black smudge
against the faded backdrop of the distant Skullmars. With a spyglass, one
could see now that there were seven columns all told, staggered in some instances behind one another. Seven distinct blazes, headed slowly their way.

It did not seem right to Corathel. Fires that large would spread and join.
But these remained separate, the space between their sooty stalks actually
widening as they neared. The foot of each column remained obscured by distance and the uneven lay of the land. As yet, the lookouts had seen no hint of
flames—not even a glow to suggest their presence. Surely, the first waves of
Illychar had reached them by now, but if so, those upon Leaven's battlements
saw nothing of the result.

His lieutenant generals shared his concerns. Odd, they called it, though
Dengyn went so far as to deem it unnatural, and proclaim it an ill omen.
Others might have agreed—were it not for the reavers' continued departure.
Given that, the majority of soldiers and civilians—knowing little about the
fires' true configuration—were quick to celebrate, giving praise to the Ceilhigh
for this Olirian boon.

Such reaction only reaffirmed Corathel's fears concerning this people's
morale. He had lived all his life in war's shade, and had learned to decipher its
every deepening chill. In this case, his gut rumbled an insistent echo of Jasyn's
observations. Should this people not soon find freedom, they would likely
surrender to madness.

Even so, he tried not to let that weigh too heavily in his decision. Ragenon
had voiced some good arguments, and Corathel might have raised several
more of his own. He meant to choose this course should it prove to be the best
available option, not merely out of desperation.

The first scouts set forth at midafternoon, charging hard from a western
postern under cover from above. Enough reavers remained to take notice, and
to drag two from their mounts while the other half dozen sped away. Their
escape brought a renewed rush against that section of the city wall, but the re-

taliation proved short-lived. Upon Corathel's witching-hour raid, the Illychar as a whole had shown no concern in abandoning the city to chase down easier prey. It seemed *that* much hadn't changed.

Another wave of scouts followed half an hour later, and another after them, setting up a relay that would allow reports to extend farther and return more quickly. By then, they rode forth almost without contest. Of the more than fifty thousand Illychar that had assailed Leaven's walls, perhaps a thousand remained, clustered mostly around the east gate. The rest had been siphoned off with ever-growing haste, leaving the way as clear as it was likely to get.

Nevertheless, Corathel waited, with eyes peeled for the return of his scouts—or the enemy. As the final decision loomed, the people's anxiety grew, both for and against the planned evacuation. A few small riots broke within the streets, while atop the battlements, soldiers strutted nervously, a mix of hope and dread reflected in their gazes. The winds shifted, so that most believed they could smell now the approach of that great, spreading smoke plume— that which heralded either their doom or their salvation. The columns that fueled it marched alongside one another like disciplined sentinels. Black and ominous, they held a desperate people spellbound, frozen with anticipation.

Another hour passed, with the sun picking its way carefully across a cloud-littered sky. The relative quiet beyond Leaven's walls struck an eerie, echoing chord in the ears of those who had listened for so long to the roar of combat. As if an entire ocean had ceased to stir.

The first scout to return came from the west. A fiery arrow announced his arrival, and a contingent sallied forth to sweep away the dozen or so reavers that blocked his way. His news brought a sense of relief. The western road was clear.

Two more arrived the same way, bringing tidings from south and east. The reavers were several leagues beyond the reach of the eastern scouts, doing battle upon the Fields of Ravacost. The roots of the smoke columns remained hidden from view, but whatever the source of those blazes, it seemed to be contained.

Southward, along the broken slopes of the Whistlecrags, they had seen only birds—mostly carrion-eaters—amid the trees.

That was enough for Corathel. After a final briefing, the barriers used to shore up the various gates were brought down, and the portals themselves opened. The main gate drew the most attention. Reavers upon the eastern slopes rushed to fill the breach, only to be hewn down by those waiting within. From the south and west, cavalrymen spilled forth, riding circuit around the city walls. All the while, lookouts scanned the horizon in every direction, wary of ambush.

When none came, the true exodus began. Their options were to march west through the mountains toward Laulk before turning south, or ride south from the main gate and cut west later along the tail of the Whistlecrags. The latter was the larger road, and likely swifter, but the former was deemed safer.

Not only would it put more initial distance between themselves and fifty thousand reavers, but, should something go awry, the mountains would help to shield them. Afterward, they would have the option of remaining at Laulk or continuing west toward Alson, should the southern road prove unnavigable to them.

A force of twelve thousand led the way, commanded by Generals Maltyk and Bannon. Behind this shield would stream some four hundred thousand souls—the populations of Laulk, Leaven, and an untold number of refugees inherited from the surrounding lands over the past months. Lar, Dengyn, and another twelve thousand troops would serve as rear guard, with every man, forward and back, doing what he could to ensure a bloodless retreat.

The first few hours were the worst. Despite his wounds, Corathel paced fretfully, and tensed every time a status report was delivered. Most of the populace cooperated readily enough; after hunkering helplessly for more than a fortnight against such ravening creatures, they were more than ready to be on the move. But there were plenty who feared leaving the last shelter they might find, and thousands of others whose infirmities brought the overall pace to a crawl. Packhorses and draft animals were in abundance, many of which balked and brayed with reservations of their own. Ragenon and the city garrison tended to these and other issues, maintaining order and safety while pressing the pace. Despite the effort, it did not seem nearly fast enough.

By dusk, however, only stragglers remained. Lar and Dengyn ushered them on their way, sweeping the streets and plazas of looters and cripples, orphans and urchins, and those who could not bring themselves to leave their homes without a stern nudge. Lar's troops did not have the time or numbers to ferret out all who might be determined to stay, but Corathel wanted to make sure that none were simply abandoned. Provided those who wished to escape were given a chance to do so, the chief general could suffer the loss of a few dregs.

But that would be up to his lieutenants. The time had come to set his own course. At the head of four thousand remaining soldiers, he and Jasyn set out through the east gate, in search of the southern road. It would be their job to divert and defend against any reavers that came sniffing back too soon, giving the bulk of their people a better chance to reach safety. If the gods were good, all would reunite at the Gaperon before entering the lands of Kuuria. If not . . .

He grimaced with every jarring stride his mount took upon that rutted road. To the east, the black shafts to which he owed his freedom rose starkly through reddened skies, a line of bruises against the setting sun. It still troubled him, not knowing what they were. A godsend, yes, but what would be the price?

He veered south as darkness fell. By then, the men in his column began to relax somewhat in their stolen freedom. Their words were few, and their voices hushed. But haunted eyes and severe frowns were giving way to relieved smiles and even rare snippets of shared laughter. Corathel was glad for them. The road to Kuuria promised only danger, and even if they were to arrive safely, they had nothing to look forward to but a long, harrowing struggle for the liberation of their lands.

Let them find solace where they may.

"The tail is clear," Jasyn reported, having ridden up the column to rein in beside him. "I ordered the east gate barred behind us."

Did we make the right choice? "I feel suddenly naked," he admitted.

"And never so refreshed," Jasyn replied cheerfully. "Siege defense is about as exciting as sweeping cobwebs from rafters."

A far cry from the trench-and-field warfare they were more accustomed to, certainly. "Best get used to it. I suspect we'll spend a lot more time languishing behind walls before this is done."

Jasyn's face soured at the prospect. He glanced over his pauldron-encased shoulder, peering to the east. "Shall we lay wager on how long it takes them to find us?"

"I seem to have misplaced my coin purse. But if you—"

"Reavers!" someone shouted.

The call came from the right forward flank. Corathel whipped his head in that direction. A small pack of Illychar was emerging from a copse of hemlock, upon a jutting ridge perhaps ten feet overhead. At a distance of thirty paces, they were already well within bowshot of the archers warding the regiment's western face. Mounts whickered as they halted, while bows and arrows came to hand.

Corathel wrestled with his own steed, eyes locked upon that shallow ridge. Elves. In the deepening darkness, against the backdrop of trees, it was difficult to discern much else. Five, six, no more. They bore weapons—spears and slings and giant longbows—but did not brandish them. A few crouched low before one who stood tall in the center.

The chief general gaped with hopeful suspicion. "Hold!"

He spurred his horse ahead. Jasyn kept to his side, sword drawn, echoing his order. Though most held their shots, a few of the archers had already loosed.

Their shafts streaked unerringly through the darkness, but the elves avoided them or swept them aside. Corathel did not slow, but continued on with his hand raised and his retinue in tow, until grinding to a halt at the base of the overlook.

A smile split his features as he looked up at Owl and his Mookla'ayans. "Should you not be halfway home to your jungles by now?"

Owl pointed and clicked his tongue, spouting gibberish.

"They could still be reavers, sir," Jasyn reminded him.

"Then where are the rest of them? Sheathe your blade." He bowed to the elf leader, who responded with an indecipherable gesture. He then addressed the commander of his ready archers. "Stand down, Corporal. These are ours."

Moments later, with greetings and pulses exchanged, they were headed south once more. Corathel ordered his guard ring to fall back, making room for Owl and his few remaining clansmen. His men obeyed with scowls and wrinkled noses in the wake of spoken protest. Even his horse seemed wary and agitated by the presence of the natives.

Corathel didn't care. Little had changed, all in all. He had still abandoned Leaven and was leaving his lands to the reavers. A perilous, uncertain trek lay ahead. His wounds still throbbed and would be given scant opportunity to heal. He had picked up a handful of savages was all, onetime enemies he could not even speak with, and whose own numbers had been cut down to almost nothing.

But it was enough to shed new light upon murky hopes, and reassure him in what had been just another dubious venture.

"You seem in better spirits," Jasyn observed. "Do you truly believe this troop can make any sort of difference?"

Corathel grinned. Though he could not justify the feeling, he was not about to fight it. On this night of their miraculous escape, anything seemed possible.

CHAPTER THIRTY-TWO

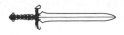

Something was wrong.

Amid the darkness . . . a whispered murmur, a briny scent, both growing stronger. But he no longer sensed such things. He lacked the form with which to do so. He had no ears, no nose—

His eyes fluttered open, and the darkness receded in a dizzying rush. He thought at once of the dream, and closed his eyes again, seeking to recapture it. Dyanne's countenance hovered over him, lingering like a lover at dawn. How beautiful her gleaming eyes, he marveled, how radiant her smile. He could still taste the fervor of her kiss, and the rapture that burned within his chest. When he drew breath, a tingling warmth filled his body. Such a glorious experience, he realized in thankful reflection, the most magnificent moment of his life.

Life.

A chill ratcheted through him, sucking the breath from his lungs. *No, not again.* Life meant pain, for himself and for others. The Illysp. He had escaped them once. He could not endure that horror to begin again.

He clenched his eyelids in refusal, searching frantically for Dyanne's departing image. She was still there, but vague now, and distant, crowded aside by a wave of other, comparably hideous figures and impressions. The memories of his life were returning, risen up like an army of ghouls. He willed them away, striving to reclaim the bliss they had taken from him. But his dream had been only that, a portrait of wishful longing, to be swept away by the throes of yet another hateful awakening.

He opened his eyes in surrender, unable to face the deluge of who he had been, the horror of his deeds . . . the atrocities he had yet to commit. He heard himself groan—

Or had he done that himself? A desperate hope took hold, as he lay blinking at the rafters of a stone-and-timber ceiling. He directed his gaze at his feet, and found them beneath the blankets at the end of the bed in which he lay . . . to the right, at a stone wall slashed through by arrow slits and soft streamers of light . . . to the left, at a closed door. His eyes seemed to obey him, but how could he know it was *his* will and not that of an Illysp inside him? He made himself blink once, then twice in succession, then three times, holding the last for a silent count of five. *Hold it*, he urged himself. *Gods above, let it hold.*

When he reached his count, he felt a smile upon his face. He let go—

And gasped to find a woman leaning over him, young and of bracing beauty, with long, red-gold hair draped to one side, soft pale cheeks without mole or blemish, and bright emerald eyes, depthless in the light of the taper she thrust toward him.

He recognized her at once.

"Your name," she prompted, before he could find words for his shock.

"I . . ." His voice was raspy, unfamiliar. "Torin," he croaked, and a wary relief flooded through him. "I am Torin."

The words echoed in his mind. *I am Torin. I am Torin.* But how could that be?

The lass seated herself upon the edge of the straw-filled mattress. Torin recoiled, pushing himself up on his elbows. He winced as he did so, feeling pains throughout his body, none more acute than the fire in his right shoulder.

"You . . . you brought the dragon down." The words slipped free before he could truly consider them. His thoughts were a tempest, questions swarming like a cloud of angry bees.

His visitor simply stared at him with those brilliant emerald eyes. Behind her, a small hearthfire crackled. A gust whistled through the arrow slits to his right, bearing the sound and breath of the sea.

"I sapped a measure of its strength," she admitted finally. "Its energy would have been regained in time, but Lorre's armies did not give it that chance."

His head stirred all the faster. Killangrathor defeated. Was it possible? The battle, the woods . . . too much, too quickly. "Why am I not dead?"

"Because I have no desire to kill you. And for the moment, at least, I've convinced my grandfather to extend you the same courtesy."

"Your grandfather?"

"Lorre."

Her answers told him nothing. His confusion was too thick. Words without meaning, blown aside by the next—

And then it struck him. "You're . . . you're the daughter. Laressa's child."

"Annleia."

A black horror filled him, clawing at his lungs and chest. Aefengaard. Her home. He had destroyed it. He had slain her mother, butchered her people. "I *was* dead," he insisted, and heard the pleading in his own voice, the need to deny it all and return to his eternal slumber. "Before . . . before . . ."

"You were possessed?" She leaned closer, and he pulled back, drawing himself up higher despite the pain. She studied him a moment, then exchanged her taper for a cup and pitcher set upon a table at his elbow. She filled the cup with water and offered it to him. "The Illysp raised you. I purged your body of its spirit."

No. Bloody gods, I don't deserve . . . He wanted to swat the cup aside, but took it in hand. "Why?"

"Because that was the calling given me. We've much to discuss, Torin of Alson, some of which may be difficult to understand, and none of which will be pleasant."

Her gaze seemed to engulf him, to swallow him whole. He closed his eyes and drank. This was not about him. This was about the Sword. It was always about . . . He opened his eyes and looked around. Even that simple movement felt clumsy and awkward. "The Sword. Is it—"

"In my grandfather's keeping. Lorre's hunters found us shortly after our . . . *meeting* in the wood. His orders were to capture, if possible, rather than kill. But there was no way he was going to leave the talisman in your possession."

"We're at Neak-Thur, then?"

"In Lorre's citadel, former seat of the Council of Rogues, I'm told. What else do you recall?"

More than I care to, he thought, staring into his empty cup. Atharvan. Aefengaard. "The wood," he said instead, and reached with his left hand to rub his injured shoulder. "You wielded magic against me."

When he looked to her wrist, she did so as well. Her lightweight dress had long, pointed sleeves. She drew back the left-hand one to show him a loop of crystals strung together on silken thread. A central crystal dominated the array, larger than those that surrounded it, teardrop-shaped and multifaceted. The room's dim light seemed to pulse within its depths.

"An heirloom," she said, "passed down by Eolin's royal mother to mine. A wellstone, it is called, in your human tongue, for it serves as a receptacle for the storage and transfer of energy. The energy I fed into you was borrowed from the dragon—far too much for your human body to contain. Had I released it all at once, it would have destroyed you."

"A safer course, don't you think?" he remarked grimly. "I nearly killed you."

"But *I* was warned *not* to kill *you*. So I had to err toward caution, releasing only a little at a time."

"A risk either way. The Sword should have—"

"The Sword will not repel a power meant to strengthen you." Her tone suggested that she was already weary of the topic. She had not brought him back from the dead, he supposed, merely to explain how she had done so.

"I was given to believe that the Vandari and their powers are no more," he countered. "You seem to know much you should not."

Annleia lowered her sleeve, hiding her wellstone from view. He wondered if she had it ready to defend against him now. Perhaps he should find out, and return to his dreams.

"My father did not lie to you," she said sternly. "Yes, we possess some knowledge of what you call magic, as all Finlorians do. But you sought answers on how to combat the Illysp, else rebuild the shattered seal between their world and ours. That sort of power, my people no longer have."

Torin frowned. She had traveled a long way, and risked her own life to preserve his. If she hadn't come to help him . . . "Then why are you here?"

"I am here because the elf I called Father is dead. I am here because my mother looks enough like one that she would not have made it through the first settlement she encountered. I am here in their stead to learn what knowledge *you* have, to learn if together we may not find a way to save both your people and mine."

Torin's stomach knotted at the reminder. *Her* people's fate had already been decided. He realized suddenly that she been avoiding that subject as much as he had. But the dreaded question was there now, in her taut face, in her focused gaze.

He could go no further until he spoke to it.

"Annleia, I . . . the dragon and I, and the other Illychar . . . we did not cross the ocean to attack Lorre."

The young woman tried to remain stoic, but her lip began to tremble, and her eyes rimmed with wetness. "Tell me."

"Annleia, you don't want—"

"They escaped, did they not? My mother was prepared. She knew . . ."

Her voice cracked, and tears began to spill. Torin wished his mattress were stuffed with blades instead of straw, that he might be cut to pieces rather than give voice to his shame.

"Some escaped," he allowed, staring again at the empty cup in his hand. "Others perished. I cannot number them except to say, too many of the latter."

The young woman wept openly. Torin sat silent, miserable, knowing how hollow and useless any apology would be.

"And my mother?"

A lump came to his throat, and it felt as if a giant fist squeezed his heart. He looked up, the horrible truth perched on his tongue. But as he met her gaze, something stopped him. It had nothing to do with fear of personal consequences. Whatever punishment she might choose, he would submit to gladly. Yet he could not imagine stealing what small hope remained to her— that which the truth would destroy.

Before he realized it, he was shaking his head. "The dragon did most of the killing, and the goblins their share. I did not see the faces of all who fell before them."

It was not a direct lie; nevertheless, he hated himself the moment he said it.

Annleia sniffed. "So she might have escaped."

Had he not found her amid the ruin of that toppled tree. Had she fled, instead of foolishly trying to buy her people time. "I imagine she had as much opportunity as the rest—though they were not given much."

The young woman searched his face a moment longer, then turned her eyes to the floor. Torin hoped she would not press him further. He told himself again that it was better to leave her question to doubt and spare her any further devastation. At the same time, he silently cursed himself for a coward, wondering if the decision had truly been made for *her* sake, or his own. By what right did he—

"She warned me," Annleia murmured softly. "She told me I could not do both."

Torin hesitated, uncertain that she was speaking to him. "Your mother?"

"The crone," she said, turning to face him once more. "In the forest. The one who carried your blood."

"My blood?" *Who could be carrying*— He froze, the witch's ravaged face appearing suddenly before his mind's eye.

"Necanicum, she called herself. I set forth of my own accord, but it was she who found me, and showed me what I must do." Annleia wiped the streams from her cheeks. "She gave me a choice: Return to warn my people, or poison your body in a manner to drive the Illysp from you."

Torin scarcely heard her, fighting instead to recall all that he could of his strange confrontation with the eccentric woodswoman. The episode seemed a hundred years removed, a blur of inane babble and superstitious ravings. *Immortal One*, she had called him. Was this why? How could she have known?

"Seems to me you made a poor decision," he said sullenly. "Why save a stranger when—"

"My decision was not made for *your* sake, but for those you are meant to save. According to Necanicum, you, Torin of the Crimson Sword, control the fates of all."

Torin glowered. For a moment, he considered telling her what he thought of the old madwoman, and of such prophecies in general. If Annleia was fool-ish enough to believe . . .

Yet such anger was misdirected. He realized that what he really wanted was to express his own remorse, to tell her that he understood her pain better than she knew. After all, he had made a similar choice to hunt for the Sword rather than return to his village, and in so doing had unwittingly let his home be destroyed, all in the name of the greater good. In some ways, he regretted it to this day—now, perhaps, more than ever.

But he could not see where knowing that might lessen her own pain, so he kept it to himself.

"And did she tell you what answers I am supposed to have?" he asked instead.

Annleia scoffed. "You are the first I know of to escape an Illysp's thrall alive. You are here to tell what none before you has had the opportunity to reveal. Would you tell me you learned nothing?"

I learned of hatred, of hunger, of reveling in another's misery . . . "The Illysp stole my mind. It used my memories and knowledge against me." He shivered at the recollection, at the hundreds—the thousands—slain. "But its own thoughts were never revealed to me."

"You walked among them," she said pointedly. "You *led* them."

Indeed, it remained difficult to believe he was even having this conversa-tion. The horror was still so fresh in his mind. He stared at his hands, still pale and slashed and scarred. He fiddled with the empty cup, remembering what it had been like—the strength, the fury. He remembered how it had felt, to see others cower before him, while shrugging aside injuries that would have felled any normal man thrice over. He could only imagine how the rest of him appeared. More significantly, he wondered if his body would ever truly belong to him again.

"I recall what I saw, and the words I spoke." A shudder ripped through him. "Their armies are everywhere—I can tell you that. Their aims, you already know. If I am to banish them, I know not how. Those answers were supposed to lie with the Vandari. But your father—"

He bit off the rest, halted by his recollection of the one who had sent him on his quest to begin with. He knew suddenly that he couldn't trust any of it, not truly.

Annleia misinterpreted his silence. "My father regrets spurning you as he did, but—"

"Darinor was an Illychar," Torin blurted.

"What?"

"From the beginning, before he first came to me." A dire hope blossomed within. "I discovered the truth only upon my return, when I walked into the trap he had set for me and my home city. He claimed then that my quest was not a lie, but . . . Annleia, I know little but what *he* told me."

He could almost see her thoughts spinning, there behind those emerald eyes. He gave her a moment to respond. When she did not, he added, "If you were to share what *you*—"

"What did he tell you of Ravar?"

"Ravar?"

She closed her eyes, whispering to herself in a language he did not comprehend. When finished, she faced him squarely, her gaze penetrating. "It seems we must begin anew—from the start this time. Share with me what you know, and I shall do what I can to fill in the holes and correct any lies."

As should have happened when he first met Eolin, Torin reflected bitterly. They clearly knew at least one thing of import that he did not. Had the elf been more receptive to his needs, how much tragedy might have been avoided?

He took a deep breath, refusing to travel that road of thought, fearful of where it might lead. "If" and "should have been" would accomplish nothing at this point. And he was the last person to be passing judgment upon others for any mistakes they may have made.

He tried to begin with the coming of Darinor, but she bade him go back even further. Unlike her father, she wanted to know how he had uncovered the Sword to begin with, and why. He owed her his life, she said, and she would have it all.

He started again by confessing his lifelong obsession with the Swords of Asahiel, from the moment he had *first* met Darinor, a mere storyteller who had shared with young Jarom of Diln the legend of the blades. From there, he gave an overview of his life as it had been, and how it had changed with the death of King Sorl, the wizard's invasion of his homeland, the revelation of his own heritage . . .

She made him go slow. Often, when he tried to brush past something, she would have him go back and fill in the details. He quickly came to sense that she was interested not so much in the events themselves, but in the effect they'd had on him. She wanted to know *who* he was, this young man who a madwoman claimed would determine the fate of their world. It was a struggle for Torin not to scoff at every turn.

It made for an easier telling, in a way, in that he did not have to pick and choose matters of relevance, allowing her to decide for herself what events might or might not have bearing on the current predicament. On the other hand, he often became irritated, being forced to dwell on meaningless trifles, or to relive choices that, in hindsight, he might not have made. His altered perspective had come to cast strange light on all his dealings; at times, he could hardly recognize who he had been, or the things he had believed.

But Annleia listened raptly, and never judged, as best he could tell. Because of that, he spoke candidly of matters he had never openly revealed to anyone before. He told her the truth of the wizard's identity as his elder brother. He told her how he had been tempted by Spithaera, and how he had decided not just once, but twice, to surrender all she asked for. Given what Annleia already knew of him, of the monster he had become, such revelations felt relatively shameless by comparison.

When he finally got to speaking of Darinor and the Illysp, he immediately began asking questions. But Annleia made him put those aside and focus on his narration. One thing at a time, she said, or they would never get through this.

So he proceeded to tell her of his voyage across the sea, and of the quest that followed. He told her what he could remember of the Fenwa and Necanicum and Lorre. While describing his northward trek, the one thing he made no mention of was the intense feelings he had developed for Dyanne. Those remained his, and his alone. He would not risk that they should ever be used against her. He would not sully them by speaking them with his unclean lips.

Annleia said nothing throughout, guarding her emotions, withholding comment even when he paused to allow it. He thought to spare her another recounting of his initial visit to her valley, but she wished to hear it all, from his view. She wept anew at the attack on one father at the hands of the other, but demanded that he proceed despite her tears.

The bedside pitcher was empty by the time he spoke of his return to Alson, Darinor's unveiling, Cianellen . . . and his awakening as an Illychar. His tone darkened, and his shame returned. Annleia cried again when he spoke of the dragon's assault on Aefengaard, leading him to reconsider his continued omission concerning her mother's fate.

Yet, on that count, he kept to his silence.

All that remained was the battle at Neak-Thur, of which she knew as much as he. But she asked him to tell of it anyway, and of their own fight in the wood.

"What happened to paralyze him?" she asked at the very end. "When he had the chance, why didn't he kill me?"

He. As if it were someone else she had struggled against, and not the very same face she was gazing upon.

He answered her as best he could, saying nothing of Dyanne, only that there were memories and feelings within him that the Illysp had not yet claimed. It had finally occurred to him, in that fateful moment, to let Thrakkon suffer their release, as the Illysp had suffered when stealing the rest.

She thanked him for that, to which Torin only snorted gracelessly. A flash of inspiration that should have come much sooner, he thought to himself. Had he been wiser, he might have seen to it that he fell victim to Killangrathor—or earlier, even, to the giant Rek Gerra and those other Illychar he had sent south against Laulk and Leaven. He should have paralyzed himself long before he had slain so many.

He deserved no gratitude.

Annleia permitted him a momentary silence, then asked, "Is that everything?"

He certainly hoped so. The afternoon sun that had peeked through the chamber's arrow slits upon his awakening had given way to ruddy sunset. His voice was hoarse, his strength gone, his emotions all but spent. Nevertheless, he forced himself to consider, uncertain, thinking back on anything he might have unintentionally missed.

Finally, he looked at Annleia and nodded.

She gave him another moment to make sure, then shook her head and sighed. "Then Darinor revealed nothing we do not already know."

Torin found that difficult to believe. "He spoke truly, then?"

"It would seem he had to, if he hoped to win your compliance and ours. He misled you only in regard to his underlying purpose, as he confessed to you in the end."

"But . . . that can't be everything." This Finlorian lass who looked nothing like one was his last hope, his *only* hope. It could not end here. "What of this Ravar you spoke of? What is that?"

Her eyes fixed upon his, glimmering with their depthless intensity. "You say you wonder why Darinor did not journey himself to find my people. Have you not recognized the truth of it by now?"

Torin scowled, realizing he had not. Nor did he care to try. He was sick of questions and riddles. At this point, they all seemed knotted together, a jumble he might never unravel.

"He didn't because he *could* not," Annleia prompted, seeing that he was about to give up.

That only confused him more. "What do you—" he began, then halted beneath the weight of her stare. Another shiver ran through him. "It . . . the sea . . . that *thing*."

"That *thing*, if the legends be true, is our only ally, *and* our greatest enemy."

Another riddle. "How can it be both? Is it an Illychar?"

Annleia laughed, though her eyes were so bright, so open, that he could see the fear within them. "It is not a creature you or I can quite comprehend, save that it hunts them. Its only purpose, its only need, is to ward this earth, this *Ia-Tamarin*, against horrors—such as the Illysp—that are not of its sphere."

Torin gritted his teeth, weary of being told by others what he could or could not understand—particularly when it seemed they were right. "What sort of fate is that?"

"A fate decreed by His brothers and sisters of the Ceilhigh, and a fate well earned. For He once sought to claim this earth, to enslave their creations to His own—and lost."

Torin felt his eyes widen. "You don't mean . . ." *The Dragon Wars.* "Is it even possible . . . ?"

"To condemn a god to physical form? According to legend, when Ravar's earthly hordes were driven forth by the Vandari and their Swords of Asahiel, the other Ceilhigh came together to do just that, imprisoning Him in the body He now wields and banishing Him to the depths of Ia-Tamarin's oceans— there to dwell for all eternity. Immortal still, but compelled forever after to defend this earth's creatures, whose lives He had deemed unworthy except as fodder for His once-mighty minions."

Torin did not even attempt to respond. He sat in stunned silence, reeling with disbelief, with wonder. The divine being who had bid His armies of dragons conquer this world . . . Could this be the selfsame creature he had encountered twice in his journeys across the sea? Could it be he had come so near to a living god?

"It was from Him," Annleia continued, "that Algorath and the Vandari obtained the Dragon Orb, with which they fashioned the seal that ended the Illysp War."

The *First* Illysp War, Torin thought, now three thousand years past—itself four millennia removed from the Dragon God's banishment, Killangrathor's exile to Mount Krakken, the close of the Dragon Wars . . . "But the Orb is destroyed," he managed at last.

"And I lack the knowledge or power with which to erect a seal as my forefathers did. Our last hope, it seems, is for Ravar to provide both."

A sudden cold gripped Torin from within. Was she suggesting he visit with such awesome majesty face-to-face? "Can He do that?"

"I know of no other course, else I would gladly seize upon it. I had hoped that you, as wielder of the Sword, might know something I did not."

That might explain why she had been so determined to find him in the first place. She would need the Sword in any case, yes. But without the skills her people had once possessed, she'd had only two choices: Seek him, or seek the sea monster, the Dragon God, Ravar.

"You say He may also be our greatest enemy," Torin recalled. "Why?"

Annleia looked to the bank of arrow slits serving as windows, toward the unseen ocean in which the monster lay. "If Ravar can help us, it will not be because He wishes to do so. He would sooner see the world destroyed, and all weakling creations of His fellow Ceilhigh with it. He hunts the Illysp only because He is compelled by a feral craving too great to resist, cursed by His brothers and sisters to act against His own wishes."

Torin shuddered despite himself, for it was a curse he understood all too well. "He hunts the Illysp, also? In addition to the Illychar, I mean."

"He sees all. Given the chance, He will *consume* all, when the hunger to do so becomes too great to resist."

"But the Illysp know this," Torin reasoned, "and will come nowhere near Him." Without Killangrathor, he realized, Thrakkon and his brood would never have dared this journey. "My own lands may be lost, but—"

"And these shores, as well," she reminded him, "for there may be no limit to the number of Illysp that clung to the minds of Thrakkon and his army as they made their flight overseas."

She means you, Torin thought sourly, *your flight.*

"It matters not," she claimed, "this land or that. When the hunger becomes too great to resist"—she paused, as if to emphasize the repeated words—"*all* will be consumed."

He kept silent, working it through while matching her inescapable gaze. "The ocean," he realized. "Can He . . . ?"

But he already knew. Having twice witnessed the creature—its strength and its sheer size—he needed no help to imagine the beast capable of raising waves that might swallow all but the highest reaches of this world. The Illychar could not be drowned, of course, but this would not be some gentle rising of the tides. These would be crushing waves that would smash and grind and splinter, triggering sinkholes, mudslides, and other devastating, earth-altering cataclysms. Lands would be ravaged, bodies pulverized and dragged beneath the sea. In the end, no coil would be spared, none left for the Illysp to claim.

"Necanicum spoke of it," Annleia confirmed. "A cleansing, by waves or by fire. I needn't tell you who she saw commanding which."

Just a mad old crone, he wanted to suggest, though even he no longer believed that. *The fates of all,* Annleia had said, to be controlled by him. For no better reason, it seemed, than that he had been the one to draw the Crimson Sword from what should have been its final resting place.

"The blade is no longer mine," he observed. "And we've no reason to believe that Lorre will return it to me—or even allow me to leave this city." He wasn't sure whether to be fearful of that, or grateful, yet it held true in either case.

"Then those are the first challenges we must overcome."

Words, effortlessly spoken. But how to act on them? "Does Lorre know who you are? Who you *really* are?"

"He does."

"And does that work *for* or *against* us?"

"You mean, does he intend to keep me here against my will." Off his nod, she said, "I don't believe so. Though, he is mistrustful of this entire situation—of you, and of me. He may wish us gone from here as soon as he learns you have awakened. Else he may decide to make sure you cannot assault him a third time."

Despite his frown, Torin would not fault the warlord were that his decision. "How long have you been here? Do you know of any others within your grandfather's camp that we might turn to?" He was thinking already of Gilden and Bardik, whom he remembered encountering during the battle. He'd been surprised to find them here—outside fetters, at least—and could not help but wonder if they were truly Lorre's men, or could be persuaded to assist him. Assuming either man had survived . . .

"Saena," was Annleia's first answer.

His thoughts shifted. "She made it back, then?" She had told him when he bid her farewell in Kasseri that she intended to return. But that had been weeks ago, and many leagues from this place. Anything might have happened.

Annleia nodded in response. "I was suspicious of her, initially—of the fact that Lorre made no mention of her from the first. Even after I learned that she was here, I was not permitted to visit her until my grandfather had briefed her in private. But the lass has such an open manner . . ." She shook her head, as if unable to explain. "She is Lorre's servant, yes, but does not seem to have anything to hide."

Torin knew how she felt, having had the same fears and reached the same conclusions, though it had taken him much longer to do so.

"Before the battle," she added, "when Lorre would make no promise to spare you, Saena helped to guide and prepare me, smuggling me into position atop the Bastion as a member of General Gilden's regiment. I cannot say that she would defy her lord outright, but she will help us again, I think, if need be."

"Gilden. Bardik. Are they . . . ?" He found himself afraid to ask. "Did they survive the assault?"

"Bardik did. He led those who found us in the wood. I can't say about Gilden. I've not heard otherwise, but I've been as much a prisoner as you over these past three days, under constant guard while the Illysp incubation reversed itself and I waited for you to awake."

Torin glanced at the heavy iron lock and keyhole upon the closed door, undecided as to what troubled him most at that particular moment. Their entrapment, yes. The missing details of who Annleia was, and of *how* exactly she had purged him, to be sure. Mostly, however, it was knowing that his former comrades had betrayed the Wylddean freedom for which they had struggled so valiantly, throwing in with Lorre and an eventual conquest of Yawacor's Southland. Granted, the warlord would not likely have spared their lives had they elected otherwise. Did that mean Chamaar and Arn and Jaik and all the rest had changed banners as well?

"Is there anyone else who might help us?" he asked.

"The soldiers you fought with all seem to have sworn genuine allegiance to my grandfather," she admitted, as if reading his thoughts. "The Nymphs, perhaps."

Her words struck him like a bucket of ice water, and he responded breath-lessly. "What?"

"Dyanne and Holly. They're the ones Lorre suggested I speak with to learn of your potential whereabouts, and the ones who then directed me to Saena. As they—and now you—told it, Saena was the last to have seen you, remaining with you and Crag after the Nymphs had bid farewell in order to travel south."

Yes, but they were only to have stopped through Neak-Thur on their way home to the Nest. If they were still here . . . "Lorre captured them?"

"They claim to have decided that the best way to keep an eye on my grandfather's movements was to remain close to his side."

The hive of thoughts that had begun to settle somewhat over the past few hours whirred and buzzed anew. *Dyanne? Here?* "I must go to them."

"What, now?"

Yes, now. Confound all else. He had less than half the answers he needed, but could tolerate no more questions, no more doubts, no more charges from witch or elf or fallen god. Dyanne was here, in Lorre's clutches. He would see her at once. He would know she was safe, free, and that at least one small portion of the world was as it should be.

"Guard!" he shouted, jerking his legs from beneath the blankets and rising to his feet.

When he swooned, Annleia reached out to catch him. "You haven't the strength," she said, as he clutched at a bedpost. "They'll look in on us at supper. Please, we've still much to discuss."

A dizziness clouded his vision, and myriad aches and pains assailed him. "None of which will matter," he insisted, gritting it all away, "until we know what your grandfather intends for us. Guards!"

A key was already scraping in the lock, and a moment later the heavy door flung open. A steward appeared, flanked by a pair of troll faces, their low-slung jaws thrust forward. The steward's eyes widened to see Torin on his feet, even sagging against the bedpost. "My lady—"

"Fetch me a page," Torin snapped. "There are friends I wish to speak to."

CHAPTER THIRTY-THREE

TORIN CRANED AND TWISTED BESIDE the windows, angling in vain for a glimpse of events outside. A crescendo akin to battle cries had been building steadily ever since the steward's departure, but the slits were too narrow to allow him a proper view.

All of which was forgotten the moment he heard the knock upon the door. One of the troll sentries, which had remained inside, rapped twice in response. Torin glanced at Annleia as she emerged from an adjacent chamber of the small suite. The trolls' lingering presence had dampened any further discussions. While Torin privately doubted their ability to understand—or their interest in hearing—anything he or Annleia might have to say to each other, the Finlorian lass had chosen to retreat to her own room and sit in sulky silence. That suited Torin just fine, overwhelmed as he was by what he had learned already, and by the expectation of seeing Dyanne again.

But it was not the Nymph who stepped through the door in answer to his summons.

It was Saena.

Torin winced as his right knee wrenched awkwardly beneath him. The injured joint was heavily wrapped, yet he had done little thus far to test it. His abrupt motions—and the stabbing pains they unleashed—nearly dropped him to the floor.

"Are you all right?" Saena asked, hastening forward.

Torin looked past the woman to those who accompanied her. He saw the steward, and another pair of trolls waiting outside.

"Where's Dyanne?" he asked.

Saena's gaze turned briefly to Annleia, then to the floor.

"Saena?"

"I'm sent by His Lordship. If you would see your friends, you are to follow me."

Her eyes finally lifted, yet she could not seem to force a smile. This was not the Saena he remembered. The realization caused a tightening in his stomach. He looked at Annleia, whose reservations shone plainly on her face.

But Torin would not be deterred. "Then lead on."

Saena hesitated. Surely, there was much she wished to say, yet she did not seem to know how to begin. Torin could hardly blame her.

At last she nodded and stepped out into the hall. Torin followed without delay. Annleia continued to prove more wary, lingering until both he and

Saena looked back at her. Finally, she joined them, staring purposefully at Torin as all four troll guards formed up alongside.

Only the steward remained behind as their group started down the corridor. Annleia's cautionary glances persisted. That Lorre felt the need for an armed escort did not bode well, but Torin would not let it trouble him. Nor would he be unsettled by Saena's uncharacteristic silence. Whatever friendship they may have formed during his previous visit, he was no longer the same person. The woman could no doubt sense it, and had every right to feel awkward.

It scarcely mattered, in any case. Until he had assured himself that Dyanne was well, he found it difficult to devote much care to anything else.

Nevertheless, he knew that Saena's voice would carry at least some weight with Lorre. Perhaps that was the impetus behind Annleia's unrelenting looks. Perhaps she wished for him to discover where they stood.

"I'm glad to see you safe," he offered tentatively.

"And I you," Saena replied, turning to regard him with . . . what, exactly? A mixture of emotions, it seemed—fueled in part by sympathy, he decided, when her eyes dipped to regard his wounded leg. "I'm not sure I understand what all has happened here."

"I haven't come to terms with it myself," Torin admitted, and wondered if he ever truly could. To die and live again . . . "I would not expect you or your lord to understand; though if he'll give me a chance, I'll do my best to explain."

Saena nodded, then fell again into glum silence. All those times in which he had been unable to shut her up, and now it appeared he might have to drag her words out of her. She certainly wasn't ready to offer reassurance. He caught Annleia's next look and scowled in response. She was welcome to make her own attempt, if she thought she could do better.

She said nothing, however, and the uncomfortable silence thickened. As the footfalls of their little company echoed amid the empty halls, a sense of grim solitude closed round. It was not until they passed near an outer ward that Torin heard again the snatches of din from outside, and decided to ask about them.

"Is the city under attack?"

"A celebration," Saena answered, without looking at him. "In honor of His Lordship and the city's recent triumph."

That put a lid on any other questions Torin might have asked. It was *his* fall they rejoiced in, and that of his devil minions. This was no homecoming, as some small, foolish part of him wanted to believe. He was a trophy, as likely as not to be executed for his crimes as part of this night's festivities.

The corridor led to a winding stair, which they descended by the light of low-burning torches ensconced upon the weathered wall. A series of halls and steps followed, all leading down into the depths of the citadel. Though he would not have been able to trace the route on his own, Torin recognized bits and stretches of it as that which he had walked weeks earlier when led from

Lorre's dungeons. A wiser man might have been alarmed by the prospect, but the only chill Torin felt was that of icy determination.

Upon reaching the outer door to the dungeons, at the base of a narrow flight of steps, they found a single giant standing post. When it saw them coming, it ducked its shaggy head beneath the opening and murmured something in a guttural tongue to those beyond. It turned back just as Saena reached the floor's landing, and nodded her through.

Torin limped down the final step and shuffled after. His knee throbbed, and he felt a sweat upon his brow despite the dank, briny cold. He hated feeling so weak and languid, and focused those feelings in a glare given to mirror the one aimed at him by the tusked giant.

But that standoff was swiftly set aside, for beyond the portal, Lord Lorre waited, flanked by another pair of giants. Though the creatures towered over him, the overlord's was clearly the more commanding presence, with his frigid stare, his crossed arms—

And the Sword of Asahiel sheathed at his waist, heartstones afire amid the gem-studded silver of the unblemished hilt.

Saena and the trolls stepped aside. Torin held his breath, braced against the terrible emptiness of Lorre's gaze. If the warlord was at all surprised to see him raised from the dead, his steely manner did nothing to show it.

"Twice now you have come against me," Lorre snapped in his crisp, imperial tone. "There are few who could boast the same. Tell me, what cause have I to spare your life a second time?"

The overlord's eyes never shifted, not even to glance at the granddaughter stood at Torin's side. His evident anger was greater than Torin had imagined.

"None."

"None?" Lorre arched a colorless eyebrow. "My granddaughter speaks of a quest, one you must complete if we are to avoid further assaults such as the one you most recently led against us. As I recall, you spoke similarly when last we met. Is this not so?"

"I am responsible for a great many ills," Torin replied. "Should you spare me, I will do what I can to set matters aright. But I cannot promise that it is within my power to do so. Nor will I make the attempt until I know my companions are safe."

The warlord's leathery face seemed to darken. "Your Nymph comrades returned of their own accord, and dwelled here under their own influence. My granddaughter has told you this, yes?"

"You will forgive me my doubts. After Warrlun's attack—"

"I had no hand in that treachery. He would have suffered long and slow, had he not found mercy at the end of your blade."

Lorre's tone was so sharp, so bitter, that Torin did not doubt the claim—and this for exacting revenge against Laressa's traitorous husband. It caused him to wonder briefly just what sort of suffering the overlord might devise for the man who had murdered Laressa herself.

"So you say," Torin responded, thinking it better that Lorre did not learn of his daughter's death. "So let me see my friends, and hear it from their lips."

The overlord studied him a moment longer, giving no hint of either acquiescence or denial. When at last he turned on a heel to proceed down the dungeon's throat, he left no indication of whether he intended to grant Torin's request.

His giant attendants, which formed a wall at the warlord's back, motioned them onward. Saena, still looking doleful, led the way. Torin glanced at Annleia, but did not care for the Finlorian's worried expression. The trolls started forward, and so did he.

They did not travel far. Perhaps a dozen strides along the central hall, Lorre stopped beside a large holding cell. Odd scuffling sounds echoed from within, which for some reason made the hairs on Torin's neck stand upright. When he drew close enough to see clearly, and heard Annleia's startled gasp, he understood why.

Through a wall of rust-flaked iron bars, he glimpsed several rows of bodies set upon makeshift biers. Each was wrapped and tightly bound in a burial shroud, watched over by a handful of torch-bearing soldiers. The presence of these armed attendants might have seemed odd, were the bodies not thrashing and writhing, struggling to tear free.

Annleia was aghast. "I warned you to burn the dead!" she exclaimed, rounding angrily upon her grandfather.

"Which we did," Lorre assured her, "by the thousands." He passed through the open cell door, taking a torch from one of the soldiers, whom he then dismissed. "But I wished to examine these *Illychar* myself," he explained, as he strolled amid the rows of animated corpses, "and thus kept a few of our fallen, so as to witness the supposed transformation and better understand the enemy I face."

A taste like bile rose in the back of Torin's throat. To willfully condemn others so . . . Either the overlord lacked any grasp of what he did, or else he was far crueler than any of the stories about him suggested.

Lorre came to a stop beside one of the bundled forms, and beckoned Torin forward. "This one," he said, when Torin stood beside him, "you may recognize."

He did not. Not through the thick layer of burlap shroud. But the very possibility appalled him. "Should I?" he croaked, while the body kicked and squirmed against its bonds.

When the warlord did not respond, Torin forced himself to seek the other's gaze.

"You wished to see your friends," Lorre answered once their eyes had met. "Here she is."

An invisible vise clamped round his chest, and everything within seemed to burst. He did not blink; he did not breathe. There could be no doubt as to who *she* referred to. Torin's devotion to her had been plainly demonstrated in the heat of battle—ending, in fact, their earlier assault on Neak-Thur. Lorre had not forgotten.

"Her companion, the smaller one, was slain by a goblin," the warlord said, "ripped to ribbons. This one," he added, his eyes turning back to the body in question, "Dyanne, she slew the beast, but perished from her wounds."

The words echoed as though from a great distance. Torin did not know whether to vomit or weep. He looked to Saena for refutation, but the woman only hung her head.

"Is there nothing that can be done?" Lorre asked.

Torin rounded on Annleia. "You must help her," he pleaded, "the way you helped me."

The Finlorian, her eyes still wide with revulsion, shook her head. "I cannot."

"Why?" Lorre pounced upon the response as if springing a trap. "Your witchcraft saved one. Will it not save another?"

Annleia pouted defensively as a roomful of eyes bored into her. For a moment, she ignored them all, then reached into a small pouch tied to the hempen belt about her waist. From within, she drew forth a small, barely budded flower. It looked something like a thistle, save that its petals, stem, and even its spiny thorns were pure white, as if all pigments had been leeched from the plant's tiny veins.

"Here is your witchcraft," she said. "A mere gosswyn, whose life juices, I was told, are poison to an Illysp spirit. Sure enough, a simple invocation—call it elven sorcery, if you must—enabled me to draw those toxins and use them to purge Torin's body."

"So let us see it at work," Lorre challenged with a measure of distaste.

"The flower can be used but once," Annleia admitted, looking apologetically at Torin. "For the invasive spirit is not destroyed, but driven out, caged now within the gosswyn—as evidenced by its blanched appearance."

"We can fetch you another," Lorre suggested derisively, turning promptly to make it a command.

"But can you also fetch a fresh sample of her untainted blood?" Annleia challenged.

Lorre's eyebrow arched. "Untainted?"

"Prior to her death," Annleia explained, slipping the flower back into its pouch. "For that is the key ingredient. Without it, the poison is incomplete, and will not work to expel the Illysp inhabiting the body."

Where hope and need had given him strength, Torin knew now only staggering dismay. Damn that Necanicum for preserving *his* blood and not Dyanne's. Damn her for not telling them plainly what they might do to defend themselves against the unspeakable. A sample of blood, a gosswyn, a Finlorian to manipulate nature's song—it mattered not how ridiculous and painstaking and impracticable it all seemed. At the least, it had provided them an opportunity.

A chance that was now gone.

"If that is so," Lorre said, speaking again to Torin, "what would you have me do, with her and the others?"

Torin did not know that he could speak the words. But he knew all too well the torment they endured, and could think of nothing more vile than allowing it to continue unchecked. He gazed down upon Dyanne's body—thrashing upon its bier—and heard himself whisper, "We must . . . we must set them free."

At that came the rasp of steel. "Do it, then," Lorre said, presenting him a long-bladed dagger.

Torin regarded him with anguish. He could not make himself take the weapon.

Lorre frowned. "Would you prefer I assign the task to one of these others?"

Torin looked around, then wrapped his fingers around the bone-handled hilt. Its surface felt smooth and cold, clammy in his palm. What was one more death? he asked himself. It seemed the only fair penance, for all that he had done: to be forced to take the life of the one he had come to prize above all others.

He peered down upon her face, where a monster's mouth sucked madly in and out against the rough layers of shroud. He tried to envision the woman he had known: her gleaming eyes, her contented smile. He fought to remember the dreams he had once had, a longing for things that could never be. He leaned close, placing his left hand gently upon her brow.

And drove the dagger through her heart.

The woman bucked and writhed, screaming out against the coarse, suffocating wrap. Other Illychar within the cell took up the muffled cry. Torin closed his eyes and held her tight, twisting the blade like a key in a lock. Horror . . . pain . . . denial . . . they flapped and tore at him like a flock of angry scavengers, each claiming a piece in the race to devour his soul.

He laid her back when at last it was finished, opening his eyes to the stain of blood welling up around his dagger's thrust. A choking rage assailed him. The blame was his to bear, yes, but Lorre's as well. Had the overlord not kept her here, she would surely have returned to the Nest—she and Holly both—to their sisters of the Fenwood, far from the havoc he had wreaked upon this city. The debt for their lives had yet to be fully paid.

He whirled, caring not for those around him, caring not for the consequences that might befall this vicious, unjust world. Dyanne's blood was upon Lorre's blade, and only the warlord's life could wipe that steel clean.

But as he came about, fully prepared to drive the dagger home, he found his own throat perched against the tip of the Crimson Sword, held firm in Lorre's ready hand.

He heard someone gasp—Saena, he thought. He did not turn to see. His eyes locked with those of the warlord, muscles rigid with grief and fury. Through a glaze of unshed tears, he peered deep into those soulless orbs. It was like staring down a long, dark well to the shadowy reflection awaiting him at its bottom. Only now did he truly comprehend the emptiness within the man, the waging of war against a guilt and pain from which he would never be absolved. The drawn, tense moment gave Torin a studied glimpse of his own future.

Should he live to see it.

Lorre was the first to blink. He then lowered the Sword, laying it back along the length of his arm to present it by its hilt. "Your Dyanne lives."

"What?" Torin rasped. He refused the proffered blade, not daring to believe.

"I had to make certain that all you've told me is true," Lorre said, "that this quest to vanquish the Illysp is indeed the only hope for all." When Torin still did not respond, he shook his arm and the Sword impatiently. "I had to know that you possess the resolve to carry out this mission—whatever that may entail—to its bitter end."

Torin let his gaze slip, first to the blood-smeared dagger in his palm, then to the body on which it had been used. "This . . . this woman I killed—"

"Served me faithfully, and died too soon. These others, as well," Lorre added, gesturing with his torch at those still struggling against their bonds. "Were your death sufficient to buy back their lives, I would make the exchange and call it a bargain. Alas, I am no sorcerer, and must suffer the blind whims of fate."

Torin let his eyes drift about the cell, embarrassed by a growing sense of relief. "Then Dyanne . . . and Holly . . ."

"Are among the celebrants outside, I'm sure. Saena should be able to help you find them."

Once more, Torin shifted his attention to Lorre's servant. Her pained look remained. Shame, he now supposed, at being a part of the warlord's deception. And something more, some underlying sullenness, that he did not immediately recognize.

He did not have time to puzzle it through. His head was spinning, his heart beating too fast. A hot anger still burned within, deep beneath the cold shock of reprieve. As bitter as he felt toward Lorre, he was also grateful. He wasn't sure if he should embrace the man, or take the Sword and use it to lop off the warlord's head.

At last, his focus turned to the talisman itself. The Sword seemed to beckon him, drawing his beleaguered spirit into its comforting depths. He followed freely at first, but recalled all too quickly the pain he had inflicted, the sorrow he had harvested, when last he had held the blade in his fiendish hands.

"A weapon like this should belong to a warrior," he uttered in due warning, "something I've never proven to be."

"Until now, perhaps." Lorre gritted his teeth in obvious frustration. "There are things I don't understand, and others I'm no longer sure of. But I still trust my instincts. If the stories I've heard are any indication, you've achieved much already that others decry as impossible. Whatever your destiny," he added, looking now at Annleia, "I am reluctant to stand in its way."

Torin took a moment to gauge the Finlorian's reaction, but found it impossible to interpret. With her grandfather similarly distracted, he reached for his blade, only to have Lorre draw it suddenly away.

"But know this," the overlord concluded. "I'll not spare you a third time.

Should you take up this weapon against me once more, of your or another's accord, I will show you what hell is before ever you find the Abyss."

Too late, Torin thought, but settled for grasping the Sword as Lorre returned it to his reach. All at once, its familiar warmth shivered through his veins. The invigorating power could not allay his guilt, and yet he had come to depend upon it in so many other ways. By now, he knew well enough that he would never again feel truly alive without it.

Remembering Lorre's dagger, he wiped its blade across his own tunic, then flipped it around and handed it back in the Sword's place. "I'm sorry for your losses," he said, and thought again of Laressa. "If I find a way for my life to buy back theirs, I'll pay it gladly, and consider it a bargain."

Useless words, poorly mimicked, yet Lorre grunted as if appreciative of the sentiment. "Good fortune, then, to the both of you." He sheathed his dagger. "See to their provisions, Saena, if you would. I expect they'll want to be on their way before I have the good sense to change my mind."

He made it sound like farewell, brusque and hurried as it was. So be it. Torin was in no mood to consult the man further—to learn of his army's status, inquire as to his plans, or even to advise him of the looming threat he surely faced from an army of Finlorian Illychar. For Torin, the most pressing concern was as it had been at this meeting's inception. The rest of this madness could wait.

"My friends first," he reminded Saena, as if any in the cell might have forgotten.

He shuffled toward her as Lorre turned away.

"What about you?" Annleia asked.

The warlord looked back, stern brow pinched in question.

"Will you not join the celebration?" his granddaughter asked him. "It is well earned."

"*They* might disagree," Lorre countered, gesturing at the roomful of bundled Illychar. "I have an army to rebuild, a city to repair, and a realm to defend. I have no time for trifles."

Torin exited through the open cell door.

"I'll remain with you, then," Annleia blurted. She glanced back long enough to catch Torin's look of surprise, then faced her grandfather again. "While Torin says his good-byes. If I may be of any help, that is."

A trick of shadow perhaps, but, for the barest of moments, Lorre's seamed face softened. "As you will," he agreed.

Torin started down the hall then, brushing past the troll guards and leaving Saena to scurry in pursuit. Despite a wealth of assurances, he had yet to confirm the fates of Dyanne, Holly, and so many others abandoned to Lorre's clutches. The power of the Sword dulled his pains and drove his step. He only hoped he wouldn't have to use it to slay the proud, inscrutable warlord before this night was done.

CHAPTER THIRTY-FOUR

THE LAST TIME HE HAD left Lorre's citadel to walk the roads and alleys of Neak-Thur, Torin had found it to be a ramshackle city teeming with sullen-eyed citizens and boorish soldiers. But that had been fresh off General Chamaar's failed attempt to recapture the Wylddean capital, and within a fortnight of the overlord's initial occupation. Now, it seemed, Southland commoners and Northland invaders were the dearest of friends, a people made one by their common victory. The tyrant had become the savior, his armies the shield that had sheltered them against the unimaginable. These inhabitants owed their lives to Lorre and his troops, and had spilled forth in droves to proclaim their gratitude.

Torin made his way among them with nervous anticipation, casting guarded glances against any who might recognize him. The chances were remote, Saena had assured him. The battle's focus—and that of the people—was upon the dragon. Despite the occasional rumor, few knew—or had cause to believe—the various accounts of the outlander king and his Sword of Asahiel having led the attack.

They had taken a few simple precautions, just in case, stopping by an armory to pick out a scabbard for the Sword, and the heavy cloak that Torin now wore. Beneath its thick, musty folds, Torin kept his hand at all times upon his weapon's hilt, both as a salve against his wounds, and to alert him of any danger.

Stealing about like some cutpurse was almost enough to give him pause. So anxious was he to reunite with Dyanne and others he hoped would be here that he had scarcely considered what their reactions might be. The more he thought about it, the more he fretted. What cause would they have to welcome him? What reason to be pleased by his return? Most, he had barely known. Even those he had once fought beside were not what he might call friends—particularly when he had tried more recently to send so many of them to their graves.

But those concerns did no more than put a hitch in his stride. A terrible risk, he knew, especially in regard to Dyanne. For so long now, she had been his only strength, her memory all that had kept him going. Should she reject or ignore him, should she dismiss him out of hand, he wasn't sure what new source he might draw upon. So be it. If only he were to see her again, he would suffer any unforeseen consequences gladly.

His focus just now was on finding her at all. "Are you sure you know where we're going?"

Saena's pout deepened. She had scarcely opened her mouth since accompanying him from the dungeons. Granted, he had done little enough to encourage conversation, but when had that ever stopped her before?

"I was told that she'd gone to the bonfire," the woman replied.

"*Which* bonfire? There is one in every plaza that we pass."

And at every corner, and in the streets, surrounded by revelers of every shape and persuasion. Around them, flocks of squealing children chased one another with borrowed brands, delighting at the way the flames whipped in the wind. Other youths acted out the roles of soldiers and monsters, with one pack even come together in a knotted pyramid to play the part of the dragon. For the moment, at least, long-standing prejudices had been forgotten. Here a man bought drinks for a band of orcs; there a drunken woman planted kisses upon a disinterested troll sentry. Everywhere Torin looked, mobs had spilled forth from homes and taverns to raise cheers and share tankards and dance with one another in unbridled merriment.

"The heart of the festival is beyond the city wall, upon the field of battle," Saena said, shouting to be heard above the thunderous press. "You'll see."

If we can reach it, Torin thought, pushing through a crowd gathered tight around a puppeteer's stage. Viewers groaned and hissed at him to clear the way, but he paid their complaints no mind. The parks and squares and roadways ahead were crammed with vendor stalls, whose owners hawked charms and trinkets and food for the masses. There were singers and tumblers and jugglers and fortune-tellers and body artists woven among them, each promising thrills no other could offer, and clogging the way for all. Torin was left to forge his path where he could.

"Dragon tooth, sir?" a cloaked codger asked him, sidling up close.

The man looked and smelled like something a rat might haul from a gutter, and Torin shied away reflexively.

"What have you got there?" Saena asked.

Torin tried to pull her along, but the peddler came between them, opening his cloak to reveal a cache of loops and pockets sewn into the lining. Tucked or slung within were a variety of blackened bone shards.

"From the beast hisself. Teeth, claws, powder of scale—"

"Ground down with what?" Torin snorted. "And those 'teeth' of yours are not half as thick as some of the dragon's smallest spines."

It was one of the few topics he *had* thought to ask his guide about, back when they were rummaging about the armory: what had become of Killangrathor's remains. Saena had quietly explained that, despite all attempts, the dead beast had proven impervious to fire. But with Torin's blade in hand, Lorre himself had led an effort to butcher the dragon and chop its bones up into so many artifacts and trinkets, to be sold and distributed as wards, charms, trophies, medicines, and more. A brigade of giants had helped, though they had dulled, chipped, or shattered scores of mauls, axe heads, and saw blades in the process. The task had taken more than two full days, and many of the resulting pieces were the size of boulders and trees. Yet there was little risk of the creature ever rising again.

The peddler offered a conspiratorial smile. "Rumor has made the beast larger and more fearsome than it really was, you see. These are genuine relics, sold to me by a friend who worked the crews what handled—"

"Either your friend was a liar, or you are," Saena snapped. "His Lordship established a special council of guildsmen to see to the allocation of all dragon artifacts."

She made to brush past, but the peddler followed. "Guildsmen make coin where they can," he sighed regretfully. "A few morsels on the side, you understand, to escape the overlord's tax. A savings to you, hmm? How about it, sir? A necklace for your sweet that none other shall have. Else this here powder, for a paste that will keep her skin forever young."

Torin glared at the other's persistence, while, beside him, Saena flushed.

"Leave us," she insisted, "before I have you arrested."

At last the charlatan bowed and melted back into the throng.

Moments later, the outer gates to the city finally came into view. Torin groaned inwardly at the sight of so many crammed together in that outer courtyard and in the curving corridor beyond, penned in like sheep. Many were not even moving, but stood bleating in place, making it difficult for those who *were* trying to pass by to enjoy any progress. City watchmen were doing their best to keep the hordes in motion, but, by the looks of it, their efforts were meeting with only marginal success.

"The festivities are liable to end before we make it through this," Torin grumbled, searching for the moon amid the high stone walls and a cloud-smothered sky.

"Must you see them tonight?" Saena asked, as if to agree. "Chances are we'll be able to catch them on the morrow, before you set out."

Torin kept his complaints to himself after that, and focused on carving as swift a path as he could through the swarm.

His worries proved grossly unfounded, as their escape did not take half as long as he'd feared. Once beyond the confines of the curtain wall, a sudden change swept over him. It came upon the roar of music and laughter, underscored by that of the sea. It came upon the air, moist with mist and thick with the threat of rain. It came as stifling smells gave way to strong, salty wind gusts. While Saena drew her cloak tighter about her shoulders, Torin drew a deep, invigorating breath, savoring these and other sensations that rushed to greet him. He could almost taste them in the air—Dynara and her Fenwa clan, Chamaar and his wedge commanders, Arn and Gavrin and all of the many rogues whose company he had shared. His imagination, surely, nothing more than the aroma of the vegetation, the flavor and caress of the ocean air. But to Torin, the living aura of those encountered here was a palpable entity, a magic borne upon the wind. He had dreamt of it often enough to sense it readily; infused with its strength, he reflexively quickened his pace.

He knew, without asking, where they were headed. Several hundred paces to the west, beyond the milling heads of a vast multitude, a tower of fire raked and clawed at the heavens, built upon a temple of logs. That was where the throngs had gathered. That was where Dyanne and the others might be found.

He made the mistake, then, of glancing to the north, to the ruined hulk of the Bastion. Even from a distance, he espied the clefts in that great wall, and the rubble yet to be swept away from its base. A lump came to his throat, and he turned his head in disgrace. It never should have happened. He never should have left. He should have been here to *defend* this people, not lead the assault *against* them.

But that was a child's reasoning. He had done what was asked of him in fulfilling his task and returning to the land of his birth. His own desires had been irrelevant.

Except, if he had followed his heart rather than Darinor's demands, would not both lands, this one and Pentania, be better off?

He looked again to the Bastion's forbidding silhouette. *Done is done.* Should the time come to atone for his failures, this image would be among those that gave him the courage he would surely need.

"This way," Saena urged.

Torin did not bother to question her. Though dismayed by the numbers amassed before him, he had begun to trust in the atmosphere around him. Regardless of his past, and in spite of his shadowy future, he could not deny the exhilaration spawned by this . . . this culmination of his fervent longing. It fostered in him the sense that anything was possible—an energy that lent strength to the power of his dreams.

The press thickened as they neared the back of a gallery erected upon a set of risers. Tumblers danced upon a stage below, performing daring aerial maneuvers that drew gasps of awe and delight from the crowds. The bonfire raged in backdrop. Torin saw now that it was built on dragon bones, cross-laid in the shape of a giant pyramid. The bones themselves did not burn, but provided a framework for the driftwood stacked high upon its ledges. One could not come within twenty paces, so intense was the heat. Beyond this no-man's-land, however, hundreds—if not thousands—surged and writhed, wrestling for a better view of events, or else engaged in drinking, dancing, and other festive pursuits.

"His Lordship's lieutenants will be in the gallery," Saena shouted in his ear, while trying to worm in that direction.

Torin nodded distractedly. It was difficult to fathom the Dyanne and Holly *he* knew pledging themselves to Lorre in any fashion. Then again, Annleia *had* made mention of them wishing to keep a close eye on the warlord's conquest strategies. What better way to do that than as members of his inner circle?

As they neared the front of the gallery, they passed an area cordoned off for entertainers preparing to take their turn onstage. Torin peeked inside a few of the tents and pavilions as he passed, seeing mummers, minstrels, performing animals, and more. Musk and perfumes cloyed the air; already, Torin could feel their sickly sweet taste in the back of his throat.

Before he realized it, he had lost step with Saena. He found her several paces ahead, looking up at the shadowed rows of the gallery from the lowermost tier. Searching for Dyanne, he supposed. He had begun to push past those come between them, muttering apologies, when his cloaked eye brushed against a familiar face.

He froze, turning his head at once. The woman stared back at him, bright black eyes pinched with suspicion.

"Torin?"

"Holly," was all he could think to say, gaping in shock.

Too late, he considered that it might not be wise to reveal himself so openly. His first clue was the throwing knife that appeared in Holly's hand.

But his gaze did not linger on the ready blade. For in the next instant, there she was, behind Holly, emerging with a pack of strangers from a curtained hollow beneath the gallery. From out of his imagination, straight from a dream, it seemed, bearing that infectious, heart-crippling grin.

The grin slipped when she turned from the others to find him standing there. A gasp of surprise escaped her lips. "Torin."

"Dyanne," he greeted, before his breath caught in his throat. She appeared precisely as he remembered her, as if immune to the time and distance—to the shadowy veils of death itself—that had come between them. Her tunic and breeches were of silk and leather, as smooth and supple as the flesh they covered. Her hair hung long and unbound. Wide with shock, her maple eyes gleamed.

The Nymph took note of Holly's aggressive stance. She slid to her kinmate's side, hand resting lightly on the pommel of her rapier. "We saw you on your deathbed," she said.

It pleased him that she would have bothered. He showed them his empty palms, then reached up slowly to lower his hood. "Necanicum dubbed me immortal, remember?"

A poor jape. Neither woman matched his meager smile.

"It's you, then?" Holly piped in that child's voice of hers. Her own eyes glittered warily. "Where is your elven girl? What are you doing out here?"

"She's with Lorre. I left them to find you."

Holly cocked her head. "Left them. Alive, or dead?"

"Stop!" Saena cried, rushing up to stand between them.

Torin glanced around, but the outburst—and the face-off that had prompted it—had gone virtually unnoticed. He turned his eyes back to Dyanne.

"I see you've found one another, then," Saena remarked.

Holly uncoiled slightly. "The elf's witchcraft actually worked?"

Dyanne laid a hand upon her kinmate's shoulder. Her gaze held Torin's captive. "You might as easily have been one of *them*," she explained in Holly's defense.

"They told me you were still here," Torin said, and wondered if she could sense the breathlessness in his voice, the feathery lightness in his head and heart. "I had to see it to believe it."

"To make sure our good overlord thinks twice about marching south," Dyanne replied.

Holly snorted. "That's *one* reason."

"Meaning what?" a bemused Torin asked Dyanne. By now, he was staring, but he could not seem to look away. After so much yearning and so much fear, it did not seem possible that here they stood, face-to-face. Every memory he'd had of her, every lost image, brought now to sudden, wondrous life.

A moment too perfect to be real.

Somewhere in the background, a troupe of musicians stopped playing, and the crowds raised a hearty applause. "That's us," said Holly. She looked at her kinmate, frowning in hesitation. Dyanne seemed to consider him for another moment, then nodded, at which point, Holly sheathed her knife and stepped forward.

Dyanne followed, brushing past him. "Wait here," she bade him. "I want to hear of everything that has happened since we parted." She then turned with a confident twist, chasing Holly through a tunnel of bodies, making her way toward the stage.

"Where are they going?" Torin asked, his gaze locked upon her departing heels.

"To perform, it seems," Saena replied.

The tumblers onstage were making their bows, stooping to collect flowers and coins tossed up at them from an appreciative audience. A few were already headed down the riser stair, where Holly and Dyanne stood waiting. When Dyanne glanced back at him, a warm flush billowed in his chest.

"Come," Saena urged. "Let us find a seat."

"She said to wait here," Torin protested.

"Would you see their act, or not? We won't lose them, if that is your fear."

Saena climbed into the gallery, displaying for the watchman a token of rank worn on a thong about her neck. Torin followed, but halted at the forward rail, wishing to stay close to ground level rather than burying himself amid those who occupied the tiered benches above. Saena flashed an irritated look before joining him.

Their routine was hardly an *act*, but rather a demonstration of their joint fighting technique. Some in the crowd might have thought it staged: two slender girls making work of a dozen men in padded armor. But Torin had witnessed such displays before against actual opponents much fiercer than these. Had the Nymphs not exchanged their arms for blunted tourney weapons, this troop would be suffering more than mere welts and bruises.

"I wonder who put them up to this," Saena said, as members of the audience gasped and cheered.

Whomever, Torin owed them a debt of thanks. For he could think of nothing more mesmerizing than watching her up on that stage, executing an inimitable array of thrusts and parries, leaps and rolls, flips and slides, alongside her kinmate. In light of their dance, he lost track of all but the rapture of this night. He knew not whether to shout or weep. Grateful he was for the reunion, but how much had he lost? How much time had he already wasted?

"Are you all right?" Saena asked him.

Her words could not dislodge his admiring gaze. He simply stood there, staring, paralyzed by Dyanne's divine charm. Though he had envisioned their reunion a thousand times over, none of the memories, dreams, or emotions to which he had clung had prepared him for the surge of bittersweet joy unleashed by this startling reality.

"I love her," he said to the wind.

Saena did not respond. Perhaps she hadn't heard. But Torin had heard himself clearly. For the first time, he had uttered the words aloud, and they now rang splendidly in his ears. A renewed sense of exhilaration washed over him, a sense of liberation at having shared the truth with someone, at last.

The audience roared as the last of the "assailants" yielded, and Holly and Dyanne took their bows. As whistles and applause rained down from the gallery, Torin smiled. His sins, his sufferings—they no longer seemed to matter. Though he might never comprehend how or why, he had been given a second chance, and was determined to make the most of it. He would prove himself to this woman, and make up for the time he had squandered. This very night, he would tell her all that roiled within his heart, that they might never be forced to separate again. The notion filled him with such hope and anticipation that his body and soul shivered with it.

He watched her as she and Holly traded their sparring tools for their own weapons belts, and the wounded around them helped one another offstage. True to her word, she headed straight toward the area in which she had left him, grinning politely at those who rushed the cordon to shower her with praise. There were suitors among them, Torin was sure, and not all of them drunkards, but she only smiled and ignored them, looking around until she caught sight of him and Saena at the gallery rail.

A bear in manacles was being led onstage. By the time Dyanne and Holly reached him, the audience's focus had shifted, and he had her attention almost to himself.

"Well?" she asked, virtually aglow beneath the wash of firelight and a thin sheen of sweat.

"Seems neither of you has lost a step."

Her lips parted, and there it was, that revealing, dazzling smile that had first captured his devotion a lifetime ago.

"Begging pardon," Saena broke in, "I must excuse myself."

Torin turned. "What? Why?"

"There are your provisions to see to," she said roughly, "and my father as well."

Something in the way she spoke raised a twinge of alarm. "Your father?"

"Was wounded during the battle," she said, confirming his fears. "He will be well," she assured him, "but I vowed not to leave him alone any longer than I must."

Before Torin could apologize, she turned to the Nymphs and added, "I can entrust him to you, can I not?"

"We'll keep him safe enough," Holly said. Her impish grin seemed part pledge, part warning.

Torin felt he should persuade Saena to stay, else offer to attend her . . . until Dyanne showed him another smile, and said, "It might be best, in fact, that we don't let him out of our sight again."

Saena scarcely received a nod as she took her leave.

"Come, then," Dyanne suggested. "Let us hear your tale."

She slipped past to lead him onward, weaving her way toward an aisle stair. Torin followed in a daze. Now, more than ever, it felt to him as if their destinies were linked, woven together by a divine hand. A trick of his own passions, perhaps, but Torin had to believe otherwise. He had to believe that Dyanne felt it too—that somehow it was meant to be.

As they climbed the gallery steps, the wind from the south strengthened. High overhead, the sky's mantle of clouds grew dark and menacing. The citizens, well accustomed to such weather, scarcely noticed. Torin smiled, basking in a soothing familiarity. The bellow of the ocean amid shrieking winds was to him a glorious harmony, while the tang and thickness of the air was like the security of his bed, wrapping him in a shield of comfort no blanket ever could.

He scanned the benches as he climbed, searching for any faces he might know. Some waved or called greeting to the Nymphs, but none seemed to recognize him. An outsider still, though that was not how he felt. He was stronger here. He was quicker, more alert. Most of all, he was happier, immersed in a sense of having found his true home. This was where he should have been born, he thought. Come what may, this was where he must remain.

"Dyanne," a voice hailed, low and even.

Torin could not place it, though it struck a familiar chord in his memory. Then he saw the tall, stone-faced man emerging from his seat among a clutch of comrades, rising in welcome.

Jaik.

The sight of the man gave him pause. Dyanne, however, showed no hesitation as she turned toward the former Wylddean wedge commander, who was urging his benchmates to make room. As she reached him, the soldier greeted her with a gentle embrace, before leaning down to kiss her on the lips.

As sudden as that, planks and timber turned to quicksand beneath Torin's feet, freezing him in place.

Holly came up behind him. "You remember Jaik, I'm sure."

Dyanne withdrew, looking back at her companions with what might have been an embarrassed grin. "Jaik, look who we found returned from the dead."

The soldier eyed Torin, his typically placid expression rippling with surprise. He glanced back at Dyanne, who nodded reassuringly, then thrust forth
his hand. "You look well, I'd say. Welcome back."

The warmth of the man's greeting was a shock in and of itself, and jolted
Torin into clasping the outstretched arm. "Jaik," was all he could think to say.

Inside, he was reeling, bent beneath a tempest of foul memories he had
done his best to forget: recollections of Jaik's lavish attentions . . . Dyanne's
evident interest in the soldier . . . a hint of attraction between the two, displayed while en route to recapture Neak-Thur, almost from the moment the
two had met.

That's one *reason*, he heard Holly suggest again.

"Join us?" Jaik offered, gesturing to the bench.

Torin nodded because he did not know what else to do. It would seem
rather uncouth of him to drive the Sword through this man's stomach. He
might have done so anyway, but for the knowledge that Dyanne would not
thank him for it.

Instead, he shuffled after Holly down the length of the bench, ignoring a
line of stares from men he did not recall. They might have been Northlanders,
whom he had fought against twice. Or they might have been Southlanders,
like Jaik, who had turned cause to save their own necks. Some smiled and
welcomed him as if they were old friends, while others nodded curtly or ignored him altogether, focused as they were on the entertainment below. The
bear onstage was doing a dance around its handler. It made as much sense to
Torin as anything else.

"I'll have those wagers now, sirs," Jaik said, grinning proudly as he followed down the row with an arm around Dyanne.

"Well fought, lass," one older man grumbled. "Lucky you are, Jaik," said
another. "You'll never convince me those men weren't bought," complained a
third, smirking at Holly, "but a right good show nonetheless."

Holly sat, then Torin, then Jaik, with Dyanne on his far side. As the last of
the debts and compliments were paid, attentions drifted back to the dancing
bear below.

"You and your dragon, you picked the wrong people to hunt, eh?" Jaik
offered quietly.

Torin winced, then glared, but held his tongue as he found Dyanne peering
at him from around Jaik's chest.

"Savage beast," Jaik went on. "We had to spill half its marrow before
it ceased to struggle, and lost ten thousand men in the process. We've been
sweeping up the rubble and burning the dead for three days now."

The man as Torin had known him had always been stern and straightfor-
ward. He did not seem to be trying to give offense. Yet Torin did not know
what the soldier expected of him. An explanation, perhaps? Yes or no, Jaik
was hardly the one he felt like explaining himself to.

"I hadn't thought to find any of you fighting for Lorre," he countered.

Jaik laughed. "That makes two of us. When I rejected Lorre's offer, I expected that was the end of me. But the old tyrant surprised me—surprised us all—by setting us loose."

"Us?"

"General Chamaar, me, Gilden and Bardik—all of the high-level commanders who came against him, and who refused to join his army. I guess he realized that a man cowed into service is not the most dependable of officers."

"So, what happened?" Torin asked. Moment by moment, he found his anger and jealousy dissipating as a result of Jaik's brotherly manner. The man did not have to be sharing any of this, yet did so without mistrust, as if they were comrades-in-arms, rather than enemies and rivals.

Or perhaps it was merely that Dyanne's presence continued to soothe him. With her looking on and listening in, eyes bright with interest and lips drawn back in a pleasant smile, how could he know anything but gratitude and delight?

"We fled south," Jaik continued, "thinking to gather our scattered forces and renew our siege. But the commanders and I, we got to sharing what we'd learned. For the vast part, those who serve Lorre do so with genuine fealty. He demands structure, discipline, but that's not the same as enslavement. The more we spoke of it, the more we realized that he offered us a life better suited to our warrior spirits—reckless and wild, yet not without order and purpose."

A great stretch in reasoning, Torin might have thought, had he not deemed long ago that Lorre was less a tyrant and more like a stern father seeking to shelter his many children from the ills of the world. Whichever, he could hardly speak to the cravings of another man's spirit, save that he and Jaik might have had more in common than he wished to believe.

"You all came back, then?" he asked.

"A good deal of us. Chamaar accepted a governorship far to the north, while Gilden and Bardik and I took up standing offers to join Lorre's vanguard, here to the south."

"Are they . . . are they here?" It was past time that he forced himself to inquire as to which of his former comrades had survived.

Jaik nodded. "Bardik is here somewhere, likely halfway through his second barrel. Lancer came out as well, but I believe his flock of nurses convinced him to return to his chambers for more rest."

Torin could not help but smile in relief. "What of Arn? And Gavrin?"

"Arn? He went his own way. Too much of a mercenary, that one. Could never sit in one place. I don't know any Gavrin."

"Yes you do," Dyanne prompted. "That weasel of a flank scout, the one who recruited us."

"Ah, him. No idea. Disappeared even before our defeat. Skulked off to the Southland, be my guess."

And a safe one at that, Torin decided. A rogue, through and through, never more at ease than among those of his own ilk. It surprised him, though, the hole he felt at not knowing for sure. "What of those whose ways you swore to defend?" he asked. "Will you let Lorre make thralls of them all?"

"Wylddeans have no oaths—or none I was ever called upon to swear. We at Neak-Thur banded together against the only threat we knew, never *really* knowing what we were fighting against. Regardless, Lorre's primary goal in taking Neak-Thur was to solidify his southern border. He's come to realize, however, that he has stretched himself rather thin. Having lost half his army here, he may have us retreat north."

"That would be wise," Torin agreed in reflex, to which both Jaik and Dyanne regarded him questioningly. "The Illychar will come again," he explained. He spoke mostly to Dyanne, not knowing how much she had shared with Jaik. "Elves, from the Splinterwood. Some five thousand, I'd say, at the least. Lorre would do well to reinforce his people to the north, and hold out for as long as possible."

"Five thousand is not all that many," Jaik mused.

"Perhaps not. Perhaps Lorre will be able to destroy them all. But it is unlikely to end there. With the Illysp, it may be that no corpse upon these shores is safe."

He should have told Lorre as much already. He likely would have, had he not been so angry and flustered at being tricked into "killing" Dyanne. Perhaps Annleia was relaying news of the slaughter at Aefengaard even now, and what it meant to have all of those Illysp and Illychar on the loose. But Torin felt now that he had to make certain *someone* knew, just in case.

"What happened?" Holly interjected. "I thought you went home to *end* this threat. Instead, you bring it back to us?"

"I failed." He thought to tell them more, to relay how, exactly, but ended up only shaking his head. "Annleia . . . she says there may still be hope. If there is any truth to her belief . . ." He swallowed, peering beyond the fire, out upon the black stain of the ocean, picturing this city, this land, this people, beneath its churning, icy cold embrace. He then turned to Dyanne, vowing, "I will not falter again."

"Then let us celebrate," Jaik proposed. He signaled to one of the passing servers, calling for wine. Coins were exchanged for a flagon and any cups on hand. Men in the row offered to share theirs for a draft, and Jaik heartily complied. "A toast," he said, when the last had been poured. "To lessons learned, friends reclaimed, and to our common strength in the battle ahead."

The cheers went up, and a surrounding knot of men and women who knew nothing of the horrors being privately discussed quaffed their drinks in merry salute. Torin took a polite sip from Holly's cup, still trying to sort through the chaos of his feelings.

Not long after, the string of performances concluded and the dancing began. The gallery all but emptied, captains and commanders and others of rank and influence within Lorre's newest city heading down to join the common masses upon the stage and the surrounding grounds. This included Jaik, who invited Torin to join him and his fellows. With Dyanne looking on, Torin was not about to refuse.

They settled upon the crowd's fringe, listening to the roar of the blaze that crackled amid Killangrathor's remains, and to the uproarious shouts of those who danced within its eerie mix of shadow and light. By then, it had become painfully evident that his comrades had gotten along in their lives just fine, and needed no rescuing. For hours, it seemed, he listened to them trade comments on matters of little import and lesser consequence. They spoke of songs and drinks and dances. They spoke of places they might like to see, and old friends they might like to visit. Jaik wanted to see the so-called Nest from which Dyanne and Holly hailed. Dyanne only smiled and allowed that perhaps one day he would.

Try as he might, Torin could not bring himself to feel cheated by their relationship. He'd had his chance, after all, and had failed to take advantage of it. Having known all along that she was more than he could possibly deserve, why had he allowed himself to dream otherwise?

Besides, Jaik remained far too disarming to suffer his enmity. As envious as Torin felt, as willing in that moment to trade lives, he could not fault the man for having taken notice of Dyanne's charms, or for having the courage to tell her so.

"Dance with me," Holly demanded at one point. He obliged her, of course, if only to remain near Dyanne and Jaik, who had already risen to do the same. There, upon the well-trampled grounds, he silently observed the woman he loved as she swayed gracefully within Jaik's arms. The ache in his chest deepened while watching her stare upward at her partner, devouring him with her priceless orbs, gazing upon his features with a rapture typically reserved for a god.

"Strange, isn't it," Holly said.

Torin glanced at his own partner, to find her looking at the pair as well. He cleared his throat. "You tell me. Is it odd having someone come between the two of you?"

"I only want her to be happy."

"And is she?"

Holly took a moment to consider. "As content as I've ever seen."

The remainder of the evening passed in a haze of music and laughter and frivolity that enveloped Torin without ever fully reaching him inside. Now and then, the couples danced, but for the most part kept to the fringe and conversed with one another while watching others come and go. Dyanne never asked for the rest of his story. Perhaps she was not as interested as she had claimed. Else perhaps she understood the inherent horror, and sensed his reluctance to relive it. When asked what his plans were, he told her only that his travels had not yet ended, that he would be forced to resume them on the morrow.

His intense disappointment continued to be tempered by the thrill of simply sharing her company again. Each time he risked a glance in her direction, he found another image to savor. Each time she smiled, whether at him or another, he grew warm with contentment.

He was enjoying one such moment when Bardik came upon them, smelling of ale and holding a woman in each arm. The commander let go of the pair in order to hug Torin in front of all, offering a hearty smile and a welcome return. *No more drink for this one*, Torin thought, abashed by the exchange.

But there were others as well, rogues-become-soldiers whose names and faces Torin had forgotten, but who had not forgotten his. Each extended the same companionable welcome offered by Jaik and Bardik. After a while, Torin was given to marvel at this spirit of undeserved fellowship. Though some may not have known of his role in the recent battle, many others clearly did. It was naught but the glee of victory, he determined, that caused them to embrace him so. None could be so forgiving otherwise.

He grew to appreciate it nonetheless. He enjoyed the fact that to these people, he was merely *Torin*, not some title to be unduly praised or endlessly prevailed upon. Small gestures, and meaningless, but they helped him to feel more comfortable, more secure in his own skin.

More at home.

When his companions grew weary, he accompanied them back to the city. The hour was late, and many had already retired to their beds, so the return trek passed almost too swiftly. Upon reaching Lorre's citadel, where Jaik was barracked and where Dyanne and Holly kept chambers, a guardsman informed Torin that his own chambers were waiting, with a letter of instruction from His Lordship and his granddaughter, and a small inventory awaiting his inspection.

Jaik was the first to bid him a peaceful rest and safe journey, shaking Torin's hand and urging him to return when he could. Holly followed, offering her impish grin and a nod of farewell.

Dyanne went last. With the fullness of life shimmering in her eyes, she reached out and clasped him briefly just below the shoulder. "Don't leave without saying good-bye."

"I won't," he promised, exhilarated by her touch. She then slipped down an open hall along with her comrades, leaving him in that outer courtyard as a rain began to pour.

CHAPTER THIRTY-FIVE

Allion's eyes were closed, but the darkness afforded him no comfort. The tumult raged in his ears, a cacophony of screams and moans, of grating steel and whistling bowstrings. The fires, fed incessantly, spat and crackled. The stench of smoke and pitch and corpses had formed a crust in his nostrils and a putrid taste upon his tongue.

The taste of war.

"Enough," Marisha scolded. His lids snapped open to find her standing over him, backlit by the orange glow of the forward blazes—their black breath an ugly smear against the evening sky. "You're exhausted. Why won't you go and rest?"

"For the same reason you won't," he said, his throat raw.

It seemed pointless to try. Even when he did manage to sleep, the combat raged in his dreams. Ghosts danced before his mind's eye, twisted shadows entangled in a web of bloodshed. Dark weapons protruded from these churning silhouettes like misshapen appendages, waved about as part of some macabre display. Figures fell, but countless others joined the fray, ensuring that the dance would continue. Ceaseless, immortal, the maelstrom was without end.

"You're of no use to anyone like this," she pressed, then looked down and glared. "I see you're not using the guard I gave you."

He followed her gaze, to where a throbbing in his hand matched the pulsing in his head. His fingers were caked with blood, stuck to where they rested against his muddy breeches. The repeated use of his bowstring had long since cut through skin and callus, leaving the flesh blistered almost beyond recognition.

"My aim suffers if—"

"Your aim will suffer a great deal more when you've naught but knuckles to draw with."

"We've had this conversation before," he reminded her.

"Too many times," she agreed. "So where is that guard?"

Allion motioned vaguely. "I gave it to one of the others. Tevarian, I believe his name was. His rotation is sleeping."

"*Your* rotation," she pointed out. "Yet here you—"

"First reserve! Form up! West flank!"

Allion leapt to his feet, propelled by instinct. Marisha, thankfully, did not try to stop him, but ducked aside behind the barricade. Amid a scramble of his fellow reserves, the hunter dashed to his left, peering over the boulder wall to the black wave of Illychar that had broken through the front lines of infantry, charged through the fire walls, and was now bearing down upon their position.

"Alight!" the crier shouted, echoing the orders of the commander on duty.

Allion swiped a pitch-coated arrow from the nearest barrel, and nocked it to his bowstring. The Illychar were closing fast, but he waited for the torch-bearers to run down the line, igniting one arrow after another until his turn had come.

"Draw!"

He grimaced as the cord cut into the ruined flesh of his fingers. Clenching his teeth, he trained his eye upon the mass of enemies that had closed already to within thirty paces.

"Loose!"

He released his flaming missile and reached for another, listening to the chorus of shrill whispers that marked the first volley's flight. He looked back as the flesh-piercing rain was descending. He could not see the faces of those who yelped and contorted as the bolts struck home. Perhaps that was for the best.

A few of the more gravely wounded seemed to hesitate, as if wondering whether they should press onward or return to the madness from whence they had strayed. Humans, Allion decided, men and women, part of the swarm that had descended upon them two days ago. *From Atharvan*, he recalled, and cringed at the sound of their screams.

But that did not stop him from loosing another arrow, and another, until finally the charge had been broken and the infantry had swarmed in from behind to seal the breach.

He lingered until the order was given to stand down, and he and his fellow reserves were dismissed. Even then, he was slow to depart, mesmerized by the thrashings of those he had helped to slay. Though gruesome, the sight of a dying Illychar never grew stale; even now, his stomach twisted with a kind of fascinated revulsion.

"Come," Marisha said, appearing suddenly at his elbow.

It was worse when seeing them up close. He had done so, more than once. You had to peer deep, past the unspeakable bloodlust, but it was there, in their eyes: the torment of an enslaved soul. It was the same pain he'd seen in Darinor's eyes on the night the renegade Entient had saved him and Marisha from the goblin Illychar . . . though he hadn't recognized the truth of it at the time.

At last he lowered his bow, and allowed Marisha to lead him away by the arm. The healer never strayed far from his side, nor he from hers. She suffered with him the perils of combat, while he suffered with her the after-horrors of injury and gore. All a consequence of their continuing pact to face whatever end together.

Back along the wall they moved—one of a staggered series of bulwarks raised by the Kuurian force over the past few days. Theirs was a defensive stand, as drawn up from the outset. With King Thelin and the bulk of the Imperial Army leading the land's refugees south to Wingport, Allion and Marisha had joined High Commander Troy and a force of twelve thousand in marching north to blockade the Gaperon against a gathering tide of Illychar, in hopes of guarding the civilian retreat. They had arrived with barely enough time to erect their walls, dig their trenches, and establish their infantry lines and rotations, skirmishing even then with an increasing number of foes trickling south through the mountain pass. By the time those early preparations had been completed, a horde of some thirty thousand commoners slain at Atharvan had descended upon the army's position.

And his nightmare had begun.

Day and night they battled, utilizing a system of rotation to keep the men fresh—which made the disparity in numbers even worse. They had brought mobile ballistae, though, along with wagonloads of ammunition. They had close to a thousand arrows for every bow, and fletchers labored continuously to make more. The Illychar, though relentless, were poorly shielded, and ill equipped to weather such a storm. Provisions were plentiful. With any luck, they might hold out for weeks.

Which we must, Allion thought grimly, if Thelin's desperate plan was to have any chance of success.

The hunter kept his head low, squinting as a coarse breeze of grit and ash and cinders raked his eyes. A river of oily black smoke followed. All about, the fires continued to writhe and belch, scorching his throat and poisoning his lungs. Soot darkened his skin and his already shadowed hopes. Difficult to control, those blazes, given the swirling of the winds here within the pass. But they were a necessary part of the defense, helping to funnel the Illychar somewhat, and to destroy those who fell. Most of the time, however, they were less a blessing and more a curse.

When the singeing cloud had passed, he let his gaze slip to the north, scanning the slopes to make sure that none of their positions had been compromised. Marisha pulled on his arm.

"No more," she said. "We'll go together."

She drew him southward, away from the worst of it. She was taking him to rest, he knew, though this time he made no effort to resist. It was his regiment's turn to do so, after all, as she had reminded him. And she was right: He badly needed it. If only true rest could be found. But the battle would follow. A man could not work himself into such a frenzy and expect to simply wind down for an evening nap. The sounds, the smells, the horrid and unforgettable images would remain, permeating his soul, turning him gradually into something less than human.

He'd found it better to remain awake, with mental wards set consciously in place. And as long as he was awake, he preferred to be of some use. Troy and his Souari lieutenants knew better than he how to stage a force for long-term, all-hours combat. Yet, from what the hunter could tell, the time never came in which additional hands were not needed.

For one task or another, he thought, as he caught eye of a team of sappers laboring to dig yet another trench. Their position to the south was secure, but was being fortified in advance for when the battalions gave way. While Troy had no delusions about pressing forward, he meant to scratch and claw for every pace of ground his troops must surrender. The longer they stayed within the Gaperon, the better, as the mountains rising on either side made it much easier to keep the enemy bottled up. Once they were pushed back upon the plain . . .

He might have hoped it would never come to that. After all, they had not surrendered a single barricade since their arrival. Against a force already three times the size of their own, superior arms and superior tactics had enabled them to hold their entrenched position.

But the decision had already been made, the exodus begun. Thus, he could take no hope in any success they enjoyed here. Amid all the clangor and bloodshed and smoke and sweat and sleeplessness, the worst was knowing that theirs had already been deemed a lost cause.

"Do you suppose Nevik has had any luck in convincing Rogun to evacuate Krynwall?" Marisha asked him.

Allion could only speculate. They'd had no word from the north, and no scout or messenger was going to break through this clog of enemies. As of now, the Illychar were not so numerous as anyone had anticipated; clearly, the swarms that had sacked Atharvan had found battle elsewhere. While good news for the peoples in the south, what might this mean for their beleaguered neighbors to the north? Had they barred the gate on their own friends?

He certainly hoped that Rogun had the sense to listen, and to lead his countrymen west before the Illychar engulfed them. Allion's family was still at Krynwall: his parents, his brothers and sisters, the friends who had survived the massacre at Diln, and those he'd made after his move to the city. He wondered constantly if they were even still alive. He supposed they must wonder the same about him.

"Either way," he replied at last, "they won't have a shield like ours. Their fortunes and ours seem to be on opposite ends of a pendulum's swing."

Marisha gave his arm a gentle squeeze. "You mustn't lose heart."

The suggestion rankled him. "Simple as breath for some," he muttered. "Not so easy for the rest of us."

"Meaning?" she asked, letting go of his arm.

"You challenge others incessantly to find their strength. Seems sometimes you forget the truth of your own."

Marisha halted, grown suddenly cold beside him. Her hand moved reflexively toward the Pendant, hidden safely against her breast. "It's yours to wear, if you wish. It has brought me as much grief as joy."

"Spare me," Allion snorted. He wasn't certain why he was unleashing upon her like this, but it was too late to back away now. "Such grief as you may have felt, you brought upon yourself."

"Oh? And how is that?"

"It couldn't be some mere heirloom, could it? It had to mean something more. It had to *make* you something, something special, and you just had to know what that might be."

"Stop this."

"A princess, perhaps. Or a sorceress."

"I'm telling you to stop."

"Well, you know now, don't you? And you were right. You're not like the rest of us. You're more than I or any of these others can ever be. And if we perish, you'll find a way to endure, won't you? Just like you always have."

Her eyes were red. Her lip quivered. She looked as if she was about to cry. Instead, she slapped him.

"There are things in this world we must bear," she snapped. "But I will not bear this. Not from you. *Whatever* I am, I did not ask for it. Nor should it make any difference." A tear *did* fall, then, and seemed to make her angrier. "Should you wish to give rein to this . . . this sulking weakness, well then, so be it. Make your excuses. Take the beaten road. And let me know what sort of happiness you find when you get to its end."

With that, she stomped away from him, making not for the tent they shared, but for the infirmary grounds, to see to those in need of her care.

Allion considered going after her, but only for a moment. Though he regretted the way he had spilled them, those words had needed to be said. They were too different, no matter how badly they tried to pretend. Better for both that he stop chasing someone whose pace he would never be able to match.

Fueled by his frustration, he turned about and marched north.

It had been cruel of him to mock the dreams she must have had as a girl. He'd had dreams of his own, when he was small. Growing up, he had listened like so many others to the legends of heroes, and craved the many glories reaped of their noble wars. Were anyone to ask him now, he might claim there was no such thing.

But it was too late to matter. Right or wrong, Thelin was headed south, in search of a new destiny. Right or wrong, Allion had asked for the opportunity to guard the king's back. A lost cause, it might seem, but *that* was his purpose here. He could not save the world, as he may have aspired to as a boy. He could not mend every hurt and soothe every suffering, as Marisha seemed determined to do even today. But if he could make even this one, small difference, he would consider it enough for his own brief, mortal legacy.

Settling in among his fellow bowmen, the hunter closed his eyes, shutting out the world while waiting for the next call to arms.

"Too many," Corathel determined, peering through his overworked spyglass at the rear ranks of the Illychar swarm choking the mountain pass.

With moon and stars clouded over by those billowing smoke plumes, a precise count was impossible. But judging by the size of that tightly packed enemy horde, the number—whatever it might be—was greater than their own.

"For our divisions, perhaps," Jasyn allowed. "Throw in our civilians, and we ought to run them over easily."

"Not without heavy casualty," the chief general argued, though he was indeed tempted by the thought. "Less than a third are even armed."

"Let them throw rocks. We're more than four *hundred*, all told. The enemy is . . . what, forty?"

Thirty, Corathel estimated. No more than thirty-five.

"We'd have them at better than ten to one," Jasyn pressed.

"And when our civilians break?" Lar interjected. The soft rumble of his voice was like that of distant thunder, deep and ominous. "They'll crush one another—and us—in their own stampede."

"I wasn't suggesting we place them in the van. Their weight at our rear would be enough to—"

"Our rear may fall prey any day now to those enemies we left behind," Corathel reminded his Second General. He lowered the spyglass and shook his head. "This people did not follow us all this way to serve as fodder—on either front."

A leaden silence ensued, until Lar said, "It appears we are trapped."

The bitter truth churned in Corathel's stomach. Three days it had taken them—three long, grinding days for those who had evacuated Leaven to be herded west through the mountains and then south to the Gaperon. Riding his own shield, farther to the east, Corathel had been sick with fear for all that might go wrong. His scouts' constant reports, though encouraging, were not enough to completely ease his mind. Only when his smaller diversionary force had reunited with the main civilian body—and the four six-thousand-man divisions that protected it—had he finally heaved a sigh of relief.

For a few hours thereafter, he'd felt as if the desperate road they'd taken might actually lead to safety. He was still hobbled by his wounds, and weakened from his long time abed, but determined to put all of that behind him. The lands of Kuuria were within reach. Once he had recombined his armies with the ten thousand sent from Atharvan to guard *that* civilian retreat, and added whatever strength King Thelin and the Imperial Council had marshaled . . . well, they just might stand a chance.

Then had come word from a forward scout of the blockade that awaited them. The sun had just set—upon the land *and* his hopes, it seemed. After leaving orders with Maltyk for the host to make camp at the Gaperon's northern mouth, Corathel had ridden ahead to see for himself what lay before them, joined by Jasyn and Lar. Together, he and his chosen lieutenants had worked their way onto this barren jut upon the Gaperon's western slopes, and found themselves overlooking what appeared to be a dead end.

"Chances are," Jasyn said, not yet cowed, "this horde is the one that bypassed Leaven. Civilians themselves, for the most part. And we've got Kuurians on the other side. Put all our strength up front, I say, and drive through."

"A grand bloody mess," Lar predicted. "But he may be right, sir. We just may have the strength to eradicate this group."

"Should we make the attempt and fail," Corathel replied, "or take too long in doing so, we'll be crushed ourselves by those on our tail." Again he shook his head. "And without a rear guard, our civilians would suffer the meat of that blow. I say again, our numbers are insufficient to both clear the way *and* shield against pursuit."

He glanced over at Owl as the Mookla'ayan chieftain gave ear to one of his handful of remaining savages. The little band had chased after Corathel when he had broken away to follow his scout to this point. Ahorse, Corathel and his lieutenant generals had outpaced their stubborn followers for a time, but the slow trek along the paths of the mountain slopes had given the fleet-footed savages a chance to catch up.

The elf's words and gestures seemed to have turned Owl's attention to the eastern ridge, across the pass. Owl nodded, but said nothing.

"What do you suppose they're seeing?" Jasyn asked.

Corathel couldn't guess. At this point, he would have welcomed any advice the savages had to offer, but trying to communicate with them always ended up giving him a headache. He had searched for an interpreter among his troops, yet hadn't been able to turn one up. Barring that, he might as easily wish for a giant bird to bear them all safely over the mountains to Souaris as for the ability to understand their barbaric tongue.

Sensing his gaze, Owl looked to him, but gave no reaction.

"It doesn't matter," Corathel decided. He turned back to the scene below, and sighed. "We'll have to think on this." As sour as Jasyn's plan tasted, their only apparent option was to redirect themselves west. Krynwall did not offer half the strength—or room—that Souaris did, and Corathel was far less confident in General Rogun's willingness to permit refuge than he was in King Thelin's. Be that as it may, he would seek word from his western outriders as to the possibility, before making a decision.

"Come," he said, rising from his crouch. "Let us claim what rest we can, and see what the dawn brings."

CHAPTER THIRTY-SIX

"Ogre!" her forward spotter roared.

General Vashen slammed the door to the primary boiler and scrambled for her seat at the helm. Ignoring her driver's worried glance, she threw open an iron viewing slat. The wash of cool air that poured through was like a mother's breath upon a stinging wound. Yet the scene beyond caused her stomach to clench.

"Full to grinder!" she yelled back at her crew.

"Full to grinder!" they acknowledged.

The drillers were already in place, working the pump handle back and forth in steady cadence. As the order was given, their pace quickened reflexively. It mattered not. Under this new, steam-powered configuration, it was up to the boiler master to determine the allocation of energy maintained by their labors.

He worked to do so swiftly, turning a series of knobs and levers that would redirect power from the wheels to the grinder. They could not surrender all momentum, of course, but given what lay ahead of them . . .

Vashen looked again through her tiny window. The ogre was still coming, a lumbering monstrosity that might been taller than their rover were it able to straighten its hunched, gnarled bulk. The stump of an uprooted tree served as its cudgel, broken roots caked with dirt and blood. The grinder was turning, but not fast enough, she feared.

"Impact!" the spotter called down, hunkering in his turret.

Vashen grasped a pair of handholds welded against the rover's inner wall. The ogre hefted its cudgel, cheered by the swarm of skatchykem around it. The weapon came down—

And was promptly ripped from the creature's grasp as the grinder roared to full strength. So stunned was the beast that it did not even attempt to move aside, but was caught headlong by the rover's drilling snout. Rocklike skin cracked and tore, and a spray of blood filled the air, some of which flew through the viewing slat to spatter Vashen's face. She closed her eyes at the ogre's bellow, under which she heard its bones crunch and splinter amid the grinder's metal tooth-wheels.

The rover's meal was soon finished, the deep, crackling thunder of its munching replaced by the high-pitched whine of barbs and teeth spinning in empty air. The warder general wiped her eyes with a sleeve and saw that the ogre's brethren were wisely clearing a path along the road, sliding to either side of the lethal grinder. Their weapons banged and raked against the outer walls of the rover's steel-and-iron shell, while the skatchykem themselves shrieked and hissed with contempt. But, for now, the rover rolled on.

"Return to wheels, three to two," she commanded, licking the scar upon her lips and tasting the ogre's blood.

"Wheels, three to two," came the echo, and the boiler master set to readjusting the rover's power ratios.

She'd had good reason to doubt, in the beginning, the success she enjoyed now. The theories presented by the outsider who called himself Htomah had *appeared* sound, but she was Hrothgari, and her people knew better than any other, perhaps, that diagrams and implementation were often separated by a wide gulf of trial and error. When King Hreidmar had asked her opinion, she had allowed only that it *could* work, not that she believed it *would*.

Had she laid wager, the only purse she would have won was that her people could make the requested modifications in the time allotted. After much discussion between these Entients and the king's engineers, it was decided that seven siege rovers would have to suffice. Given what they might be expected to go up against, Vashen herself had argued for no fewer than twice that number. But *time*, Htomah had kept insisting, was their greatest enemy, and had to be taken into account.

Seven days for seven rovers. The Hrothgari had completed them in six. But there would be no time to test them—no chance to make further modifications or to learn if the Entients' powers could be trusted. To get them out of Ungarveld, the rovers had been constructed in segments, floated on barges along rivers from beneath the earth, and quickly assembled under the light of moon and sun. All would have to work as planned, for there was no going back.

It was for that reason that Vashen had insisted upon captaining one of the rovers herself. Her most natural place, others had argued, was at the head of the Hrothgari army as it led their people south. But the best hope for their safe emergence was a successful diversion. If their small pack of siege rovers failed to provide that, the Hrothgari's main populace would likely be caught out in the open and fall quickly to the very fate they were risking so much to avoid.

As primary commander and first defender of Ungarveld, the warder general would not let that happen.

She had selected each of the crews herself—no easy task given the number of uncertainties involved, and considering that she did not wish to strip the army of its leaders. Fortunately, it was not necessarily warriors she needed. Each converted mole required a team of operators, but the great hope was that few would be required to wield hammer or blade. She took officers as captains, engineers as drivers and boiler masters, warders as spotters and hurlers, miners as pushers and drillers, and general laborers to fill out support positions and to serve as reserves. For each rover, more than two dozen dwarves rode within, keeping the war machines churning day and night.

And so they had for more than a week now, rolling south and west across the eastern half of Tritos. At its heart, each rover was still an enclosed handcar. Wheels and grinder were driven now by a steam mechanism of valves and rods, pistons and boilers, rotating cogs and spinning flywheels, as laid out by Htomah—generating a strength of energy that no team of dwarves could match or maintain while pumping manually on the seesaw lever arms. The problem was the scarcity of fuel available to them to keep the fires burning and the boilers steaming. That was where the Entients' sorcery—and Vashen's greatest fears—came into play. For it made no sense to her that the fires would continue burning without wood or coal, or that the boilers' water supply should remain full with but a few drops of sweat and the occasional rain shower to replenish it. Yet Htomah and his friends had claimed to have tied the renewal of these fuels to the dwarves' labors. So long as Hrothgari on the pump levers maintained their endless push-pull cycle—pushers on the wheels, drillers on the grinder—the rovers would continue rolling and chewing along.

"Long enough to rendezvous in the south?" she had asked Htomah skeptically.

"If you do as I say, yes."

Only now, after eight full days, did she truly believe him. She had even given up trying to understand how they managed it, and simply accepted the Entients' work for its results. Her chief concern now was in dealing with the skatchykem that had assailed them for the past three days. A handful at first, her foes now stretched far and wide beyond her spotters' range of sight. Should any of their vessels suffer a failure—mechanical or magical—at this point, its passengers would be stranded within this sea of enemies, left to starve and rot until the skatchykem tore their way inside and raised the dead up as their own.

Small wonder her nerves had grown tighter and tighter over the past few days. It had been bad enough before, praying to Achthium that so many complex mechanisms would hold strong against the rigors of movement over such rough and varied terrain. With thousands of enemies now battering them day and night, trying to get at those seen to be riding within, it seemed but a matter of time before the assault exacted a critical toll.

"Made short work of that one, eh?" her driver shouted, loud enough to be heard over the hiss of steam and churning thrum of machinery.

Vashen stroked the forked braids of her chin beard and gave him a nod. She was already hoarse from shouting commands, and would likely be deaf before this ordeal was done. Htomah had failed to warn them about the forge-like conditions she and her crew would be called upon to endure. The shrieks and squeals and groans of metal, the roar of fires, the whir of spinning teeth, the grinding of studded wheels over mud and stone and corpses, the rhythmic huffing of the pushers and drillers, the snarls and grunts of the hurlers whose job it was to pepper the enemy with missiles so as to tease and torment and draw them on . . . all was magnified by the thick plates of iron and steel that shielded them now from certain death, creating a cacophony that raged endlessly inside her skull.

At the same time, she had come to cherish these sounds. For they were the breath and heartbeat of the monster in which she rode, a living creature of fire and metal shambling its way inexorably across the land. Should its pulse cease, so too would hers.

Given the latest exchange, however, her confidence was soaring. That ogre had presented the fiercest test yet, and had scarcely caused her rover to shudder. Doubtless, the blades and teeth of her grinder had suffered damage as a result; mincing one ogre did not guarantee that it could devour another. But she liked their chances better now than before. With any luck, the skatchykem would take note, and do better to clear a path henceforth.

So long as they do not clear away altogether. Strange, that they hadn't done so already. They seemed to have been summoned, as Htomah had promised, by the pillar of smoke risen from each rover's tail. After three days of bitter failure, however, she would have thought they might stray in search of easier prey. It left her to wonder if the Entient had worked some additional sorcery to fuel their obsession, or if their madness truly ran so deep.

Not that such frustration was inconceivable. It must be vexing indeed, she thought, to be able to crawl all over one's enemy and yet fail to crack its shell. For all its armored protection, her force's pace was . . . ponderous. Were it not for the swarm of foes, she could have crawled alongside without sweating a drop.

Which was more than she could say riding inside. The air was hot and stifling within these iron walls, clouded with a haze of dust and smoke. *'Tis no worse than some of the caves back home*, she reminded herself, and drew strength from the thought. The shadow-earth in which she had been bred and raised was leagues behind her—a prison, despite all that her kin had shaped and fashioned and constructed within. The wide world awaited, and she would make it her own.

She shut her viewing slat with a determined grunt and clambered back down to renew her inspection of the boilers, nodding and grinning at the crew members she passed. The fires burned as hot as they had eight days ago, upon setting forth. The sparks struck and fanned beneath the floor by those working the pump levers up and down, up and down, seemed indeed capable of fueling the Entients' sorcery indefinitely. Or was it the other way around? Either way, she saw no cause for her persistent suspicion that Htomah had hidden something important from her.

Her boiler master, Duggarian, was wiping his brow as she came upon him. He greeted her with a scowl.

"Is something amiss?" she asked him.

He shook his head. "Nothing I can see," he grumbled over the engines' roar.

She patted his shoulder in understanding. Dugg had grasped Htomah's designs quicker than most. But he was even worse than she about accepting results whose cause he did not comprehend.

"You fret too much over what cannot be helped," she said. "If they could have explained it to us, I'm certain they—"

"We're using up water too fast," he replied impatiently. "I've been adjusting the cutoff to minimize unnecessary flow loss, but at our current rate, we're going to run dry long before we reach the southern mountains."

It was Vashen's turn to scowl. Her gaze shifted to a set of pipes leading up to the roof of their rover, where gutters had been carved to collect and channel rainwater into the feeder tanks. "Could our friendly parasites have impaired our gutters?"

"I don't see how," Dugg snorted. "Even if the brutes were to recognize their function, I've not seen the weaponry that would be needed to damage the troughs. I'd sooner believe that the old man's . . . *spells* are losing strength."

"He assured us that wouldn't happen, not so long as we had even a trickle to keep them fed."

"We've not had a good rain since starting out," he reminded her. "Might be he was counting on it."

She could not argue there. She and the king's engineers had questioned Htomah and his friends endlessly, it seemed, but there was still plenty about this venture that remained unknown. The Entient himself, Vashen had sensed, did not have all the answers, and had served up hopeful assurances, in those cases, rather than share his doubts.

But there was nothing to be done about that now.

"We'll make do," she promised him. "Might be we'll all have to sweat a mite more, else cut our ale rations and burn that."

Dugg harrumphed. "I'd sooner *double* those rations, and let the beast choke on what my own body can't keep."

"There's that, too," she agreed. "And a pity it would be. Just in case, pray for rain, hmm?"

He shook his head, and she moved on. Hurlers busied themselves at the arrow slits on either side, firing darts and jabbing with spears at those who poked futilely back at them. The openings were little more than ventilation holes, angled downward so that the dwarves inside could attack from above while those below were left to aim and scratch at the inner ceiling. She would have enjoyed causing a few more casualties, even knowing as she did that they would only rise anew. Alas, she would have to settle for the destruction of those who ventured too close to her grinder. Those ones, at least, would not haunt her again.

The grinder roared as if in response—once, twice, in quick succession, finishing its victims almost before they could scream. Mere morsels, those. Humans. She had learned to tell simply by the pitch of the whirring drill teeth. Though far outnumbered among this horde by the various races of Eldrakkar and Gorgathar, humans were the weakest and most clumsy, and thus the last to clear her rover's path as it cored its way through their thick, jostling press. Her fool enemies would push and shove to get close, then push and shove to get away. Those who tripped and fell or failed to squirm past the others were caught by the grinder—which often seemed to draw as much delight as anger from their fellow skatchykem.

"Any messages?" she asked as she came upon her courier. Her people had long ago devised a system of relaying messages in the dark through the use of their glowstone lanterns, using the dimmer knobs to send staggered flashes of light as signals. A similar system had been implemented among each rover and its crew before setting out, to ensure communications between the separate vessels.

"All is well, at last report," Tonra replied. The smooth-cheeked Hrothgari was one of a half dozen other female dwarves aboard this, the lead siege rover, and one of Vashen's oldest friends. She seemed to sense the warder general's frown without turning to see it. "Have you word to relay?"

"Only to keep close watch on their water supply," Vashen said. "I would know if Duggarian's concerns are shared by the other boiler masters."

"At once, General."

Vashen left her to it, pausing to peer out a rear viewing slat, which afforded a glimpse of the black cloud chugging skyward from her rover's chimney. A pall it was against the clear blue heavens she had dreamed of for so long, yet another sign she had come to rely upon. So long as that smoke kept burning, the bulk of the Hrothgari should be safe, given the cover they needed to sneak southward. That had been Htomah's plan, anyway, and the one that Vashen and her king's people had agreed to. Though much could still go wrong, she preferred to focus on making it work.

The grinder feasted, the rover thrummed, and Warder General Vashen rode along in the forgelike belly of her shelled beast, bearing death to her enemies, and hope for a better future.

IT IS NOT TOO LATE, an inner voice whispered to him. *Turn back now, and all may yet be forgiven.*

Htomah shut his eyes, and breathed deeply of the crisp mountain air, trying to quiet the promptings within. So certain he had been that this was the course he must take—so certain that he had risked not only his own future, but those of his fellow Entients: Quinlan, Jedua, and Wislome. After tracking him to the Hrothgari city of Ungarveld and learning of his plan, they had decided to support him in his efforts, lending him even greater confidence than before. Upon launching the siege rovers and setting forth with the rest of the Hrothgari nation in tow, he had felt nothing but peace and determination.

But that was more than a week past, before he and his host had crossed the forsaken wilderness of southern Partha and reached the Aspandel Mountains—returning him to the doorstep of his former home. Now, all he could think of was the wedge he had driven through their sacred order, of the irreparable and far-reaching ramifications of his choices. Did the good he intend truly outweigh the unforeseen ills that must surely result?

"Lost our way, have we?" a voice grumbled.

Craggenbrun. The Tuthari must have followed him after realizing how long he had been gone. So deep was he in his own reflections that he had failed to sense the other's approach. "You should be resting," Htomah chided him quietly. "A long day lies ahead."

"And another after that, I'm sure. The camp stirs. Have you found our path?"

Not a path, but a crossroads—the last he would come to. Continue west, and he would pass through to the lands of Kuuria, where the Hrothgari might unite with the realms of man in battle against the Illysp. Veer south, however, and he would find himself on the trail to Whitlock, where he might beseech the mercy of Maventhrowe and their brethren—that he might renew his divine oaths and resume his all-important studies.

"I've not seen you think twice on which direction to take," Crag pressed. "Not once. And our choice here seems clearer than most. What's wrong?"

Wrong? Htomah nearly smirked at the other's obliviousness, and at his own inability to fully explain his dilemma to any but another Entient. In simplest terms, he had erred in coming this way. He had never anticipated that the temptation to turn back could be so great.

It is not too late.

But it was. He had led these people out, herding them from their caverns and tunnels to take part in the struggles of an unfamiliar world. Not merely an army of warders, but the entire Hrothgari nation—male, female, and child. Having listened to Htomah's pleas, they had emerged completely, under royal order of King Hreidmar, to join forces with the humans besieged upon the surface-earth. A desperate decision, but due to their own minor run-ins with the Illysp, and given a lack of options, the Hrothgari had agreed to seek the shelter of the human cities and lend their military strength in a united defense, hoping to earn the trust and gratitude of their neighbors.

Htomah had led them to believe it was possible.

He could not abandon them now.

"Come," he sighed, rising from the log upon which he had sat in solitude since before daybreak. Even then, his gaze clung with reflexive longing to the southerly track that stretched away among the jagged, crumbled slopes. With a concerted effort, he tore his eyes from that path, triggering a profound hollowness deep within. "Let us march."

Crag fixed him with a skeptical look, as if dissatisfied by the lack of a true response. *Always wary, this one.* Htomah could not fault him for it, but neither would he burden the dwarf with riddles and mysteries beyond mortal comprehension.

"Good day for it, leastwise," the Tuthari said. "Last time I passed by these mountains, rains and mudslides nearly buried me—and that to the north, among her foothills."

Htomah grimaced at the reminder. That they had suffered not a single downpour since journey's inception spoke ill for Warder General Vashen and her siege rovers. He turned his gaze to the north, searching leagues and leagues of open sky and finding only the barest wisps of cloud. So as not to add undue alarm, he had led them to believe that sweat and waste fluids would be enough. Those served a purpose, yes: Burned as exhaust, they filled the air with a scent that would help to lure the Illychar and fuel their blood-lust. But additional water would be required to fuel the boilers themselves. He had assumed there would be rain aplenty during this, the spring season. Thus far, he had been wrong.

Yet Crag's observation was correct. Showers here, in the mountains, would have made the path much more treacherous than it already was. Were it humans that followed him, rather than dwarves, Htomah never would have risked crossing this way. But even the smallest Hrothgari possessed a strength and toughness that few humans grew to match. For them, this was the quick-est road, made safer by the fact that they had it to themselves.

"One man's blessing is often another's curse," Htomah remarked, turn-ing east along the trail that would lead them back to the Hrothgari camp and his fellow Entients who watched over it. There was nothing he could do for Vashen at this time. To call forth a stream of lightning was relatively easy, given the nature of its composition. But it was no simple task to coax rain from the sky. Perhaps, when the rovers drew closer, he and his outcast brethren could manipulate the winds so that a few storm clouds might brew. Perhaps.

By that time, his own host should be safely over these mountains and into Kuuria. That was where the true battle would take place, he knew. He had seen before leaving Whitlock the way in which the tides of this war were moving. And he had mankind's actions in the recent War of the Demon Queen as a model. Souaris was where his flock would gather while seeking to weather this storm. At Souaris, this people, too, would be as safe as it could be.

Just a few more days, he hoped, barring misfortune. The going thus far had been easier than any had reason to expect. Even with the siege rovers to cover their movements and hide their true intent, Htomah and his brethren had expected to encounter ambush or resistance of some kind. Keen senses and powers of persuasion enabled them to sweep from the roads they traveled the rabble and strays who might give them away, but they had found precious little need. He had not yet decided whether he should be pleased by this, or alarmed.

For now, then, he and his splintered faction of Entients would stay the course. Overseeing this people's safety allowed them to keep watch of these lands shared with their own flock—without directly involving themselves with their human charges. In that, he might continue to hope that when his task here was finished—when he had seen to it that the Illysp failed to claim all—he might return home, rather than fade away into exile.

Even though, in his heart, he knew he had just faced his last chance at redemption, and turned the other way.

CHAPTER THIRTY-SEVEN

THE EARTH STIRRED, A WHISPER of thunder rising from within.

Corathel paused, lowering the spoon held halfway to his mouth. He could see upon the faces of his lieutenants that they felt it, too. All kept silent, listening, until the pebbles at their feet began to dance.

"That's no outrider," Jasyn warned.

Corathel dropped the bowl of cold oaten porridge he'd been sharing with his division commanders, and snatched up his sword belt. Soldiers in their nearby squads took note, and the murmurs of alarm began to spread.

"To your posts," the chief general ordered his lieutenants. "Silent muster. I don't want a panic. Ninth Cavalry upon the western ridge. All others to await my command. General Jasyn, take the Fourth. General Lar, with me."

The division commanders snapped to obey. An attendant came racing up with Corathel's battered breastplate, but the chief general waved him off, signaling for his horse instead. Moments later, he and Lar were galloping in the direction of the growing thunder, flanked by a pair of mounted runners, and with Owl and his Mookla'ayans giving chase. *Let it not be Illychar*, Corathel prayed. *Not yet. Not now.*

"Sir!" Lar shouted, pointing with outstretched arm.

Corathel saw it: a lookout, ahorse, scampering down from his perch of scrub and boulders. The chief general's own steed whinnied as he turned its head sharply to intercept.

"Heavy horse," the lookout reported breathlessly. "A company at the least, maybe two. Alsonian banner, led by a Parthan crier flag."

"Was it one of ours still carried it?" Corathel asked.

"Sir, yes, sir. I held long enough to be sure. Sergeant Dunnel, if my eyes serve."

Fair news, or so it seemed. He had sent Dunnel out just last night, after what he had seen of the reavers clogging the southern pass. There hadn't been time for the sergeant to become a reaver himself.

"Carry on. Bear word to the encampment. Orders unchanged. I'll send a runner with any further command."

And off he spurred once again, bearing now a twinge of hope amid the fear. Could it be they had found friends at last?

As the trail he rode emptied out onto the main highway, they were all but on top of him: scores of armored riders, in livery of brown and green and gold. A cloud of dust billowed in their wake, forming a veil against the distant horizon. And there, out ahead of the central column, the flag his lookout had spied, the red-on-black falcon of his homeland.

He could have smiled, had he not then seen the leader of that host. Encased in black, and with a dark-hued stallion barded to match, the unknown commander drew eye like a bloodstain on fresh linens. His sudden, upthrust fist might easily have been an attack signal; Corathel felt it like a punch in the gut.

The oncoming riders, however, slowed in response. Only the leader and a small detachment pressed on, a few lengths behind Sergeant Dunnel. Corathel breathed a private sigh of relief, and held pace until his outrider reined up before him.

He had barely received the sergeant's salute when the other newcomers came to a sudden, skidding halt, sending a wave of dust washing over the chief general's party. Corathel squinted against the grit as he looked them over. The leader wore a visored helm, his eyes hidden within its darkened recesses. His armor was a heavy plate dominated up and down by lines of flared ridges, with reinforced clefts designed to ensnare an enemy's blade. Bladebreaker, as the design was known, though, for most men, its cumbersome weight and treacherous balance made it all but unsuitable for battle. Corathel listened to the wearer's breath sawing in and out through vertical mouth slits.

"I would speak with your chief general," a shredded voice echoed from within that mask, "the one called Corathel."

Sergeant Dunnel cleared his throat. "With respect, sir, I present Corathel, chief general of the Parthan Legion, and Lar, lieutenant general of the Fourth Division."

The leader raised his visor at last. Flint-gray eyes peered out from beneath a broad forehead, taking in Lar's size as if measuring an opponent. They then turned to Corathel.

"Is that so?" he asked. Without the visor to obstruct it, the man's voice was clear and unbroken, full of meat and stone. "Begging pardon, but you are not what I had imagined."

"And may I have *your* name, sir?" Corathel replied, even though, at this point, he knew.

"General Rogun, chief commander of Krynwall, and acting regent of Alson." He gestured to the man on his right. "My right hand and commander-in-waiting, Zain."

At least he hasn't named himself king, Corathel thought. He glanced momentarily at Rogun's lieutenant, who wore no helm, only a smirk.

"You keep odd company, General, if you'll forgive my saying so," Zain offered.

Corathel glanced back as Owl and his brood came sliding up behind him, their olive, tattooed skins bristling with horn-and-stake piercings. "I'll accept stranger yet, should they prove even half as useful. How many are you?"

"I bring four hundred riders," Rogun said, "as many as can be spared of two thousand set down as an eastern front, twenty-five leagues west of here. The front is quiet, and my men grow bored. When your rider found us, and claimed you could use some help, I decided it high time we came to where the fighting is."

"High time indeed," Corathel agreed. The personal slights he would tolerate, but he was rankled by Rogun's flippant tone, after all his people had endured. "I wonder that this aid did not come sooner."

Rogun's scowl, after he had seemed so pleased with himself, was an abrupt and startling thing. "I've been seeing to my own. We are here now. Take us or leave us."

"Has my sergeant apprised you of our situation?"

"You seek to break through to the south, from what I'm told, though I might question why."

"We make for Souaris. Our civilian populace—"

"Shall have the city to itself. Have you not heard? Kuuria is deserted. The Imperial Council seeks to lead its people overseas, and has bid us do the same."

Corathel felt a sudden lack of breath. "Impossible."

"So said I, but I have it from Baron Nevik, who has proven his loyalty. And with fewer than ten thousand men at my command, I've not the strength to stand alone. My own people are well on their way, led by Nevik, shielded by the bulk of my army. The eastern front I spoke of was established to defend their exodus against enemy pursuit."

"Just as Thelin holds the Gaperon," Corathel realized. "He is stalling, no more."

For but a moment, he seemed to have Rogun's sympathy. Then the stern-faced general proceeded to lay out his options. "Your people can flee westward to join ours, else attempt to punch through the Gaperon and flee south. Either way, the *men*"—he spat—"of Pentania are in full retreat."

Corathel did not want to believe it. But he, too, trusted Nevik, and had no real cause to doubt Rogun's account. The Alsonian general had shown already an inability to mince words, and did not seem one to shy from fact. Though he looked, Corathel saw no guile in his counterpart's eyes, only cold, implacable truth.

All of a sudden, the Parthan chief general felt the full weight of his weariness, the assault of every buried wound. He had been fighting so hard . . . and to what end? There would be no valiant stand, no reclamation of his lands. He had given his entire life for the glory of Partha, and had not even known when setting foot upon its soil for the last time.

"It would seem the clearest road for our civilians is to the west," he allowed. "Will they find succor among the brave souls of Alson?"

"You know Drakmar's young baron as well as I. They will be treated as his own."

Corathel nodded. "Then they shall be readied at once. I have others, however—"

"A final caution," Rogun interjected, "before you make that choice."

The chief general raised an eyebrow.

"Reports from Gammelost say the western seas have been unseasonably volatile, of late. Two weeks ago, a tidal wave tore down her seawall. Should another such wave strike, the harbor itself will be devastated, her fleet destroyed."

Corathel's jaw fell slack. "Have the very gods arrayed against us?"

"Wind and water, at the very least. As great a threat as the reavers, perhaps, but I leave it up to you."

"The ocean *may* swallow us," Corathel decided quickly, helplessly, "but the Illychar most certainly will. And we've no guarantee that the southern seas will be any gentler."

Rogun nodded smartly. "You spoke of others," he prompted.

"The rest of my people, already in Kuuria—or so I hope. I would see them given a chance to depart as well."

"Theirs is the more beleaguered land, I am sure," Rogun granted. "My victory against Darinor's host at Krynwall seems to have chased his reavers south and east. Those making for the western shore will need but a token force to escort them."

Corathel looked to Lar. "Enabling the rest of our men to relieve pressure on Thelin's blockade by striking at the backs of those foes who now bear down upon them."

"Further drawing the enemy's focus," Rogun added, "which will serve the westward retreat, as well. Should that be your desire, my riders stand ready to charge."

Corathel gazed again upon the columns of horse reined up at the Alsonian general's back. Four hundred, Rogun had said. Not nearly enough to overcome the odds his troops would face should they make this attack. But his own men were anxious for it, and Rogun had not led this force across twenty-five leagues merely to deliver a report that could as easily have been entrusted to his outrider.

He glanced at Owl, though the savage could not advise him, then looked again at Zain, who continued to smirk as if this were all some frivolous amusement.

"If it's blood your men are thirsting for," the chief general decided, "I will gladly show them where to find it."

THE BEGINNING OF THE END, thought Allion, as he scrambled from the trench in pursuit of the others. *The more they take, the faster we give.*

After nearly three days of successful defense of Kuuria's northern border, the archer had heard talk among several of his comrades that Thelin's exodus was a mistake. The king had lost his mettle, some whispered. The premature death of his children and heirs—not to mention the near calamity befallen his proud city at the hands of the dragonspawn—had sapped their ruler's strength and made him frail before his time. If so few could hold out against so many, here behind makeshift bulwarks, what cause had Thelin to fear for the mighty walls of Souaris?

You shall learn soon enough, Allion had reflected whenever their gossip reached his ears, though he had kept his morbid sentiments to himself. Such confidence would be needed in the days and weeks ahead. He could have told them that this force of human Illychar they withstood was but rabble compared to the hordes of elves and goblins and ogres and giants he knew to be out there. He could have explained how time would never again favor them, and that if Thelin and the Imperial Council had waited any longer in coming to a decision, they would have lost their already dubious chance at gathering and outfitting the countless vessels that would be required to bear this people out to sea. He might even have confirmed for them the rumors that a dragon had been reborn, and that, should the creature happen to return, it might destroy them all as it had Atharvan, without being winded by its effort.

He'd found it easier to remain silent, however, to let the soldiers around him buoy one another with ignorant bravado, even if he himself could not partake of their false hope.

And then, sometime in the hours before dawn, a pack of Illychar had stolen upon one of the cliffside anchor positions, overwhelming those who held it. According to the officers Allion had spoken to, none knew how the vile reavers had managed it. Some rumored that the company commander had gone mad upon learning his son had been killed in the previous day's fighting, and had launched an unauthorized incursion to recover the body—thus weakening his defensive position. Others claimed that the company's ranks had consisted of one or more reavers all along, and that these had finally found an opportunity to compromise the entire regiment. Whatever the truth, the position had been lost, and the army's flank forced. The entire forward line had folded as a result.

They had barely reassembled behind the next barrier when it, too, was breached, this time by a mad rush straight up the center. Archers rushing to converge from either side had ended up feathering as many friends as foes— and the friends went down much easier. Troy himself had put an end to that debacle, giving the order to retreat to the next bulwark.

Now, that line, too, had fallen. Allion could not yet say why. But the command to displace had filtered down from the east, and he knew better than to ignore it. When a tidal wave was rising, one did not stand still to see where it would fall.

The sun overhead had not yet reached its midday brightness. Three lines lost, all in a matter of hours. Even Allion, in his bleakest of moments, had not imagined this. They were giving ground faster than their sappers and engineers could secure their fallback positions. With every trench and bulwark claimed, the enemy seized valuable weapons and stores and artillery that the defense could scarcely afford to surrender. The great blazes with which they had attempted to destroy the dead and keep the reavers at bay had been all but stamped out. Weariness and despair were beginning at last to exact their critical toll, while the Illychar only gained in strength and madness.

When Allion stumbled, it was all he could do to raise himself to his hands and knees. He did not even remember sprawling to the earth, yet there he lay, as though in a drunken daze. He stared stupidly for a moment at a scattering of arrows flown from the communal quiver he had thought to snatch from the trench before fleeing. His body felt leaden and useless. Too long without sleep. Too long without hope.

Too long without Marisha's touch, her voice, to lend him strength and purpose.

He surveyed his surroundings, turning his head slowly, thinking he might find her. He hadn't seen her since their quarrel, some sixteen hours past. Already, it felt like days. His tongue grew thick as he recalled the words he had uttered, and his heart began to boil. Perhaps he needn't have spoken at all. Clearly, she meant to punish him, but that only made him angrier. His feelings had not been groundless, his fears not without merit. If she expected him to seek her out to offer an apology, she stood to be sorely disappointed.

A pair of arms seized him about the waist. *Marisha*, he thought, *Marisha, I'm so sorry* . . .

With a yank, the arms drew him to his feet, and held him while he swayed unsteadily. He turned to find not Marisha, but one of his fellow bowmen: Tevarian.

"Come," the lad bade him, slapping him on the chest. "It's a long crawl on hands and knees."

Allion could only wince in response. The struggle no longer seemed to matter. Not when he had already thrown away that which was most precious to him—for fear of its eventual loss.

Then a horn sounded. Its moaning blast was followed hard upon by another.

"What's this, now?" Tevarian wondered aloud.

Allion had no answer. Soldiers looked to be charging now in both directions, north and south. The horn sounded again, and this time there were others to echo its signal. Two stern blasts. An advance. But had they not just been signaling a retreat?

"Our command is unraveling," Tevarian muttered. "Are we coming or going?"

Others seemed to share his uncertainty. Wherever Allion looked, soldiers caked with blood and soot milled in evident confusion. Half were still trying to flee. Half were spoiling to fight. None seemed to know what their true orders were.

But the horns sounded again. And then again. Bit by bit, shattered ranks began to form up. A cavalry squad thundered past, riding for the blockade line they had just abandoned. One of them stopped to bellow at a pack of retreating swordsmen to turn about and follow.

Another rider came up behind that one, pale hair blown by the wind. "Bows! I need bows!" Troy shouted. When Allion raised his arm, the high commander spotted them and galloped toward their position. "Where is your unit? I need advance fire. We ride to recapture our line."

"We were ordered to fall back," Tevarian said.

"Are you wounded?" Troy asked.

Allion felt himself shaking his head. "What's happened?"

"Lookouts signal that the enemy rush has slackened."

"Slackened?"

"Something has drawn the reavers' attention. I know not how long it may last. I go to press our advantage." He noticed then the sprawl of arrows littering the ground. "I would have your bows, if you are able."

Allion immediately bent to gather up the quarrels. The abrupt motion made him light-headed, but his shame was enough to drive away his stupor.

Troy merely smiled. Even in this, the high commander appeared to be enjoying himself, as if he knew something Allion did not. "See you at the front."

The soldier's steed left them choking on a curtain of dust. Tevarian helped him to collect a few more arrows, then clutched his arm and drew him again to his feet.

"That's enough," the lad said. "There will be barrels where we left them."

Allion nodded and shouldered the quiver. Several of his platoon members, whom he had been chasing south, were returning, and caught sight of him. He motioned for them to hurry.

"False alarm, was it?" one of them asked.

"Else this one is," Tevarian replied, clapping the man's shoulder as they fell into formation.

Allion kept pace alongside. The first few steps were the worst; after that, he found his stride. While he did not share Tevarian's zest, he wasn't so blind or wasted as to misrecognize a ray of hope. Slight as it might prove, it would seem better than succumbing to the cold and the darkness—like a streamer of daylight to guide a drowning man to the surface.

If only *she* had been there to help pull him free.

He resisted the urge to look, hardened by his pride, focused on his duty. *Draw, aim, loose. Draw, aim, loose.* His only task, until this nightmare gave way to oblivion.

If Marisha wished to claim her apology, she would have to find him before then.

CHAPTER THIRTY-EIGHT

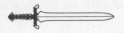

TORIN MARCHED IN A COCOON of silence. Annleia strolled beside him, but he paid her no notice. His eyes were locked upon the moist earth, where a glistening layer of dampness steamed beneath the warmth of the sun's rays. Within the resulting mist danced images of Dyanne. Memories, fantasies, he savored them all, fearing each to be the last picture he would ever have of the woman he so cherished.

It had taken hours of reflection to grasp the consequences of all else. But he had understood immediately the simple fact that Dyanne was gone. Two days ago, he had stood before her and accepted her farewell, walking away without any reason to hope he might see her again.

He still wasn't sure how he had let it happen.

She had eluded the pages he'd sent to notify her of his departure. She had then eluded *him* as he made his own rounds through Lorre's citadel. The keep had been cold and quiet, with many having just settled down after a long night of celebrating. Saena, who had woken him, had complained of causing a stir, but had surrendered to his wishes and led him in his search.

He had all but given up hope, venturing down to the stables . . . where they had found her waiting for him. A yawning Holly stood with her, the pair of them come to wish him well.

Torin had refused, at first, to say good-bye. He had not finished savoring her company. He doubted that he ever could. But how to bring himself to tell her so? *How can you not?* an inner voice had demanded. This was his last chance, his final opportunity to admit how much he ached to hold and to soothe her. He understood it instinctively. Surrender now, and he would lose her forever. Remain silent, and he would have to live with that emptiness for the rest of his life.

"It's not too late to join us," he had said. "Wherever we end up, I'm sure we could use your skills."

Dyanne had laughed. "Of that, I have no doubt. But your companion tells me you are most likely bound for your homeland."

Homeland. Once upon a time, perhaps. Pentania had been the birthplace of his life, his dreams, his first love . . . everything he was or had wanted to be. But this was where he now belonged. She and Holly and Jaik and Bardik and so many others had shown him that. Their unanticipated acceptance of him the night before had shown him the shadows of possibility, of the experiences he could have enjoyed, of the delights that might yet be his.

Annleia had approached them, then, else he might have raised any number of feeble arguments about how nothing was certain. The breach he must find a way to seal lay upon Pentania's shores, yes. And he had indeed left those realms in much more dire straits than these. But his fiendish actions made him every bit as responsible for this land as that. *Ask me to do so*, he had thought, *and I will stay.*

"Pentania is too far away," she had remarked instead. "*My* people, *my* fight, is here.

"But take this," she had added, before he could summon a protest. "A token of esteem, lest you forget us altogether." Draped from her fingers upon a thin, vine-woven necklace was a pendant of black amber. "I had it made for Jaik," she admitted, and, for a moment, her eyes had lowered along with the gemstone. "But I'd rather you take it, since I can fashion him another."

He hadn't anything to say to that, and so had bowed low enough to let her slip the ornament around his neck. When she had finished, and he saw her smiling at the way the polished jet hung in place, he had wanted nothing more than to reach out and seize her in his arms. The time had come to amend his childish silence and allow the decision regarding their relationship to lie with her. Fear and hesitation had cost him everything before. He would not let them cheat him again.

Even in that moment, however, he had realized how unfair that would be: to bid her choose between him and Jaik when he had nothing to offer her. And so he had faltered, thinking not about what he stood to lose with his persistent silence, only how grateful he was that she should bestow upon him this small symbol of her regard.

"Would you like to talk about it?"

The coaxing words, though softly spoken, pulled Torin from his reverie. When he looked up, he half expected Dyanne to still be standing there in front of him. Instead, his gaze found Annleia's as she strolled alongside, peering over at him with gentle concern.

"About what?"

"You've done nothing but brood since before we left. Makes me worry that there's something you've not told me."

Her visage was one of impatience, as though she had grown tired of his sullen silence. Yet there was no hardness in her countenance, no accusation in the soft furrows of her brow. Though unswayed by reproach, he found her imploring gaze much more difficult to ignore.

But what might he tell her? Would she hear of that first morning following his reunion with those at Neak-Thur? How he had awakened with pierced chest and flaming lungs, seething in private anguish over what he had lost? How, without the balm of Dyanne's physical presence, he had been left with only the raw, stinging truth of the fact that he had returned too late? Would she hear of how he had tossed and turned, cursing his many wasted opportunities and wishing, pleading—to the light and to the darkness, whichever might answer—for but one chance to go back and reshape his destiny?

Or perhaps he might tell her of the agony he had endured since. How more than two days' march had done nothing to dull his torment. How each morning, he awoke with a surge of emotion he didn't think his heart could contain. How he wished it would simply rupture, that he might feel no more of the empty ache that choked him from within. Raked by bitterness during the day, beset each night by the demons of what could have been, he fought a constant struggle to memorize Dyanne's words, her sweet touch. All the simple moments she had granted him, all the meaningless gestures . . . Now that they were behind him, only the pain seemed real.

Annleia did not need to hear any of that. Such feelings were petty and self-ish, and meant less than nothing in the larger scheme of what lay ahead. He would not be mocked or chided for having them. Nor would he seek sympathy or solace where none could be found.

"Are your wounds troubling you?" his companion prodded.

His knee, though heavily wrapped for support, throbbed with every step. Invisible nails held his shoulder in its socket—and even they failed now and then to keep it in place. His heart thumped sickly within his chest, twisting and contorting through a series of involuntary convulsions.

"My wounds," he grumbled, "are better than I deserve."

"If you're hurting, we can rest. Else, I can mix you something for the pain."

I need the pain, he realized. His travels were leading him away from Yawacor and the dreams he had hoped to realize here. Grief was his strongest reminder of those he had left behind, a consort to his memories. When one faded, he feared, so too would the other.

"I would sooner have my wits on these trails," he replied. "These paths can be treacherous."

When preparing to leave Neak-Thur, Annleia had asked to be shown the nearest pass east through the mountains. A strange course, Torin had thought, until realizing that they couldn't bloody well summon Ravar upon the western shore, where every seaside villager within fifty leagues might see Him. So they had ridden south and east with a lone guide, having declined any further assistance. Torin sensed that, had Annleia requested it, Lorre might have sent half his army to accompany them. Tempting as that notion had been, even Torin understood what little good a show of such force would ultimately do them.

Upon reaching the foot of a pass carved by the Tanir River, their guide had warned them one last time that it led only to an inaccessible cove. Unless they had a vessel awaiting them there, they would do better to continue south, through the Dragonscale Cleft and on to Razorport. Annleia had thanked the man for his counsel, and bid him a safe return, leaving them to venture up the pass alone.

Torin had questioned that decision, also, remembering all too well how unforgiving this mountain range could be. Yet the map they had been provided was well drawn, and the snows that had made this stretch of the Dragontails impassable months before were all but melted. They had encountered no blizzards, and no avalanches, just high-rushing streams amid vales and meadows of verdant green. Earlier that morning, they had found the headwaters of the Tanir as it tumbled down out of the cliffs, and had soon thereafter slipped across the pass's summit. Strong winds had assailed them, whistling down off the adjacent peaks, and for a time, the paths had indeed grown steep and narrow, with startling glimpses of deep-throated chasms to either side. But the worst of that, even, appeared to be behind them. For as their winding course resettled amid the treeline, the slope softened, boulders and rockslides ceased to threaten, and the winds tapered off amid the rising forests.

"I've led you this far," Annleia reminded him. "I won't let any ill befall you now."

Her smile was wasted on him, and faded quickly. Her gaze, however, refused to let go.

He turned away from it, reaching reflexively for the jet pendant hung high upon his chest. Dyanne's unexpected gift to him. A tangible memento, for which he was grateful—though even *it* seemed but a searing reminder of the joy that had so briefly been his.

"I hope this is not about *her*."

Torin felt a flush crawl up his cheeks. Embarrassment, that she should see right through him. Anger, that she should consider it any business of hers. He let go of the pendant, and tightened his grip on the Sword, making sure to keep his eyes on the path ahead. "It feels wrong," he said, "leaving with so much unfinished."

"The best way to serve your friends is to see the Illysp seal restored. Whatever debts remain thereafter must be settled later—just like those you owe *my* people."

She may as well have slapped him in the face. He would rather she had done so, for when he looked, he found that she had made the comment with more pity than accusation. She still saw him as a victim in this—how, he wasn't sure. But the ease with which she had apparently forgiven him only sharpened his own sense of guilt. He thought back to her comment, her fear that he was withholding something from her. Which of course he was. Something she deserved to know. Something he could not quite bring himself to tell her.

"We could go in search of them, you know," he offered. "Your people. The ones who . . . the ones who survived. I could help you find them."

"The best *I* can do for *them* is to finish what I was sent here to do, making certain you succeed in your quest." Her depthless gaze seemed to swallow him whole. "Our paths are the same now, yours and mine, until the end is decided."

Once again, she left him speechless, uncertain how to respond to such focused intensity. "Will you know where to find them?" he managed finally.

"I will know where to look. Part of me would sooner do so now, I assure you. But you cannot summon Ravar on your own. He may choose to present Himself to you, or He may not. Only I can make sure, and I mean to do so."

"Is it some enchantment, then? Some spell your people hold over Him?"

One of her hands moved within her cloak, coming to rest on the handle of a longknife sheathed at her waist. "A pact, as I understand it, between Him and the Vandari, made ages ago at the close of the Dragon Wars. In accordance with the one He made with the Ceilhigh to safeguard this world from outside threat."

Torin scowled. "Then what makes you think you can contain Him?"

"Contain Him? He is in no way my thrall, if that's what you are thinking. I know only that He must answer my summons, just as He must honor His divine charge, else face the fires of oblivion."

Torin could think of few things she might have said that would have been less reassuring. All this time, he had assumed the creature was somehow beholden to her will. As difficult as that had been to fathom, he could not comprehend taking the risk otherwise. If Ravar's Olirian peers would not stop Him from scouring this earth with the ocean's waters, why should they prevent Him from butchering a pair of insignificant mortals beforehand? Would it not give the Dragon God special pleasure to drag the last known Sword of Asahiel into the ocean depths?

On the other hand, he had sailed across the sea safely not once, but twice before. Ravar had let him pass in peace on the voyage west, and had ignored him altogether on the voyage east. By that reckoning, the creature was not his enemy.

Of course, he had not forgotten his last encounter, aboard Killangrathor's back. If the leviathan believed him to still be an Illychar . . .

He closed his mind to the thought, remembering well the cavernous gullet that had loomed up beneath him like a gateway to the Abyss. Their path was set. They had no other. There was no one else they might turn to for the answers they so desperately needed. Had it been otherwise, they would not have come this far.

"If Ravar can aid us," Annleia insisted, "we shall make him do so."

Though she hid it well, Torin read the fearful veneration in her features.

As you say, my lady.

He remained silent after that, and Annleia let him be, seeming to focus her attention on the path ahead. With the river behind them, their route had become much less clear. There were no roads or signs, only meltwater gullies and narrow game trails. Torin left it to his companion to set the pace and determine their course. Though she knew this region no better than he, she showed no great difficulty in navigating it. She seldom hesitated, rarely consulted their map, and never did she ask his input. Yet somehow she maintained an easterly tack over a winding and oft-splintered series of slopes and footpaths and streams, while skirting all dangers or any obstacles that might cause them to backtrack or divert. At times, Torin wondered how she managed it, only to remind himself that she had been raised a Finlorian, and was possessed of skills he did not understand. Likely as not, she simply asked the trees.

Now and again they came upon the tracks or discards of the various hunters, trappers, and other Wylddean frontiersmen known to trek this mountain wilderness. But none of these appeared recent, and not once did they encounter another human soul. Birds and squirrels and insects seemed in endless supply. He spied wolves and rabbits and a great bull elk that nearly startled him from his feet before drawing close enough for Annleia to stroke its mane. When thoughts of venison steaks and sausages entered Torin's mind, the animal snorted and took its leave.

Their lunch consisted instead of a broadleaf salad filled with sprouts and mushrooms and a sprinkle of nuts. A far cry from fresh elk meat spit-roasted slow and tender, but tasteless was better than foul, and anything was better than nothing at all. They consumed it in a clearing that bore signs of having served before as a campsite, though the rain-washed fire marks on the ring of stones looked to be seasons old. Torin stared at them as he ate, so as to escape his companion's gaze and thus remain alone with his inviolable reflections.

"It must be a great comfort, to be able to eat again," Annleia ventured.

Torin glowered at the old fire pit, though all at once he felt his jaws begin to slow. The simple act of feeding himself was indeed something he had taken for granted. Were it not for the woman across from him, he might never have been able to do so again.

"And your color is returning much swifter than I might have imagined."

He was indebted to her; that much was certain. Present misery notwithstanding, he would forever be grateful for the second chance he'd been given—no matter how painful, guilt-ridden, and ill-fated his new life promised to be. And yet . . .

What did he truly know about this woman? Only what she had told him, which was little enough. He didn't care for the fact that she knew his entire life's story, while he knew next to nothing about hers. It further gnawed at him that she should absolve him so readily, or that she should show no fear at sharing this trail with him alone, when she might have allowed her grandfather to send at least a few soldiers in escort. None of these, perhaps, was enough to warrant his mistrust, but why should he put his full faith in her when so many others of late had played him false?

"Do you feel any different?" she asked. "From before, I mean. Did the Illysp . . . *scar* you in any way?"

She could see the cuts and scrapes and bruises for herself. And she had already inquired as to his wounds, and made mention of his physical recovery. So what was she *really* asking?

"You don't need to speak of it if you don't wish to," she said. "But it would seem important to know if . . . whether it affected you in other ways."

"Are you trying to ask if I've gone mad?"

"There are horrors yet that lay ahead," she replied carefully. "And you've already experienced a great deal."

Perpetrated, you mean. Was her sympathetic view meant to heal him in some way? Or did she truly not understand? "Men are strengthened by the trials they overcome. Is that not so?"

"Else worn and weakened by damages unseen, until even a lesser hardship is enough to break them."

Torin spat a nutshell from his salad. How was he to answer *that*? He knew not what strength of will he had left, or if his possession might return to haunt him in unforeseen ways. Wasn't that *her* province? To tell *him* how these sorceries worked?

"I am neither witch nor elf," he replied. "I cannot fathom these matters as you do."

"That's not what I—"

"I passed your grandfather's test, did I not?" he snapped. "I am prepared to do whatever is asked of me. If you'd rather seek another who might serve better, then by all means, take the Sword and do so."

That quieted her. She even looked away, granting him a temporary relief from that soulful gaze of hers. For all of that, he did not feel better. He had treated her crossly, he knew. *No more than she deserves, with inquiries such as those. Have I been* scarred *in any way?*

But his anger curdled in his stomach. For nearly three days, he had done naught but grunt and murmur when required, scowling as if he might somehow change the world by doing so. Annleia had given him all the time she could. With luck, they would reach Yawacor's eastern shore this very night. It was not a battle they would face, if the gods were good, but near enough that they should make ready as if it were.

And that meant gauging the condition—both mental and physical—of one's comrade.

He might have apologized, but wasn't sure how. It seemed pointless, besides. What understanding could the pair of them come to that might possibly prepare them for what lay ahead?

Still, he had to say *something* to dispel the guilt of his outburst. Frustrated by her questions, he decided to turn them back on her. After a moment's thought, he settled upon one that might help put one or more of *his* concerns to rest.

"Darinor told me in the very beginning that a body's essence is enslaved by the Illysp that possesses it." He looked up to find Annleia's waiting gaze and patient expression. "If I am the first to be purged, as you say, how would he know this? Aside from being a victim himself, I mean."

"I did not claim that you were the first Illychar ever examined. My ancestors made extensive studies of those they battled, and our kind has never been so blind as yours in matters of body and mind and spirit. They would have shared what they knew with Algorath."

That made sense enough, Torin supposed. He wasn't certain where to go from there. "And the gosswyn?" he decided, staring at the pouch upon her waist in which it was stored. "If the Illysp that claimed me is trapped within, why keep it? Why not grind it into dust?"

If confused by his abrupt shift in thought, Annleia did not show it. "Because I was instructed to preserve it."

"For what purpose?"

"She did not say, or would not. Only that there may come a time when it is required."

"She. Necanicum."

Across the clearing, his companion's eyes glimmered. "Yes."

He wished now that he hadn't broached the topic. He rather preferred thoughts of the Dragon God to those of the mysterious woodswoman. Annleia had told him already that the former Fenwa had passed away upon delivering the phial of his blood and her instructions on how to use it. To have made that journey, to have forfeited her life to see his restored . . . The whole matter raised questions of prophecy and foresight that he had found much easier to brush aside as insanity.

He shook his head. "What was she, do you suppose?"

"A witch, if I am to hear you tell it." Annleia smiled wanly. "Mine are not the only people in this world to channel nature's forces. As to what force guided Necanicum, I cannot say, though *its* purpose was clearly to further *yours*."

An unsettling prospect, in more ways than he cared to count. Another life for which he was responsible . . . A fate foreshadowed—and perhaps even predetermined—so soon after he had weaned himself of such childish beliefs . . . A world of powers and energies affected by *his* choices, *his* actions, *his* failures . . .

"Would that some force simply tell me what I must do," he huffed.

Annleia frowned, the first truly sour look she had given him. "Would you pretend not to know?"

"I *thought* I knew when I unearthed the Sword in the first place. Clearly, I was wrong."

Her sun-dappled features smoothed. "Ravar will tell us."

Else devour us. Or both. But he kept that to himself. His gaze slipped to the Sword's pommel, then to the flaming heartstones that lined its grip and crosspiece. "You've magic to summon a god," he said. "Have you none to unlock the Sword's fire?"

He could sense Annleia shaking her head. "Only the very first Vandari—those who accepted the divine talismans from the Ha'Rasha—were given to know how to do so."

"So Darinor told me, though it still seems you must have *some* idea. Can one magic be so different from another?"

"What you call magic is simply the manipulation of natural energies that exist in the world—both around and within us. But just as some rivers flow swifter than others, making them difficult to ford, the Sword is a vessel of such magnificent power that anyone seeking to direct its flow would have to possess a strength beyond mortal reckoning."

"But mortals *have* wielded them," Torin insisted, "and commanded that power."

"If we are to believe the legends, yes." When he gaped at her, she added,

"I do not say it is impossible, merely that I cannot fathom the strain exacted upon the wielder."

"Strain. Like that which you bore when stealing Killangrathor's life force."

Annleia nodded. "Patience versus passion—the fundamental theory governing magic's use. Exercising patience, I was able to briefly absorb a measure of Killangrathor's fury. But I had to let it go through a release of passion—which I did against the Illysp who controlled you."

It was still me. I have the injuries to prove it. Was he to bear no culpability whatsoever?

"Consider how you breathe," she continued, misreading the scowl upon his face. "Inhale, exhale. All of life—and therefore magic—is ebb and flow, the transfer of energy from one state to another. Nothing is created or destroyed without a consequence of equal measure. It is how the universe maintains its balance. Without this balance, everything around us, all of this—our very existence—would fail."

"Everything?"

"Think of it. Push, pull; rise, fall; defend, attack; action, reaction. None of these exists without its antithesis. Yet few who practice magic exercise patience in a measure equal to their passion. The resulting imbalance is why most sorcery—in any form—exacts such a toll. Physically, yes, but mentally and spiritually as well."

Her words brought to mind an image of his brother, so hate-filled, consumed with vengeance, intent on sharing his pain with others—personal cost be damned.

Annleia went on. "Some can maintain the imbalance longer than others. Dragons, for instance, are the purest form of the material elements, the perfect embodiment of their strength and power, which is why these creatures have such an affinity for—and command over—the fundamental laws that govern their use."

"*Had.* I was led to believe Killangrathor was the last."

"Just so, perhaps. And had strength aplenty to fuel his wrath. Yet even he, I imagine, was a creature much wracked in life, living with an inner torment only hinted at by the external scars. A dragon, according to my people, *was* the greatest creature to have ever lived—envied for its majesty, yet pitied for its life's curse as perhaps the most passionate creature throughout time and creation."

And once tried to exterminate your kind, he thought. *Twice now, actually.* She seemed to have forgiven *that*, as well. "So how does one learn to . . . influence this flow of energy from one source to another?"

"The ability is within you, the secrets locked within your own mind. You must merely learn to free them. Tokens and artifacts—such as my wellstone—can serve as aids. Sound vibrations, incense, ritualistic movements—all can help the individual to attain the necessary focus. There is no single, universal answer. Nor could I simply teach you a quick word or gesture and expect you to be able to call forth power as I might, using the same. It is a discipline like any other, requiring study and practice. No different than swordplay, really, only the work is less physical, and more mental and spiritual."

"My head hurts already," Torin complained.

Annleia laughed, a quick, delicate burst. "So does mine, endeavoring to explain. No one has all the answers, especially since much of it is subject to an individual's point of view. Higher beings than you and I have been working at it since the beginning of time. The critical thing to remember is that one cannot expend passion without exercising the patience required to restore what is lost. Nor can one hoard power through endless patience without a release of passion. An extreme of either measure is destructive and, for even the most powerful beings, ultimately fatal."

Torin mulled it over. "I don't see where that is of much help concerning the Sword."

"Perhaps it isn't. What little I know of the talisman stems from legend—and from you. But I have a strong notion of how power of *any* kind works. If you would have my guess, it's that the Sword is governed by many of the same principles I've just shared."

Then the weapon was truly beyond him. If what Necanicum had told Annleia was to be believed, their hour had grown short already. He did not have time to solve the mystery of the Sword *and* riddle through the inner workings of his own mind.

Annleia spoke as if sensing his thoughts. "In any use of magic, the first step, along with desire, is to believe you can do it. With true faith, most anything is possible."

"A pleasing notion," he granted, then set to finishing his meal. The conversation had done nothing to rouse his spirits. No matter what he believed, Dyanne and Neak-Thur were still behind him; while only Ravar and a forbidding future lay ahead. The sooner he resumed his cursed trek, the sooner he would be done with it.

Annleia's words, however, lingered in his thoughts as she led him from the clearing. She was trying to strengthen him, he supposed, the way Marisha always had. The notion irritated him. He was not some child in need of constant encouragement. The doubts and pains and questions that plagued him were well earned. Trading them all away for a few hollow platitudes would not serve to bolster him in whatever he must do. She and others seemed to think that his melancholy made him incapable. True or not, he wasn't going to armor himself with false smiles.

Yet his sense of guilt persisted. Annleia had suffered in this, as well. She might not know the truth concerning her mother, but she had learned just days ago that her people had been brutally attacked, slain, scattered. Hers had already suffered a calamity she was working now to help others avoid—and she was doing so without any of his self-indulgent brooding. A kinder man might be doing more to comfort and strengthen *her*.

Events at Neak-Thur had left him disoriented; he had gained and then lost so much. But he need look no farther than his current companion to find his focus. He was alive for one reason: to atone for the pain he had unleashed upon this world. He could tie his head in knots trying to guess how, exactly. He could puzzle over Necanicum's actions, and wonder at what else she may have known. He could bemoan Dyanne's feelings for Jaik and imagine how their lives might have been different . . .

Or he could follow Annleia's lead and seek to clear his heart and mind as much as possible, summoning his courage and putting aside all else of lesser import. If it was madness she feared, she had reason to do so. For within the shadow of the next coastal twilight, he was to confront the physical eminence of a banished god.

CHAPTER THIRTY-NINE

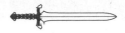

CORATHEL'S MOUNT REARED, SNORTING AND flailing at the pack of reavers converging against him. The creatures came ahead anyway, Parthan once, but no longer. With feral shrieks and lust in their eyes, brandishing clubs and staves, mauls and axes, they bore down upon a man who for years had battled to keep them safe—as if to punish him for failing to do so.

The chief general drew his dagger. He could not yet wield his sword with any strength or skill. His wounds from Leaven were still too fresh. It hurt to ride, to breathe. He searched the dust-filled clangor around him, questioning his decision now to leave his guard regiment behind . . . wondering how these reavers had managed to penetrate so deep, so fast . . . thinking it might not be too late to turn and flee . . .

Then they were upon him.

Again his horse reared, its ironshod hooves connecting this time with the head of his lead assailant. Bone crunched and caved, and the human reaver crumpled. Another aimed its polearm at the horse's heart. Without thinking, Corathel whipped his dagger end over end, impaling the reaver through its throat.

A third jabbed at him with wooden spear. Unarmed, the general leaned forward, then back, then swept his cloak around the shaft, entangling its thrust. He fought to wrestle the weapon away, but its wielder was too strong, and threatened to pull him from his mount. While he was thus occupied, a foe's maul struck a glancing blow at his back, an axe swing just missed his thrashing steed's neck, and the reaver with his dagger in its throat reentered the fray, sputtering blood with every hiss and grunt.

When the elves came bounding in, Corathel knew he was finished . . . until first one of the human Illychar fell, followed swiftly by another. All of a sudden, the spear hung lightly in his hand, weighted only by an arm—severed at the elbow—that still held fast. He worked swiftly to unwrap the twisted folds of his cloak, knock the appendage away, and bring the weapon's fire-hardened tip to bear, but, by then, the last of his attackers lay upon the ground, swarmed over by a trio of Mookla'ayans whose knuckle-fanning blades rose and fell beneath a spray of blood.

To one side, Owl presented him his discarded dagger, the stain of its victim already wiped clean.

Corathel nodded his gratitude as he sheathed the weapon, then turned yet again as an ominous rider drew up beside him.

"I see now why you keep them around," Rogun said through his visor. His black, bristling bulk, there amid the shouts and screams and choking cloud of dust, gave him the appearance of some monstrous fiend of the Abyss. "Your horse bleeds," he added.

Corathel looked. Rogun's devil of a steed sniffed at the wound as if drawn to its smell. A long gash along its foreleg, though it did not appear terribly deep.

"Who among us doesn't?" the chief general countered. Rogun, it seemed. The Alsonian general's armor bore plenty of nicks and scrapes, but did not appear to have been pierced or bludgeoned in any notable fashion. When finished looking the other over, he asked, "How fares the advance?"

"Your foot has assumed the main thrust. Your cavalry and mine ward the flanks now, while leading staggered sorties to puncture any phalanx seeking to form up against us. By and large, the enemy continues to engage us in blind, headlong countercharge. Mere vermin, these ones. Thus far, the battle is a rout."

The chief general bit his tongue at the word "vermin," knowing that Rogun made reference to their foes' lack of soldiering capabilities, and intended no slight against the Parthan people. At least, he *hoped* that to be the other's meaning. When Commander Zain, riding beside his general, flashed his ever-present smirk, Corathel became much less certain.

"Catching your breath, then, are you?"

"Just plugged the breach that led to your little melee," Rogun answered. "Saw the straits you were in and came back to lend a sword. Your vine-skins beat us to it."

"Sir!" a voice hailed, and Corporal Darros, commander of the squad charged with the chief general's protection, came spurring forward at the head of his unit. The corporal bulled near with drawn blade, interposing himself between Corathel and Rogun. He gave the latter a long, stern look. "Sir, shall we return to your command position?"

The chief general had left them to secure it, while riding down to redirect a reserve company that had turned south instead of east. He might have sent a runner, but hadn't had the time to express the order in relay, and wanted to make certain that this time, the company commander received the proper orders. As it was, the endangered flank had crumpled too soon, and much more severely than Corathel had anticipated. Thankfully, Owl had not been far behind, and Rogun had seen and responded to the danger, else matters might have grown truly ugly.

"The front is in good hands, General," Rogun assured him. "Perhaps you should indeed return to the safety of your ridge."

Corathel glared. There was a note of condescension in the other's voice, he believed, but without seeing the man's face, he could not know for sure. Either way, the worst of his aches and pains stemmed from serving an observer's role when, in an offensive such as this, he should have been leading the charge.

But Rogun, Darros, Jasyn, Maltyk, Lar—all of them were right. It made no sense for him to be in the thick of the press when he could scarcely hold his weapon. Nor did he wish to risk the lives of Owl and his few remaining elves unnecessarily, and he knew that where he went, they would follow.

"The legion has made steady progress," he agreed, pointedly assigning credit to his own lieutenants and those they led. Rogun's riders were swiftly proving invaluable, yes, but he wasn't ready to give Commander Zain and his smug smile the satisfaction. For all the ground their troops had gained, the enemy had yet to break before them. Perhaps, when the day was won, he would grant them their due.

"But the task is not yet done," Rogun finished for him. "Not by half. If the general and his guard would pardon us, my riders and I shall see what we can do about that."

With that, Rogun tipped his helm in salute, then wheeled his charger about and set off for the front lines.

Corathel very nearly followed, but ground his teeth and resisted the urge. *The battle goes well*, he reminded himself. With fortune's favor, his legion's remnants would not stop until reaching the Kuurian troops holding the southern blockade, eradicating this enemy force. So long as final victory was theirs, he cared not who claimed glory in the end.

He turned at last in the opposite direction. His personal guard—both Mookla'ayan and Parthan—ringed him protectively. Soldiers hailed and saluted as he rode past, and he did his best to nod and grin and bellow encouragement to all. Whether leading from the front or commanding from the rear, he had their respect, which in turn fueled his own determination. The reaver swarm was thick and relentless. Hours of brutal conflict lay ahead. But he would not fail this people as he had at Atharvan. He would see their stolen bodies reclaimed, their enslaved souls laid to rest.

It was all he could hope to achieve. Half his land's populace traveled south even now, looking to board whatever vessels they could and set sail for foreign lands. The other half marched westward with the same goal. Fortune, it seemed, had already deserted them.

This day, if this day only, would belong to them.

"A SLAUGHTER PIT, IF YOU'RE asking me," Crag muttered.

That it was. Even from this distant, bird's-eye vantage, Htomah could hear the cries, smell the blood, and taste the horror of those who struggled within the pass below. Though smoke and dust soiled the air, neither could mask the chaos and brutality of his human flock waging war against its own.

Beside him, Hreidmar nodded. "And where are the rest?" the Hrothgari king wondered aloud. "Where are the Eldrakkar, the greater Gorgathar and Sahndamar? I see only men."

"There must be other battles, as well," Htomah allowed, glancing at Quinlan.

"Then how do we know this is ours?" Hreidmar asked.

His people's moment of choice had come. They had left their halls within the shadow-earth, yes. They had trekked day and night for more than a week across a land that most could scarcely recognize. But this was the true turning point, the moment in which the Hrothgari would reveal themselves to the larger world after centuries of isolation, else shy away and seek another path. Were they to elect the former, as Htomah intended, there would be no turning back.

"The plan was to deliver your people to Kuuria," Htomah reminded him, "to join in the human defense. Would you turn about now, while standing upon the threshold?"

"We could go around," Crag pointed out. "We needn't force our way through the middle of this bloodbath."

Ungar Warder Thromb, serving as primary commander in the absence of Warder General Vashen, agreed. "The *drumguir* appear to have the advantage already," he observed, speaking primarily to his king. His term for the non-Illychar humans had no direct translation from Gohran to Entian, but Htomah approximated it to mean *flat-skinned giantlings*. "To join them here and now would pose unnecessary risk, Your Glory."

"Their advantage would be that much greater," Htomah said, "with your army's aid."

"Perhaps we should wait," suggested Ungar Warder Thayre, another of Hreidmar's military advisors. "We see the battle, but do not yet know its flow."

"Every moment you wait brings death to those you would claim as allies," Htomah maintained. His tone was calm, yet firm. "And each fallen ally makes for another enemy you must face."

"Allies," Hreidmar mused. "I wonder, will they recognize us as such?" His question did not seem to be directed at any of his counselors, but toward the gusting breezes there upon the mountain ledge.

Thromb grunted. "More likely they will think us skatchykem ourselves, Your Glory, given that none of them has seen a dwarf in his lifetime."

"Else they may recognize the truth, yet dub us cretins and savages and despise us anyway," Crag huffed. Meeting Htomah's frown, he added, "I've seen it before."

"And knew it to be a danger before setting out," Htomah reminded the Tuthari.

He turned from Crag to look upon the others. He could not fault them their hesitation. Dealings with humans were what had led to this people's self-imposed exile to begin with. The fear that their appearance here might only spark a three-way war between human, Illychar, and dwarf could not be categorically dismissed. But the cost of inaction, at this juncture, was too great to ignore.

"Your Glory, loyal advisors, these perils did not sprout with the rising of the sun, but are risks you undertook in search of a greater dream. The chance you seek, it is here before you. These men are not the same barbarians who drove you and your forebears underground centuries ago. They are, as you, fighting now for their very existence. Take this opportunity to prove yourselves as friends. Demonstrate your noble intent, and you will find yourselves welcome. I must believe that. *You* must believe that. Elsewise, there is no cause for hope."

Those who regarded him did so with only doubt and suspicion mirrored in their eyes. Hreidmar himself never turned. Gnarled fingers combed through his striped beard, fondling the jewels nested therein. Winds whistled amid the bare, craggy stone, snapping at Htomah's robes. A vulture screamed overhead.

"Mayhap you would be so good as to serve as envoy," the king suggested, rounding at last. "You and yours at least look the part of friend, and are more likely to meet with kind reception. Mayhap you can explain to them our desire for common strength and fellowship, and . . ."

He trailed off as Htomah looked again at Quinlan and then shook his head. "This is as far as I and my kind are permitted to go. We have taken our own risks in coming this far. To step any farther would guarantee for us a dire consequence."

Thromb scowled. "You ask the same of us, do you not?"

"A significant reward awaits you," Htomah said, "should you overcome the intervening challenge. The choice for us is not so well balanced. Our natural place is amid the shadows. We have little to offer and less to gain by stepping fully into the light, yet stand to forfeit all that we are should we do so. We dare not make that sacrifice"—*if we have not already*, he thought—"for what small difference we might make as soldiers here."

"You mean to leave us, then?" Crag asked, glowering.

"We mean to observe the battle," Htomah clarified, "but will not intervene unless we must. My brothers and I will reconsider our own path once we are certain that yours is settled." Perhaps they would seek to return home and beg apology of their order. Perhaps they would call upon its members to engage in further, more direct action. He could not know until he had witnessed the results of this initial effort.

"I begin to understand why your own people bear you such little faith and tolerance," Hreidmar said. His tone was not unkind, but the way he turned his back on the pair of Entients left little doubt as to his frustration.

"If we *were* to strike," Thromb hazarded, "the most effective course would be to drive a wedge straight into the enemy flank. Grind them down, as planned, and we would then find ourselves trapped between drumguir forces north and south. If the old man is wrong . . ."

He left the rest unsaid, giving Htomah another opportunity to interject. The Entient declined to do so. He had given his opinion. The ultimate decision had to be theirs.

Their advance company watched in silence for a time, as streaks of clouds scraped past the sun. In the valley behind them, through a long, narrow draw, the Hrothgari army awaited its orders. Among its stout warriors, the young and the elderly were left to ponder what their fate might be. Jedua and Wislome stood with them, lending what guidance and assurances they could. Htomah hoped that they were doing a better job than he.

"That charge is losing strength," Crag noted.

So it was, and had been for some time. Whereas surprise had given the northern force momentum in its southerly attack, the Illychar clogging the floor of the pass refused to flee. Even if they had wished to do so, they had nowhere to run, save into the wall of spears and earthworks at the southern end, or up into the slopes and cliffs hemming them in on either side. They were cornered, and lashed back at their assailants as if they knew it. The longer the battle wore on, the more fatigue would play a factor against those who were subject to it. As with any fight against Illychar, this one had to end quickly if there was any hope of it ending well.

Still, Htomah held his tongue, resisting the urge to rush Hreidmar or his counselors to judgment.

"So," Crag pressed in his stead, "what's it to be?"

Thromb flashed the Tuthari a look of annoyance, then glanced at Htomah as if fearing a subterfuge between them.

Crag glared. "Attack or reroute—I ain't caring which. But we'd best be about it," he insisted. "Don't need no graybeard to tell us that."

"No," Hreidmar agreed, "we don't." He turned from the ledge to fix Htomah with a critical eye. "'Tis walls of stone you promised my people, and walls of stone they shall have."

"Souaris is yet many leagues from here," Htomah said.

"Unless the enemy gives me no choice, I do not battle until I've some assurance they'll be safe." His speckled eyes glanced purposefully at the slopes rising to either side.

Htomah shared a long look with Quinlan, until Hreidmar lost patience.

"General Thromb, make ready to divert."

"Aye, Your Glory."

Thromb and Thayre turned as one to follow their king back toward the draw. Crag lingered, his expression sour, before finding their heels.

Behind them, Quinlan finally offered a slight nod.

"As Your Glory most surely noticed . . ." Htomah called out. He then paused, permitting his fellow Entient a moment to reconsider. When Quinlan did not, Htomah rounded slowly to find the pack of dwarves peering back at him. ". . . if there is one thing these mountains have no lack of, it is stone."

CORATHEL GRIPPED THE SPYGLASS IN his sweaty fingers, squeezing so hard his knuckles ached. He could see catastrophe unfolding, yet was powerless to prevent it. Wracked with tension, all he could do was grimace in denial from afar.

After more than an hour of slow, steady progress, the tide had turned. For a time, his troops had held it at bay, but that time had passed. No longer able to hold their lines, they had allowed the front to splinter. Little by little, the reaver swarm was digging northward in widening streams. Some of his men could barely lift their weapons against foes that came howling against them with undiminished strength and fury. All reserves had been deployed, but it did not seem enough to make a difference. A roiling sickness in his stomach hissed and spat the truth.

They were losing this battle.

The east flank was ready to buckle. Reavers along that side had taken to the slopes. With lighter weapons and little to no armor, they were able to scamper much faster than his own troops in a race to gain the higher ground. As a result, they had circumnavigated the deadlocked front and were pouring around to weaken it from behind. The Ninth Cavalry had fought to drive them back, but their steeds were ill suited to the terrain. Corathel had called them off, and redirected a foot battalion to shore up the collapsing wall before it was too late.

The command had fallen upon Dengyn, of the Fifth Division, who was just now reaching the point of conflict. The Fifth General and his current battalion were as fresh as any upon the field . . . but that did not seem to matter. The reavers hissed and yowled and hurled their stolen bodies into the teeth of Dengyn's phalanx. Incredible, that they should move as they did, these reavers. They were civilians, after all, untrained, lacking in fitness and discipline.

Like any rabid beast, they did not seem to care.

Dengyn and his soldiers, however, understood the critical nature of their assignment. Though they lacked Corathel's overview of the battlefield, being pulled from an advance to shore up a flank could scarcely bode well. So they drove onward against that thickening rush as if the lives of all behind them depended on it, unaware of just how true that might be.

Reavers upon the slopes hurled rocks and dislodged boulders, caring not whether it was the enemy or their own kind crushed underneath. Upon the floor of the pass, they wielded bills and scythes and crude polearms against sword and axe and shield. Like foaming waters they poured, against an iron shore determined to throw them back.

Blood gushed, commands echoed, steel hacked and scraped and rang. The shore was winning. Reavers fell to either side like ocean spray, shrieking and flailing. Their maniacal frenzy was no match for the fierce, calculated discipline of the Parthan Legion.

Or so it seemed.

He was about to look away when Dengyn went down. One moment, the Fifth General stood tall and strong, bellowing orders, removing the head from one victim with a single swipe of his broadsword. The next, a reaver found him, plunging a rancher's pike through the commander's back. The reaver wielding it was on its knees—assumed dead a moment before. Dengyn gaped at the slash in the creature's stomach, at its entrails dangling to the ground, before focusing again on the rusted iron tip sprouted from his own chest.

Corathel felt as though the shaft had gone through *him*. It should have. He gritted his teeth as Dengyn did, clenched his spyglass as Dengyn tried feebly to raise his sword, then watched the division commander fall uselessly to the earth.

A pair of soldiers at Dengyn's back came along with axe and mace and made pulp of the reaver's skull. But the damage had been done. Dengyn, a seasoned veteran, done in by a bloody rancher. Up and down the line, similar confrontations were having ill effect, causing the advance to falter. Push past a wounded reaver, and, half the time, the fiend would rise again from behind. Turn to finish the deed, and its bloody kin would pile on from in front. His troops could not seem to form phalanx or schilltron tight enough to keep these reckless animals at bay.

A battle standard went down. And there, another. Like all before, the assault wavered. As it failed, reavers snatched up weapons from the fallen. Some claimed helms and wore them as trophies, squealing in feral triumph. For his own troops, there was only disbelief, fatigue, despair.

What more can be done?

Then came an unexpected surge from the southern front, pushing north. In the moment that it took Corathel to adjust focus, he feared it to be a vein of enemies widening amid his columns. The first vein he spied, though, was a column of horse—Rogun and his riders, retaking the front. Which in turn allowed . . . Lar, he now saw, to spearhead a shift to the east, a counter meant to stem the gash in the legion's side.

An undeniable pride began to boil within as Corathel watched the rusty-haired giant of a man rally those around him. He could not hear the Fourth General's bellows—not at this distance, and not over the intervening din—but knew them well enough by their effect. As Lar's mouth opened and his barrel chest heaved, soldiers raced to form up at his side, gaining courage with every stride.

What *had* been a flagging jumble of doubt and confusion was once again a fully formed wedge of battle-hardened soldiers. A chill of savage euphoria rippled up Corathel's spine as Lar practically dove into the enemy swarm, great axe cleaving with every swipe. He was smeared and spattered already with the blood of his victims, and fountains of it were rising around him. Reavers clawed and bashed and jabbed with their blades and clubs and staves, while others rolled and flung their stones. But, in that moment, Lar's strength and ferocity surpassed their own. All around, soldiers found their faith, reclaimed their spirits, and battled with renewed vigor to push the enemy back, back, among the scrub and scree and gullies of the Gaperon's eastern wall.

The chief general finally exhaled, and drew fresh breath in relief—until he swung his lens back toward the front. The lines there were not faring so well. Frayed, fragmented, straining or tearing at almost every possible seam. Men and horses were screaming, dying. Some were trying to retreat, to catch their breath, to beg quarter of a merciless foe. He could find neither Jasyn nor Maltyk, of the Second and Third. He glimpsed Sixth General Bannon, but only momentarily, before a wind-driven smoke cloud obscured his view.

Ranchers, he thought again. *Crofters, bakers, chandlers, butchers* . . . If he could not trammel and destroy these, what hope had he to resist the savage hordes yet to descend from—

"Sir!"

Corathel spun. Corporal Darros was pointing. The eastern flank, again. *Not Lar*, he prayed. If the Fourth General had fallen . . .

Then he saw, and he felt his heart in his throat. A new wave bearing down upon them from high amid the hills. Five thousand. Ten. More.

How? he wanted to scream. From where had these . . . ?

His mind did not complete the thought. "Corporal," he said instead, "sound the withdraw."

His tongue felt thick and leathery, his throat raw. It would be Atharvan all over again. They would flee and lose a good share of men in the process. Those left behind would be raised as reavers, while the rest of them sought to regroup elsewhere—with Rogun's rear guard in Alson, perhaps. When they returned—*if* they returned—he would set about killing friends, compatriots . . . Dengyn.

The blaring horns drove spikes of torment into his ears, echoing his shame, his folly. He had known better than this. The numbers had seemed even enough, yet numbers were all but meaningless against a foe that would not yield, would not tire, would not—

"Corporal, the east flank, what are they . . . ?"

But he could see it clearly for himself. Across the length and breadth of the field, lines and columns were reversing course, slowly but steadily forming up for the retreat as the order reached them. Lar, however, had delved too deep. He and a string of those who had followed were some thirty paces up the slope, still seeking to drive back the circling reavers, and establishing a defensive wall.

"He means to deflect their rush," Corathel muttered angrily, clenching his jaw. It was the right decision. It was what *he* would have done in Lar's stead.

And then he was riding, spurring his mount to a gallop down the rise. Darros and his guard ring followed. He did not have to look to know that Owl would be sprinting after, bounding and weaving through their clouds of dust. He would be sacrificing their lives along with his own, if it came to that. That was their choice to make. His was to ensure that more capable men were not dying in his stead.

"Fall back!" he shouted, as he reached the floor of the pass. "Inverse column! Wheel and cover! Fall back!" On and on, he shouted maneuvers. Here a "steady full," there a "hook and roll." The last thing needed was panic and more chaos. He would not tolerate a stampede. But the day was lost, and the time come to salvage what they could.

His pace slowed as he wove and cantered through a clotting press. He had hoped to reach Lar, but realized he would never do so in time. Rumbling and skittering over naked escarpment and steep, snaking trail came an avalanche of bodies. Their movements were not quite human, their blocky forms either hunched or stunted. Whatever their nature, their numbers continued to stream down from the heights, a trickle become a flood. The mushroom of soldiers sprouted up on the east flank would surely crumble beneath its flow.

Corathel cried a useless warning as the forces were set to clash. Only, the dreaded impact never came. For some reason, the avalanche shifted direction, driving not into Lar's phalanx, but veering south and west and charging hard into the reaver lines.

Even seeing it for himself, Corathel dared not hope. A ruse it must be, he thought, some trickery meant to forestall their retreat and lure them on again in full.

He let his current orders stand and finished pushing his horse on up the slope to where Lar waited. The Fourth General turned toward him with a bemused expression, looking ever taller beside the squat, bearded figure standing next to him.

"Sir," Lar greeted in a winded voice. "Dwarves."

Corathel had never seen a dwarf. Not a true one, anyway. Only the stunted human half-folk who were at times referred to as such. Now and then, he had come across one of these who had taken to the part for show or fair, wearing a jerkin overstuffed with random lumps for that gnarled appearance, and hiding his face behind a shaggy, goat-hair beard of outlandish size and thickness. Not so, here. The figure before him was knotted and growth-ridden, true, and wore a thicket of a beard to put any bramble nest to shame. Yet there was nothing about his presentation intended to be comical; neither did Corathel mistake it as such.

"*Grell graggen hoke,*" the dwarf grunted. His eyes held a grim confidence that matched well his gruff features.

The chief general could only nod. "I don't suppose we've much chance of finding a Gohran translator among us just now," he mumbled at Lar.

Before his lieutenant could respond, the dwarf answered. "I said, you're a mite short to be this one's commander, ain't ya?"

"I saw you coming, sir," Lar explained. "He bears greeting and word from the leader of this host."

"From the king hisself," the dwarf clarified, as scores of his comrades continued to thunder past. "And your man here's telling me you're the leader of this one."

"I am," Corathel affirmed. "And you are . . ."

"Friends, if you'll have us. Else I'll be sounding this here horn and we'll be leaving the lot of you as ya were." A knobby hand patted a curved horn draped over one shoulder.

"No need for that, I assure you. But how did you . . . ? Where—"

"Later," the dwarf said, reaching back to unsling his axe. The squares of metal armor riveted upon his brigandine clanked as he moved. When he brought the weapon about, Corathel saw that its head was as big as the one wielded by Lar. "There's killing to be done, and it seems to me your troops are moving in the wrong direction."

The chief general glanced at his lieutenant, who merely nodded to where an army of dwarves continued to plow as they pleased through the reaver ranks, digging furrows long and wide. A secondary line had formed up all along the base of the slope, securing the eastern flank for good and all. Corathel found himself thinking back to the stories he'd heard as a youth. A dwarf's strength and stamina was fabled. Even the females, it was said, boasted thrice that of an average human male.

"Shall we to work?" his newfound companion urged. "His Glory ain't intending to save any for the laggards."

The dwarf turned an eye to Owl. Corathel watched the pair nod at each other in unspoken courtesy.

"Corporal, belay the retreat. All ahead march." He felt a smile upon his lips. "Seems our day is not yet done."

CHAPTER FORTY

THE COVE LAY EMPTY. OVERHEAD, a pocket of clouds caressed the round, radiant moon. A lamenting wind whistled amid the trees, scraped across crags in the seaside bluff, and combed the choppy surface of the ocean that grumbled below. All else was still, quiet. Yet Torin dared not breathe.

Annleia nudged him, rustling the foliage of their thick woodland shelter. Torin scowled, but never removed his gaze from the rocky beach. Beneath the shadows of the forested mountainside, the sea brewed patiently. Incoming waves were being shred by buried rocks and hidden boulders, ripped into foam and spray. Broken ledges glistened in the moonlight, wet from the salty surf. From their ridge above, Torin and Annleia watched it all, and waited.

"It's out there," Torin whispered, crouching deeper within the clammy underbrush.

"Do you see something?" Annleia asked, eyes wide as they searched the black breakers.

He studied her momentarily. Even in the pale moonlight, her emerald orbs shone deep and bright. "No," he admitted, then looked again, out beyond the shore. *But I feel it.*

"We must go down to meet Him," Annleia said.

Torin managed to nod. His heart raced, fingers gripping the hilt of the Sword. At last, he shifted his gaze from the sea and turned to his companion.

"I'll follow," she offered.

He led in the direction she indicated, skulking through the underbrush along the forest's edge. Damp leaves and wet branches slapped at him as he passed. Though mindful of his footing, he kept an eye at all times upon the ocean's roiling surface, watching wave after wave be lured to the craggy shoreline. The sea would then recoil, sputtering in displeasure while licking its wounded swells. Seconds would pass in which the ocean drew another heaving breath, and a fresh billow would crash forward with renewed fury. Each time, he knew, the minced waters bore away tiny grains of the weathered shore—the eternal exchange between land and sea . . .

Upon reaching the narrow path that wound down the bluff, he paused for a steadying breath, then stepped out into the open.

It required his full focus to navigate the muddy, sandswept trail, which in some areas had been eroded completely by wind and rain. While aiding one another in half treading, half sliding down hundreds of feet along that steep, uncertain descent, he was almost able to forget their purpose in doing so. Only as it leveled off near the bottom did he look back up and realize how far they would have to climb when this night's meeting was finished.

Provided they were given the chance.

"Closer," Annleia urged quietly. "We have to reach the water's edge."

The woman herself seemed in no great rush to do so. She continued to wait behind him, as if his feeble body could provide her some kind of shield against that which they must face. Torin looked beyond the dunes and debris piled at the base of the bluff, out past the deserted, stone-and-pebble beach to where dark waves continued to wrestle with shoreline rocks. His muscles knotted, and he found himself holding his breath. He felt naked here. The surf's assault upon the unyielding shore was deafening at this level, its crush a thunderous echo within the cove's horseshoe walls. *Intruders*, it seemed to roar. *Infidels*. Had they valued their lives, they would not have come.

He drew the Sword, and took what comfort he could from the warmth it unleashed within. With a white-knuckled grip, he started forward.

After that, his legs seemed to move irrespective of his will, dragging him ever closer to that dark, foaming tempest. Half a step behind, Annleia matched him stride for stride. Together, they stepped and stumbled over sand and sea-weed and stone. Charging breakers loomed nearer, threatening to consume them, but invisible undertows held the sea's fury in check. When at last the waves reached forth to soak his ankles, Torin felt Annleia's restraining hand upon his arm, and he gladly halted his progress.

Another eternity passed as he stared out upon the surge of onrushing waters, and at the rise and fall of distant swells. Despite the Sword's warmth, his bones were shaking.

"How do we summon Him?" he asked.

When he received no response, he turned to his companion, and found her wide-eyed and trembling as she, too, focused upon the sea. "With this," she said.

Without looking at him, she reached within her cloak and drew forth the longknife he had seen her fondle but never use. He only glanced at it, at first, afraid to turn his eye from the ocean . . . but found his gaze whipping back.

"Where did you . . . ?" he began, and could not finish.

"I thought you might recognize it," she confessed, shifting her own gaze at last. His was fixated upon the thinness of the blade, the soft curve in its length, the way the moonlight glimmered upon its perfect edge. "The weapons he wielded, young Kylac, they looked something like this, did they not?"

Almost precisely. Kylac had carried one longsword, two shortswords, and an array of daggers and throwing knives. All had borne handles of wood and leather, complete with disc-shaped crosspiece. The grip on this blade was unremarkable—a tightly wrapped thong of hemp and leather. But the blade, so sleek and slender, with just a hint of pearl-like gleam. . .

"You knew," he said, the words sharp with accusation.

"I suspected, based on your account of their strength, of where he found them, of Killangrathor's demise."

"Do you know why?"

"Killangrathor would sooner destroy himself than face them? Not truly. Though we may be about to learn."

Torin frowned, finally pulling his eyes from the blade to find hers.

"It came from Him," she explained, her gaze flicking toward the ocean. "A spine, from the body of Ravar himself. Given the Vandari as a means by which to call to Him in our need."

A spine. Kylac had claimed to have found his in an isolated cove in the northern Skullmars, an ocean away. *Thousands*, the youth had said, *some the size o' spears*. Torin himself had seen these weapons at work and had witnessed their unlikely strength. *I's never even chipped one, never even nicked the edge of a blade*. Not against stone or demon or dragonspawn. No weapon of steel could be hammered so thin yet withstand such punishment. To envision the leviathan he knew wearing these as a saber rat wore its coat of quills . . .

"You might have shared this with me before," he said, staving off a shudder.

"You did not seem much interested in speaking to me on this or any other matter," she reminded him. "Nor is the mystery of Killangrathor's suicide vital to our purpose here."

Vital? Perhaps not. But after carrying that and other riddles around in his head for so long, *any* understanding was like a soothing balm upon an open sore. Knowing *how* and *why* things were happening helped him to feel more a participant in these struggles, and less a victim caught in their flow.

"It may not be so irrelevant to Him," he cautioned, "if Killangrathor was truly the last of his breed."

Annleia swallowed, and their heads turned as one, back to the pounding waves. The lesser wavelets continued to splash and churn about their ankles, drawing sand and pebbles from beneath their feet as if to root them in place.

"I suppose we must find out," she said, a mere whisper against the roaring surf.

She brushed him gently aside, then took two more paces toward the sea. She bent carefully to her knees, cloak snapping in the wind, waves dragging at its hem. He saw her eyes close, and her lips move, murmuring as if in prayer. Slowly, she raised her left arm, clutching the knifelike spine by its makeshift grip, its tip pointed to the earth. When she could stretch no higher, her words stopped, and her eyes opened.

Her arm came down in a blur, blade streaking across the black like a shooting star. While Torin tightened his grip on the Sword, Annleia let go of the spine, leaving it embedded in a rock upon the stony shore.

The ocean roared, the wind moaned, and the earth seemed to shudder. Annleia glanced to the heavens, as if anticipating a bolt of lightning from overhead. But the skies did not answer, remaining pale and vast and empty. A series of gusts reached down to finger a narrow thong left hanging from the spine's hilt, then unfurled it like a flag. When the breezes lost interest, they dropped the strap into the froth of an incoming wave.

Torin held his breath as if it would be his last. He no longer felt the biting cold of the onrushing wavelets. Like curious children, they curled and splashed around the implanted spine and the feet of those who had placed it there, then rushed back to speak of their discovery to the ocean that had spawned them.

The ocean did not seem to care.

Dread anticipation gave way to hollow relief. Perhaps the Dragon God would not answer their summons after all. So be it. They would find another way. Better that, he thought, than to have to face that monstrous titan again.

He was about to express as much to Annleia, when all of a sudden she stiffened. He felt her reaction more than saw it, an awareness through the Sword. His eyes saw well enough the rest.

In slow, steady motion, the entire sea seemed to heave, swelling as if to drown the horrified viewers. Annleia stood, and Torin rushed forward, thinking to grab her and flee. Then the waters parted, and from the ocean's womb lifted a glistening black reef. As this submerged ridge continued to rise, rivers and falls cascaded from hidden crevices within its jagged skin. Looming above them, the reef soon looked to Torin like another cliff, another mountain, eclipsing the moon as it ascended skyward. Mercifully, it remained outside the cove, far too immense to fit within . . . yet still it rose, until suddenly, impossibly, the mountain's underbelly was revealed—it, too, breaching the water's surface.

Beneath, the ocean seemed to disappear, sucked into the void left by the creature's emergence. And Torin, left far from the surf's edge as the waters receded, wished now that he had drowned.

And so you shall, before all is done.

The words reverberated through his chest, through his mind. An inner voice not his own.

Waves of passion. Waves of torment. They will engulf your heart, your head, your lungs. You will choke and sputter and beg release as they crush and grind your soul, Asahiel.

The voice was thunderous and primordial and unrelenting. It gripped him like a giant fist around his rib cage. Ravar. The Dragon God was speaking to him.

An audible groan rattled the cliffs as Ravar arched His gargantuan form, bending His cavernous maw toward them. Though too vast to fully explore, His silvery, eel-shaped torso was armored in reefs of black coral and limestone. From these dripping cliffs hung forests of seaweed, along with countless creatures of rock and shell still clinging to their underwater homes. An entire world, Torin marveled, an entire world hidden from man had risen to greet them.

"I came as soon as I could," Annleia snapped.

Her words startled him almost as much as Ravar's had. At the same time, the defiance in her tone confused him.

Twilight descends, I told her. Yet only now does she summon, rank with fear and mortality. She is too few, too late.

He speaks to both of us, Torin realized, *at the same time, yet independently.*

An infinity of voices, an infinity of ears. Eleahim I am, Asahiel, and shall forever be.

Torin feared his knees might buckle as the creature's stench washed over him. A stench of brine, of deep-sea growth and rot, of timelessness . . . Who was he to stand before such majesty? A worm. A gnat.

Less, Ravar suggested. The creature's head had settled so that it now walled off the cove's entrance. Its eye, a black pearl too small for its body, fixed upon him, gleaming with depthless knowledge and boundless perception. Its gaze pierced him, impaling him with awe, riddling him with despair. In half a heartbeat, Ravar saw everything he was and was not, his every deed, for good and for ill—and was amused by it.

"Then it will cost you nothing to share what you know," Annleia replied to some unknown statement.

She was trembling visibly now, despite her boldness. He wondered what exactly Ravar was telling her. He thought to put his arm around her, to comfort her, but could scarcely breathe, let alone move. His life, his struggles, his successes, his failures—all meant nothing. Only his blade, the Sword of Asahiel, was worthy of such a magnificent presence, and even it felt somehow inadequate. He could see now the hundreds, thousands of spines protruding from Ravar's armored flesh, worn like stubble. A hail of Crimson Swords would not scratch the behemoth before him, could in no way mar its titanic surface. Holding the weapon even now, Torin felt suddenly foolish.

A candle in your palm, its power wasted, Ravar agreed. *A boundless inferno nonetheless, waiting to be unleashed. Given a true wielder, its power could consume a form even such as mine.*

Torin might have scoffed. Could a god lie? Would Ravar attempt to deceive him?

Deception, artifice—devices of the weak, tools used to grasp or shield. My existence is without need, without fear.

Even that, Torin wasn't certain he believed. Annleia had described Ravar as a prisoner, condemned and shackled. Would He not break those bonds if He could? Would He not return—

My life endures, Asahiel. Were you not listening when Vandar told you?

Vandar, Torin thought. *Annleia?*

The Finlorian paradigm is rudimentary, but will serve. Balance. To keep me chained to this earth in physical form—even as an immortal—the Ceilhigh, as you know them, must divert a measure of my everlasting essence elsewhere. They do so constantly, eternally, to ensure my compliance with their chosen sentence. Mountains, winds, waves, and countless living creatures above and below this earth bear now my strength and my legacy. Anchors, yes, but each carries a piece of me throughout their lives, and I theirs. When one chain breaks, another is forged. I am both bound and unbound, forever.

Mountains. The image of a fiery volcano came to mind. He did not know if he had thought of it himself, or if Ravar had put it there, but he echoed its name aloud.

"Krakken." It was the first word to escape his lips since the Dragon God's emergence. "Your power is what gives it life, dominance over the rest of the Skullmars."

A whit, no more. A latent force that drew Killangrathor, when he sought sanctuary from those who hunted him. A power that he, as my child, was able to stir.

The mention of Killangrathor sent a fresh chill rippling down Torin's spine. He glanced at Annleia, and found her peering at him with beetled brow, as puzzled by his words as he had been by hers. Then her face lit with understanding.

"Do you riddle with him as you do me?" she demanded of the creature. "If time is so short, do not fence with us. Tell him what he must know."

Ravar continued to hover, great gills sucking vainly at the salt air as He breathed now through His lungs. There was no expression in His great, craggy face, only the skitter and squirm of crabs and cockles and sea flowers. Yet Torin could feel His mockery all the same.

Do I bore you, Asahiel? Is there something else you would know?

All and more. Too many questions to grasp. Yet, despite Annleia's protest, and despite Ravar's obvious taunt, he was not yet ready to let go of this one.

The dragonspawn, he thought, keeping his thoughts from his elven companion. *They were yours as much as Killangrathor's.*

Bound and unbound, forever.

The Sword's warmth billowed as Torin felt an anger curdling within. Not Ravar's, but his own, fueled by the Dragon God's snide, spiteful manner. So many dead, mutilated, devoured . . .

Such minuscule lives you lead. A breath, no more.

Yet it is the dragonspawn that are dead, he thought, anger spilling over into defiance. *As is the one who birthed them. The last of your children, was he not?*

So he believed. So all of you believe.

The ambiguity took him aback, but he refused to dwell on it. He glanced at Annleia's longknife—Ravar's spine—embedded upon the drained shore. *It must gnaw at you,* he countered, *to have spawned such weakness—a creature that would sooner succumb to death than fight for its right to exist.*

He felt Ravar's derision as a tightening in his chest, and wondered if he might have gone too far. But they would be dead already, he felt, if the monster cared enough to make them so.

You have never stood in the presence of your creator, came the Dragon God's reply. *Nor can you begin to fathom the soul-wracking anguish and humility should you be confronted by even one lash fallen from Her brow.*

I am but a man. Men are weak. Dragons were meant to be strong. To be so fearful as to kill himself—

Ravar's spines rattled—whether in response to him or Annleia, he could not say. *There are fates worse than death, Asahiel. Killangrathor understood this. The acids that ravaged his skin and stopped his heart are like infant oils when held against the fires of oblivion.*

Torin considered that for a moment, if that was really all there was to it. *Oblivion. And is that what* you *face, should you refuse to aid us?*

I will play my part in this, Ravar assured him, *however I must. What is yet to be decided is, will you?*

Annleia was looking at him again, this time with a worried expression. Whatever she was hearing, she did not seem pleased.

"Tell me of the Illysp," he said aloud, thinking to unify their conversations once and for all.

Have you not learned enough?

"I would know where they came from, how to send them back."

Where they came from? Ravar echoed, and Torin felt suddenly as if he had stepped out over a precipice. *I shall show you.*

The world went dark. Torin did not remember closing his eyes, but when he opened them, the cove, the Dragon God, Annleia—all of it was gone. He stood instead amid a charred wasteland. Oven winds baked the arid landscape, stirring dust and soot with every howling gust. The air was black and foul, and choked him when he tried to breathe. He covered his mouth and nose to ward off a nauseating stench that seemed somehow familiar. Then he heard Ravar's disembodied voice within.

On their own plane, the Illysp were beings who could shed their physical coil and exchange it for a new one. They could do so at will, as often as they cared to, and thus live forever.

The sky flashed, a parade of lightning dancing from cloud to cloud. Torin whirled and spun, seeking shelter from the grit that pelted him.

But the coils themselves were not unlimited. Exhausting their most precious resource through war and waste, the Illysp became naught but fleshless spirits, hungering for so much as a taste of what once belonged to them in abundance.

A raindrop fell, burning his skin like acid. Torin glanced up, and another struck his eye, gouging as if it were a bead of molten steel.

Here, they have found a new source, albeit bodies to which they must commit for life. Regardless, the hunger for flesh, for the sensations it brings, is too great for them to ignore. Physical life, even a mortal one, is a temptation they cannot resist.

The rain began in earnest then, a drizzle at first, then a downpour. Trails of smoke drifted from his clothes, while his flesh began to steam. His search for shelter became frantic, as he gripped himself against the searing agony. But the desert surrounded him. He had nowhere to run, and the rain was falling faster. He tried to duck beneath his cloak, but the garment was already in tatters. Then he saw his hand. The skin had melted, and was sloughing away to reveal muscle and ligament and bone. As he watched, a finger fell off. Drawing a deep breath that nearly gagged him, Torin screamed . . .

. . . and found himself within the cove once more. The sea's windborne spray lashed his face, and he swiped at it in a reflexive panic. Salt, not acid. He stared at it upon his fingers, gasping in relief to find them whole.

"Enough, I say!" Annleia was shrieking, all taut muscles and clenched fists. She then turned to find Torin gaping, and stomped toward him as if to make certain he was all right. He blinked once, twice, and held up his hand to ward her off. With the other, he strengthened his grasp upon the Sword.

This realm, too, might end the same. Given rein, the Illysp will resort again to chaos and butchery in the ultimate, maddened pursuit of self-preservation.

Torin shook his head, still dazed from his brush with that feral world. Would the Ceilhigh, the creators of *this* world, truly allow that to happen? How could that be?

As ruler of your people, do you harvest every grain and tube grown within your nation's fields? Do you rush to defend against every storm, every poacher, every vermin? The Ceilhigh are cultivating an entire maelstrom. They have scant cause to dedicate themselves to the concerns of a single world or the lives crawling upon it. They left caretakers for that, avatars, when their creations were fresh and young. Ha'Rasha, whose calling was to guide and nurture and oversee this realm in its infant stages. But that time is past, and the Ha'Rasha all but extinct, having returned in one form or another unto the great Var-Rahim.

Not all, Torin thought, reminded immediately of Cianellen.

A child, as you learned, of whim and fancy and coquettish curiosity. She and her kind may play upon this world, but long ago ceased to affect it in any meaningful way.

Leaving you.

Leaving me. My punishment, as it were, for seeking to shape a history my brothers and sisters thought better left to its natural course. For taking part in this world's struggles, I condemned myself to forever doing so—an avatar, in my own way, since that, in effect, is what I chose to become.

The answer to your question, then, Ravar continued, *is yes. As sole warder against this infestation, I would stand aside if I could. I would follow the lead of the Ceilhigh and leave this realm to rot. I would give it over to the plague that elves and then humans unleashed.*

The creature's great bulk clenched. Spines bristled. Ledges of reef and barnacle cracked and crumbled and splashed into the waters beneath. Another slow groan slipped through the eel-like lips, its rumble seeming to fill the dome of the sky.

But I cannot. Even now I feel them, skittering upon the surface like roaches upon mine own skin. Illysp, Illychar, their form makes no matter. I cannot resist the growing hunger planted in me by my brethren of the Ceilhigh. I must rid myself of their pestilence, though I would see your sufferings continue . . . if only a while longer.

To end it all now would be a mercy. Ravar knew this. He was going to hold out for as long as He could. He was going to give them as many chances as possible to fail. Only when they were battered and broken and had nothing left would He do His part and sweep it all away, and let the world begin anew.

"You will do as you must, then," Annleia said. "As will we."

She glanced back at him for confirmation, and Torin gave it, nodding with as much confidence as he could muster. "The seal. How do we restore—"

Forget the seal, Ravar urged. *Would you vanquish this menace before I do? Then close the rift between these worlds and destroy the Illysp utterly.*

Torin regarded Annleia at the same time she turned toward him. The expression she showed him might have been his own.

"Is that even possible?" he asked. "If so, why didn't the Vandari destroy the rift the last time? Why did they seal it up instead?"

Once Sabaoth was slain, Algorath was charged with precisely that: the rift's destruction. He need only have commanded the Sword's full power, but could not do so. The seal was created to mask that failure, a construct of Finlorian magi, Algorath's Sword, and the Dragon Orb, which I was obliged to provide them. A patch, I warned, but they could see no other way.

Neither could Torin. If Algorath, an Entient, had failed to unlock the Sword's fires, then what chance did *he* have?

The answer to that lies within. Words of instruction do not equal faith. Nor am I given or required to make men into avatars. The key to the Sword is something the wielder must divine for himself.

The nebulous answer did not surprise him. His gaze dipped to study the talisman, to watch the swirl of flames within its lustrous blade. "And if I cannot?"

Should the Illysp be locked away, how long before they are once again unleashed? I have but one more Orb to bestow. How will your progeny survive without one?

"Perhaps one of them will find a way to do what I cannot."

And perhaps the talisman will again be lost to the enemy when the seal is breached—and this time fail to be regained. The Vandari might die out completely. You would leave your kind naked, defenseless. You would leave it to me to save them.

By eradicating them, Torin thought glumly.

"If he should succeed," Annleia asked, "if he should unleash the fires of Asahiel and destroy the rift, what are we to do about the Illysp and Illychar already set loose?"

They will know, when the time comes.

"They?" Annleia echoed. "Who are *they*?"

All who played a part. Granted, their actions, like yours, cannot be guaranteed. One choice will be to aid you. The other to let the world fall.

Annleia was clearly unsatisfied by the response. But Torin found it a moot issue. Try as he might, he could not foresee himself succeeding where Algorath had failed. To believe otherwise would be a childish vanity, and would be to wager too many lives in the bargain. Better to attempt what had been done before, and thus could be done again.

Ravar disagreed.

You must not leave this sickness to fester. You must do as Algorath should have, and destroy it.

Torin faced Annleia. Though she peered at him with that imploring gaze, he could not imagine what she expected of him. "If I cannot?" he asked again.

You must.

Raise his hopes only to have them dashed again? Why? To provide amusement for a fallen god? "If I cannot"—he made it a statement this time—"surely, there is another way."

Annleia's gaze fell, as if his stubborn refusal somehow disappointed her. Her reaction caused his own frustration to billow, but before he could speak to it, he felt again Ravar's sneering derision, like screws upon his chest.

So be it, Asahiel. It shall be given to Vandar to carry my Orb, to banish the Illysp to the well beneath Thrak-Symbos, and to construct a seal as her forebears once did. Since none other might comprehend and execute the magics involved, it is upon her shoulders that this burden will rest.

Torin looked to her in apology, but Annleia had already turned away, her focus upon the Dragon God's unblinking eye.

"I am ready," she said.

Torin could only stand there and grind his teeth, flush with a guilt from which he saw no relief. Did she not understand how foolish he would have to be to saunter off under the assumption that he could bring the Sword's divine power to bear? It was only prudent to know their every option. Besides, it was not as if he would let her go off and do this alone. He would be there to ward her every step, to lend what skill he could to the quest she was being given. Together, they would see it done.

It occurred to him suddenly that Ravar's voice had gone silent. Annleia was still looking at Him, gripping herself against gusting winds. Every now and then, she would nod or shake her head or glance again in Torin's direction. Clearly, the pair of them were still communicating, but saw fit to leave him out of it.

"Am I to not know how this will happen?" he asked with some irritation.

Annleia only waved at him to be silent, intent on catching words he could not hear.

I can share only what did *happen, Asahiel, little of which you will believe, and less you will understand. If you mean to be her warder, let your focus be on the path you must tread.*

No small matter, that, Torin acknowledged privately. Pentania remained a long way off—a voyage of at least two weeks with favorable winds, added to the time it would take them to travel to a port and find a ship. Afterward, it—

"Ravar has agreed to carry us," Annleia announced.

Torin blinked in surprise. Either the Vandari had read his thoughts, or she and Ravar had reached the same point in their own conversation.

"He . . . has He now?" Torin stammered.

The titan moaned, and Torin's bones shivered. Not the most settling of prospects, though better than some he had heard this night. While he had no real way of knowing, he suspected the snaking leviathan could swim faster than any ship, without threat of being becalmed or misdirected by squall. Assuming the beast did not drown them, He might even convey them directly to Pentania's treacherous eastern shore—upon which no vessel of wood and sail could safely land. Once there . . .

His grudging enthusiasm faltered, then slipped away. Once there, who would lead them through the ruins?

I will deliver you upon the southern shore, to where your people battle their last. There you will find your guide—one you will recognize.

Torin perked up at once. "Kylac?" he blurted. "Has Kylac found his way back to us?"

The Eternal Youth treads upon another path. In this, he cannot aid you.

The sudden, certain hope, dashed so quickly, left him raw with disappointment. The mere possibility led his gaze back to the spine embedded near his feet, so much like the weapons Kylac had fashioned for himself. *The Eternal Youth*, he mused. What did *that* mean? Was it meant to reflect—

A new suspicion gripped him, as sudden and certain as the last. "Is he one of yours?" Torin asked. "Is he one of those who bear your legacy?"

Kylac Kronus is one whose prowess is fed by an endowment of my divine strength—sapped from me by my fellow gods.

If so, it would explain much. Kylac's speed, his skills, his warrior's anticipation . . . won through years of training, yes, yet preternatural nonetheless. A paragon of finely honed—and seemingly divine—potential.

"If not Kylac," Annleia pressed, "who is to guide us? How will we know them?"

His appearance will leave no doubt. Already, he hunts for you.

A dubious reassurance, Torin thought, sobering quickly. But he couldn't well hope to navigate that labyrinth by himself. His prior trek through the buried halls of that city had been a meandering one, marked by trial and error. Doubtless, his trail would have been further obscured by the many Illychar to have—

His thoughts froze with yet another jolting realization. So obvious, had he only thought far enough ahead to consider.

"The ruins themselves are guarded, are they not?"

Along with your guide, the south holds those who will perish in your stead.

Torin shared another look with Annleia. His mouth felt suddenly dry. "And why must any be asked to do that?"

But the answer was evident. The Illysp would not take the defense of their portal lightly. They had ambushed Darinor. They would be lying in wait for him as well.

This is the course you have chosen. Would you now choose the other?

The Sword. Once again, Ravar was taunting him, baiting him. Torin refused to bite.

"An army, then," he decided. It would *have* to be, if Annleia was to be given a fair chance.

As many lives as you mean to sacrifice.

Torin scowled. "Are you saying all who accompany us will be lost?"

I say, wager what you will, numbers will not save you.

Torin gnawed on that a moment, disliking its taste. "Can you describe the dangers our company will face?" He knew of one already, which they would have to battle past or seek to avoid. But he had to assume there would be others as well.

Your peril lies threefold, Ravar confirmed. *Against them, I offer these warnings: A spider's web does not forbid entry, but escape. For one to press forward, the rest must be consumed. The greatest danger is that which lurks unseen.*

Torin repeated them quickly in his head, mulling them over while committing them to memory. He did not trust in Ravar's willingness to repeat them—or anything else He had shared.

The more he considered them, however, the less reason he found to hope.

Hope is impotent. It is deeds, with or without hope, that will save you.

True enough, Torin supposed. Sometimes, a man's only recourse was to keep moving. "I suppose I must ask, then—"

Time wastes, Asahiel, Vandar. You have so little left. Should you question me unto eternity, I will yet have puzzles to share.

"He's right," Annleia said. She turned and plucked the longknife from its bed of sand and sea stone. The earth gave another shudder, and Ravar another moan. "We'll sort it out on our way."

So be it. He had more than enough to digest just now, and felt sufficiently ill because of it. Perhaps Annleia had made better use of her questions, and would have some small encouragement to lend.

With the spine tucked away, the elven woman began picking her way cautiously across the naked beach—still stripped of its tide by Ravar's emergence. After a moment of peering vainly into the Dragon God's distant eye, Torin sheathed the Sword and followed.

The exposed tidal flat was a rugged stretch of boulders and loose stones, all of it gritty with sand and slick with ocean growth. It took them some time to reach the end of the visible reef, stretching just beyond the cove's mouth. Ravar's immense bulk shifted closer to meet them, grinding and scraping as He aligned Himself against the shore.

Annleia waited until He had settled, then scaled His hide as she might any other coral rock formation. *She hides her trepidation well*, Torin thought, and he was determined to do the same. Trying not to breathe too deeply of Ravar's overwhelming, unfamiliar stench, he clambered after her from hold to hold, wary of the many jags and spiny growths and concealing crevices. He spied crabs and other clawed creatures hidden amid those holes, as well as beds of oysters and mussels growing in clumps. *At least we won't starve*, he thought.

He took special care to avoid the leviathan's spines, which sprouted forth like a forest of mismatched trees. Some were no longer than his forearm, while others easily reached twice his height. Most were filthy and salt-stained, coated like so much else with algae and barnacles. But he had no delusions about their razor sharpness, even in their natural state.

At long last they crested Ravar's side and worked their way toward the ridge of His back. Looking north and then south along that line, Torin saw only more of the same: a bizarre jungle of scale and spine and coral, ravaged in its appearance, yet inhabited by urchins and sea stars and a thousand and more scuttling creatures he did not recognize. It might have been the ugliest terrain he'd ever seen. Or else the most beautiful.

Take hold.

Torin did not expect a second warning. But he knew not where they were expected to lie. Annleia, however, quickly found a nearby grotto with a larboard opening, and called him over to join her. Its floor was carpeted with sea moss. The moss was wet, and soaked through his breeches the moment he sat, but he supposed he would have to get used to that.

Uncertain of what to expect, he gripped the edges of the grotto, though the sharp coral dug into his palms. Annleia, who had sat down behind him, cinched her own arms about his waist.

No sooner had they settled than the earth beneath them lurched and twisted, detaching from the shore. He had anticipated worse. Even though Ravar swung His head to starboard with a serpentine thrust, His flesh rippled so that the momentum seemed to dissipate within the vastness of His form. This was no ship they sailed, Torin reminded himself, but a mass bigger than many an island.

Ravar dipped lower into the black waves on either side, sending the ocean's waters rushing back into the cove. But that was behind them. Ahead, they found themselves skimming along just above the windblown crests. As their speed increased, so too did the gale of their passage, whistling through gaps in the grotto wall. Torin could scarcely feel the behemoth's snaking movements—as deep and widespread and powerful as the sea's own currents. The eastern horizon was dark and bleak and boundless, instilling a sense of isolation both fearful and wondrous. With night all around and the taste of spray upon the wind, he felt a stirring of the same exhilaration and freedom that sailing had first taught him.

To his left, however, the coastal face of the Dragontails veered north and east in a ragged line, craggy features limned in moonlight. Growing smaller, with every passing heartbeat.

An undeniable ache took hold in his chest. It made no sense to him, that he should feel so strongly about a place he had scarcely known. Yet here he had found faith—those who trusted in him when he did not trust in himself. Here he had found hope—aims and aspirations for a life he had never before imagined. Here he had found love—a woman who had shown him with a single smile why men were given life. He had not asked for it to happen, yet his heart had somehow tethered itself to this place and people. To separate himself was like tearing it out by the roots.

Still, better to endure the grief of bittersweet memories, he supposed, than to have never known either.

So many to cling to. So many images to defend against the immutable decay of time. He couldn't possibly retain them all, and time alone could tell which would remain. If only he had something more to grasp them with, something more than fallible mind and fickle heart.

His hands let go of their unnecessary hold on the coral walls. His left formed a fist around Dyanne's pendant, her once-radiant fire reduced already to this mere ember. He would channel his efforts, he decided. All else would live through her memory, and her memory through this small token.

It was more than he might have expected. It would have to suffice.

Annleia's arms slipped from around his waist. "I'm going to take some rest," she said, her voice in his ear. "You might do well to join me."

"Should we not share what we learned while our thoughts are fresh?" He turned as she rose.

"My thoughts are anything but fresh," she said, her expression weary. "Nor, I daresay, are yours."

A maelstrom, more like. He held his tongue against any claim to the contrary, while Annleia moved away to curl up against the back of their little cave, her cloak wrapped close about her.

I suppose I should go and keep her warm, Torin thought, before realizing that, with their coral windbreak and Ravar's internal heat, the surrounding cold posed little real threat.

His fingers released Dyanne's pendant and slipped to the hilt of the Sword. *Its power could consume a form even such as mine.* As boundless as the sea, but only in the hands of one who commanded it. He would do his best, of course, but when had his best ever truly been enough?

He looked to the ocean for an answer, soon losing himself in the rhythm of its swells.

CHAPTER FORTY-ONE

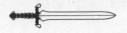

Allion did his best to keep his eyes forward as he made his way through the dwarven encampment. Hrothgari, the gnarled envoy had named them. Allies and saviors, when judged by their actions. But in that early morning mix of red light and flickering shadows, with their misshapen limbs and their stern, suspicious gazes, they looked to Allion more like ghouls.

Thus far, victory within the Gaperon had been a somber affair. The fires had surged with the dawn, feasting upon the bodies of the slain. Ash and cinder rained down amid gusting winds. The fighting had ended, the Illychar defeated—save for a few stubborn pockets entrenched upon the rocky slopes, and the occasional rising of a wounded one feigning death amid the carnage. It was mankind's first real triumph since Rogun had quashed Darinor's initial uprising at Krynwall. Yet, with all that Allion had seen of the aftermath, the outcome still tasted of defeat.

He had thought to spare himself the worst of it, to remain behind the Kuurian blockade and serve the wounded carried in for treatment. Perhaps he would find Marisha and try to make amends. But he was still with Commander Troy, out near the front, when the dwarven herald had found them, escorted by one of Troy's own runners. The Hrothgari king, Hreidmar, had invited the various leaders of this impromptu coalition to meet with him. With only cleanup remaining, the time had come to take stock, greet their new friends, and plan their next maneuver.

Troy had agreed, and, before thinking the matter through, Allion had begged permission to accompany him. Too late, the hunter found himself wending past heaps of bloodstained corpses—not only of men, but of women and children. While some Illysp might seek only the strongest physical vessels, as Darinor had once claimed, there were plenty of others, it seemed, who would settle for whatever was available. And once possessed of an Illysp frenzy, none could be spared.

He had known it, he had seen it, though not on this scale. The Illychar he had battled before now had mostly been races of another age, many of them deemed monsters already. But this slaughter had come against their own, against innocents fallen at Atharvan. It made the atrocity of the wounds required to hew them down a second time all the more sickening.

Not that he could ignore the damage they had inflicted in turn. Wading through the still-simmering sea of bodies, he had suffered the anguished groans, the twitching limbs, the crawling wounded who writhed about, not yet realizing they were dead. These were the worst, he decided, those who clutched at severed stumps or punctured organs with one hand, while clawing at his feet with the other. More than once, he and Troy had paused to lend aid or comfort, but for every one that might be saved, they encountered a dozen whose moaning pleas would be answered only by disease or blood loss. The hope and fear that shone in their eyes, coupled with Allion's sense of helplessness, was enough to etch another scar in the wall of his heart.

Reaching the Hrothgari muster area had been of no great relief. The dwarves had weathered the battle better than most. Even those who had been maimed or injured bore their pain with tight-lipped determination. But Allion was immediately uncomfortable in their presence. His eyes seemed drawn to their deformities—the spurs and lumps and awkward angle of their appendages. He guarded his reactions, yet they seemed to sense his pity and dismay all the same. Their tart, indignant stares suggested as much. Some might only have been wary. Others regarded him with outright disdain.

Still, they parted before him without contest, deferring to the Hrothgari messenger who led them. So Allion kept pace with Troy, who seemed perfectly at ease, and dared not look back. He could sense the path closing behind them, making him mindful of his every breath and glance, understanding now why Hreidmar had invited them into *his* camp rather than wait to be invited into theirs.

Just ahead now, a clutch of boulders climbed a shallow rise. A pack of sentries formed a wall before the opening. These did *not* appear in any rush to step aside.

Their escort turned his head. "His Glory's warders will unburden you of your weapons."

Again, Troy uttered no protest. He had already agreed to leave his mount behind, sending it off with one of his grooms. As naked as Allion felt without his bow, he handed the weapon over along with his arrows and knives. They would do him little good at this point, anyway.

The *warders* watched him with disgruntled expressions. Then again, so much of their face was hidden behind those bristling, unkempt beards. Underneath, they might have been smiling, for what little he could tell. All he really had to go by were the knuckled brows and dark, agate-colored eyes. Given these, even the broadest grin would have done little to soften their overall bearing.

He forced his misgivings aside and even managed to nod at one of the warders as they parted before him. These were not his enemies, he reminded himself. They had proven that already. His mistrust in this instance was undeserved.

He followed Troy up the narrow footpath, feet scuffing upon a layer of pebbles. His boots were soaked with gore, stiffened leather turned soft and malleable against his toes. His ears rang with the distant clangor of swords and shouts, while his nose fought to reject the pervasive stench of smoke and sweat and rotting flesh. He wondered idly if he would ever smell clean air again, or glimpse a sky unstained by soot.

Troy's sudden chuckle caught him off guard. "Mercy's shade. Can that be who it appears?"

Allion looked up to take in the scene. The council had started without them, but came now to a murmuring halt. Bodies crammed the boulder-studded meeting ground—dwarves mostly, but the hunter realized quickly enough whom Troy had spotted.

"General!" he exclaimed, as Corathel turned to face them. "You're alive!" He hastened forward, all else forgotten, until their guide reached out a twisted arm that stopped him after his second stride, nearly taking the wind from his lungs.

"*Tagge grem*," the dwarf rumbled, "*hig marren groat, Tobarri. Drumguir aute.*"

His words were directed at a dwarf flanked by sentries and perched upon a boulder, who wore jewels within a striped beard. Hreidmar, Allion supposed. Heads turned to gauge the Hrothgari king's reaction.

"Friends of mine," a rising Corathel assured the dwarf leader. Hreidmar inclined his head, and their escort lowered his arms. The Parthan general approached, limping noticeably. His armor was dented, his clothing torn, his flesh battered and bloodstained. His face seemed a mesh of scabs and bruises.

"Allion, Commander," he greeted with a grim smile.

"I should have known," Troy said, clasping the other's arm. "Who else would be mad enough to—"

"U'uyen?" Allion gasped. An apparition, surely, slipped from the crowd's perimeter to appear at Corathel's back. But there was no mistaking the Powaii chieftain's lithe movements, his towering height, that crown of sharpened stakes. "How can it . . . ? Is it really you?"

Cwingen U'uyen made a chittering noise and drew a pair of fingers in a line across his chest.

"You know this one?" Corathel asked Allion.

"It's him," was all the hunter could think to say at first. "The one who led our search for the Sword. The one Kylac told you about, when you and I first met." His mouth was racing now, his thoughts almost feverish. "Where did you . . . ? What's he doing here?"

"I couldn't say. He and a pack of his kind saw us safely from Atharvan. Been snug as a sword belt ever since. I've lost count of the number of times he's saved my life."

Again, U'uyen gestured, while his mouth made strange clicking and popping noises that Allion could not begin to decipher.

"Is Kae not here?" the hunter asked. "Or someone else who might tell us what he's saying?"

Corathel shook his head. "We've discerned no more than his name. Few among us care to attempt even that. We've been calling him Owl."

"He is pleased to see you," a voice called over at them. Allion turned with the others to see who had spoken, and found it to be Hreidmar.

"You understand him?" Corathel asked.

"His general meaning. I've not heard the Illian tongue in decades, and theirs is a unique offshoot of that, even."

With the entire assembly—and their king in particular—staring back at him, Allion became suddenly self-aware. As shocked and delighted as he was by these unexpected reunions, this gathering, he knew, was meant to serve a greater purpose.

"Begging pardon," he offered, glancing between his friends and the dwarf king, "I did not intend a distraction. Only, I had feared these comrades dead."

Hreidmar waved the apology aside. "Your familiarity with one another should hasten these proceedings. You are commanders from the south?"

Troy stepped forward, then bowed crisply. "Troy, named high commander of the Imperial Army of Kuuria by King Thelin of Souaris. My companion is Allion, regent of Krynwall—the capital of Alson."

"Former regent," Allion corrected. He looked again at U'uyen, who hovered protectively at Corathel's shoulder.

Hreidmar beckoned them closer. Corathel led them to the flat shelf of rock on which he'd been seated upon their arrival. Behind them, U'uyen slipped into the shadow of a nearby boulder.

Hreidmar waited until they were situated, then fixed his gaze upon Troy. "Is it true, then, what this one's been telling me?"

Neither the king's somber tone, nor the gruff stares of the many dwarves in attendance, could hold Troy's familiar half smile at bay. "What has he told you?"

Corathel answered. "Word is, Souaris has been abandoned."

"Assaulted from within." Troy's smile had vanished. "The Imperial Council deemed her walls unsafe, given the nature of this enemy."

"You fled," Hreidmar stated plainly.

"I serve as my king commands, guarding the exodus of my people—and many a refugee from throughout Pentania—from these lands."

Allion turned to Corathel. "Those I marched with from Atharvan—your citizens, your soldiers—went with them, to blaze a trail across the sea."

"They will be reaching the coast by now," Troy added. "At last report, they were just a few days out."

A chorus of complaints broke out among the dwarves, in a tongue Allion did not know. Hreidmar raised a fist to quiet them.

"My kin came forth to fight, not sacrifice themselves to the mercy of wind and wave."

"And we're indebted to you," Troy said, "make no mistake. Our defenses were crumbling. Your timely efforts have won us a reprieve."

"Temporarily," Corathel muttered. When the others looked to him, he explained, "This was a mercy killing, no more. A chance to lay past failures to rest. The true threat is still en route."

"How many?" some dwarf asked.

"Fifty thousand, at the least. All of a much deadlier variety than that faced here."

"The Imperial Army alone can muster that and more," Troy observed.

"My warriors number greater than twelve thousand," Hreidmar added.

"And the Parthan Legion stands at better than twenty, discounting our night's losses, and without including those to the south," Corathel said. "It matters not."

Emboldened by the growing count, Allion was confused by the sudden turn. "But . . . we outnumber them."

"At first glance, perhaps," the Parthan general allowed. "But ours count no better than half—and more likely a third or a fourth—given their need to battle in shifts, while the enemy comes continuously at full strength. And the fifty we face might well be a hundred, two hundred, before we are finished, since many will have to be killed several times over ere their coils are finally destroyed."

The momentary joy Allion had felt at seeing Corathel and U'uyen again, the hope their appearance had fostered, seeped away like water through parched earth. He could sense the truth in Corathel's words. How many times had they witnessed it? As King Thelin had pointed out, the underlying threat was not the Illychar, but the spirits that raised them—over and over again.

"As loath as I am to admit it," Corathel said gravely, "I cannot fault Thelin or his councilors the decision they've made. If the Illysp were no more, then perhaps—just perhaps—our numbers might stand sufficient. Barring that, it seems we are hopelessly outmatched."

Hreidmar's beard rustled. He seemed to be grinding his teeth. "We were led to believe your kind was stronger than this. We believed there was still a chance."

"And there is," Allion heard himself say. Upon realizing that he had drawn the assembly's attention, he spoke up. "If it's survival you speak of, there are lands aplenty, I imagine, far grander than this one."

"With perils of their own, I do not doubt," Hreidmar countered. "And should this plague we seek to leave behind gain in strength, there may come a time in which we'll wish we'd done more to stamp it out when presented this opportunity."

"Looking back," Corathel said, "I fear the opportunity was never more than a mirage."

Again the Hrothgari grumbled among themselves. Some looked or gestured angrily to the eastern slopes rising overhead. Allion peered in that direction, shielding his eyes against the brightening sun, but saw only cliffs and fissures and clinging growth. He was more concerned with Corathel and all that the chief general must have endured to have soured so completely on their chances. Once again, false hope had given way to only deeper despair.

As the arguments grew louder, with Hreidmar sitting still in silent appraisal, the approach of a fresh envoy drew Allion's gaze. When he saw who accompanied the herald, his chest tightened with an odd mix of fear and pride.

"I do pray I've not missed the festivities," Rogun boomed in sardonic greeting.

The envoy bowed. "*Tobarri, big drumguir gragmel. Rogun, dar Alson roke.*"

"How many leaders do you men require?" Hreidmar asked of the three already present.

Rogun ignored the king's comment. "Well, now," he said, staring squarely at Allion, "venturing a bit close to the fire, aren't we?"

"Good of you to join us, General," Allion replied. "How fares Nevik?"

Rogun stepped near, a bristling hulk in his suit of spiked steel. His face was streaked with sweat, his armor spattered with blood and grime. Ribbons of flesh, clumps of hair—even a smashed and severed finger—had been trapped in its bladed ridges.

"The baron's message was received, if General Corathel has not yet told you. He leads Alson's remaining populace westward to Gammelost and any other port they may find." The Alsonian general seated himself beside a pair of dwarves, who quickly made room. "What *have* I missed?"

"Rogun, is it?" Troy interjected. "A man of reputation."

"And every word of it true, I suspect." The general snorted. "Yours are the colors of Souaris. Commander Troy, could it be?"

Troy nodded, then offered his hand. "It appears I must thank you for coming to our aid."

"A small part, my contingent played," Rogun said. Braces scraped as he grasped and then quickly released Troy's forearm. "Save your thanks for the brave fools of Partha. And you, fair liege," he added, turning to salute Hreidmar. "I would call your arrival blessed, were it not known that whatever gods may be have long since forsaken us."

"Scant difference our coming has made," Hreidmar remarked, nodding stiffly. "We venture forth to defend this roach nest, only to learn that the roaches have already fled."

"It's what men do best," Rogun granted, "scurry from place to place, seeking shelter and comfort to be won with the least amount of struggle. Water?" he asked, eyeing a nearby skin.

Hreidmar nodded, and the skin was passed. Rogun unstoppered it, sniffed twice, then took a deep swig.

"Would you stay and fight?" the Hrothgari king asked.

The general wiped his mouth. "For what spoils these lands can offer? No."

"But they are yours."

"And were another's before my forebears took them. Is that not so?" He quaffed another mouthful. "Field and river and forest mean little enough to me. It is the *people* I'm sworn to defend, and my people have decided to flee. I'll not force any to remain against their will."

"If they were to reconsider," Hreidmar pressed, "if they were to stand strong, might they win? Your counterparts tell me no. They would urge my kind to desert alongside yours."

Allion stiffened as Rogun looked upon him with a sneer. The general would make them out to be cowards, all three. His own fear, Allion would not deny, but Corathel and Troy had earned better.

"I say only that I have fought two battles against these creatures, and won them both," the general said finally. "I know not what greater strength they have in store, but these are proud men seated before you, whose courage I'll not question. They'd not allow their people to seek peace and prosperity elsewhere, I think, if they held any reasonable chance of providing it."

Allion could only look on in wonder as Rogun finished draining the waterskin. The general had not exactly supported their assessment, only claimed them qualified enough to make it. Yet even that small concession was more than the hunter would have anticipated.

"And what do *you* seek, General," Hreidmar questioned, "if not peace and prosperity?"

Rogun tossed the empty skin back to its dwarven owner. "Most fight for what they may find when the warring is done." His countenance hardened. "For the rest of us, battle is its own reward."

A prolonged quiet ensued, while Rogun and Hreidmar faced one another and the commotion of the battlefield cleansing continued.

"General Corathel," the Hrothgari king grumbled at last, "how long before this dire host is upon us?"

"They've fallen behind range of my outriders," Corathel admitted. "I do not yet understand what has captured their attention. It may be that—"

"A diversion, sent by my people. If all goes to plan, they will reach this ground in four, five days. Your suggestion?"

"To finish burning our dead, refortify our position, and make sure that any who would find peace fly south as swiftly as possible."

"Commander Troy?"

"Those are the orders I've been given. If possible, we are to initiate a gradual fallback to join the exodus, once word is received that the majority are away. I confess, I do not expect to set eyes upon the sea."

"Allion?"

The hunter was somewhat startled at his inclusion, more so given Troy's blunt appraisal. "I . . . What of your kin? Back home, I mean. Wherever that is. Can they evacuate in time?"

"It seems we must soon find out. General Rogun?"

"And what of U'uyen?" Allion barreled on. "And *his* kin? Are they to fend for themselves?" He glanced back at where his Powaii friend stood, a silent sentinel amid the mountain's shadows. The sounds from the battlefield were his only answer.

"I've made my position clear," Rogun replied. "The choice to fight or flee is an individual one. Might just be that those of us who stay will prove victorious, and will then have these lands to ourselves—to share with the cannibals, it seems."

If intended as a jape, no one—not even Rogun himself—laughed.

One of the dwarves sitting nearest Hreidmar mumbled something at his king.

"Ah, yes," Hreidmar replied, "can any of you tell me, is the enemy still in possession of a Sword of Asahiel?"

Allion looked to Corathel, then to Rogun, both of whom seemed to be pinning this one on *him*.

"I was warned we may have to face one of these legendary blades," Hreidmar continued. "Was that a lie?"

Allion found his tongue, though the forming words unleashed a foul taste. "Its bearer flew off upon a dragon. To my knowledge, neither weapon nor monster has been sighted since."

The king's eyes widened. "A dragon? Killangrathor?" His dwarven pack murmured, while Hreidmar himself glanced up at the mountain pass from which his army had poured. "No mention was made to us of *that*."

"With any luck," Allion added bitterly, "they've been lost or destroyed."

"Luck?" Rogun echoed. "In that case, it is too much to hope."

"The prevailing opinion, it seems." Hreidmar shook his head. "I have heard enough for now. I thank you for your counsel, but must ask for time to confer with my own." Again, he glanced at the pass above, causing Allion to wonder what might be up there. "Are there any of you we missed?"

The generals glanced at one another. "We represent the surviving nations of these shores," Corathel answered. "Unless there are others like yourself we're unaware of."

The Hrothgari king grunted. "None that can redirect this tide, it seems." His sour gaze drifted once more to the eastern heights. "But let us speak again later."

"I HAVE THEM," RANUNCULUS ANNOUNCED.

Maventhrowe cocked his head, but did not turn. He sat at the edge of the natural stone bridge that spanned his favorite subterranean grotto. A school of silverthorn had gathered, groping blindly for the bits of food the white-haired Entient was feeding them in that lightless cavern. "They are close, are they not?"

"Here, within the mountains. Not two days hence."

"Returning, perhaps?"

Ranunculus snorted, stepping forward to the edge of the bridge. "Hardly. They created an earthshield, to conceal a portion of the Hrothgari."

"Ah, is that what I felt." It sounded like a statement. "Have the Hrothgari placed themselves in danger, then?"

"Their army joined the humans in battle in the Gaperon."

Maventhrowe sighed. "While Htomah and his followers shielded the gentler folk from scouting eyes."

"Yes."

Had they not done so, Ranunculus might still be searching. An Entient might hide himself from scrying, but could still be viewed while in the presence of another. Ranunculus had first caught up with the renegade Htomah in the halls of Ungarveld. Once his former brother had convinced Quinlan, Jedua, and Wislome to join him, however, the four had fashioned a web thick enough to hide not only themselves, but any with whom they might come in contact.

For a time, he had traced the signature of their expended power westward across the Parthan plains. Yet he had sensed all along that something was not right. Eventually, he had been able to bring the truth into focus. The use of power there was residual only, fueled not by their continued efforts, but by the labor of a team of Hrothgari. And while Ranunculus had been chasing that rabbit, Htomah's renegade faction—and the rest of the Hrothgari nation, it seemed—had slipped away beneath their impenetrable shroud.

That shroud, however, had been ripped to shreds with the expense of power required to build and maintain the earthshield. In sheltering the Hrothgari so, the fools had lit a beacon so bright that Ranunculus had scarcely needed the scrying chamber to pinpoint their exact location.

A pair of silverthorn reached a singular piece of food at the same time. Each slapped furiously at the other to claim it, sending ripples throughout the slow-moving stream.

"The Hrothgari will follow the humans south," Ranunculus predicted, as the struggle broke off and Maventhrowe's silence persisted. "It has become their only choice."

"An unfortunate one," Maventhrowe declared. "Thelin is about to reach a dead end. Those who join him will find the enemy at their backs, with nowhere to run."

Ranunculus clenched his jaw. One folly after another—on their part, as well as those they watched over. Perhaps they deserved to lose these lands to the Illysp.

"Summon our brethren," Maventhrowe said. "Those who remain to us on the council. We must prepare to set forth. The time has come to settle this rift in our order once and for all."

"Let them go," Ranunculus argued, speaking of Htomah and his faction. "We have wasted too much focus on them already." He was not even sure why Maventhrowe had charged him with keeping eye on their movements in the first place. They had been forewarned. Let them pay the agreed-upon price.

But Maventhrowe shook his head. "They have gone too far." He turned his head at last, sapphire gaze aglow. "I believe I understand now what Ravar intends."

Ranunculus failed to mask his surprise. "And?"

"And we cannot deal with Him until we have dealt first with our own. Htomah's games must end. You and I and the others, we must attend to this personally."

Ranunculus did not care for the feeling that settled in his stomach. It seemed impossible, what the other was suggesting. They might be renegades, but Htomah, Quinlan, Jedua, Wislome—they were still his brothers.

Yet Maventhrowe was his trusted leader, the most aged, the most wise. Given that, Ranunculus was ill prepared to protest such a weighty decision.

The white-haired Entient rose, brushing his hands clean of the remaining food particles, watching the silverthorn splash one another in a sudden frenzy. "Come, they may seek to evade us. We have little time to spare."

Ranunculus felt the other's hand upon his shoulder, but did not immediately turn to follow. All of a sudden, he could not take his eyes from that thrashing school of fish, its members beating viciously against their own.

CHAPTER FORTY-TWO

ALLION TIED OFF ANOTHER FLETCHING, wincing as the slender thread bit into his bandaged fingers.

"You should let me do that," Tevarian suggested.

The hunter just shook his head as he examined his work. An arrow's vanes were its most critical feature. He could make adjustments for a shaft with too much spine or bend, a short length, a faulty notch, or an improperly weighted head. But a fault in the fletching could produce an unpredictable pitch or yaw that would not be revealed to the shooter until the missile was already in flight.

Satisfied, he traded the completed arrow for another of the naked quarrels Tevarian had prepared. With that came a set of goose feathers—split down the middle—for him to choose from. Allion looked at the shaft from all angles, and weighed its balance across his fingers.

"Thumb and a half," he said, assigning the desired feather length. "No," he added, seeing those his companion reached for. "The darker ones. There."

"Beats fire duty in any case, no?"

Allion grunted, taking a closer look at the feathers once he had them in hand. He'd never heard it said that arrow-making was not tedious work. Thankfully, however, they as archers were much better suited to that than to digging pits, dragging bodies about the battlefield, or tending to the fires that filled the one while consuming the other. After two days and nights, those assigned to do so were still cremating the remains of the fallen—more than forty thousand in all. On this, the dawn of the third day, that effort had taken on an increased sense of urgency. Whether notching shafts and splitting feathers as Tevarian was doing, or matching components and lashing them all together, Allion felt blessed not to be a part of it.

Only, he was, of course. For if any dead remained come afternoon or nightfall, he might have to start putting these fresh-made arrows to use before he had intended.

"Seems they must be making strides," his companion added cheerfully. "Smells better of late. Either that, or I'm becoming accustomed to it."

It helped that Allion had picked a spot upwind of those communal pyres—albeit for reasons that had little to do with scents and breezes. His gaze lifted momentarily, reaching toward the primary healers' pavilion, erected some thirty paces downslope to the east. Among the many nurses and aides scurrying about in attendance, he caught sight of Marisha—tunic soiled and bloody, hair tied back, working feverishly to address the needs of hundreds of wounded whose only real reason to go on living was to rejoin their hopeless struggle.

"Or," Tevarian continued, "it might just be the air is less foul without all them dwarves about."

Allion ignored that one, while notching another feather to the tail of the shaft. He'd been as unsettled as anyone by the sight of so many gnarled little bodies—most especially those of the women and children. A human born with such deformities was often deemed a misfortune, a malady, or worse. That such a people should exist and continue to propagate seemed almost cruel. But he understood as well the narrow-sighted arrogance of such an opinion. Judgments such as Tevarian's were the true cruelty. By any indication, the Hrothgari were neither troubled by, nor ashamed of, their appearance. And it was widely accepted that dwarves had been around longer than any human could recall. What gave man any greater right to life and freedom than they?

Mostly, he was amazed that an entire nation of such people had shared these shores with his own kind all this time, without anyone knowing it. It led him to wonder who or what else might be out there in a land and a world over which he'd been taught that mankind had long since gained dominion.

"What do you suppose the chances are His Majesty will actually make room for them to set sail?" Tevarian asked.

Having never met the Souari king, Allion had no way of knowing. But Troy had pledged his assurances that Thelin would welcome Hreidmar's refugees as he had all others, and sent a quarter of his remaining force in escort. It seemed only fair, given that Hreidmar had pledged the vast majority of *his* warriors to the continued defense of the Gaperon, thereby covering the retreat of all headed south.

"I would hope that Thelin treats them as well as they've treated us," Allion replied.

He still remembered how his jaw had dropped to see those dwarf families streaming forth from the mountain pass. He had worried there would be no time to send for them; yet, as it had turned out, they had been there all along, tucked away somewhere in those higher elevations. Perhaps their home lay somewhere within. Regardless, the Hrothgari consensus, after less than half a day's discussion, had been that, if room could be afforded, they should set sail from Pentania alongside the beleaguered nations of men. With Troy's concurrence, Hreidmar had quickly sent for the remainder of his people, some twenty thousand or more—young and old, male and female, nonwarriors all—who had passed through the human encampment to the collective astonishment of those who had lived all their lives without seeing a single dwarf of any nature.

Tevarian snorted. "They make for good workers; I'll give them that."

That went without saying. The warriors Hreidmar had kept here with him numbered roughly ten thousand—less than the initial number of Kuurians Troy had brought from Souaris. Yet they had already dug more trenches and erected more bulwarks in two days than Troy's army could have in a week.

Whatever else anyone might think or say about these Hrothgari, the chances for survival in the next battle had increased tenfold due to their ingenuity and labors.

"And will be holding the front lines," Allion reminded his comrade. He gritted his teeth as he finished wrapping another set of vanes and secured the thread with a double clove hitch. "Seems we should be focusing on *our* task, so that they have the support needed to carry out theirs, no?"

"Yes, sir," Tevarian agreed, somewhat sourly. "I meant no disrespect, sir."

Allion shook his head, stealing another glance at the nearby healers' tent as he handed back the arrow. In doing so, he dropped the next shaft handed to him.

Tevarian snickered. "Who's losing focus now?"

Allion scooped the unfinished quarrel from the dirt and examined it. The head on this one was heavier than the last. "Two thumbs," he decided.

Tevarian selected a trio of half feathers, but held them back at the last moment. "Something happen between you two?"

The hunter scowled. "What do you mean?"

"The lady, Marisha. The pair of you were inseparable. Now, you steal glances, yet look away whenever she turns in your direction."

Allion snatched the feathers from Tevarian's hand. He could feel his face reddening, and lowered it quickly to his work. "She has duties to attend to, as do I. And you're falling behind," he added, with a quick nod at the other's pile.

Tevarian chuckled. "Just thinking I might help, whatever it is."

The hunter chose not to respond. He had hoped Marisha would come to him following the last battle. She hadn't. The longer she took to do so, the more bitter he became. Each day, he had placed himself nearer her vicinity, thinking that if she would only step out partway to meet him, he might offer apology for the rift come between them. But her continued, willful avoidance had made that much less certain. Were she to come to him now, he no longer knew *what* he would say.

Regardless, his issues with Marisha were of little import at this juncture, and certainly none of this lad's affair.

They worked without speaking for a time, listening to the all-too-familiar roar of the distant blazes, whose ashen plumes drifted northward like a veil against the horror yet to come. Picks and shovels dug at the earth, men and dwarves shouted, wounded within the pavilion groaned. Now and then, the din was punctuated by the shriek of a crow or vulture. It was a sign of progress that most of the winged carrion-eaters had since moved on—though many still hovered in clouds about the peaks of the pass, as if waiting for the true feast yet to come.

On a shallow plateau, east toward Marisha's pavilion and a bit farther north, a command area had been established for the coalition leaders. Allion saw most of them conferring now. Troy, Corathel, and the unmistakable Hreidmar had gathered at sunup, along with a smattering of aides and lieutenants and advisors. Of the major generals, only Rogun was absent, having led a mounted contingent northward with the intent to harry the enemy swarm once it reached the mouth of the pass, and to direct the relay of scouts sent to mark its progress beforehand. To Allion's knowledge, there had been no reports yet on how any of that company fared.

The thought was interrupted by a pounding of hooves. He and Tevarian both turned to see who was coming at such a frantic pace. A courier, Allion realized, arriving from the south. Though the road was clogged with workers and carts, the rider galloped and swerved ahead, shouting for the rest to make way. Even after nearly impaling himself on a sharpened log shouldered by a pair of dwarves, the fool did not slow. Allion frowned, then stood, recognizing the color and gilded edge of the messenger's sash.

This word came from King Thelin.

"Wait here," he told Tevarian.

Without looking back, he hastened toward the command area. He glanced aside only once, to see if Marisha would take note. She had heard the courier, all right, pausing to watch as it thundered past. In its wake, there was a moment in which hunter and healer were left peering at one another—though the distance was too great for Allion to know if her eyes were fixed upon him the way his were on her. Whichever, she quickly turned away, to refocus on her work.

Allion began to jog. Already, the messenger had dismounted at the base of the command plateau and was presenting himself to its sentries. The guardsmen allowed him to pass without delay.

They did the same for Allion, once he reached them. For whatever reason, he continued to receive the respect and privileges accorded to the coalition's most senior officers. With barely a nod, he scampered on up the slope toward the meeting already in progress.

He arrived breathless and disheveled, sweat beading upon his brow. The others paused, their faces an array of worried confusion, angry denial, and grave disbelief. One or two nodded at him. The rest were yet overcome with shock.

"Proceed, Sergeant," Troy commanded, wearing no hint of his customary smile. "How did this come about?"

The messenger eyed Allion a moment longer—a woman, he was surprised to realize, though her head was shorn. She turned back to Troy. "His Majesty had every assurance from Governor Kardan that all was being prepared in accordance with the council's decree." Like many a courier, she spoke in steady tones, her emotionless words clipped and precise. "By the time we reached Stralk, those assurances had ceased, along with all other communications. Forward scouts soon returned with news of the city's desertion."

Desertion. The word struck Allion like a blow to the stomach.

"Not a ship is left?" Troy asked.

"Barges, ferries, skiffs—nothing that will serve to bear a man across the sea. Of that variety, Wingport is bereft."

A dwarf with salted beard, whom Allion did not recognize, spat. "Ours is already off to join yours. You telling us now they got no place to go?"

"At present, His Majesty's intended escape is cut off. I spoke with your flock," she said to the unknown dwarf, "after encountering one of their Kuurian outriders. They have been warned. By now they have either pressed on, or are awaiting your command. I did not linger long enough for them to decide."

"The ships," Troy pressed. "Where are they? Where did they go? I want every detail."

"Our sweep at Wingport revealed hundreds of stranded citizens. To a man, the tale is roughly the same. The exodus was not to begin until His Majesty's arrival. But word leaked, and the people panicked. Merchants began packing their ships with possessions and setting sail in the dead of night, overwhelming the few city guardsmen who warded the docks. Governor Kardan sent ships to bring them to heel and close off the harbor, but half of those deserted. People soon feared that with the horde of refugees en route, there would not be room enough for all. The governor himself took to sea when it became clear the runaway tide could not be stemmed."

The images spawned a hollow coring that worked its way up into Allion's chest. Wingport emptied, fled, in advance of Thelin's arrival. Women and children left ashore in favor of wealth and provisions. Other vessels sailing away half empty, rather than risk being overrun. A cowardly governor who had taken flight rather than face the cost of his ineptitude.

A nation of trusting refugees—numbering in the hundreds of thousands—abandoned.

"Can the king's people turn back?" Allion asked. But he knew the answer as soon as the words had left his mouth. *No.* Not with the Illychar force nearly upon them. A multitude that size could not reroute with the necessary swiftness. And where would they go? Alson was too far, and Gammelost had not half the ships to ferry so many. The very attempt might give rise to another panic. It might well be that Nevik was dealing with one already.

"His Majesty considered returning to Souaris," the courier replied, "but decided it too late when he received word relayed from here, the battlefront. Instead, every civilian who can serve as laborer, along with every soldier that can be spared, has followed His Majesty on to Wingport, to begin work already on a new fleet."

Even Allion, who knew nothing of shipbuilding, understood that it could take weeks, months, to gather the raw materials, draw up designs, assemble these ships, and rig and supply them for a prolonged sea voyage. It might go swifter, with so many dedicated to the cause. Then again, many of these workers would be raw, unskilled, and might only end up in one another's way. Anxiety would run high, and tempers short. A monumental undertaking under the best of circumstances, it seemed nigh impossible here.

"In the meantime," the courier continued, "those who cannot lend aid in some capacity will take shelter at Stralk."

Southern Kuuria's most defensible city, Allion knew, and within fair distance of the coast. Thelin would see that her walls were amply garrisoned, with the rest of the Imperial Army ready to drop their saws and hammers and reclaim their swords at a moment's notice. It would not be enough. If they could not have withstood the enemy at Souaris, they would not survive at Stralk.

The people of Kuuria, and all those who had joined them, were doomed.

"We will hold the front for as long as necessary," Troy assured his king's messenger. "Though it may be wise to send another division or two our way."

"His Majesty means to do so if you require it, Commander. In the meantime, he asks the opposite. I am to bring any who can be spared south with me, men with which to bolster the construction efforts."

The assembly grew heated. Hrothgari grumbled in their little packs, with snarls and gestures that made Allion grateful he could not understand their words. Low-level officers in both Kuurian and Parthan colors murmured and bickered, while their generals gritted their teeth in stony contemplation. Allion looked around until he caught sight of U'uyen, lurking nearby, never far from Corathel's side. The Powaii chieftain's eyes were bright and inquisitive, his mouth a fierce line made fiercer by the pair of tusklike stakes that pierced his lower lip. Allion wondered how much the Powaii chieftain could possibly understand of what was happening around him. He wished there were a way for him to find out what the elf was doing here, so far from his own.

Troy shared a long look with first Corathel, and then Hreidmar, before speaking up loud enough to quell the surrounding voices. "I might suggest a trade," he said. "I've men here who are too haggard and battle-weary to contribute much more in combat than they already have. A change in both task and scenery might serve them well."

"My own have always cared more for building than warring," Hreidmar added. "And while ships are hardly our specialty, it might not hurt to have a few more of ours spearheading the construction effort."

"It is unfair for the Hrothgari to risk so many of their warriors here," Corathel agreed. "While they would be sorely missed, let us send a team of them south, and ask for reserves of our own kind as needed."

Allion wasn't certain he liked the idea. Better, he thought, to hold ground here within the Gaperon for as long as possible. And allowing their numbers to be siphoned elsewhere did not seem the best way to go about that. On the other hand, his understanding of tactics and troop deployment was much too limited to second-guess men who had been doing it all their lives. If they felt that emphasizing escape over defense was the answer, and trusted in Thelin to send fresh troops north as needed, then he wasn't going to argue.

"Craggenbrun," Hreidmar said, and the unfamiliar dwarf who had spoken earlier grunted in acknowledgment. "I grow short of battle commanders. Any chance you would be willing to lead this contingent for me?"

"I'd rather wring another neck or two, truth be told," Craggenbrun mumbled. "But I'll serve as needed."

"I've no abundance of officers myself," Troy admitted, looking slowly from face to face. "Allion," he said finally.

"Sir?"

"I would send an envoy who will see that His Majesty appreciates our own predicament, and one who will ensure this Hrothgari troop is well received. I've no reason to believe it won't be," he added, his gaze catching those of Hreidmar and Craggenbrun, "but just in case . . ." He turned back to Allion. "You are well known, and well respected. A man of heroic standing. What say you?"

Allion very nearly refused. Limited as his battle skills might be in this kind of frenetic, ebb-and-flow-style warfare, he did not wish to be asked again to step away while others did the dying for him. Besides, his place was with Marisha, and he knew right away that she would never—

But wait. It might make sense for her to go as well, to shepherd this batch of wounded south while the battle had hit a lull. She could always return for the next wave.

All at once, he saw it as a way to force her hand, to close this new gulf between them. She had sworn to remain by his side as he had sworn to remain by hers. Separation within the same camp was one thing. But if he were to accept this charge and journey south, she would have to follow.

Wouldn't she?

He glanced back at her pavilion. It was worth the risk, he decided. He would not ask her to come. He would let her decide on her own, and thus learn where they truly stood. Should she follow, he might be persuaded to reconcile—and, if nothing else, would stand a better chance at keeping her safe. If she chose to stay, well . . .

He turned to Troy and nodded. "I will go," he said.

"Prepare a dispatch," Troy said to one of his aides, "to be sent under royal sash."

"You've a carrier before you," the messenger reminded him. "I'll set forth as soon as the response is formalized."

"You will rest, Sergeant," Troy said. "I'll have a fresh rider to go with fresh steed." Seeing the proud, surly glint in her eyes, he added, "I shall have further need of you before long, I promise you."

"What of Nevik?" Allion blurted. "We should bear him word—and warning—now, while the pass is clear." He hoped again that the baron and those he led were not dealing already with the same misfortune. "He may even be able to help in some way."

Troy's expression did not seem hopeful. "It will be done."

At that, everyone seemed to have something else to do, and somewhere else to be. Allion received a nod from Corathel before the chief general was drawn into a private conference. Most of the others ignored the hunter completely. He was about to set forth himself when Craggenbrun trundled over to him.

"Allion, eh? You the one what killed the dragon? Torin's friend?"

"I . . . What do you know of Torin?"

"Met him in Yawacor. He's the one what brought me here. He spoke proud of ya during the voyage."

Allion had learned next to nothing about Torin's adventures in that western land. The battle at Krynwall had come between any stories his onetime friend might have been able to tell. And by the time the battle had ended . . .

"Sorry to hear of his death," Craggenbrun offered. "Lad had some fire in him."

Allion felt his own face darken. *Torin is an Illychar*, he almost snapped. *It's he who wields the Sword and freed Killangrathor; he who started all of this by unearthing the cursed talisman in the first place.*

Instead, he only grunted and glanced away. When he looked back, the dwarf had moved on.

His own thoughts shifting already to other matters, Allion did not bother to follow.

FROM HIS PERCH HIGH UPON the Gaperon's eastern wall, Htomah eyed the new movements of the allied forces below, curious and somewhat concerned to see such a sizable departure of Hrothgari warriors, headed south.

"What do you make of it?" Quinlan asked him.

Htomah could only shake his head. It had been two days since his last audience with Hreidmar, two days since he and his brethren had lowered the earthshield formed of the surrounding peaks and watched the Hrothgari king lead his people down from the mountains. Their plan at the time, from what Hreidmar had shared, had been to lead their families south with but a small escort of warriors, while the rest remained to blockade the pass against the next wave of Illychar. By the looks of things, something had happened to change the latter part of that.

"This was not in their plans," he replied solemnly.

"Little of this has been," Quinlan remarked.

It was not a rebuke, exactly, but held the weight of one against Htomah's sagging shoulders. After so much risk, so much struggle, his efforts were amounting to naught. He felt he should be doing more, else moving on. There was a degree of danger in remaining here, exposed. The four of them had discussed it. But they had discussed also what few options they had. They had elected to remain because it seemed clear that this was where the seminal struggle would take place. The next step in the preservation or eradication of humankind upon these shores would be taken here, at the juncture of these mountain ranges, when the rabid horde that the Illychar had become sought to force its way against those determined to repel it.

He felt it coming. He sensed its impending arrival.

But it was no longer mankind alone that he worried for. As Quinlan had indicated, he was also beholden to the Hrothgari, for having led them on a trek that had not exactly gone to plan. Instead of battling for their freedom behind the walls of Souaris and other proud cities, they were fighting only for time enough to flee this island continent like rats. Upon returning to Htomah after the alliance's victory, Hreidmar had been ill pleased, demanding to know if his kind had been willfully used and misled. Htomah had listened patiently to the accusations before denying them all and expressing his own disappointment at the unforeseen developments. After the private council with his fellow Entients, he had gone on to assure Hreidmar that he would watch over the coming conflict, and would intervene if he must to ensure that as many Hrothgari as possible would be spared. Hreidmar had expressed a chill gratitude, yet Htomah had heard others grumbling even afterward of having been deceived.

"Do you suppose they mean to tell us what this is about?" Jedua asked.

Htomah continued to stretch his gaze, searching the camp and the movements of those within. "I imagine they would have sent someone already, had they deemed it worthy of our attention."

"Else they may have washed their hands of us," Quinlan observed.

"Or determined that we should be able to divine the truth on our own," Wislome added.

Any one of which was cause for concern. Even between the four of them, they were severely limited in what they could discern at this distance. If the dwarves believed otherwise, they were mistaken. For the dwarves to think them helpless or uncaring would also be in error. Their little band might yet do much to sway the outcome—as it seemed now they must—but only if granted a better understanding of all that was happening, and why.

Htomah crouched back on one knee, and sighed. "Perhaps it is time for me to venture down there in person."

"Consider that unwise," came a familiar voice, from near at hand.

The words sparked a chill like lightning, which rippled down his spine. He heard his friends spinning about, one of them—Jedua—even gasping in alarm. Htomah himself hesitated, then stood and rounded slowly.

He did well to bury his dismay. The speaker, Maventhrowe, had revealed himself already. What Htomah had not anticipated, what he might never have believed prior to this very moment, was that the head of their order had brought with him seven senior members—the entire rest of the council—to this mountain crag. Under a masking shroud they had come—Barwn, Sovenson, Prather, and all the rest—their faces as stern and pale as death.

"Why?" Htomah mustered the courage to ask. "Would I be subjecting myself to greater penalty?"

Maventhrowe's gaze was steady, impassive, even now. "Would you ask me to explain the consequences of your deeds? The additional strain this order has been called upon to bear?"

He knew well enough. But he had never meant for it to lead to this. The entire senior council, drawn from its duties. Not in memory had that happened before, not since their order had migrated to these shores. The implications were staggering. And yet . . .

"Our purpose is a senseless one," he claimed, "should we neglect our first and most solemn calling. To believe otherwise is an inflation of our own importance."

Maventhrowe's faction had formed a wall, leaving Htomah and his pinned against the open ledge of that mostly barren outcrop. The numbers were two to one against them. He could feel Jedua, Wislome, and Quinlan looking to him, to see what he might do. They were as stunned by this turn as he. Whatever additional pursuit they may have feared, none could have imagined this.

"So you have been saying for months—for longer than that, even," Maventhrowe replied. "Yours has always been a soft heart, my friend. Too soft, perhaps."

Htomah continued to steel himself. His face was a stony mask. Beneath his cloak, his flesh was tight, his muscles rigid. He continued to calculate the odds, the choices before him.

"All I have done," he said, "is lead a people from hiding and protect them from almost certain slaughter."

"And made what difference, truly?"

Htomah wavered. As always, the head Entient saw right through him, right to the core of his hopes and fears. "I am prepared and willing to accept sole responsibility for my actions," he acceded. "Only, forgive our brothers the small part they played, which they did out of honor and respect for their elder."

Maventhrowe let that notion twist for a moment in the swirling, mid-morning wind. "You speak of pardons, my friend?" he said finally. "Those must come later. We have come to bring you to justice, yes, but not in the manner you seem to fear."

Htomah frowned. What game was this now?

"Ranunculus tells me you have taken extreme care not to violate the exact stipulations placed upon you by the council: to forgo any direct interaction with the members of our human flock."

Htomah answered slowly. "I have. Though I might yet do so if—"

"You might have done so much earlier, were you not set upon this other path."

Set upon? But—

The slightest glimmer shone in Maventhrowe's eye. Htomah's stomach tightened, the threads starting to pull together. All those weeks of insisting upon a course of action to aid mankind against a threat he and his Entients had inadvertently helped to unleash. The council's steadfast, nearly unanimous refusal. Maventhrowe's sudden, almost inexplicable edict that he was to make no human contact . . . narrowing his focus to those who were *not* human, but who might be able to assist mankind—and themselves—in some way.

But was it true? Could Maventhrowe have been goading him into treading this path from that very moment?

"It seems to me," Maventhrowe said, reading into Htomah's silence, "that any true effort to rein you in should not have been led by he who was most sympathetic to your cause."

Htomah glanced at Quinlan, who appeared mostly befuddled. With that, his own suspicions were confirmed, all doubt removed. Maventhrowe had known what he was doing, first in sowing the seeds that would lead Htomah to the Hrothgari, and then in allowing Quinlan to be the one sent in pursuit. The head Entient, then, was not nearly as blind to the unfolding chaos as Htomah had feared. Though the question remained . . .

"Why? Why succor me in this, if it was a path you would have rather I not taken?"

Maventhrowe smiled wanly. "So that you would not undertake a more disastrous one. You were so impatient, so dead set on action. The harm caused here—by all of you—is little enough when compared to the havoc you might have wreaked elsewise."

"Time lay critical," Htomah insisted, vexed anew. "It still does—more so now than if we had responded earlier. Yet now I learn you kept us preoccupied even longer, on a course you presumed would afford us little. What, then, have you come for? What do you mean to achieve with all of this?"

"We have come because the final piece of this conflict has fallen into place—something you yourself would have seen, had you waited long enough."

Htomah scowled, wondering what that might be. All at once, it struck him. "Ravar," he said breathlessly.

"I have descried His purpose in this, from the words shared between those who have met with Him. Our Sword-bearer, Torin, serves now a quest ridden with lies."

"Torin? But he was killed, possessed. Unless . . ."

"You have missed much, my friend. Torin is shed of the Illysp influence, yet even now stands to do as much harm as good. We must prepare ourselves for his choice, for if compelled to act as I believe we must, it will needs be with a strength united."

The tension had fled Htomah's body, his limbs gone slack with surprise, disbelief, at these revelations.

"Will you join us, my brothers?" Maventhrowe asked. "Will you renew your faith in my guidance? Will you follow me now on a journey of significant peril and even greater magnitude?"

"What of Killangrathor?" Quinlan countered abruptly. "The Hrothgari were told that the dragon was raised as an Illychar, to wage battle against us."

Hreidmar had indeed been quite furious at that, Htomah recalled. Though the dwarven king had held careful check on his composure, it had infuriated him to learn that they had not been warned of the monster's emergence. The honest answer, of course, was that Htomah and his pursuers had set forth from Whitlock before that particular calamity had unfolded. In light of other misjudgments on his part, however, Htomah could not fault Hreidmar or his people their intense skepticism.

"Killangrathor has found his peace," Maventhrowe replied, setting that fear to rest. "His shadow will not threaten us, though there are others that shall."

"The Hrothgari," Htomah said, glancing back at the valley floor. "I vowed not to abandon them."

Maventhrowe's thin smile turned sad. "For good or ill, the fortunes of dwarf and man are now inextricably tied. What they might do for themselves may well be determined here. What good *we* might do them must be determined elsewhere."

Htomah felt a rending within. For too long now, he had been tugged in different directions by similar needs. Like a frayed rope pulled taut, ready to snap.

"I need your strength, my brother," Maventhrowe insisted. His focused gaze seemed especially bright and piercing amid the crisp mountain air. "The end comes, and it comes swiftly. Will you go with us to meet it?"

Htomah glanced at his fellow renegades, then at the wall of brethren he had betrayed—blindly, it now seemed, when before he had thought himself the only one able to see. "The outcome hinges upon the Sword-bearer's quest?"

"Though he does not fully realize it, yes."

"And are we to aid, or to hinder?"

"The answer to that will depend greatly upon him."

Nothing more would be revealed, Htomah realized, until he had made a decision. Though frustrated by the other's staunch evasiveness, he imagined it must be so.

"To the end, then," he agreed, and wondered immediately where that might take them.

CHAPTER FORTY-THREE

DO AS YOU MUST, ASAHIEL.

A shallow surf churned about Torin's feet, chewed to foam by the jagged limestone shore. The Sword felt unusually heavy in his hand. He stared into Ravar's great, unblinking eye. At this proximity, it engulfed him, a doorway into the Abyss.

He turned to look at Annleia, who stood nearby, but saw only sullenness in her guarded features.

The Orb is needed, if she is to do this. Ravar's soundless voice reverberated within his head, within his chest, carrying the weight of eternity. *She cannot go forward without it.*

That much had been explained to him. What *hadn't* been explained, what he found just as difficult to fathom, were the unspoken consequences of mutilating a living god.

A token it is to me, no more, Ravar insisted. *I will not be blinded so easily.*

There was no escape from that depthless, penetrating gaze. Ravar's eye, though small for His body, stood taller than Torin. The leviathan lay half submerged at the shore's edge, eye lowered so that the waves crashed and surged about its base. The other—on the opposite side of His gargantuan head—was naught but a hollow socket, crusted over with barnacles. The Dragon Orb, Torin had been sickened to learn, came from just that: the eye of the Dragon God. That was why He had but one more to give.

Only, *give* wasn't the correct term. Ravar had made it quite clear that they would have to take it.

Hesitation merits you nothing. Why wear her trinket around your neck, if not to remind you of that lesson?

A sudden heat filled Torin's veins. He went rigid, then drove the Sword into the center of that giant eye, ripping downward. A clear jelly gushed forth. Despite His bold taunts, Ravar clenched, His titanic form stiffening in pain and denial.

It was too late to stop now. Torin dug deeper, carving through the gelatinous mass toward the eye's center. His stomach roiled, and he feared it might betray him. For a week now, he'd had nothing to eat but mussels and oysters and other, creeping shellfish—whatever they could harvest from Ravar's body. There had been no fuel for a fire, save for some dried clumps of seaweed, so they had eaten their meals raw. Just as well, since their water had run out three days ago, forcing them to subsist on the juices trapped within the meat and shells of the sea creatures they fed upon. Though he'd kept it all down, his stomach's strength wasn't what it normally was. There was little Torin was looking forward to more than roasted meat and a flagon of springwater.

The sooner he was finished here . . .

He felt it now, a strange pulse through the Sword. Of its own will, it seemed, the blade angled wide of where he directed it. The talisman understood his intent, as always, and would not let him damage the true prize with all his hacking and slashing. He turned his head and drew one last deep breath before plunging into the ravaged eye, groping with his free hand. He came upon it almost at once: the hardened, marble-like object that nested at the core of Ravar's remaining eye.

The Dragon Orb.

He sheathed the Sword and wrapped both arms about the Orb. It was large enough that his fingers did not quite touch as he embraced it. With his own eyes clenched protectively, he scraped and tugged until the Orb came away against a slurp of protest.

Torin stumbled backward swiftly, wading through the spilled vitreous, nearly tripping when he reached the shore. He managed to hold his feet, but spun at once and dropped to his knees within the surf. He set the Orb down carefully, then scooped up a double handful of ocean and hurriedly scrubbed his face.

He came up spitting jelly and seawater, eyes stung by salt. Annleia was beside him now, one hand resting upon the Orb. Pearl black, like the nest from which it had been torn, with a surface as smooth as polished glass.

Ravar moaned. Torin looked over his shoulder, dripping, at the ruin of the Dragon God's eye. It was no longer black, but gray and clouded. Half of its jelly lay like a mudslide amid the churning waves, leaving the once-rounded cornea to sag like a windless sail. A handful of tiny crabs had scuttled forth already to inspect the damage.

You have what you need, the monster told him. *Go and make what use of it you will, what use you can. Pray this is the last you see of me, Asahiel.*

On that much, Torin readily agreed. Relief turned to alarm, however, as the behemoth's head lurched skyward. Torin's neck craned after, and he was momentarily spellbound as this lord of the deep hovered like a reared serpent and snorted at the briny air. Slowly, He began to sink.

"We have to move," Annleia urged.

Torin snapped out of his thrall. Already, the waves had climbed from his ankles to his knees. He helped Annleia to scoop up the Orb, then took it himself, thinking he might move faster alone. She did not argue, but led the way. He hurried after as best he could, slogging awkwardly through the churning waters, scarcely able to see by stretching his neck and chin over the Orb's crown. Though he felt the ground rising beneath him, the tide seemed to follow as it rose.

Twice he stumbled, once falling to a knee. But he grimaced and held on, staggering stubbornly ahead. Only when he finally caught up to Annleia, perched atop a sandy shelf, did he pause as she did to peer back at the sea.

Ravar had gone. In His wake, the ocean roiled and spat, fighting to restore its more natural rhythms. White-capped waves rushed in all directions, crashing into one another and sending geysers of spray skyward. Overhead, the stony heavens seemed to press heavily, hunkered down upon the world.

With Annleia at his side, Torin waited for the Dragon God to breach once more, to offer one last glimpse of His awesome presence. Even now, it did not quite seem real. They had spent eight days upon His back, crossing the ocean in less than half the time that might have been required by sail. Yet it seemed more likely that it had all been a dream than that they had actually ridden that awesome form, spoken with it, been charged by it to shut away the Illysp before He destroyed them all. It felt as if they might still be standing upon Yawacor's shore, rather than Pentania's. Despite the wracking chill of sea-soaked clothing on this overcast morn, it warmed him within to imagine it so.

A stray gull winged out upon the waters from some cliffside nest, shrieking at the empty sea in challenge. Other seabirds began to follow, no longer frightened, apparently, by what had driven them off. Torin watched them for a moment, then glanced down at the Orb resting in the sand at his feet.

It was the only reminder he needed as to what had actually occurred. The warmth drained from his blood, and he shivered.

"We should build you a fire," Annleia suggested, "and dry those clothes."

Torin shook his head. "We need to keep moving," he argued, teeth chattering. "I'll keep just as warm, and we won't be wasting time."

Annleia frowned. She had been doing that a lot, lately, ever since their conversation with Ravar in that isolated cove. Something in her perception toward him had changed that night. He had tried to get her to admit it, but had been unsuccessful thus far. The more he had pried, the tighter she had closed up against him. Soon enough, he had surrendered the attempt. She had any number of valid reasons to dislike and mistrust him. The only wonder was that she had not shown him a colder shoulder before.

She looked now as if she might insist on drying him first, but shook her head instead, as if to indicate that the choice was his. His eyes followed hers to the Orb.

He wished at once for a sack or net of some kind with which to carry it. Though the talisman was surprisingly lightweight, its sheer size made it cumbersome. Nor was it going to grow lighter across the many miles and leagues that stood before them. And yet, he wasn't going to get anywhere while complaining about it.

"Wait," Annleia said, as he knelt to scoop it up.

"For?"

"There is a better way. Ravar explained it to me, just last night."

Torin scowled, but decided not to argue. The Dragon God had shared not a single thought with him during their voyage. No more instructions, no more taunts, no more riddles. Not until they had reached this isolated stretch of coast upon Kuuria's southern shore had that silence been broken. He had asked Annleia more than once if *she* had managed to coax anything further from Him, but all she had admitted before now was, *I have tried.*

Then again, she hadn't yet revealed to him all that she had learned during their initial conversation back in the cove. Of that he was convinced. Her evasions had been obvious, with statements such as: *You know what He wants you to know. Let that be enough.*

It seemed he had little choice.

He stepped back, allowing her room to approach the Orb without him hovering over her. He wondered what she intended. Some form of magic, no doubt. In his eyes, so much of her was defined by its use.

He hugged his shoulders, arms across his chest, in a feeble effort to ward off the cold. The wind had picked up, blowing sand, bending blades of sword grass, knifing through his wet tunic and breeches. Whatever she meant to do, he hoped she could finish quickly.

She knelt beside the Orb, legs folded beneath her, and placed her hands upon its surface. She spoke to it as she might a child, soft and soothing. Her tone was singsong, her words archaic. Though he understood none of it, Torin found his muscles loosening in response, his eyelids growing heavy. Were this a better time and place, he might have curled up for a moment's nap.

Nothing discernible was happening with the Orb. Perhaps this was a waste of time after all.

"I can manage as far as Wingport," he insisted. "Once there, we can . . ."

He trailed off as he noticed sweatlike beads forming upon the Orb's surface. He glanced at the sky, but saw no rain. Nor did it appear to be ocean mist or gathering dew. The beads were growing larger, bubbling up from within, already joining to form streams and droplets that trickled down around the spherical edges.

Neither pearl nor glass, after all, but a porous surface filled with at least some manner of fluid. It seeped out faster now, from all around, darkening the sands beneath.

But once it was gone . . .

"How will you restore it?" he asked.

Annleia responded this time, albeit without turning or opening her eyes. "A few tears are all that is required. Hush, now."

As these *tears* drained, the Orb began to shrivel like a dried fig. Torin thought of another question, but decided to respect her wishes and remain silent. While the Orb continued to shrink, his thoughts shifted instead to the manner in which it would be used—or how it *had* been used, if he was to recall Ravar's emphasis. To trap the Illysp and Illychar, Algorath and his Vandari followers had first closed all tunnels into the cavern in which the rift had been opened. A lone opening was left, high in the cavern ceiling, an altar constructed, and the Dragon Orb planted upon it. Magic, fueled by the power of the Sword, was used to activate it, bringing the seal to life.

But that did not explain how every last Illysp and Illychar had been lured into the cavern to begin with. That was where the Orb's power truly came into play. Like the lens of a spyglass used to direct and magnify the sun's rays, so was the Orb used to focus the light spilling from the interplanar cleft through which the Illysp had come, and to seek out all beings native to that realm. Once sighted, Illysp and Illychar alike were drawn into the Orb via magical rents, then spit out below, into the darkness—sealed away for as long as the Sword held its power.

When Annleia had first explained this to him, she had done so slowly, uncertainly, as if only to measure her own understanding of what was expected. He had asked her to explain it again several times since, until he finally felt as if he grasped the overall concept. Even so, Ravar had been right: To Torin, it all sounded rather unlikely and incomprehensible. But it was all they had, and better that than a futile reliance upon his own limited command of the Sword's powers.

Besides, there was really no need for him to understand the specifics of it, the magics involved. He had his own concerns in simply getting them there—in overcoming the warnings that Ravar had laid out for them. He would let Annleia worry about the rest.

The Orb had shrunk already to the size of a pumpkin—and the transformation showed no signs of slowing. The smaller it became, the faster it shriveled, weeping freely now in thin cascades. When it had reached the size of a pinkfruit, Annleia uncorked her empty waterskin. Hefting the withered Orb in one hand, she held the skin beneath it, to catch the underlying runoff.

At last, when the Orb was no larger than an apple, the flow of its tears bled away to a trickle. Annleia's waterskin was perhaps half full when she replaced the stopper and let the skin hang back in place.

"Better," she proclaimed.

Torin could only shake his head in wonder, his amazement shadowed with skepticism. The Orb no longer bore any resemblance to the glasslike sphere he had first laid eyes upon in the ruins of Thrak-Symbos—the one he had inadvertently destroyed. This looked more like a fist-sized walnut, all dry and wrinkled and misshapen. Easier to carry, sure, but had it been weakened in any way? Or would it still serve as needed when the time came?

Too late now. The task was already done. Time now to turn their attention to the next.

Annleia found an empty drawstring pouch and placed the Orb within. She stood, then, and secured the artifact at her waist, leaving behind a patch of wet sand and sloughed jelly. When she looked at him, her features were solemn, expectant.

"To the north, He said."

Torin nodded. Wingport. *Your friends will be found there*, Ravar had told them. *Do not expect a warm welcome.*

An unnecessary caution. Torin had not forgotten that when last he had flown from this land, he had done so after laying waste to one of its greatest cities. Had any survived that slaughter, tales of his treachery would have spread. They would think him foe until he proved otherwise. Some might not even be willing to grant him that chance.

But he had to believe otherwise. This was still his homeland, whether or not it felt as such. He still had friends here. They could not *all* have been killed.

It did worry him, though, to learn that Wingport was where his reunions would begin. What would any of his people be doing so far south? Souaris was where he would have expected to find those still battling for survival. Or had the legendary City of Man already been overrun?

He would find out soon enough, he supposed, as he fell into step alongside his companion. Whatever the truth, he could scarcely imagine it to be worse than some of those already faced.

There was no road here, only windblown sands and grasses abutting the rocky shore. They followed the ridgeline as it jagged northward, listening to the billow and crash of waves at their feet. Whenever he dared, Torin would snake a glance out to sea, still searching for some further sign as to Ravar's course or heading. Alas, the ocean seemed to have swallowed Him whole, its depths the only bed large enough to contain Him.

Annleia remained silent, eyes forward. Torin did nothing to disturb her. He had already approached her in every way he knew how. Instead, he worked to recall and sift through all that she *had* revealed to him of her private conversations with the Dragon God. There wasn't much. In the early going, while he had been learning of Killangrathor and the means by which the Ceilhigh kept Ravar chained, Annleia claimed to have received little more than taunts and admonitions. The Dragon God, she had told him, had kept insisting that she was too late. When she had pressed Him for what He knew, Ravar had scornfully replied that *what He knew* would shred her heart and tear her mind asunder. He had gone on to accuse her Finlorian ancestors of an excess of pride, reminding her that it was their arrogance and vanity that had unleashed the Illysp to begin with.

Upon hearing this, Torin had understood why she had been in no rush to recount it. Even so, he had hounded her to go on.

"He told me yours is the roiling heart," she had said, almost accusingly, "the one that will decide the fate of all. He said also that you would refuse the charge He gives you."

That had taken him aback, though it had made clearer the source of her aggravation. It also irritated him, to think that Ravar had predicted his response.

"My charge is to defend you," Torin had replied, "to see you through to the end. I have not refused that."

He had thought that might cheer her, but it hadn't. They had gone some time without speaking after that, before he had returned to her and asked what she had learned later on, about restoring the seal.

"He told me how the threads of power must be woven," she had said. "He further warned me that magic, even to those most knowledgeable, is mysterious and unpredictable, often behaving with a will of its own."

This, along with the Orb's purpose, was the extent of what he had been able to draw from her. Day after day, he had made some follow-up attempt, by turns coaxing and prying. Yet, what more she knew she refused to tell. Her hesitation, he felt, betrayed a lack of confidence. He could relate to that easily enough, and so had sought to reassure her.

"You solved Necanicum's riddles," he had reminded her. "You'll solve Ravar's and those of His Orb, as well."

Her responses, when given at all, had been delivered with little enthusiasm, only a quiet resignation. Torin tried not to judge her. Was he not the one whose attitude constantly left others doubting his ability to persevere? He had seen her strength already. He had to trust that, when it mattered most, she would find what she needed to accomplish her task.

"What was it like?" she asked him suddenly.

He looked over at her in surprise, reflections scattered upon the wind. His body was still rigid with cold, his teeth still chattering. "Wh-what was *what* like?"

Her eyes found his, bold and bright. "The possession. You still haven't told me."

As quick as that, Torin lost interest in her conversation. "I relayed everything that happened," he argued.

"But not how it felt."

This again? Could she not guess? What bearing did any of that have now, anyway?

His scowl softened, however, when he saw the unexpected concern reflected in the elf-woman's countenance. A game, perhaps. Else an attempt to draw from him the secret *he* still kept from *her*. Yet it didn't feel that way. Once again, she alluded to his crimes without allegation. Once again, her tone suggested that she did not hate him for what he'd done, even though he hated himself. He was still confused by this undue compassion. He might have dismissed it as a Finlorian trait, but recalled even now what little charity her people had shown him before. Whatever its source, perhaps the time had come to show her some gratitude—or at the very least, a similar respect.

"I suppose the worst was not knowing what would happen next," he admitted. He stared ahead, unable to meet her gaze, his hand wringing nervously upon the Sword's hilt. "Each deed seemed more terrible than the last. And where would it end?" He shuddered. "I had come to fear that it never would."

Annleia was quiet, reflective. "I'm sorry you had to endure that. I feel sorry for anyone who does."

Torin bit back an incredulous retort. Sorry? For others, yes, but he had no right to pity himself. Not after what he had done. Not after what he continued to do. In tracking him down and purging him of the Illysp spirit, Annleia had rescued him from a destiny that even now remained too horrid to recount. And how did he seek to repay her? With lies. Kindly meant, but lies nonetheless.

"No one who knew me was safe," he said, to break the uncomfortable silence. "Everyone I had ever come in contact with was at risk. The Illysp, they take special delight in the torment of their hosts; of that I'm convinced."

Annleia reached up to rub the back of his head, a gentle, comforting gesture. Torin nearly recoiled. His intent, if anything, had been to warn her, not attract further sympathy.

"Be that as it may, you're now my warder, and the only one I have." She smiled. "So I guess you're stuck with me."

Torin only stared, uncertain what to say. She had a lovely smile, he decided. Not like Dyanne's—so bold and bright and able to light his soul afire—but shy and soft, heartfelt and alluring. Strange that he hadn't noticed it before.

She looked forward again, removing her hand from the back of his head. Only then did he realize that he might have been staring too long. He hoped that she hadn't mistaken his reasons for doing so. It might complicate matters should she believe he thought of her in that way. He *didn't*, of course. His every fiber belonged to Dyanne, and felt as if it would forever. He was indebted to Annleia, yes. And he could not truthfully deny a certain fascination at the unassuming manner with which she carried herself—this exotic maiden with power enough to help fell a dragon, yet gracious enough to pardon his unmentionable transgressions. But he had no interest in her beyond what service he could offer in setting things right—first with the seal, and later, perhaps, in finding her people.

He owed her that much and more.

"We'll veer west once we reach that treeline," Annleia offered, ending the uncomfortable silence. "That should help shelter us from this wind, without having to surrender the sun."

Torin nodded, though he was not much concerned with freezing to death. Sword or no, that would be too easy—and better than he deserved. After all the ills he had committed, after the trouble of seeing him raised again, the Ceilhigh, he felt sure, had a more fiendish end in store. And as tempted as he might be to defy them by falling on his blade, his guilt demanded that he keep pressing forward, to whatever fate his own deeds had wrought.

Clenching his teeth against the cold, against the past, against the impossibility of what lay ahead, he strode along dutifully, not knowing which secrets should trouble him more: Annleia's or his.

"Rover down," Tonra announced somberly.

Vashen bit hard upon her scarred lip, holding back a string of curses that might have made Achthium blanch. He had ceased already to watch over them. No need to stoke His wrath.

She felt the eyes of her crew upon her, awaiting her response. Their dismay and fury were palpable, thickening the already sultry air.

"Tighten formation," she decided, nearly choking on the words. "All ahead, maximum lean."

There was a moment of tense silence from her crew members, though she was not likely to hear any mutters over the grinding, screeching thrum. Perhaps they hadn't heard her command.

"Courier? Relay orders."

Tonra swallowed. "At once, General."

Vashen turned to the others. Even those busy at their tasks were peering back at her, their sweat-streaked faces pallid and grim.

She scowled. "We knew this might happen. You have your orders."

One by one, they shifted to obey, one or two with lingering glares. These were not all military, she had to remind herself, but conscripted laborers. She made a mental note of those whose reactions were the most bitter, the most distraught. They were the ones she would have to be wary of in the coming days.

When that was done, she turned back to the rearward viewing slat, hoping that a fresh look might alter what she had seen. They had known this *might* happen, but that didn't mean they—herself included—had been prepared for this choice.

Especially not now, as she watched the skatchykem swarm the stranded carrier like ants upon a captured crumb, its smoke tail trailing uselessly skyward.

"Warder General?"

Brokk. Captain of her hurlers. His brother Tegg was a driver inside the rover she had just ordered abandoned.

"Yes, Captain?" It hurt to speak. Her throat was parched, her tongue leathery and swollen.

"Given time, they might be able to start it up again. If we were to go back, and circle up—"

"We would all be stranded together."

"Even so, our strength would be greater—"

"Our mission is to push south. His Glory may yet have need of us. Our personal feelings cannot outweigh the greater good."

Brokk's angry features tightened. "They're still alive in there."

"And will have to fend for themselves for as long as they can." She knew as well as he what that meant, but forced herself to continue. "The enemy may disperse before cracking their shell. Else, we may be able to return for them—which I'll gladly do, given permission. For now, the rest of us press on as commanded."

Brokk seemed unwilling to let the decision stand. His hand flexed upon the haft of his polearm, used to prod attackers from the shell of their own rover—often gutting a beast or two in the process, for all the good it did. Vashen herself was unarmed, save for a dirk sheathed in her boot. But she forced that thought aside. She would not let it come to that.

His horror and frustration were no greater than her own. It was not as if their friends had been mortally wounded in some way. Rather, the magic had failed them. They had been rolling along now for more than a fortnight, and still without a drop of rain. Dugg had made all the adjustments he could, sharing the results of his tests and strategies with those of his fellow boiler masters. They simply didn't have enough fluids to keep producing steam. Rations had been apportioned equally before setting out, but, due mostly to the varying use of the grinders, each engine and crew had consumed these fuels at different rates—especially in the beginning, before the potential shortage had been discovered.

The rover carrying Brokk's brother had been the first to stall, but it would not be the last. And though they had already entered the pinch of ranges dubbed by their people as Achthium's Tongs, it might take them days to traverse the length of the pass. Even if they were to keep full power at the wheels and shut down their grinders—which might only encourage the skatchykem to pile aboard and thus slow them further—there seemed scant chance any of them were going to complete this next leg, let alone reach the preappointed rendezvous at Souaris.

"I thank you for questioning me in private, Captain, and not within ear of the crew. But the decision is made. All who accompany us knew the risk. So long as we keep moving, we hold the enemy's attention. Draw up short, and there's no predicting how many scatter—or in what direction."

That splintering, she feared, had already begun. While a significant swarm continued to assail them, the skatchykem she had worked so hard to distract had been lengthening southward for nearly a day now, leaving the slower-paced rovers behind. A blessing, perhaps, but after contending with them all this time, she knew better. If even a portion of this horde was moving on, it could only be because it had found another, likelier target farther ahead.

"I will not assume His Glory and our people are safe," she continued. "I will buy them as much time as I can." And if they were already under attack, then further distraction was pointless, and she had all the more reason to hurry to their aid while her grinders still worked. "Are my orders understood?"

His eyes were angry, sullen. He glanced toward the viewing slat, as if he might catch some final glimpse of his brother.

"If you must weep, Captain," she said, "report to Master Duggarian. I'm quite certain he could make use of any tears."

Brokk stiffened, gave her a withering look, then marched back to his post. Shoving past a pair of hurlers, he thrust his polearm through one of the murder-holes with a vengeful cry. Good. Perhaps he would return with a blade dipped in skatchykem blood.

She moved to find Duggarian, who sweated beside the boiler. "Bleed me," she said, rolling up her sleeve.

Dugg frowned. His cheeks and pate were blistered, his beard singed. "You were bled just last night. With what scant liquids we have, you can't hope to—"

"That was a command, Master Duggarian, not a request for counsel."

Her friend's face pinched to one side, left eye squinting, the lip beneath curling up in a half snarl. "At once, General."

He continued to mutter, but did as he was told, slicing a new gash across her wrist and turning it over a collection bowl. She sat quietly as it drained.

Now and then, one of her crew would glance over at her. The look she would give in return sent their gazes skittering away.

She would see them to Souaris if they had to wring her body dry. Better that than the hell to which she had just consigned Tegg and his rover crew.

She closed her eyes, wishing her doomed comrades swift passage and eternal flight amid the bellows winds of Achthium's Earthforge. She prayed they would not become skatchykem. She prayed they would choose to burn first. Let the entire belly of their rover become a blackened furnace. Let the enemy pick and claw its way inside to claim only ash.

She lay back, wondering what her own crew's choice would be, should she fail them. For now, she listened to their huffs and grunts amid those of their armored carrier, battling still.

From beyond, the enemy's triumphant howls dug like slivers beneath her skin.

CHAPTER FORTY-FOUR

Saws wheezed and hammers rang, punctuated by every manner of creak, squeal, and shout that Torin could have imagined. From the central district and its governor's manse high atop the coastal bluff, down to the encircling horseshoe harbor, Wingport swarmed with untold thousands of men, women, children, and service animals, all in steadfast activity. Their numbers spread even beyond the city, to the north and west, where teams attacked the sheltering forests like an army of termites, stripping the hillsides bare.

Wingport, it appeared, was readying to take flight.

It hadn't taken long to confirm that suspicion. Coming up from the south, he and Annleia had encountered no guard patrols, only work crews hauling bushels of raw hemp with which to weave rope. Torin had observed their efforts for a time, then hailed them from a distance and asked if he could lend a hand. The response was brusque, but accepting: Unless he was a reaver, no hand was being turned away.

Keeping the Sword carefully concealed in the folds of his cloak, he had introduced himself to the crew's foreman as a fisherman from a tiny hamlet to the south. Hadn't been any reavers in his quiet corner of the world, Torin claimed, but with all his neighbors pulling up stakes and moving north, he had finally relented. He and his sister, he amended, once he'd made certain that these men were no Illychar. Annleia's presence seemed to put an end to their lingering wariness. Hands let go of weapon hilts, nerves relaxed, and the team went back to work.

From there, he had learned quickly enough about Wingport's treachery and King Thelin's failed exodus. The thousands gathered here were refugees, one and all, working alongside soldiers borrowed from the northern front to construct seaworthy vessels. Those too weak to contribute were holing up at nearby Stralk, the most defensible southern city of any reasonable proximity.

"And those who refuse to flee?" Torin had asked. Matters might have been worse, he supposed, but the truth as it stood had left him aghast. "Surely, some are more frightened of the sea than the Illychar."

"And will be drowning themselves in its breakers, mark my words, when the reavers come."

Torin would not wager against it. Not when he knew that the Illychar had yet to muster their full strength. Or had they? Might Itz lar Thrakkon's secret reserve force have been the one to trigger this desperate retreat?

And desperate it was. Futile, really. When he had looked to Annleia, he'd seen that even she understood as much. For all the obvious reasons, yes, but more so for the ones these people could not possibly know.

They had begged leave once the delivery had been completed, heading off, they said, in search of friends from their former hamlet. The crew chief, a Kuurian sergeant, hadn't tried to stop them—whether because he lacked the authority, or because he did not wish to displease Annleia, Torin wasn't sure.

Since then, they had been working their way toward the governor's manse. There seemed little enough reason to visit the docks and shipyards up close. It didn't much matter what progress was being made on those skeletal hulls. If Thelin commanded twice as many ships as needed, and was already setting sail, the end result would be the same.

According to Ravar, the sea was to be their doom, not their salvation.

"Will this Thelin believe any of what we have to tell him?" Annleia asked.

Torin pulled his thoughts and gaze into focus. "I cannot promise that he will. The less we actually have to tell him, the better, I would guess."

"Then perhaps we should be looking for someone else."

Who? Torin nearly asked, but realized it to be an unfair question. She knew no more than he concerning the guide and escort they were to find en route to Thrak-Symbos. Or so she claimed. In either case, he didn't wish to provoke her. The sense of withdrawal and isolation shrouding her over the past week had continued to slacken throughout that morning, lifting like a fog. It felt almost as if the greater distance between her and their time with Ravar, the less troubled she became. Whatever the reason, he was relieved to see her spirits climb, and did not wish to dampen them.

His, on the other hand, had only grown more somber. For some reason, traipsing among these inhabitants of his former land had made him both nervous and grave. It was an unwelcome feeling that had nothing to do with any spoken words or the disinterested looks that passed his way. It went deeper than that, to an inner sense he couldn't quite place.

"We may as well start at the top," Torin said, limping slightly as he climbed the uneven cobbles of that steep, winding hill. "If King Thelin is actually here, as they say, then he is the one who must be warned. I know of no better way to . . ."

He trailed off as he realized she was no longer listening to him, her attention diverted by the sounds of a company descending toward them from around a sharp bend. He wondered why she should be more fascinated by this troop than any of the others seen coming and going throughout the city . . . until their actual forms came into view from behind a rugged retaining wall.

Dwarves.

Torin nearly tripped. None they had spoken with had made any mention of dwarves among them. Then again, it had never occurred to him to ask.

His hand slipped reflexively to the Sword's hilt, even as his thoughts flashed back to when he had met his first dwarf, Crag, back in Yawacor. The Tuthari had come to them in hopes of reuniting with his Pentanian cousins.

Torin had warned him then that there *were* no more dwarves living on these shores, to which Crag had scoffed: *Precisely what the Hrothgari would have you humans believe.*

"Craggenbrun?" Annleia gasped

Torin glanced at her, then traced her stunned gaze to the head of that dwarven column. His own breath caught in his throat when he spied the pepper-bearded dwarf scowling back at them. He looked exactly like—

Crag's eyes widened, sharing their surprise. "Lei?" He started toward them, mouth agape. "Lei, what are you—" The dwarf faltered as his gaze shifted to Torin, probing his drawn cowl. "Torin?" A flicker of excitement lit his features, and he resumed his approach. "How? They told me ya were killed—"

The Tuthari drew up short, noting Torin's hand where it lay inside his cloak upon the hilt of his weapon. A shadow of alarm passed over his bearded face, dousing his initial enthusiasm. In the next breath, his axe was in his fist, ripped from its sling with a leathery rasp.

"Crag, no!" Annleia shouted, stepping forward with hands upraised.

Torin was careful to keep his where they were. Crag's company numbered more than a score. Already, its members were fanning out behind their leader, hammers, picks, maces, and other weapons unslung.

"Dead, Lei," Crag growled in renewed warning. His eyes remained locked with Torin's. "That's what they told me."

"And they told you true, but he is not what you fear."

Crag glanced at the elven-blooded woman, a fresh dread blooming in his gruff features. It was not difficult to read. If Torin *was* what the Tuthari feared, might she be, as well?

Annleia lowered her hood. She looked back at Torin, gesturing for him to do the same. Moving slowly, Torin released his grip and reached up with both hands to comply.

"Back!" Crag barked at those dwarves who began to inch past him.

In the distance, the ocean hissed and rumbled. Strangers along the roadway were now taking notice of the confrontation. A few scampered away, up or down the hill. Most froze in place, gawking.

Crag gnawed his lip for a moment, then stepped forward. "Your wrist, Lei."

She offered it to him, drawing back her sleeve to reveal her wellstone bracelet. He met her gaze in unspoken question, but remained focused. His relief a moment later was palpable. He gave her arm a friendly squeeze, then pulled her protectively behind him.

"Now yours," he said to Torin.

Torin held forth his arm, trying not to focus on Crag's axe while the dwarf grabbed hold of him. A knobby thumb pressed tightly against the tendons of his wrist. "You found your people, I see."

Crag's crushing inspection became a welcoming clasp. "That I did, lad. Like I told ya I would." He spun back to Annleia, leaning upon his axe head while reaching out with the other arm to catch her enthusiastic embrace. "Aw, child, I'm so sorry. You'll never know."

Only then did Torin realize that Annleia was weeping, her body shuddering as she clutched that of her friend.

He remained silent, doing nothing that might disturb them. Instead, he looked back at the pack of dwarves, most of whom appeared every bit as uncomfortable. One or two nodded at him. The rest continued to glare.

At last, Annleia withdrew. Though tears streaked her cheeks, a broad smile warmed her face. "I can't believe we found you."

Crag scowled. "Was it me ya was looking for, then?"

Was it? Torin wondered. Could Crag be the one Ravar had claimed they would find? Certainly, the Tuthari was more likely than most to believe—or at least accept—what Annleia had come here to do.

"I never even imagined it," Annleia admitted, shaking her head. She leaned over for another quick hug, which only added to the dwarf's evident confusion.

"Well then, how . . . What *has* brought ya here?" He glanced at Torin. "And why did they tell me ya died?"

Torin opened his mouth, then realized he had no idea where to begin.

"Ours is a lengthy story," Annleia answered for him, "best shared elsewhere, I think."

"What can you tell us about matters here?" Torin asked, thinking it crucial to learn just how much time they might have.

"What don't ya know?" Crag asked. "Ain't it plain to see?"

The Tuthari sounded gruff, as always, but there was an unmistakable gleam in his eye. He was genuinely pleased to see them both, Torin decided, and a measure of his own anxiety swiftly drained with the realization.

"They say our armies battle at the Gaperon," Torin said.

"Those that ain't here," Crag snorted. "When I left 'em, troops up north were still awaiting the enemy's arrival. Most are here, working on our escape." He seemed to spit the last of this, as if critical of the decision. Or maybe it was just his reluctance to set sail again so soon after his last voyage.

"King Thelin," Torin said, peering toward the crest of the hill. He could see the upper roofline of the governor's manse almost directly around the corner, peeking above the roadside ridge. "Is he here?"

Crag nodded. "I just came from a council briefing. Come to rattle his head, have ya? Sour taste, this seafaring business. You've brought better hope for all, I trust."

Had they? Torin wasn't sure. He felt confident that their current efforts were a waste. But what use was there in telling them that without providing a positive alternative?

"Some might call it that," he hedged finally, gaze drawn by a fresh trample of booted feet marching in unison. "Others may say . . ."

He stopped as the vanguard of the new company cleared the bend. Kuurian infantry, by their colors, led by a cadre of Souari royal guard. One of the onlookers who had scampered away moments ago was with them. A lookout, disguised as a civilian. He knew it the moment the man leaned toward the company's commander and pointed in Torin's direction.

"Hold!" the commander shouted.

Torin took an involuntary step back, holding up his hands in a gesture of faith. The Kuurian force doubled pace, thudding toward him.

When their weapons came free, Crag stepped forward to shield Annleia. His monstrous axe swept up as if it weighed no more than a willow switch.

"That's close enough, I'm thinking," the Tuthari warned.

The first wave slowed, but continued to approach, backed by a spreading line of infantry. Though clearly outnumbered, Crag signaled to his accompanying dwarves, who turned at once to form a defensive line of their own.

"Stop!" a new voice cried out.

Torin looked to the retaining wall. Atop its ridge, a dozen archers had gathered, bows flexing. Among them . . .

"Allion," he breathed in relief.

"Stay as you are," Allion snapped back. "These men have leave to feather anyone who moves."

Torin blinked in surprise. Beside him, a growl rose in the back of Crag's throat.

"I checked 'em, you doddard. They ain't the enemy."

"Then they won't mind being taken into custody," Allion countered.

His friend's arrow, Torin noted, was aimed directly at him. His chest itched with the certainty of it.

"Good of you to remain vigilant," he replied. "Come, then, examine us for yourself. I assure you, we are at your mercy."

"Surrender your weapons," Allion demanded. "Then we'll see."

Crag's eyes were flitting back and forth, measuring odds. When the Tuthari's gaze met his own, Torin shook his head.

"And how do we know *your* men can be trusted?" he asked.

"I've not buried any of *them*."

So his earlier assumption was true. Allion was the one who had attempted to preserve his remains there in Diln. It seemed he was going to have to explain much that he had hoped to avoid. "As you wish, then. I'll not resist."

Allion scowled in obvious, understandable mistrust, but nodded at the commander below. A gloved signal sent two men forward, who promptly relieved Torin of the Crimson Sword. Its silver, gem-studded hilt captured a splay of light from the afternoon sun, causing an awed murmur to sweep among the growing mass of roadside viewers.

The talisman was passed on to another team, allowing the first pair to turn to Annleia.

"She ain't armed," Crag said.

"I've a dagger and longknife," she corrected. "Though I'd prefer you be the one to hold them."

Crag gave the soldiers another threatening look, then found the blades

Annleia had mentioned. He stuffed one at a time into his own belt with his free hand, keeping his axe at the ready.

"Gonna examine them, then?" he asked irritably.

Allion ignored him. "Bring them," he said to the troops upon the ground.

Ropes were brought forward to bind Torin's wrists. He said nothing, only stared up at his friend with open regret.

"Any man lays a finger on her will be counting by nines hereafter," he heard Crag snarl.

"Your bold tongue does them no favor," Allion called down.

"And I'm thinking your iron skull might make for a fine whetstone. So why don't we resolve this with a mite more speed and courtesy, eh? The lass is *my* ward."

Allion grimaced, but nodded again to the ground commander. The procession started forward—Torin flanked by soldiers, and followed by Crag, Annleia, and their pack of dwarves.

"I'm pleased to find you safe," Torin shouted up at Allion, when the hunter finally relaxed his bow.

His friend fixed him with a chilling stare. "Welcome home."

Sunlight dappled the inner courtyard, seeking purchase amid the plants and fountains and statues. A ceaseless struggle, for clouds hung across the midday sky like cobwebs over a neglected world, while the shadows of wind-blown trees shifted as if to smother the light where it lay.

The garden seemed well tended, filled with flowers and vines and the fresh scents of spring. And the sea, of course. Even here, deep within the governor's manse, Torin could hear its restless groan and smell its briny breath. A sheltered place, all in all, quiet and peaceful, untouched by the chaos that so marred the world outside. A small piece of paradise, he thought, in a dying realm.

He turned at the sound of steps upon the gravel path. A herald approached, flanked by a pair of sentries. The same trio had left them moments earlier at the edge of these grounds, bearing the Sword ahead. They did not carry it now.

"His Majesty will see them," the herald announced.

The commander of their unit gestured. Torin, his wrists still bound behind his back, was seized by the arm and dragged forward. Crag and Annleia were to his right. The company of dwarves had been refused entry at an earlier checkpoint. If Crag insisted on accompanying the girl into the king's sanctum, he'd been told, he would do so alone. He had even agreed to surrender his axe, though Torin would be surprised if the Tuthari did not carry some other, hidden weapon.

Hopefully, he would not have to find out.

Their ring of captors was twenty strong—the king's own—all bearing naked halberds in addition to the swords at their waists. As they marched, boots crunching on the walkway of crushed limestone, Torin saw archers appear along the corniced eaves overhead, arrows nocked and ready.

Even paradise had its thorns.

He resisted the urge to turn and acknowledge the one at his back. Throughout their trek, Allion had refused to let him out of sight, keeping his own arrow ready. Torin thought his friend would have found that to be unnecessary by now, but Allion would not be coaxed into relaxing his stance—not by the unit's commander, and certainly not by Torin himself. He had refused even to communicate, ignoring Torin's kinder entreaties and scowling murderously at a pair of attempted japes. Truth be told, the hunter's aggressive vigilance was beginning to wear thin.

They turned a corner past a flowered hedgerow taller than their heads. Here, the path widened, but ended quickly at a natural alcove formed by the wraparound hedge wall. A sculpted fountain burbled in backdrop, with a pair of curving stone benches set before its basin. Upon one of these benches sat a woman Torin did not recognize. Her long, dark hair was streaked with silver, and hung like a veil over her face—turned down to regard the Sword, which lay across her lap.

Thelin stood beside her. The Souari king looked up to receive them. The woman did not.

Their company came to a halt. The forward guardsmen took three more strides, then turned crisply, parting to either side of their king.

"This is . . . unexpected," Thelin said.

From the other's stony mask, Torin could read little of the king's feelings. He did not see pleasure among them.

"You were killed at Krynwall, or so they say. I have later, eyewitness accounts of you leading the assault that devastated Atharvan. Yet my own eyes have you standing before me, thrice-examined and deemed living—truly living. So tell me, which of these tales is false?"

"All are true, Your Highness."

Thelin's eyes darkened. His face appeared much thinner than Torin remembered, his cheeks high and hollow. It lent him a grave, shadowy look. "How can this be?" he demanded. "Have you found a cure, then, against the Illychar madness? A way to restore the corrupted dead to life?"

For a moment, the woman's head rose. Her eyes lifted to meet Torin's, blue eyes tinged with hope.

Torin did not have time to explain the unique circumstances of his resurrection—not even what little of it he believed he understood. "The witch who saw my life restored gave hers in the process," he said. "It is too much to suggest we might duplicate her efforts."

Behind him, Allion scoffed. "Bloody fortunate, eh? And why should *you* be so favored?"

A bristle crept along the back of Torin's neck, but he kept his tongue caged. The woman's gaze lowered.

"And your friend?" Thelin asked. "Who is she in all of this?" Apparently, he, too, deemed Allion's remark little more than an angry taunt. Or perhaps the king was simply perceptive enough to realize that Annleia's was the true importance.

"She is the one I was sent to find," Torin said, peeking over at her. Annleia gave a slight nod. Crag glared. "She is the only one who can save us from the Illysp."

"*Sent*," Allion echoed, "by Darinor, you mean." He circled around from Torin's back and into view, arrow still nocked. "The same Darinor who orchestrated almost the whole of this calamity."

Torin spared his friend a sour glance before refocusing on Thelin. "Darinor feared the very knowledge she carries, the slim chance she represents. Were he here, he would seek her death, else have you detain her until it was too late."

"Neither of which is gonna happen," Crag growled.

Thelin's brow curdled. "Your quest was in search of elves, as I was told, living Finlorians. She hardly bears the look of one."

"Appearances can be deceiving," Torin said, a bit too curtly.

"Hence the reason you are still bound," Thelin countered.

A rising frustration drummed within Torin's chest. "I allowed myself to be bound, Your Highness."

"As I have *allowed* you to live," the king snapped, "when it might have been safer to riddle you on sight as others here suggested."

Torin looked again toward Allion, who still seethed with a barely bridled hostility. Then the woman rose from her bench, Sword in hand. She placed a calming hand upon Thelin's rigid arm as she stepped forward. The king's wife, Torin decided, Loisse. He couldn't know for sure, for in the time he'd spent at Souaris—even after their victory against the dragonspawn—the queen had chosen to remain secluded, in mourning over the death of her children. But who else could this be?

"What would you have of us?" she asked.

"My lady?"

"Your purpose. You mean to thwart our enemy, but the enemy does not yet plague us here—not those we can see, anyway."

The face of the fountain standing in backdrop was sculpted with twining eels, water spouting from their jagged mouths. Torin thought of Ravar, and wondered how much to say.

"Our journey carries us to the very heart of this scourge," Annleia answered for him, "to the wellspring from which it was spawned. We seek those who might help to show us the path."

"And why should they be found here," Thelin grumbled, "among those of us who know only what little you tell us?"

A fair gripe, Torin had to admit. "We have only recently learned the truth ourselves," he said, placating. "You are the first we've come to share it with."

"And what is that?" the queen asked.

When Torin looked into her eyes, he realized he had fenced as long as he could. He took a breath. "Annleia must be allowed to restore the seal that I destroyed. All else is feint and posturing."

Allion snarled. "Men braver than you are dying, likely as we speak. You call that *posturing*?"

Thelin raised an arm. One of his guardsmen stepped forward to place a restraining hand upon the agitated hunter's shoulder. When the king spoke, however, his own jaw was clenched.

"I have dispatched sloops north to those fleeing Alson, west to Yawacor, south in pursuit of Wingport's runaway citizens . . . begging help from any quarter. Nearly a million souls labor now to build the fleet I've vowed shall deliver them from this forsaken land. Is it all in vain? Am I to tell this people there is no hope?"

Torin had heard whispers of the western exodus, led by Baron Nevik. None seemed to know how the baron and those with him fared. Torin wondered how long either populace could hold on—especially if rumor of the truth were to spread.

"What Your Highness tells his subjects," Torin replied carefully, "is not for me to determine. Let their labors persist, if it serves their spirits. Only, be warned that the Illysp have just cause to fear the sea, and so do we. It is my companion's quest that will make the difference. Help us, if you can, else let us be on our way."

Allion laughed derisively. "Like that, you say. Your Highness, the Gaperon is closed by now. They would never make it to the Skullmars from here. Nor should we risk losing the Sword, now that it has been returned to us."

"The Sword is the key to the seal," Torin argued hastily. His friend's words had triggered an alarming memory of his detention by Emperor Derreg at Morethil, before dragonspawn had overrun the city. They could not afford to be similarly waylaid here.

"Then send it with another," Allion said. "Your Highness, Your Grace, we cannot trust it in *his* hands."

Annleia spoke up at once. "It must be Torin who accompanies me—he who drew the talisman from its vault to begin with."

Thelin shared a long look with his wife. It was widely held that the Souari king trusted his queen's counsel more than any other's. Witnessing it now provided a truer appreciation for the depth of the king's commitment.

"Marvelous though it is, I see not what great good the weapon does us here," Loisse admitted. "If drawing it loosed this ill, and replacing it may bottle it up once more, I see scant reason to forestall the attempt."

"Your Grace," Allion tried again, "we know nothing about this waif who claims to be an elf. And Torin has failed us too many times to—"

"Faith can be perilous," Loisse countered crisply. "But there is also a danger in seeking to control matters one does not understand." She studied Torin closely, as if hunting for some hidden flaw. "Give the man his blade," she said, handing the Sword to her husband. "Let them carry it to the front. Perhaps, if nothing else, it will lend our armies courage as it once did."

Torin, somewhat relieved, looked to Allion, awaiting the next protest. It came at once.

"Your Grace, you cannot truly believe—"

"What I may or may not believe bears little relevance," the queen insisted. "We will build our ships and set sail. Either this maiden will succeed, or she won't. We will learn the truth then—and hope to be long gone should your fears prove out."

Thelin considered. "What would *you* have us do," he asked Torin, "while we await the outcome of this dubious expedition?"

"Her Grace has already outlined a most practical course," Torin said, bowing slightly. He wasn't sure which had swayed her: logic or inspiration. Either way, she seemed to be his only friend in this. "There is little enough those here can do but wait," he continued, "and it would serve no purpose for them to turn idle."

"Yet idle they will be, according to you," Allion groused. "Laboring pointlessly, blind to the knowledge that you and you alone command their fate."

"Not alone," Thelin mused. "We will prepare a company, I think, to escort you—at least as far as the Gaperon. Perhaps you, Master Allion, would care to join that party."

The hunter looked as though he would sooner spit than share the road with him, but Torin could also see what both men were thinking. A company to escort him, yes, but also to make sure he did not stray or revert to his Illychar ways.

"I go, too," Crag interjected, eyeing Allion distastefully.

"Captain Wynn will see to the arrangements," Thelin said. "Captain."

The commander of the guard unit saluted. "Sir."

"Release him."

Wynn signaled. A pair of hands worked roughly at the knot binding Torin's wrists, pulling it free.

"Your weapon," Thelin said.

Torin stepped forward, resisting the urge to rub his burning wrists, or to cast wary glances toward the guardsmen and archers marking his every twitch. When he was within a pace of the king and queen, Thelin extended the Sword, locking gazes as he did so. The proud city of Souaris had weathered centuries, and her latest king looked as if he had weathered each of them with her. As mistrustful as all had been, Torin thought, there was much they hadn't compelled him to explain: the source of Annleia's knowledge, the means by which she would rebuild this seal, what would become of the Illysp and Illychar already set loose. Either they didn't believe a word of what he'd shared, or he could take it as another sign of their utter desperation.

With one hand on the hilt and the other on that gleaming, fire-filled blade, Torin bowed in unspoken promise, and stepped back.

"Captain," the king said, as if Torin were already forgotten, "a word, please."

Torin's gaze shifted to Allion. The hunter was glowering. A thumb brushed the fletching on his arrow, betraying his continued anxiety.

"They say the greatest deeds are those hailed as impossible," Loisse said, drawing Torin's attention. Her tone was soft with resignation. "I suppose we shall soon find out."

CHAPTER FORTY-FIVE

CORATHEL WRENCHED HIS BLADE FROM the reaver's chest, a spray of blood painting his forearm. With a feral grunt, he shoved the soulless creature aside and shifted to meet the next. A troll, its lower jaw missing, thundered down upon him, brandishing a bloodstained cudgel. It launched the weapon at Corathel's face, a heavy, gusting swing under which the seasoned general ducked easily. Upon an armored knee, Corathel thrust his own sword upward and into the roof of the troll's damaged mouth. The beast convulsed as the blade minced its brain and shattered the top of its skull, ruptured vessels spilling in rivulets down the length of sharpened steel.

Shielded by the creature's dying bulk, Corathel took a moment to catch his breath. When the full weight of its corpse began to slide forward, the general stood and twisted, dumping the fresh carcass to the blood-smeared earth. Hefting his weapon with burning shoulders, he spun to the ready.

His men were still behind him—those who still stood—grappling with opponents of their own. Ahead, a wall of elven Illychar had formed at the rear of the trench, trapping those who had been the last to flee. Corathel ripped into them with a growl, hacking one elf across the midsection and removing the head of a second as it turned to face him. Their comrades closed on either side with a collective hiss, but his own fellow soldiers barged in at his heels, lunging to intercept, allowing the chief general to press onward.

Near the base of the trench's rear slope, he spied Bannon at last. The lieutenant general had battled to the end for his wing of the northernmost line, lingering so that others might escape. When seeing from afar that the reavers were cutting his regiment off from behind, Corathel had raced in to relieve them.

He was too late. Even as he watched, Bannon was laid flat upon the blood-soaked mud. The fallen commander glanced reflexively to the right, but his severed sword arm had fallen just out of reach. When a troll's foot pinned him at the chest, his gaze swiveled back in time to catch the full, bludgeoning force of a descending cudgel.

Corathel howled—in fury, frustration, and to lend fresh hope to the slain Bannon's faltering troops. He skidded down the slope with reckless abandon, parrying what blows he could and trusting his armor to deflect the rest. He felt old wounds opening, and new ones overlapping those, but he didn't have time just now to acknowledge them.

He planted himself before Bannon's body, driving back a pair seeking to haul it off by the ankles. The troll who had struck the final blow was nowhere to be seen. Corathel took a moment to glance at his friend's face—now a mashed ruin within its crumpled half helm.

He glanced up as an elf slipped past his trailing guard. The reaver's twin blades clamped and twisted, wrenching the sword from Corathel's grasp. He let it go, reaching for his dagger instead. Ducking a scissor strike, he ripped a wide seam in the elf's gut. As the reaver peered down in surprise, one of its own shoved it aside. Corathel met this next opponent with a forearm to the face, heavy bracer crushing its rotted nose and blinding it with unbidden tears. He whirled then, in time to puncture an artery in a third elf's thigh. While it snarled at the resulting fountain, a Parthan blade erupted through its chest, driven through from behind.

The chief general let that one slump to its knees, turning back to the blinded one, which snorted and clawed at its broken face in irritation. Reddened, tear-filled eyes managed to focus as Corathel's dagger flayed its throat.

It, too, was then shouldered aside, by the same elf it had shoved past—the one that had first disarmed him. One of its blades was now missing. Its entrails hung from their cavity, black and withered and foul. Still it came forward, hefting its lone weapon, its face a promise of pain.

Corathel brandished his dagger, fueling the reaver's focus, drawing it on. It never saw the Mookla'ayans that closed on either side. One took its arm at the shoulder. The other sent its head rolling across a pile of bodies upon the trench floor.

"Your sword, sir."

Corathel sheathed his bloody dagger and accepted the blade, offered to him by one of his soldiers. He swiped at the mud clinging to its hilt, before looking up again.

"Down!" he yelled, seeing the form barreling in at the other's back.

Again he was too late. The troll's cudgel met the right side of the youth's face, crushing it like a harvest melon. Corathel lunged as the soldier dropped, his full weight behind the point of his sword. With unnatural agility, however, the troll sidestepped the blow, and all his weapon did was draw a thin line across the reaver's hardened side. By the time he caught himself and turned, the troll's weapon was raised, while his own dragged heavily upon the ground.

A thrown spear punctured the beast's arm, in advance of an approaching thunder. Corathel and his adversary turned as one. A hard-charging soldier slammed into the troll's side. The beast withstood the blow and threw an elbow to fend off the next, sending both men reeling. But a stampede followed. Not Parthan, but Kuurian. Following the route Corathel had carved, its members continued to pour in, clearing the trench of enemies, sweeping the troll and its kind underfoot.

Corathel stood aside, ringed by his own, chest heaving. A week's reprieve from combat and travel had bolstered his recovery from earlier injuries. In the days between their elimination of the first army of Illychar and the arrival of this one, he'd regained much of his fighting strength. His endurance, however, was but a shadow of what he was accustomed to. He was going to have to ease his pace, else find some hidden reserve, if he hoped to still be standing come battle's end.

Then again, at the rate the reavers were advancing, he needn't expect the battle to last all that long.

"Time to move out, General," said Troy, ridden up on a lathered courser.

Corathel nodded, too worn and winded to argue. He signaled to his troops to begin the withdrawal. He did not yet know how many were left, as opposed to the number who would never escape this trench. Already, Troy's fire crews were setting the ground alight, touching off barrels of pitch set in place for that purpose. The Kuurians who had cleared the area were falling back beneath the renewed Illychar press.

He would make his counts later.

As he scrambled back up the slope, he checked the heavens in measure of their progress. They battled beneath a sky of fire and ash, the sun smoldering in pockets of toasted gray clouds. If not mistaken about the orb's position, the fighting was not yet a day old. He shook his head. Too soon to have surrendered their forwardmost barricade. The bulk of the enemy force had yet to even reach them, according to General Rogun and his team of advance scouts. Most were still wrangling with the Hrothgari siege rovers, said to be grinding their way south through the pass. After all he'd heard from Hreidmar and others about these unique war engines, Corathel was anxious to see them in action. But he never would if their coalition continued to give ground as they had here.

He wondered if Bannon had been thinking the same. Perhaps that was why the Sixth General had waited so long, rather than signaling the retreat when there was still time. A foolish mistake, in hindsight. All knew that stronger entrenchments lay farther south, due to the positioning of armaments and the broken nature of the land itself. Even with the Hrothgari among them and a week to prepare, they could do only so much to shape the terrain. The lieutenant general should have trusted in their fallback positions rather than fight so stubbornly to maintain this one.

Too late now, he thought. His phrase of the day, it seemed. Perhaps he needed to push himself a bit harder, rather than allow himself to slow down.

A pair of Hrothgari went running past, back toward the trench, bearing more fuel for the fires. The loads upon their backs looked to be larger than the dwarves themselves. Corathel wished now that they'd kept a few more of their kind. In exchange for the five thousand sent south as shipbuilders with the one called Craggenbrun, King Thelin had dispatched nearly eight thousand of his own men north, more than doubling Troy's surviving count. Yet from all Corathel had seen, he'd sooner pit five thousand dwarves than eight thousand men against this savage swarm, and consider himself fortunate.

He could only hope that Craggenbrun's crews, along with the families of Hrothgari sent south before, would make as much difference to the southern effort as they might have made here.

The number of corpses littering the earth began to diminish as the distance between himself and the lost trench widened. The carnage was horrific, though he'd seen worse—and likely would again. He wondered how many they had lost in just this short time. All told, their coalition numbered in the realm of forty thousand. With more and more reavers filtering southward, he could soon expect to be outnumbered. When that happened, only the narrow terrain and the strength of their determination could save them.

Within, the general's emotions blazed. But he kept the fires in check, refusing to let them cloud his judgment. A soldier did not long survive without passion and instinct, yet did well to keep them reined. His own ability to balance rage and rationality, as war required, was perhaps the best way to explain his continued survival.

That, and blind, cursed luck.

He had nearly reached the funneled opening in the next barricade when a shouted alarm spun him about. Owl—U'uyen—was the first to turn with him, and to point out the team of giants careening down from a western ridge.

Descending directly into the flank of Troy's trailing contingent.

"Mother's mercy," Corathel muttered, then called to his regiment, "Form up!"

In the next breath, they were sprinting back the other way. Bad enough that he would have to find a commander to replace Bannon. He was not going to let Troy fall, as well.

Too late, his fears taunted, as the swift-striding giants hewed into the Kuurian column. He growled the thought away and used that anger to quicken his pace. Horses and riders shrieked and squealed. The giant Illychar carried axes and hammers and greatswords taller in some instances than the men they were wielded against. How their pack had slipped up and around without warning from the lookouts was not plainly apparent, but the gnawing question would have to lie set for now.

Blood filled the air in beaded ropes and sudden sprays. Troy himself was on the ground, amid severed chunks of horse and man. He seemed not to notice the club-wielding giant standing over him. The creature barked with savage laughter, reveling in the slaughter. When a wounded soldier stumbled toward it, the giant sent the man sailing with a single, meaty crunch. Troy turned at the sound, but could do no more than raise an arm as the brute took overhead aim against him.

Corathel spurred himself forward, refusing—like the coalition forces dug in behind him—to accept the inevitable.

DARKENING CLOUDS ROILED AGAINST THE gray slate of the sky. The Falcon's Hour, Torin estimated, barely midafternoon. Yet, with that thundering cover, it seemed closer to dusk. The brewing storm hailed from the south, blown up from the coast upon their company's heels. When it finally broke, things were going to get wet in a hurry.

The wagon bed in which he rode creaked and jostled beneath him. Uncovered, he noted again. But then, it hadn't been provided for their comfort.

Crag didn't ride horses. Annleia's only experience doing so had been a short jaunt from Neak-Thur—and she would not be separated from her Tuthari companion in any case. And as for himself . . . he wasn't to be trusted with a horse. More than two hundred Kuurian soldiers surrounded them—for their protection, the company commander had suggested, but the whole thing felt to Torin more like a prisoner detachment than a guard detail.

Their departure from Wingport had been a hasty one, made promptly after their audience with Souaris's king and queen, just hours ago. With all that lay at stake, they hadn't the luxury of prolonged debate. Nor would a day or two have made any difference, Torin suspected, when it came to convincing Thelin, Loisse, Allion, or anyone else of the truthfulness of Annleia's purpose. Torin was still wrestling with the unlikelihood himself. He couldn't well expect the others to pin their hopes on it.

All they cared to understand was that letting him take the Sword north—and into battle—might help to embolden the soldiers at the front and relieve some of the pressure bearing down upon them. Though this was not his primary goal, Torin certainly meant to find out.

He looked to his left as Allion, riding ahead of them, peered back with a sour glance. Since setting forth, the hunter had spent most of his time trailing their wagon, where Torin could feel the man's suspicious gaze boring into him. Now and again, however, his friend would push forward to whisper with the company commander, positioned at the heart of the column. Even then, he refused to let Torin out of his sight for long.

"Perhaps you should go and speak with him," Annleia said.

He turned abruptly, her voice catching him off guard. She sat on the wagon bed's right-side bench, Crag at her shoulder. He sat alone across from them. Fodder and stores lay heaped upon the floor. It wasn't much. Between theirs and the other carts, they carried just enough provisions for their unit, and only for a couple of days.

"Who?" he asked, feigning distraction.

Heavier wagons were set to follow, to help provide longer for this company and the extra divisions Thelin had promised to send in pursuit. Before parting, Torin had urged the king to send reinforcements northward to further fortify the Gaperon. The shipbuilding effort—even if successful—would take weeks, if not months. Based on a more detailed report by Crag, such time would not be won by the few already set in place to guard their backs.

Annleia gave him a disapproving frown. "Your friend. There should not be this gulf between you."

Nor would he have imagined it. Not from Allion. "The man is entitled to his feelings."

"As you are to yours. Ill will festers in such silence."

Perhaps she was right. He could sit there all day and pretend to be unaffected by Allion's cutting remarks, or he could seek to assuage the bitterness between them before it became too much to overcome.

"Go," Annleia urged. "It might be your last opportunity to do so."

True enough. He had experienced already life's unexpected ebbs and flows—seen how, without warning, its tides could pull people apart and carry them off in separate directions. Allion was too close a friend to let go without at least seeking to settle matters between them.

He knew also that they had only so much time before the entire company was urged forward again at full pace. Such rest periods promised to be short and infrequent. Were their horses able to gallop the entire distance, he had no doubts that they would be doing so.

He glanced at Crag, whose pinched expression showed only a general distaste. Annleia, however, nodded encouragingly. Perhaps she only wanted some more time alone with her dwarven friend, Torin thought. If that was the case, he wouldn't refuse her.

After tightening the sword strap slung across his shoulder, he swung a leg over the wagon bed's wall and dropped to the side. The driver glanced back at the motion, then farther back at a pair of watchriders who urged their mounts forward. Torin paid them no mind, but strode swiftly ahead, outpacing the slow-rolling wagon and the scores of walking steeds that formed their company.

His escorts reined up close. "May we be of service, sir?" one of them asked.

"Just stretching my legs," he replied, staring ahead.

At that point, Allion turned and saw him coming. The hunter scowled and pulled his own mount to a halt. "Something wrong?" he demanded, as Torin neared.

"Thought I might have a word with you."

Allion's horse snorted. The hunter looked as if he wished to do the same. "Concerning what?"

Torin kept marching, passing his friend by. Allion turned his steed's head and kicked in alongside.

"Where are you going?"

"The Gaperon, or so I'm told." It was difficult to keep the annoyance from his voice. "Must these soldiers share our every word?"

Allion, still scowling, signaled to the warders, who backed off, but remained alert, eyeing Torin like vultures. "Is the wagon not comfort enough for you? I'm afraid it's the best we have to offer—and far easier than riding in armor and saddle."

Torin passed over the first retort that came to mind. He hadn't come to be drawn into a fight. "Such hospitality is better than I deserve," he agreed instead. "I'll do my best to reward their sacrifice in the coming battle."

"Will you? Or will you have already run off with this *elf* of yours?"

It took even more effort, this time, for Torin to keep his eyes forward and his tongue in check. His own presence might well warrant Allion's enmity, but Annleia's most certainly did not. "Where's Marisha?" he asked abruptly, thinking to catch his friend off guard. Aside from that, he had put the question off too long already. "Is she safe?"

Allion turned briefly to glare at him, before fixing his gaze northward once more. "She's serving as healer to those on the front. Having been away, I cannot tell you if she still lives."

To Torin, the answer was a relief. He'd feared she might have fallen already, and that *that* might be the true cause of Allion's distress.

Perhaps he wasn't far off, for the hunter seemed even more bitter and frustrated than before when adding, "What else would you have of me?"

"Blazes, Allion, I'm only trying to apologize for the ill I've caused, and to learn what I must do to make amends."

"*Amends?*" The hunter shook his head with a brittle laugh. "How can you speak of amends while you continue to make the same mistakes?"

"And which mistakes are those?" Torin asked, shifting his eye toward his friend.

Allion met his gaze this time, glaring down at him from the saddle. "If you had only learned to accept life as it comes, rather than constantly chasing after childhood dreams, none of this would have happened."

Torin frowned, puzzled by the claim. "If I had ignored the dreams," he said, thinking of those fostered by the Entients, "I never would have found the Sword."

"And had you not found the Sword," Allion remarked primly, "you would not have unleashed the Illysp."

"What of the Demon Queen?"

"We don't know *how* that might have turned out. I don't recall the bearer of the Crimson Sword crushing his leg in Killangrathor's lair."

A fair argument, perhaps . . . though, without the Sword, they may never have met the Entients and learned of the dragon at all. Either way, the threads were too closely intertwined to believe that one change in events would not have altered others.

"By the same token," Torin countered finally, "it was you who helped to slay Killangrathor. And had the dragon not been killed, it never would have become an Illychar."

Allion's glare turned poisonous. "Would you have rather let the dragon-spawn roam free?"

"Of course not. You did what you had to, what you believed was right at the time. As did I. No one could have foreseen all that would result."

The hunter scoffed. "Is that how you wish to justify it?"

"I'm not seeking to *justify* anything. I'm only—"

"You're doing what you always do, challenging fate in pursuit of some ideal future that doesn't exist. You refuse to accept the ordinary, as if you're somehow better than the rest of us. And your actions have brought ruin to us all."

Was that how all of this had happened? He had indeed made certain choices, early on, to reach for a grander future than that afforded by the safer, more certain path. But was it wrong to reach for the extraordinary if the known path offered only a dead end?

"Even now," Allion pressed, "you think to save the world in one fell swoop, rather than join the slower, more difficult struggle the rest of us must face. Your only commitment is to your own glorified aspirations, leaving others to take up your share of the common burden."

Perhaps his friend was right. Contentions sprang to mind, but they seemed petty and self-minded, one and all, their only potential purpose in redirecting blame. If that was all Allion was willing to discuss with him, then Torin was clearly wasting his breath.

"You seem to have already decided, then, upon my lack of value in the upcoming battle. Hopefully, the rest of these men are not similarly discouraged."

"You're no hero, Torin. I was there, every step, when you recovered the Sword, remember? I know what you did and what you *didn't* do. You cannot ask me to take heart in a legend I know to be false."

Torin had heard enough. "The tale isn't written yet," he said, then turned on a heel and headed back toward the trailing wagon.

The pounding in his chest soon reached his ears, his blood envenomed with the sting of truth. He didn't need Allion to tell him that he was hardly what the bards would sing about. He didn't need his best friend to bring to light all his darkest fears. He'd received a warmer reception in Yawacor, from mercenaries and cutthroats and those he had barely known, than from the one person he might have expected to welcome his return. He wasn't sure what it might take to satisfy his former friend, but he doubted now if even his death would be enough.

"Did it not go well?" Annleia asked, after he had climbed back up into the wagon bed.

"Perfectly," he huffed, without looking at her.

She remained silent for a moment, then added, "It does you no good to hoard your misery from the world."

"It does the world no good for me to share it," he snarled, glaring now across the way. Catching the stern look Crag gave him, he forced his tone to soften. "I've sown misery enough, don't you think?"

He looked to his own hands then, clenching them together with a molten determination. She knew no more than Allion. But he would show them both soon enough. To the Abyss with her and Ravar and their restoration of the seal. That road was far too perilous to risk on such an uncertain outcome. Instead, he would give Allion the commitment he was seeking. He would show them all just how well versed he had become in the harvesting of death and sorrow. They wanted a battle? He would give it to them, with all the pain and fury that Itz lar Thrakkon had bred within him. It would be a conflict for the ages, the kind in which true legends were forged.

One way or the other, he would make this next confrontation his last.

CHAPTER FORTY-SIX

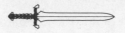

THE SILENCE PEALED LOUDER THAN thunder.

It wasn't *complete* silence, but after weeks of deafening clangor within their iron-shelled rover, it seemed as such. The steam-powered engines had gone cold and quiet. Her team no longer labored at the pump handles, for their efforts availed them nothing. For a time, there had been the raucous howling and banging and clawing of those skatchykem seeking to pry their way inside. But most had since moved south to engage easier prey. After that had come the rains, a downpour so violent that it rang like pebbles upon the ceiling. The waters, funneled down to the boiler, had effectively replenished their drinking stores, but had failed them in their attempts to start the rover back up again. When the boiler had gone dry, the fires fanned by the pushers' labors had failed as well, and no flame of their own would take hold as that one had. Evidently, whatever sorcery the Entients had worked would be required anew if they hoped to bring the rovers back to life.

Until then, they were stranded, hunkered within a cocoon of their own making, with nothing now but to wait and pray for some manner of deliverance.

"Do you think they've forgotten about us?" Tonra asked.

Vashen shook her head, not so much in answer as in frustration. *Most* of the skatchykem had pushed south, but not all. Every now and then, a pack would come crawling back to probe the seams of their shell. The fighting that raged without sounded muffled and distant, yet was near enough that a single shout of warning would be sufficient to bring a fair portion of that enemy host swooping down upon them.

"How does the cave cat hunt the shield lizard?" she mused in reply.

"By waiting for the lizard to stick its neck out," Dugg answered. "Which it must do eventually," he added gruffly, "else suffocate in its own shell."

Vashen winced. Perhaps she should have taken care to choose a more hopeful image—even if none could more accurately describe their own predicament.

"We've rations enough for a few more days," her driver observed. "May as well wait it out, see if they give us a mite more breathing room."

"It's as quiet now as it's likely to get," argued Brokk. His tone was venomous, his stare accusing, as it had been since they had left his brother Tegg behind. "We should break now."

Vashen wasn't sure which made more sense. Whenever she thought too hard on one course or the other, her head began to float. She glanced down at her hands and wrists, bound against the raking slashes used to drain her blood in a vain attempt to keep her rover moving. Perhaps Dugg was right, and she had lost too much. She felt stronger than she had a couple of days ago; the rains had done that much for her. If only they'd come a few hours earlier Achthium's trials seemed right cruel, at times. But then, steel wasn't forged amid blossoms and snowflakes.

"His Glory will learn what happened here," Vashen declared bravely. "He will not abandon us."

"As we did not abandon the others?" Brokk asked, mocking. Others amid the crew stiffened uncomfortably at the challenge, but the hurler captain pressed on. "You know we're on our own. Why else would you have positioned us as you did?"

He was right, she supposed, on both counts. Hreidmar would first have to learn of their situation. Even if he did, there was no assurance of a rescue attempt. Doing so would demand that many be put at risk for a relative few. Faced with the same choice, she had left two more rovers behind as she had the first, pressing on with the remainder because she felt she must. When it had become clear that even those rovers were failing—her own included—she'd had them close ranks and drive east to the very wall of the mountains. Should they be forced to flee their vessels, better to scatter up the slopes than through the enemy-choked floor of the pass.

"What few rations we have, we're likely to need," Brokk continued. "And my muscles are going to rot with all this sitting around. If I must fight for my life, let me do so while I can still heft pole and hammer."

Vashen eyed him squarely. Did he think she felt any differently? Blind passion was fine and good, but survival was a game of wits as well as will.

"Do the rest of you feel the same?" she asked her crew. None responded directly, but as the silence lengthened, she shifted her gaze to gauge their expressions. Her answer soon became clear. "Tonra," she said, hope and fear blooming in the nest of her stomach, "relay word to the others. We make plans to emerge at sundown."

THE MIDDAY SUN SHONE FAINTLY behind a grim cover of cloud. The air was chill and moist from the previous night's showers. Its feel reminded Torin of Yawacor, where the next rain had never been far behind the last. The smell of ash blanketed the earth. Fine weather for a battle, he thought. Crisp and invigorating.

A good day for killing. A good day to die.

He'd spent the past two days in a roiling silence, making no further effort to approach Allion or anyone else. He'd answered questions from Crag or Annleia when pressed, but had done so with frigid grunts and minimal eye contact. His fury may have cooled, but not his resolve to eradicate these Illychar one by one—or perish in the attempt. Even now, with the thunder of their battle cries ringing in his ears, he felt no fear, only a simmering desire to unleash his hand against them.

He couldn't actually see them yet. His company was still skirting the southern face of the Tenstrock Mountains, whose rugged folds formed a wall against the slaughter raging within the Gaperon itself. The land about was broken and stepped, rising and falling in an unpredictable array of gnarled mounds, knifing gullies, and steep, sheer-faced plateaus. All he could truly discern, based upon the tempest of howls and clangor of arms, was that the battle had reached the southern mouth of the pass, as if ready to spill south upon the shattered plains.

An ill sign. Though no one bothered to confer with him, he could read the dismay in their faces. The coalition forces, as he'd understood it, had dug their forwardmost trenches miles to the north, closer to the Gaperon's gullet. To have been forced back this far after just a few days of actual fighting did not bode well.

Their wagon was halted at the next checkpoint, and Torin, Annleia, and Crag unloaded from its bed. A much smaller contingent accompanied him now, led by Allion and a bearded envoy sent to them by coalition command. They'd already cleared two other checkpoints before this one. By now, word of his arrival was running well ahead of him. He saw it in the eyes of those he passed: sentries and soldiers and cooks and nurses and handlers and runners—an endless variety of fighters and camp laborers who took pause to mark his coming with sidelong looks and anxious whispers. Torin avoided their gazes, caring nothing for their wonder and suspicion. He didn't need them to trust or welcome him, only to make way.

The farther they went, the thicker the press became. Many were injured, all were exhausted, debilitated by the relentless conflict. Little by little, Torin sensed something new building around him: hope. A spark only, but fanning gradually, causing the palm that rested upon the Sword's hilt to tingle. Queen Loisse had been right. Her troops needed this. They needed to reclaim, if only briefly, a glimmer of mirth and triumph. To see that it was happening, and that he was the cause, served as an infectious reminder of what this struggle was about.

Under a mounting wave of expectation, he set his eyes forward and continued ahead.

"Ho!" a voice hailed.

Torin glanced around until he spied a filthy, half-armored figure striding toward them.

Zain.

General Rogun's commander-in-waiting wore his reptilian smile, beady eyes glittering like those of a weasel in a bird's nest. "So it's true," he said. "Sorl's son has returned from the Abyss."

Up ahead, Allion frowned, but spared the commander a nod. Their party continued its march. Zain fell into step alongside, leaving a troop of mud-spattered Alsonians behind.

"Is the general here, then?" Torin asked.

"Conferring with high command," Zain replied, "lending our regiment a much-needed rest." His gaze found Annleia. "There's a pretty one. Angel or devil?"

"She ain't one of your camp followers," Crag growled, "if that's your meaning."

"No? Pity." Zain's smile broadened, both chivalrous and predatory. His attention shifted back to Torin. "So, is the Great Fiend as ugly as they say?"

"Handsomer than some," Torin muttered.

Zain chuckled. "As I suspected. Welcome back, boy." He stopped, surprising Torin with a quick salute, then grinned at Annleia and turned back toward his men.

Torin's gaze stretched after him momentarily, after which he simply shook his head.

A tent rose before them. One of the sentries stepped inside the shadowed entrance flap, announcing their arrival, Torin supposed. He emerged a moment later and beckoned them forward.

The detachment of guardsmen halted. The envoy bowed and held the tent flap open for Allion, Torin, Annleia, and Crag to enter.

The interior was lit with lanterns, candles, and the diffuse light of the sun. The smell of blood and dirt and medicinal herbs created a sickly sweet potpourri. Near the center of the tent, stood over a crude wooden table, two men awaited them.

"General, Commander," Allion greeted dourly. His breath caught as his eyes adjusted and he took a full look at Troy. "Blazes. Good to see you took care of yourself in my absence."

The high commander's face was bruised and knotted. His left arm was splinted, his torso and one leg wrapped in gauze. His armor lay in a pile beside a nearby cot, where a pair of attendants were working to scrub it clean and beat out the dents with hammer and chisel. "Better battered than dead," he replied hoarsely, turning gaze to Torin. One eye was swollen shut. The other was painted red with swollen vessels. "Though, for a time there, I might have argued otherwise."

Allion gestured to his charges. "Torin, Crag, Annleia. You received your king's message?"

Troy nodded, studying Torin with that damaged eye of his. "Come to rid us of this scourge, we're told."

"And just in time," Rogun jeered. The general was in full, bladed armor, looking and smelling as if he'd been rolling in a mound of offal. "En route to Thrak-Symbos, we hear. Pray tell, how do you mean to drive the rats back into their hole?"

Annleia responded before Torin could. "'Tis the task we've been given," she said, as if that were explanation enough. "We bear artifacts that make it possible."

Rogun snorted. "Magic."

"The Illysp are not natural to this plane," she said. "It is not by physical means that they will be vanquished."

"Seem real enough to me," Rogun argued, picking a scrap of flesh from his shoulder and flicking it to the earth. "Though the men they've trampled will doubtless be relieved to hear it."

"We're here to serve," Torin offered, "in whatever manner is necessary." Annleia scowled. "The Gaperon is sealed, is it not?" he pressed, weathering the heat of her stare.

"There are other passes," Crag reminded him, "east through the Aspandels."

"That is our road," Annleia insisted.

"And a dead end, until you find me one who can navigate the ruins," Torin responded curtly. "General, Commander, my blade is yours."

He felt Allion peering at him, seeming suddenly uncertain. When he looked over, however, and their eyes met, the hunter's mouth snapped shut and his expression became petulant.

"A pet dragon might prove more useful," Rogun said. "Lost yours, did you?"

"And angered its sire. Trust me, General, you have no wish to meet Him."

Rogun raised an eyebrow, more amused than curious. Torin expected Annleia to say something, but the elf-woman had gone cold with silence. Instead, it was Troy who replied, "Trust, in these times, is a precious commodity."

It was the same as with Allion, he realized. They were not certain they *wanted* his help. They were not sure they could rely on it. And why should they? Up until now, he had failed everyone's expectations, including his own. Well, the time had come to put to rest the doubts that had haunted him throughout his life. If his existence was to signify anything, he would have to define it now.

"That I might do more harm than good, is this what you fear?" he asked. "With respect, Commander, seems your forces are already on the verge of defeat. Trade me weapons, if you must. Arm me with seed cones. But do not ask me to watch from afar when I might do much to help stem this tide."

Allion scoffed, clearly unimpressed. Both Rogun and Troy regarded him bluntly. Annleia was the first to speak.

"You swore an oath. You cannot forsake our task."

"Then find us a guide, Annleia, as Ravar said we would. Until then, I'll not sit idle, waiting for the stars to align."

Her lips tightened, and the intensity in her eyes nearly caused him to retract the words. But he set his jaw and gripped the Sword's hilt, refusing to do so. When it appeared she might say something more, she turned instead and strode from the tent. Crag followed, leaving him with a long, pinch-eyed glare.

He must think I'm right, Torin thought, *else he would have spoken.*

Allion, strangely, looked as if he might go after them, but stood his ground.

"Are you so eager to return to the grave?" Rogun asked when the pair had gone.

"If that's what it takes."

The general's moustache twitched, the corner of his mouth turning up with just the barest hint of a smile. "In that case, you'll ride with me."

Torin wasn't sure how to respond. Slight as it seemed, it might be the most respect Rogun had ever shown him. As with Zain, he had to wonder if this acceptance was some sort of game being played at his expense. The general did so enjoy keeping others off their guard.

"Where's Corathel?" Allion asked, when it seemed Troy was not going to argue. "Seems *he* should have a say."

"The chief general is in the field," Troy answered. "Those siege rovers our Hrothgari spoke of finally arrived, only to stall in the pass. Corathel has led a host north to hazard a rescue of those stranded within."

Torin frowned. He'd heard of these mysterious *rovers* from Crag during their ride from Wingport. Some sort of mining-cart-turned-siege-engine. Expected to be a powerful weapon against the Illychar, it seemed they had become a liability instead.

"We have decisions to make that cannot wait," Rogun added.

Troy grimaced. "The Thornspur," he said, turning back to the table and a mound of maps spread across its surface. "You were going to suggest . . . ?"

"Surrender it," Rogun answered flatly.

"The bluff is secure. Why would we—"

"The *bluff* may be secure, but little else is." An armored finger jabbed at the table. "We can hit them harder by tearing down Bannok's Fist."

Torin knew the name. A mighty dam near the headwaters of the Shia River as it tumbled out of the Aspandel Mountains, helping to turn that torrent on a southern course. Even *his* breath caught at the suggestion.

"But that would mean . . ." Troy began, then trailed off, peering closer at the sketches before him.

Allion stepped in for a closer look. Torin, though tempted to join them, thought it better to remain where he stood.

"Loose the river," Rogun explained. "Let it do the work we cannot."

"The Spur is our last significant toehold upon the Gaperon. Without it, we'll be forced to displace to the southern plain, and will lose ground faster than ever."

"So we fight upon the plain. The defenses are already in place. We might hold the Spur, but the lowline along Morgan's Harrow is fraying, and our anchors at Hokkum Spire and Tonner's Fang will not last the day. As those break and shear, the enemy will encircle the Thornspur like a noose."

Despite the more obvious implications, Torin could conjure only a vague sense of the precise strategy being discussed. The terrain's features were mostly foreign to him, and he'd received only the barest briefing from Crag on the coalition's defenses. And much of *those*, set in place before the Tuthari's departure south, had already been overtaken, losing all relevance.

"What about the rovers?" Troy asked, while gingerly rubbing his bruised chin. "With where they pulled up, the Shia is likely to drown them."

Rogun shrugged. "We lose what, four-, fivescore? For which Corathel means already to risk more than six hundred. Better that we crack the dam now and force him to withdraw the attempt."

"You would flood the pass?" Allion asked.

"As much of it as we can," Rogun admitted. "And buy ourselves more time with that than by clinging desperately to its mouth."

"Bannok's Fist is five hundred years old," Troy lamented. "It was one of our forebears' first great achievements."

"Might as well take it with us," Rogun remarked, unmoved. "Let the reavers build their own dam, if they wish it."

A heavy air settled over the tent. For several moments, the only sounds were those made by the attendants, scuffing and banging at Troy's armor. Beyond, the din of battle roared like the restless sea.

"There is some sense to the strategy," Troy allowed finally.

"And a good deal of need," Rogun urged. "Dither, and we'll pay a heavy price."

Alson's general had always been a man of action, Torin knew, with little tolerance for the weighing-out of possible consequences. Why guess at results when one could simply measure the truth and react accordingly? It was the man's greatest strength, at times, but carried with it the potential for disaster.

"I'll set a company of sappers in place," Troy yielded reluctantly. "But it doesn't happen without my direct command."

"And in the meantime?" Rogun asked.

"We hold the Spur, and give Corathel what time he needs."

CHAPTER FORTY-SEVEN

CORATHEL PEERED CAUTIOUSLY THROUGH THE thicket of scrub that lined the hollowed ridge. A hundred paces below, the four rovers lay in their gully at the base of the slopes, motionless drill snouts pointed outward. Forgotten, it seemed, by the sea of reavers that had choked them upon their arrival. Thousands, there had been, though all their weapons and bodies had seemed incapable of stalling the rovers' coring, methodical advance.

Yet stalled they had, backed into a corner like sentinels pressed by an angry mob. King Hreidmar had been unable to tell him why, exactly, hazarding only that they may have misjudged their fuel supplies. Whatever, without their grinders, the Hrothgari crews had found themselves bitterly pressed by the adversary they had baited for so long. Their machines shielded them, but how long could they last?

Without being asked, Corathel had taken it upon himself to reach the iron rovers, to help the dwarves inside escape the Illysp's wrath—just as they had done for him and the people of Leaven.

"Why are we waiting?" asked Jasyn, crouched beside him.

Corathel raised a finger to his lips. His own words were a coarse whisper. "Unearthly quiet, wouldn't you say?"

Jasyn shrugged. "Lar knows how to draw a foe's attention."

And was doing an admirable job of it now. Corathel had caught glimpses of the fighting across the pass, on the western slopes, while he and his own half battalion skulked northward along the upper reaches of the eastern wall. The reavers were so focused now on the trenches and bulwarks set in place on the valley floor that they hadn't noticed the hundreds crawling high around each flank, navigating a series of crevasses and ravines and washout trails. That Lar's attack had begun at the appointed spot, and at almost precisely the estimated hour, indicated that his half battalion, like Corathel's, had progressed without undue surprise or difficulty.

"So why do I feel ants crawling along my spine?" he asked.

His lieutenant looked him over. "Come to feed upon the lice nesting in your hair," Jasyn suggested. "When was the last time you bathed?"

"When did the rains end?" Corathel muttered, keeping his eyes on the rovers below.

Jasyn permitted him a moment of silence, then asked, "Would you have us wait until dark?"

Ideally, yes. But the decision had already been made to execute this maneuver as swiftly as possible. They had no guarantee that the enemy would not drift back this way in greater numbers, making the escape that much harder to spring. By nightfall, it might be too late.

Besides, Lar had already engaged—a diversionary offensive used to draw the northern strays away from the rovers' position. Though it seemed to be working almost *too* well, it was in fact working. Sitting around now might only waste that effort—especially since there was near as much danger of being spotted while waiting here as there was in slipping down below.

"We have the element of surprise," he said, denying his misgivings with cold fact. "We'd be fools to wait and see how long it lasts."

Jasyn nodded, though he, too, looked around now with a greater deal of caution than before, having learned some time ago to trust his commander's instincts.

"We'll close to that lowermost overhang," Corathel decided. Vacant as the area appeared, putting their troops on the ground, as originally planned, would only attract unnecessary attention. "Where's our envoy?"

"I'll fetch him now."

Jasyn scurried off, leaving Corathel alone beneath the ridge's curled, scrub-grown lip. The nearest fighting was hundreds of paces off, and aimed the other way. Around the rovers, not an enemy was in sight. He could not have prayed for better circumstances. And yet, his back continued to itch with invisible warning.

He looked for Owl . . . and found the elf huddled with his four remaining Mookla'ayans upon a higher ridge. Perhaps *they* were the cause of his distress—with the way they kept sniffing and glancing about. He'd not seen them do that before. It made them seem nervous.

Aside from that, he scarcely noticed them anymore. Like his own shadow, he just assumed they were there, and had yet to be disappointed.

When Jasyn returned, he did so with Ulgrenshem, one of Hreidmar's own advisors. The dwarf had an especially large knot beneath one eye, leaving only one good one with which to see. *A dwarf is beautiful in that each is unique*, Hreidmar had boasted during one of their council sessions. *You humans all look the same, with your bluff faces and smooth skin.* Perhaps so, but fine good that beauty would do if Shem, here, could not watch his own back.

"Take him down," Corathel commanded his lieutenant. "The rest of us will be right behind you."

"Not too close," Jasyn said. "They'll think us all Illychar, reeking the way you do."

"I don't imagine my kin inside smell much better," Shem grunted, missing the jape.

Jasyn drew his sword with a rasp. That gleam Corathel had come to recognize sparked within his friend's eye. Whatever blood must be spilled in this, he hoped the Second General did not go looking for it.

As the pair slipped past in a crouch, he turned attention to the southerly lines of Parthan soldiers strung along behind him. A relay of hand signals had them all moving forward once more, following him down the slope. His steps were slow, deliberate, emphasizing stealth over speed. By now, the men who trailed him were well practiced at it.

Even so, their muffled scrapings sounded like trumpets in his ears. His pulse was pounding. Something wasn't right, though it still seemed he had no choice but to press on.

By the time he reached the lowermost shelf of rock overhanging the silent rovers, Jasyn and Shem were picking their way amid the shale and scree that carpeted the gully. While Jasyn took up a watch post, the dwarf slipped up to a slatted opening in one of the steel-and-iron hulls. Corathel cast about, waiting breathlessly.

After several moments, a series of lights flashed from a knobbed protrusion near the tail of the chosen rover. One by one, the other three flashed a quick acknowledgment. Shem stumped over to Jasyn, who looked toward Corathel's position and hefted his sword in salute.

A hatch in the side of the first rover opened with a sharp squeal. Corathel winced and scanned for foes, but again saw no sign of enemy alarm. Perhaps his nerves were simply strung too tight, after all.

Other hatches opened, and Hrothgari ventured forth. Most took careful stock of their surroundings before stepping down, weapons in hand. Gradually, they began to form up beside Shem. Some were pale-faced, others sooty. Several appeared worn and cramped, while the rest greeted their comrades from the other rovers with grins and handclasps. Even at a distance, Corathel sensed their obvious relief.

When all were freed, they began filing up the broken path that Jasyn had descended to reach them—a narrow, crooked defile filled with boulder shards and other, smaller stone fragments. The loose earth crunched beneath so many heavy feet, further testing Corathel's fraying composure. While Jasyn led the way, Shem remained at the bottom, speaking with another—a female, given her smooth cheeks. Corathel wondered if she could be the warder general Hreidmar had hoped would be among them.

He was still wondering when a new rumble overcame that of the marching dwarves. Jasyn must have heard it, too, for the Second General turned his head sharply to the north. The line of Hrothgari hesitated alongside.

A moment later, Corathel's fears came to life in the form of a reaver host, hundreds, perhaps thousands strong, headed south, coming apace.

He motioned to Jasyn to hurry. The nearing enemy had not yet spotted them, but *would* as soon as it rounded the next jutting crag.

He sent signal back to his men. Archers to form up. The tail end of the retreat was going to need cover fire. As the command echoed silently and his troops shifted into position, he turned back to mark the horde's approach. Where had these ones come from? Why had they been held back?

The answer did not elude him for long. These were fresh, he realized, spying Kuurians and Parthans among them. A batch of dead from three days ago who had escaped the torch—ushered along by the elves who must have watched over them during the incubation. Condemned to die a second death, this time at the hands of their friends.

He cursed their timing. Another hour, maybe less, and his half battalion would have been safely away, sneaking south along the same trail that had brought them. They might have been able to pull this off with no worse than blisters upon their feet.

A useless lament, as the leading reavers came around the mountain's bend and caught sight of the rovers. The escaping dwarves were spotted immediately after. With a howling uproar, the enemy pursuit was on.

All of a sudden, Owl was at his side. Corathel gave signal, and the first wave of arrows was loosed. The reavers did not slow, but continued to close swiftly, jostling and trampling their own kind in their fevered haste. A second volley was loosed, followed by a third. By then, Shem and his female comrade were scrabbling up and out of the defile, aided by Jasyn, who then paused at the trail's mouth to scream at the enemy in challenge.

"General!" Corathel roared.

Jasyn spun about, then stopped again to shove a boulder into the cut. It kicked off a minor rockslide, but nothing that was going to stop their pursuers for long.

"General Corathel," Shem wheezed, "Warder General Vashen."

"We're indebted to you," Vashen greeted, glancing at Owl before gripping Corathel's hand.

"Not just yet," Corathel said, then called again for Jasyn to join them.

The Second General came scampering up with a dusty smile. "Might be a long hike back, with them on our tail."

"Take the van. I'll command the rear guard. Maintain the high ground, whatever else."

Jasyn's eyes turned, venturing up the slope.

"General, your orders."

"Here come your ants," Jasyn said.

Corathel spun, and his stomach lurched. Not ants, but giants, pouring down from the heights—just as they had against Troy days ago. How creatures so large and numerous had hidden themselves upon ground that his companies had marched right over might forever remain a mystery. But there was no great riddle as to why. The enemy had known they would be coming, or, at the very least, that the stranded dwarves would eventually attempt to emerge. With no return now to the safety of the rovers, the trap had been sprung.

"Wedges!" he roared. Already, his officers had seen the new threat, and were bracing to meet it. Corathel glanced back at the reavers clawing up from below, realizing reflexively that it was not merely ill luck, but Illychar cunning, that had held them in check until this very moment.

"Watch yourself, General," Jasyn bade, then scooted on up the trail. Not twenty paces ahead, he lunged to catch one of the barreling giants midleap with the spiked pauldron worn over his left shoulder. Howling, he bore the creature to the earth, as blades on both sides began to clash and sing.

Like a great worm, the battalion line began writhing its way up the slope and south along the return trail. There was no help but to fight their way past the giants as quickly as they could. If they allowed themselves to be pinned down, the horde giving chase would surely annihilate them.

"Seems you were better off below," he murmured to Vashen apologetically.

Beside him, the warder general hefted a spiked hammer. Her blue eyes seemed to sparkle. "After what we've been though, you don't know how good this is going to feel."

She hastened forward. With another glance behind him, Corathel drew his sword and gave chase, Mookla'ayan guard at his side. A giant neared. He believed he recognized it as that from which he had narrowly rescued Troy days before.

When he saw its tusked smile, he became certain of it.

THE OGRE SNARLED, A BULBOUS, growth-ridden tongue licking at its own drool. Seething with an Illysp's fury, it lumbered up the hill, hefting a bloodied club. A pack of elves filled its wake like feral-eyed scavengers, set to feast on whatever scraps were provided.

"Arrows won't slow that thing," Torin warned.

Zain ignored him, hand upraised as he sat atop his mount. When the ogre and its company closed to within a dozen paces of the barricade, the hand lowered. "Loose!"

Shafts flew in a piercing cloud. Most of the elves danced aside, fluid-quick. The ogre raised an arm to shield its face, but kept marching as arrowheads clattered off its bony hide. Perhaps a dozen managed to penetrate its arms, legs, and chest, but the brute pressed forward, heedless. As the shower ceased, it lowered its arm and thrust forth its gnarled face, unleashing a stone-rattling roar.

"Enough," Torin spat, and shoved through an angled gap between schilltrons. Sharpened tips scraped at him, but he ignored them as he did Zain's shout. The Crimson Sword flared in his hand as he scampered down the slope, gritting his teeth in answer to the ogre's challenge.

The creature chose a roundhouse swing, low to the earth as if scything wheat. Without slowing, Torin sprang sideways onto a rock and used the added height to leap the blow. The ogre's eyes met his as its head rolled from its shoulders.

As he touched down again, the elves surrounded him. In their eagerness, they pressed too close. With just a few spinning swipes, he left half a dozen of them on the slope in pieces, either dead or hissing in helpless contempt. Another pair lunged at him, but he cut one in half at the waist and the other deep across the chest. A spear then came at his back. In a single whirling motion, he swatted the shaft aside with the flat of his blade, then buried its flaming tip in the elf's stomach.

The ogre's headless body toppled. Three elves remained, but they skittered back down the slope, seeking easier prey.

Torin glared at them, chest heaving with feral ecstasy. He tasted blood on his lips, but not nearly enough to satisfy him.

"Soldier!" Zain shouted. "Return to line!"

Finding no more challengers, Torin turned back toward his unit. As he climbed, he peered down the length of the ridge along which their phalanx had been settled. Morgan's Harrow, Rogun had called it. Heavily pressed at the lower, western elevations. Yet here he stood, just below the Thornspur, a towering, broad-faced bluff serving as an unbreakable anchor upon the eastern heights.

"We should be down there, Commander," Torin growled, as he shoved his way back through the narrow opening some of his wide-eyed comrades helped clear for him in the stake line.

"We all have our assignments," Zain argued from his saddle. "And yours is not to go leaping ahead of this regiment."

"Would you have waited for that beast to tear down our entire barricade?"

"You're fortunate you weren't feathered in the back. You're hardly fitted to take an arrow."

That much was true. He'd chosen to suit up in only bits of armor: lightweight shoulder plates, vambraces to protect his arms, cuisses and greaves upon his legs, and a studded leather brigandine over his torso. Others might think him mad, but the Sword kept him safer than any heavy armor, which he knew would weigh him down and impede his motions. This cobbled array of metal plates—a stripped-down version of the Parthan style—allowed him the mobility he expected to need.

Of course, that was when he'd thought himself assigned to the thick of the battle line, not set upon some shelf. Below, Rogun and others were engaged in all manner of strikes and counters, seeking to disrupt the enemy flow. Torin should have been down there among them, leading such maneuvers, not standing here in occasional defense of one of the coalition's most secure positions.

"I might as well be carrying an arrow or two in my gut, for all the good I'm doing atop this ridge."

Zain regarded him with blunt appraisal. "It does no good to hold the outer lines if you mean to let the inner fall. The general knows what he's doing."

And I'm his king, Torin wanted to blurt. But he wasn't, of course. Not in any meaningful way. He glanced around at his fellow soldiers, Alsonians all. Most were giving him a wide berth. They were certainly wary of him, but he did not yet have their respect. And he wasn't likely to win it by usurping their command.

Alone, there was only so much he could do—ready as he was to find out.

"Have a look," Zain said, beckoning westward. Torin, the Sword still aglow in his hand, stepped near. "There, just above the second cut. If the line breaks where the general expects, we'll be the first to close upon the gash."

"If he knows where it will break, why not reinforce it now?"

"You have to grant them their small gains here and there," Zain said. "Channels their focus and helps to funnel their advances. Otherwise, they press the whole line at once, and there's no telling where it snaps."

Torin frowned. He saw the sense in the strategy. He did *not* understand why he wasn't a more direct part of it.

"We hold a position of strategic importance," Zain insisted, "in more ways than one. I need you fresh, not wasting yourself over every minor challenge."

"I'm beyond weariness," Torin boasted, hefting the Sword.

Zain smirked. "I hope so. The battle will find its way to us. Wait and see."

There was little left but to clench his jaw in frustration. If Zain had the right of it, then Torin owed it to his comrades to play his assigned part. But that wasn't how it felt. He feared that if they wanted him here, it was because they thought it an area in which he could do the least harm should he turn against them, or fail in some way. Had he not just shown them how wrong they were to shackle him so?

He left the commander astride his horse and turned back to the barricade. From far below, scores of elven Illychar were bounding up the escarpment. He was at first surprised by their thickening numbers, then recalled those who had scampered away moments ago. Evidently, his actions had captured the enemy's interest.

Zain trotted up behind him. "Perhaps you would be good enough to sheathe that beacon of yours for now," the commander suggested. "Before you manage to redirect the entire battle's flow."

Let them come, Torin thought. He hadn't considered that the Sword might prove a lure, as it had against the dragonspawn. Perhaps that was something they could use to their advantage.

Nevertheless, he sheathed the blade as asked, conceding for now that it was best not to unbalance whatever strategies were in place. He had waited this long. If necessary, he could wait a while longer.

He took up one of the surplus bows instead. The barricade was well stocked. Here, near the Thornspur, weapons and ammunition were plentiful, largely because men were scarce. A single soldier could do the work of many from such an elevated vantage, so long as his stores held out.

There wasn't much use in aiming, Torin soon discovered, for a singular elf often proved too lithe and quick. He and his comrades settled instead for maintaining a general rain through which few danced unscathed. Those who did were eventually slowed by the schilltrons, and felled at the stake line.

A Kuurian reserve unit poured down from the bluff to lend aid against the sudden press. Catapults turned upon the heights, and helped to trigger rockslides that further set the enemy back or kept them pinned. Dust and screams filled the air. Little by little, the rising flood lessened to a trickle.

Whenever the action waned, Torin would turn eye to the greater conflict raging in the valley below. There, close-quartered combatants chewed back and forth. Like the waves of any rising tide, the enemy's forays ebbed and flowed, but were deliberate in their progress. Torin's muscles soon ached, grown taut with bitter anticipation. He could not help but chafe at being restrained. Here at last was his chance to prove himself, yet how could he do so while watching from afar?

And then it happened. A series of horn blasts drew Zain's attention. "Riders!" he shouted. "Double wedge! Flank drive! On my command!"

A nervous chill bloomed in the pit of Torin's stomach. The line along Morgan's Harrow had broken, almost precisely where Zain had shown him. Illychar were ripping through, unchecked. Coalition reserves were racing up from the south to blunt the charge, but such a flow, unstanched, would spread. Enemies would sprout up among their regiments like weeds among cobblestones, weakening the entire defense until it crumbled from within.

As promised, their time had come.

Torin raced for the horse picket. The animals were barded and prepped. They seemed fresh and eager. He wondered if they were as ready to die as he.

Within moments, the cavalry line had formed. Torin reined in beside Zain, who studied him before lowering the visor on his helm and raising his sword. "We stay together," the commander's faceless voice echoed privately. His sword fell, and he shouted to all, "Charge!"

Down the ridge they thundered, into a black river of shrieking forms. A pair of elves awaited him with bladed halberds. He tried to turn his steed's head, but did so amid a fountain of blood. The beast whinnied, its dying weight crumpling beneath him and crushing at least one of its killers. Torin kicked free of the stirrups, tumbling into the depths of the press.

He hit hard, legs kicking against a startled enemy, damaged shoulder wrenching partly from its socket. His mouth filled with mud and gore. For a fleeting moment, he felt he must surely drown.

Then the Sword flared in his hand. Its fire coursed through him. He yanked his arm into place and came to his feet swinging. A tempest surrounded him, shrieking with hurricane winds. But he was the eye in the midst of that storm, a perfect center of raging calm.

He lashed out with arcs and sweeps and lunges, given over to a dreadful euphoria. It no longer amazed him. He no longer questioned his ability. Hack, duck, spin, parry, dodge, slice—an instinctual dance without wasted motion. Blades, shafts, armor, bone, limbs—none so much as slowed the Sword's slashing edge. Crimson flames spurted from the blade with every stroke, shielding the weapon against damage, stain, or blemish. They flashed so rapidly that it seemed the blade and all around it might catch permanent fire.

The same fire had already engulfed him within. He was both lost and perfectly attuned. He knew precisely where he stood. He felt every motion around him. Their charge had cut deep. Already, the enemy drive was faltering. It no longer seemed to matter. All he cared about was the unbridled surge of power rushing through him, controlling and yet obeying him. All that mattered was knowing none could withstand the divine energies he had unleashed.

The surrounding press thickened. His focus cored inward. Enemies assailed him with hate and lust and madness, yet those same emotions welled up from within. Unbidden memories fueled his feral cravings, of those who had used or manipulated or offended him in some unforgivable manner. Chief among them: Itz lar Thrakkon. He wanted to howl, recalling the helplessness he had felt while in the clutches of his Illysp self.

He was helpless no longer.

With each kill, Torin felt ever more alive. A goblin came at him, and went away shrieking. An ogre waded in from the side, only to end up grasping at the severed stumps of its legs. In their eyes, he continued to see the ghosts of former enemies. There had been others before Thrakkon. The wizard Soric, the renegade Darinor, the bandit Traver . . .

This last caused a shift in his thoughts and a wringing in his heart. All of a sudden, his focus was on those he had lost, friends and companions he had failed. Their faces flashed in his vision. Some, he had barely known. Others had meant more to him than he could fully comprehend. If only he could bring back those who had given their lives. If only he could return to those left behind.

They came and went, all but Dyanne. The Fenwa Hunter stood beside each of them. No matter where he turned, he met with another image, another memory of their time together. He might have laughed. He did not even know why he felt for her as he did. There was her stunning beauty, her confident bearing, her infectious smile . . . yet these but scratched the surface of how she made him feel, about himself and the world around him—a trove of emotions he could scarcely look at, let alone examine, given the intensity of their luster.

Whatever their source, he'd been a fool to guard them so. An oyster hoarding its pearl, he'd left it to her to pry open his unspectacular shell. She hadn't. And what might have been a treasure, if revealed, would forever now be his to choke on.

Illychar encircled him in a grinding crush. He slew one, then another, and another—hacking, hewing, dismembering in cold, remorseless fury. How hard would it have been, he wondered, to open his mouth and reveal his heart? What could that have cost him? What was he left with now that he'd been so afraid to lose?

He felt as if perched upon a precipice, and realized abruptly that he must check his emotions. He could not afford to be carried off by them as he had before. Already, he was drifting northward into the heart of the Gaperon, leaving the defensive lines behind. Part of him wanted nothing more than to continue on, scouring the earth of any who rose against him. But striking out alone had led only to defeat and capture in battles past. Not this time.

This time, he would remain with his companions. He would be their anchor, helping them to hold their lines. He would carry all—not just himself—to victory.

Behind him lay a bloody swath of mutilated corpses, swept under already by a trampling rush from all sides. Grimacing in lustful defiance, he began making his way back along that path. Coalition soldiers rallied to his side, faces awash with courage and awe.

He heard Rogun's voice. "Zain! Hold the breach! Torin, with me!"

Torin turned his head and spied the Alsonian general, still mounted atop his rearing stallion. The horse was dangerously lathered, and bleeding from a dozen wounds. A wonder it hadn't yet been killed. Grooms and stable boys back at Krynwall had claimed it an immortal hell-beast. Perhaps their superstitions were true.

He recognized, then, the source of Rogun's alarm. While the line had pinched in upon itself to defend its wound, another had opened farther west, at the anchor point of Tonner's Fang. The troops there had been flanked and surrounded upon their squat plateau by a brigade of giants, who must have made their incursion while the coalition's focus lay elsewhere. Lose the Fang, and the line here would become like a sail without a mast.

Rogun wasn't waiting, but charging ahead, shouting at his troops to clear a path while relying heavily upon his armor to deflect any blades that raked at him. Torin gave chase afoot, making his way west along the front, strafing the enemy as he went. A slick tangle of severed limbs and bloodied trunks lay strewn upon the ground—already sodden and treacherous from the previous day's rain. Upon the heights, the earth had at least had *some* opportunity to dry. Here, daylight scarcely touched a slough of mud and blood through the constant, writhing stampede. At times, it was like fighting in quicksand; at others, like dancing across a mound of wet stones. For many, a single false placement of toe or heel proved fatal.

None of that could slow Torin's pace. He leapt and slid and spun, but with a flawless balance born of his preternatural awareness. So long as he held his focus, no earthly obstacle could come between him and his goal.

Rogun, however, was already climbing the plateau, his steed's hooves digging their way up the rise. For a moment, Torin regretted the arcing path he had taken along the face of the battle line. For all the damage he had inflicted, the swarm continued its press, unabated. He might have done better to follow the general through the parting ranks of their own men, and thus reach the Fang more quickly.

He growled and sliced and continued on, refusing to bemoan another decision made. He'd already wasted half his life, it seemed, wondering vainly where a path not taken might have led.

Reaching the Fang's jutting face, he finally turned south, seeking the nearest trail to its heights. He chose a narrow, crooked track upon the eastern flank swarmed over with Illychar. Some fell back against him, dodging missiles hurled from defenders above. But those defenders, it seemed, were quickly overwhelmed, for the line of assailants soon pushed steadily up the knifing switchback. Torin went with them, carving through those that turned to confront him, reducing their weapons and bodies to scraps of raining dead-wood.

He crested the shelf to find Rogun hard-pressed. A pair of giants seemed to have him trapped near the promontory's edge. Kethra Dane, Torin realized with a sharp breath. Leader of the Illychar host he had met in the Whistlecrags before setting off for Mount Krakken. And with her, Rek Gerra, her lieutenant, who had tried at the time to rip him from his mount.

They seemed to be attempting much the same here. Dane was prodding at Rogun's steed with a metal pike, while Gerra took axe-swings at the general himself. A clutch of Kuurian foot soldiers were involved in the skirmish, helping to draw Gerra's attention, but Rogun was hollering at them to clear, to leave him and secure the ridge.

All of a sudden, the pair of giants reversed focus, with Dane making an abrupt lunge at Rogun. His horse saved him, rearing up to deflect the blow and beat against Dane's chest with bloody, ironshod hooves. Dane staggered, but Gerra took advantage of the opening with a swing that bit halfway through the stallion's corded neck. The animal found its legs, but only for a moment. With a gargled trumpeting, it foundered and crumpled, spilling its rider to the earth.

Though Torin was already racing in that direction, he knew Rogun was finished. If his horse hadn't crushed him, the weight of his armor would hold him pinned until Dane or Gerra finished the job.

Instead, the general bolted upright with a flourish. Gerra, who had turned to swat aside a pair of Kuurians, wore a look of shock as the general's sword plunged into his stomach. The giant then snarled, belting Rogun across the face so that his helmet went flying. For a moment, it seemed the general's head must have still been inside—but only until the angle changed, and a leaning Rogun pulled back, ripping his sword free.

By then, Dane had returned, to press Rogun with a jabbing charge. The general was forced to leave Gerra behind.

Torin swept in.

Rek Gerra spied his approach. Recognition flared in the Illychar's eyes. A moment's confusion gave way to eager fury. The giant bore down on him, monstrous axe descending from overhead. But Torin ripped the Sword across in a wiping motion that severed the giant's forearm. He followed that with a pair of diagonal swipes—up, down—in a blindingly swift crosscut pattern. Hip to shoulder, shoulder to hip, the cuts went all the way through. By the time Gerra looked down, his body was sliding apart in four, wedge-shaped pieces.

Torin spun to find Dane. The giantess appeared to have vanished amid the melee. Rogun was still on his feet, trading blows with a ring of enemies. He was singularly suited to the task. When enemies hacked at him, the jutting ridges of his armor redirected their strikes into reinforced grooves, where, with a twist, he would snap a weapon haft or yank it from its wielder's grasp. His face was purple with exertion and rage. Even now, he bellowed commands, trying to organize those who battled to resecure the plateau.

The Illychar at the general's back shrieked and squealed as Torin ripped into them, sweeping the bloodstained ground. Some leapt from the Fang's edges rather than face him; the rest were left wishing that they had. There weren't enough in all the world to bring him the retribution he craved, the revenge he so needed for a lifetime of prior failings.

With the north-facing promontory cleared, he spun back to where he had last seen Rogun. Kethra Dane had returned. He thought her a boulder, at first, until she uncurled herself at Rogun's back. The general was parrying strikes aimed at him by another giant downslope. He had no idea its leader was there.

"Behind you!" Torin roared.

Rogun ducked a hammer blow from his opponent and brought his sword down hard upon the outside of the creature's knee. The Illychar toppled with a wail upon the ruin of its leg. But Torin's warning went unheard, unheeded. Instead of turning to face the new threat, Rogun hefted his sword for a killing blow.

Dane skewered him through the back.

The giantess snarled triumphantly, twisting her pike's shaft. Its tip had punched clear through Rogun's torso. Her tusked grin only widened, yellow teeth gleaming with slaver, as Torin descended upon her.

She yanked on her weapon . . . but its head snagged on the front of Rogun's armor. Her grin faltered. She let go of her pike and tried to sidestep his charge, but Torin knew precisely where she would be. His first swipe relieved her of her entrails. When she bent as if to collect them, the Sword split her skull down the center.

He looked to Rogun. The general was on his knees, studying the red-painted shaft where it protruded from his stomach. When Torin approached, his gaze lifted, glimmering with amusement.

"Such fine armor," he said wistfully, blood spilling from his mouth.

Then he fell, another corpse to be trampled underfoot.

Torin scarcely paused. There were yet too many adversaries atop the Fang. When he glanced farther west, he found Hokkum Spire similarly beset. If he was to reclaim that distant anchor position, he had to finish securing this one with all haste.

To either side, the lines were splintering. He spied not one, but a pair of widening breaks. Rogun had been right. It seemed the coalition had held already as long as it could.

Yet he was still alive. The Sword still burned bright in his hands. Odds be damned, he wasn't finished.

As if in answer, there came a shuddering rumble. Somehow, Torin knew what it signified, even before he looked to the east and the heights of the

Thornspur. Soldiers were streaming south atop that towering bluff, displacing from their positions along its northern rim. A torrent of water was gushing across those abandoned grounds, unleashed from a cleft in the mountains even higher up. The command Rogun had urged from the outset had been given.

While others murmured in awe and uncertainty, Torin felt his heart sink.

Troy had just surrendered the Gaperon.

CHAPTER FORTY-EIGHT

AWE TURNED TO CHEERS AMONG the coalition forces as the Shia River came roaring down upon the heads of their enemy, channeled northward by the natural depressions of the land. The flood did what they themselves could not: force the enemy into a sudden retreat to avoid being swept away. Those spread along Morgan's Harrow were spared, save for windblown gusts of river spray. With the bulk of the Illychar retreating north or racing toward higher ground, only a thin, ragged wave now remained to press the southern entrenchments.

Frontline soldiers fell upon these with renewed vigor, seizing the sudden advantage. The Illychar, without benefit of reinforcements, fought like cornered badgers, but succumbed swiftly. Their shrieks, and those of the ones being engulfed, raised a cacophony that punctuated the river's continuing roar.

Nevertheless, the coalition's fallback had already begun. As of now, the Shia was a churning wash that gutted the land and devoured anything in its way. When it settled, however, it would do so within its ancient bed along the base of the eastern slopes. Thousands of Illychar would be killed in the torrential crush, but not all. The survivors would regroup, and come again. The dead, when hauled from the river, would rise and rejoin them. This time, the defenders would not have the heights of the Thornspur upon which to anchor their already tattered defenses. Survival depended now on banding together south of the pass, behind the trenches and bulwarks set farther south upon the broken plain.

To remain within the Gaperon was suicide.

Torin stood his ground upon Tonner's Fang. A cold numbness crawled through his veins as he watched so much of the carnage be swept up in the Shia's wake—buried by the river's own, scouring form of butchery. Rogun's strategy had worked, but the general himself had not survived to witness it. The coalition had bought itself time, but doing so would become ever more expensive in the days and weeks to come.

At best, a hollow, fleeting victory.

At worst, the end.

A few around him were leaning on their swords, swallowing much-needed breaths as they, too, beheld the sudden, violent turn. Their inaction, along with his own, rekindled his fury. Beneath the Fang, battle still raged. He might yet make a difference. If not, he might still leave himself bleeding upon the field, having exhausted every ounce of his will in a final, defiant display.

He spun about with a snarl, only to find Zain riding up the Fang's slope. The commander-in-waiting faced him, then turned to where General Rogun lay among the slain. Torin hesitated as Zain dismounted and removed his helm.

"Bring the body," the commander ordered a team of his men.

The soldiers moved to obey. Torin studied them a moment longer, then started past.

"Where are you going?" Zain asked, catching hold of his arm.

Torin pointed with the Sword at a line of Illychar still digging southward, past the rise. "There are still enemies to be thrown back."

"Don't bother," Zain said. "They won't make it past the rear lines."

The commander was likely right. But that would scarcely satisfy the volatile mix of emotions still churning within.

Torin wrenched free of the other's grasp.

"They're running mad," Zain called after him. "You'll never catch them. It's over."

Sword in hand, Torin marched down the slope, Zain's final proclamation echoing ominously in his ears.

It's over.

Not yet, it wasn't.

For a time, he lost himself in the continuing slaughter. He fought for those who had been killed. He fought for those whose lives might yet be preserved. Mostly, he fought to ward off the harrowing, encroaching truth, that this struggle, like all others in his life, was futile.

But the enemy trail led him only so far. Most of the Illychar that had escaped and might have circumnavigated the river's rush chose not to pursue the retreating forces, but to linger upon the western slopes of the Gaperon, securing and retrieving slain coils. So Torin hunted southward after those that had broken through the lines. Without burden of position or assignment, he carved his way freely, painting himself in blood and grime. As Zain had predicted, however, many were brought down before he could catch them, ringed and hacked apart by reserve units set down to defend the allied encampment. By the time dusk began to settle over the war-torn region, the coalition's withdrawal was nearly complete, and the enemies among them all but dried up.

A courier found him, and bade him to a command council. Torin nearly cut the man in half. To discuss what? Another defeat. Another round of stratagems, none of which would avail them anything more than they had won this day.

He went with the youth anyway, not knowing where else he might go. It occurred to him that he might try to find Annleia. For some reason, the thought of seeing her brought him comfort. Confronting her with his failure did not.

Soldiers saluted as he passed. Others made an effort to raise a cheer on his behalf. Torin ignored most of them, and glared sullenly at the rest. The string of cheers soon grew silent.

The command tent felt almost empty without Rogun's domineering presence. A somber Zain seemed uncomfortable in the general's stead, something Torin would not have expected. The dwarf king, Hreidmar, still lived. As did Troy, of course, who had sat out the most recent battle on account of his injuries. Third General Maltyk stood representative of the Parthan Legion's sad remnants. By this, Torin determined that Corathel and his other lieutenants, Jasyn and Lar, had not yet returned. He wondered how much time would pass before they were presumed lost.

Allion was present, as well, but chose not to favor Torin with his gaze. Nor did Torin seek it.

"You fought well today," Troy said. "By all accounts, there are many who owe you their lives."

Torin glanced at Zain, who nodded. *It's over*, Torin heard the soldier say again. Neither Maltyk nor Hreidmar offered a reaction. Allion continued to study what looked to be a diagram of the present trench configuration.

"We cannot win," Torin replied. There, he had said it. Something within seemed to tear.

Hreidmar snorted.

"No," Troy agreed bluntly. "But we can hold. A month, a week, a day. Whatever time and hope we can provide, we will."

Torin regretted already his compliance in coming here. Hope? What hope?

"His Majesty's reinforcement divisions will arrive within two days," Troy went on. "Will you still be with us?"

So *that* was why he'd been summoned. To be asked again a question he had already answered.

Only, the fire he'd felt before had gone out of him, his conviction reduced to embers and ashes. What difference had his efforts this day truly made? A stretch of earth held here and there a few moments longer. A handful of lives, perhaps, saved. What did that matter, with all set soon to be consumed?

"Our fates shall be one and the same," he remarked tonelessly. It seemed the only promise he could give.

Troy accepted it. "Commander Zain has recommended you be given General Rogun's position of command."

Allion looked up with a frown.

"Rogun's riders are much more familiar with the commander than they are with me," Torin argued. "*He* should be their new general. Make whatever other use of me you will."

Allion turned back to his defense map.

"Partha's legion stands in need," said Maltyk, speaking to Troy as if Torin himself were not present. "Especially if Corathel is delayed in his return."

Or fails to return at all, Torin thought morosely.

Either way, the air in the tent felt suddenly stifling. Nor did it seem like he truly needed to be here for a decision to be made on his behalf. "If the commanders will excuse me," he said stiffly, "I'll take a moment to wash while you debate my next assignment."

"Let me call for an attendant," Troy offered.

"I'll fare well enough on my own," Torin assured him, turning toward the exit flaps.

He acted as if nothing were amiss as he brushed past the sentries. And yet his head was spinning, his stomach roiling. The open air did little to help. As the crest of the sun dipped below the western horizon, he half trudged, half stumbled his way up a shallow rise. Upon reaching the top, he collapsed to one knee. He drew the Sword, but its warmth seemed as diffuse as the fading, dusk-choked daylight.

It's over.

He thrust the blade's point into the earth, and watched the soft glow of flames that arose. His forehead lowered until it touched the pommel in defeat.

It's over.

He did not understand the malady taking hold, but could not deny its effects. His entire body ached, wracked from within. He needed to retch, but could not seem to do so. He wanted to weep, but no tears would come. A wringing hollowness gripped him, as if some primeval force were turning him inside out.

How had this happened? He had always tried to live nobly, to conduct himself with selflessness and honor. So why did he continue to reap only failure and disappointment for himself and those around him? How had all his yearnings, all his efforts, come only to this?

His hand clenched the Sword's hilt, seeking to choke the answers from the talisman's flaming depths. But the truth lay buried, like the secret of the fires themselves. Those damned, crimson fires . . .

His knee throbbed; his shoulder ached. Buried scars welled up amid fresh wounds, until a lifetime of cuts and scrapes and bruises seemed to assail him all at once. Worse was the brewing sting of failure that came with it. Every heartache, every rejection, every setback he had ever known seemed to be pushing toward the surface with taunting, gut-wrenching force. As the pain began to overwhelm him, he gritted his teeth and fought back, clamped down against an eruption of madness.

"This is not the end," someone said.

He turned his head just enough to catch Annleia's gaze. The bubble of agony subsided as she approached, replaced by the emptiness he'd felt a moment before.

"If I may?" she asked.

He searched quickly for others. She had come alone. He wasn't sure what difference that should have made, but it struck him as faintly invigorating.

"You are wrong to lament today's defeat," she continued, stepping closer. "A courageous struggle, but meaningless."

Torin glared. For one so perceptive, how could she fail to understand? He'd left all he was upon that battlefront, all he'd ever hoped to be. For him, this had not been just another skirmish, but the culmination of his life's purpose.

"Meaningless?" he echoed, choking on the word.

"Our true objective remains to the east, whether our armies stand here, or if still within the Gaperon."

Torin looked away, shaking his head and giving her his back once more. "Another failure, Annleia. Like all that have come before. What difference does it make who is right, you or Allion? No matter how I choose to fight, the result is the same."

"Too often, failure is a choice, used by those who would evade further challenge."

Had he the strength, Torin might have laughed. "Choices? Oh, I've made plenty enough of those. And been wrong, as you say, time and again."

His decision to seek the Sword in the first place had permitted the destruction of Diln. Drawing the blade had unleashed the Illysp. Accepting Darinor's charge to find the Vandari had very nearly cost them this war before it had truly begun. Even his decision to forfeit his life for Allion's had proven to be an egregious error—the worst of all, perhaps. Thinking back, he wondered if Cianellen hadn't tried to warn him. Had she foreseen the devastation that would result? If so, he hadn't bothered to listen.

"Yet in each instance," Annleia pressed, "you made the best decision you could with what you knew at the time. Is that not so?"

He dimly recalled voicing that same argument with Allion. It sounded now like self-justification, as the hunter had claimed. "Don't try to label me innocent, Annleia. You have no idea what I've done."

"I know you to have a kind and dutiful heart. I know that you have confronted every challenge set before you, no matter the personal risk. I know that you have sacrificed—"

"Sacrifice?" he balked, no longer able to control a simmering fury.

"Not once have you—"

"Sacrifice?" he repeated, his voice becoming shrill.

"Both great and small, whatever was required."

And suddenly he was on his feet, spinning angrily, lashing out. "Your mother is dead!" he roared, brandishing the Sword at his side. "I killed her! *She* is the one who sacrificed. She offered up her life to help cover your people's retreat, and I took it!"

He stood over her, teeth clenched, his chest heaving. The Sword flared in his hand. Annleia's face was a mask of horror. Here, at last, he would have from her the loathing he deserved.

Instead, her eyes began to water, and her legs crumbled beneath her. Torin might have caught her, but reaching out would have been yet another affront. His heart fell as she sat upon the earth, legs folded awkwardly, downcast eyes peering into her lap.

She remained like that for a long moment, sobbing quietly. Her right hand reached out to grasp the wellstone cupped within her left. He had already lost the will to tell her the rest: that he had left Laressa behind in that valley, her body intact. Likely as not, Annleia could determine that for herself.

He felt his sword arm lowering. His gut churned, sickened anew. The acid silence grew thick. But what was he to say? *I'm sorry?*

"I should have told you before. I had no right . . ."

His words trailed away as she shuddered. A moment later, he thought he heard her speaking—the faintest whisper, a prayer in her Illian tongue.

"I knew," she said finally, without looking up. "Somehow, in my heart, I already knew."

He hesitated, then crouched before her, laying the Sword upon the ground.

"No," she said, swiping at her cheeks. "This, we do not share." Her gaze fell upon the Sword. "Pick that up."

"Annleia—"

"Pick it up," she commanded again, eyes fixing upon him. They seemed just now to burn with an otherworldly fire. "You have had your say. Here is mine. I will not betray my mother's gift by letting it go for naught. Nor will I allow you to use it as an excuse to give up. Would you atone for your sins? Then you will do so, by accompanying me as Ravar bade you. You will stop dwelling on the past, except to draw from it what strength you need to press forward and make things right. We will use this as further fuel to do what we must."

He could feel her resolve—immutable, radiant. Why didn't *he* have that kind of strength? Why was he so quick to wallow in misery and defeat?

There was no way to refuse her, even if he had wanted to. And, in that moment, he didn't. In that moment, with her soul-enslaving gaze and those petulant lips, she could have demanded anything of him, and he would have surrendered it heedlessly.

"We still need a guide," he managed softly.

Annleia blinked. "Crag has been working on that. His Hrothgari cousins do not know the ruins themselves, having long avoided them as unholy ground. But none could be better at bringing us to them. Once inside, we'll have to make our way as best we can."

Torin nodded. Her spell over him had broken. Even so, he felt a lingering connection that hadn't been there before, as if some tiny spider had woven a single, delicate thread between them. For the first time, he felt truly bound to her in this, no matter the cost or consequence.

He licked at his cracked lips, and came away with the taste of bloodshed. He realized again how he appeared, caked head to heel in gore and grit. It reminded him of the pretense under which he had left Troy and the others.

"I should tell the commanders," he said, eyes falling upon the Sword. He scooped it up into his palm. "I told them I would stay and fight."

"Shall I go with you?"

He shook his head. "Find Crag. See what sort of escort he can put together to defend us along the trail." He stood. Annleia held forth a hand. He looked at it, awash with guilt, then helped her to rise. "Remember Ravar's words," he added. "About those who accompany us."

Annleia nodded. "Any who join us will be forewarned." She started to turn away, then added, "Find a stream. You truly are filthy."

She said it with just a hint of playfulness, he thought, though she did not look back as she set off down the rise. Either way, Torin could only marvel anew at her unflagging charity.

He was about to sheathe the Sword when he caught sight of a disturbance amid the camp lines. A company was returning from the front—and a sizable one at that. Torin wondered what it could mean. From what he knew, all rotations from the day's conflict had been completed, battle-weary units replaced already with fresh reserves.

As they neared, however, he recognized them by their armor as Parthan, and his heart leapt.

A forward detachment made for the command tent. In the near darkness of cloud-smothered stars and sooty campfires, Torin could not tell who stood among them, save that the party consisted of both men and dwarves. He hastened down the rise, choked with anxiety, but needing to find out which of his former friends still lived.

"General!" he hailed, to those who came upon the sentries warding the tent's entrance. At a distance, he still wasn't sure, but the one who led them looked enough like Corathel to—

Torin froze as the group turned. A few looked about, still searching for the caller. Others had found him right away, including a towering pair of thin-limbed figures whose olive, tattooed skins all but blended into the surrounding night, but whose eyes shone with an animal gleam. Now that he saw them, Torin was suddenly transfixed.

"Torin," Corathel greeted grimly. "I had word of your return. I'm sorry I was unable to meet with you before . . ." He trailed off as Cwingen U'uyen stepped forward, sliding past the general and his aides and lieutenants. A trio of Powaii also came forward, to stand with their chieftain.

Torin stood slack-jawed as U'uyen clacked and chirped, his strange speech punctuated by slicing gestures.

A moment's silence followed.

"Allion tells me you know each other," Corathel offered, a forgotten voice from behind U'uyen.

"He was my guide," Torin breathed at last.

His appearance will leave no doubt. Already, he hunts for you.

In the murmur of the encampment, he imagined he heard the ocean, and that somewhere within, Ravar was mocking him.

CHAPTER FORTY-NINE

With dawn's first gray light, Torin was finally able to peer down from the mountain and catch a glimpse of what he was leaving behind. The night before, while he and his company climbed the slopes under light of stars and glowstone lanterns, the pass below had been shrouded in darkness. Now, however, he could see the river, reforging its path along that ancient bed. To the west of that, the Illychar were a writhing swarm, busily collecting and warding the bodies that would serve to replenish their ranks. From there, looking south from the Gaperon and over a rugged stretch of stone shelf and grassy plain, he could still make out the lines and columns of the coalition's defense, settled uneasily behind a twig nest of trenches and bulwarks and fortified rises.

So quiet, he thought. So different from being down there, amid the carnage. From this god's-eye vantage, he could almost imagine it all to be but pieces in some child's game.

Behind him, he could feel U'uyen's gaze. Since their reunion, the Powaii chieftain had scarcely let him out of sight. Given Corathel's tale of how U'uyen and his clansmen had come upon the chief general and been defending him ever since, Torin had at first worried for his chances of swaying the Mookla'ayans to his cause. A needless concern, for it seemed *he* was the one U'uyen had truly been seeking all along.

"He was shown a vision of the chief general," Annleia had explained upon joining them, interpreting for U'uyen himself. "Corathel, he was told, would eventually lead him to you."

"But why search for me at all? How could he have known?"

"He was sent by . . . Her With Amethyst Eyes," Annleia had answered, struggling with her translation of the native's speech. "She visited him in a waking dream. In it, she showed him the fate that would befall his people should he refuse her task. He was honored to accept the charge, to be chosen among his people to help fulfill a long-standing prophecy."

A chill had crawled up Torin's spine at the telling. He'd met only one person with amethyst-colored eyes, one person whose continued involvement would account for so much—while at the same time raising new questions that, in all likelihood, no mortal could answer. That was how she lived her life. That was how she had worked from the very beginning.

Others in attendance had scowled or scoffed or called it savage gibberish. Corathel had accepted the news stoically, admitting that he would miss having the natives around, and bidding Torin see them well cared for. None but Torin himself, it seemed, were unnerved by the further implications.

"Did she tell him what his purpose was?" he had asked. "Did she give hint of *our* purpose, or the perils we must face?"

"She told him what he needed to know," was all Annleia could gather from the Powaii chieftain in response.

By then, Torin had been virtually aghast. "How easy would it have been for Corathel and me to miss one another? Did we ever have a choice? Does U'uyen? Nearly all of his original company are dead. How can he—"

"He's here," Crag had grumbled, "able and willing. The sea slug was right. Ain't much use in dwelling on it further."

Fine, Torin had thought bitterly. Forget the nagging, unanswerable questions of fate versus will that he had once thought put to rest. But, to him, stumbling across U'uyen would seem to validate all else that Ravar had told them. And if the Powaii was to be his guide . . .

"Ravar warned us that numbers would not save us," he had reminded Crag later on, when the Tuthari had introduced him to the score of Hrothgari set to join them in escort. "For one to press forward, He said, the rest must be consumed."

"You're thinking I've forgotten? You're thinking Lei had me hide that bit from them? My kind, we don't shirk a task due to foul weather or ill omen. I ain't saying we disrespect such things, only that, if there's a chore needs doing, we brave the elements to see it done."

"I don't want to hike east over a trail of fallen friends."

"And I'm saying, we don't go, might be you fail to find your way at all. Whatever the danger, I owe that lass and her mother a great favor, after what I did to them. Seems you do, too."

With a lump in his throat, Torin had wondered if the dwarf spoke only of Aefengaard's fall—of which he'd been told—or if Annleia had also shared with him the truth about Laressa. Torin didn't think she'd done so. Otherwise, the Tuthari's ire would have been much greater.

Or would it? In that moment, he'd been struck again by the inexplicable forgiveness granted him by those he'd met in Yawacor, versus that meted out so grudgingly by his closer, truer friends of Pentania. And Crag was one of the former.

"It be my decision to make," the Tuthari had gone on to say. "And these have all been given their own. They know the risks, and what's at stake. Children they ain't. Don't treat them as such."

That was where the discussion had ended. In Torin's mind, however, it had been churning ever since. For the most part, he had forced aside the many reflections on matters over which he had no control. Yet there was still the journey itself, and the dangers to be overcome. These, he had been mulling constantly throughout the night: *A spider's web does not forbid entry, but escape. For one to press forward, the rest must be consumed. The greatest danger is that which lurks unseen.*

The first clearly suggested an ambush. For this, he hadn't even needed Ravar's warning. He knew already of the goblin swarm that lay amid the Skullmars. It was from the ranks of this brood that he, as Itz lar Thrakkon, had culled the company that had flown with him across the seas. Two dozen, he had taken, from the thousands left behind. He had spoken of them already with Annleia, and she had agreed: If this was not the web Ravar referred to, then she shuddered to think what was.

The second and third warnings, however, were beyond his full understanding. If only *one* could press forward, it would have to be Annleia. None other could use the Orb to rebuild the seal. Did that mean Torin himself would have to surrender the Sword to her and send her off to finish her task alone? He wasn't sure he could abandon her like that—not while he still drew breath.

Nor had he had much success envisioning this "unseen" foe to which the third warning referred. Who could know what sort of creatures had emerged alongside the Illysp from that wasted world? Or did the threat reference the Illysp themselves? So long as they hadn't taken mortal form, what harm could those feral spirits truly inflict?

A nearby motion drew his attention. He turned, as did U'uyen, to find Annleia approaching the overlook upon which he stood.

"Did you sleep?" she asked him.

"Some." He wasn't entirely sure that was true. It seemed he'd tossed and turned upon the cold ground throughout the predawn hours in which they had finally determined to get some rest. The demons he grappled with would permit him no peace.

She stepped up to the ledge beside him, to gaze down upon the Gaperon below. "You're not thinking of going back, I hope."

He shook his head in steadfast reassurance. "Only wishing for another clue in unraveling Ravar's riddles."

"Patience," she said. "You seek to ford a river before passing through the jungle."

Torin frowned, but when he glanced at her, his frustration melted. Her eyes, directed west, were red and puffy, swollen with spent tears. As useless as *his* efforts at sleep had been, he could only imagine the torment that had marred hers.

"Should we wake the others, then?" he asked.

"We seem to be safe, at the moment. There's no telling how long that might last. Let them rest while they can."

One of the reasons they had started out last night, amid the dark, was to make sure they were well into the mountains before the Illychar had a chance to perhaps sneak up and close off the passes. Corathel's run-in with giants during his rescue of Vashen's rover crews had made them all doubly nervous. To hear the chief general tell it, only the Shia's sudden flood, which had all but wiped out the hordes of Illychar giving chase, had enabled his regiment to survive that ambush.

Torin waited for her to say something more. When she did not, he allowed his thoughts to drift. Truth be told, he'd been happy to trade the relative comforts of the encampment for the cold, barren elevations of the western Aspandels. The news of his impending departure had not been well received. Though the coalition commanders had done nothing to chide him openly, their disgruntlement was plain. Torin had grown tired of it. He did not fault them their feelings, yet fretting over them had availed him nothing. Let them keep their judgments. He had other, more critical matters to attend to.

His irritation had been strongest with Allion. Upon reentering the command tent with Corathel and U'uyen, he'd learned that his friend had already known of the elf's presence. Allion could have told him of U'uyen way back when he had first reunited with the hunter in Wingport. Or else, he certainly might have done so during the briefing with Rogun and Troy before the battle, when Annleia had admitted their need for a guide to lead them through the ruins. Perhaps sharing this news would have made no difference in Torin's decision to spurn Annleia and join the battle. U'uyen had already set forth with Corathel, after all. But it burned him to know that his friend had held his tongue, letting him think there was no other option but to risk the Sword and Annleia's quest, when he might have let either of them know that the guide they required was most certainly among them.

It had left him to wonder if there was truly anything left to salvage of their former friendship—or any of the others he had once enjoyed upon these shores.

A chilling breeze whistled over the naked ledge, tossing Annleia's hair and scraping like a razor across his own cheeks. High above, banks of clouds scudded ponderously across the sky, driven relentlessly by parent winds. Though the rising sun continued to etch out small details, a dim moon had not yet surrendered to its light.

In the same soft glow, Annleia's fluttering locks reminded him of autumn leaves, tinged orange and russet and gold. Her cheeks, so full and smooth and devoid of blemish, bore a gentle, windblown rouge. Undeniably attractive, this one, though it had never mattered enough for him to acknowledge it before. Peering at her now through the corner of his eye, he saw traces of the same exotic beauty Laressa had possessed, the blush of her elven heritage shining through.

"I should thank you," she said suddenly, feather-soft amid the morning quiet. "For telling me."

Torin winced. He wondered which she had sensed: his subtle attentions or subtler thoughts. Whichever, the crisp mountain air seemed thinner than it had a moment before. "I never should have lied to you. I should have told you from the start."

"You wished to spare me. I understand."

Was that the only reason? It seemed now like there may have been another, like some part of him hadn't wanted her to think ill of him.

"Had I known earlier," she added, "I might . . . It might have changed things."

She seemed hesitant, uncomfortable. Why should that be? *He* was the one who had done grievous wrong, and then tried to hide it from her.

She turned to examine him. "Sometimes, the truth can be too sharp to handle, and one must wait for the callus to build."

Callus? What was she really speaking of? "You are much too forgiving," he offered thickly, staring back at her.

Annleia held his gaze. Her own felt somehow imploring. "Now and again, one has to be."

Her words, as well as her lingering look, seemed almost cryptic. He might have questioned her, but knew not what sort of answer to seek. Before he could decide, his attention was drawn to a heavy stumping along the path behind them.

"Everything all right?" Crag asked.

Torin and Annleia both turned inward, brushing into each other in the process. He hadn't realized how close they really stood. Suddenly, he was aware of nothing else.

"Just considering the road to come," Annleia replied.

Crag fixed them both with that pinched, sour expression of his. "Vashen's rousing the others. Scouts are already moving. We'll see this road better once we're on it."

At that, he wheeled about, headed back toward the shallow caves in which they had slept. With the way Annleia hesitated, Torin wondered if she might have something more to say to him. Instead, she only sniffed and followed after Crag, without so much as a backward glance.

Torin lingered but a moment, then traced her steps, U'uyen and his trio of Powaii falling in alongside.

Do you mean to leave again without even saying good-bye?"

Allion froze, heart in his throat, hand deep in the leather sack in which he was arranging his meager provisions. He spoke without turning. "How did you know I was—"

"I didn't. Tevarian asked me to come and speak with you. He claims to be tired of your sulking."

Tevarian. Had the young archer been standing there, Allion would not have known whether to embrace him or throttle him.

"This," Marisha said, "I did not expect. Has Troy assigned you some new mission, then?"

"Troy does not yet know," Allion replied. He resumed his preparations, though he was no longer paying much attention to his own actions. "This is something *I* have to do."

"You mean to pursue Torin." She paused, as if giving him a chance to deny it. When he did not, she added, "May I ask why?"

He stopped his rummaging, turning at last to face her. Her hair was disheveled, her eyes dark-pooled and weary. Smears of her charges' blood coated her arms and dress.

She had never looked more beautiful.

"Because I cannot in good conscience let him run off to do this thing—and risk bringing further disaster to us all."

Marisha lifted an eyebrow in surprise. "Do you mean to aid him, or stop him?"

"Did you see him?" Allion asked. "While he was here, did you speak with him?"

"I heard word of his coming. It seemed . . . I thought I might . . ." She hesitated, then shook her head. "Our paths did not cross. Whispers now are that he left during the night, to return to where the Illysp were first unleashed."

"I swore to destroy him, Marisha. Back when we led the refugees from Atharvan, I swore to see him punished for the harm he has caused. Seeing him again . . ." He paused, seeking the right words to explain. "I can't rid my mind of the image of him atop Killangrathor. I can't convince myself that he won't turn on us again—willfully or otherwise. I mean to make sure he either succeeds or perishes."

He waited for her expression of dismay. He waited for her to castigate him for even thinking of such a betrayal, let alone admitting it aloud. Instead, she held herself emotionless, arms crossed, the sun rising at her back.

Finally, she said, "And you mean to do this alone?"

"We both know how precious every sword is here."

"Any road these days is a perilous one. A man cannot watch his own back at all times and still expect to cover ground."

Perhaps she was right. He could take it up with Troy when advising the high commander of his departure. A single scout or two, perhaps, might not be missed—not with Thelin continuing to send reserves north as needed.

"I'll go and gather my things," Marisha said.

Allion felt his jaw drop, though his heart gave another leap in its cage. "Marisha—"

"Save your breath, Allion. This is nothing to do with us. I've been a part of this misadventure almost from the beginning, and I would not miss the endgame. Knowing Torin, he'll require encouragement every step of the way. And if he should falter . . . well, we'll do what we must."

The hunter was speechless. Her conviction should not have surprised him. Ever since he'd known her, Marisha had been seeking her true purpose, hoping to affect the world in some larger way. She had thought her father might be able to show her, not realizing the man was dead before he ever found her. She had no one, now, to show her what her life might mean. If she was to find that path, she would have to forge it herself.

But that thought only stirred the painful bitterness that had overcome him before.

"What if I cannot keep pace?" he asked.

Marisha frowned. "What do you mean?"

A rising heat loosened his tongue, enabling him to abandon caution at long last. "With your life, with your destiny. When I finally falter, will you simply leave me behind?"

His chest drummed while he awaited her response. It seemed an eternity before she knelt with him, hands reaching up to cup his face. "Fate has no more control over us than we allow," she said, imprisoning his gaze. "And I'll not permit mine to take you from me."

There was nothing to do but kiss her, and so he did, feeling a passion within him swell. He could not know if she meant it. Today's vows were often the source of tomorrow's lies. But tomorrow would have to await its turn.

"How will we find him?" Marisha asked, when finally he let her break free.

"I've not lost my tracking skills entirely," Allion said. "I think I can follow a day-old trail of some twenty dwarves. Besides, we know where he's going."

"Together, then."

"Together," he agreed, and kissed her again.

CHAPTER FIFTY

Torin's party crossed the summit of the Aspandels around midmorning—at about the same time a choking cloud cover finally lost its grip on the sun. The warm rays, Torin decided, were a welcome relief, despite the sheen of sweat that covered him. A measure of added heat seemed a small price to pay for the sense of rejuvenation wrought by the sun's boundless, life-giving radiance.

Indeed, as he crossed that eastward threshold and began his descent, the wall of peaks rising at his back helped to provide a sense of leaving the unimaginable chaos of recent weeks behind. An absurd notion, when those he meant to defend were still trapped behind that wall, and the road he traveled promised challenges every bit as harrowing. But with the vast bulk of the Illychar at his back and an ocean of sun-dappled forest flooding the lower horizon, he could almost bring himself to imagine that this world might have a future after all.

His Hrothgari escort set a cruel pace through the maze of draws and defiles and switchback mountain trails. Sometimes, it seemed to Torin that they went out of their way to choose the most rugged, hazardous, and trying stretches they could find. Even so, he refused to complain. U'uyen and his clansmen loped alongside without discernible effort. Annleia, though lacking the dwarves' strength and the elves' agility, never once gave voice to any discomfort she might feel. Aches and injuries notwithstanding, Torin was the only one among them in possession of a divine talisman that helped soothe such hurts while lending vigor and endurance. With it, he was determined to carry on *at least* as well as his companions.

He believed that he could have done so even without the Sword. He'd learned as an Illychar just how resilient a human body could be. Granted, an Illychar vessel did not need breath or blood to keep it moving—two fundamental limitations of the living. But even these limits, he'd come to understand, were as much mental as physical. So he continued to push himself as Thrakkon had taught him, beyond what he might expect his body could endure, forcing it to respond.

As the hours crawled by, he discovered yet another source of strength—one he could not have predicted. He was to be Annleia's defender, but she somehow made him feel as if their roles were reversed. She kept to his side at all times, while the others in the company gave the pair of them a comfortable berth. On open ground, their escorts surrounded them in a wide, defensive circle. When forced into single file by narrow tracks and trails, the group separated to guard them fore and aft. Even U'uyen and his Powaii chose at most times to settle back and watch them from afar.

Within this halo of privacy, he could not seem to shake free of Annleia's attentions. She questioned him constantly, asking him for details about his former trek to Thrak-Symbos, as well as countless other, less significant things. She asked him about his childhood, about his life in Diln. She asked him who he had dreamed of becoming, long before events and choices had come together to shape him. She asked him about foods and melodies and merriments, wanting to know which had been his favorite, back when there had still been meaning in such simple delights.

In many ways, she reminded him of Saena, the servant of Lord Lorre who had plied him with all manner of trivialities during their ill-fated search for the overlord's daughter. Annleia's tone was not as frivolous as Saena's had been, and yet, one might never have known that she was speaking with the man who had butchered her people and condemned her own mother to a fate worse than death.

Torin himself could not forget it. Nor could he absolve himself so easily. All those horrid deeds had been perpetrated by *his* hand. Malevolent spirit or no, he'd had a choice all along, the power to overrule its command—and been too late in doing so.

It was for this reason that he made himself answer her every question, when he would have much preferred to redirect the tide. The fascination he felt for her continued to grow with every word, every smile, every unnecessary gesture of undeserved kindness. Having set aside so much of the anguish with which he had wrestled upon first meeting her, having come to terms as best he could with who and what he had left behind, he found himself wanting to know more about *her* childhood, *her* family, *her* tastes and dreams and desires. But how could he ask about any of that without dredging up the horrific truth of what he had done to destroy it?

Left alone, he might have found it easy to slide into a distemper of remorse and self-pity. But his companion would not allow it. With her earnest, congenial nature, she made sure that he was never allowed to dwell long with such thoughts. Now and then, he wondered at the cause, if perhaps there was some secret motive behind her efforts. Most of the time, he simply appreciated her comforting presence, and tried to think back on when it had first become so.

They marched until dusk, then continued on through the eastern foothills by the light of their Hrothgari lanterns. The Kalmira Forest loomed large beneath them, its fringes crawling up the slopes as if to embrace their arrival. Having had little discussion with Crag or any others that day, Torin assumed that they meant to settle upon the forest floor before stopping for the night.

Instead, their Hrothgari scouts located a broad, flat shelf overlooking the treetops, with a sheer, cliffside backing and only a single approach from below—a splintered crevasse both steep and narrow. Highly defensible, the ridge was an obvious choice once Torin saw it. Even before the sentries had been posted, he began thinking kindly of his chances for a few hours of honest sleep.

In setting camp, there was little for him to do that some pairing of Hrothgari hadn't already seen to. Cookfires, snares, camouflage—all and more were under way, it seemed, before Torin could consider them.

"A relief it is to be traveling with those adept at doing so," he commented to Vashen, looking to see where he might lend a hand. The warder general grunted and went about her business.

There were not even any pack animals to tend to. Each dwarf carried provisions enough for three, should the journey take a week. Mules would have been slow and cumbersome, and horses sore-pressed over such mountainous terrain.

"See to your rest," Crag told him, "else you'll be wishing ya had in the days ahead."

After supper, during which he listened to the team leaders discuss their plan for the morrow's trek, he found himself alone again with Annleia. Unbidden, she had taken a seat close beside him as he studied the Sword's hilt, mesmerized by the play of light cast by a nearby watch fire, coupled with the endless swirl of flames within its ruby heartstones.

"It's still a marvel to me," he admitted, "every time I hold it. That I should be allowed to touch an item of such magnificence . . . it seems . . . blasphemous."

"I find it hard to imagine the talisman in anyone else's hands."

It was the kind of statement she had been catching him off guard with all day: flattering, disarming, yet so out of place with their present circumstances that he couldn't help but question her sincerity.

"You say that because I'm the only choice you've been given."

"I'm saying that your retrieval of the Sword was certainly no accident. Even you must admit that. Besides," she added, eyes agleam, "you wear it well. A handsome blade for one of the more handsome men I've seen in my travels."

Torin scoffed to hide his embarrassment. "I fear the weapon's brilliance has blinded you. Else you haven't traveled nearly enough."

Annleia pinched his arm. "I meant that as a compliment. You should be gracious enough to accept it as such." She stood. "Sleep well, Torin."

"Peaceful dreams, Annleia."

THE NEXT MORNING, TORIN DISCOVERED quickly that something was wrong.

He had once again awakened early, though feeling better rested than at any time in recent memory. Determined to be of some use, he had set about mixing porridge over one of the resurrected cookfires. When it was warmed, he carried it over to where Annleia stirred beside Crag.

"Breakfast?" he asked her.

She glanced up, then quickly looked away. "Not for me."

Torin's smile slipped. "You'll like it. I promise."

"I'm not hungry, thank you."

"I am," Crag grunted, digging for a spoon.

Though she continued to evade him, Torin searched Annleia's expression, his own a worry of confusion. He shifted to set the kettle down before Crag. "Is there something else I can—"

But Annleia had already risen to her feet and was slipping away, eyes downcast.

"Is she feeling well?" Torin asked Crag.

"Why wouldn't she be?"

Uncertain of the dwarf's tone, Torin let the matter lie.

His concern persisted, however, as the company struck camp and made its way down from the foothills, to be swallowed up by the Kalmira Forest's thickening canopy. Instead of trekking beside him, Annleia chose to march near the front of the column. If she spoke with anyone, it was with Crag, and then only sparingly. Her sullen behavior seemed a strange departure from that exhibited throughout the previous day. Torin found himself thinking back on their prior interactions, hoping he hadn't wronged her in some new way or otherwise caused offense. If so, he could not think what it might have been.

After a time, he resolved not to worry about it. Since when had it troubled him to be left alone? In any case, his job was not to pry into her private thoughts, only to see that she remained safe.

Even in that regard, however, he soon began to feel rather useless. With all these protectors around, what did she truly need *him* for? Why did he not simply give her the Sword now and let her do as she must?

Such gnawing frustrations began to weigh heavy as the day lengthened and Annleia maintained her new distance. Perhaps it had nothing to do with him. Perhaps the forest had reminded her of her scattered people and her desire to return to them. Whatever the reason, he saw no need to disrespect her unspoken wishes, nor any right to demand an explanation.

So why did he continue to obsess over her?

From time to time, he did manage to distract himself with other reflections. Past, present, or future, none offered any solace. He could only wonder how Lorre and others were faring in their battle to contain the Illychar unleashed from Aefengaard . . . if Nevik and the northern peoples of this land had managed to set sail . . . if Troy and Corathel and the southern coalition would be able to hold long enough for him to ensure that Annleia repaired his mistake . . . if she would even be able to do so.

What had felt yesterday like a journey of fresh hope seemed now but a long, slow, painful reminder of all he had lost or allowed to be destroyed. Here he was, surrounded mostly by strangers, seeking to undo what had once seemed his greatest achievement. Even if his mission proved successful, what then? He no longer had a home. His friends and family were all dead or possessed or alienated. Even Allion, like a brother since childhood, had turned his back on him. How could anything Torin did now possibly account for all of that?

Forest shadows lengthened. Twilight descended. His troop continued on until midnight, then stopped finally beside a narrow tributary of the Emerald River. Annleia did not spare him a single word as camp was set and a quick meal consumed. Not once did Torin catch her even glancing in his direction.

Selecting an area on the opposite side of camp in which to unfurl his bedroll, Torin settled down and waited for sleep to come, doing his best to focus on more important matters.

HE AWOKE IN SOUR SPIRITS, cramped and groggy from a fitful slumber. Yesterday's rancor still festered in the pit of his stomach. The day had not yet begun, and already he was anxious for it to end.

The Hrothgari were stirring. U'uyen crouched nearby with his trio of clansmen, engaged in quiet discussion. Torin cast about for Annleia, but didn't see her. He didn't see Crag, either, so he assumed they were together, that Annleia was safe.

With a quick word to one of the sentries, he headed out of camp, north along the river stream. The forest was shadowed and cold, the underbrush slick with dew and swimming in morning mist. But Torin felt in need of a crisp bath if he was to make it through this day.

The stream's waters were even colder than he had expected, yet he gritted his teeth and immersed himself completely, scrubbing furiously at the film of dirt and sweat upon his skin. In the process, he seemed to discover half a dozen nicks and scars he hadn't known he had. His flesh seemed to be covered with them.

He emerged wet and shivering, though not nearly as refreshed as he had hoped. The Sword's warmth offered only meager comfort as he stood dripping, glaring disconsolately at his pile of soiled clothes. He wished now that he had taken the time to wash and hang them the night before.

He had only barely laced up his breeches when he heard Annleia's voice.

"Here you are," she said, hiking toward him through the foliage. Crag stumped along behind her. "You shouldn't wander off alone."

"Just heading back," he assured her, somewhat gruffly.

Annleia continued forward. It was clear that she, too, had come from bathing. Her hair was still wet, her skin pink and fresh. She marched right up to him, smelling of some kind of wildflower, and rubbed some of the clinging water from the back of his close-cropped hair.

"Next time, bring a guard," she scolded.

Torin regarded her suspiciously, reaching up to where she had touched him. He didn't know how to respond. "Is there something wrong with the back of my head?" he asked finally, recalling that she had used that same gesture before.

"I'm still not accustomed to men with hair," she admitted. "None of the elves I grew up with had any."

"I can shave it clean, if that would please you."

"Not at all," she said, with another quick rub. This time, she added a smile. "I like it the way it is. Don't you, Crag?"

The Tuthari snorted. "Dashing. Are we finished here, then?"

The pair accompanied him back to camp, where they consumed a hurried meal before resuming the journey east. Whatever malady or concerns had driven Annleia from him the previous day appeared to have passed. She was his closest companion once more, and seemed to regard him as hers. They traveled quietly much of the time, alert for any sign of enemies. The rest of the time, she peppered him with questions, as she had while they'd made their way down from the mountains. After yesterday's solitude, Torin found himself happy to answer just about anything, so long as it kept her near him and his darker thoughts at bay.

There was little he felt uncomfortable sharing with her anyway. He had already confessed to her his life's story and let her judge him for it. Having shed the terrible burden of his secret about her mother, there was nothing left to hide. He still felt awkward about prying into *her* past, but, so long as only she was listening, he regarded his own as an open scroll.

Even when she began asking him about Marisha—and later, Dyanne—he found himself speaking openly of his feelings for each. Difficult as it was at times to understand his own inconstant emotions, he described them as best he could, ever more flattered by Annleia's seeming interest. He did not believe it to be of a romantic nature, and would not have known how to react otherwise. But the mere fact that she should want to know things about him that had no discernible bearing upon their quest helped him to feel as though he *wasn't*, perhaps, the most detestable man alive.

"And it doesn't bother you?" she asked at one point, "that Allion and Marisha—your friends—developed their relationship behind your back?"

"How could it? I practically forced them together." Though it still felt strange, his only regret was not knowing sooner of the bond his friends had formed, so that he might have felt free to express his own feelings to Dyanne.

"And Dyanne . . . Would you return to her if you could? Would you tell her this time how you truly feel?"

He resisted the reflexive urge to reach for the pendant Dyanne had given him in farewell. "If she has found happiness," he said, thinking carefully, "that is enough for me."

Annleia gave him a long, searching look, but did not challenge his claim.

They forded the trunk of the Emerald River near midafternoon, to the north of where it branched east and west along its southerly course. Soon after, Annleia separated from him again. When she did not return after another hour, Torin strode forward to join her—only to find her unreceptive to his efforts at further communication. The chilly turn left him wondering again what he might have said or done to frighten her off. Or perhaps it was something he *hadn't* done. He thought to question her more directly, but with Crag and a handful of Hrothgari within earshot, he did not want to risk starting an argument over so tiny an issue.

On the other hand, they only had so many days left before reaching the coast. Should they not be taking every opportunity to discuss what needed to be done? Granted, so much of it was puzzles in the dark. But those puzzles were not going to solve themselves.

Perhaps she felt that his advice could only confuse her. Perhaps she needed this time to herself to prepare in her own way for the forthcoming challenge.

Perhaps he should forget about her and concentrate on doing the same.

A long, lonely afternoon gave way to a long, lonely evening. He should have been grateful that they hadn't yet come under attack. He should have found peace in the presence of his comrades, whose expertise spared him a great deal of guesswork on this trek. All he need do was follow along and try not to stumble upon the roots and knobs and tripping ground cover. Instead, he found himself wondering constantly what Annleia might be thinking, and why she chose to keep it from him.

His own disposition soured further when, an hour or so before midnight, the forest fell away suddenly on either side in a charred swath of trampled deadwood. Black boughs carpeted the land like battlefield leavings. Stripped and stunted boles poked forth like grave markers from an ashen earth. Across this ravaged wasteland, a chill wind blew sullen and mournful.

The trail of the dragonspawn, Torin reflected dourly. Even now, two full seasons later, the devastation wrought by that unholy brood seemed complete and inescapable, a scar from which the forest might never fully heal. Marisha's home had fallen to that scourge, and with it the kindly healers who had nursed him back from the brink of death. He had all but forgotten—parts of a past that should have haunted him forever. It all seemed now as though it had happened to someone else.

As he picked his way across that nightmare landscape, however, his eye drew here and there to the budding shoots of fresh vegetation. The more he searched, the more such signs he saw. Rotting logs were slick with new moss. Nightbirds hunted insects come to nest amid the decay. Merely the first cries, perhaps, of a world reborn, yet enough to make him wonder if, with time, success against the Illysp might allow life to replenish what he had stolen from it.

To his initial horror, Vashen decided it to be a good place to set camp. There was plenty of debris with which to erect shelters and defenses, she said, and the near-naked terrain would give them a clear view of any unwelcome approach. At this point, it seemed nothing out there was hunting them, but the warder general wasn't going to start taking unnecessary chances.

Torin did not care to explain to them that lying here would feel like lying with the ghosts of those he'd slain. So he bit his tongue and assisted his dwarven comrades in making the area more suitable. He considered approaching and working alongside Annleia, but she'd made it quite clear by now that if she wanted his company, she would seek it.

The mood around dinner was somber, the enveloping night a shroud of wary silence. Torin gnawed on a tasteless strip of dried meat, drank his helping of stew, then bid good night to those near him.

The sky was mostly cloudless, so he eschewed the lean-tos and laid his bedroll beside a downed log some distance from the group—hoping that the farther he was from Annleia, the less tempted he would be to let her rule his thoughts. With a steady pace and such long hours, they were making swift time, even through the forest. He had only two more days, perhaps three, before—

"You shouldn't sleep alone so far from the fire," Annleia said.

He turned to find her hauling her own roll of blankets up after him. While he stood there staring, she arranged her bedding next to his, then crawled within, behaving as if nothing could be more natural.

"You're not going to leave me here freezing, are you?" she asked after a moment.

Torin tried not to think too closely on what he felt in that moment. It did no good to consider it. Instead, he lay down beside her, careful not to slide too close.

Annleia shifted nearer, pressing herself up against him. "We'll be back in the mountains tomorrow," she said. "Last night we'll have of soft woodland floor."

Torin did not want to think about *that*, either. The Skullmars were not a place he had ever hoped to return to. Then again, he had not hoped for any of this.

He said nothing, and within moments was listening to the soft, rhythmic breathing of his slumbering companion. He was almost reluctant to shut his own eyes, to allow this evening to end. When finally he fell asleep, he did so wondering which side of her the morrow might bring.

HE STIRRED WITH A KISS from the morning sun, a brush of warmth that infused his soul with hopeful longing. He opened his eyes slowly, carefully, looking to where Annleia had slept beside him. She was already gone.

A shadow slipped over him, as a bank of clouds enshrouded the sun's beacon. The light had come only to tease him, it seemed, to offer a taste of its treasures before flitting away with them.

By the sound of things, he was the last to awaken this morning. He sat up and rubbed his eyes. When he looked out across the encampment, he found Annleia tending the contents of a steaming kettle.

He approached her tentatively, mulling through a list of possible greetings, seeking the most innocent. "I've slept too long," he said.

She grunted with mock disappointment. "You're actually a few moments early. I decided it was *my* turn to wake *you* with breakfast."

"I can go back."

"May as well eat, now that you're here." She offered him a smile. "Just don't blame me if it's still a little cold."

He sat down on a stump across from her, and watched her busy herself with the porridge. He seemed to have found her in favorable spirits. Suddenly, his worries to the contrary seemed unfounded and immature.

He might have lowered his guard too soon. With breakfast ended and the day's march under way, the swings in mood began. Or so he viewed them. He could not read into her heart or mind, but he knew not how else to character-ize her unpredictable and sometimes abrupt shifts in behavior. Playful, almost daring, advances would be followed by long periods in which she became inexplicably aloof. One moment, she would not stop staring at him. The next, he could have lit himself afire and scarcely garnered a glance. Altogether, he could make no sense of it.

The forest seemed to thicken with his confusion. U'uyen led them now, seeking a trail, Annleia informed the company, that he had followed before. The hour was difficult to gauge, with the sun screened so thoroughly by the woodland mesh, but Torin judged it to be early afternoon when that trail was found. A *tunnel*, really, that Kylac Kronus had carved through a near-solid wall of underbrush when last Torin had trekked this way.

The Eternal Youth treads upon another path, Ravar had said of his young friend. Torin could not help but wonder: What *had* happened to Kylac? Would he ever see his friend again? He smirked as he recalled the boy's infec-tious confidence, wishing he had some of it now—not only for his looming confrontation with the Illysp, but in dealing with Annleia. Kylac, he was quite certain, would have advised him that no matter—and no woman—was worth such a headache.

And yet, he continued to waste hours, it seemed, wrestling privately with the many reasons Annleia might have to treat him so. Any number of them might explain one set of behaviors or the other, but he could think of nothing that would account for both.

Each persisted nonetheless, alternating throughout the afternoon, as fickle as the mountain winds. She warmed to him for a time after they had emerged from the suffocating woods and onto the desolate trails of the southern Skull-mar foothills—enough so that Torin barely reflected upon the awesome maj-esty of Mount Krakken hulking to the north amid the pile of broken peaks. Later, the mountain seemed his only companion, a looming, mocking pres-ence. Though dormant, it was worse now, Torin thought, than before. For he now understood the ominous feeling that caused his stomach to tighten.

The power of the Dragon God was among them.

He did find one thing in which to take heart. The path they now traced was well to the south of the valley in which that army of goblin Illychar lay in wait. Though it was possible they had grown tired of their vigil and spread forth to join the slaughter, Torin felt it unlikely. Were the creatures unwilling or too impatient to serve the appointed role, they never would have accepted it. Since they had, they would see it done. And Torin, knowing where they hid, held reasonable hope that his company might be able to escape their notice.

The *rest* of the afternoon, and on into evening, Torin thought back glumly on the past few days, trying to recall each shift in Annleia's behavior and its potential cause. He found it to be a vexing, fruitless endeavor.

More and more, he faulted only himself. The sole reason her withdrawals troubled him, he decided, was his growing tendency to indulge too deeply in her imagined affections. Upon each lingering look, each flattering word, each unnecessary physical contact, Torin found himself wondering if there wasn't something more behind it. He assured himself otherwise. He tried to deny that her flirtations moved him at all. But whenever he caught himself smiling, he could invariably trace the cause of his momentary satisfaction to something Annleia had said or done. Given this, he found it impossible not to look at her in a new light—going so far as to think more positively of what his future might hold should he survive this quest. For all he'd lost or thrown away, was she not someone who might help him to fill the void?

A question you've no business asking, he chided himself—even before U'uyen caught him staring at Annleia as the company settled down, finally, within a pebble-strewn mountain hollow. A stream meandered nearby, thin-running and choked with silt. Torin nevertheless used it to refill his waterskin, as an excuse to escape U'uyen's knowing scrutiny.

What did it say about him, he wondered, that the question should even find purchase in his thoughts? What of his feelings for Dyanne? What of Annleia's butchered people? What of the task he'd come here to complete?

How, with all of that, could he possibly be concerned with whether or not Annleia might care for him?

Even then, as he admitted privately the truth of his disgruntlement, he found himself watching her, a moth making study of a flame. Only when she laid herself down near Crag was he able to look away, resolved to riddle himself no more this night.

When he turned, he found U'uyen's eyes beaming at him, wolflike in the darkness.

CHAPTER FIFTY-ONE

In the dead of night, the Illychar found them.

The fiends were already within the camp when the first scream woke him—knifing through the silence of his dreams. Torin lunged from his bedroll, tearing the Sword from its scabbard. Its eager, billowing warmth could not quite chase the chill that raked along his spine.

The whirring black forms seemed to be everywhere, their shrieks like daggers in his ears. A pair of Hrothgari had one trapped against a boulder—or so it appeared, until it lashed out at them, blindingly fast, impossibly strong, flaying their throats after slapping their weapons wide. Blood spattered against stone, inklike in the near darkness of moon and stars and low-burning watch fires. The goblin left its enemies choking as it moved on.

Two more dwarves rushed to meet it, and were swatted aside almost as swiftly. Then Torin was there, Sword raised, its crimson aura blazing. The creature's eyes burned with reflected light an instant before its torso was split in triangular halves.

All were awake now, in a mad scramble for their lives. Torin forced himself to draw a steadying breath, to quell his reflexive panic and attune himself to the conflict. Five—no, six—goblins remained. The northern sentries lay motionless upon their ledge, killed before they could raise the alarm. He scanned the slopes farther up, but the host he dreaded was not there.

Still, half a dozen goblins was more than enough to dispatch a score of dwarves caught unawares in the middle of their slumber. They should have been more secretive, Torin thought. They should have banked their fires and trusted to the night to hide them from prying eyes. Of course, had the goblins happened upon them anyway . . .

Already, the Illychar sought to scatter the few piles of burning brands, while the Hrothgari formed rank around them. The fires were perhaps the best weapon they had against these creatures of the dark, the only reason his company wasn't battling blind.

He pushed boldly into the center of camp, hollering in challenge. A pair of goblins closed on him from either side, their snapping, batlike maws lathered in blood. Their approach was blurred, each a whipping cloud of leathery wing and flailing limbs. Barbed claws reached for him—

And grasped at air as he stepped forward and back again, ducking one strike, leaping another. He slashed, spun, drew back to avoid a lethal swipe, then raised his blade to intercept another. Sinewy flesh parted like strands of webbing. Hooks and horns were sheared away; bones cracked and splintered.

A wash of crimson light flashed upon horrid expressions of agony and hatred as his wounded enemies retreated into the surrounding darkness.

He did not give chase, for others were already screaming down upon his position. Two, then three, then four, Torin welcomed them with a feral snarl. Better that they engage him than his friends. He thought of Annleia, but could not sense where she might be. He heard a shout, however, that sounded like Crag. If the Tuthari still lived, Torin assured himself, so, too, did Annleia.

That suspicion was confirmed when a radiant light came bursting in from behind him, into the back of one of his foes. A white fire took hold of it, sending up trailers of black smoke. The light flared again, and another goblin found itself wreathed in sudden flame. Torin cut this one down before it could flee. The first had already done so—directly into a wall of dwarves. Though it lashed out at them in a terrible frenzy, they refused to give way.

The tide had turned. As Torin slew another, the last of the four who had converged upon him surrendered the fight, spinning away with a wail and a flourish.

He turned to help the dwarves, but their foe already lay upon the ground, a hacked-up, smoking ruin. He found another—one of the earlier pair that he had wounded—surrounded by the Powaii. One of the elves was down, but U'uyen and his remaining pair of clansmen had slowed the goblin with strikes of their own. It huffed raggedly, seeking an escape from their tightening noose, swiping out now and again only to suffer another spear-prick from behind. A bear in a pit, that one, its baiting nearly finished.

He spied only a pair of survivors. Each was tearing up the slope, tracing a twister's random path across the ravaged terrain. A ray of light from Annleia's wellstone touched the trailing one, but the creature only screeched and stumbled before regaining its balance and flapping on.

Torin considered giving chase, but understood right away that he lacked the speed to catch either one of them. Nor could he know for certain what might lie in wait for him if he did.

He turned slightly as Vashen came up beside him, one side of her face a glistening red stain. "Off to warn their kin, I'll wager," she spat, as if sharing his thoughts.

Torin looked back to the Powaii. Their quarry had finally fallen. Spears rose and fell as the creature arched and flapped upon the earth, letting loose a chorus of hideous screams.

"Lookouts," Torin agreed. "Else they'd not have scattered so easily."

Annleia ran up to them, her wellstone glowing faintly. She clutched Torin's arm, her expression worried as she looked him over in search of wounds. She then glanced at Vashen. "Your face," she gasped.

Blood pulsed from the gouges in the warder general's cheek. Vashen wiped angrily at the mess. Putting her back to the fleeing goblins, she shouted, "How many are we?"

"Ten," came the answering cry, which ended in a pained grunt. Torin turned to find Brokk, Vashen's primary lieutenant, who dropped to one knee, holding an organ that had slipped from a gash in his side. "Perhaps nine," he amended, looking strangely at his find.

Vashen cursed under her breath, moving toward Brokk and the rest of her Hrothgari company. Crag took her place with Torin and Annleia at the edge of camp.

"More than half our escort," the Tuthari growled under his breath. His great axe was still in hand, though he stared disgustedly at its clean edge. "And this from but a handful of the black devils."

"If any more were in the area," Torin offered by way of solace, "they would have finished the job."

"May be," Crag allowed. "But make no mistake. What you're watching there is an alarm being sounded, back through the passes. The rest'll be en route."

Torin knew it, and swallowed thickly. So much for evading notice. Ravar's words haunted him. *A spider's web does not forbid entry, but escape.* And they had most certainly wiggled the first strand.

He looked up at U'uyen, hunched over the remains of his fallen clansman. The Hrothgari were seeing to their own. *For one to press forward, the rest must be consumed.* His stomach sickened.

"Come," Annleia bade them. "Looks like we're to be getting an early start."

Upon the slopes, a departing goblin shrieked its own, savage lament.

The sun was slow in rising that day, as if unable to draw free from the quagmire of night. By the time it crested the shattered horizon between him and the eastern coast, Torin had already grown sick of the aches—both mental and physical—that weighed upon him.

They had burned eleven bodies before setting forth from the site of the goblin ambush. Brokk had made Vashen put him down alongside the others who had been slain or mortally wounded. His own wound might not have killed him for days, but killed him it had, he'd insisted. He wouldn't be able to keep up with them while it bled and slowly festered, and the company could not afford to hold back.

"Besides," the dwarf had said while arguing with his warder general, "I'm rather sure Tegg is waiting for me."

A brother, Torin had learned later, left for dead in the first rover to have stalled, way back in the northern Gaperon. "Gave the order myself," Vashen had added morosely.

Torin had attempted a feeble apology, which only seemed to make the dwarf angrier.

"We left our hole in the earth to fight," she had snapped, "and are seeing this as a better way to do it. Just be sure you and the elf-lass do your part when the time comes."

Brokk would have been the twelfth given to the flames, except that the Powaii had not allowed *their* companion to be burned. Instead, they had retreated into a ravine to carve his body into unusable pieces, which they left to be fed upon by scavengers. All but the heart, Torin had noticed, watching their ritual with a mix of fascination and revulsion. That, they divided among themselves.

"For his journey in the afterlife," Annleia had explained. "That the strength of the departed may be bolstered by them who carry on."

She had marched at his side throughout those dismal, predawn hours, clinging to his arm and leaning close. Torin didn't know if she was trying to *lend* support or *draw* it, but regretted that he did not have more to offer. He felt guilty for having thought harshly of her before.

With the rising of the sun, however, most of the surviving members of his party seemed to regain a measure of their fighting spirit. Subdued silence gave way to happier stories about their fallen comrades. Torin only heard what Crag or Annleia would translate for him, but understood it all to be some form of ongoing eulogy. The bones and ashes were likely still warm, he marveled, and already this people had mustered the strength to press forward with unfettered determination. He only wished he could say the same.

As it had before, the road he traveled on U'uyen's naked heels merely skirted the southern Skullmar peaks, bearing them over and through what were truly just foothills. Only, these foothills were as monstrously tall, steep, and jagged as any other full-fledged mountain range Torin had trekked through. Trails were narrow; winds were sudden and strong. Pits and fissures abounded, gaping hungrily on all sides. Slow, steady, cautious of their footing and wary of enemies they now knew had been—or soon would be—alerted to their presence, Torin and his companions crawled on.

He resolved not to spend this day fretting over Annleia as he had the bulk, now, of the past week. An easy vow to make while she clung to him, or involved him in her every word. But she left him, of course, as had been her pattern of late, moving ahead or dropping behind to engage in private thoughts or discussions with other members of the party. Whenever he caught her frowning, he would assume that it was at him, though he could not say why. Either way, it seemed odd that she should exclude him from anything, or feel the need to separate herself from him when they had bound themselves to one another—or so he had thought—for the purpose of this quest.

Eventually, his resolution crumbled. Once again, he became as frustrated with her as he was by the uncertain perils that lay ahead. Such bitterness was made worse by his failure that morning to better defend the others, and by the imminent threat of attack. But it all came back to Annleia and her bizarre pattern of approach and withdrawal, leaving him increasingly determined to understand why.

At times, her whole focus seemed to be on coaxing him from his shell. Yet the moment he began to emerge, she startled and drew into hers. It had gotten to be that when she *did* converse with him, he examined carefully every thought seeking to pass through his lips, worried that something in his words or tone might cause her to sour.

It seemed to make no difference. No matter how cautiously he spoke, her moods continued to swing erratically, more often and more abruptly than before. Having puzzled over her behavior too much and for too long already, he had quite grown sick of it. Let her decide, one way or the other, if he was to be her companion or just an oaf forced upon her by circumstance. Whatever her choice, at least he would know his place, and would be able to stand in it without further confusion.

Such feelings, though largely purposeless and juvenile, made the passing hours feel like days. The treacherous winds and challenging terrain didn't help. Each time a rogue gust threatened to topple him or another member of his company from a precarious perch, Torin would mutter to himself in silent frustration. Each time a bend or rise gave view to only the next bridge or valley or defile, he would wonder if they were but traveling in hopeless circles. Half the time, he would end up looking to Annleia—near or far—as if this were all somehow her fault.

It wasn't, of course. And he had no right to be cross with her for any of it—not even for the hurt and bewilderment her capricious actions caused him.

Not after the inexcusable suffering *he* had caused *her*.

A bloody sun disappeared into the teeth of the mountains behind them. Shadows lengthened, and color and warmth drained from the world. Now and then, Torin thought he tasted the sea upon the wind, and hoped they were drawing close. He did not even want to think about the blisters upon his feet, or whether his belabored muscles would ever be allowed to mend. All he wanted was for this damnable journey to be ended, for the circle of his life's misdeeds to close.

Before midnight, they came at last to a bridge of stone Torin recognized. It wound its way through a narrow defile whose floor was slowly being devoured by a widening chasm. This was it, he thought, the final tunnel before they reached the coast. He hadn't recognized anything else, but he felt certain about this.

Sure enough, at the other end of the wind-chewed path, the horizon opened up, the moonlit sky touching down upon the silver stain of the ocean. He half expected Ravar to be waiting for him, to choose this very moment to unleash His wave of cleansing devastation. But the sea appeared empty. Evidently, the Dragon God wished for him to suffer a while longer.

It took them another hour to descend from the heights, and another after that to creep up near the site of the hole through which Torin had last entered the ruins.

The view made him blanch.

What *had* been a tiny pit—through which he and his former companions had lowered themselves one at a time to a rubble-strewn hall far below—was now a gaping cave mouth yawning downslope toward the still-distant ocean. A tumble of boulders spilled inward against the lower lip—a landslide, but expertly laid, providing a natural stair for those seeking to enter the cave's depths.

·"Hrothgari work," Vashen muttered. "Was a team of ours helped craft that exit."

Exit. Of course. It was not for intruders like himself that the opening had been widened and a ramp laid, but for those creatures trapped within to more quickly and easily reach the surface. How else would trolls and ogres or even elves have clambered free? Flown up from below by goblins?

He knew not why the truth should bother him, except that it reminded him of how poorly he had thought this through. He had envisioned scurrying down by rope as before. He had envisioned stealing silently through the ruined depths on U'uyen's heels. He understood now that this was to be nothing like last time. Though he might try otherwise, he had absolutely no idea what to expect.

U'uyen spoke.

"He asks if we are to go down now, tonight," Annleia whispered.

Torin swallowed. *For one to press forward, the rest must be consumed.*

"As I recall, it's another three hours' march to the catacombs," he said, "and that's without surprise or incident." He looked to the sky. He still had a couple of hours before midnight, but they'd been on the march now since the Vulture's Hour, well before dawn. As precious as time had become, and as badly as he wanted this to be over, it seemed foolish to proceed without at least *some* rest.

"At dawn, I'm thinking," said Vashen. She eyed him critically, trying to determine, Torin thought, if he appeared up to the challenge. "We'll sleep close—though not *too* close—and double the watch. We enter at first light."

The members of their company glanced at one another. No one raised any objections. It seemed the decision had been made.

They retreated farther up the slopes, spreading themselves amid a smattering of scrub and boulders. They divided into threes: U'uyen with his clansmen, Torin with Crag and Annleia, and the surviving Hrothgari as three separate trios. Each group was to stay tightly knit, yet apart from the others, so that if one fell under attack, the rest might still get away. No fires would be lit this night. They were to become as still and silent as the rocks themselves.

There were a few arguments this time as to which strategy made the best sense, but they were quickly put to rest. Torin himself had little feeling one way or the other. And even if he had, he would have been hesitant to trust it.

So he settled down with Crag and Annleia as Vashen wished, saying little to either, praying for *and* dreading the coming of dawn.

CHAPTER FIFTY-TWO

"Are they down there?" Marisha asked.

From their overlook near the crest of the mountain pass, Allion continued to scan the coastal valley below, squinting in the near darkness. "Hard to say. I don't see any fires."

Then again, considering the remains of the skirmish he and Marisha had come across that morning, it was altogether likely that Torin's company would elect *not* to draw such attention to themselves again.

"Would they have entered the ruins already? It seems they're long overdue for a rest."

Allion could only shake his head, uncertain. The pyres he had encountered shortly after dawn had marked the last campsite set down by Torin's company. After eighteen more hours, or near enough, he and Marisha had found no other—and Torin and his escorts had been on the move even longer than that. Surely, now that they had reached the coast, they would take what rest they could, so as to enter the ruins fresh.

On the other hand, their company had maintained a punishing pace since leaving the Gaperon. In moving so swiftly, they had done nothing to disguise their trail, making it easy for Allion and Marisha to chase along at full stride. Even so, the pair had failed to gain any real ground in their pursuit. A lead of roughly seven or eight hours had been whittled down to two, if Torin was encamped somewhere below. If he had decided to press on to the finish, his lead might be closer to four or five—long enough to have reached the catacombs, perhaps.

"Perhaps we're too late," Marisha said, as if sharing his thoughts.

Allion glanced at the dim gathering of stars overhead. How were they to know? They'd seen or heard nothing to indicate a change of any sort in the universal fabric of things. Whatever sorcery was to suck the Illychar back into their hole had either happened invisibly, or not at all.

"We won't learn the truth by sitting here," he determined finally. It would take them another hour or two just to descend to the beach below. If they were to have any hope of catching Torin before he entered the ruins, they would have to make that descent tonight, and hope for the best.

Marisha gave him a lingering look of concern.

"We did not come all this way to hesitate now," he said.

She took his hand and gave it a squeeze. He could almost feel the strength and stamina coursing through her veins. Some of that was the Pendant, he knew, though he was no longer certain as to how much came from the talisman and how much from her own iron will.

He flashed her a reassuring smile, then turned from the overlook, back toward the main path.

He took but two steps before halting in confusion. Where the mouth of the pass had been, he saw only a pinnacle of stone. He glanced about to regain his bearings. The defile they had passed through was still there, but the cut leading down to the beach had been plugged as if by a giant boulder shaped to fill the breach. What could have possibly—

Beside him, Marisha gasped. Allion turned, and forgot to breathe as he saw them. Two, four, half a dozen, their brown robes blending into the darkness.

He shifted, retreating a step, until Marisha gave him a warning tug. Daring to take his eyes off the first group, he found a second at his back. Seven, this time. Thirteen in all. Too many.

A flurry of questions came to mind, but his tongue would not respond. His instincts told him that it didn't matter. He knew without asking that he and Marisha would be permitted to travel no farther. He could tell by their rigid stance and predatory gazes.

The hunters had become the prey.

With deceptively slow movement, the newcomers formed a ring around him. He had long forgotten most of their names, but knew they shouldn't be here. He realized then that his eyes had become fixed on those of their leader. When he tried to reach for his bow, he found his muscles unresponsive. Too late to hide. Too late to flee.

He could not even voice a challenge as their circle closed, chilling eyes aglow.

TORIN WAS STILL AWAKE, STARING skyward, when Annleia sat up from her bedroll.

"Are you sleeping?" she whispered.

He had to turn to make sure she was addressing him, rather than Crag. "No," he answered.

"Will you walk with me?"

Crag, seated against a nearby boulder, shifted attentively. "Ain't ya walked enough today?"

"I need to speak with Torin," she explained. "Alone."

The Tuthari leaned forward, moonlight revealing his scowl. "Vashen said not to separate. I'm thinking she's right. Least of all you two."

"Please," she said, then looked back to Torin. "I don't think this can wait any longer."

Torin felt a nervous flutter in his stomach, exhilaration tempered by a strange sense of foreboding. He leaned up on an elbow, returning her stare for a moment. "All right."

"I don't like it, Lei," Crag grumbled.

"I don't expect you to like it," she said, rising, "only to trust me."

The Tuthari's scowl settled upon Torin as he, too, threw his blankets aside. Though he understood the dwarf's concern, Torin was much too curious to deny Annleia's request.

"Don't go far," Crag practically growled. "And don't be gone long."

"You have my word," Annleia said, then took Torin by the arm and led him away.

She drew him north and west, down toward the jagged shore. She said nothing as they walked, and Torin let her keep to her silence. He couldn't shake the eerie feeling that whatever lay behind this was not something he wished to hear.

After straying several hundred paces from their encampment, Torin glanced back, certain that Crag would not approve. Before he could say as much, Annleia began to hum—a soft, slow tune he did not recognize. Torin stopped, peering at his companion in surprise. Instead of pulling away, she turned in to him, wrapping her arms about his shoulders in a loose embrace.

For a moment, he did not know how to respond. When she began to circle, he did so with her, putting his arms about her waist. She leaned closer, and so did he, until their foreheads touched. Her hair, soft and feathery, brushed his face. Her song echoed tenderly in his ear. They swayed and turned to its melody, dancing as if alone in all the world. A warmth spread through Torin's veins as he savored every soothing sensation. Nothing mattered beyond her sweet sound, her fresh scent, the serenity of her touch. Had he the power to make a single moment last forever, he would have done so then and there.

All too soon, her voice trailed into silence. She slowed, and Torin, though reluctant to do so, relaxed his arms, allowing her to pull back a half step.

"Thank you," she breathed.

Torin, transfixed by the heartfelt intensity in her eyes, could only shake his head in wonder. "I don't understand," he said.

Annleia looked at her feet. Once again, Torin feared he had said something wrong, destroying the moment. "I'm not sure that I do, either." She took his left hand with both of hers. One held his fingers. The other lightly traced the lines on his palm. "What is it you want?" she asked, her gaze lifting.

He'd been wanting to ask her the same question. Having it turned upon him caught him off guard—as did the vulnerable, beseeching look in her eyes. Torin found himself blinking in response. *Want?* What did anyone want? Peace. Freedom from obligation and strife. A chance to bring joy to the lives of others, and perhaps even find some himself. *Someone to care for*, he thought, and who would care for him in turn. A chance to love and be loved.

But he could not bring himself to say any of that. It all seemed selfish and unimportant, undeserving of his consideration given the larger issues at stake.

"I wish I could remember," he said finally, glancing away.

Annleia seemed to sag with disappointment. "You know that I care for you," she said, and Torin's gaze flew back to her in surprise. "Your passion . . .

it's daunting at times, yet easy to admire. I see all you have achieved, and can only imagine what more you are capable of. Yet you must understand . . . my mother, and my people . . ."

Torin closed his eyes and nodded. He did not need to hear her say it.

"When this is over," she pressed, "I mean to find them—those who are left. I must do that before I can even consider what else the future might hold . . . for me . . . for us."

Torin's emotions could scarcely keep pace with her words. As she had all that week, she seemed to be opening up and withdrawing from him at the same time. "So let me join you. We'll find them together. I owe you that and more."

"I'm not sure it would do to be accompanied by . . . by—"

"He who slaughtered them."

Her look tightened, becoming somewhat stern. "By one who is lost himself. You said it already. You don't know *what* you want . . . or who."

Torin's reply lodged in his throat. Returning with her would mean returning to Yawacor. Annleia's conflicted feelings about him stemmed not only from what he had done to her people, but from the fact that he had not yet let go—not fully—of Dyanne. *If*, somehow, someway, a choice were presented, which would he make?

He stood silent for a moment, listening to the crashing of waves and wondering if this admission of hers could be the cause of her erratic behavior over the past week. He did not believe so. It simply wasn't important enough. Whatever she might or might not feel for him, whatever he might or might not feel for her, what did it matter when measured against what they had come here to do?

"Surely we could have held this discussion for tomorrow," he said, his voice husky with suspicion. "By then, it may not matter."

Annleia looked at the ground, suddenly evasive. "It's a lie, Torin."

"What is?"

"The magic to siphon the Illysp and to rebuild the seal is beyond me," she confessed, forcing herself to meet his stunned gaze. "It is beyond anything I might learn in the time allotted us."

"But . . . then why . . . ?"

"That was why Ravar insisted the Illysp must be destroyed—they and their portal. But you refused to believe it could be done, that the Sword's power could be unlocked. So He gave me this other charge, one He knew I could not complete, to compel you along the path you seemed so reluctant to follow."

Torin felt himself shaking. His hand fell upon the Sword's hilt, but drew no comfort. His thoughts were a maelstrom of disbelief.

Annleia went on. "I was to continue the lie until the last moment, when nothing would remain but need—a sense of urgency powerful enough, perhaps, to force your hand." She glanced at where his palm gripped the hilt, then pressed her gaze upon him. "But I no longer wish to deceive you. It did not seem fair that I should—"

"Fair," Torin echoed hollowly.

"Know that I believe in you, and that I will be at your side when it comes time to do what you must."

Torin scoffed at the words, cruel understanding dawning at last. All her encouragement, all her probing behavior, all her gestures of faith and support . . . a lie. What he had mistaken for signs of affection were merely a part of her ploy, an effort to help him find the confidence required to gain true command of the Sword. How could he have thought otherwise? She had forgiven him when he could not forgive himself, urging him instead to focus only on the path ahead. She had plied him constantly with affirmations he did not deserve. At long last, it all made sense.

He shook his head, bitter, angry, frightened at the truth. They had come all this way . . . allowed Brokk and the others to give their lives . . . for what? To lay it all upon his shoulders as before. To see him attempt something they already knew could not be done.

"You still don't see it," he hissed accusingly. "I'm not some kind of chosen one. You're playing games with people's lives."

"I've done as Ravar bade me."

"Ravar," he blurted in exasperation. "And why not? The creature cares so much for us, after all. Why *wouldn't* we trust His every word?"

Annleia frowned, displeased by his mockery. "I did as I felt was right. Do not ask me to bemoan my choice, as you so often do yours. I have wrestled with it long enough already."

"And what would you have *me* do, Annleia? You say you don't have the power to rebuild the seal. You're telling me now that you never did. And I'm telling *you* that the power of the Sword is beyond me. That much, I warned you from the beginning."

"Necanicum believed otherwise. So does Ravar. So do I."

Torin could have plunged a pair of daggers into his ears, so tired was he of listening to such baseless prattle. "Yet no one can tell me how," he growled. "A secret since the Dragon Wars and the time of the first Vandari. Seven thousand years, Annleia. I am no elf, no wizard, no avatar. I am nothing but a man, and at times scarcely that. How can you put this in my hands and trust that a few gentle words will enable me to overcome the impossible?"

"Because it seems your greatest adversary is your own self-doubt, and I see no cause for it. What is it you're afraid of?"

And in that moment, he knew. With her standing so close, her soulful gaze studying him as if she meant to devour him, it became clear to him just why his insides were tearing.

He swallowed and shook his head, burying the truth within. Once again, it made no difference to their struggle, and thus didn't matter. "You're telling me the world will drown if I fail," he offered instead, shaking his head at the inherent absurdity. "I should think my fears would be obvious."

"Nothing about you is obvious," Annleia huffed. "You sulk and you brood and you live inside yourself, keeping all else at arm's length. I can't decide which frightens you more: the hurt you might do others, or the hurt you might receive. Either way, you must learn to trust in the strength of those around you. You must learn to trust in your *own* strength. That you have survived what you have without doing so is a testament to your potential."

Torin looked away, up to where he sensed movement amid a cluster of broken rocks. He welcomed the distraction. "I think Crag's up there, watching us."

"I'd be shocked if he wasn't," Annleia said, without turning to check.

"We should head back."

She did not respond right away, continuing her silent scrutiny of him while he pretended not to notice. What was she searching for? he wondered. What did she expect to see in him that could possibly make a difference at this late juncture?

The same held true of *his* feelings for *her*. He considered sharing them, but wasn't entirely sure what they were right now. Neither did he think it worth her time or his to figure them out. Even if he could, what would that achieve?

"Ravar *did* claim that the answer to the Sword lies within," she offered finally. "Perhaps something down there will trigger your understanding."

"Perhaps."

"I'm still here for you," she stressed again. "Together, we'll find the answer."

More likely, we'll find ourselves Illychar, he thought, and wondered how much easier it might be to burn their bodies now.

But that obviously wasn't what she wanted to hear.

"I suppose I should thank you for telling me," he said, recalling her words to him the morning after he had confessed to Laressa's murder. "Come now, before Crag breaks his neck stumbling about in the dark."

IT WAS MIDNIGHT BEFORE CRAG'S snores filled Torin's ears, letting him know that the time had come.

He rolled over to double-check Annleia's breathing. Soft. Deep. Rhythmic. He watched her for a moment with an ache in his chest, then shoved that feeling deep and crawled from his bedroll.

He moved slowly, quietly, careful not to disturb his slumbering companions or to alert the dwarven sentries Vashen had set in place. There were three in all, one from each cluster of surviving Hrothgari. Torin had made sure to note their scattered positions upon returning with Annleia earlier, knowing even then what he had to do.

For one to press forward, the rest must be consumed. Well, the burden he had thought to avoid was his once more—and his alone. There was no longer any reason for the others to accompany him. Granted, Ravar's warnings might have pertained only to Annleia's quest and not his own. But he couldn't make himself believe that, and saw no need to let his comrades take the risk.

The more he had considered it, the more his resolve had grown. While feigning sleep, he had thought back upon Ravar's charge to Annleia, trying to determine if the Dragon God had lied outright, or merely allowed him to mislead himself with false assumptions. He was fairly certain it was the latter. Ravar had never claimed Annleia could execute the magic needed to restore the seal, only that *none other* could. He hadn't told Torin what *would* happen with the Orb, only what *had* happened in the past. Torin had simply accepted the possibility because he was so anxious to deny all others, making the actual deception as much his own as anyone else's.

Either way, he had made himself sick already with guesses over Annleia's feelings, Ravar's true intent, and more. He had even puzzled briefly over the timing of Annleia's revelation. Was she scared of entering the ruins? Had she told him the truth so as to encourage the course he was now taking? He had ended their conversation before she could explain any other reason she might have had, and had elected later on to keep the issue to himself. The best way to answer this and all other questions—indeed, to put an end to everything, one way or the other—was to accept the truth and fulfill his task.

Even though he still had no idea how he might do so.

His pace quickened as the distance between himself and the camp grew. He still crept carefully, crouched low, mindful of his footing upon the treacherous terrain. He had only the light of moon and stars to go by. He would not yet risk the glow of the Sword serving as a beacon. He had brought with him a length of rope and a skin of water, leaving all else behind. He suspected that he would not even need these. His only concern was how to navigate the maze of corridors without U'uyen to lead him, but he intended to give it his best effort. Easier that, he imagined, than solving the Sword's riddle—if it should truly end up that he needed to. Part of him held out hope that the weapon's fires would respond unbidden, unleashing themselves against whatever foul force awaited. The weapon had surprised him numerous times in the past. Perhaps it might do so again.

When he neared the now-gaping hole in the earth, he paused to collect himself. A rust-colored stain encircled the moon, casting all in a grim light. Looking back, he saw no one following. Ahead, to the west, a bloody ocean churned against the grating shore, its distant horizon as bleak and mysterious as his own. He watched the surf roll in, recede, then roll in again. The tide was rising, steady and inexorable, as if to signify the coming end.

At last he rose from his crouch and slipped down between a pair of boulders. He cast glances left and right, his neck skin crawling. *A spider's web does not forbid entry, but escape.* He hoped at least half of that was true.

He circled wide, coming around to the massive ramp of loose stones laid down against the lower rim. There, he paused again, but could see nothing of what lay within. All he heard was the wind and the sea.

After hesitating for as long as he dared, he drew the Sword and slid forward.

He had only barely set foot upon the ramp when he sensed movement to one side. He froze, the Sword's light flaring with his alarm. In its light, he saw the shadows of three figures striding forward from amid the surrounding rocks, unafraid.

U'uyen and his Mookla'ayans.

Torin lowered his blade, breathing a sigh of relief. At the same time, he wanted to throttle the Powaii chieftain, knowing full well why they were here.

For one to press forward, the rest must be consumed.

"Go back," he said.

U'uyen stared.

"Go back," Torin repeated, pointing a finger up the slope.

Neither the chieftain nor either of his kin said a word. They simply padded down amid the rocks until they stood beside Torin at the lip of the entrance. Before Torin could try again to express his desire to proceed by himself, the natives started down the ramp.

Torin shook his head. There was obviously no way to escape them at this point. And, in truth, he still needed them. As fearful as he was of the sacrifice they seemed intent on making, it might mean the death of all should he try to navigate the ruined labyrinth on his own.

Still he waited, hoping they might stop to turn around—or at least look back. He waited until he could no longer see them in that engulfing darkness.

With a deep breath and a final look at the moonlit heavens, Torin hefted the Sword and followed.

CHAPTER FIFTY-THREE

BEYOND HIS GLOBE OF CRIMSON light, the blackness remained impenetrable. Ahead and to either side, Torin could scarcely make out the shadowy forms of his Mookla'ayan guides, who paced along at the farthest edges of the Sword's glow. *Like swimming the ocean floor,* he thought, *cold and blind, not knowing what hunts us . . .*

He fought to remain alert, to keep his senses attuned to his uncertain surroundings. Even with the Sword, he found it difficult. A numbing exhaustion had set in, both physical and emotional, in the hours since he had entered the ruins. His head and heart were still reeling. Annleia cared for him. She had said as much—even if he wasn't certain he could trust the words. At the same time, she could not bear to be with him. Not before she had discovered what remained of her people. Not until the both of them took some time apart from each other to consider their true feelings.

In the meantime, it was up to him to vanquish this bane. *Close the rift between these worlds and destroy the Illysp utterly.* That had been Ravar's command to him. In His own spiteful manner, the Dragon God had even offered reassurance concerning the Sword. *Its power could consume a form even such as mine.* But how was he to unlock it? *The answer to that lies within . . . The key to the Sword is something the wielder must divine for himself.*

He had been thinking of that more than anything else. For if he failed here, whatever future he might salvage would be short-lived. Despite his anguish and confusion, despite his fear of ambush, he studied the Sword as he marched, watching the play of its inner flames and reviewing the times in which he had seen them unleashed, seeking vainly for a clue as to how he might will them forth.

The first had been against the jailor at Leaven, who had attempted to pry a heartstone from the Sword's hilt. Torin might trigger the talisman's defenses in a similar fashion, he supposed, but would likely destroy only himself in the process. After all, he and his companions had watched the unfortunate thief be consumed before their eyes—bones, dagger, and all—while they and their surroundings had gone virtually unscathed.

The presence of magic offered better hope. Spithaera's attack upon the ramparts of Morethil had shown him that the Sword would not allow itself or its wielder to be touched by preternatural assault. Torin had used that lesson to save Marisha's life—and his own—in the Demon Queen's lair. Even before that, he had used it to cut through and burn away the illusory door with which Spithaera had warded the entrance to her cave. If it could destroy one door . . .

Yet Ravar had described the portal as a rift. He was to somehow *create* a seal, not burn one away. Even if this doorway was of a magical nature, how could a weapon meant to *open* wounds be used to *close* one?

It couldn't. Not without the Sword's full power, anyway. Were the weapon's basic properties enough, Algorath would have put them to use before.

Which inevitably brought him back to the primary question: how to unleash those inner flames. A maddening cycle—particularly since he had examined these matters in his mind countless times already. But he couldn't stop. He couldn't let go. As ill suited as he was to solving this riddle, there was no one else.

His only solace came from his silent comrades, who continued to lead him bravely along his prior path. Or so he assumed. Sections of it were completely unfamiliar to him. During his first trek through this labyrinth, his small company had wasted hours traveling one way, then another, doubling back, turning around, and doubling back again. Not so this time. U'uyen had evidently memorized the most direct path to the catacombs through the city's warren of halls and corridors and interconnecting passages. More than once already, Torin had given silent thanks to the steady elf for his unerring guidance. For, as he had feared, all traces of his former steps had been scoured away by the legions of Illychar who had no doubt combed the ruins for days, even weeks, before finding their way to the surface.

In a way, the fiends had made it easier for him. In places where he and his friends had originally relied upon ropes and stairs, the Illychar had built crude ramps or even punched through walls, eliminating the need to climb and descend as often as he had before. There was a great deal more rubble and dust to wade through, but the sure-footed Mookla'ayans were doing well in finding the safest, most efficient path, allowing Torin to concentrate less on their march, and more on what lay at its end.

Now and then, however, he would come across a chamber he remembered clearly—such as the feast hall in which they had entered or the dance hall in which one of the marble staircases had crumbled beneath him. At such times, he couldn't help but marvel at the way his memories would come billowing forth like a cloud of dust. It seemed a lifetime and longer since he had last made this journey, and yet there were parts of it that might have happened only yesterday. It caused him to think of his other adventures, and the memories he had already begun to leave behind. To Dyanne and others, he wanted so badly to hold on. But would he be able to cling to their fast-fading images without similar reminder?

The question arose anew as they entered a small chapel, marked by its rotted benches, a crumbling altar, and broken statuary. Its fragmented remains, miraculously preserved, had been further smashed and splintered by the Illychar hordes, but Torin felt certain that this was the same prayer room that adjoined the royal cathedral.

He was getting close.

The thought sent a tingle up his spine, and the Sword's aura brightened. U'uyen glanced back at him, then proceeded forward.

Sure enough, their path led them through a priest's private quarters and down a long, narrow corridor that bypassed a series of empty chambers. A ruined cathedral awaited them at its end, and beyond that, a foyer, with new passages branching off in three different directions. The one U'uyen selected led down a battle-scarred hall, capped by a large archway. Torin recalled having wondered before at the damage sustained in this section. Looking again at the mangled gates that lay strewn about this opening to the royal catacombs, and thinking of the thousands upon thousands of vacant grave beds below, he suddenly had a clear picture of the truth.

Like the assault that had convinced King Thelin to abandon Souaris, Thrak-Symbos had fallen from within.

Through the arch and down the stair they went, the four of them now pressed close. An earthen floor lay at the base of the rough-hewn well. U'uyen hesitated, as if stung by the memory of the "devil's bite" that had once warded the curving hall beyond. But the removal of the Sword had eliminated that and all other magical snares set in place below to thwart would-be treasure hunters and keep the Illysp seal intact. The portal was clear.

Torin tried to take the lead, convinced that he knew the way from this point on, but U'uyen and the others held him back. All three elves tightened their grip upon the hafts of their weapons, giving Torin pause. U'uyen's eyes seemed to gleam with solemn warning.

Then they were through and into the cavernous, dome-shaped crypt serving as the entrance hall to the catacombs. Here, a central slab lay covered with rags, with earthen debris piled at its base. Toppled suits of armor kept watch from the encircling walls, alongside the skeletal remains of past adventurers too far gone to be raised as Illychar. Torin glanced at the floor to his left and found the shattered pieces of an ancient iron blade that had once masqueraded as the Sword of Asahiel. A cruel illusion—and not the last his life had offered.

A number of tunnels led from the crypt, branching off into an almost limitless web of intersecting grave-rings and burial chambers. Fortunately, they did not have far to travel before reaching the shallow alcove that Torin had believed to be an ornamental inlay, but that had actually covered an access tunnel to an even deeper level of the complex. The portal had been widened considerably. By the looks of it, an ogre might be able to pass through while barely stooping its ugly head.

One of the Powaii sniffed and said something to U'uyen. The chieftain's reply was short and quick. All three looked at Torin before entering the sloped passageway, delving deeper into the darkness.

The lower burial corridor stretched away to either side. They turned left, ignoring the empty niches that had once served as deathbeds, and soon passing the first of many large, wormlike holes in the rock walls. Torin wondered what had become of the pack of serpentine lizards that had previously infested these tunnels. Basilisks, Annleia had called them, upon hearing that portion of his tale. Most likely, the emerging Illychar had slaughtered them, else chased them all away.

Even so, he held the Sword tighter, his flesh clammy as he ventured past ring after ring of grave-lined passages and through one central crypt after another. On this occasion, there was no telltale light to illuminate the one he needed. The blue-glowing slab of granite that had blockaded the antechamber in which the Sword and seal had rested had been dispelled. Still, he knew the crypt before he came upon it—knew it by the chill in his blood, the rank smell in the air. He saw its gaping maw just ahead now, and felt it beckoning to him as if in challenge.

His Powaii warders slowed, but did not halt. They could feel it, too. Like him, they were wary, but understood the senselessness in hesitating now.

They crossed the threshold, leaving the corridor behind. The cavern opened up around them. Torin could no longer see the walls, only the insistent blackness that enveloped the Sword's aura of light. He willed it outward, straining to see more. The Sword responded. A mound of rubble filled the floor, broken from the ceiling during Kylac's fight with the basilisk. Buried emotions were stirred. He remembered his fear, his fury, as he had battled beside the warrior youth, thinking it to be his last act upon this earth. He saw again the struggle as it had played out: Kylac's whirring blades, the creature's whiplike movements, the blasts of lightning launched from its mouth. As real now as it had been then. And yet, something felt out of place . . .

U'uyen circled left, and Torin followed. His stomach clenched when he saw it: the vacant doorway to the crypt's antechamber. In the darkness beyond lay the shattered Illysp seal. One way or the other, his journey was set soon to end.

He continued forward bravely, defiantly, feet crunching upon the scattered bits of debris at his feet, while his senses continued to scream in unheeded warning.

The final doorway loomed nearer, grew larger, a demon's throat opening wide. Instead of entering, U'uyen stepped past, and took a defensive stance against possible pursuit. Torin glanced back into the main chamber, but sensed nothing.

He waited for the others, but they joined their chieftain in blocking off the doorway. Torin frowned, yet decided at last to have a look within.

The chamber of the Sword was much as he remembered it. Smaller than the parent crypt, yet spacious enough that he could only scarcely see the walls, still riddled with basilisk holes. He remembered how the beasts had fled when the seal had been destroyed—the foul gust that had chased them away and simultaneously signaled the Illysp rebirth. Shivering at the recollection, he looked to the center of the room, to the pit that now lay where an altar had stood—crowned by the Dragon Orb and the Sword of Asahiel. This pit, like so many others, had been gashed wide, and a pile of stones stacked against its inner lip. A ramp by which the denizens of a prior age had climbed into man's own.

For him, a descent into the Abyss.

He took his first step toward the gaping floor-cleft when he heard the scraping, skittering, of metal against stone. His heart spiked with recognition, then froze with fear. He looked to the holes in the surrounding walls, but the sound did not come from there. It came from farther out—the crypt itself.

He scampered toward the doorway blocked by his Powaii comrades. The rasping had grown louder, echoing from every niche and corner. He suddenly realized what was missing from the scene of his prior battle.

The carcass of the slain basilisk.

U'uyen nudged him with an elbow, a clear indication to go back. Torin ignored it, gazing with cold dread at the first of the basilisks that emerged writhing from their holes. They did not approach right away, but rather waited for others to appear. The chamber was quickly flooded with them, hissing and snarling, silver skins reflecting the Sword's bloody light.

Torin recognized the dragonoid intelligence in their eyes—along with the madness that now gripped them. Illychar. By their patient positioning, he could see that they were sniffing for additional intruders, as well as sealing off any escape for those already pinned.

U'uyen pressed a hand against his chest, shoving him back toward the antechamber, more insistent than before. Torin understood what was being asked of him, but knew as well that three Powaii could not possibly repel this swarm of creatures for long.

"You need me," he said.

A scintillating energy blast rocked the chiseled doorframe in response. Rock fragments rained down upon his head. The forward basilisks came in a frenzied rush. Torin acted almost without thought, hacking into the stone above, bringing it down in chunks. Thankfully, the elves understood his intent, and backed away from the sudden shower, into the antechamber. More lightning struck the growing mound and the wall around it, but that only further weakened the wall and ceiling, causing it to crumble faster.

He, too, had to back up, as blocks and boulders tumbled. Grit filled his mouth and clawed at his eyes. A stone bit his ankle, which flared with pain. He slipped and staggered and would have fallen backward directly into the room's pit, except that U'uyen caught his arm and held him aloft.

While he perched there, suspended, the Powaii chieftain peered into his eyes and pointed down into the opening. Torin glanced at it, then looked back to the barrier he had just helped to create. Little more than a curtain, probably, to creatures accustomed to coring through solid rock. Already, he could hear them on the other side, scrabbling to get through.

One came shooting forward, then, through the existing hole to one side of the door. U'uyen's kin were on it as its head poked free, spears digging into its brain. The creature howled and thrashed, but their hatchet knives slit its throat, leaving it to gargle on its own screams.

Another basilisk immediately fought to wrestle its way in, but the body of the first blocked its way. Already, the Powaii were working to pile rocks to further impede its efforts.

U'uyen chirped, pointing again at the pit over which Torin hung.

"You cannot stall them for long," Torin tried to explain. He shook the Sword in his free hand. "We'll fight them off together."

One moment, the elf's touch was leathery, his hold firm. The next, he let go.

And Torin fell.

He arrested himself quickly enough upon the bed of rocks piled up within the pit, though his body cried out with fresh pains as it rolled over the jagged edges. His first thought as he gathered himself was to charge right back up to the aid of his friends. As he got to his hands and knees, however, he was already thinking that perhaps U'uyen was right. Even if he stayed to fight, he and his companions might be overrun. *For one to press forward, the rest must be consumed.* And he had to press forward, like it or not. He hadn't come to do battle with the rift's guardians, but to close the rift itself.

Nevertheless, he did climb high enough to peer over the pit's rim for another look. As his head poked free, he could hear the basilisks outside snapping and snarling at one another, lashing out in their frustration. The dam of loose rock rattled and shifted as they dug at its far side. A lightning blast broke through, followed swiftly by a twisting maw. A Mookla'ayan spear found and pierced its throat, seeking to make its body just another block in the makeshift wall.

U'uyen turned to scowl down upon him, even as the creature squirmed on the tip of his spear. Torin accepted then that he was causing more danger to his friends in delaying than in forging ahead. He glared right back at the elf, then spun about, peering into the well at his feet. Clenching his jaw in anger and defiance, he started down, to challenge whatever hell awaited.

CHAPTER FIFTY-FOUR

Torin tread cautiously at first, mindful of his step upon the tower of loose stones. The echoes of conflict from above, however, spurred his pace, until he was slipping and grinding his way down the crude stairway, focused only on reaching the bottom. His growing momentum soon carried him into a tumbling, headlong roll, full of grating pains that punished him for his recklessness.

He came to a skidding halt, battered and dizzy within an ocean of swirling blackness. He closed his eyes for a moment and gripped the Sword tightly, calling upon its soothing power. The pains quieted, and the world around him steadied.

He rolled himself to one side and climbed gingerly to his knees, coughing on the dust he had stirred. Blood streamed from a gash in his head, but he had no time to be concerned with minor wounds. In the halo of the Sword's light, he saw the base of the rampway behind him. In all other directions . . . nothing. The darkness appeared boundless, save for the scabrous floor at his feet. Which way was he to turn?

He decided to follow the angle of the ramp and hope for the best. Gritting his teeth against the pain of injuries to hip, knees, and ankle, he forced himself to stand and begin hobbling in that direction. It hurt to breathe, so he did so sparingly. His stern gaze knifed forward, seeking to cut through the black folds that smothered the path ahead.

Now and then he looked around, skin crawling with the eyes of invisible enemies. *The greatest danger is that which lurks unseen.* He listened for sounds of approach, but the only movements he heard were his own—along with the faint shrieks of the basilisks above. Was it merely Ravar's warning that had him on edge?

Then he sensed it: a quaking in the floor, like the rumble of a distant landslide. Only, there was a rhythm to this vibration, an undeniable ebb and flow, tidelike in its churn. He stopped for a moment, then veered to his right, toward what felt like the source. As the disturbance in the earth grew stronger, he hastened his pace.

But the natural cavern seemed without end. He began counting paces, in case he should find cause and opportunity to retrace his steps. One hundred, two hundred, three. Still, the den to which the Illysp had once been banished stretched away on all sides, a seemingly infinite void.

Voices in his mind whispered at him to turn back, telling him that he was moving in the wrong direction. And indeed, he no longer felt certain that he was tracking the soundless quake at his feet. He was lost, with nowhere else to turn.

He paused, doing his best to shut the voices out and to reattune himself to the only marker he had. With more desperation than confidence, he forged ahead.

Just a few steps later, he came at last to one of the cavern's walls. A dead end, it seemed, but at least it gave him another anchor for his bearings. Over-riding the nagging voices of despair, he turned left this time, following the wall's jagged course, still in search of the unknown vibration.

He came across a gaping cleft in the cavern wall—an open-air portal framed with massive blocks of exotic craftsmanship. The doorway itself was immense, stretching skyward beyond his red-tinted vision. But Torin knew what he had found. He recalled Darinor's explanation of how the ancient Finlorians had brought about the rift to begin with. It had been an attempt to reach into the afterlife, to touch the realm of the departed, the divine. For such an effort, a temple would have been erected, or something akin to one. Amid the desolation of this underground desert, this doorframe alone had the feel of a palace.

And the vibration he felt was flowing from within.

He hurried inside, all but heedless of the inherent peril. Let his foes spring what traps they would. He would carve his way through, one by one.

The corridor he marched down was lined with columns and statues. He did not take time to study them, only to make sure that none posed or hid any threat. Inner doubts continued to scratch at him, but he blew them aside with an air of focused determination.

The cavernous gullet stretched on. It was considerably colder here, the darkness so thick he could almost feel it against his skin. He no longer needed to follow the vibration. He could smell his goal, marked by the same rank fetor that had escaped the pit above when he had first drawn the Sword. *The stink of their world*, he thought, recalling the unforgettable glimpse Ravar had shown him.

Frustrated by the endless length of the tunneling corridor, he broke into a trot. He found himself wincing, but otherwise ignored his body's stabbing protests. Before long, he perceived a dim light flashing ahead. The colonnaded gallery was at last coming to a close, abutting an inner portico whose face was punctured by a single, diamond-shaped doorway.

The gentle quaking—as well as the faint light flashes—lay somewhere beyond.

He climbed the portico steps with a pair of leaping strides, then slowed before entering the doorway—just enough to tighten his grip on the Sword. With a deep breath, he plunged inside.

He hadn't imagined hell's heart could be so beautiful.

It sloped down before him in a series of terraced risers, a subterranean amphitheater smaller than he would have imagined, given the immensity of the temple that held it—yet undeniably magnificent in its artistry. Fluted pillars, twining arches, bas-reliefs of stunning scope and intricate detail, gave the chamber a soft, exquisite, Olirian feel. Gems studding the walls and sconces, the suspended cressets, and the domed ceiling, twinkled like stars, reflecting a dim, pulsing radiance.

Though, when he looked to the source of that radiance, his soul shivered with the horrid truth.

It lay upon the floor of the crescent-moon arena, reclined against a marvelously sculpted backdrop. Diamond-shaped, like the doorway behind him, its edges formed by a low stone wall. A well that reminded him of the pool in Spithaera's lair. Only, he saw not water in this pool, but a vortex of inky clouds, lit by flashes of thunderless lightning. With each rhythmic pulse, the pool's glow filled the chamber—

And Torin's heart with dread.

By the fear it fostered in him, he knew that this was it: the portal he sought, the rift between his world and that of the Illysp. Born of mortal vanity, it had bred only punishment and madness. That much hadn't been his doing, but he felt as though it was. It reminded him of all the mistakes he had made in his own life, all the suffering he had caused. Every selfish thought. Every fell deed. He didn't know why, or how it could be, yet understood instinctively that his own sins and failings were a part of the force spilling through the fabric of that unnatural fissure.

He swallowed thickly, then started down the aisle stair before him. Mesmerized, horrified, he placed one foot before the other, forcing himself to look now and then from side to side in search of enemies. The Illychar were too cunning to abandon their portal into this world completely. Seeing it there, unguarded . . . it didn't feel right. Despite his revulsion, he felt drawn to that rift in a way he couldn't describe: an almost insatiable need to explore its depths. The army of goblins, the basilisks . . . their numbers might have filled the arena, and it would not have seemed enough to ward such a rare and divine treasure.

Before he knew it, he stood upon the amphitheater floor, just below the portal's angled rim. Though he peered inside, he could see nothing beyond its smoky curtain. He felt its light upon his face, sensed its vibrations in the earth. The deepest blackness he had ever known, punctuated by those forked flashes—each of which seemed to claw at his heart and mind, bidding him to shed his mortal coil and become one with the primordial.

A loathing overcame him, a sudden need to destroy this construct, himself, everything. It was no longer about saving his world or his friends. Worms . . . gnats . . . *Less*, Ravar had said, and the Dragon God had been right.

His lip curled back in a snarl. Muscles flexed as he climbed onto the pool's rim and tightened both hands about the Sword. He raised the talisman overhead, tip pointed down. The same stance with which he had killed Laressa. He laughed madly at the recollection, then drove the blade down with all his might, into the soundless fury of that churning cauldron.

A blinding explosion rocked the cavern and sent Torin hurtling backward.

Disoriented, waking as if from a daydream, he sat up to see what had become of the rift. His blade had struck nothing tangible, yet the portal's stormy surface had erupted. The black clouds were roiling faster, and the lightning pulsed now at a frenetic pace. The arena, dimly illuminated before, was filled with such brightness that Torin could scarcely make out the edges of the rift's containment wall. Reflexively, he lifted an arm to shade his eyes, hoping that the Sword's power would shield him from the portal's violent throes.

As the moments passed, however, the lancing light did not diminish, but continued to intensify, each pulse seeming stronger than the last. A shrill, inaudible whistle pierced Torin's mind, and a horrifying realization began to suck the breath from his lungs.

He hadn't *destroyed* the rift.

He had enlarged it.

He looked to the Sword as if it had betrayed him. He remembered this sensation, this sinking feeling of dread. It reminded him of his final confrontation with Darinor, in which he'd learned that he'd been tricked into completing a critical task for the Illysp. It was that same, sickening realization that in everything he had been told, in all he had been led to believe, he had been deceived.

Lies, the inner voices shrieked.

Ravar. It had to be. *Close the rift between these worlds and destroy the Illysp utterly.* And Torin, pawn that he was, had set forth with blind trust to do the creature's bidding.

Lies.

He fought to shut the voices out, but they would not be silenced. A reflection of the portal's raging surface, his mind became a tempest, in which cruel possibility spawned terrifying certainty. It all seemed so clear to him now; how had he missed it before? His final quest to eradicate this plague was but a fiendish scheme to destroy what little barrier had remained between the two worlds. Only Ravar and His fellow gods knew what Torin's foolishness had unleashed.

Lies.

And who had led him to the Dragon God, but Annleia? His stomach knotted. Had she truly been a part of it? The whistle grew louder, faster, more shrill. Of course she had. Hers was the guise that had won his trust, charming him with kindness and beauty and talk of Finlorian magic. He couldn't know what had prompted her actions—revenge, perhaps—but the deceit had begun with her.

Lies.

He thought of their dance on the beach above. He recalled her exotic song, her moonlit face . . . and hated himself for becoming enamored with her. How could he have been so foolish? How could he have trusted her, a stranger, so easily? So many times, he had stared directly into her eyes, and rather than recognize the truth . . .

A vision of her gaze steadied the spinning in his head. Those emerald orbs, that petulant smile—for him, a haven, a sanctuary of compassion in a dark and callous world. Rarely in the course of his life had he beheld such strength of innocence. As pure as a dawn's first rays, Annleia had become an embodiment of love, of hope, of divine splendor—all the sacred virtues that had been chased from this vile world. Despite his confusion, despite being lashed by so many harrowing doubts, Torin would carry at least one conviction to his grave.

Annleia was no servant of the Illysp.

He shut his eyes, focusing on that simple truth. For a moment, the maddening whistle quieted, losing its grip upon his mind.

But he could see the portal's violent radiance, even behind closed lids. When he reopened them, the mental chorus struck again, with the fury of a dragon's breath.

Lies!

The message throbbed in Torin's head, mocking him and his foolish faith. Annleia had misled him about her charge, after all, proving already that she was not above deceit. Was there another he was missing?

Lies!

That she cared for him—that must be it. He had suspected it as soon as the words were spoken, mistrustful of her motives. Hope alone had prevented him from fully accepting it before.

Lies!

What did that matter? he demanded furiously, trying again to find steady ground within the maelstrom of his thoughts. He had come to vanquish the Illysp. U'uyen, Corathel, Dyanne, and countless others were still struggling to repel that threat. He needed to focus. He had to find a way . . .

Lies!

Were they even still alive? Some of them, perhaps. Surely not all. And who was deceiving whom? Whatever Ravar's actual designs, Torin could do no more. His attack on the rift had succeeded only in speeding his enemies' entry into this world. Without command of the Sword's fires, he was powerless, helpless, hopeless.

Lies . . . Lies . . . Lies . . .

He looked to the talisman, still clutched in his hand as he lay upon the arena floor. Its light had died to a glimmer. Though he tried to concentrate, defeatist thoughts continued to flay his thinning determination. He no longer knew what to believe. With the rift flashing before him, he knew only that the horror of his mistake had never felt more real. If even his achievements had been failures, then it stood to reason that his life could end no other way.

And why should he care? He had lost them all: Marisha, Dyanne, Annleia. He had bound himself to each, in one fashion or another, finding just enough happiness to better know misery and despair. Annleia had asked him what he feared. The answer had been too selfish to utter, almost too simple to believe.

What did it matter to save the world if he found himself alone in the end?

Yet that was how he felt. He had alienated his friends. He had failed to take his chance with Dyanne, and Annleia had already decided to leave him when this was over. There was no one else to turn to, no one who could grant him a reprieve from his hateful existence.

Alive or dead, all that remained for him was a cold, barren torment.

Torin shuddered in the darkness, succumbing to its chill. He couldn't think; he couldn't breathe. No memory, no passion, could justify this grief, yet it would not be driven away. The longing, the remorse, and the pain remained, clinging to his heart like a starving, slashing predator.

Sitting forward, he let go of the Sword and placed his head in his hands. His face was wet. He pulled back to find tears—actual tears—glistening in his palms. He looked at them strangely, then laughed, scornful of his own weakness. His feelings were childish, senseless, grossly insignificant in light of his struggle. How could he indulge such self-pity while the future of so many others depended on his actions?

But he was tired of resisting, of fighting vainly to ward off the inevitable. With nothing left to give, and nothing left to gain . . .

He looked back to the Sword. It was not too late to end his own suffering, to hew himself down in ultimate defiance of the Ceilhigh's fiendish schemes. If he could but summon a final twitch of strength . . .

His hand moved reflexively to the pendant Dyanne had given him. A symbol of how close he had once been to a bliss he could scarcely imagine. The piece of black amber felt like a razor in his clenched palm. He recalled the bittersweet pain he had felt as she had placed it around his neck, this parting token—a pale candle with which to remember the sun. Worthless, and at the same time priceless . . .

He relaxed his grip and massaged it with his fingers, tips brushing its smooth planes and gentle ridges. Back and forth it spun, while the lightning flashed silently around him and he listened to those shrieking voices of inner despair. If only he could turn back time's sands, he would return to her and confess the truth of his feelings—back when the opportunity had been his. But for one more chance . . .

Once, twice, his nail caught upon the pendant's outer edge. Scarcely aware of himself or his actions, he held it up for a closer look. Sure enough, there appeared to be a hairline crack encircling the jet's perimeter, dividing face from back. He hadn't perceived it before, but then, the piece appeared so simple, he had never studied it that closely. Now that he did . . .

His gaze narrowed, scrutinizing. There, at the top, upon the clasp. A row of four tiny slits, cutting across the larger line's path.

A hinge.

Torin frowned, even as a strange excitement stirred in his stomach. With trembling fingers, he pried open the locket.

To discover a portrait of Dyanne, peering back at him from within.

For a moment, he simply stared, stunned by his find. In the portal's garish light, he could see every minuscule detail. The image was small, but had obviously been etched with painstaking care and precision. The soft-flowing hair, the mysterious eyes, the full-bodied lips—pursed with a hint of mischief . . . All had somehow been captured, just as Torin had remembered them.

A fresh warmth spilled suddenly from his chest. Tears of desolation gave way to joyful disbelief. Here, finally, was something tangible, an image that would not disintegrate into the untouchable recesses of his mind. At long last, he had a talisman to cling to, a physical memory of the woman he most truly admired.

Lies! the voices shrieked anew, over and over again. But the truth lay there in his palm. He might tell himself it was a trick, another deception to which he had foolishly fallen prey, but as he blinked and stared and blinked again, the image remained. He even forced himself to close the locket—despite his fears—and open it again.

Dyanne was still with him.

And just like that, it no longer mattered that Annleia had rejected him. It no longer mattered that Dyanne herself was an ocean removed—or that she had found contentment with another. What he felt for her . . . no one could take that from him. No one could strip that away.

Even in the throes of possession, an enemy to all, the passions of his own heart had held strong—had in fact been the key to his liberation. Somehow, he had failed to grasp the inherent lesson. That he might never be allowed to explore his affections seemed suddenly inconsequential. They remained his, invincible, eternal. Though he held no sway over the feelings of others, his own love, his own devotion, would forever be his to control.

Lies!

Yet, amid that endless tumult, a buried warning now echoed. *The greatest danger . . . The greatest danger . . .*

. . . lurks unseen.

Torin looked up, gazing into the portal with a flicker of renewed understanding. Each flash . . . the birth of another Illysp, perhaps? He felt certain now that it was they who assailed him, in such high concentration as to sap the will of even the strongest adversary. He recalled having considered—and dismissed—that possibility before. Annleia had been right about him being his own worst enemy. The self-doubts he carried were like livid embers to these fiends, from which they easily stoked the flames of despair.

He had underestimated the threat they posed. Even now, having determined what he was truly up against, he challenged his own logic, and questioned his conclusions. How could he make such assumptions? Who was he to define the supernatural?

But he refused to tread that path again, focusing instead on the peace and self-assurance that now flooded his veins. For once, his strength swelled from within, and he reveled in the magnitude of that power.

He reached for the Sword. Its light flared with his resurgent passion. He marveled that it should do so, as though it fed upon his emotions as much as it fueled them. *A candle in your palm*, Ravar had told him. *Given a true wielder, its power could consume a form even such as mine.*

What, then, did he lack? What, that he might use to tap into that boundless inferno?

The answer to that lies within.

Within . . .

He still clutched the locket, as a ward against his raking doubts. Though quieted, he could hear them even now, tearing at his resolve. But the warm waves unleashed by Dyanne's image continued to flush through him—not unlike the sensations imbued by the Sword. What might it mean, that both had the ability to so stir his soul?

His gaze delved into the glowing blade, mesmerized anew by the tendrils of fire swirling within its depths. He thought again of Leaven's jailor . . . of Spithaera's assaults . . . then pushed those images from his mind, deciding to look at it another way. Annleia had spoken of passion and patience as the guiding principles to any power—even the Sword's. Patience to draw and hold, passion to direct and unleash. To unleash . . .

The answer was there. He could almost see it, flashing like a lure amid the depths of his consciousness. Why could he not grasp it?

With hope and doubt vying for control, he pushed both aside in favor of a numbing detachment. In the glittering emeralds that adorned the Sword's hilt, he saw Annleia's eyes . . . in its gleaming silver, the dazzling purity of Dyanne's smile . . . in the radiant heartstones, an inferno of unrequited feelings.

Love . . .

Pain . . .

Peace . . .

Desire . . .

The swirling fire . . .

Buried power . . .

And then, suddenly, he understood.

CHAPTER FIFTY-FIVE

I AM CWINGEN U'UYEN, SON OF *the Powaii. I do not suffer death, I earn it.*

He clenched his jaw, biting back a scream as one of the basilisks tore off his remaining foot. He bucked with agony, but a pair of the creatures lay atop him, pinning him where he had fallen. They had already taken his arms—one had been chewed to the elbow, the other to the shoulder. Struggle though he might, his battle was ended.

His brothers—Oobolso Bwinem and Getarin Ta'alo—had succumbed before him. But their valor had won them labors swift and light in the journey to come. His passing, like theirs, promised to be a transcendent experience with far-reaching impact, and in that, he took great pride.

He only hoped now that their shield had stood long enough—had given the Sword-wielder the time he needed. That was what the Lady had asked of him, and the charge he had accepted. The basilisks were simply too numerous. The most stubborn ones had fought to grind through the rubble-filled doorway, or begun chewing fresh holes in the surrounding walls. But the rest had been clever and patient enough to snake around, seeking the many holes that fed into this antechamber from the outer tunnels. Once surrounded, he and his brothers had found their end.

They had met it bravely. Only Ta'alo had cried out—and that for Bwinem as the lightning had struck. He, like U'uyen, had held his tongue as the creatures devoured him—obeying their hosts' natural instinct to mine a victim's body for minerals as they did the stone they typically fed upon. *Let them do so,* U'uyen thought. The longer his own body kept them occupied, the better chance Torin would have.

A pressing numbness began to soothe the fire of his wounds. His vision brightened unnaturally. He could still hear the basilisks snapping at one another, but their snarls had grown distant. He wished he could think of some further way to stall or distract the pack that had slipped already into the pit. Instead, he sent a final thought out to Torin.

Fear not the embrace of darkness. Fear not . . .

In the growing brightness, he glimpsed a pair of amethyst eyes.

I am Cwingen U'uyen . . .

TORIN CAME TO HIS FEET, Sword in hand. He faced the portal squarely, squinting against its harsh glare, raising the blade so that its tip was aimed at the heart of that otherworldly tempest.

He shut his eyes then, the better to focus on what he was feeling within.

He thought of Dyanne and all that she meant to him. He thought of Annleia and the confidence she had given him. There was nothing he wouldn't do, nothing he wouldn't give, to defend them from harm and sadness. He allowed that selflessness to churn inside him, felt it giving rise to a noble desire, a willingness to sacrifice all to bring but a smile to their radiant faces. The Sword flared with the strength of his passion . . .

It wasn't enough.

He feared for a moment that he might be wrong, that the understanding he had come to was vain and false, when a forgotten voice echoed in his head.

Fear not the embrace of darkness. Like the stars at night, we need the shadows to see the light.

It was something U'uyen had said to him, a parting message delivered after their retrieval of the Sword. He didn't know what caused him to think of it now, but saw in it the obvious truth.

He dug deeper, as he had after his battle at the Gaperon, recalling that moment of supreme disappointment. Buried wounds resurfaced, a life's collection of scars ripping wide. Pain . . . shame . . . bitterness . . . He did not fight to quell the feelings this time; he welcomed them, allowing them to wrack, strip, tear him all over again . . .

He felt a fire in his chest. His blood began to boil. It all churned together now—love, hate, joy, anguish—came raging to the surface. He fanned that inferno with mental images, memories of what he had gained, what he had lost—all of the experiences that had shaped his life and served to forge this creature he had become. He grimaced with the effort, but willed the torrent of blazing passion into his arm, his hand. The Sword's heartstones seemed to sizzle in his palm. He embraced their power, felt them open . . .

And rather than draw upon their fire, pushed at it with his own.

A river of flame erupted from the polished blade, a searing streak that blasted into the radiant portal. Though blinded, Torin heard the resultant explosion, its thunderous howl shaking the arena. A titanic backlash threw itself against him, but Torin roared in response, smothering it with his own, matchless fury.

The portal's light flared into darkness. Crimson flames billowed within its stone rim, filling the arena with a bloody glow. Torin's bellow echoed amid the benches and walls, until it seemed a thousand voices screamed down upon him.

At last, he relented, lidding his emotions. The fire drew back into the Sword as suddenly as it had been unleashed. The blade, however, continued to glow as never before, pulsing with radiance to the rhythm of his beating heart.

Torin studied the rift—an empty well of melted bedrock—then looked to the Sword. So obvious, now that he knew. The strength of the Sword was fueled by the wielder. He'd been told that before, but never grasped what it meant. It meant that, despite all its perfect glory, the Sword was merely a conduit for the will and desire of a being who was decidedly imperfect. *He* was the bellows that fanned its flames, *his* passions the wind that drove them.

The Sword simply amplified those passions and channeled them into physical form. Like a fire-breather at a city fair, who spat his oils across a tiny flame to ignite a roaring burst.

A symbiotic relationship, yes, but one that began with him. The Sword provided endless stamina and supernatural awareness, not through some latent divinity stored there by the Ceilhigh, but through his own need and desire. By magnifying his emotions to a divine scale, such mortal limitations were all but stripped away. That the Sword should bestow such energy and take nothing in return was merely an illusion.

His ears perked at a scraping rumble, reminding him that his task was far from finished. With a final look at the steaming portal, he whirled toward the arena exit. He hadn't gone ten paces before the basilisks came pouring through in a frenzied rush. Torin strode forward to meet them, simmering with rage and excitement, taking pleasure now in the cacophony of Illysp voices that filled his mind with fury and despair.

The clues had been everywhere; he simply hadn't recognized them. Why could some, such as fellow soldiers on a battlefield, draw strength from the talisman's mere aura, while others, such as patrons in a crowded tavern—or even those who unknowingly handled the blade—remain oblivious to the same? Because so much depended on the qualities a person projected onto it. Though divine in nature, the talisman was no more wondrous than the viewer believed it to be.

Words of instruction do not equal faith, Ravar had said. Torin now knew why. Trying to explain the internal mechanism by which he had gained control of the Sword's fires would not have been enough. It was something he had to feel. A casting aside of all hesitation and doubt. An embrace of everything within him—strength and weakness, pride and guilt, courage and fear. A willingness to accept and reveal to the world his deepest passions, including those he was most ashamed of and would ordinarily keep hidden. For all were required in order to realize the full measure of his own being, to forge a will that knew no limit, no pretense. Only then could he meld thought and desire into one unquenchable torrent of power.

He did so now as the basilisks reached him. Once again, the Sword erupted, spewing its divine fire in a concentrated stream. The nearest basilisks vanished with hardly a shriek of protest. Those farther back blackened, curled, and flew away in wisps of ash. A lightning blast came from the left, and another from the right, but the Sword's flames reacted as Torin did, spreading forth to intercept them.

The bolts were consumed.

At that, the remaining beasts tried to scatter, slithering and clambering over one another and the surrounding benches in desperate haste. Torin simply willed the fire after them, sweeping his sword arm from side to side. The river of flames responded, splitting off into forked streams when necessary—chasing, immolating, until all that remained of its victims was an acrid haze and the sharp echo of severed screams.

It ended all too quickly. Again, Torin forced himself to withdraw his assault, letting the fire settle back into the polished blade, the gleaming heart-stones, his thundering heart. He found himself dizzy from the outpour of emotion, yet flush with the raw power still churning within. It rolled through him as though he stood beneath a waterfall, washing in sheets over his neck and shoulders, one wave after another. With such euphoric strength, he could raise mountains from the earth, or melt the highest peak into oblivion. Anything he might ever wish for could now be his.

Anything but what you most desire, he reminded himself, as he descended the portico steps in a rush and ran on down the temple corridor. He might raze this earth until only he and Dyanne remained, but that would not make her love him. Nor would Annleia admire him for doing so. He was still exactly who he had been before: a mix of charity and greed, of bravery and cowardice, of trust and jealousy. That he could manifest such feelings as a physical fire used to create or destroy at will made him a dangerous adversary, perhaps. But would those he cared about think any better of him for it?

One of many questions he could not yet answer. There was still much to learn, and more to be done. For now, he wanted only to reach those he had left behind, as quickly as possible.

He did not count his steps as he burst from the tunneling corridor and into the outer cavern. He could sense exactly where he was, and where he needed to be. The Sword's glow pushed forth ahead of him, shoving back the darkness. A frenzy of voices still raked his mind, but he had numbed himself to all fear, all doubt. They were just another fuel to be burned. They would not paralyze him again.

A blast of lightning sizzled through the blackness. More basilisks, their maws bloody. Torin did not slow. He sought them out, one by one, and sent a spear of fire hurtling after them. Some hissed; some shrieked. Some attacked; some ran. All died.

The ladder of stones appeared before him. He scampered up its loose face with sure strides. His injuries stabbed at him, but could not bring him down.

He climbed from the pit, knowing already what he would find. U'uyen and his Powaii were gone. Only the pools of their blood marked where they had fallen. Consumed, as Ravar had warned. He cast about, hoping one or more had managed to slip away, but all he saw were the carcasses of the basilisks they had slain in his defense.

Torin ignited those remains with an explosive vengeance. He stood amid the conflagration, feeling the heat of his own wrath wash over him. The Illysp danced in his mind. Their presence stoked his fury. They, too, would one day claim mortal bodies, and when they did . . .

With the chamber cleansed of its creature coils, Torin set forth. This deed, he knew, was not yet finished, and he still felt a surge of passions smoldering within.

CHAPTER FIFTY-SIX

IT WAS THE THUNDER THAT awoke her, even before she felt Crag's urgent touch upon her shoulder.

The look in his eyes was enough to draw her to her feet.

She glanced east, to find the sun peering tentatively over the ocean's horizon. The clamor she both heard and felt came from the west, as if the mountains themselves were stirring.

"Where's Torin?" she asked.

Crag shook his head. "Fool lad ain't here."

Annleia's stomach pitched nervously. "What do you mean? Where did he go?"

"Our elves are missing, too," announced Vashen, coming up behind her with five of her Hrothgari. "Would they have entered the ruins without us?"

Anxiety spawned dismay. "We have to go after them."

Vashen looked up at the mouth of the pass. Already, the first of the Illychar were streaming over its lip, trumpeting their arrival with shrieks of bloodlust. "Goblins," she spat. "As Torin warned. Headed for the ruins, no doubt."

"Then let's get moving," Crag suggested.

"Won't any of us make it far before they catch us," one of the Hrothgari grumbled.

"We stage a diversion," Vashen ordered, as the last three dwarves scampered close. "Maybe win the Tuthari and his elf-maid a bit more time." She turned upon Annleia, eyeing her bluntly. "If you're to work the magic, why would they have left you behind?"

Annleia understood the warder general's suspicion—and the choice being given. The Hrothgari would surrender their lives to provide her at least some chance of reaching the Illysp portal, even knowing that without the Powaii to guide her, such hope was all but futile. She could not allow them to do that, not when she remained uncertain as to what aid she could truly be to Torin in his struggle.

"It's not up to me," she admitted. She turned to Crag in apology. "I told Torin last night. His is the power that must save us."

"In that case," Vashen replied, her tone critical, "I'd say we've served our purpose. Give the word, elf-woman, and we'll see what little we might do to distract that horde. Otherwise, I'm for taking what shelter we can amid these rocks, and hope that your Sword-wielder knows better than we what he's doing."

Annleia did not care for her options. But she wasn't about to condemn these others for her own foolishness. For a moment, she watched the Illychar approach, a black tide streaming down the scarred slopes, the swiftest and strongest leading the way. Vashen was right. She had done all she could. It was time now to trust in Ravar's plan.

"Torin chose to do this alone," she said. "It is too late but to believe in him."

Vashen snorted, and immediately signaled her team to move out. They were already north of the enemy's position, but were far too close to the ruins to escape notice once the goblin swarm had descended. Annleia hesitated, looking back toward the ruins' cave mouth, but allowed a scowling Crag to drag her along in pursuit of the others.

They moved quickly up the beach, higher into the foothills, and into a thickening cover of boulders. Annleia kept stealing glances south, amazed at how quickly the goblin Illychar were racing down that mountain pass. Their numbers were staggering—a force of thousands. Even if Torin had destroyed the rift, even if he had found a way to unleash the Sword's fires, what was he to do against *that*?

When she and the others had wedged their way into a narrow, scrub-grown crevasse, Annleia felt Crag pulling her down. There they huddled, the last of them together, peering down upon the barren, rock-littered shore. The once-distant clamor had become a resonating rumble as the goblins reached the beach, shrieking and clawing like a single, giant whirlwind.

She nearly cried out when its tip came into view, though it remained hundreds of paces east of her position. By chance or by design, Vashen had picked a vantage point that afforded a mostly unobstructed view of the ruins' entrance. Though Annleia could not quite see the cave mouth itself, she watched with abject horror as the whipping cloud of goblin Illychar began to funnel its way—scores at a time—into the earth.

A spider's web does not forbid entry, but escape.

"Achthium's mercy," Vashen muttered.

After a time, Annleia had to cover her ears against those gargling shrieks of hunger and torment. No sound the damned might make could echo as shrill or terrible. And still they came on, until the very earth began to groan.

That groan grew into a new rumble, muted, born somewhere underground. It must have been that the majority of goblins had entered the ruins, she thought, dragging their thunder below—though she estimated that fewer than half had actually done so. She became further confused when there came an unexpected commotion around the cave's mouth: a shifting and squawking among those fighting to enter and those who looked suddenly as if they were attempting to flee.

The subterranean roar grew louder, and the ground began to quake. In the near darkness, the spot of earth around which the goblins swarmed appeared to glow red. A trick of the dawning sun, she thought.

Until a blinding flash sparked a geyser of crimson fire—erupting skyward as if to ignite the heavens.

. . .

A MERCILESS TRIUMPH BURNED IN his chest as Torin climbed from that smoking hole. Unthreatened, he allowed the Sword's flames to withdraw. The dawning sun bowed upon the horizon, as if in deference to a fire as great as its own. And no wonder. For his heart was a forge of emotions, a well of strength, an unquenchable passion. Awash with a euphoria not experienced by anyone in millennia, he felt as godlike as any mortal could become.

That feeling only intensified as he looked around at the scrabbling swarm of thousands upon thousands of goblin Illychar that blanketed the rugged coastline. They could not flee him fast enough. They could not . . .

The scattering hordes began to turn back. For just a moment, his lungs tightened. He knew how they must see him, with the fire gone out. One man, alone within their midst. A coil to claim, else a morsel to shred. He had startled them, was all, his conflagration catching them unawares. Seeing now what they had run from only fanned the coals of their hatred.

Torin stood motionless as the storm gathered and closed. There were more than even he had remembered—too many, perhaps.

He did not want to let any escape.

The nearest were within thirty paces, twenty, ten. Their fetor enveloped him; their stabbing cries pierced his ears. In their eyes gleamed an insanity he was beginning to comprehend. Ecstasy . . . agony . . .

Deep inside, it churned, billowed.

The Sword's fire flashed forth. He spun, sending it out in a circle. Flames spread along the shore in lancing streams, each of which blasted through an enemy, then continued on to devour another. Hair and skin, teeth and bones—consumed without prejudice. Scores, hundreds, their lives snuffed in an instant.

The rest came on, a rabid surge from all directions. Torin willed them forward, shivering with laughter, with love, with hate . . . with madness. His newfound power seemed without end. He couldn't wait to return to the southern battlefields, to meet his enemies as he had before, to demonstrate for all the world his true, terrible nature.

He felt himself slipping away and did not care. So many had scorned him, he knew, so many who had mistaken humility for frailty, kindness for weakness. Let them gaze upon him now, if they could. For the only frailty he saw was in those who dared to rise against him; the only doubt, that which flashed in his foes' eyes an instant before they met with annihilation.

A gradual shift took root inside him, a hollowing sensation that sent coring pains throughout his chest and limbs. He felt the strength of his fires weakening, turning back as if to eat at him within. He gritted his teeth, resisting all the harder, but that only seemed to speed the tilting of power.

The Illychar drew closer, flying in from all angles, and he could no longer seem to move fast enough—or reach far enough—to stop them all. Doubt, that shade of his past, came creeping back in. Had he exhausted his emotional reserve? Was there in fact a limit to his strength?

Strangely, the balance shifted once again, the outer fires roaring with renewed vigor. *Like the stars at night . . .* he realized, glancing up at the predawn skies. He needed them both, confound it. Pride *and* humility. Strength *and* weakness. He could not be one without the other. Seek to banish one, and its antithesis withered alongside.

Still so much to learn, he thought, fighting to steady his focus, to find a middle ground between vanity and self-loathing. Competing images swirled within his mind: those that fostered pity, followed by those that inspired vengeance; those that caused him to smile, followed by those that made him want to weep. He set them to chasing one another in an endless cycle, using them to maintain the balance that seemed to be required.

He soon understood, however, that even this was a challenge he could not maintain forever. His doubt had been correct in one respect: The wellspring of his emotions was fast running dry. A chilling numbness was stealing through him like ivy over a castle wall. A renewal was needed, a fresh inspiration. No matter the desire unleashed by his various memories, he could not keep recalling the same ones over and over and expect them to yield the same potency.

He looked around, still spinning, still trailing streamers of fire. Thousands of his enemies had been incinerated, yet thousands more remained. *Too many*, he thought again. Only, this time, he wished more would take flight. Many had done so, but not nearly enough. The rocky beach was still swarming with attackers bent on assault. Alone, he could not destroy them all.

In that moment of bitter acceptance, his time ran out.

He felt the ominous rising, even before the ocean's growl became a spitting roar. A pillar shot skyward at the edge of the coastline, darkening the reddened sky. Sheets of water and spray fell away from its sides, revealing the horror that Torin already knew lay beneath.

Ravar.

The Dragon God's shadow engulfed the beach, and His great maw fell after. With startling swiftness, the leviathan struck the stony shore, swallowing scores of Illychar with a single, snapping bite. At the same time, a tidal wave swept over the earth, crushing even more Illychar before hauling them off to a watery grave.

An awestruck Torin withdrew his fires in a posture of defense. But Ravar's wrath seemed focused on the Illychar. Hundreds disappeared as His cavernous maw lashed out again and again. Others were ground into pulp as the creature's unfathomable bulk—with its armor of limestone and coral—grated over them. Within moments, the roiling sea was filled with both the battered and the dead, mangled bodies flailing amid ribbons of flesh and splinters of bone.

The goblins took flight, winging frantically in all directions, desperate to escape the leviathan's ravening. Torin and his Sword were all but forgotten as the majority flocked westward, seeking the safety of the mountain slopes.

Drive them to me.

The command resonated in Torin's mind. Though wary and exhausted, he didn't dare disobey. Once more, he leveled his blade and sent flames shooting from its radiant surface. He did not attack his enemies directly this time, but rather formed a conflagration that rushed up the mountainside ahead of them, a line set to corral the Illychar and stem their retreat.

Some plunged headlong into that fiery wall, to emerge only as cinders and wisps of smoke. The rest turned, hissing and screaming with rabid fury. Torin advanced toward them, holding as many as he could in place, incinerating those who came too close. Gradually, he began to herd them back toward the water's edge.

While Ravar lunged forth to devour them, Torin battled the strain of blocking their escape. It was hard enough to keep his feet as he marched toward the sea. The earth shuddered, rocked time and again by the Dragon God's thrashing movements. As goblins flew at him, he was forced to summon flame tongues to destroy them, without allowing gaps in his primary wall. But he had to hold strong. He could not allow Ravar's hunger to go unsated.

Iron sinews bulged from his forearms. Veins ripped across his skin like tiny bolts of lightning. A molten sweat seemed to sear the flesh from his face and arms. The deafening tumult raked his ears—the roar of flames, the hiss and shriek of enemies, the churning of the ocean, Ravar's groans and earth-shattering assaults . . . while in his mind, he heard only the thunder of his own raging desire.

The sounds continued to echo even after the slaughter had ended. Torin opened his eyes when he felt waves slapping at his feet. Only then did he realize he had closed them. Almost the whole of the goblin army was gone, its few dregs having fled up the slopes. The only other traces lay all around, smashed upon the earth or cradled by the settling sea.

It's finished, he thought, and allowed the fires of the Sword to slip back into their gleaming sheath.

Not yet, Asahiel.

Reminded of its hulking shadow by the chill that came over him, Torin gazed upward at the hovering Dragon God, and fell to his knees in the crimson surf.

CHAPTER FIFTY-SEVEN

Torin waded through a fog of dizziness. He looked from Ravar's mountainous form to the waves crashing around him to the fires in the Sword's blade and heartstones. He felt utterly drained. If Ravar meant to challenge him now . . .

Again you flatter yourself with undue importance, came the scornful reply. *But look, Asahiel, and tell me what you have truly accomplished.*

He forced himself to turn eye back to the west, tracing the flight of those few remaining goblins scurrying upward into the pass. A grim understanding began to cut through his confusion. The rift may have been closed, but . . .

His thoughts reached across the miles to friends and regions unseen. By now, the coalition blockade had likely been breached, if not destroyed. If so, then those at Stralk, Wingport, and other cities were no doubt fighting for their lives, hunkered behind their feeble defenses. Nevik and the rest of Alson would be out to sea, or wishing they were. All was still lost unless he could somehow cleanse these shores—and Yawacor's—of the Illysp already set loose.

"You must give me more time."

And delight I would in your continued struggles. But the Illysp are innumerable. I can tolerate them no longer.

Torin still wasn't certain how scouring the earth would silence the Illysp spirits—perhaps by eradicating the physical minds in which they whispered their fell urges. Whatever, that was Ravar's concern. His was in finding another, less devastating way.

But how? How could even the Sword's fires be used against an enemy he couldn't see?

Though he knew the creature read his every thought, Torin could not help but consider instigating now the conflict he so dreaded. For the only sure way to prevent Ravar from unleashing His full fury would be to destroy Him first.

See to your friends, Asahiel, before you do anything rash.

He cast about and, sure enough, spied the members of his company rushing down the beach toward his position. Annleia led, dashing along at a dangerous pace upon the slick, jagged ironshore. Crag fought to keep up, but was falling steadily behind. Farther back trudged Vashen and her Hrothgari, weapons drawn, necks craned skyward at Ravar's impossible majesty.

Annleia stared not at the Dragon God, but at Torin, as she approached. He forced himself to his feet, uncertain of his feelings, but well aware of the fresh spark that her arrival lit within him.

By the wild look in her eyes, he thought for a moment that she meant to throw her arms about him. Instead, she slowed as she reached the surf line, and finally stopped, awe reflected in her features.

He could almost see her thoughts spinning, her lips itching for some proper expression of her feelings. At last, she gave up and looked instead to Ravar. "He did what you asked of him," she said. "Tell us what more must happen, and I will see it done."

She was the one who had thought to ask about it beforehand, Torin recalled: what was to become of the reigning Illysp should he manage to destroy their portal. That question, the one he had been so quick to dismiss, had suddenly become of paramount importance. What was the answer Ravar had given?

"You spoke of *they*," he remembered vaguely. "The ones who would help us." He looked to Annleia for acknowledgment. She nodded fiercely before turning her glare upon Ravar.

Or not, the Dragon God replied. *That is their choice, their challenge.*

"Then at least tell us who *they* are," Torin demanded, shaking the Sword at his side, "that we might sway them."

See to your friends, Asahiel, Ravar repeated.

Torin frowned, looking back at those drawing near. Crag splashed through the surf, looking none too pleased with any of this. Vashen and the others were still a hundred paces out, wary, uncertain. What could any of them have to offer that they hadn't already?

He was about to voice this question aloud when he caught sight of the others.

They came in a tightly knit cluster, angling down from a more southerly position at the base of the coastal foothills. Torin squinted. He could not yet make out their identities, but if judged by their slow, methodical pace, they were no Illychar. Whomever, they were lucky to have escaped the enemy swarm—and his far-ranging conflagration—alive.

He glanced at Ravar with curiosity and suspicion, but the Dragon God only hovered silently, His great neck swaying almost imperceptibly in the strengthening wind.

Torin turned and headed up the beach, thinking to meet the new arrivals. The members of his company fell into step alongside. Annleia and Crag followed closely; the rest gave him a comfortable berth, while casting more than a single lingering glance at the monstrous leviathan at their backs.

Instead of continuing toward him, the newcomers veered toward the entrance to Thrak-Symbos's ruins. As they did so, Torin realized who they were. A twinge of surprise overcame him, drowned quickly by mingled waves of expectation and displeasure.

By the time he came within hailing distance, they had formed a wall at the edge of the ruined cave mouth, and there stood waiting. They were not alone.

With them, Torin found Allion and Marisha, whose own presence spawned a momentary confusion that he quickly dismissed as inconsequential.

"I might have known," he said, eyeing the Entients sourly. They were all there, the few whose names he remembered, and many he did not. He fixed his gaze upon their white-haired leader's, who stood center among them. "Is this as you planned, then?"

Maventhrowe looked at Ravar, looming at the coast's edge, before smiling thinly in response. "Would that we were capable of dictating such forces and events. No, Sword-bearer, we did not plan for this, no more than you did. But we have watched, and we have seen. Of all the possibilities to unfold, you have brought forth the best for which we might have hoped."

Torin's frown deepened. Though subtle, he sensed the wariness, the relief, in those he faced. While they indeed seemed pleased with fortune's turn, a shadow of darker intent still lurked about them.

His doubts must have shone clearly, for a familiar gray-hair—Htomah, if recollection served—hastily added, "We come as friends, whatever else you may think of us."

Torin glanced at Allion and Marisha, stood near the end of the line beside a glaring Ranunculus. He still wasn't sure how their presence fit in here, but saw little sign of friendship within their stares. Awe, yes. Beyond that . . . shame, and a grim boldness. Like the Entients, they had journeyed here with unsettled purpose, Torin decided, a double-edged sword that might have fallen either way.

He looked back to Htomah. "It's not your friendship that I require, but whatever aid you're here to lend. How much do you know?"

"The rift is closed, is it not?" Maventhrowe asked.

"It is. But the Illysp that remain—"

"And do you still carry the Dragon Orb?"

Torin looked with Maventhrowe to Annleia. "Yes," she said. "But I do not have the power to use it as my forebears did."

"Of course you do not," Maventhrowe replied kindly. "It is how I knew the task set upon your shoulders was little more than a ploy, that the true charge must be the one Ravar gave Torin from the first. Were he to fail—"

"The rift is closed," Torin repeated, impatient. "So, what now? Can you command the Orb's magic?"

Maventhrowe slowly spread his arms, indicating his fellow Entients. "Together, it seems we must."

"But how will you draw them," Annleia demanded, "when the light from their world can no longer be used to seek them out?"

The key to their dilemma. Ravar had described the Orb as a lens. But the light was to have come from the portal itself. Without that . . .

"A summoning like your ancestors performed is no longer possible," Maventhrowe admitted. "But the Orb is all-seeing, as Ravar is all-seeing." He nodded respectfully toward the silent leviathan. "We need only to show it what we seek—in this case, Illysp souls." His smile became almost mischievous. "Unless you spurned the woodswoman's advice, you carry one of those, as well."

The gosswyn, Torin thought. The one Annleia had displayed during their confrontation with Lorre in the overlord's dungeon. The one in which she claimed to have caged the spirit of Itz lar Thrakkon. Necanicum had warned her to keep it, that there might come a time when it would be required.

Once again, it seemed, the witch had been right.

Annleia's hand went to one of the small pouches at her waist. She gave Torin a long, searching look before she finally nodded.

Torin returned his attention to Maventhrowe. "So the flower will enable you to spy them through the Orb. How do you then destroy them?"

"A transference of energy along the opened sightways." The Entient's great white mane shook slowly back and forth. "Only, no energy *we* could summon would be powerful enough to eradicate so many."

Torin stared for a moment into those brilliant blue eyes, considering that which Maventhrowe suggested. "Is there anything else you require?"

"Once it begins, you must not pause until it is finished, for there will be no second chance."

Torin hefted the Sword, and brought a sheath of flames dancing to its surface. "Then let us begin."

Annleia drew forth the Orb. Torin measured the Entients' reaction, but none showed any concern at its withered, shrunken appearance. With those assembled looking on, the last of the Vandari uncorked the skin in which she had collected some of the Orb's tears, and used them to wash the artifact's surface, murmuring softly all the while in that exotic, singsong tone.

Within moments, the Orb began to glisten, then swell. As he waited, Torin glanced now and then at Ravar, to see if the Dragon God had anything to add, any clue to offer as to whether this was the proper course. But the leviathan remained still, silent—the grim presence of a headsman waiting for sentence to be passed.

Questions filled his mind with every fleeting moment, as nagging and insistent as the parade of breezes sweeping that desolate shore. He thought to ask more about the process laid out by the Entients, but didn't. Strange as it all sounded, he didn't much care *how* it could work, only that it *would*.

The sun had cast aside a blanket of clouds and slipped fully from the ocean's bed before Annleia stepped back, leaving the Orb to lie upon a nest of broken rocks. Its restoration appeared complete. Not only had it grown to its original size, but its skin had smoothed so that the dawning skies reflected brightly against the black-pearl surface.

Maventhrowe came forward to make his own inspection, running a single hand lightly over the glasslike sphere. He gave Annleia an encouraging smile. "The gosswyn," he said.

Annleia, who seemed suddenly weary, reached into her pouch. Torin tensed as the thistle-like flower came into view. Except for its complete lack of color, it still appeared alive and healthy—not dry and dead as he would have anticipated. Seeing it again, he recalled having wanted her to grind it into dust. Even now, a part of him might have taken satisfaction in doing just that, so intense was his loathing at the mere sight of it.

Upon accepting the gosswyn, Maventhrowe spun it slowly in his fingers, studying it from all sides, grimacing as he did so. He then looked to Torin. "When you are ready."

Torin strode forward. The Entients closed round, brushing all others aside. Annleia tried at first to stay within their ring, but Crag helped draw her back. The rest—Allion, Marisha, Vashen, and her Hrothgari—seemed content with observing from afar.

Maventhrowe set the gosswyn atop the Orb, then laid his hands flat on either side—palms down, digits splayed, thumbs and forefingers touching to form a central, tear-shaped gap. "When I signal to you," he said, "stab here to pierce the Orb's heart, but do not yet call upon the Sword's fire. You will know when it is time."

Torin nodded smartly, anxious for this to be ended.

"When it is time," Maventhrowe cautioned again.

One by one, the remaining Entients placed their hands upon the Orb's surface, their fingers forming an intricate webwork. As he watched them, Torin was reminded of their ancestors' study of the Sword—of the secret he had uncovered that they had not. Even now, it scarcely seemed possible—not only that the answer he had come up with was true, but that it could be so simple. How it could have eluded so many for so long, including those whose understanding of such things was much greater than his, remained a mystery. But perhaps that was it. Perhaps they had been looking too hard down the wrong paths, as he had. Everyone saw the Sword as a font, a cask waiting to be uncorked. And the more they looked, the farther they moved from the obvious truth: that its wielder was the true source, the weapon itself merely a filter.

Maventhrowe closed his eyes and began to hum. The other Entients followed suit, matching their tune to his. Inside the Orb, invisible veins flashed now with streaks of light, as if a thunderstorm brewed within. High above, the skies darkened and churned, mirroring that internal conflict.

While waiting, Torin turned his own focus inward, stoking the passions he knew would be required. As drained as he had felt, his emotions, it seemed, were remarkably resilient. It didn't take much to set them to seething once again. He thought of the victories he had known, as well as the many times he had felt beaten and helpless. Neither mattered now, save that, together, those moments had culminated in this one. His triumphs, his failings—his deeds, for good and ill—all would weigh out now to determine his lasting legacy upon this world. If ever he had anything to give, to take, he must do so now.

Lightning crackled overhead, and thunder pealed. Before him, Maventhrowe's eyes snapped open, glowing a brilliant, phosphorescent blue. Torin looked to the space between the Entient's hands, where the pale gosswyn rested. A host of flickering energy streams danced just beneath it, like roots set down deep inside the Orb.

With a growl, he plunged the Sword through the flower's throat, severing bud from stem. All at once, a chilling revulsion swept through him, as if Itz lar Thrakkon had been set free to lay stripping siege to his mind. Despite Maventhrowe's earlier instruction, Torin nearly unleashed the Sword's fires then and there in order to drive back the raping assault. He would not suffer that again. He would destroy himself and all else before falling victim again to that infernal madness.

But he was no longer dead, he assured himself. He was thus safe from Illysp possession. It was not Thrakkon's intrusion he felt, but something else. A distant sense, perhaps, of the suffering still out there. A kinship with those enslaved as he had once been.

A mere taste of the hunger, the hatred, the horror he had set free, glimpsed through the eye of a living god.

That feeling crawled over him, through him . . . tugging, clawing, beetling beneath his flesh. An itch he could not scratch. A writhing pain that would not be soothed. He wanted it to stop. He *needed* it to stop. Their pleading voices filled his mind . . . a whisper, a roar . . .

He looked to Maventhrowe, but the Entient shook his head. Torin clenched his teeth. The Orb's veins had already ignited, flashing crimson with the fire that burned along the buried length of the Sword's blade. Torin ached, trembled, fighting to hold back the flames that roiled within, when all he could think of was bathing himself in their cleansing fury.

Without warning, a stroke of lightning touched down upon the Sword's hilt. Though startled, Torin was wound too tight to let go. The bolt became a stream, dancing upon the pommel, growing stronger, brighter, as additional lightning threads descended . . . twined together . . . forming a tether between the Orb and the heavens' boundless expanse. The connection drew taut—

And Torin summoned the fire.

In a blink, the center of the Dragon Orb filled with flame. Crimson tongues erupted from the Sword's hilt, shooting skyward along the cascading river of lightning. The skies themselves seemed to ignite, with scattered streamers of fire-laden bolts spewing in every direction, as if to spread across the globe.

CORATHEL LOOKED WITH DISMAY AT the widening breach in the southern line. That particular line was to have held throughout the night *and* the next day. Well, the new day had not yet dawned, and already it was time to order another critical displacement. Stay any longer, and the entire battalion might be hemmed in, making today's struggle its last.

Does it matter? an inner voice whispered insidiously. He had lost count of the number of holes in the coalition defenses—enough that only half of the ever-growing Illychar army still pressed them here upon the Kuurian highland. The rest had swept southward, to engage a staggered series of reinforcements deployed by Thelin. While battle was yet carefully orchestrated in specific areas, the war in whole had degenerated into chaotic melee. What good was holding this valley when the enemy had had time enough by now to reach the sea?

A glancing strike jerked the general's attention into an enemy's face. The larger picture was forgotten as he lost balance, tripped up by a mud-spattered corpse. One of his own, he thought, until he hit the earth and caught sight of its fire-blackened face. At some point, the dead man had been Parthan, yes. But he had fallen this day—and perhaps others before—as an Illychar.

If there was consolation to be had in that, Corathel didn't know where. His own assailant stood over him, hefting a pole-axe for the killing stroke. Trapped by the jostling hordes and the awkwardness of his landing, winded by his ceaseless efforts and unsure in that moment why he had struggled even this long, the chief general simply peered into the eyes of the foe to which he had finally succumbed, congratulating the creature with a silent curse.

Where axe and curse met, however, the sky ripped wide in a scintillating burst. A moment later, when he realized that he was still alive, Corathel opened his eyes. Lightning. The clouds were filled with it, like a bloody web laid across the heavens. Strands were falling, as well. All around, bodies crumpled, as bolts rained in fiery flashes, striking men dead where they stood.

A *hail of fire*, the chief general mused—dazed, blinded, thinking that perhaps he had perished and found the Abyss after all.

KING THELIN LEANED UPON THE tower parapet, clutching his wife's hand. Together, they stared eastward, noting the sun's attempt to rise. A ritual of theirs over the past few days, ever since a horde of Illychar had descended upon Stralk's walls and it had become clear that any sunrise might be their last.

"My regiment awaits," he said finally.

Loisse squeezed his hand. "Their numbers have increased during the night," she observed.

The dispassion in her voice weighed heavily upon his heart. All their plans, all their struggles . . . all for naught. The storm they had sought to avoid had come, and it seemed now that there was nothing more but to delay the inevitable. "I regret, now, leaving Souaris."

"The risk was worthwhile—necessary, even."

"But to be fighting here, like this . . ." His hand swept out over the shadowed hillside at their feet. The majority of troops he'd held in reserve battled even now upon that shredded ground. With the city itself crammed full of refugees, there simply wasn't room to place more than a token garrison inside. As of now, their defenders still outnumbered the enemy descended upon them, but it would not be long before those tides shifted irrevocably. "We should be home."

"We are together," Loisse said. "If this is to be the end, that is all that matters to me."

Thelin gritted his teeth. Despite being rebuffed time and again, the Illychar armies reached forth incessantly, carving at the ranks of his men like surf upon the beach. He wondered if Wingport was still able to defend itself—if at least some of his people had managed to cast off and sail away. He wondered how long he had before the coalition fell completely and the rest of the Illychar he'd heard reports about came swooping in. He wondered how much longer he would be forced to gaze upon this trampled, blood-soaked terrain, smell the piles of bloated and smoldering corpses, listen to the pitched clangor and the agonized screams of those claimed by the growing onslaught . . .

"I should go," he said, and this time his wife only nodded, making no attempt to stall him.

Until he turned, and the heavens shattered.

Loisse's hand clamped down hard, freezing him in place. He turned to find her crouched low, realizing only then that he had done the same. A spectacular, blood-red lightning storm raged overhead, highlighting the seams of the sky. But if that were so, then the very dome of the world had cracked, for wherever he looked—

Down it poured, then, in splintering streaks, hundreds at a time, so fast that his eyes could not keep pace. Many of these bolts stopped in midair—within the city and without—terminating in a puff of red fire. The rest flashed down upon the heads of individuals, killing with a touch. They forked through walls and windows, through timber and iron and stone. Their fury was everywhere, a fiery tempest that knifed across the land with indiscriminate frenzy.

Beside him, he felt his wife trying to rise.

"Stay down!" he yelled, fighting to shield her body with his own.

"Look!" she hollered right back. "It doesn't touch us!"

Cringing against the incessant strikes, and still wrestling with his wife, Thelin nevertheless managed to peek between merlons long enough to glimpse the truth of her words. Though lightning flashed amid the tightly packed ring of Kuurian troops, its touch resulted only in those strange, fiery puffs. At the same time, the surrounding Illychar were dropping by the scores, as if some invisible hand were simply reaching out to snip their puppet strings.

"Ceilhigh," Thelin breathed. "Could it be . . . ?"

Amid the earth-rending thunder, the shrieks of the Illychar rose to a desperate, furious pitch, as they, too, recognized the disparity. Some turned that rage against their enemies, while others fled. It did not seem to matter which route they chose, for none moved swiftly enough to escape the unnatural storm.

Loisse stood. Thelin rose slowly beside her, still looking at the raging sky, still fretful. His queen gave a grim smile.

"Impossible," she said, and grinned fearlessly as death's fingers flashed down among them.

"We're too late," the ship's captain grumbled.

Nevik gripped the bow rail in frustration. Wingport's harbor lay just ahead, across a dark expanse of coastal waters. Behind him sailed a small fleet of empty ships, brought round to the southern shore in answer to Thelin's plea for help. Their passengers from Krynwall had been deposited onto islands off the western coast, agreeing to wait there while others were ferried from the mainland. With luck, these offshore staging grounds would provide safe haven from the Illychar until enough ships were available to bear all across the seas.

The best that could be done, under the circumstances, Nevik assured himself. But the ship's captain was right. Wingport was already under siege. From the lookout's reports, a defense force was doing its best to close off the highway north of the seaport and there waylay the bulk of the enemy tide. Battle was at its thickest there. Yet the struggle had spilled already into the city streets and onto the wharves themselves, where soldiers and civilians alike had been working to construct a fleet of their own. Any attempt to sail in now would be to leap headlong into the mounting slaughter.

"We cannot just leave them," Nevik growled to the wind.

Many of these people were his, after all, refugees brought from southern Alson earlier in the conflict. The people of Drakmar, Palladur . . . *Ghellenay*. He had promised her he would return. When he'd ridden north from Souaris to warn Rogun of the Kuurian exodus, Palladur's baroness had remained behind to tend the flocks. He could not abandon her now.

The captain spat. "We tie up there, we risk being overrun and losing our own ships. Stranding ourselves alongside won't be helping them, and won't be helping those trusting in our return."

"I'm aware of the risks, Captain. I'm also aware—"

The sky flashed, and a booming roar rocked the decks. Nevik clenched in terror, staring inland as streaks of red-tinged lightning carved up the heavens and slashed across the earth.

A great wail arose from the shore. Even at a distance, in this unholy light, he could see men falling, their souls snatched away in fiery, quicksilver streams.

"Mother's bounty," the captain whispered breathlessly. "What hell is that?"

Nevik could scarcely tear his eyes from the knee-buckling display, but finally managed to do so. The sky above their heads, here upon the ocean, was veined with red streaks, like some great, bloodshot eye. And yet, their masts, their sails, their men—all were untouched by the flickering bolts that raked the ground ahead. Whatever unnatural force had spawned this squall, it seemed to be concentrated on the land, not on the sea.

"Your spyglass," Nevik demanded, gripped with a sudden suspicion.

The captain, gaping, did not respond until Nevik seized the item from his hand. "Still wish to sail into that?"

Nevik's fingers trembled as he drew focus upon the harbor, the inner quarter, the northern road. Elves, goblins, ogres—coils of the enemy—cut down in waves. But where the defenders hunkered . . .

He might have been wrong, misled by desperation, but neither would this be the first time he'd seen an entire army felled by mystical means.

"At full speed," he said, handing back the spyglass. "While we have them on the run."

THE FIRE RAGED, TAKING HIS heart, taking his soul.

And still it wanted more.

Torin continued to feed it everything he had, determined not to falter. The strain was like nothing he could have fathomed, as if his every fiber were being pulled in opposing directions. He sensed now the outpouring of energy Maventhrowe had described. The lightning streams that bore the Sword's fire skyward were only the beginning. Once overhead, they reached out across the land, into the depths of the nearby ruins—across the sea, even, to an unfamiliar, mountainous region of Yawacor. Wherever an Illysp hid, a fire-laden bolt flashed down—through stone cairns, earthen graves, and any other barrier—to immolate the fleshless creature forever. Thousands, millions, had already perished, ripped from the coils they had claimed, else obliterated before ever knowing the taste of mortal flesh. An ocean-spanning cataclysm, facilitated by the Dragon Orb, yet fueled now by his will alone.

His agony was matched only by his ecstasy. The ripping, scouring assault—upon the Illysp, and upon himself—was well deserved. As the power drained him, he let himself feel the weight of every life the Illysp had claimed. The deaths at Atharvan, the slaughter of Annleia's people, his own possession . . . This was the closest he would ever come to atonement. The suffering he had caused would never be undone, but there was an inherent justice in being called upon to bear it once more before banishing it henceforth.

Even so, it felt already as if he had reached beyond some spiritual limit, and there was no telling how much longer he must endure. To maintain the assault, he had to dig ever deeper within himself . . . to where his emotions flared brightest. It was there that he found those who had sacrificed all for him: from his mother, to fish-eyed Cordan, to U'uyen and his Powaii clansmen. It was there that he found those who had raised him, instructed him, or befriended him in some way. There, where he was not just an individual, but the sum of all those who had meaningfully impacted his life.

As before, he found particular potency in the memories of those he had loved. The smiles, the surprises, the tenderness . . . but also the false hopes, the bitter farewells, the wrenching heartache of dreams unfulfilled. Whether by outright rejection or a chance not taken, it was the losses that drove him. And the closer he had been to happiness, the more those wounds bled.

His stomach churned, and his head began to reel. *Take it all*, he thought. He did not need happiness—not when it came with such torment. He did not need love—whatever that proved to be. Let it all vanish in a flaming vortex. Let his past be reduced to cold ashes and gray embers. He was an instrument of devastation, no more. A pitiless, feral craving.

There will be no second chance.

He didn't need one. He didn't want one. Not with Dyanne. Not with Annleia. Not for the life he had led. To the Abyss with who he had been. To the Abyss with who he might be. Let both burn for eternity with the specter of his broken dreams. There was nothing to hold back—and no reason to do so. All that mattered was feeding the fire. Though it blackened his heart . . . Though it ate his soul . . .

In the depths of a ravaged mind, he heard himself scream.

As suddenly as that, the Illysp were gone. The pillar of lightning withdrew, its connection severed. Torin, in a final furious burst, ignited the Orb itself. The Entients fell away as it melted into the ether—taking the gosswyn with it.

With nothing more to consume, he let the fire die. All at once, a crushing emptiness gripped him.

Which he felt hardly at all.

CHAPTER FIFTY-EIGHT

Annleia was the only one to approach, pushing through the loosened ring of Entients to peer up at him with concern. "Are you . . . ?" she began, but faltered at his expression. "Is it over?"

Though raw with expended emotion, Torin still felt the Sword's power—*his* power—coursing through him in pulsing waves, begging release. He looked to Ravar. The Dragon God moaned gently—a sound that nevertheless rumbled across the sky. His great neck, hefted high, slid deeper into the frothy swells, until only His head remained above the waterline.

"You have fulfilled a greater promise than any of us in the beginning could have anticipated," said Maventhrowe. "I do believe that Ravar shall return now to His rest, and we to our duties."

Like that, Torin thought. It felt to him like there should be more. For all that had just happened to conclude so abruptly . . .

"Is that all you would say to him?" Annleia asked.

"What more would you have of us?" growled Ranunculus.

Annleia frowned.

"An apology," Htomah surmised. "Is that it?"

Torin felt Annleia's gaze upon him. Her unnecessary worry confused him. "They have served their purpose," he said. "Let them go."

"And we expect that you will continue to serve yours, wherever it leads you." Maventhrowe smiled, adding, "No matter your future deeds, I suspect they shall bear watching."

At this, the head Entient directed a knowing glance at Htomah. After, the group's members began to turn away, one by one, each with a nod of farewell.

"You will not call upon me to relinquish the Sword?" Torin asked, all but daring them to do so.

Maventhrowe paused, showing again that steady, all-knowing smile. "I am not so foolish as that."

"A prize it would be for your studies."

"Indeed. Though we shall learn far more, I think, leaving it in your hands. Be mindful of its use, Sword-bearer. The greater the power, the greater the consequence."

For a moment, it seemed the Entient meant to expound upon that warning. Instead, he turned to face Marisha, who stood silent within his shadow, clinging to Allion's arm.

"You, child, have further questions."

She tensed, blinking at him with doe eyes. "Questions?"

"As Algorath's scion, you seek answers to a legacy you cannot yet fathom, answers that only we can provide." He held forth his hand. "If you so desire, come with us, and I will grant that opportunity."

The blinking stopped. Marisha stared, transfixed by the Entient's gaze, clearly tempted by his offer. Beside her, Allion had gone rigid. Even at a distance, Torin sensed the hunter's sudden, gripping fear.

"I . . ." She paused. Suddenly, she, too, had become aware of Allion's distress, judging by the look she gave him. "How long would we—"

"There would be no *we*," Maventhrowe explained gently. "Do you recall what Darinor told you of our ways? An unprecedented chance I offer you—requiring mutual sacrifice great and small—in the interest of expanded horizons. Some traditions, however, cannot be broken, as you would come to understand. If you are to let go these anchors," he added, glancing at Allion, "better to do so now."

"In that case," Marisha replied, "I have all the answers I need." She abandoned the Entient's gaze to stare into Allion's. "What more there is to know, he and I will learn together."

If disappointed by her rebuff, Maventhrowe did nothing to show it. "May that be enough." He bowed, then turned with his flock, leading them up the beach.

For a long moment, no one spoke, as if waiting for better privacy from the departing company. Finally, Allion bent to whisper to Marisha. Torin missed what was said, for Annleia chose that same moment to break her own silence.

"The Powaii," she said. "Did they . . . ?"

Torin glared at Ravar, then shook his head.

"I still can't believe you went in there without me."

"Without *us*," Crag corrected, drawing near. "Might have made a difference."

As if the blood of the Powaii hadn't been enough, Torin thought, but left it unsaid as Allion stepped close, Marisha still clinging to his arm.

"We would have joined you, as well," his childhood friend offered. "I don't know what all happened here, but . . . I should have known you would find a way."

His grudging tone did not match the sympathy of his words. "We arrived late last night," Marisha added for him, as if to soften the air. "But the Entients . . . they held us back."

"Fed us some riddle about arriving too late," Allion said, "or else too *soon*, depending on the outcome."

Too late to be of any help against the portal, Torin supposed, or the basilisks, or the goblin horde—or all three, perhaps. Too soon? His gaze trailed after the Entients' retreating forms. Too soon to work the Orb's magic, most likely. Until he had shown them that he could summon the power of the Sword . . .

It caused him to wonder what other action the mystics might have taken, had circumstances unfolded differently. Of course, the same held true of the pair of former friends still standing before him. He shook away the thought. It didn't matter. He never had to know.

"Will you be returning with us, then?" Marisha asked, with an uncertain glance at the rest of his company.

Torin considered, looking first at her, then at the lingering scowl upon Allion's face. "I'm afraid I must travel first to Yawacor. I've still some debts to settle there." He said this without so much as a glance in Annleia's direction. Thankfully, she kept silent. "Should I return," he went on, "I'll expect to find Nevik sitting Krynwall's throne—or if not, then yourself, perhaps."

Allion snorted. "I've had my fill of regency. But we'll appoint someone suitable, if that is your wish."

Torin nodded curtly. Still gripping the Sword, he made no effort to extend a hand in parting. Nor did Allion, he noted.

"So this is farewell?" Marisha asked.

"I presume Vashen will escort you." In this case, he *did* look back, seeking the warder general's confirmation.

Vashen grunted. "If we're truly finished here, me and mine will return to our people. May as well journey together."

"And you with them, Craggenbrun," Annleia said softly.

The Tuthari shifted in surprise. "Not a chance, Lei. I go with you to find your family. I owe that much and more—"

"You owe me nothing, dear friend. Neither are you beholden to my people."

"You forget what I did, Lei. Your mother—"

"Forgave you almost immediately," Annleia reassured him, with a quick glance at Torin. "She wished for you to be happy, to find a home among your own kind. That place is here."

Crag regarded her sourly before shifting a glare to Torin. For a moment, his stern gaze slipped back and forth between the pair, as if wary of some subterfuge. "You'll see to it that she finds the others?" he demanded finally.

"I will serve her wishes in all things," Torin vowed.

That only caused the furrows in Crag's brow to deepen. Torin had no desire to deceive the dwarf outright, but decided that he would do so, if it came to that.

Crag surprised him by accepting his answer. "You know I do the same, Lei."

"I know. Which is why you will remain. I will miss you, though."

She bent to embrace him. Crag gripped her in his powerful arms, though he continued to glare at Torin over her shoulder. Upon releasing her, he said, "I learn you let some ill befall her, you'd best run far and fast, flaming sword or no."

"She came a long way, Crag. She'll do fine."

"Taking the slug again?" he grumbled at Annleia.

"It is why He waits."

Crag's face wrinkled again as he considered the floating leviathan, which groaned suddenly.

"He knows your thoughts," Annleia cautioned, "and would choose not to suffer your threats."

"Smarter than it looks, then." He looked her in the eyes. "Safe voyage, Lei."

"Be well, Craggenbrun. *Uum darrow mi*. Do not think this a forever good-bye."

The Tuthari merely shook his head at that, then turned to the others. "While the day is fresh?"

Vashen stumped over to join him, her Hrothgari forming up behind. When she stood before Torin, she dipped a slight bow.

"*Graggen du mard*," she said to him, then, to Annleia, "Keep each other well."

"And you," Annleia replied. "May all your morrows shine bright."

Nods, grunts, a few lasting stares. That was all the more Torin had to suffer through before the dwarves took their leave, Allion and Marisha in tow. He wasn't sure if it was the look he gave that kept all at a distance, the volatility of the blade in his hand, or something else altogether. But there were no real smiles, no handclasps, no embraces. They simply went on their way, as he preferred.

Time soon to be upon his.

Annleia stepped up to his elbow as he watched the others depart. "You do not truly mean to accompany me, do you."

A statement, not a question. "You said before that you would be better off alone. The reasons you gave . . . nothing has changed."

When she did not reply, he turned to face her. The deep stare that awaited him was as compelling as any he had ever received—enough to cause the barest flutter in his chest. Perhaps he was wrong. Perhaps she hoped that he would argue for her to change her mind. If so, she was going to have to speak the words. She knew well enough that he had nowhere else to go, nowhere else he would rather be. She had spurned his offer once already. He wasn't going to beg.

"Take the Sword, at least," he urged.

Annleia's incredulous chirp was part laugh, part grunt. "The Sword could belong now to no one but you."

"You are the last of the Vandari," he reminded her, as he presented her the blade.

She pushed it away, her eyes never leaving his. "I am a link only, between the old and the new. Their secrets, their responsibilities, are yours."

"Secrets can be passed on. I can tell you—"

"You could *tell* me," she agreed, "but we spoke of this before, remember?

Knowing how magic works is not the same as being able to summon it. And the need would have to be dire indeed before I would even attempt to wrangle such power."

His gaze slipped to the glowing blade. She was right, of course, more so than she knew. Better that she keep to her mother's wellstone, its energies drawn from an external source. Better that she never expose herself as the Sword required, or experience its full, devouring nature. He winced to even imagine it. Kindled by her love, her hate . . . Feasting upon her every shame, her every desire . . .

"Remember the Entient's warning," she said, her soft voice cutting into his thoughts. "Remember also what I told you of passion and patience. Destroyers each, if you do not keep them in balance."

"In that case, you may not wish to keep Him waiting much longer." His eyes shifted to indicate Ravar's titanic presence, waiting patiently to bear her home.

Still she hesitated. "I must know first that we will see each other again."

Had he felt any less numb inside, Torin might have laughed. Was this parting not *her* decision? He almost pitied her her conflict of emotions.

Almost.

"I'll not try to predict the future," he said. "Nor will I stand here and make promises I do not know I can keep."

"Then promise me this, at least. Promise me that you will not let the past prevent you from seeking future joys. Life is full of glorious horizons. Often, the best are saved for last."

Torin nodded mechanically, while gnawing irritably at her words. On what grounds did people so often assume the future would be better than the past? Was it merely an excuse to press on when the best, it seemed, had already gone by?

"Come," he said. "Let's not let Crag think that something is amiss."

He began his march without waiting for her reply, but found her falling into step quickly enough. Neither spoke a word as they navigated the rock-strewn terrain, though he felt her gaze lingering upon him more than once. As they neared the tideline, he veered north, angling behind a jutting rock formation that would help to hide them from the view of their departing companions. Ravar, attuned to his every thought, snaked slowly in that direction.

You do mean to bear her safely, do you not? Torin asked the leviathan.

See to your own course, Asahiel, before you think to question mine.

"Will you give me no clue as to where I might find you?" Annleia asked, coming to a stop on the reef beside a shallow tide pool.

"You found me before. Should the need arise, I'm sure you can do so again."

That elicited another squeak of protest. Her eyes sparked, then softened. With no more warning than that, she stepped close and wrapped her arms around him.

He still held the Sword, and so squeezed her briefly with his one free arm. Annleia hung on. For a long moment, she held him tight, as if genuinely reluctant to release him. When at last she pulled away, she did so slowly, staring into his eyes with that conflicted sense of longing.

Torin did not know what else he might say, and so reached forth to brush her cheek. Annleia clutched his hand momentarily, her emerald orbs shimmering, then spun away in a swish of red-gold hair.

Without turning back, she splashed a trail across the reef toward the waiting Dragon God. Torin himself turned to make sure that Crag and the others were out of sight, then watched her scale the leviathan's ravaged hide. Much of the clinging sea-growth had been broken away during His assault, but enough remained in patches to provide food and shelter for her voyage. If Ravar had truly agreed to this, Torin assured himself, then nowhere else in all the world would she be as safe.

It occurred to him then that a farewell to the Dragon God might be in order, no matter their actual feelings toward each other. Easier said than done.

Your Entients wished me peace at journey's end, Ravar offered helpfully.

Then I bid you the same.

The Dragon God seemed to scoff. *And I tell you what I told them: As long as your kind hold dominion over this world, my sleep will not be a lasting one.*

Even before His passenger had found a perch, the monstrous creature slid farther out into the frothing waters. His immense torso twisted, head snaking to the south. Torin quickly lost sight of Annleia amid the forest of coral and spines, but felt her peering back at him in silent farewell.

While the Dragon God sliced an unerring furrow through the sea.

LONG AFTER THEY HAD ESCAPED his view, Torin stood in place, a cold sense of finality taking root as he listened to the wind and the waves and studied the rise and fall of the ocean swells. Annleia was gone. Whatever he might have offered her was not enough when measured against the demons she carried. So, that was that.

All for the best, he assured himself, reaching up to fondle Dyanne's locket. For without the elven woman clouding his head and heart, he was closer to where he'd once been—closer, perhaps, to where he should have been all along.

Still, he could not shake the lingering image of Annleia's eyes, those orbs wherein had lain his last chance for happiness. Never again would he gaze into them and find the hope, the wonders, they had so briefly offered. So much promise, resulting only in emptiness.

Even so, he would forever be indebted to her, he knew—not only for cleansing him of Thrakkon's influence, but for her faith and companionship on the road that had followed. So brief, it now seemed. Despite the bittersweet outcome, there was little for which he might trade their common adventures.

Such dark times, he marveled, made somehow wonderful.

Nothing lasts forever.

He'd had his opportunity.

Gone.

As with Dyanne, all that was left to him, all that he would ever know, was the longing.

Another memory.

Another season in the Abyss.

CHAPTER FIFTY-NINE

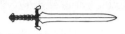

"IT WAS A LOVELY CEREMONY," Marisha remarked.

Their small group stood in an antechamber to the food hall in which last night's coronation dinner had been held. Only a few score had attended: friends and noblemen from within and without Alson. Many of the same had gathered again this morning, and were waiting behind closed doors for the new king to join them at breakfast within.

King Nevik inclined his head graciously. "A modest affair, by any measure."

That, it had been, Allion thought. With so much pain and devastation still fresh in everyone's hearts, it hadn't seemed appropriate to hold any kind of lavish, drawn-out celebration. Some within the Circle had argued against crowning the new king at all, claiming that it was far too soon to be seen as moving forward—that doing so was somehow disrespectful to those who had fallen. The prevailing opinion, however, was that there was no better way to put to rest so many lingering doubts and set forth on the long road of healing than by formally anointing he who would preside over the slow, arduous restoration ahead.

"Tastefully done," Corathel agreed.

"A bit *too* tasteful, if anyone's asking me," Jasyn added. "I'll expect much more feasting—and much more drink—at the royal wedding."

Nevik seemed to blush behind his thick beard, and cast a nervous glance at Ghellenay beside him.

"His Majesty has many pressing concerns just now," the baroness offered dismissively, though Allion did not miss the gleam in her eye. "Let us not burden him yet with such trifles as the choosing of a queen."

"In any case," Nevik offered, after clearing his throat. "I should think you'll find ample reason to celebrate in the weeks and months to come. All know that King Thelin will accept the imperial mantle in time. And there is your own people's monarchy to consider."

"When will that be decided, by the way?" Marisha asked, with a teasing look at Corathel.

"Not for some time yet, I'm thinking," the chief general replied.

Allion understood his friend's reservations. Galdric's sons had yet to be discovered—alive *or* dead. Still, with as much time as had passed since that fateful flight from Atharvan, there seemed little reason to hope. The land of Partha—struck harder than any other by the Illychar—needed for that very same reason, he believed, to usher in quickly a dawn of recovery.

"The cries for *King* Corathel follow you everywhere you go," Allion observed.

"He knows," Jasyn said. "He chooses not to hear them."

"*You're* the king's blood," Corathel countered, "not I."

That caused a moment of silence, in which those assembled turned to the Second General in obvious surprise.

Jasyn seemed abashed by the sudden attention. "A cousin's nephew only. Or is it a nephew's cousin? I can never quite remember."

"But you *are* of royal lineage?" Marisha asked.

"It's not something I take pride in."

"Joined the army by choice, fool that he is," Corathel snickered. "Could have had a long life as some court advisor or palace cretin."

"No longer than the rope I'd have been compelled to hang myself with," Jasyn groaned.

Nevik smirked. "I trust we'll be among the first to hear, once you've sorted it out. Shall we eat?"

"Ours is packed for the road," Corathel said. "I'm pleased to have borne witness to your coronation, my friend, but I really must be seeing now to the affairs of my country."

Nevik bowed. "I understand. Thank you for making the trip." Under the watchful eyes of his guardsmen, he clasped the chief general's forearm, then wrapped him in a powerful hug. He did the same with Jasyn. "Give my regards to Generals Maltyk and Lar."

"And mine," Ghellenay added, as she embraced the Parthan representatives in turn. "Our people would not have been spared without your valiant efforts."

"And you?" Nevik asked, shifting his attention to Allion. "I know how anxious the two of you are to set forth."

"Our horses are being readied this very moment," Allion confessed. "Like the generals here, we just came down to pay parting respects to the new king."

"Gods, my lady, do you hear that?" Nevik asked Ghellenay. "They speak to me as if I've become someone else altogether."

"You are our lord and king," Marisha reminded him.

"I am your friend," he corrected, with a sweeping glance to include them all, "your brother, in battle and blood. Any favor I'm given to grant you—any of you—is but a debt repaid."

"Is there nothing we might do to persuade you to stay?" Ghellenay asked.

Allion shook his head. "The summer is fast upon us. Best to begin our rebuilding now."

"Anything more you need, then," added Nevik, an assurance in his unquestioning tone.

"If so, we shall come and beg Your Highness's favor," Allion answered with a sly smile.

"You'll do so often, I hope," the king replied, pulling the hunter into his embrace. "Diln is but a half day's ride, from all I hear."

"You'll grow sick of our visits, I'm sure," Marisha said, as she took her turn at farewell.

"Impossible," said Ghellenay, "but do try."

The doors to the food hall opened, and an attendant poked forth his head. "Ah, my liege. I was about to send a page."

"Until we see one another again," Nevik said, ignoring the interruption, "be well, my friends."

THE FOUR OF THEM REMAINED together as they made their way to the stables. En route, they came across General Zain, whose battlefield promotion had been officially upheld upon his return to Krynwall. It was not a position he had ever wanted; he had been much more comfortable in Rogun's shadow. Already, however, he confessed to having developed a taste for it. It amused him, he said, the way in which his men—and women—worked harder than ever before to please him.

"Irrepressible," Allion muttered, as they left the weasel to his salacious smirk.

"The sort of spirit this land needs right now," Marisha soothed. "If need be, Nevik will keep him in line."

As they reached the stables, another unexpected visitor awaited them.

"Stephan," Marisha greeted warmly. "So good of you to see us off personally."

The chief seneschal bowed, though the look he gave her was somber. "Master Allion, might I a word?"

"Don't you have duties within the palace?" Allion replied warily.

"A moment is all I ask."

"We'll see to the horses," Marisha offered, and drew both Corathel and Jasyn away.

Allion waited until they had gone. "What troubles you?"

"It's just . . . I can't help but wonder . . . Are you certain he's not coming back?"

The hunter did not have to ask whom the other referred to. Stephan had been brooding over Torin ever since the former king-to-be's story had been relayed to him. "Of course I'm not certain," Allion sighed. "Torin himself was not. But I know the man better than anyone. If you still doubt his wishes—"

"It's not his wishes I doubt, sir. I just wonder at the haste with which we carried them out."

Allion fought hard to suppress a weary groan. Why did so many—or anyone, for that matter—still concern themselves with Torin's fate? Despite the account he and Marisha had delivered upon their return, all of Pentania, it seemed, ran rampant with rumor, spread by those who refused to believe that the wielder of the Crimson Sword would have chosen on his own not to return. Some said he had been killed. Others storied that he had been dragged into the Illysp's realm. And still others posited that he had been consumed by the same mysterious force he had used to vanquish the reavers from their midst.

A small measure of the populace, to be sure, yet such rumors fanned the sympathies of many more, like Stephan, who seemed to think that a hero was somehow being dishonored. Obviously, they knew little to nothing about Torin's true role in all that had transpired, else they would have saved more of that sympathy for themselves.

What truly gnawed at him, however, no matter any particular man's beliefs, was that it should be an issue at all. So much remained to be done in making safe the return of Alson's refugees, in helping their neighbors to pick through the rubble, in washing out the stains of so much death and bloodshed. Why should one man—who could be seen as responsible for so much of it—merit more than a passing concern?

"The baron is a fine man," Stephan added, as Allion's silence lengthened, "but—"

"The *king*, you mean. And a better fit for the office than Torin ever was—as Torin himself suggested many a time."

"He was never a very prideful man," Stephan agreed. "But neither did he ever shirk his duties. Whatever the need, he gave everything he could to fulfill it, and was unafraid to seek the guidance or opinions of others."

Allion glanced away to find Marisha and the pair of Parthan generals approaching slowly, saddled horses in tow. "He was a good friend to you, Stephan. He afforded you a respect that Sorl and perhaps others did not. But let me assure you this: What was done here is for the best—for Alson, for Torin, for all of Pentania. If not now, you will see it in time." He clapped the man's shoulder and turned to the others. "Ready?"

When Marisha looked at Stephan, her smile became uncertain. "Is everything all right?"

The chief seneschal kept his sullen stare upon Allion. "In time, my lady. In time."

A WARBLING WIND BLEW OVER him in sharp gusts, raking the barren summit. His was a treacherous perch, given the loose nest of jagged rocks in which he sat. One false lean, and that wind might send him skittering out over the cliff's edge.

To a fate determined, at least.

The view before him was of everything and nothing. The ocean swept toward the sky until it was impossible to discern where one ended and the other began, their conjunction veiled by a mist hanging on the horizon. Far below, waves rolled onto the shore south of the bluff like spreading paint. The chill air scraped dully at his flesh as he listened, unblinking, to those waves' churning roar.

He was unsure of how much time had passed. Weeks. A month, perhaps. He hadn't eaten or drunk in all that time, and had scarcely slept. He should have been dead. But he could feel the fires of Asahiel swirling inside him, sustaining him. They were as much a part of him as breath and blood, an enduring tempest awakened within.

Yet they could not answer the question that most plagued him: the road he must travel. More than once, he had wondered if this was how Kylac felt—to bear such vast potential without any clear sense of direction. A victim of the winds due to his own, seemingly limitless choices.

And so the days had slipped past in aimless wandering amid this mountain wasteland, his time spent largely in reflection of where he had been—thinking *that* was where he would find his clues as to what lay ahead. Thus far, he had gained no true focus. Since he'd first drawn the Sword, his life had seen as many peaks and valleys as the Skullmars around him. He had scaled heights undreamed—only to learn what he would never have. If there were lessons to be found in that, he had yet to discover them.

There was the Sword itself, of course, which he imagined he must now put to some great purpose. But whose? For what gain? His answer to the weapon's riddle had only made its power that much more inscrutable. He wasn't certain that he trusted it, any more than he trusted himself. Its volatility was tied now to his own mercurial nature. Had this world not suffered enough of that already?

He gripped the hilt of the blade where it lay in his lap, shuddering at the wash of heat unleashed by the talisman's heartstones. It flowed swiftly through his palm, his neck, his spine. A boundless inferno, since his emotions might be drained, but never extinguished.

Or could they? Much of his confusion, he felt, stemmed from the lingering effects of the Sword's use against the Illysp. The memories with which he had fueled those assaults had become somehow lifeless. The images were still there, but their emotional influence had diminished, leaving him to feel as if his life had belonged not to him at all, but to someone else. In looking to the past, he came away now with little more than a numbed sense of regret. So many poor decisions, so many pivotal moments that he wished to relive . . .

But it was too late for that. Detached as he was, he understood there was no going back. Not to Alson and those he had unwittingly betrayed. Not to Yawacor and those with whom he had belatedly discovered such unexpected kinship. Guilt would not allow that he impose himself among any he had so wronged.

Which left him with what? He had no other desires he could recall. The remainder of his goals lay amid the glittering shards of his past. Their luster would not die, yet they were irretrievable, barely recognizable. All he had were those deadened memories, carried now by some faithless stranger wearing his skin.

If only he could find it in himself to be angry. Surely there were others who shared responsibility for this desolate state of his. His brother Soric, Spithaera, the Entients . . . Had their deeds not forced his hand? What of Darinor and his lies, Eolin and his stubborn refusal, or Cianellen and her subtle manipulations? How might his destiny have differed without their damning influence?

But such questions—such accusations—held no purchase in his thoughts. Life was but a web of interactions, forcing each man to mark well his individual path, lest he become entangled. He would not use the strands laid forth by others as an excuse for his circumstances.

If his life was to be deemed a failure, he had no one to blame but himself.

A stab of irritation knifed through his inner haze. Even he was tired of such self-indulgent brooding. His endless introspection had played no small role in his unlocking of the Sword, but that purpose had already been served. Kylac had never sat around, waiting for his life's meaning to present itself. Time and again, the youth had set out to find it.

And what if Annleia had been right? The future offered nothing if not hope. As his own journeys had proven, one never knew for certain what treasures lay beyond the horizon.

He opened Dyanne's locket, taking a moment to savor the image within. Perhaps his former life had truly slipped away, never to be recaptured. Like all ends, however, this could serve as yet another beginning. Beyond this island lay a vast world never short on troubles, he thought, his gaze returning to the sea. Instead of dwelling on his past, why not venture forth as Kylac had to confront the unknown?

With luck, he might even find the missing youth . . .

Or better yet, himself.